A Rose to the Fallen

APRIL BOSTIC

authorHOUSE®

AuthorHouse™
1663 Liberty Drive, Suite 200
Bloomington, IN 47403
www.authorhouse.com
Phone: 1-800-839-8640

This book is a work of fiction. People, places, events, and situations are the product of the author's imagination. Any resemblance to actual persons, living or dead, or historical events, is purely coincidental.

First published by AuthorHouse 3/26/2010

ISBN: 978-1-4389-0259-3 (sc)

Printed in the United States of America
Bloomington, Indiana

This book is printed on acid-free paper.

In flight of day a lovely rose
Did speak by subtle sway
And stirred a heart so long lain dead
No flower could ever stay.
But embers did to fire aglow
And whispered soft affection
And bared a breast to open light
In trust and insurrection.
How to know the honest heart
Would blush the lovely rose?
A teardrop fell in shame and guilt,
No blush did it propose.
But only tender souls may touch
In magic born of heart
And dare to dream of times to come
When they're not far apart.
For all we have in life is Love,
To give, to share, enhance;
Would you deny ourselves
A hope? a prayer? a chance?
And so my honest heart does ask
In lines of rhyming prose
If I might share my love with you,
My sweet and lovely rose.

~Richard Lee Orey

Acknowledgments

To my wonderful mother who supports my dream to have at least one book published in my lifetime. Well, I believe it's never too late to turn a dream into reality. To my younger sister who never hesitated to give me encouragement. Even though I know you won't read my book because it's a romance and that's not your cup of tea, I hope you display it proudly amongst your massive book collection. And lastly, to my friend Cora who said I should get a book published and make one million dollars. The former would definitely be a blessing…the latter would just be a bonus.

Prologue

HE HEARD MUMMY COME INTO his bedroom this morning. And even though she interrupted the really fun dream he was having with *Her*, he still didn't want to open his eyes. Because if he *did* open his eyes, he couldn't talk to Her as much as he could when he was asleep. But Mummy was good at getting him to wake up, and she whispered in his ear a promise to make his favorite banana pancakes for breakfast. He could already smell the bananas and cinnamon, and it didn't take long for his azure eyes to shoot open and a toothy smile to appear on his youthful face. Today was starting out to be a happy day.

When he sat up in bed and looked out of his bedroom window, he was even happier when he realized it wasn't raining. Not that he minded the rain. You couldn't make adequate mud pies if the earth wasn't moist enough. But he did prefer the sunshine. Since it was a sunny day, he hoped Mummy would take him to the beach. Going to the beach meant building a massive sandcastle, digging for seashells, and playing in the ocean of course.

It was definitely a happy day when he went to the loo because he didn't have to hold himself and hop up and down in the hallway while he waited for his older brother to finish first. He had the loo all to himself this morning.

While the boy was eating his favorite breakfast in the kitchen with his family, he asked his mother, "Mummy, can we go to the beach today? Pleeease?"

He was elated when she agreed. "Sure, love," and smoothed his light blond hair affectionately.

Once she turned around to walk back to the stove, and he made sure no one else at the table was watching him, he whispered to Her, "We're going to the beach today."

'Yay! I like the beach!'

But then the day wasn't so happy when Grampy fell out of his chair at the kitchen table. Nanny and Mummy both yelled in surprise and tried to wake him up but he wouldn't open his eyes. Daddy rushed over too and blocked Grampy from his view. After that, there was a lot of confusion. He saw Mummy on the phone; frantically telling someone on the other end that her father was unconscious and to please send help. The boy sat motionless in his chair with his banana pancakes now cold and sitting in a puddle of syrup. He was frightened, and he wished his older brother hadn't already left for school so he could explain to him what was going on.

He could tell Mummy was frightened too, and she told him to go back to his room. As she gently nudged her second-born son out of the kitchen, she tried to make her voice sound reassuring. "Don't worry, love. Grampy is alright; he's just really tired and he fell asleep at the table."

The boy's small feet only made it halfway to his bedroom before he walked back towards the kitchen. But he didn't go in. He peeked around the corner and he saw the police and some other men come into the house. Everyone was gathered around Grampy who was still lying unconscious on the kitchen floor. He could hear Mummy and Nanny crying and it wasn't long until the men took his grandfather away on a little bed with wheels. "I think Grampy is hurt. The bobbies just took him away," he whispered to Her.

'Don't worry, Grampy will be alright.'

He was sitting in the hospital waiting room with his short legs dangling off the edge of the blue plastic chair. He started swinging them back and forth as he watched many different people pass by him. His eyes widened in curiosity when he saw a sleeping man being pushed in a wheel chair. He continued to watch as the man was pushed down the hallway and the boy wondered what it would be like to ride on one of those wheel chairs. As he looked around the waiting room he noticed a lady wearing a pink shirt sitting across from him. She was reading a magazine and she was still wearing her bedroom slippers. A man with black hair and a mustache was sitting two seats away from the lady. He was watching the television but his knees wouldn't stop bouncing up and down.

He wanted to talk to Her again, but he couldn't because Daddy was sitting next to him. He never spoke to Her when his family could hear him because they didn't understand that She was real. And sometimes his older brother would tease him if he caught him talking to Her. Mummy said it was alright for him to have an imaginary friend, but he knew the girl's voice that he heard in his head wasn't imaginary.

He remembers when he heard her voice for the first time. He was just a wee baby. But he couldn't form words…and neither could she…so they just exchanged gurgles and squeals. But when he got a little older, he realized that there was someone he could hear but couldn't see. And soon…they began speaking to each other.

The boy turned his head and looked past his father. He saw Nanny crying and wiping her nose with a tissue. Daddy had his arm around her and was saying comforting words to try and make her feel better. He looked up at his father's face and he turned his head and smiled wearily down at his son as he ruffled his platinum hair.

Mummy went to the vending machine but when she returned, she had more than a cup of tea in her hand. "Here darling, I got you some paper and crayons," she said quietly as she handed her son a few items to keep him occupied. "Why don't you draw a nice picture for Grampy? I think he'd like that." The boy took the paper and crayons from his mother while she gave him a warm smile. Her nose was still red and her eyes were still watery. Poor Mummy. He didn't like to see her so upset.

Just as the boy put the blank sheet of paper on the unoccupied chair next to him, a doctor approached his family. The doctor was speaking to them in a hushed voice but the boy could still hear what he was saying. But just because he could hear him, didn't mean he understood. He had a feeling it wasn't good news because no one looked happy. But he couldn't help but wonder if Grampy was feeling better. The doctor walked away and Daddy and Nanny followed him into a room.

He was about to hop off the chair and follow them, but Mummy spoke. "Stay here and draw your picture for Grampy." She knelt down in front of her four-year-old son and smiled. "I'll be right back. I just want to see how he's doing. The doctor said he's awake now."

The little boy's eyes, which were identical to his mother's, lit up instantly at this happy news indeed. "I wanna see him too, Mummy!"

She sniffled and smoothed his hair in her own motherly way again. "I know, love. You can see him in a little while. Just draw your picture, okay? Be a good boy." He smiled back and nodded. Mummy gave him a tight squeeze before she stood up and walked quickly towards the room he saw Daddy and Nanny enter moments ago.

"I'm gonna draw Grampy the best picture ever," he said to himself.

'Oooh! Draw me too,' she said excitedly.

"Okay." He opened his box of crayons and set to work on his picture. He drew himself and his family but when he was about to draw Her, he realized he had a problem. "What color is your hair?" When she answered his question, he pulled out the crayon that best matched her hair. He wrote his name on top of the drawing of himself and his family's names above each of their heads. Then he realized he had another problem. "What's your name?"

'I can't tell you.'

The boy scrunched up his face in confusion and spoke louder than he intended. "Why not?!?"

'Because…he said I can't.'

"Who's *he*?"

'I don't know. Some man just whispered in my ear and told me not to tell you.'

The little boy sighed in frustration. "Fine, I'll just call you Rosie 'cause your hair is the same color."

She laughed in sheer delight. *'I like Rosie.'*

Someone sat next to him while he was engrossed in his artwork. He briefly looked up and he was met by a pair of friendly brown eyes. The nurse's round face was framed with dark curls and the boy thought that she smelled like dish soap. "Your mum asked me to keep an eye on you." She gave him a kind smile but the boy averted his eyes back to his drawing. He was much too busy to pay attention to her.

With his masterpiece now finished, he got up from his chair to give Grampy his picture. He walked slowly with it cradled against his chest. Another nurse smiled at him as she passed and told him he was a 'cute lad'. He stood in the doorway to Grampy's hospital room and saw him lying in bed with Nanny and Mummy sitting on either side of him.

Daddy was sitting in a chair next to the bed and he was rubbing his hands together as if they were cold. But he didn't look cold; he still looked sad just like Mummy and Nanny.

Then for some reason, his little feet wouldn't move any further. He couldn't walk into the room and give Grampy his picture. The boy was about to call his grandfather's name and perhaps that would alert him that he was there. But he didn't have to speak, because Grampy finally set his eyes on the small child standing quietly in the doorway.

The old man gasped and his eyes widened in surprise. His reaction caused everyone in the room to turn their attention towards the little boy. Grampy seemed like he wanted to say something but all he could do was stare at his grandson in astonishment.

Now the boy was confused. Why was Grampy staring at him like this? Did he not recognize who he was? The boy couldn't speak either; he was still frozen on the spot with his drawing pressed against his shirt. Finally his grandfather spoke, but he still sounded amazed. "Oh Mary mother of Christ. I can't believe what me eyes are seein'."

"What is it, Dad?" Mummy asked urgently.

An expression of concern appeared on Nanny's face as she looked back and forth between her grandson and her husband. "Charles, what's wrong?"

It was then that Grampy smiled at him. The boy smiled back and his feet moved a tiny bit. He took a few more steps until he was close enough to see Grampy's eyes welling up with tears. But why was he sad? Was he not happy to see him? "My beautiful boy," he said in a trembling voice. "Thank you."

All of a sudden, the smile faded from Grampy's wrinkled face and he closed his eyes. There was a loud beeping sound coming from something in the room. Mummy and Nanny began yelling again and they were trying to wake him up. Daddy stood up swiftly from his chair and the little boy could no longer see his grandfather's face. He jumped in surprise when the dark-haired nurse rushed into the room and pushed him aside. She made him drop Grampy's picture and he watched it flutter silently to the floor. The boy kept his eyes on his masterpiece as more feet trampled over his family and their smiling faces. And Her...holding his hand while they stood on top of the green hill with the yellow sun shining brightly above them.

"I'm scared, Rosie. I wish you were here with me," he whispered. He could feel the tears pricking at the back of his eyes and before he knew it, they began trickling down his cherub cheeks.

Me too, she whispered back. Now he couldn't be sure, but her voice sounded sad too. Today was not a happy day.

Chapter 1

'It's in your moments of decision that your destiny is shaped.'

~ Anthony Robbins

It was Thursday, September 28, 2006 when I received the phone call that would change my life forever. I just got home from grocery shopping when my house phone rang. I didn't answer it on the first ring because I needed to hurry and put the ice cream in the freezer. Its consistency had already turned into that of a milkshake just from being in the sweltering trunk of my car. After I closed the refrigerator, I picked up on the second ring.

"Hello?"

"Hey Bridget, it's Autumn." Autumn is my best friend. We met on a social networking site called MySpace a couple months ago, and even though our personalities and lifestyles are as different as night and day, it didn't take us long to form a genuine bond of friendship.

"Oh hey, what's up?"

"I tried calling your cell but you didn't pick up. Did you turn it off or something?"

"No, I didn't turn it off. I probably didn't hear it ring. Why, what's up?"

There was a pause. "Ummm...what are you doing tomorrow night?"

"Nothing really. Why?"

"Can you come over to my place? I'm having a little get-together. Just a few friends...you know, nothing big."

"Yeah, sure. I'd love to!" I always enjoyed hanging out with Autumn. Whenever she has parties at her house, she's always a wonderful hostess. One thing I loved about her was her ability to entertain.

She paused again but this one was longer. "I want you to meet someone."

I had a slight feeling where this conversation was heading but I wanted to give Autumn the benefit of the doubt. "Who?"

"A friend of mine."

"Would this friend just happen to be a guy?"

There was another pause on her end. "Yeah. So?" I knew it! We were heading down *this* road again. In the past month, Autumn introduced me to about half a dozen guys. She claimed that my love life lacked variety but I was convinced that she was totally clueless about what I looked for in a man.

I sighed. "You're not trying to hook me up with someone are you?"

"Okay, but this is---"

I had to interject for a moment because I guess she didn't remember the last few guys she introduced me to. "Autumn, I told you I don't want to be hooked up."

"Why not?"

Now I had to refresh her memory. "Why *not*? Because the last guys you introduced me to were real assholes." My brain quickly flashed back and the men Autumn introduced me to in the past went by like a slide-show. I quickly began to remember each of their faces and each of their unflattering qualities which put up red flags in <u>Bridget's Book of Dating Do's And Don'ts</u>.

"Hey, I'm sorry alright? But this is different. I really think I found your soul mate."

I couldn't help but to start laughing. My exhaustive search for Mr. Right has left me pessimistic about finding someone special and my faith in finding my soul mate was diminishing like a candle with the wick almost completely spent. I went into my living room to sit down because I had a feeling this was going be one of those debating conversations I often had with Autumn. I would say 'to-MAY-to', and she would say 'to-MAH-to'. "My *soul mate?!?*" I just couldn't stop laughing because the whole idea sounded ridiculous. Once I composed myself I asked, "Autumn, why do you think he's my soul mate?"

"I just know he is, okay. Please trust me on this."

"See, now I don't want to come over. I don't feel like meeting another one of your *friends*."

"Bridge, you're really gonna like him."

"That's what you said about the others." I'll admit, Los Angeles is full of beautiful men but the quality of them had left a sour taste in my mouth. I wasn't what one would call a *bitter* woman; I was more of a realist.

"No, I really, *really* mean it. He's exactly your type Bridge...blond hair, blue eyes, tatts, absolutely beautiful---"

"He's probably a player."

She paused again. "Well...kinda. But the girls always know what they're getting into. It's not like---"

Autumn's audacity to think that I should actually take her seriously was just too amusing so I started laughing again. I couldn't believe that someone I considered a best friend would want to introduce me to a 'man-whore'. I was so shocked that I had to say, "And you want me to *hook* up with him? Are you crazy? Wait, are you drunk?"

"Bridge, listen to me okay. He has girls he messes with but we've been friends for awhile, and he's told me on numerous occasions that he'd settle down with one girl if he could find the right girl. He's not afraid of commitment or monogamy; it's just that he hasn't met anyone he wanted to give his heart to. *Please* meet him. Did I mention that he's British?"

This time I had to pause because I have a 'thing' for Brits. I paused for awhile because I seriously had to think about this. Would I be wasting my time *again*? Was he really beautiful like Autumn described? Was I really going to entertain the idea that Mr. Right could exist? Was he really my...soul mate? I concluded that there was only one way to find out. I sighed again. "Okay Autumn, I'll meet him."

"Great!"

"But I *swear*...if he's a jerk...I'm never listening to you again!"

"Okay, deal."

"Alright, well I have to go and put my food away. What time should I come by tomorrow?"

"Um, like around eight o'clock."

"Alright, I'll be there."

I was about to hang up when I heard her yell, "Wait, Bridge!"

I sighed. "What?"

"Wear something really cute. And wear your hair down. You look so sexy when your hair is down."

"Fine," I gritted through my teeth. "Wait a sec, can you send me a picture of your friend? And what's his name?" I would love to get a preview of this mystery guy since I just committed myself to yet another 'hook-up'.

There was yet another pause on her end. What was up with her today? "His name is Tristan and I'd rather you be surprised. I think you will be." She gave a very sly laugh, and before I could say anything else, she quickly said, "Later girlie," and hung up.

What did I just get myself into?

I started thinking: *Tristan, huh? Well this Tristan better be something special.* I swore I wouldn't let Autumn introduce me to any more guys because she obviously didn't know what I liked. I hoped this time would be worth it; worth getting all dolled up. I was going to *kill* her if Tristan wasn't what she said he was. Then I started to regret what I just agreed to because I hated going back on my word.

After I put the groceries away, I went into my bedroom closet to look for something to wear tomorrow night. It's Los Angeles, California and it was unusually hot for this time of year so I chose a white and pale pink cotton sundress that showed a little bit of cleavage. Then I pulled out a cute pair of pearly pink strappy wedge sandals that had about a one-inch heel. As I was looking through my jewelry box for some nice accessories, I started wondering if Autumn had already told Tristan about me. Did he know he was going to be introduced to me? I wonder what he said. Did she show him a picture of me? I started to get nervous like the kind of nervousness you feel when you go on a blind date. And really, that's exactly what this was...a blind meeting.

I couldn't sleep at all that night and I kept trying to picture what Tristan looked like. I prayed to God that he would be a nice guy and that he'd be attracted to me because pale, red hair and freckles doesn't appeal to everyone.

I was still thinking about him when I woke up the next morning. After I brushed my teeth, I was looking at myself in the mirror and I kept telling myself: *Yeah, this will be good. I'll just be myself and Tristan will like me.* God, I just hoped he wouldn't turn out to be a dick.

In the evening, I was getting ready to go to Autumn's apartment and I had the sudden urge to call and tell her I wasn't feeling well. I started to pick up the phone but then I thought: *No, she'll see right through that lie.* Needless to say, I ended up going over there...after I sat in my car for twenty minutes debating with myself. When I knocked on the door, she opened it on the first knock and I couldn't help but wonder if she was waiting by the door.

"Bridge! You're here!" she said excitedly. Oddly, she closed the door behind her and we were both standing in the hallway. Autumn was dressed casual in a pair of black low-rise jeans and a white halter top with spaghetti straps. Her bleach-blonde hair was styled in her usual page-boy hairstyle and she was sporting a couple black and silver bracelets. Her eye makeup was still as dramatic as ever but I was glad she went easy on the lip gloss.

I looked at her with a confused expression. "What's the matter?"

"Nothing. Just..." She started biting her black painted fingernails and looking at me intently.

All of a sudden I started to get a little concerned. "What? Is Tristan here?"

"Yeah, he's here."

I realized that even though I didn't really get to ask questions about Tristan, I was curious as to what information he knew. "What did you tell him about me?"

She gave a short laugh. "Don't worry, I just told him good things about you." She was smiling and giving me the once-over. "Oh my God, he's gonna fucking love you! You look soooo pretty."

I smiled back. "Thanks." Then I thought out loud, "Why did you close the door?"

Autumn shifted on her black Vans sneakers with the little white skulls and put a hand on her hip. "'Cause I don't want him peeking out to see if it's you. He's been watching the door all night."

"Really?" I said with wide-eyed astonishment. Then I looked at her questioningly and asked, "So...can I come in or what?" Autumn's hazel eyes were looking at me with this weird expression like she wasn't sure if she wanted me to come in or for Tristan to come out here.

"Yeah, you can come in. I'll introduce you." Right at that moment, I felt a warm flush bloom inside me and I could feel myself getting nervous. My palms were a little sweaty so I quickly wiped them on my dress because I didn't want to shake Tristan's hand with clammy hands. Yeah, that would've made a nice first impression. As I walked into her apartment the music was blasting, there was smoke in the air, and people were standing around; mostly with drinks in their hands, laughing, talking, and some people were hanging out on the sofa. I still couldn't spot this 'Tristan' person and I honestly forgot Autumn's description of him. She was walking in front of me as we walked towards her kitchen. Her kitchen was so small that it couldn't accommodate a table and chairs. For some reason, I was looking at the floor as I walked so I didn't see who we approached. The next thing I knew, I heard her voice and I looked up.

"Bridget, this is Tristan. Tris, this is Bridget."

You know how some people describe the world actually coming to a complete stop and the only thing in focus that's actually moving is you and this other person? That's exactly what happened. I looked up and I swear, I didn't notice anyone else in the room but Tristan. He was absolutely gorgeous! And he was *definitely* my type. He was tall...about six-feet if I had to take a guess, and he had golden blond hair which was cut short but tousled in a very sexy way.

I continued to survey his handsome face. Blond eyebrows with pretty cerulean eyes underneath that were framed by long lashes. There was a real intensity behind his eyes and his gaze caused me to shift on my feet nervously. I swallowed thickly when my eyes darted to his sensual and *very* kissable lips. Tristan had a strong, masculine jaw and the cutest dimple on his left cheek that I've ever seen. He was smiling at me and he definitely debunked the stereotype that the English have bad teeth.

His attire was very common for a lot of young guys today: a black tank-top which showed off the strong, sculpted muscles in his arms. He wasn't skinny; he was lean and his arms were scattered with tattoos here and there. I had a strong feeling he liked the color black because of the rubber necklace and matching bracelets he was wearing; even the stud in his left ear looked like an onyx gemstone. Below his black shirt were faded-blue baggy jeans and on his feet were black Converse Chuck Taylors. Overall, I thought he looked very good. He was holding a Guinness beer bottle in his hand and I couldn't help but notice his long, piano fingers. The sexual part of my female brain started to imagine all the things his beautiful fingers could be capable of.

Once I finished my physical appraisal of Tristan, I found my voice. "Hi," I said meekly. I managed to smile at him but I knew I looked like a deer caught in headlights because he gave a short laugh.

"Hi. It's nice to finally meet you, Bridget." He had a boyish voice, but Oh my God…his British accent was orgasmic. "Autumn's told me a lot about you." I thought: *Oh really? I wonder what she told you.*

"Oh really?" I said out loud. "I hope it was all good things." I turned my attention to Autumn and she was looking back and forth between me and Tristan with an expression that told me she was really ecstatic. She looked like a little kid on Christmas morning.

"Of course," he said. And he flashed that brilliant smile of his.

"Well, I'll leave you guys to chat," Autumn said lightly. She walked away and left me and Tristan standing there…halfway in the kitchen and halfway in the living room. All of a sudden he started staring at me again…directly in my eyes. I felt fidgety and I noticed my palms were sweaty again. I started to think that it was a good thing I didn't shake his hand. But I was also wondering about his opinion of me because I noticed his eyes begin their scrutiny up and down my feminine form. I guess now it was *my* turn to be appraised.

Tristan took his time looking me over, and once he was satisfied, his eyes met mine and he broke the uncomfortable silence between us. "So… you want a beer?"

"Sure." I smiled again but this time it wasn't a nervous smile. It was one of my genuine 'I-think-I-may-like-you' kind of smiles. Tristan walked over to the fridge to get me a beer and I couldn't help but watch him. I swear the man is the definition of 'sex on legs'. Even the way he moved was turning me on. He had a swagger but I could tell it was just natural confidence.

He came back over to me and handed me a Guinness beer. Yuck, I hate Guinness. But I didn't tell him that. I thanked him and I drank it anyway. After all, he was being polite. I noticed he was just staring at me again so I figured I needed to get the conversation going. Ugh, this started to feel like an interview. I wondered if I should start asking him all the standard questions like: 'Where are you from?' 'What do you do?' Then I really started wondering about what he did and how old he was. I began to realize that Autumn didn't actually tell me any pertinent information about him.

I sighed internally and thought: *Well...here goes nothing.* "So Tristan, how long have you been in The States?"

"Since I was eighteen." I looked at him expectedly like: 'So how many years is that?' He caught on quickly because he added, "Five years."

"Oh. And uh, what do you do for a living?"

"I'm an actor. Well...I'm *trying* to be an actor." There was that dimple again. "What about you?"

"I teach fourth grade."

"Oh *that's* right. Autumn told me you were a teacher." He gave me the once-over again and then he grinned. "You don't look like a teacher." I wasn't surprised by his comment because I received that response a lot whenever I told anyone about my profession. Then I was suddenly aware of the fact that he seemed to know more about me than I knew about him. In the back of my mind I plotted to get revenge on Autumn for this.

"Yeah, yeah, I know. I get that a lot." I laughed. My brain seemed to press an internal rewind button and I started thinking about the fact that he was an aspiring actor. I looked down at the floor and mumbled quietly to myself, "Autumn didn't tell me he was an actor."

Tristan heard exactly what I said. "What *did* she tell you?" And he smiled at me again. I swear I could get lost in those sky blue eyes.

"Actually not much. She just told me about you yesterday. She said she wanted me to meet you and that you were beautiful." I gave him a coy smile.

He grinned and cast his eyes down shyly. When our eyes met, he said, "Hmmm. That's odd, 'cause she talked *a lot* about you." Then he looked up at the ceiling with an expression like he was talking to himself and murmured, "Wait, no...I was asking all the questions and she was answering them."

I couldn't hold back my surprise. "Really?!? I mean..." I let out a nervous laugh.

"When I saw your picture, I knew I wanted to meet you." She showed him my picture but wouldn't show me his? What the hell was up with her? I couldn't help what came out of my mouth next.

"She showed you a picture of me?!?"

His next words really shocked me. He grinned and said, "Actually, I saw you on MySpace. I saw you on her top friends and I clicked on your profile."

For a moment, I was speechless because Autumn didn't tell me that either. I had a strong feeling that Tristan probably mentioned seeing me on her MySpace but why didn't she tell me anything about him? When I finally found my voice, I gave him a shy smile and then I found Autumn's floor to be very interesting. "I didn't know you saw my profile." I looked back up at him and laughed lightly. "Autumn didn't tell me that and she wouldn't show me a picture of you. She said that she wanted me to be surprised."

He smiled charmingly. "Well...*are* you?" Oh, he was good. He was *real* good. Flirting already, are we?

"I sure am." At that moment, I started to imagine how easy it must be for him to attract the opposite sex.

We spent the rest of night chatting, laughing, and mildly flirting. It was amazing how natural it started to feel after such a short period of time. I started to feel very comfortable with him and the feeling seemed to be mutual. I noticed how at random moments he would just stop talking and stare intently into my eyes. Man, this guy could be intense. And I noticed him giving me the once-over on numerous occasions. He was actually very sweet, and I loved listening to him talk. He seemed to like asking me questions about myself rather than talk about himself. Every time we'd get into a string of conversation about him, he'd answer me but follow up with questions about me.

He also started complimenting me. He took a few strands of my auburn hair between his long fingers. "You have beautiful hair." My throat went dry as I watched him run his fingers through from the roots to the tips. My scalp tingled and I suppressed a slight shiver of pleasure. I could already feel my ears getting hot. I went cross-eyed for a moment when he tapped my nose gently. "And I like your freckles." It was too late; I was blushing. Talk about being 'tickled pink'.

After making me blush furiously, I didn't mind telling him that I liked his tatts. That's when he actually started telling me the history behind each of them. I was touched to know that the one on his right ring finger was his mother's name. As he was showing them to me, I couldn't help but think that a pair of angel wings would look absolutely divine spanned out on his back.

My first impression of Tristan was that he reminded me of a fallen angel. He had this almost inhuman beauty but he seemed oblivious to it. I couldn't detect an arrogant bone in his entire body. And judging by his extremely casual appearance, he didn't seem like one to obsess over vanity. But I was fooling myself because a man as gorgeous as him has definitely been made aware of his good looks; probably as soon as he hit puberty. I could just imagine what his mother had to go through with all the teenage girls calling the house.

But since he was showering me with compliments, I felt that he deserved a few in return. After the presentation of his body art, I said, "You really have beautiful eyes. I've never seen a shade of blue so vibrant." Tristan grinned but I was a little disappointed that I couldn't make him blush too. I tried again by saying, "I have a thing for British guys, you know; especially blonds." His ivory skin still didn't change in hue. I was actually fine with that because I think I blushed enough already for the both of us. "I always wished I was a blonde," I confessed.

In response to my confession, he really put some icing on the cake by telling me, "I think you look perfect with red hair." He added a dashing smile behind that one.

After about three more Guinness beers and half a box of pizza between us, we headed out to the backyard to talk more privately. Autumn lived on the first floor of her apartment building so she had access to the backyard. We sat down together on a white plastic loveseat and he turned to face me. He was staring at me again, but this time it looked like he was contemplating his next words.

"Did Autumn tell you *why* she wanted you to meet me?" I began to panic because I wondered if I should I tell him the truth and risk having him laugh at me? Wait, hold on. He'd really be laughing at Autumn because she's the one who was talking all that 'soul mate' crap. I decided to tell him the half-truth.

"Yeah, she said that we might like each other."

"Oh." He suddenly got quiet but he was still looking into my eyes.

I gave him a perplexed look. "What is it?" And then I touched his bare arm. Wow, his skin felt really nice. It was warm and smooth and I found myself wanting a more in-depth exploration. He scooted closer to me and held my hand in his. Oh my God. That's when I noticed something strange. His hand seemed to fit mine and I couldn't help but to look down at our joined hands and smile inwardly.

His voice was soft when he said, "Promise you won't laugh if I tell you this?" I thought: *Well, well, well. Maybe Autumn told him the same bullshit she told me.*

"I promise." I gave him my most beautiful smile. "I cross my heart." Then I made the crossing motion with my free hand; right on top of my left breast. Tristan watched the motion intently.

"She ringed me the other day to tell me about a dream she had. She was out of breath and was like...going mental. At first I was worried like, 'What the fuck is wrong with you?' She told me that she had a dream about me and it freaked her out.

She was queued up in this coffee shop and she heard crying. It sounded like a child crying. She turned around and there was this little boy in the corner of the shop and he was crying. No one seemed to notice him 'cause people kept going about their business. She thought that was weird that no one said anything to the boy. So she walked over to him and knelt down in front him. He was covering his face and crying into his hands. She asked him what was wrong. Why was he crying? Was he lost? At first he didn't answer her. It was like he didn't notice she was there. Then he stopped crying and looked up at her. She said the little boy looked like he could be my son or something. He looked like me. He pointed to his heart and said, "I hurt. I hurt." She said he had a British accent. She asked him if he wanted her to get a doctor. Then he said, "I need the red hair girl. I need the red hair girl." Then he started crying again. She said at first she didn't know who he was talking about. But then she said something clicked in her head. It was you. She told me you're her only mate with red hair. And that's when she noticed he had a tatt on his finger. The same one I have, on the same finger. And she realized the little boy was me.

I've told Autumn before that I'd like to settle down with one person. You know, fall in love...have a girlfriend...all that good stuff. But I just haven't found that special someone. A lot of women I meet don't understand that I can't devote all my time to them. I'm busy a lot...you know what I mean? And one time when I was drunk, I told her that my heart aches sometimes." He laughed. "I can get all sentimental and shit when I've been drinking." Then Tristan looked away from me and dropped my hand. His voice lowered when he said, "That freaked you out too, huh?"

I was speechless. No wonder Autumn was acting all weird on me. No wonder she believed that Tristan was my soul mate. But why didn't she tell me about the dream? Why did she only tell Tristan? I said, "Yeah, that was weird." Then I spoke softly when I asked, "Do you believe her... I mean the dream? Like, that you needed to meet me?"

Tristan turned around and faced me, and at that moment our eyes locked on each other. The look he gave me was the most intense one he'd given me all night. He moved closer to me so that we were probably an inch apart, and that's when I noticed he smelled *so* good; a very masculine scent like smoke, mint and something woodsy mixed with the smell of freshly laundered clothes. He caressed my cheek with the back of his hand and whispered, "Yes I do, Bridget."

I won't deny that I wanted him to kiss me. To hell with the fact that we just met...I wanted him to. I was feeling sentimental myself so I said, "I think I needed to meet you too." He flashed his beautiful smile at me again...with that cute dimple and all.

Needless to say, the kiss never happened that night. It was probably 3AM when I told Tristan that I had to go home. He looked upset but I gave him my phone number and told him to call me some time. He said he definitely would and he gave me his. I needed to find Autumn to tell her I was leaving so Tristan and I went back inside to look for her.

She was standing by her stereo talking to someone, and how she could hear them above the loud music was beyond my comprehension. When she saw me approach, she perked up, excused herself from her company, and came over to me.

"I have to go, Aut," I said to her. As soon as I said this, I saw her expression change to disappointment. She looked over at Tristan who was standing next to me, and then she looked back at me.

"Awww, why?" She whined.

"Because it's late."

"But it's the weekend and you don't have to work." I felt Tristan shift next to me and I could feel his eyes on me, so I chanced a glance at him. He looked hopeful and he was smiling at me. I could already feel my resistance slipping but I tried hard to stick to my guns.

"I can't I---"

"It's too late for you to drive home, Bridge. I know you're tired. Hey, you can crash here. Tristan is crashing on my couch." She smiled as if saying that would further persuade me.

"So...what...you want me to crash on the couch with him or something?" I laughed but they were both silent; just looking at me as if to say: 'Why not?' Oh hell no! I just met this guy; even though deep down I would love to snuggle up next to him. I lied with a straight face and said, "I can't, Autumn. I have things to do tomorrow." Then I turned to Tristan and said, "I had a great time, Tristan. It was really nice meeting you. And I meant what I said before...give me a call me some time. Maybe we can get together." I took one of his hands in both of mine and smiled up at him. He was staring at me again and I was beginning to find it a little unnerving.

Then he seemed to come out of his trance and realize I was talking to him because he said, "Don't worry...I will." To my surprise, he stepped closer to me and I found myself in his warm embrace. My arms began to encircle around him and for the next few seconds, we just held each other. For one short moment, I was lost in this new boy named Tristan. And I swear...I could've stayed right there in his arms. It felt so comfortable... so safe...and so right. A part of me was actually disappointed when he released me. "Let me walk you out?" He was being such a gentleman that it actually warmed my heart.

After saying goodbye to Autumn and some quick goodbyes to the few people who were still lingering around, Tristan and I walked out to the parking lot. When we got to my car, I unlocked the driver's side door and he actually opened it for me. I turned slightly to look at him and he was grinning. "Thanks," I said shyly as I got into my car. Once he closed the door, I rolled down the window. Then I looked up at him and smiled. "Well, see you later handsome."

He leaned down so that we were face-to-face and he spoke in that orgasmic British accent of his, "See you later...red hair girl." Then he gave me another beautiful smile. I honestly don't think I could ever get tired of seeing him smile.

I couldn't help but to smile back and it stayed glued to my face the whole ride home. It wasn't until I was driving home that I remembered my MySpace profile was private. If Tristan said he was able to see my pictures, then I must've accepted his friend request. I planned to check my friend list tomorrow. If he *was* one of my friends, the idea of checking out his profile and being able to talk to him online made me very excited. Even though, talking to him in person was no comparison. When I got inside my apartment I was still smiling and I honestly couldn't stop until I finally shut my eyes to sleep.

That night I dreamt of me and Tristan in a coffee shop. I was sitting on his lap, his arms were around me, and he was whispering in my ear. I don't recall what he was saying but I'm sure some of it was naughty because I was giggling like a schoolgirl. I had my arms around his neck and we were gazing into each other's eyes. His beautiful azure eyes captured me in a spell and his wonderful scent engulfed my senses. Suddenly, his head started to move closer to mine and I began to meet him halfway. Our lips were a mere centimeter away when he whispered against my mouth the only words I *do* remember him saying: "There's something going on between us."

I had no idea how right he would turn out to be.

Chapter 2

I HAD SUCH A WONDERFUL dream about Tristan that I was content to let the dream last forever. But then I looked at the clock and realized I just wasted half of my Saturday in bed. It's not normal for me to sleep late and wake up in the afternoon. Last night I stayed out until almost four o'clock in the morning drinking bottles of Guinness beer. I should've known better. I know what Guinness does to my stomach.

On the other hand, it was kind of worth it because I met a beautiful, amazing guy named Tristan. Where did this guy come from? England apparently. I believe one day God was having a spectacular day and said, 'I think I'm going to create Tristan Hathaway today!' The more I talked to him and the more I got to know him, I realized there wasn't anything I *didn't* like about him. He was so down-to-earth, charming, charismatic, and just plain real. He didn't apologize for the fact that he cursed a lot and had a mouth like a sailor. I appreciated that because I found his honesty to be very endearing. He wasn't what I expected at all and it didn't hurt that he was so pleasing to the eye. He was one of the most beautiful men I've ever seen. Tristan was just...too good to be true. Well, there was only one way to find out for sure.

Now, should I call him first or wait for him to call me? Isn't that like one of the most difficult decisions one makes after meeting someone? I was pondering that very question as I was walking into the kitchen to get some breakfast. Wait, scratch that...lunch was more like it. I happened to glance over towards the phone and I saw the light blinking on the answering machine. I walked over to it and noticed there were three messages. I had a feeling one of them was from Autumn wanting to know how it went with Tristan. No doubt she already got the scoop from him since he *did* crash at her place last night. I wondered what he told her about me. I was hoping at least one of the other two messages were from him. As I pressed the 'PLAY' button I was secretly praying that I would hear his voice. The first message was a damn telemarketer; skip to the next one. It was Autumn (I knew it!)...talking at full speed!

Bridge! Oh my God! You have to tell me what happened with Tristan. How did it go? Do you like him? Did you feel like you guys were clicking? What do you think of him? Bridge, he REALLY likes you. He just kept talking about you and asking me all these questions about you and saying how pretty you were and that he wants to get to know you better. See, I told you. I told you that he was your type. I saw how you two were looking at each other. Oh my God, this is gonna be perfect. He's the one for you. I mean it. Okay well, call me back. Like as soon as you get this message. Alright bye.

I won't deny that I was elated at this news. Tristan really liked me? He couldn't stop talking about me? I must've made a good impression on him. I couldn't stop grinning. Maybe I *will* call him first. That is, if this next message isn't from him. I pressed 'PLAY'.

Hey Bridget, it's Tristan. [Pause] I know you're probably asleep. I can't believe I'm up at this hour. Anyway, um, ring me when you get a chance. Maybe we can hook up later. Alright then, cheers. Oh wait, um...I had a really nice time with you last night. I forgot to tell you that before you left. I can't get you out of my head. Anyway...I'll talk to you later then. Cheers, love.

After the message ended, my mouth dropped. He called...and he called me *'love'*! And he wanted to hook up later? Hold on wait, last night I lied and said I had things to do, didn't I? Damn, I guess I'd just have to lie *again* and tell him that I already finished my errands and I could meet with him. I couldn't help but wonder if this was going to be like a date.

After I ate some lunch, I called Autumn back. She was ecstatic on the phone and talking a hundred miles per minute. "Bridge...oh my God! I was hoping you would call me back. I wanna know everything. Do you like Tristan? What do you think of him? Do you think you guys were clicking?"

"Aut, calm down," I laughed. "Just pause and take a breath, okay."

She laughed. "I'm sorry, I'm sorry. I'm just so excited for you."

"Yeah, I can tell."

"Okay," she breathed. "I'm calm now. So, what did you think of him?"

"I really like him."

"Awesome!"

"And you were right. He's definitely my type."

"See, I told you." I could hear the smugness in her voice.

"He left me a message asking if I wanted to hook up with him later."

"Oh shit! He called you back *already*? Damn. That's unusual. Usually a week goes by before a guy will call you back…if he even calls back at all."

I felt relieved and kind of special that Tristan was eager to speak to me again. The same giddy smile from last night crept up onto my face. I found myself eager to speak to him too. "Yeah, so…I think I'll call him back." I paused and said slyly, "As soon as you let me get off the phone."

"Say no more," she said briskly. "I'll talk to you later." I thought she was about to hang up, but she said these last words to me with rapid speed: "Let me know what happens." *CLICK*

I went back into the bedroom to get my cell phone since that's where I put his number. I was nervous and I was thinking of what to say to him. After a few moments of debate, I decided to just keep it short. I dialed his number and his phone rang a couple times. Then I heard him pick up. Oh God.

"Hey you."

"Tristan? It's Bridget."

"I know." I could *hear* him smiling.

"Oh. Um, I got your message." I paused and he was silent. "Um yeah, we can hook up later. What did you have in mind?"

"I don't know. It doesn't really matter to me. I just wanna see you." I almost dropped the phone.

I blushed and laughed lightly. "I want to see you too. Um, okay…well did you want to meet and have a drink somewhere?"

"Yeah sure, we can do that."

Tristan and I discussed the when and where of our planned meeting together. I was keeping to my word and trying to keep the conversation short so I said, "Well, that sounds like a plan to me. I'll see you later then?"

"It's a date." He paused for a beat and then I heard him say my name. "Bridget?" Uh-oh. What's he doing? He's supposed to say 'see you later' so we can hang up.

"Yes?"

"I meant what I said when I left you that message. I can't get you out of my head. When I woke up this morning, you were the first thing I thought about." Wow, I couldn't believe he just admitted that. I was quiet again; not on purpose but because I really didn't know what to say. He caught on quickly because he said, "You don't have to say anything. I just wanted to tell you that. Okay, I guess I'll see you later."

"Wait Tristan!"

"Yeah?"

"I thought about you too when I first woke up," I admitted. I couldn't believe what came out of my mouth next. "I actually had a dream about you last night." I slapped myself in the forehead because I didn't intend on revealing that. But he had already heard it so there was no going back now.

"Oh yeah? I hope it wasn't a creepy one like Autumn had."

"No, it was nothing like that. But it did involve a coffee shop. We were at a table and I was sitting on your lap, and you were whispering in my ear."

"What did I say?"

"I can't really remember. The only thing I do remember is that you said there's something going on between us."

"Hmmm...I think there is." Very perceptive of him. Then he asked, "What do you think?"

"I don't know." Damn it, I just had to be an idiot. Why didn't I just say 'yes'? I slapped my forehead again.

"Well, I guess I'll just have to make you see, won't I?" This guy was *good*. I was blushing again and my hands started sweating. Why were my hands sweating from just talking on the phone?

I let out a nervous laugh. "I guess so." I paused again and there was more silence on his end, so I decided that I had to stop talking now. "Okay, well I have to go and uh, do some stuff. So uh, yeah..."

"Yeah...I'll let you go. Cheers."

We hung up with each other and I flopped down on my bed breathless. I must have a major crush on this guy. I don't get it. I was relaxed with him last night and now I was acting like we just had an awkward sexual episode with each other. He's already proven to me that he's perceptive so I know he picked up on the way I was acting on the phone. I just hoped he wouldn't mention it tonight. Tonight! Just at that moment, I realized that I had to figure out what I was going to wear. Even though we weren't meeting until much later, I didn't want to be late for our date because I couldn't find anything to wear.

I went in my closet and frantically searched for something cute and flirty. I decided to go a little more casual this time and wear a nice pair of vintage-looking low-rise jeans and a white Abercrombie & Fitch top that had a baby doll fit. I pulled out my white sling-back espadrilles shoes and decided that I would deal with putting together some accessories right before I leave for the date. I remembered that I still had to go to the gym so I decided to kill some time by working out. Nothing eases tension like a good workout.

After I finished working out and showered, I decided to run a few quick errands before I headed home. By the time I got back home, it was an hour before I had to go and meet him. Shit! I needed to hurry so I got dressed and did my hair and makeup. I decided on keeping the accessories simple so I wore my thin silver chain with a cross pendant, silver hoop earrings, and a white bangle bracelet. Before I left, I sent a text to Tristan telling him that I was on my way and he text me back saying he was already there and that he'd be waiting for me.

Tristan and I agreed on meeting at a local bar & grill that we were both familiar with. When I got inside I noticed a big sign that read: ***KARAOKE NIGHT - CONTEST WITH PRIZE!*** I started to wonder if I could get Tristan to perform a duet with me. As soon as I visualized it, I laughed at myself. Would he be willing to humiliate himself for me? I was standing next to the hostess podium looking into the dining area to see if I could spot my date. I didn't see him there so I walked over towards the bar area; no sight of him there either. I was going to ask the hostess if she'd seen him but she wasn't at her station. Then I thought that maybe he went to the men's room. Just as I was heading back to the waiting area to sit down, someone came up from behind me and put their arms around my waist.

I shrieked, "Ahhhh, what the---" Then I recognized the scent. Tristan laughed and placed a soft kiss on the side of my neck.

"Glad you could make it," he said. He let go of my waist and moved around my body to face me. He was smiling so beautifully at me, that for a moment I was speechless. My eyes quickly gave him the once-over and I noticed he decided to keep it casual too. He was wearing a black t-shirt, blue baggy jeans, and black boots. He was also sporting his black rubber necklace and matching bracelets again. He had some other wrist-wear too; including a watch. His hair was the same but I noticed that he changed his earring. Today it was a small silver hoop. What a coincidence. Then I noticed that he was looking me over too. Our eyes finally met and he grinned. "You look beautiful."

I immediately started blushing. Then I smiled and waved my hand dismissively. "Oh, I just threw this together." I laughed. "But thanks, you look nice too." What he said next really threw me for a loop.

"I love it when you blush." Then he reached out and touched my hair. "You did that a lot last night." He started looking into my eyes again. He did *that* a lot and I reminded myself to ask him about that later.

Finally the hostess came back to the podium and Tristan walked over to her and asked if we could have a booth. She seated us right away and gave us our menus. We sat down together and what began was one of the most revealing conversations I had with him so far. We were both looking at the menus when he glanced up at me and said casually, "I just wanna tell you that I don't normally do this."

I looked up at him. "Do what?" I was actually intrigued as to where this was going.

"Go on...you know..." and he gestured between us, "dates."

"Why not? Don't tell me you can't get any." I laughed. What did he mean he doesn't go on dates? That's preposterous!

He laughed. "No, it's not that. It's just...when I meet someone it's like..." He paused and looked up at the ceiling with a thoughtful expression. Then he looked at me and explained, "Okay, it's usually like this: I go somewhere and I might meet a bird..." I looked at him in confusion because of his choice of word to represent the female gender. When he noticed my reaction, he gave a short laugh and corrected himself. "I mean a *girl*..." He paused again before he continued. "And if we dig each other...we get the talking, drinking, and flirting...you know...whatever. Usually towards the end of the night we're both pretty fucked up and we come to this agreement that we wanna...you know...

shag." My eyes widened; almost involuntarily and he dropped his gaze and started playing with the corner of his napkin.

Our waiter came over, interrupted us and took our order. After I ordered the southwestern chicken fajita and Tristan ordered the smoky cheddar burger with French fries, he looked back at me and said, "I sort of tell them straight up what I'm looking for. Nothing serious, no strings...just some fun. They're usually cool with that. And yeah, we may hook up more than once for a bit of fun but I don't really..." He paused again and looked down at the table, but I was hanging on his every word. What exactly is he about? Then he looked up again and leaned towards me. He took my hand and started rubbing the back of it with his thumb. He had a serious expression on his face when he said, "I don't ever *pursue* anyone. I don't really have *girlfriends*. I've never claimed anyone as mine and had them claim me. Since I've lived in The States, I've never introduced anyone to my mates as my girlfriend. I mean, I had girlfriends back at school in Brighton but nothing serious. I'll admit to you Bridget...I'm a bit of a slut."

Wow, I wasn't expecting him to say that. I replied, "A *slut*, huh?" I sighed and started looking around the restaurant because for some reason I couldn't look at him. Maybe it was disappointment in his confession. I didn't mask the irritation in my voice when I blurted out, "Why are you telling me this?" His next words shocked me.

"'Cause I don't wanna have any lies between us. And I want more than just a shag with you. I really fancy you, Bridget. After getting to know you and spending time with you last night, I realized that all I wanted to do...was to see you again. I wasn't lying when I said I couldn't get you out of my head." He picked up my hand and placed a light kiss on the inside of my wrist. His nose lingered there for a moment like he was breathing my scent. I was so blown away by his words that I was speechless.

I don't know how much time had passed because the next thing I knew, our food was being placed in front of us. We ate and talked more but the conversation turned to less intense topics such as our childhoods and our families. During our meal, he had a couple beers and I had a dirty martini. We skipped on the dessert and just relaxed in some playful banter with one another. I was curious to know the answer to this question so I asked, "What does your mom think about the girls you 'mess' with?" I did the quote marks gesture with my hands.

"She's never met any of the girls I 'mess' with." He did the quote marks gesture too. "Even when I was in school, she never did. They weren't the type of girls you bring home to mum." Wow, talk about honesty.

"Really? So you've never introduced a girl to your mother? *Ever?*" I couldn't believe it. I know my eyes were probably popping out of my head and my mouth was agape, but I couldn't help it. Why would he never take a girl home to meet his mother; not even once? Of course, Tristan didn't cease to amaze me with his answer.

"I've never met a girl who was worthy of meeting my mum." Ah-ha! So he's a Mama's Boy! Instead of being turned off by that, I was surprised to find myself thinking that was quite endearing. I smiled at him and then I started nibbling on the olive from my martini. I wasn't looking at him while I was doing this but he was determined to have my attention for this next bit of information. He leaned over towards me again and put his index finger under my chin. He lifted it gently so that we were looking into each other's eyes. Then he said, "The only way I would introduce a girl to my mum is if I considered her my girlfriend." He gave me a pointed look of some sort; like he was hinting at something. At that moment I wished his next words would be, 'I want you to fly to Brighton with me and meet my mum.' God, I think I was falling already; despite his admission to being a slut. Maybe I could get him to kick that habit and be monogamous with me. Autumn said he's not afraid of commitment; it's just that he hasn't met the right girl. Was I the right girl?

All these confessions from him were too intense for me to handle right now. I needed to breathe. Plus the look he was giving me was making me blush again. I felt warm, sweaty, and slightly aroused. Oh God, he was undoing me with his eyes. I couldn't take it. He started smiling at me again and I think it's because he noticed that I was flushed. I had to get a moment away so I abruptly told him that I had to use the ladies room.

I walked as fast I could towards the ladies room and when I got inside, I rushed into an unoccupied stall to compose myself. I kept telling myself to take deep breaths. I sat on the toilet just to close my eyes and catch my breath. What was this boy doing to me? I was feeling completely different than the way I felt yesterday with him. What's wrong with me?

I left the stall and went over to the sink. As I looked at myself in the mirror I noticed that my face and neck were still flushed. I went to get a paper towel and ran it under the faucet. I patted myself lightly with the cold, wet towel to cool myself down. After I decided I was relaxed enough to continue our date, I left the bathroom and returned to our booth.

When I walked back to the booth, Tristan wasn't there. I scanned the room for him and I saw him standing in the crowd in the area where they were holding the karaoke contest. I made my way over and stood next to him. He put his arm around my shoulders and smiled down at me. I couldn't help but smile back and I put my arm around his waist. Then he kissed the top of my head and I started to think how sweet it was that he was so affectionate.

A middle-aged man wearing a turquoise polo shirt, tan shorts, gray socks, and brown shoes was on the stage singing a horrendous version of Madonna's 'Like a Virgin'. He was sweating because I saw the stains developing in his armpits. And he obviously didn't know any of the lyrics because he was staring at the teleprompter the whole time during his performance. Why on earth would he choose that song? Then I looked over to the side of the stage and I saw this large spinning wheel with different colored sections and words written in the sections. It reminded me of a lottery wheel. "Tristan, what's the wheel for?"

"You spin it, and whatever song it lands on, that's the song you have to sing."

I couldn't help but to laugh because that explained everything. It was at that moment that a rush of bravery flowed through me. I extracted myself from Tristan and announced, "I'm going up there."

He gave me a huge smile. "Go for it, love."

I made my way towards the stage and I saw a few other people standing to the side waiting in line to speak to a woman sitting at a table. I went over and stood in the line. The closer I got to the table, I could see that the contestants were signing a paper (probably their names) and the woman was giving them a ticket. When I finally made it to the table I realized my assumption was correct. I signed my name and the woman gave me a ticket with the number eight on it. She briefly told me the rules and wished me luck. I stood there through a couple more horrendous performances, one so-so performance, and one 'you should audition on *American Idol*' performance.

When it was my turn, I walked up on the stage and the MC said, "Hey, a pretty redhead. How are you doing tonight little lady?" I thought: *Okay buddy, enough with the introductions. Let's get on with it.* I heard a few wolf whistles from the audience and I looked out into the crowd. I noticed that Tristan had moved up from where I last left him and he was now standing right next to the stage. I guess he wanted a front row seat to my performance. He smiled and winked at me. For some strange reason I hadn't lost my confidence and I was ready to give this amateur performance everything I had. I walked over to the wheel and gave it a good spin. The wheel went round and around and then it started to slow down and become less of a blur. What would be my fate tonight? BAM! It stopped on Nancy Sinatra's *'These Boots Were Made For Walkin'.*

Fate seemed to be in my corner that night because I already knew the lyrics to that song. I gave the best performance of my karaoke career. Every now and then while I was singing, I would single Tristan out and sing directly to him. Some people in the crowd were cheering me on and whistling; Tristan included. After I finished my performance, I gave a very dramatic bow and exited the stage. I heard someone yell out, "Encore!"

I made my way through the crowd and back over to where Tristan was standing. He gave me a big hug and when he pulled away from me, he was beaming. "That was the best karaoke performance I've ever seen! You fucking rocked!"

"Thanks," I said breathlessly. "I hope I win."

"It's in the bag." Then he kissed me on the cheek.

He still had his arms around me and he was looking into my eyes. All of a sudden, I found myself mesmerized. The moment was interrupted because an attractive young man with messy brown hair and clear blue eyes came over to me and said, "You were really great. I think you're going to win this thing. That was the best rendition of that song I've ever heard." Then he flashed a smile at me that revealed two rows of straight, white teeth.

"Thanks a lot," I said. I looked up at Tristan and I saw his jaw twitch. His brows were drawn together and he was looking at the guy through slightly narrowed eyes. Was jealousy rearing its ugly head? I couldn't help but to feel a little flattered. The guy looked at Tristan with a blank expression and walked away. That's when I felt his grip on me tighten. Yep, he was jealous.

There was one more contestant who performed after me. It was an older woman singing Michael Jackson's *'Billy Jean'*. She wasn't that great in my opinion and I heard a few people around me laughing.

It was finally time for the announcement of the winner. The MC went back up on stage and said, "The winner of tonight's karaoke contest is…number eight! Bridget!"

I gasped, "Oh my God!" I was honestly surprised. I thought my performance was okay but it wasn't as good as that *'American Idol'* hopeful.

"See…what did I tell you?" Tristan said with a smile. "Go on…go up there." He gave me a gentle nudge and I walked up onto the stage. The MC congratulated me and gave me a gift certificate for two free meals.

Tristan and I went back to our booth to order a couple more drinks. We decided to use the gift certificate to pay for tonight's meals but Tristan paid for our drinks. I left the tip on the table and then we got up to leave. After a few more congratulatory remarks from some other people, we headed out to the parking lot.

When we got outside, I began absentmindedly walking towards my car and Tristan was walking next to me. Once we got to the rear of my car, he stopped. I turned towards him and saw him pull out a pack of cigarettes, take one out, and light it. Then he took a long drag.

"You smoke? I didn't know that." I remembered that he didn't light up once last night so I added, "I didn't see you smoke last night."

He let out a slow puff of smoke from his mouth into the sky and then small wisps of smoke from his nose. God, he made smoking look sexy. He looked down at me and said, "I didn't need to last night." Without taking his eyes off me, he took another drag and exhaled the smoke away from me. "When I was with you, I didn't even think about it. I didn't have one craving. I was so wrapped up in---" He abruptly ended his sentence and began looking at me strangely.

I was just standing there…almost entranced…looking up into his azure eyes. I saw some of the smoke still lingering around his head. I stepped closer to him and I felt a light breeze sweep through my hair. Right at that moment, he flicked his cigarette away and closed the distance between us. He put one arm around my waist and lifted his other arm to run his fingers through my hair. He held me close and then he said softly, "I was so wrapped up in you, Bridget. Does it bother you that I smoke?" A worried expression appeared on his face.

"No, not really. I don't care." What was I saying? Usually smoking turns me off. Then a little voice in the back of mind said: *You can help him to quit.* I was feeling so comfortable with him; just being in his arms... just being in his presence *period*. He brushed my cheek with the back of his hand and smiled at me. I reached up and put my palm to his cheek; it was warm and smooth.

Suddenly, the pad of his thumb gently caressed my bottom lip and he whispered, "You beautiful redhead...what are you doing to me?" Then to my complete surprise, he leaned down and captured my mouth with his. The kiss was soft but wanting; almost needy. He had both of his hands on either side of my head as he slanted his mouth over mine twice and ran his tongue across my bottom lip. I opened my mouth slightly and let him taste me with his tongue. I tasted him and I was expecting to be a little repulsed because he just smoked a cigarette, but I wasn't. For some strange reason I could hardly taste it.

My arms encircled his neck but then I lifted one hand and ran it through his blond hair. He wasn't wearing any product so his hair was really soft. At that moment, his hands moved from my head to my waist and he pulled me tighter against him. I could feel the masculine hardness behind his jeans right against my belly. His body felt so good that I couldn't help but moan softly into his mouth. I heard him moan too, and his kiss became deeper and more intense. The next thing I knew, he pushed me up against my car. He moved his pelvis slightly and ground himself into me. He moaned into my mouth again and his hands reached down and grabbed my butt. Something strange happened then. I could feel myself getting lost in his kiss. My hands began to roam everywhere but then I felt like someone doused me with cold water. We were outside, in a public place, and I was willing to bet that we had attracted a few on-lookers.

I broke the kiss and we were both breathing hard. He looked at me with a charming smile and said, "I behaved for you." I was shocked when I detected the underlying pride in his tone. Did he call this kiss behaving? Pushing me up against a car in public and having his way with me?

"Huh?" I said with an expression of confusion.

"I usually never leave a bar sober but I didn't wanna get drunk with you tonight. Actually, the thought never crossed my mind." There he goes again with that honesty. He noticed the confused expression on my face and started laughing. I smiled at him and then I glanced over his shoulder. My earlier assumption was correct because some people were watching us. Then he said cryptically, "Am I embarrassing you?" How the hell was he able to read me so easily? He didn't let up. "I pay attention to you, you know. I watch your face and read your expressions." *Now* he was reading my mind.

"Is that why you stare at me all the time? You give me these intense looks like you're..." I cast my eyes towards the ground to hide my eyes from him. "Looking into my soul or something." This time I was being honest because that's exactly what it felt like.

"I can't help it, Bridget. It's just..." He gently cupped my face in his large hands and made me look at him. "I think you're *so* beautiful." He was doing it right now; looking deep into my eyes...my soul. "Does it make you uncomfortable? Tell me and I'll stop. I mean, I'll *try* to stop." He grinned and tilted his head to the side to regard me.

And right at that moment, I decided I wanted him. And I don't mean just for tonight or for awhile. I mean I wanted *him*...all of him for as long as he'd have me. I wanted him to claim me as his and for me to claim him as mine. I wanted to be his girlfriend and I was determined to be. I said, "No, I don't want you to stop." He must've been rubbing off on me because the next thing I said was very un-Bridget-like. "And fuck the people watching, just snog me." And he did. While I was completely lost in our kiss, I concluded that Tristan was a fantastic kisser.

During our commenced 'snog-session', the responsible part of my brain said that I needed to cool things down before we ended up moving way too fast. Fortunately, this time we both ended the kiss.

Before we parted ways, Tristan said, "I would like to see you again tomorrow, but I have to get up early 'cause I have a few appointments lined up with some casting directors."

"Oh. I'll probably be busy too; working on my lesson plans."

He stepped closer to me and cupped my cheek in his warm hand. "I'll let you know what my schedule will be for the week as soon as I find out." I could feel him rubbing my cheek gently with his thumb. I leaned into his touch and covered his hand with mine. Our gaze locked suddenly and his voice dropped. "I wanna see you again, Bridget." He rendered me speechless and my voice was lost somewhere in the air. All I could do was nod. "Would it be alright if I came over to your flat some time during the week?"

I mentally slapped myself again. God, this boy was truly mesmerizing. I cleared my throat before I replied, "Yeah, sure." A smile spread across my lips when I added, "I'll even cook for you."

Tristan laughed lightly. "And I'll bring dessert."

He started to walk away but a curious thought entered my mind so I asked, "What kind of dessert?"

He turned around at the sound of my voice and laughed again. "Not telling," he responded slyly. Then he just winked at me and his cute dimple made itself known on his left cheek. I couldn't pass up his offer. After all, tonight was just a prelude for my plan on becoming his girlfriend.

Chapter 3

I DIDN'T HEAR FROM TRISTAN for a few days so I assumed he was busy. It was Wednesday and I had just come home from the gym when I heard my cell phone ringing in my purse. I didn't even bother to look at the Caller ID because there was only one voice I wanted to hear on the other end and I was secretly praying it was him. As soon as I flipped my phone open, I heard, "Hey, it's me." It was Tristan, and I was so happy he called me because I was hoping he didn't lose interest in me already.

"Hey sweetie, how have you been?"

"I'm alright. You know...I'm so sorry, love. I'm a real shit. I know I told you that I'd ring you but I've been really busy. I meant to ring you sooner but I didn't get the chance. And then when I *did* get the chance, it was really late and I didn't wanna wake you up."

"It's okay, I'm just glad to hear from you. I was hoping you didn't forget about me." I laughed.

"I think that's impossible." Tristan always seems to know what to say to make me blush over the phone. "Hey, I was thinking---"

"Yeah?"

At first he didn't say anything and my mind started racing. Did he want to go out again? It was late Wednesday evening and I still hadn't started grading the math quizzes. I remembered that he said he wanted to come by during the week and I agreed to make him dinner. Oh God, what would I make him? My food supply was dwindling.

"Are you busy right now?" There was a hopeful tone in his voice and I was sorry I had to crush it.

"Actually I am. I'm usually busy on the weekdays because I'm grading papers or working on class stuff. Why, what's up?"

"Oh, okay. I was just thinking that maybe I could stop by." He paused again. Then he said, "I really miss you." I couldn't stop the grin that appeared on my face. At least I knew I wasn't suffering from his absence alone.

"I miss you too but tonight just isn't a good time. I'm really swamped." At that moment I started regretting my chosen profession.

"Hey, it's no problem. I understand. So what day would be best for you?"

"How about Friday evening? I'll be free then." There was silence on his end for a minute and then I heard him sigh. Uh-oh. I wondered if he was busy that day. I secretly hoped he wasn't because I didn't want to go a week without seeing him. I quickly said, "Why, is Friday not good for you?"

"No, it's not that. It's just...I have to wait two more days to see you." He laughed. "I sound kinda obsessed, don't I?" Tristan was just too sweet for words. I thought I was the one feeling secretly obsessed. I thought I would start going through 'Tristan-withdrawal' if I didn't speak to him soon. Apparently, he was feeling similar.

I laughed too and said, "No, you don't sound obsessed. And I know it seems like a long time."

"Actually it is. I haven't seen you since Saturday. Ah fuck, I *do* sound like some love-sick bastard." He laughed again. "But alright, Friday it is. What time should I come by?"

"I'll be home by 4:00, so any time after that would be good."

"I'll be there at 4:01."

I laughed again. I was so flattered by how much he wanted to see me. Then a part of my brain remembered that I promised to make him dinner so I asked, "Tristan, do you like Italian food?"

"Yeah, I do. Why?"

"No reason," I said in a sing-song voice. "I just wanted to know." I decided I was going to wow him with my special lasagna.

"Oh *that's* right. I'm gonna be treated to a home-cooked meal, right?"

"Yes you are." I was a firm believer in the motto: *'The way to a man's heart is through his stomach.'*

"I haven't had that in a long time. I'm really looking forward to it. Well, I gotta run babe but I promise to ring you tomorrow. Now that I've heard your voice, I need to talk to you again." All of a sudden the volume of his voice lowered and his next words sounded like he was talking to himself. "Fuck...*listen* to me." He paused again and then he said, "Alright, talk to you later, love."

"Okay, take care." I was about to hang up when I heard him speak again.

"Bridget?" Uh-oh, here we go again. He just *didn't* want me to hang up with him. Honestly, I thought that was so cute.

"Yes, Tristan?" I smiled on the outside but on the inside, the suspense was killing me.

"I really enjoyed our date. I hope I didn't turn you off. You know... with the things I said. When I got home, I kicked myself in the arse 'cause I couldn't believe I told you about my sexual habits. I was all like, 'Why the fuck did I tell her?' Then later that night as I was lying in bed, I realized why I told you." He paused for a minute, and once again he had me hanging on his every word. I guess he took that as a sign to continue so he said, "It's 'cause I wanted you to hear it from me rather than from one of my mates. Or worse, from some bird I shagged. I just like you so much that I wanna be honest with you. I want you to know me. And I want you to like me 'cause you like who I am; even though there are some things about me that are..." He paused again. "Well...fucked up."

I was so shocked by his heartfelt confession that I put my hand to my heart in dramatic fashion like they do in the movies. One thing I really liked about Tristan was his sincerity. He was real and straight up with me from the beginning. I found it shocking at first because he was unlike any guy I've ever met. A lot of men I meet aren't really themselves. I'm usually meeting their 'representative' or they let me see only the good aspects of themselves. Tristan wasn't the type to give 'too much information' but he said enough to let you know what he was truly about. I had to give him reassurance that I still liked him despite the fact that he admitted to me on our date that he was a bit of a slut. I was deep in-thought for a moment but I guess I paused too long and it began to worry him because he said softly, "Bridget? Please say something."

His voice brought my head out of the clouds and I spoke. "Tristan, I still like you. I really do. And you didn't turn me off. Okay I'll admit, at first I was a little turned off but then…I just didn't care. And believe me when I say that I want to know you. Because just from knowing what I do already…I like who you are." I started to feel a little embarrassed at my own admission of feelings so I said, "That sounded cheesy, huh?" I laughed to ease my embarrassment in the conversation.

"No, it's not cheesy at all, love. That actually makes me feel better. I'm just happy that you still wanna be bothered with me."

"Are you kidding me!?!" I was shocked that he said that. Still be bothered with him? The man who I think is the most beautiful male I've ever seen. The man who kisses me like I've never been kissed in my life. The man who shares his feelings with me even though we just met. The man who looks into my soul. "Tristan, I'm going to *bother* with you for as long as you want me to. Believe me, I have no intention of bailing out early."

This time he was the one who was silent, and I wondered if *he* was blushing on the other end. When he finally spoke, he totally blew my attempt at being sentimental out of the water. "I'm so glad to hear you say that 'cause I'm making you…my *first* pursuit." Was I hearing things? Did he say he wanted to pursue me as in…start a *relationship?* Did he want me to be his…*girlfriend?*

My heart was racing so fast that I couldn't speak. Then something in the back of my mind reminded me that I still had a pile of quizzes to grade. Oh God, how would I concentrate after digesting all this new information from this gorgeous man? How would I make it until Friday? I had to end the conversation now before I said something too embarrassing. I let out a nervous laugh and said, "Wow, I wasn't expecting you to say that. I uhhh…really have to get back to these papers. So um… I'll…talk to you…tomorrow?" Now he was causing me to stutter. There seemed to be no relief for the way he was affecting me.

"Yeah…sure, love. You have a good night, okay? Sweet dreams." Sweet dreams indeed.

"You too, sweetie. Bye." We hung up with each other and I practically died on the spot. I was perplexed about the coincidence between the last night we were together and I decided that I was going to try and be his girlfriend. And now tonight, he revealed to me that he actually wanted me to be. Something was *definitely* going on between us.

The next day after work, I went to the grocery store to get the ingredients for the dinner I was making for Tristan. I also stopped at the liquor store to pick up a nice bottle of wine. I wanted to make a good impression since this was going to be the first time he's been to my apartment. Not to mention, it was going to be the first time he tasted my cooking. That evening he called me as promised. We chatted for awhile and I gave him directions to my apartment. By the end of the conversation we were both excited and looking forward to seeing each other.

I rushed right home on Friday without saying goodbye to any of my co-workers. Anyone who tried to stop me on my way out received a quick wave and a rushed, "Sorry, gotta run!" I actually got home a lot earlier than four o'clock so I decided to change my clothes and then start making dinner. I wanted to wear something a little sexier so I put on a sleeveless, black stretch knit dress with a V-neckline that hugged my curves in all the right places. The hem of the dress was two inches above the knee. I wore a pair of heels but I made sure they weren't too high. I topped off my ensemble with a thin gold chain with a diamond-accented pendant and I wore my diamond stud earrings that my father bought me last Christmas.

I washed my face and redid my makeup, and then I brushed out my hair that was pulled up in a ponytail. I was just finishing up by putting on a touch of lip gloss when I heard the doorbell. A sudden feeling of anxiety came over me but I quickly squashed the feeling and ran to the door. I didn't open it right away because I wanted to compose myself. Tristan had a way of making me feel warm, flushed, and bothered. I looked out the peep-hole just to be sure it was him and I saw him standing there. He was craning his neck to the side to look into my window. I laughed quietly to myself and then I opened the door and stood in the threshold.

He quickly turned his head when he noticed the door open and his face lit up with this magnificent smile. "It's 4:01," he announced. We both started laughing and I poked my head back inside to look at the clock on my cable box. It was actually 4:02 but I figured he'd been standing there for a minute. I started to think to myself: '*This boy is amazing!*'

I looked back at him and smiled. "It's nice to see you again." We embraced each other for a few moments but I noticed he was holding me with one arm. When he released me, he placed a quick kiss on my cheek. He was wearing a gray t-shirt underneath a black leather jacket that was zipped halfway. He also had on black baggy jeans and the same black boots he was wearing on our date. He had the 'bed-head' thing going on with his hair which looked totally sexy and he was still wearing the silver earring. I happened to glance down and I noticed he was holding a motorcycle helmet in one hand.

I looked past him and sitting in front of my apartment in the parking spot next to my car was a bike. Not a bicycle, but a *bike*. And it was hot! It was black and lime green with a touch of silver in some places. I saw the word 'Kawasaki' on the side. The wheels were green too and the bike looked like it had just been washed because it was gleaming. I also noticed that his helmet matched the bike. I couldn't hold back my surprise. "Is that yours?!?"

I ran past him and went to get a closer look at the bike. He came over to me and said, "Yeah, that's me." He was grinning as he watched me admire his mode of transportation.

"I didn't know you rode a bike," I said as I absentmindedly ran my hand across the seat. "Actually, I never ask guys what they drive because I always thought it made me sound superficial or something."

"I wouldn't care if you asked me. It's an honest question, isn't it? I mean, it's not like when we first met, the first thing out of your mouth was 'what kinda car do you drive?'" He mimicked my voice at the end of his sentence which caused me to burst into giggles.

After I finished admiring his 'ride', we went back inside my apartment. He stopped to regard me and said, "As always...you look beautiful." It didn't take long for the flush to creep up onto my face and neck.

"Thanks, sweetie. You look nice too."

He began looking around my living room in amazement. It really wasn't much to look at, but I guess he was impressed by it. He must have realized there would be a home-cooked meal for him soon because he sniffed the air and said, "Mmmm...something smells good. Is that dinner?" He looked at me and smiled.

"You are correct." I smiled back. Then I took his helmet from him and put it on a side table. He removed his jacket and just as I was about to take it, he quickly removed something from one of the inner pockets. He did it so fast that I didn't see what it was. I took his jacket and told him to make himself comfortable. He sat down on the sofa and started looking at the decorative seashells I had on my coffee table. While his attention was occupied, I quickly snuck into the dining room to light the candles I had placed on the table earlier while I was cooking. If I was having dinner with him, I was going all out.

When I came back into the living room he had moved from the sofa and he was admiring the pictures I had on a shelf above the television. He picked one up and I noticed he was staring at it intently. I came over to his side and leaned over to see the picture. It was a photo of me as a child with my parents. I watched him run his index finger over my face in the photo. Without taking his eyes off the picture he remarked, "I see you get your red hair from your mum."

"Yeah, I look like Pippi Longstocking in that picture." I laughed. I was wearing a pink dress in the photo and my hair was in pigtails.

"Who's Pippi Longstocking?" he asked with a confused expression.

"You don't know who Pippi Longstocking is?" He shook his head. "Oh, she was this little girl who had red hair and it was in these two pigtails that kind of stuck out and...never mind. It's stupid." Right at that moment my brain realized that something was missing. Suddenly, my eyes widened and I hit him on the arm playfully. "Hey, where's dessert? You forgot it, didn't you?"

At first he looked guilty but suddenly he gave me a very sly smile and said, "I'm sorry, love. I'll make it up to you...I promise."

I pouted a little and said, "Hmph. Well okay, I'll let you slide this time."

He was determined to make it up to me now. "As a matter of fact..." He reached behind him and pulled a flat, thin, square object from his back pocket and handed it to me. It looked like a CD case. "Here."

I took the mysterious package from him. "What's this?"

"A home movie." He smiled widely and had a look of excitement on his face.

"A home movie with you in it?" I pulled the disc from the case and examined it; it was blank.

"Yeah, and my older brother Jake and some of my mates back in Brighton. It's pretty old. It's from back in my teen days." Oh, I just *had* to watch this now. I think he sensed my excitement too because he quickly went back to sit on the sofa while I rushed to pop the disc into the DVD player.

I sat next to him on the sofa and he put his arm around me. Something inside me was elated at the fact that we were snuggling on the sofa watching TV. That simple act meant the world to me. We watched about twenty minutes of Tristan & Co. acting like a bunch of rowdy teenagers on camera. He pointed his brother out to me and I noticed how similar they looked. There was also a part in the video where they were filming inside Tristan's house and I caught a glimpse of his mother and grandmother. His mother seemed to be tolerating the boys' behavior but his grandmother was not having any of it. I couldn't really understand what she was saying because she had a heavy English accent. Tristan was kind enough to interpret what she said because I kept asking repeatedly, "What did she say?"

Overall, I enjoyed seeing him in the environment where he grew up. I was heavily engrossed in the video and I was laughing a lot. But I noticed that Tristan seemed to be watching me and my reactions rather than watching the video. The next thing I knew, he moved closer to me and started nuzzling my neck. At that point, my attention on the video had completely disappeared.

I moved my head to the side to give him more access and he began to scatter soft kisses up my neck and across my jaw line. One of his arms was around my shoulder and the other was across the front of my waist. At that moment, I knew he wanted to 'snog'. I didn't disappoint him because I angled myself to face him, closed my eyes, and leaned in for a kiss. As soon as my lips touched his, he repositioned his arms so that they were both wrapped around me. I was leaning on him and I had one hand running through his hair and the other on his shoulder.

I felt him add more pressure to the kiss and I took that as I sign that he wanted in. I flicked my tongue out and lightly licked his lips. His mouth opened and his tongue met mine. We caressed each other's tongues and I wrapped both my arms around his neck. His hands were in my hair now; massaging my scalp. He deepened the kiss and I felt his tongue exploring my mouth. One of my hands dropped down and started making its way up his thigh. At that moment, I felt one of his hands caress the side of my breast and move towards the front where my nipples began to harden.

I was just about to swing my leg over his lap and straddle him, when I remembered the lasagna was in the oven. I ended the kiss but my mouth was less than an inch from his. My eyes were still closed and I whispered against his lips, "I have to check on our food." Then I quickly got up and dashed into the kitchen.

Fortunately, the lasagna was done and it didn't burn. I took it out of the oven and put it on the counter to cool a bit. Since dinner was ready, I went to tell Tristan that we could eat. I went back into the living room to see that he had turned off the video. His head was leaned back against the sofa and he was looking up at the ceiling. He was sitting exactly the way I left him.

I walked around to the front of the sofa and stood in front of him. He looked miserable. I gave him an apologetic look and asked, "Are you okay?"

Tristan chuckled and replied, "That was a dirty trick." We both started laughing.

"I'm sorry. The good news is that dinner's ready."

He took his time getting up and I could tell he was struggling with a hard-on. I really did feel bad but I couldn't let our dinner burn.

He followed me into the dining room but he stopped when he noticed the table setting. A huge smile lit up his face and he said, "Awww, babe. You didn't have to do this." A white lace tablecloth was covering the dining table. I had place settings for two; including goblets, plates, and silver utensils. I put a white porcelain vase in the middle of the table that contained a dozen red and white fake roses. There were two lit candles in brass candle holders on either side of the vase. I even had linen napkins rolled in white porcelain napkin holders.

"Have a seat and I'll bring you your food." I felt like adding 'my prince' at the end of my sentence.

He was still smiling and admiring the setting when he said, "Oh, I can make my own plate." He started to walk towards me as I was making my way into the kitchen, but I turned around and put a hand on his chest to stop him in his tracks.

"Oh no you won't. You're my guest." I walked over to one of the dining chairs and gestured for him to sit down.

Once he was seated, I went into the kitchen to get the bottle of wine and corkscrew and then I brought it back out into the dining room. I placed it on the table and asked Tristan to open it. His eyes widened and he exclaimed, "You got wine too?!?" He laughed and added, "I won't let you get drunk on this." Then he said in a quieter voice, "I'll try not to get drunk too."

The next things I brought out were the garlic knots and the Caesar salads. Tristan remarked that he felt like he was in a restaurant. I went back into the kitchen for the last time to get the lasagna. When I walked back into the dining room, Tristan had already started munching on his salad. He looked up at me with a guilty expression. "Oh, was I not supposed to start eating yet?"

"Sweetie, if you're hungry…by all means…eat." He watched intently as I put the lasagna in front of him. "I hope you like it." I put a serving on his plate and he took a bite. I watched with anticipation to see his reaction.

He chewed his food for a few seconds and swallowed. Then he closed his eyes briefly, looked up at me and said wistfully, "Bridget, this is…the best lasagna…I've ever had…in my life!" He didn't even wait for my response; he just started digging in.

I couldn't help but to smile at his compliment. "I'm so glad you like it." I sat down and poured the wine into both of our goblets. Then I served myself and we made a toast to our hopeful future. It wasn't long until we got into a comfortable ambiance of eating, talking, and just enjoying each other's company.

After we both had our fill (Tristan had about two and a half fills), we were still sitting at the table. Tristan leaned back in his chair comfortably, rubbed his stomach and said with an air of content, "I could get used to this." He looked at me intently and a smile slowly crept up onto his face. Then he straightened his posture and put his elbows on the table. "You're a really good cook, Bridget. I can't cook for shit and none of my mates can cook." Then he looked up at the ceiling with a thoughtful expression. "And from what I hear…none of their girlfriends can cook either." His eyes met mine and he leaned towards me to take my hand and entwine our fingers. "I guess I'm the lucky one." He was looking deep into my eyes again and he wore a serious expression.

I reached out and caressed his cheek and we were both quiet for a few seconds; just gazing into each other's eyes. No words needed to be said because our eyes conveyed everything we needed to say to each other.

After awhile, we decided to get up. Tristan helped me clear the table and load the dishes into the dishwasher. Strangely, the whole routine felt so normal to me; like it was something we did all the time. I even caught myself casually saying, "So, do you want to have a smoke now?"

He had a plate in his hand that he was about to pass to me, and he had a confused look on his face. "Huh? Why'd you ask me that? Do I look like I'm craving one or something?" He looked down at himself as if I said he had something on his shirt.

I smiled at him as I took the plate from his hand and put it into the dishwasher. Then I turned towards him and explained. "My dad...he used to smoke. And after dinner he would always have a cigarette. I just thought it was something that smokers do. You know..."

A look of understanding appeared on Tristan's face. "Oh yeah. Yeah, I would actually." We finished cleaning up the kitchen and I had him follow me into my bedroom.

When I opened the door, he realized what room it was and he started looking around curiously. He was walking around my bedroom, tapping his index finger on his chin like an inspector would when they're checking out a house. He stopped next to my queen-size bed and looked it over. Then he turned to me with a sly grin and remarked, "That's a nice bed you got there. It's very spacious...and roomy." He sat down on it and started waggling his eyebrows at me. He looked like he was about to lay down so I rushed over to him and grabbed him by the shirt.

"Oh no you don't mister! Over here." I guided him outside onto the balcony. He looked surprised when I followed him out there and sat down on a folding chair that was placed against the window. He stood on the other side away from me and lit up his cigarette. We chatted for awhile until he put it out on the bottom of his shoe and flicked it over the side of the rail.

He walked over to me and I stood up to face him. That look came across his features; the one where he looks like he's searching for something in my eyes. His eyes began to scan my face and suddenly he put his hands on my upper arms and asked, "Do you like living by yourself?" I wasn't expecting that question and I wondered what made him think of it.

I looked down for a moment and then I answered, "Yeah, I guess so. I mean, I like having my privacy and it's better than when I was living in a dorm." He looked satisfied with my answer and began to rub my arms with his hands as if he were trying to keep me warm. I slowly slid my arms around his waist and closed the gap between us. He took this as a sign that I wanted more physical intimacy so he leaned down and kissed me.

This time we seemed to sense what the other one wanted so we both opened our mouths invitingly to taste each other. Again, I could hardly taste the cigarette. I could feel the intensity of the kiss and the way his hands were roaming all over my body. My hands went underneath his shirt and I began caressing his bare skin. It was warm and I could feel his muscles shifting as he moved. His hand crept up my thigh and he pushed the hem of my dress almost up to my waist. I couldn't help myself, so I brushed my hand across the bulge in his jeans. His grip on me tightened and he moaned into my mouth. I added pressure to my hand and began rubbing him, and I felt his manhood grow and become harder with each stroke. One of his hands reached up and cupped my breast, and his other hand...the one that was on my thigh...had moved and was gripping my left butt cheek. That's when I began to feel a draft and I realized my panties were exposed.

Once again something in my brain registered that people could be watching us. I wouldn't be surprised if there were peeping-toms in the neighborhood. I broke the kiss and tried to distract him. I was breathless when I said, "I'm getting a little chilly." My distraction worked, because he released me and opened the balcony door.

When we were both warmly inside, Tristan didn't waste any time picking up where we left off. He put both his hands on either side of my head and kissed me deeply. I loved the way he kissed because there was an almost possessive nature about it. My hands lifted up the front of his shirt and I was running my hands up and down his chest. He steered me towards the bed and we both collapsed onto it.

He was lying on top of me and I could feel his erection pressing into my abdomen. I wiggled my body a little to cause some friction and then I grabbed his butt and pressed him harder against me. I was surrounded by Tristan's masculine scent. It was intoxicating to my senses and it washed over me and covered me like a downy blanket. I relished the feeling. He ground himself into me a couple times and whispered against my neck, "Ohhhh Bridget. You feel so fucking good." Then he started scattering light kisses on my neck, my collar bone and the top of my breasts.

Suddenly, I felt him reach down and lift my dress. Whoa! We had to slow down. I wasn't ready for *that* yet. I put my hand on his; the one that was creeping up my thigh and said, "Tristan, I can't sweetie."

He looked up at me with a confused expression. "Why, what's the problem?" I think I just doused him with cold water. He shifted his position and supported himself on his arms so that we were face-to-face.

My hands seemed to be a magnet for his hair because I immediately started to slowly run my fingers through it as I spoke to him. "I want to...believe me I do. I mean, I *really* do." He looked like he was about to speak so I quickly said, "But I don't want to rush things with you. I know what happens when I do and I always regret it later. I don't want to regret anything I do with you. And God, you feel so good on top of me right now and I love the way you smell." I sighed heavily and closed my eyes for a moment. Then I opened them again and regretfully rejected him. "I promise we will...just not tonight okay?"

He looked away for a minute and I thought he was upset. I moved my hand and laid it on his cheek to turn his head to face me. I looked at him curiously and asked, "Tristan, are you angry?"

He laughed softly and reassured me. "No love, I'm not angry." He caressed my cheek with the back of his hand. Then he slid off me and laid down beside me. He propped himself up on one arm to regard me for a moment while his other hand was making small circles on my stomach. It tickled but it felt so comforting. "It's okay, I understand. Really I do. I wanna wait until you're ready. The last thing I want is to make you uncomfortable or feel obligated." He bent down to softly kiss my lips. After he kissed me, he lingered there for a moment and gently rubbed his nose against mine. My heart burst at how tender he was being. Then he looked into my eyes and said softly, "I'll follow your lead."

I sat up slightly and turned on my side to face him. I moved closer to him and nuzzled my head underneath his chin. I wanted to display tenderness towards him too, so I kissed his Adam's apple. Then a naughty idea entered my mind so I murmured against his neck, "You can spend the night though." I heard him chuckle. "As long as I don't feel any poke-poke in the middle of the night." He laughed harder and I felt it vibrate in his chest.

He wrapped his arms around me and we laid there; he still fully dressed and I with my dress riding halfway up my thighs. I hooked one of my legs over his and snuggled up to him as close as was humanly possible. I was content to just lay there with my body molded against his and breathe his unique scent. I started to think of how easy it would be to fall in love with him. I put my hands underneath his shirt again and stroked his back because I just wanted to feel his warm skin. I heard him groan and then he said, "You're not making this easy, love. But I'll behave myself."

I think I was beginning to fall asleep but I heard myself ask, "Do you promise?"

Tristan kissed the top of my head and held me tighter against him. He was rubbing my back in the most soothing way. The last thing I heard before I drifted off into dreamland was him whispering, "I cross my heart."

⚮

A FAMILIAR FEELING CAME OVER me as I was waking up from a deep and pleasant sleep. I felt like someone was holding and protecting me from all the bad things in the world. I felt like I did when I was a child during a thunderstorm. The thunder would rumble loudly and the lightning would crack in the sky and illuminate my bedroom. I was afraid that the lightning would come through my bedroom window and electrocute me. I would hide my head under the covers, and wish for it to go far away and never come back. The storm became a monster in my youthful eyes.

When the fear became too much to bear, I would run into my parents' room and climb into their bed. That was the only time I did this. I would squeeze myself between them and my mother would wrap her arms around me while I buried my face in her bosom. She never said anything to me because she knew why I was there. She would feel my little body trembling, and she would soothe and comfort me. I knew with my father in the room too, the bad thunder and the mean ol' lightning wouldn't get me. He would protect me too. Sleeping with my parents during thunderstorms always made me feel warm and safe.

That's the way Tristan made me feel as I lay cradled in his arms. His scent comforted me and the warmth from his body soothed me. I felt like no one could hurt me as long as I had his strong, tattooed arms to protect me. No wonder I fell asleep so quickly last night. As my brain slowly registered that it was Saturday morning, one of my eyes slowly opened. I started to realize the changes that must have taken place some time during the night. Tristan kept to his word and didn't disturb me with any sexual advances. But I did notice that he removed my shoes and covered us both with my comforter.

For the first time in my adult life, I don't think I shifted once during sleep. My head was still nuzzled underneath his chin and my hands were still on his bare back. I also noticed that there was a lot less clothing on him than there was when we first laid down together. He was shirtless and bottomless except for a pair of boxer shorts. Because we were embraced so closely, I could feel his 'morning wood' nestled right between my thighs. He was fully-erect and I felt a little moisture in the crotch of my panties. I was shocked at first but then the mature part of my brain remembered that it happens to men sometimes while they sleep.

He draped his leg over me at some point while he was sleeping because I felt the tiny hairs on his leg tickle my leg. I couldn't help but to feel flattered by his possessive gesture. If not for his boxers and my panties, there wouldn't have been anything to prevent him from slipping himself inside me. I guess that was the closest we were going to get to having sex.

Suddenly, I thought about how nice it was to share my bed with him. I really didn't want to move because our bodies molded together so perfectly but I knew we had to get up.

When I started to wiggle my body a little to try and extract myself from him, I heard him moan and mumble a few words. He had practically wrapped himself around me and I had to figure out the best way to remove myself from his tangled web of arms and legs. I removed my arms from around him and pushed lightly at his chest. He didn't budge. Then I said hoarsely, "Tristan, wake up. It's time to get up. Come on, sweetie." I pushed him again but this time with more force. His body moved a few inches but he still didn't release me.

His chin was resting on top of my head and I heard him say sleepily, "Mmmm...no Bridget. Sleep. Stay sleep, babe."

I kissed his Adam's apple and tried to bribe him into waking up by saying, "I'll make you breakfast. I'll make you whatever you want. You know I'm a good cook." I pushed him again and he finally loosened his hold on me. I climbed out of bed and went into the bathroom.

After I took a shower, I put on my bathrobe that was hanging on the back of the door. I went over to the sink to brush my teeth. I opened the medicine cabinet to get my dental floss and when I closed it, I saw Tristan enter the bathroom...completely naked! It was at that moment I realized I didn't lock the bathroom door. He walked past me, brushed his hand across my lower back, and went to stand in front of the toilet. I was standing there in a trance; watching him with my toothbrush idle in my mouth. The next thing I knew, he lifted the toilet seat and started to pee. Whoa! Wait a minute here! I know we're comfortable with each other but I wasn't expecting all this. I pulled the toothbrush out of my mouth and exclaimed, "Hey, what are you doing?!?" Duh, I knew what he was doing but I felt I needed to make him aware of the situation.

Tristan looked over at me and smiled. Then he said very nonchalantly, "What's it look like I'm doing? I'm taking a piss."

"Yeah but...don't you want some privacy? I mean---"

A confused expression appeared on his face. "Why would I want privacy? I don't care if you see me piss."

He obviously didn't care about me seeing him naked either. I was utterly speechless. I'm a shy person when it comes to bathroom habits. I don't even like anyone *listening* to me pee, let alone watching me. I turned away from him and resumed brushing my teeth. I knew Tristan was finished because I heard the toilet flush. I'm a grown woman and I've seen naked men before so why was I feeling embarrassed to see him naked? Then I realized that once we saw each other naked, we would be totally exposed and vulnerable to each other. There's no hiding anything when you bare it all.

Tristan came over and stood next to me. "You got a spare?" He motioned towards the toothbrush I had just placed back in its holder. I bent down into the cabinet under the sink and pulled out a brand new toothbrush. I handed it to him and for some bizarre reason, I felt hypnotized. I just stood there watching him brush his teeth. We didn't speak for a few moments after he was done; we just gazed at each other. I honestly felt like I was under his spell. I felt like I would do anything he asked of me and without hesitation. Suddenly, I realized I had a golden opportunity in front of me and I wasn't passing it up. I was going to admire him in all his naked glory.

Tristan stood there almost motionless when he noticed me appraising him. His expression was open and clearly readable: 'Go ahead and look.' The primal nature in both of us suddenly emerged. I was a female and he was the male who wanted to mate with me. It was almost like he was giving me an invitation to see his quality. My eyes devoured him completely. He was so physically perfect that for a minute I thought maybe he had some work done.

I already knew how smooth his creamy vanilla skin was, but seeing him naked made me aware that it was almost flawless. The golden halo of hair on top of his head took on a 'bed-head' kind of state and I found that the look actually suited him. His blue eyes were a little puffy from just waking up but he looked adorable…almost boyish. The tattoos on his body made him look like a fallen angel who had a passion for body ink. His chest was hairless and I could see the lean muscles pronounced in his pectorals. His stomach was flat and his six-pack abs were clearly defined. He had dark blond hair scattered lightly around his navel, which began his 'treasure-trail' that led down to his 'treasure'. His penis was actually appealing; I've never seen one like it before. He was definitely blessed but not overly huge. It was the same color as the rest of his body but the head was flushed slightly pink. It was flaccid and it hung perfectly straight, without a bend to either the left or right. His sac was heavy and covered with the same dark blond hair. He had lean, muscular legs that were dusted with short blond hairs and he had perfect average-sized feet.

I was in awe of this beautiful creature that God created to grace this earth. I started to feel very emotional and I wished to tell him exactly how beautiful he was but something inside me prevented it. Tristan brought me out of my reverie because he suddenly touched my bathrobe. Then he touched a few strands of my wet hair. His eyes caught mine and he frowned. "You took a shower already?"

I looked up at him and I wondered why he looked upset. I couldn't help but to look confused. "Yeah, I did. Why?"

"Oh. 'Cause you know…I thought we could…take one together."

I began to look around the bathroom; averting my eyes from him. Now I didn't mind seeing *him* completely naked but I was feeling insecure about myself. I wasn't sure I wanted to fully expose myself to him yet. He still looked upset and I didn't like the hurt look in his eyes, so I put my hand on his cheek and caressed it gently. He didn't take his eyes off me and he leaned into my touch. God, he was pulling at my heartstrings. "I'm sorry, baby. Maybe we can shower together another time. I woke up and you looked so peaceful, so I thought I would just let you sleep for as long as you wanted." I gave him a very sympathetic look. His expression still didn't change and I felt like I needed to lighten the mood. After all, it was our first morning together. I smiled and laced my words with sarcasm when I said, "Hey, haven't you ever heard of modesty?"

He looked taken back for a minute; probably at the unexpected change of subject. Then he smiled back and gave a short laugh. "What's modesty?" He looked up at the ceiling with a thoughtful expression. "I can't say I ever heard of it."

I started laughing; partly due to his response and partly because I made him smile. I continued to unload my sarcasm on him. "Yeah, I bet you haven't. I bet you're the type of person who walks around naked when there's company in the house, huh? You're a regular exhibitionist, right?"

What Tristan did next touched a place inside my heart. He doubled-over, and the sight of this beautiful man's genuine laughter made me realize how badly I wanted to become a permanent part of his life. I honestly felt I could be content if all we ever ended up being was friends. I just wanted him to stay where I would always be able to be in his presence. If I was honest with myself, I would admit to what I was beginning to feel for this wonderful British boy.

When Tristan gained his composure, his face was still flushed from laughter. He said, "Yeah, that's about right. It's funny 'cause I think all my mates have seen my arse at least once; whether they wanted to or not." I didn't read into the latter part of his statement, I just smiled and shook my head. Suddenly, his expression turned serious. He closed the gap between us and put his arms around my waist. Oh my God, his naked Adonis form was pressing against me. It took every ounce of self-control to keep myself from running my hands all over his body. My hands started to itch with the desire to reach out.

He spoke to me and his eyes were burning into my soul. "Bridget, listen to me, love. I don't care if I'm sleeping. The next time you wake up to take a shower, *please* wake me up too. Before I fell asleep last night, I was kinda hoping we'd shower in the morning. I was actually gonna ask you if you wanted to. I wanted to wash your body..." He started to gently rock me back and forth in his arms. "And I wanted you to wash mine." My eyes widened at his confession. "And I know what you're thinking." Yeah, he probably did. He seemed to be very in-tune with me. "Remember I told you I'd follow your lead. Whatever you want to happen, that's what will happen. I promised to make love to you when you were ready and I meant it." I seriously doubted that sex would not have taken place if we were to wash each others' bodies in the shower. As a matter of fact, I was willing to bet my life on it; not because I didn't trust him...I didn't trust myself. I desired him greatly and I knew I wouldn't be able to resist him much longer.

And as suddenly as it appeared, it disappeared. His expression turned less serious and his cute dimple made itself known on his cheek again as he grinned sheepishly. "I guess I should go put my clothes back on, huh?"

I followed him back to my bedroom so he could get dressed, but I sat on the bed in my robe and waited patiently for him to finish. He watched me with an amused expression because he probably knew I wasn't going to get naked in front of him. I tried not to stare, but my eyes kept finding their way back to his gorgeous male form. But Tristan was a gentleman, and he eventually left the room and closed my bedroom door to give me some privacy.

It was late in the afternoon and we were both practically starving. Tristan insisted I heat up the leftover lasagna because he enjoyed it so much. After we ate, we spent the rest of the day lounging around, watching TV, talking, and just enjoying each other's company. We also started a few more make-out sessions but I kept them under control as to not go back on my word and actually have sex with him.

The more time I spent with Tristan, I started to realize how nice it was to share my personal space with him; to invite him into my home and treat him as if we were--- No, I wouldn't let myself start that train of thought. It was too soon and I still wasn't *exactly* sure I was his girlfriend yet.

Time seemed to pass quickly while I was having fun with Tristan. By the time evening approached, a massive headache unexpectedly crept its way into my skull. I took some Excedrin but I wasn't feeling any relief. It was around 8PM, and Tristan and I were on the sofa in complete silence. I was lying down with my head in his lap and he was softly stroking my hair. The only sound that could be heard was the early autumn wind blowing outside and rustling of the leaves on the tree in my front yard. My eyes were closed because the light in my living room was causing a pulsing sensation in the back of my eyeballs.

Suddenly, his cell phone rang and the sound made me cringe. He chatted with this mystery person for a few minutes and then he hung up. I mumbled, "Who was that?" Ouch. I decided that I wouldn't speak for the rest of the night.

His voice sounded excited. "That was my bro. Him and some of our mates are at a pub and he wanted to know if I would make an appearance." He laughed, and although I loved his voice, my headache caused any sound to feel like a hammer against my temple. I didn't respond to him, and I felt him bend slightly and move his face close to mine. His scent engulfed me and I felt momentary comfort from my pounding headache. This time he whispered, "Love, you're really hurting, aren't you?" I nodded very slowly. The next thing I knew, Tristan picked me up gently and carried me into the bedroom.

He laid me down on the bed and covered me with my comforter. I curled up into a fetal position and put a pillow over my head. I heard his footsteps, and then I heard him click the light-switch and turn off the light. The mattress dipped and I felt him crawl under the covers. He scooted closer until he was in back of me in a spooning position. He removed the pillow from my head and I felt him slip his arm around my waist. He kissed the back of neck twice and then nuzzled his head next to mine. Tristan was making this too easy...too easy to fall in love with him.

I knew from the tone of his voice earlier that he wanted to go the bar. I didn't want him to feel like he had to spend his entire weekend with me. He did have friends and a life outside of me. Plus, I was feeling like shit and I didn't want him to feel obligated to stay and nurse me. My voice was so soft that it was almost a whisper. "You can to the bar. I'll be okay, baby. Besides, you've been with me all day and all of yesterday evening. Go be with your friends, sweetie. I'll just go to sleep." Deep down inside of me I wanted him to stay but I honestly wouldn't have been that upset if he left. I knew Tristan usually partied on the weekend and I knew he couldn't be happy being cooped up in the house with me.

He didn't say anything at first. Then I heard him kick off his shoes and they landed on the carpet with a 'THUD'. I smiled inwardly because I assumed he was staying. He confirmed my assumption and I heard him whisper in the darkness, "Bridget, you just don't get it...do you, love? You're in pain and I'm not going anywhere. You're my girlfriend...and you come first." I felt him lean over me and kiss my lips. He didn't miss or fumble and I was surprised he could find them in the dark. "Go to sleep, babe. I'll be here when you wake up."

I wanted to kick myself for the way I reacted to his words. I was thankful that the room was dark and he couldn't see my face. I tried to control myself but my emotions overpowered me. My lips started to tremble and tears pricked at my eyes. I let a few of them fall and they made little wet spots on my pillow. I no longer had to wonder...because I heard it as clear as day. Tristan called me his girlfriend.

Chapter 4

WHEN I WAS IN HIGH school I was semi-popular and well-liked. I was a cheerleader but I didn't really travel in the same social circle as the rest of my squad. The same went for college. I was never a party girl and I've never been a heavy drinker. You'd never catch me doing shots or dancing on tables after getting drunk on Tequila. Nothing has really changed since I've been on my own. I have a few close friends and whenever we hang out, I'm usually the designated driver. I mean, I do enjoy a martini or a glass of wine every now and then, but I'm not the type of person who needs to get drunk in order to have a good time. To be honest, I've never been drunk in my entire life.

There were a few times when I was hanging out with Autumn and I almost succumbed to the peer pressure to drink heavily. Autumn is a natural-born party girl and whenever we go to bars or clubs, she always attracts a lot of attention. She seems to thrive on it but I think it's just part of her personality. She's very outgoing and people like to be around her.

Tristan is very similar in that respect. He's very popular and whenever I go out with him, it doesn't take long for people to surround him and want to be in his presence. He's very charismatic and personable. And because he's so attractive, he seems to have a lot of female friends. When I first realized that, it bothered me a little. But then I remembered that he admitted to being a slut so I'm sure he kept some 'friends with benefits' along the way. Since Tristan and I agreed to be honest with each other, I told him how I felt about all his female 'mates'. He quickly reassured me that those types of relationships were broken because he was now in a serious relationship with me. Since Tristan was friends with these girls before he met me, I didn't feel like I had any right to tell him to stop. As long as they respected our relationship and Tristan didn't stray back to his old ways, I was totally secure.

In addition to attracting attention when he goes out, he also gets invited to a lot of parties. Sometimes I wish I could check his calendar just to see how he's able to have free time to spend with me. Between his work schedule and his social life, I was truly amazed.

Mr. Popular came over to my apartment the Friday evening before Halloween and invited me to be his date to a Halloween party. When he came over, I was watching television because I was completely bored out of my mind. Truth be told, I didn't even have a third of the friends that he had so it wasn't often that I got invited anywhere. We were sitting on the sofa, and because I thought the party was that night, I immediately became excited.

"Sure baby, I'd love to go! But I have to get a costume first."

"Actually, it's tomorrow night."

I deflated inwardly. "Oh. And where is it?"

"In West Hollywood."

"So, what are you going as?"

While we were chatting, Tristan grabbed the remote and started flipping through the channels. His eyes were still fixed on the screen when he replied, "I have no idea. I really wasn't gonna dress up."

"What?!? Tristan, you can't go without a costume. I mean, it *is* a Halloween party."

He smiled and looked over at me. "I didn't dress up last year." Then he looked up at the ceiling with a thoughtful expression. "Oh wait, I was wearing a skeleton t-shirt." He gave a short laugh.

I smiled back at him. "Well, this year you're going with *me* and you're dressing up." It was my turn to look thoughtful because I started thinking of ideas for his costume. "Oooh! What about a Victorian vampire? We can dress you up like Lestat or something."

Tristan looked at me like I had insects crawling out of my ears. "Huh? Uh, that's a little elaborate, don't you think? I like to keep things simple, babe."

For the next few seconds I continued making costume suggestions for him and he casually rejected each one while he flipped though the channels. And just when I was about to take my ideas to a whole other level and ask him if he'd let me dress him up like a girl (after all, he's already pretty) I heard him mutter, "Fucking pigs." I glanced at the television and saw that his channel surfing landed on the show 'COPS'. A moment later the strangest thing happened; it was like a light bulb went off in his head. He looked over at me again and said excitedly, "Babe, I know what I wanna be!"

"What?"

He started chuckling and then he smiled widely as he finally made a decision. "An inmate."

I sputtered, "What? You mean, with the black-and-white striped jail uniform?"

"Nah, that's corny. I mean a *real* inmate. You know, with the orange jumpsuit that has the prisoner number on it." I don't know if Tristan started visualizing it or what, because he started laughing harder. His laughter was contagious and I was actually picturing him in a prison uniform. All of a sudden, he turned off the television and quickly stood up. "C'mon babe, let's go see if we can find one."

His enthusiasm started rubbing off on me and I replied with equal excitement. "Okay, well let me go get my purse." I went into my bedroom to retrieve it and when I came back to the living room, Tristan had already put on his coat and was holding mine out to me.

As I was putting on my coat he said, "And we can find something for you too."

When we walked into the party and costume shop, it was packed with people. At first I was surprised but then I remembered that it was the weekend before Halloween and a lot of people threw parties during that time. Plus, Tristan and I were like the rest of the people there: last-minute shoppers. It actually didn't take us long to find his costume. We found an orange prison jumpsuit with the short-sleeves and long pants. After he grabbed his costume, he smiled and said, "We have to get cuffs to go with this."

We went down another aisle and found his handcuffs. That's when I asked innocently, "What about the chains that go around your ankles?"

Tristan started laughing. "Do you want me to trip and fall on my face? How am I gonna walk with chains on my ankles?" I started laughing too. He was looking around the aisle when he asked, "What do you wanna be, love?"

I was so wrapped up in his costume, that I hadn't given any thought to my own. "I really don't know."

We started to wander around the store for a few minutes when out of the blue he said, "We should go as a couple."

"Oh, you want me to be an inmate too?" The idea of being a prisoner with him made me smile. My imagination began to run wild and I imagined us breaking out of prison together.

"Nah, that's no fun." As we continued to walk, he was tapping his middle finger against his chin. "Hmmm...what about...a bobbie?"

I scrunched my face up in confusion. "A *what?*"

Tristan smirked at my British ignorance. "A *cop*, babe."

I nodded in understanding and smiled sheepishly. "Oh, okay."

"No wait." He turned to look at me and a sly smile crept onto his face. "A *corrections* officer. Yeah, and I'm your inmate." He came over to me and put his arm around my waist. "What do you think, love? You can punish me if I misbehave...and you know I will." He waggled his eyebrows at me and pulled me closer. It seemed as if he was totally unaware of our surroundings because his face started to slowly inch closer to mine like he was about to kiss me.

Even though he seemed oblivious to our surroundings, I was fully aware that we were in a crowded store. I pulled out of his embrace and said with much zest, "That's a great idea! I wonder if they have one!"

We looked around a little more and to my surprise we found an adult female corrections officer costume. When I looked at the picture I couldn't help but notice how sexy it was. It was a gray and black patent leather dress but the top was cut low and the hem was *very* short. On the left breast there was a badge that read: **Department of Corrections**. It also came with a black baton, handcuffs, a black belt with a chain and keys, and a black cap. I said seductively, "What about this, huh? It's kind of kinky, don't you think? And you won't need your cuffs because they're included with the costume." Almost as an afterthought I said excitedly, "Oh, and I know Autumn has some go-go boots I can wear to match this!"

Tristan came to stand next to me to get a closer look but for some reason, he didn't find any humor in the costume. He wasn't speaking so I looked at him but he was still looking at the picture. When he finally spoke, I noticed the enthusiasm he displayed moments ago seemed to disappear. "Uh...yeah...that's good. As long as no one can see your knickers." I picked up the package that contained the costume and as I started to walk away, he gently grabbed my arm. His action caught me by surprise so I looked at him questioningly and he said quietly, "Just stay with me at the party, alright?" I gave him a confused look and before I could stop myself, I nodded my head in compliance. Then he let go of my arm and put his hand on my lower back as we walked towards the cash registers. He was quiet again while we stood in line and I couldn't help but wonder why he asked me to stay with him. Was he being jealous and possessive because it sure sounded that way.

It wasn't until after Tristan left my apartment that evening and I was lying in bed that I mentally slapped myself. Why didn't I ask him why he said it? Maybe it was because I already knew the answer: he wanted to make sure that no other men tried to flirt with me. At that moment, my earlier question was answered. He *was* being jealous and possessive. I just hoped that it wouldn't cause a big problem in our new relationship.

The following evening, I was getting dressed for the party when Autumn came over to bring the boots for my costume. They were actually knee-high, black patent leather with chunky platform heels. Since she was invited to the party as well, she was dressed as a gothic Lolita. Her costume was sexy, yet cute and the black corset and tutu she was wearing fit her perfectly.

After I put the boots on to complete my ensemble, we were both looking at ourselves in my full-length mirror. Because I'm not blessed with a voluptuous bosom, Autumn suggested that I wear a push-up bra. The bra had the desired effect but then I couldn't help but notice how much cleavage I was showing. I started feeling self-conscious and I tried to pull the top up in a futile attempt to cover my exposed breasts. But that just shortened the hem of the dress even more.

When Autumn saw what I was trying to do, she swatted my hands away. "You're supposed to show your tattas, honey. The whole outfit is meant to be *sexy* remember?" And she pulled the top back down.

I instinctively covered my chest with my hand. "Yeah I know but... geez."

All of a sudden, her hand flew up to cover her mouth as she gasped. "Oh my God! Wait until Tristan sees you!" She stood back so she could admire me and then she started laughing. "He's gonna make you stick to him like flies to shit."

My eyes widened at her statement because I remembered Tristan's 'request' last night. Autumn seemed to know Tristan very well and as the realization hit me, my eyes began scrutinizing her and I wondered if she was ever one of his 'friends with benefits'. I thought Autumn was very pretty and she and Tristan had similar personalities. Ever since I met Tristan, I found him to be the male version of Autumn. I couldn't help but to assume they became friends quickly when they first met. The two of them probably clicked immediately. But were they really just friends first? I wasn't going to ask because I felt it was none of my business but I was eager to know the truth.

She was actually adjusting her cleavage to expose *more* of herself when I asked quietly, "Hey Aut, have you and Tristan ever..." She turned from the mirror to look at me. "You know..."

She looked at me expectedly. "What?"

I sighed. Then for some reason, I couldn't look her in the eye. "Have you ever slept with Tristan?" I chanced a glance at her and I noticed she wasn't meeting my eyes either. Her mouth was slightly open and she was looking around my room. I also noticed that she was hesitating to answer. We were both quiet as I walked over to my bed and sat down. I looked over at her again but her expression didn't change.

When her eyes finally met mine, she pursed her lips before she said, "Ummm...why are you asking me this?"

I sighed again. "Look, I know that Tristan has a lot of female friends. And I'm like 99.9% sure that he's slept with a lot of them. I just want to know if you were included."

"Yeah, but why? You know how much he---" She abruptly ended her sentence and I looked at her quizzically.

"What?"

She quickly backpedaled. "Nothing." She slowly walked over to where I was sitting and sat next to me. She didn't say anything for a couple seconds; she just looked at me. Then she asked, "Bridge, will knowing the truth make you feel better?"

"Feel better?"

"Yeah. Like, does the desire to know eat away at you? Does the question keep you up at night?"

I continued to look at her with a confused expression. "Uh, no. I just want to know because---"

"Because *why*, sweetie?" Suddenly, she turned her body to face me and put her hands on my shoulders. Her expression and her voice softened when she said, "Bridge, sometimes it's not good to know *everything* about a man's past." She sighed. "You already know that Tristan was a slut. Can't you just leave it at that? Does it really matter who he was a slut *with*?"

Immediately after she finished speaking, I knew Autumn was purposely avoiding my question. And I had a feeling she was doing that because her answer was affirmative. I also knew that the reason she didn't want to admit the truth is because she didn't want to hurt me. Deep down inside me, I knew I would be upset if she admitted that she was sexually involved with my boyfriend in the past. I considered her to be one of my best friends and at that moment, I realized that she and I had the same understanding about best friends: you don't hurt them. And rather than lie to me...she didn't answer the question. I knew she wasn't going to, and I realized we were actually wasting time because Tristan would be coming over shortly.

I decided it was best to just drop the subject so I smiled at her and replied, "Yeah, you're right. If I knew every girl that Tristan slept with, I think it would affect my sanity." I laughed lightly. "Not to mention, it might put a strain on my relationship with him and I don't want that to happen." Autumn didn't reply; she just nodded in agreement.

About twenty minutes later, Tristan arrived at my apartment. When Autumn and I saw him in the orange prison uniform, we both busted out laughing. The front of his shirt had a prison number and the back read the same words as my costume. I noticed that he had rolled up the short-sleeves so that all the tattoos on his arms were visible. It was a good idea because the tattoos really made him look like a prison inmate. He laughed along with us but I noticed his full attention was on my costume because his eyes kept roaming all over it. If he didn't approve, he didn't express it. All he said was, "You two look fucking hot." Then he moved closer to me and said, "Babe, do you think you could make my face look like I got the piss beat out of me?" He opened his palm to reveal a small tube of fake blood. "I got this and thought you could add some blood. You know, like around my mouth or something. Or maybe you could make it look like my lip is bleeding."

I reached up and took his head in both my hands while my eyes scanned his beautiful face that I was about to falsely bruise. Then I smiled and said, "Sure, I think I can make your face look like a slab of raw meat." I laughed again.

Autumn chimed in excitedly, "Ooh! I can help too!" Then she snapped her fingers and said, "Shit, too bad you didn't get any of that prosthetic stuff so we can give you a swollen eye or a fat lip."

They followed me into the bathroom and I sat Tristan down on the toilet lid while I worked my magic. The best we could do with my makeup was make his left eye and cheekbone appear black-and-blue. We used the fake blood on the corner of his mouth and on his bottom lip. When we were finished transforming his lovely features, Tristan inspected himself in the mirror. He gingerly touched his face as if the bruises were real and remarked, "Yep, I look like the screws really did a number on me." Then he turned around and kissed me on the cheek. "Thanks, love."

"You're welcome, baby. But uh, what's a screw?" One special benefit to dating a Brit was that I learned a lot of British terms.

For a split second, Tristan's light blue eyes glazed over with unmistakable lust and his eyes greedily roamed my body again. I was surprised when he replied seductively, "You are." I looked at him in mild confusion because *now* I thought he meant 'screw' as in 'having sex'. As always, he noticed my expression and laughed. "A corrections officer, babe. I believe you Yanks in the pen refer to them as hacks."

A look of understanding came over me and at the same time Autumn whined, "Heyyyy, what about me? I did some shit too, you know." She cast her eyes down dejectedly.

Tristan laughed and hit her playfully on the arm. "I'm sorry, Aut. Thank you."

When Autumn raised her head to meet Tristan's eyes, she smiled widely and hit him back. "You're welcome, you wanker." He was forgiven, and the three of us shared another laugh.

We decided to take Autumn's snow-white Acura RSX to the party and when we arrived in West Hollywood, she pulled up to this moderately-sized mansion. We walked up to the door and when we rang the bell, we were greeted by a pretty transvestite. He was tall and he was wearing a long, straight blonde wig that looked quite humorous considering he had thick, brown eyebrows. The fuchsia dress he was wearing clung to his masculine body and his fake boobs. I was very amused by the black fishnet stockings and leopard-print high-heels. As I looked at his face, I noticed that his makeup wasn't half-bad and someone had accentuated his beautiful sea green eyes. He smiled and his voice was very friendly. "Hey guys, glad you could make it. Come on in."

I noticed that he was having difficulty walking in the heels and I laughed softly, but Tristan heard me and nudged me with his elbow. I looked up at him and he smiled knowingly. Our host seemed to assess each of us because he said, "Let's see...Aut, you look sexy, yet very cool." He nodded in appreciation. "I like, I like." Then he looked at me, but he tilted his head to the side and a confused expression appeared on his face. "Have we met?"

I was about to reply, when Tristan chimed in first. "Oh shit, you know I don't have any fucking manners, mate. This is Bridget." Then Tristan turned to me and said, "Babe, this is Chad Campbell."

I still didn't get a word in because immediately following my introduction, Chad wobbled closer to me and exclaimed with wide-eyes, "You're Bridget?!?" Even though I was smiling, I was looking at him like he was slightly crazy. "Oh wow! So you're Tristan's girlfriend, huh?" He started laughing but I noticed his eyes giving me the once-over. "I can't believe it. When he first told me he had a girlfriend, I thought he was just drunk." He continued laughing. "But I must say, you look very..." He paused and I noticed him glance over at Tristan. Then his eyes darted back at me and he finished his compliment. "Nice." Chad's actions struck me as odd and I wondered if he looked at Tristan to check his expression; to make sure he didn't say anything to me that would offend him.

I took advantage of the moment of silence and replied, "Thank you, Chad. And it's nice to meet you too. I must say, you look very *pretty*."

He beamed in obvious appreciation. "Thanks." Then his eyes turned back towards Tristan and he exclaimed once more. "Dude, that costume is perfect for you! Whose idea was it?"

Tristan looked positively proud of himself when he answered. "Mine."

"And with your tatts and the makeup...man, you really look like a convict. I guess the cops beat your ass, huh? Or maybe another inmate?" Chad seemed like he couldn't contain his amusement.

Tristan gave a very sarcastic laugh. "And you really look like a fucking ponce. Who did *your* makeup, huh? Did you do it yourself?" He stepped closer to Chad and fondled his fake boobs. "Nice tits, mate." They both started laughing and I noticed for the first time that Autumn disappeared.

I was standing there looking around but I heard Chad say to Tristan over the loud music, "You know dude, you really could be wearing this." He grabbed Tristan's shirt between his fingers and snapped it. "I hope your luck doesn't run out on you one of these days. Well, maybe now that you've got yourself a girl, you'll calm down." I looked over at them but they weren't paying attention to me. I walked closer and I heard Chad say quietly, "How many strikes is it now?"

I took one more step and right at that moment, Tristan noticed me. He spoke to Chad in a hushed voice. "Shut the fuck up, Campbell. Bridget can hear you."

By the time Chad noticed me, I was standing right in front of them. I looked up at Tristan and said flatly, "Too late." Then I peered at him curiously and asked, "What does Chad mean by 'how many strikes'? Are you in some kind of trouble, Tristan?"

Tristan stepped away from Chad and put his arm around my waist. He pulled me close to his body and at first he didn't speak. He wore a serious expression and he just looked into my eyes. I found myself getting lost in them again and the party in the background began to fade out of focus. I was grateful when he finally spoke because he actually broke the spell. "It's just that I've been arrested before, that's all." He averted his eyes from me and looked down at the floor. "More than once." Before I could reply, he took my hand and his expression seemed to lighten. "Hey, c'mon. Let me introduce you to some people."

Tristan introduced me to more of his friends and after we had some food, we went over to the dance floor. Akon's *Smack That* was blasting and Tristan and I were dancing very intimately. He was grinding against me and I wasn't doing anything to discourage him. Whenever we're together, it's like just the two of us exist and we quickly become enraptured by each other. I was having an amazing time dancing with him and he would make me laugh because every now and then he would smack my butt.

Chad was holding a costume contest a little while later, and I was pleasantly surprised when Tristan walked away with the award for 'Closest to Individual's Personality'. When he was announced as the winner, he gave a very humorous, yet vulgar acceptance speech which had mostly everyone laughing.

During the course of the night, I stayed by Tristan's side because I had no idea where Autumn had wandered off to. Chad's house was so big, she could've been anywhere. And since I really didn't know anyone else, I decided that my best bet would be to stay with my boyfriend. While I was with him, he consumed alcohol like there was no tomorrow. I think I had about one beer but I watched him drink a few of his friends under the table. I was actually surprised that it took him a long time to finally become inebriated. But when he did, it was a very humorous sight to see.

When I noticed Tristan get to a point where I didn't think he could stand up by himself, I spotted an unoccupied loveseat and dragged him over to it. We sat down and he leaned his head back against it and closed his eyes. I was worried that he would fall asleep so I called his name and lightly slapped his cheek. He immediately opened his eyes and looked at me in a drunken haze. "Huh? Don't worry, love. I'm not sleeping." His words were slurred and for some strange reason, his British accent was even more pronounced. His eyelids drooped heavily, a sexy yet drunken smile appeared on his face, and he moved closer to me. He put his arms around me and began to nuzzle my neck. I heard him inhale deeply and his voice was muffled when he said, "You smell so fucking good." Then he looked up at me and it took a tremendous amount of will power to keep myself from laughing in his face. He was gazing at me under half-closed lids and the makeup on his face was smeared. I was willing to bet that most of it was on my neck. "Babe, if I was really locked up...I'd want a conjugal visit with you." But he didn't say 'conjugal'. In his drunken state, he actually said 'con-zha-lul'. He started placing light kisses on my face and in between the kisses he said, "You'd visit me, right?"

I chuckled softly and decided to humor him. "Yes baby, I'd visit you. But conjugal visits are only for inmates who have wives."

Tristan ceased his kisses and looked into my eyes. His voice turned as serious as possible considering the state he was in. "Then we'd just lie and say you were my wife." And just like that, the seriousness dissipated and he became flirtatious once more. He rubbed his cheek against mine as if he were a giant feline and then rested his head in the crook of my neck again. "If I was in jail and you were my screw...you'd come in my cell, right? You'd let me shag you, wouldn't you?" Once he said that, I couldn't contain my laughter any longer but he didn't let up. "I'd shag you right on that little fucking cot. Or maybe up against the cell bars." He looked up at me again but this time his eyes roamed over my body again. "All the inmates would probably wanna shag you dressed like that. Bridget, you look so fucking sexy that I just wanna..."

I was looking at him in pure amusement but the next thing I know, he leaned over and captured my mouth in a deep kiss. He surprised me even further because the kiss wasn't sloppy; it was firm, demanding, and I actually felt the intensity in my toes. His warm tongue swept through my mouth and I tasted a cocktail of alcoholic beverages. We both ended the kiss because we needed to come up for air. Then all of a sudden, he removed his arms from my around body and cupped my face. His tone turned serious again when he said, "I'd probably have to shank someone if they touched you though."

His statement caused me to look at him with wide-eyes. Was he really serious or was that the alcohol talking? Just as I was about to reply, I felt someone grab my arm. I looked up and I saw Autumn pulling me to my feet. "C'mon Bridge, I want you to meet some folks!" Once I was on my feet, Tristan suddenly stood up and grabbed my other arm. For a couple seconds, they both had me in a slight tug-of-war.

Tristan exclaimed loudly, "No Autumn! She's with me tonight!" But he didn't say her name correctly. He actually said 'oddom'.

Autumn looked at Tristan like he was insane and quickly released me. Then she walked over to him and pushed at his chest which caused him to fall back onto the loveseat. "Relax there Mr. Hathaway. I'll take good care of her." She took my arm that was now free from Tristan's grip and started guiding me out of the room.

I turned my head to look back at Tristan and he was sitting on the edge of the loveseat yelling, "You better make sure no blokes try to touch her naughty bits! 'Cause if they do, there's gonna be some fucking con…se…qu…" I knew my baby was trying to say 'consequences'.

As Autumn and I were leaving a very drunk Tristan behind, she laughed and remarked, "Tris is a fucking train wreck!"

She actually took me downstairs to where Chad had an indoor pool. There were a lot of people down there mingling and I saw some people were swimming in the heated pool. I knew it was heated because I saw the wispy steam coming off the surface of the water. Autumn introduced me to some people and we hung out by the pool for awhile. Then we went back upstairs to hang out with some other people. It was probably about an hour since she abducted me from Tristan, that a frantic brunette approached me and said breathlessly, "Hey, your boyfriend is about to get into a fight!"

I looked at this mystery girl in shock and Autumn and I quickly followed her. I could hear Tristan's voice with his British accent yelling, "SAY THAT SHIT AGAIN YOU FUCKING TOSSER! I'LL RIP YOUR FUCKING THROAT OUT! COME OVER HERE AND SAY IT!"

When we finally arrived on the scene, I was torn between being concerned and being amused. Chad had his arms around Tristan's waist and was holding him back but he wasn't wearing his wig. It must've fell off because I saw it lying a few feet away from him and his natural brown hair was exposed. He was also wearing one shoe and it seemed as if Tristan was stronger than him because Chad's feet were sliding across the polished floor as Tristan inched closer and closer to his intended target.

I looked across from them and a guy dressed like a football player seemed to be the target. He was about the same height as Tristan but noticeably bulkier. He had spiky brown hair, a square jaw, and those two black marks under his eyes that real players use to eliminate glare. He pretended to be shivering when he retorted back to Tristan, "Oooooh! I'm soooo scared. Go and play with your boyfriend, blondie!"

I quickly assessed the situation and I stepped into the space between Tristan and his opponent. As soon as I did, the football player roughly grabbed my arm and put his other hand on my butt. I whipped my head towards him and he said brazenly, "Hey Red, how'd you like to put those cuffs on me?" Then he licked his lips and gave me the once-over.

In that same second, I yanked my arm out of his grasp and slapped his face. He chuckled in amusement and the Fiery Redhead inside me emerged like a phoenix from the ashes. "Don't you fucking touch me!"

He rubbed his cheek and smiled. "Awww, c'mon Red. Don't be like that."

"Look asshole---" I fell short of completing my sentence because I saw a sudden movement in the corner of my eye that caught my attention. I looked over at Tristan and what I saw honestly made me feel sorry for anyone who decided they were bold enough to cross him.

Tristan's blue eyes were practically blazing and the drunken man I left earlier had disappeared; now he looked completely lucid. When this guy grabbed me and touched my 'naughty bits', Tristan literally freaked out. He ripped himself from Chad's strong hold which caused the shorter boy to stumble and fall to the floor. I heard a few people gasp in surprise and I stood there in complete shock. Tristan looked directly at the football player and spoke with one single intention. "You're fucking dead."

It took exactly two seconds for me to turn my head towards the football player and see him slowly inch back, and turn my head back towards Tristan and see him approach menacingly. But Tristan didn't charge forward; he was calculating his movement like a predator would against a competing predator. For the first time since I've known him, I saw how intimidating my new boyfriend could be. While I was watching the violent scene about to unfold, something in my mind realized that no one else was intervening to try and prevent the fight; not even Chad and it was *his* house. I felt like I had to stop Tristan from getting his face bruised for real...even though I knew he'd probably cause most of the damage. Then I started thinking about what Chad said earlier about Tristan and his 'strikes'. Oh God help me if the police had to come and take him away.

I immediately approached Tristan and did the first thing I could think of to distract him: I kissed him firmly on the lips. To my relief, it worked because I felt him kiss me back. With my lips still pressed against his, I quickly put one end of the handcuffs around my wrist and snapped the other end on his wrist. He broke the kiss to look down at what I just did. Then he looked up at me and was about to speak. I spoke first and said softly, "Just come with me, baby. You need to cool off." Surprisingly, he complied with me and we started to walk away, but not before I heard Chad yell at the football player and tell him to leave.

While we were walking, I noticed Tristan began to stagger again. I guess he was still drunk after all. I guided him upstairs and we approached an open door which led to an empty bedroom. I took the keys off my chain and released him from the handcuffs.

We went inside the room and he actually made it to the bed before he collapsed on it. I closed the door and then I sat on the bed next to his legs. When I looked over at his face, I saw that his eyes were open halfway and he was gazing at me. I scooted up the bed until I was sitting closer to his body and I started threading his soft blond hair through my fingers. I made sure the pads of my fingertips massaged his scalp and he made a sound of contentment and closed his eyes. I knew he was calm and when I spoke, my voice was gentle. "What did that guy say to piss you off, sweetie?"

His eyes were still closed and he mumbled when he talked. "He was talking about how you looked. I heard him say that he wanted to see you get yourself off by putting your stick thing in your cunt." He paused and attempted to correct himself. "I mean...your vagina." But Tristan didn't say 'vagina', he really said 'vej-ine'. "So I said, 'Oi! That's my girl you're talking about you fucking arsehole!' and he was all like, 'So what'." He paused again. "I was about to show him exactly *what*."

I laughed and shook my head after I listened to Tristan explain what caused him to turn psycho and defend my honor. "Thanks for defending me...even though I *do* look kind of slutty."

He sat up slightly and looked at me. Then he tilted his head to the side to regard me beneath lowered lids. His speech was still slurred when he said, "I don't care what you're wearing, babe. I'll always defend you."

I smiled warmly because he was being so sweet and I gently caressed his face. "Awww, baby." He smiled back at me and just as I was leaning closer to try and kiss him, he fell back onto the bed. I looked down at his still form and his eyes were closed again. But this time I realized that he actually passed out. I bent over my defender's sleeping body to take my kiss and then I snuggled up close and put my arms around him. Being that close to Tristan always soothes me, so it was only natural for me to fall asleep.

The next thing I remembered was someone poking me in the shoulder. I opened my eyes and realized the sun was shining brightly through the opened curtains. I heard someone chuckling above me and I looked up and saw Chad looking down at me and Tristan with an amused expression. He was dressed in men's clothes and his hair was wet like he just took a shower. My voice was thick with sleep when I asked, "What time is it?"

"A little after twelve-thirty," he replied in a voice still laced with glee.

"Is Autumn still here?"

"No, she left last night."

I rubbed at my eyes and suddenly I heard Tristan's hoarse voice next to me say, "If you're looking at her knickers Campbell, I'm gonna fucking kill you." Right after he said it, I felt Tristan's hand on my partially exposed rear end. Even though I just woke up, that didn't stop me from flushing in embarrassment. I quickly reached down and tugged the back of my dress.

Chad started chuckling again but he quickly stopped and replied innocently, "I wasn't looking...Scout's honor." He put up some other finger gesture that was in no way related to the Boy Scouts. Somehow I doubt the 'one-finger salute' was very honorable.

Tristan was complaining of a hangover as he tried to remove himself from the bed. It actually served him right for all the drinking he did last night but I didn't say that to him. Instead, I asked Chad to take me and Tristan back to my apartment.

When we got there, I made him a pot of strong coffee. He was sitting at my dining room table with his head resting on his arms. Every now and then, he'd lift his head to take a sip of the coffee. I sat in a chair adjacent to him and watched him in utter amusement. Seeing Tristan with a hangover was very new to me. At one point he looked up at me and said, "I'm sorry for the way I was acting last night. I was so fucking drunk." He tried to laugh but he winced and grabbed his head.

"It's okay, Tristan. You weren't *that* bad, except of course when you were about to beat up that jerk. But I'm glad it didn't escalate into a physical fight."

He took another sip of his coffee. Then his voice turned hard when he said, "I don't like anyone disrespecting you, love. And I won't hesitate to kick any bloke's arse if they do. I don't care who it is. I'm sorry, but that's just the way I am."

I wasn't used to having a man so protective of me and I was actually flattered. But I wanted Tristan to know that I've held my own for a long time. "That's sweet...really. But I can handle myself."

Tristan looked up at me again but this time the look in his eyes was different. I didn't see any post-drunkenness clouding his vision. And when he spoke, his voice was very roguish with an underlying sexy hoarseness. "Yeah, I know you can. I saw how you slapped the piss out of him. You're a fiery little redhead, aren't you?"

A sexy grin appeared on my own face when I replied, "That's one stereotype I *definitely* live up to."

All of a sudden, Tristan stood up and I was surprised when he walked straight over to me and pulled me up from my chair. He quickly wrapped his arms around me and kissed me passionately. His mouth was so warm because of the hot coffee and I took delight in exploring it with my tongue. He moaned softly into my mouth and I felt him spring to life and rub his hardness against me. I grabbed his butt to press him harder against me and I rubbed against him in return. God, this boy felt so good. When he ended the kiss, he spoke in the same raspy voice, "That shit turns me on. Seeing you put someone in their place. As long as you're not angry with *me*." Before I could respond, he swooped down once more to continue his assault on my mouth.

We needed to come up for air and when we did, I took that opportunity to ask, "Tristan, what about your headache?"

A sly grin appeared on his face. "What headache?" Then I heard him drop something on the dining room table. It made a clanking noise and when I looked over towards the sound, I saw my silver handcuffs lying there. He kissed my lips to garner my attention and then he spoke in a very natural, seductive tone, "Make sure you don't lose those."

I smiled affectionately at my devilishly handsome boyfriend. As I gazed into Tristan's azure eyes, I started thinking about how different but alike we were. I was honestly surprised to discover that we both have a fiery temper. But I never would've imagined that someone like me would end up with a British 'bad-boy'. I'll admit that I used to fantasize about it but I never thought it would actually come true. Tristan pressed his soft lips against my forehead and I realized that I no longer had to dream…because my reality was so much better.

Chapter 5

HOLIDAYS ALWAYS MAKE ME NOSTALGIC. I have a significant childhood memory for just about every holiday. One fond Thanksgiving memory I have was when I was ten years old. It was the last time I was with my great-grandmother. That year my whole family celebrated the holiday at my grandparents' house in Oregon. My nana lived there too and I remember her telling me stories about when she was a little girl back in the 1910's. Her stories would always fascinate me, and me and my cousins would sit around her feet and listen in wide-eyed amazement. I will never forget Nana and her wonderful stories.

This Thanksgiving I was going to my parents' house in Sacramento. Tomorrow was the holiday and my mother called me after I got home from work to remind me to bring the pumpkin pies. She used to make the pies every Thanksgiving but one year I asked her to show me how to make them. Then one day out of pure curiosity, I began to experiment with her recipe to make my own *special* recipe. To my surprise, both my mother and father agreed that my version tasted better than Mom's original. Ever since then, I was in charge of making the pumpkin pies for Thanksgiving.

I did remember about the pies and I was getting the ingredients out of the fridge when I started thinking about Tristan. I started to wonder what he was doing for the holiday. Since he's British, I wasn't sure if he even celebrated Thanksgiving. Plus, with the exception of his brother, the rest of his family was in England. Then I began to realize that we really haven't spoken about our holiday plans. Right at that moment, I felt like a bad girlfriend. I was going away tomorrow and I didn't even tell him.

I was about to pick up the phone and call him when I heard the doorbell. It was Wednesday evening and I was dressed for baking. I expected to get flour, pie filling, and any other kind of pie ingredient on me. I was wearing an old, over-sized UCLA sweatshirt underneath a pink and white checkered apron which read: *I'd tell you the recipe, but then I'd have to kill you.* An old pair of faded-blue jeans and fluffy pink slippers rounded out my frumpy ensemble. My hair was in a ponytail and I knew I had a bit of flour on my face because some of it landed on me when I sprinkled some onto my cutting board. Basically, I looked a mess.

I was a little irritated at being disturbed because I had baking to do but I wiped my hands on my apron and ran to the door. I quickly looked into the peep-hole and I saw a familiar head of blond hair. And just like that…my mood changed. I started to feel giddy like a schoolgirl whose crush is coming over for a study date. My mood was changing like the tides because next I became self-conscious about my appearance. I cracked the door open and poked my head out. "What are you doing here?"

Tristan looked surprised at my question. "Do I need a reason? I'm sorry love, I just wanted to see you." Then he looked at me curiously. "Why are you hiding from me?" He stepped closer to me, put his hand in the space between the door and the frame and pushed. I didn't put up any resistance and the door opened. As he was taking in my appearance he said, "Wow Bridge, what *have* you been doing in there? Having a bake sale or some shit?"

I gave a nervous laugh while trying to make myself presentable. Then I stepped to the side to let him enter. He came in and I closed the door, and then I turned around to face him. I took his helmet from him and put it on the side table. This table seemed to be the regular spot for it whenever he came to visit. I watched him take off his coat and hang it in the hallway closet. I was touched by the way he was becoming so familiar with my apartment.

I took a moment to look over my boyfriend and I saw that he was wearing his signature style…t-shirt, baggy jeans, and boots. His t-shirt was black and the front had some graphic and words from a rock concert but I couldn't make it out because it was faded. His jeans were coincidentally the same color as mine and he had on tan Timberland boots. He always had the 'bed-head' look going on with his hair whenever he took off his helmet. It actually made him look even sexier and my fingers itched to run through it. After I snapped myself out of my admiration of him, I remembered his sarcastic question. "No, I'm not having a bake sale but I *am* baking."

He closed the closet door, came over to me and kissed me firmly on the lips. When he pulled away from me, a curious expression crossed his features. He brushed something off my cheek and looked at it on his hand. "I can see that. What is this…flour or something?" He put his hand up and showed me the white powder on his palm. I laughed inwardly because I knew I had flour on my face.

"Yeah, I'm making pumpkin pies for---" At that moment, I remembered I had to tell him about Thanksgiving. Then I immediately started worrying that he would be upset with me for telling him my plans at the last minute. I had a feeling that he could see my train of thought like you change the channels on a television. He was watching my face intently so I knew he saw it. Tristan has always been honest so I decided that he deserved nothing less from me. "I'm making pies for Thanksgiving." He didn't say anything; he just looked at me as if he were waiting for me to explain further. "Yeah…um, I'm going to my parents' tomorrow for the holiday and I always bring the pumpkin pies."

Then he smiled at me and I was suddenly relieved. "You know what? I forgot tomorrow is Thanksgiving."

I was happy that he wasn't upset but I was curious about this question so I asked, "You don't celebrate it? It's because you're British, right?" Just as the questions came out of my mouth, I felt ignorant. What a stupid, uninformed assumption I just made. But then I remembered that Thanksgiving really *is* an American holiday.

Tristan didn't seem offended. He actually looked amused; probably amused by my ignorance. "No, I celebrate it. Well, I do ever since I've lived in The States. Sometimes one of my mates invites me to spend it with their family, but usually it's just another day for me. I'll admit that I do look forward to all the food that Rick brings home though." He gave a short laugh.

I started to wonder if he had already received any invitations. Truthfully, I wanted to spend Thanksgiving with him and introduce him to my parents. I figured there was only one way to find out if he was available. I gave him a hopeful look and asked, "So...do you already have plans for tomorrow?"

Tristan has the ability to charm the socks off me. It's like he always knows exactly what to say to make me want to jump on him and have my way with him. His cute dimple made an appearance on his cheek, and he moved closer to me and put his arms around my waist. My God, the man's scent was intoxicating. And his words were like butter. "Even if I did...I would cancel my plans and spend the holiday with you, love. I'd rather be with you anyway. You know you're my favorite person." The pies could wait. I needed to bask in all that was Tristan for awhile.

Tristan offered to help me with the baking and he stayed until I took the last pie out of the oven. He wrapped them himself and put them in the fridge for me. Before he left, I told him that I would pick him up at his house tomorrow afternoon so we could drive to my parents' house. He asked me if he should bring anything and I told him to just bring his gorgeous ass to the front door when I ring the doorbell.

That night I called my mother to tell her I was bringing a guest. I wasn't specific about who I was bringing and she was immediately suspicious. Whenever I speak to my mother on the phone, she always asks me if I'm seeing anyone. I'm only twenty-four years old but she already pressures me about grandchildren. So you can understand my anticipation to see the look on her face when I introduce her to my new 'boyfriend'. In addition to being anxious, I was also dreading the possibility that she might embarrass me in front of him. My mother has always come across as a bit of a snob which causes me reluctance whenever I introduce *anyone* to her. She's the wife of a very successful physician and the head of the advertising department for a prominent cosmetic company. I wasn't nervous about Tristan meeting my father because he's very laid-back. He's never been one of those fathers who make your boyfriend pee his pants whenever he meets him.

In addition to being somewhat 'uppity', my mother was also a fashion critic. I kept that in mind as I was getting dressed Thanksgiving afternoon and made sure I wasn't *too* casual. After I was done getting ready, I went into the kitchen and took the wrapped pies out of the fridge. I was putting on my jacket when I decided to call Tristan and tell him that I was on my way. I called his cell phone but he didn't answer, so I tried his house phone and his roommate Rick answered the phone.

"Hey Rick, is Tristan there?"

"Hey, what's up Bridget? Yeah he's here. He's uh...in his room... getting dressed." Rick started chuckling and I wondered what he was laughing at.

My curiosity got the best of me. "What's so funny?"

"Huh? Oh, you'll see when you get here."

"O...k...well, tell Tristan I'm on my way."

When I got to their house, I saw Tristan's black and lime green Kawasaki in the driveway behind Rick's midnight blue Ford Mustang. I went up to the door and rang the bell. Rick answered the door and he wasn't wearing anything but a pair of blue-and-white checkered boxer shorts. About a month ago, I came to the conclusion that most of Tristan's friends were attractive. Not as attractive as him in my opinion, but they definitely attracted more than their fair share of the female population whenever they traveled in a pack. Rick was tall, muscular, and had dark brown hair with eyes to match. His hair was longer than Tristan's and it was in a shaggy cut that curled on the ends. He also had thick dark brows, a five o'clock shadow, and a very seductive-looking mouth.

Rick moved to the side to allow me to enter and when I walked into their living room, I noticed the place didn't look like they cleaned much since the last time I visited. There were empty pizza boxes and other assortments of take-out boxes and fast-food bags scattered around. I also saw lots of empty and half-empty beer bottles and cans. I even saw a few dirty clothes on the floor and I recognized one of Tristan's t-shirts. This house definitely belonged to a couple of young bachelors. Rick was looking at me with a huge smile on his face, and his expression looked like a child who just did something naughty and *wanted* you to see it. I looked at him questioningly and he simply said, "He's in his room."

I went to Tristan's bedroom door and knocked. He gave me permission to enter and when I came in, he was standing motionless in front of a full-length mirror. What I saw truly shocked me; he wasn't dressed *at all* like himself. He was wearing a long-sleeve white button-down shirt with a black and navy striped tie. His shirt was tucked into a pair of black trousers that looked tight and uncomfortable. He was also wearing black dress shoes with pointed tips. His hair was combed neatly...with a part on the side! And I noticed he wasn't wearing an earring. My eyes were wide and my mouth was hanging open in utter amazement. This was not the Tristan I was used to. I stood next to him and spoke to him in the mirror. "Why are you dressed like that? And where did you get these clothes? Are they yours?" He didn't give a response. Maybe he was as shocked as I was at his appearance. I placed my palm on his cheek and turned his head gently to face me. I looked into his eyes and my voice was slightly concerned. "Are you alright, baby?"

The only thing he said was, "Do you think I look alright to meet your parents?"

Now I finally understood. I couldn't help but feel flattered that he went through the trouble of making himself look so...unlike *him*, just for my parents. I took his arm and made him follow me over to his bed. We sat down on it and I ruffled his perfect hair to give him his 'bed-head' style. Then I smiled at him and said, "Tristan, listen to me, sweetie. I want you to be *you* when you meet my parents. Dress however you want. I know you're not comfortable wearing this." I looked down at his shoes and laughed lightly. "Please change into something more comfortable. I'll wait for you in the living room, okay?" Then I got up and went into the living room to wait for him.

After I cleared some of the junk off their sofa, I sat down and waited. Rick came right over and sat down next to me. He was smiling again and he looked like he could no longer hold in what he wanted to say. "So... how'd you like Tristan's get-up?" Then he busted out laughing.

I smiled back at him. "Did you put him up to it? Are those really his clothes or did he borrow them from someone? I know they're not yours because you two don't wear the same size."

Rick could hardly contain himself when he answered me. "I have no idea. I woke up and went into his room to ask him something, and I saw him putting on the tie. I thought I walked into the '*Twilight Zone*.'" Rick's laugh was contagious and soon we were both sharing a laugh over Tristan's sudden transformation.

Tristan came out of his room about fifteen minutes later looking more like himself. He also looked more relaxed, but he had a smirk on his face when he saw the identical look of surprise that was on me and Rick's faces. Rick spoke first. "Now *that's* more like it bud. You had me worried there for a minute." Tristan was wearing a black t-shirt underneath a zipped black hoodie with gray inner lining. He had on blue baggy jeans and black boots. I noticed he combed his hair again, and he was wearing his silver hoop earring and his black rubber necklace.

I walked over to him and hugged him tightly. I kissed him lightly before I whispered against his lips, "Glad to have you back, baby." We said our goodbyes to Rick and then we left.

When we got to my parent's house, Tristan carried the pies and we walked up and rang the bell. This Thanksgiving was going to be very small; just me, my parents, and Tristan. I sensed some tension reverberating from my boyfriend so I glanced over at him and noticed his jaw was set hard. I placed my hand on his arm and said in a soothing voice, "Just relax, Tristan. They're going to love you." I gave him a reassuring smile and his face seemed to relax.

My father opened the door and I heard Tristan inhale quickly. My father greeted us with a warm smile and gave me a big hug. When he released me he said, "Bridget, sweetheart! It's so good to see you again. Happy Thanksgiving! Oh, your mother's in the kitchen." Then he looked over at Tristan and his eyes widened. "And who's this strapping young man?" I looked over at Tristan and he was grinning but I could tell he was still nervous.

"Dad, this is Tristan." I paused intentionally. "My boyfriend."

My father's toffee eyes widened in surprise. "Oh…I see. Well, nice to meet you, Tristan." He went to shake Tristan's hand but stopped short when he noticed he was carrying the pies. "I would shake your hand but I see you're carrying my little girl's pumpkin pies."

This time Tristan spoke. "Nice to meet you too sir."

"Oh, call me Dr. Monahan. And I see you've got an accent. Are you English?" His eyes widened in surprise again. "My girl's got herself an English gentleman?" He laughed and I noticed the crinkles in the corner of his eyes. I knew he was genuinely happy when I saw the crinkles.

"Yes sir…I mean Dr. Monahan." At that moment, I heard my mother's voice coming from the kitchen.

"Brad, is that Bridget?"

"Yes Sharon, it's her and her…*guest*." My father winked at us and opened the door wider for us to enter. He took the pies from Tristan and said, "I'll just put these in the kitchen. And sweetie, show Tristan around, will you?" Then he walked away towards the kitchen.

That's when I saw my mother rush out. She was wiping her hands on her apron and smiling brightly. When she reached us, her emerald eyes looked over at Tristan and her smile fell for a second. I noticed it, but I wasn't sure if Tristan did.

She gave me a big hug and then she looked over at Tristan again. I could tell she was wearing one of her fake smiles. Without taking her eyes off him she asked, "And who's your friend, honey?"

I was feeling so happy and proud to say what I was about to say. "Mom, this is *my boyfriend* Tristan." And I purposely stressed the words 'my boyfriend'.

She quickly gave him the once-over and said with false kindness, "I see. Well, welcome to our home Tristan." My mother's behavior was causing me to wonder what problem she had with him. Couldn't she see how absolutely beautiful he was?

Surprisingly, Tristan mustered up enough courage to actually say more than one sentence. "Thank you Mrs. Monahan. I'm so glad Bridget invited me. It's nice to finally meet you and your husband. Bridget's told me a lot about you." He gave my mother his magnificent smile and a part of me felt that she didn't deserve to receive it because she wasn't exactly being genuinely warm towards him.

Once we were done with introductions, I showed Tristan the rest of the house. Eventually my father caught up with us and took him into the living room. They were watching TV and talking, and my father seemed to get him to relax because I heard the two of them laughing. I knew I wouldn't have to worry about my father embarrassing me; it was my mother I had to worry about. And sure enough, she didn't disappoint.

I was in the kitchen helping her with the food and she didn't mention Tristan until we were about to start bringing the food out into dining room. I was putting the cranberry sauce in a serving bowl when she finally spoke. But when she did, it was like she had been holding in her comment all day. "So, where'd you find him?" Her tone suggested that she thought Tristan was some stray dog I picked up off the street.

I immediately became defensive. I tried to keep my voice low as to not have Tristan and my father hear, but I felt my self-control slipping with every word. "What do you mean, *where did I find him?*' He's not some animal I picked up off the street, Mother! He's my boyfriend! And for your information, we *met* through a mutual friend."

She didn't look surprised at my outburst. She simply shrugged and replied, "I was only asking, Bridget."

I went over to her and whispered harshly, "What's your *problem* with Tristan anyway? I saw how you were looking at him."

She gave me a condescending look and clucked her tongue. Then she laughed softly. "Oh come now, Bridget. He's *English* right? Honey, he looks like...Euro-trash to me." Now I was outraged. How dare she say that about Tristan! She didn't even know him and she barely spoke to him. I opened my mouth to unload my rage but she put a hand up and continued. "I'm sure he's a nice boy and all, it's just that I would've expected you to choose someone a little more..." She looked up with a thoughtful expression as she tried to carefully choose her next words. "Refined. Yes, that's it...more refined. I mean, darling he looks like one of those boys who hang out at the mall. How old is he anyway...like nineteen, twenty?"

I was grinding my teeth together in anger because of her cruel words. I had so much I wanted to say and most of it involved a string of curse words, but I didn't speak to my parents that way. The only thing I said to her was, "For your information, he's twenty-three! And how *dare* you call him trash! You don't even know him and you hardly spoke to him!" I walked away from her and grabbed the bowl of cranberry sauce. When I was almost out of the kitchen I turned my head and added, "Dad likes him!"

The atmosphere surrounding Thanksgiving dinner was surprisingly calm. Tristan and my father seemed to hit it off really well. They both had a love of soccer, or as Tristan called it: 'footie'. My mother didn't really speak to him unless he asked her a question. Tristan is very perceptive and I knew that he knew my mother didn't care for him too much. I started to get really upset because her attitude towards him was not justified. I didn't see a problem with the way he looked and he certainly wasn't Euro-trash.

After we had dinner and dessert, we all helped to clear the table. My mother wouldn't let me and Tristan help with the dishes and I was glad because I didn't want to be around her. Tristan noticed the change in my mood and asked me if I would come outside with him while he had a cigarette.

We went outside on the front porch and I sat on the porch swing while he stood nearby and smoked. I was quiet and deep in-thought because I was still mulling over what my mother said about him. He didn't speak to me until after he put his cigarette out. Then he came over and sat next to me on the swing. He took my hand and entwined our fingers. He looked into my eyes and said, "What's the matter, love?" The sound of his voice and his endearment broke my defenses and I started crying. He quickly wrapped his arms around me and started rubbing my back. Then he whispered, "It's your mum, isn't it? She doesn't like me, does she?"

I was sobbing through my tears but I managed to say, "No, and for *hiccup* no good *hiccup* reason." I was making his shoulder wet with tears but I knew he didn't mind.

He released me and wiped the tears from my face. "I kinda figured she didn't like me 'cause she wouldn't talk to me." He chuckled and continued. "She wouldn't even look at me. But hey, it's okay babe. At least your dad seems to think I'm an alright bloke." Even if my snobby mother thought Tristan was 'trash', he was *my* trash.

I gave him a sad smile in return. I composed myself enough to speak without sounding like a sobbing mess but my voice was shaky. "She didn't even give you a chance. She just took one look at you and formed an unwarranted opinion. God, she just makes me sick sometimes."

Then he said something that made me realize how lucky I was to have him. "Don't be upset, love. I don't really care anymore if your mum likes me or not. Honestly, this is the best Thanksgiving I've ever had." He tilted his head to the side and smiled beautifully at me. "I spent it with my girlfriend."

I blushed furiously and tried to look away from him but he wouldn't let me. He put his hands on either side of my face, looked deep into my eyes, and kissed me. His kiss was so tender and loving that I felt myself leaning into him. We wrapped our arms around each other and continued to kiss like there was no tomorrow. I held him tighter and at that moment I decided that no one's opinion of him was going to stop me from lov--- Whoa, wait a minute! Was I falling in love...right now? Right on my parent's front porch? Suddenly I got scared; scared of my own feelings and emotions. I pulled out of his embrace and stood up. I made the decision that it would be better if we both left Sacramento. "Tristan, I want to go home."

My father was upset when I told him that we were leaving but I knew that he knew the reason why. Tristan was still polite to my mother; the woman who couldn't stand him for no good reason, when he said his goodbye. She tried to look apologetic towards me but I just brushed her off.

Tristan and I were pretty quiet on the ride back. I was still too upset to talk about my mother's behavior. He probably knew exactly how I was feeling so he didn't ask any questions. Honestly, I was so disappointed in her because all she ever talked about was how she wanted me to find someone special. Then when I did find someone special and introduced him to her, she couldn't accept him with open arms. I thought parents are supposed to want their children to be happy. Couldn't she see how happy I was with him?

It wasn't until we arrived back in Los Angeles that he finally spoke. "Bridget, don't take me home."

I turned to him with a questioning look and asked quietly, "Why not?"

He smiled at me and said, "I wanna be with you tonight. Your mum didn't ruin our Thanksgiving. The night's not over, love." And he waggled his eyebrows at me; always the naughty flirt. Surprisingly, I started to feel better. I actually felt elated at the idea of spending the rest of the holiday alone with *my* favorite person.

When we got back to my apartment, Tristan informed me that he was still hungry. That actually amazed me because of all the food we ate at my parents' house. Since we brought one of the uneaten pumpkin pies home, I cut him a huge slice and served it to him as he settled himself on the sofa. For some reason, the apartment was chilly so I turned on the heat, and took a colorful hand-knitted throw out of the hall closet. The throw was old and it was made for me by my nana before she passed away. When I joined him on the sofa, I snuggled up next to him and covered us both with the throw. Tristan turned on the TV and handed me the remote before he started to dig into his probably sixth helping of pie.

I flicked through the channels and my eyes caught the beginning of one of my favorite romantic movies: 'The Notebook'. I let out a sound of joy and looked over at Tristan with a smile. My smile wavered slightly when I realized that he may be dreading the fact that he has to suffer through another one of my 'chick flicks'. But I was pleasantly surprised when he grinned back at me; his mouth full of pumpkin pie, and nodded in approval. Midway through the movie, he surprised me again when he put a forkful of pie in front of my mouth. I looked up at him and he smiled widely in encouragement before I took a bite. Tristan sharing with me warmed me even more than Nana's throw so I snuggled even closer to him. I was content being surrounded by his unique scent and the familiar scent of the throw. All the sadness I felt earlier today seemed to vanish by Tristan's simple, kind gesture.

All through the movie, he shared his pie with me even though I only had about three bites because he devoured it quickly. When the movie was over, I yawned and gave a good stretch. I noticed Tristan was pretty quiet throughout the entire movie but when he finally commented, what he said totally shocked me. "That's what I want to happen with us." I looked over at him with intrigue and he smiled. I could see a real tenderness behind his eyes when he continued speaking. "I want us to die in each other's arms."

I was spellbound by his azure gaze and he rendered me speechless because I had no idea he wanted to spend his last moment on Earth with me…and in such an intimate way. The thought of taking my last breath while he took his, was so tragic yet so romantic. He reached out to caress my cheek and I leaned into his gentle touch and relished his warmth. I closed my eyes and I could feel my heart swelling with an intense feeling that I haven't felt in so long. But I noticed something different this time. This time I was powerless to suppress the feeling. I've always allowed myself to love my boyfriends freely without putting any restraints around my heart. I think that's the reason why I fall in love so quickly. But I've learned that loving men that way usually leaves me alone to pick up and mend the shattered pieces of my heart. When I first decided I wanted a relationship with Tristan, I was cautious with my heart and I constantly had my guard up because I was afraid of being hurt again. But something magical happened when Tristan said he wanted to die in my arms. I believe there was a hidden message behind his words, and it was almost like his heart was calling to mine but giving me a gentle reassurance at the same time. His heart was telling me that it was safe to love him.

When I opened my eyes, I spoke softly because my heart was still fluttering in my chest. "Tristan, that is so romantic, baby. I had no idea you felt that way."

He shocked me even further with his response. And there was a real intensity slowly filling his beautiful orbs. "Bridget, you have no idea how I feel about you."

He was right…because I really didn't. But I was beginning to realize how I felt about *him*. All of a sudden, that protective guard was raised to shield my heart from his. I quickly changed the subject when I said, "I'm kind of tired so I'll probably be going to bed soon. Did you want me to take you home now?"

I chuckled softly when I noticed he had some pie filling on the corner of his mouth. I leaned over to wipe the food from his mouth with my fingers and I made sure that he saw me put those same fingers in my mouth. My actions didn't go unnoticed because he looked into my eyes and grinned. After I finished cleaning him, he darted his tongue out to lick the spot. "I made a mess of myself. I guess I couldn't help it 'cause I'm telling you babe…that pie was delicious!" Then his expression turned more serious and he lowered his voice. "And no, I don't want you to take me home." I looked at him curiously and he said, "I wanna spend the night with you." My eyes widened in surprise and he added, "And I promise no poke-poke in the middle of the night." I laughed and he flashed me a wicked grin. "That is…unless you want me to." I laughed harder.

Tristan didn't disturb me with any sexual advances that night and I appreciated that he respected me so much. I remembered back to what he told me in the car on our way home and I realized that he was absolutely right. The only person whose holiday was ruined was my mother's. She had the opportunity to get to know Tristan and see all the wonderful things in him that I see. But instead, she insulted me and my heart's choice and caused me to leave on bad terms. I wasn't exactly sure when I would be visiting them again.

In the dark and quiet of my bedroom, I fell asleep easily in Tristan's embrace but I dreamt of Nana. Her face was still heavily wrinkled, her hair still snow-white, and her smile still full of unconditional affection. I will always love my Nana and her stories at Thanksgiving when I was a child will always be a fond memory of mine. But this Thanksgiving, I got to spend it with my amazing, handsome, British boyfriend named Tristan. And that was simply the dearest to me.

Chapter 6

ALL MONTH I'VE BEEN TRYING to decide what to get Tristan for Christmas. The problem wasn't that I didn't know what to buy him because he has everything; the problem was that he was one of those people who didn't have many interests. Don't get me wrong, he has interests; just not the kind that you can actually buy a gift for. He doesn't collect anything, he doesn't watch much television, and he's not into electronics or electronic gadgets. I just recently talked him into buying a new cell phone because his was so outdated. And he's definitely not into fashion. His wardrobe is very limited; mostly consisting of a variety of t-shirts, sweatshirts, and jeans. I know he's really into movies but I couldn't even begin to think of what DVD's to buy him because his collection was already massive. Basically, Tristan's interests were acting, soccer, drinking, smoking, movies, hanging out with his 'mates', sex, and me; not necessarily in that order.

It was the Thursday before Christmas and the start of my holiday break. I was practically pulling my hair out while I frantically searched the busy mall for the right gift for him. As I was passing different stores, I kept repeating the same phrase over and over in my head: *What would Tristan like?* This was going to be our first Christmas together and I wanted to get him something special. My mind was racing when all of a sudden, a memory flashed before my eyes. I remembered seeing he and Rick heavily involved in a videogame, and for a moment I started thinking along those lines. Then I remembered that they seemed to have a whole video gaming area set up in the living room; complete with these space-age chairs that hooked up into the game console. I quickly dismissed the idea because I started thinking that buying a videogame for Tristan was a bit infantile. I started listing his interests in my head again. Public schoolteacher pay isn't all its cracked up to be, so I was on a budget. I know Tristan is into music but he doesn't buy CD's because he burns them from the music he downloads onto his laptop. I was back at a dead end.

I was wandering around a sporting goods store looking for things related to soccer, when my cell phone rang. "Hello?"

"Babe, where are you?" It was Tristan and he sounded a little on-edge. But thank God he called me because now I could ask him what he wanted for Christmas. Since I've always been the kind of person who likes to surprise others with gifts, I didn't ask him specifically what he wanted.

"I'm shopping at the mall. Why, what's wrong? You sound like something's wrong."

"Oh no, nothing's wrong. It's just…I really need to talk to you. I went to your flat but you weren't there." I loved it when Tristan used British words.

"Oh. Well okay then…what's up?"

"No, I need to talk to you in person. When will you be home?" I was thinking: *Probably never, if I can't find a gift for you.*

"Um, I don't know…I'm really---"

"Bridge, it's important." His voice sounded urgent. I guess I could leave now, come back to the mall tomorrow and continue my search. That is, if he doesn't tell me what he wants first.

"Okay, well I'll leave now and be home in a little while. I'm not that far." I paused for a few seconds. "Are you *sure* you're alright?"

"Yeah, I'm alright. I'm sorry if I'm freaking you out or whatever. I just need to talk to you about something."

"I understand. Oh, before I go…what do you want for Christmas?" He better not say what I think he's going to say.

He gave a short laugh and said, "I don't know…surprise me." Damn it! I guess I'd be coming back to the mall tomorrow.

When I pulled into my parking space in front of my apartment, I saw Tristan's bike in the space next to mine. I happened to look towards my front door and I saw him sitting on the steps. I started to wonder how long he was sitting there. I got out of the car and he came over to me. I gave him a peck on the lips and said, "Hey baby, how long have you been waiting for me?"

He just smiled at me and said, "I never left."

My eyes widened in shock. "What?!? You mean, when you called me---"

His smile spread even further across his sensual lips. "I was right here." I was really surprised and couldn't stop gaping at him. Whatever he needed to talk to me about must be really important.

We went into my apartment and took our coats off. He followed me over to the sofa and I looked at him expectedly. The suspense was killing me. What was so important that it made him sit on cold cement steps in the winter and wait for me? He took one of my hands in both of his and started rubbing it. Then he looked at me and said, "I'm going away for the hols." I looked at him with a confused expression. What's 'hols'? As always, he noticed my expression and quickly added, "The *holidays*... you know, Christmas."

He was going away? Suddenly, the thought of not spending Christmas with him made me very upset because it was the one thing I was really looking forward to. Then I started wondering how long he would be gone. At that moment, I started missing him already. My face fell and I asked quietly, "Where are you going?"

"Home...to Brighton. Me and Jake are gonna visit Mum and Nanny, and see a few of our mates. You know, to catch up. We haven't been there since..." Then he looked up towards the ceiling with a thoughtful expression. "Since the beginning of summer."

I took my hand out of his grasp and looked down at my lap. I couldn't understand why he didn't want to spend Christmas with me. I didn't want to feel selfish; he was visiting his mother and grandmother after all. And they *are* more important. But still, I couldn't help but to feel hurt. Without looking at him I asked, "When are you coming back?"

He gently grasped my chin and turned my head so our eyes would meet. He was smiling; his blue eyes were bright, and his voice was soft... almost tender. "On New Year's Eve. Bridget...I want you to come with me, love. I want you to meet Mum." Once again, my eyes practically popped out of my head. He wanted me to meet his mother? Already? I was shocked, flattered, and scared to death all at the same time. Then the weight of his invitation really hit me. I would be the first girl he's introduced to his mother....*ever!* The realization was too much for me and I abruptly stood up. Tristan stood up too, and he put his hands on my upper arms and turned my body so that I was facing him. His eyes searched mine and he wore an expression of concern. "Are you alright, Bridge? You seem a little..."

My eyes were still wide and my mouth was agape, and I know I was worrying him because he frowned. I took a few short breaths and my head began to nod on its own. Then finally, my voice returned but it was small and meek. "Okay."

"We're leaving tomorrow morning."

I scoffed in disbelief because I was a little put-off at such a last-minute invitation. Before I could express my displeasure, he apologized immediately. "I'm sorry, Bridget. I know it's last-minute, but it's 'cause of my brother's schedule. The trip was originally planned for last week and I was gonna ask you sooner but something came up with Jake. Then we were just gonna cancel the whole trip 'cause he didn't think he could get time off but eventually he was able to. It was only this afternoon when we finally decided to go." After he finished explaining the reason behind this last-minute trip to England, he said, "To show you that I really *am* sorry, I'll help you pack."

Tristan left my apartment after we finished packing my luggage. But before he did, he told me that he and Jake would be picking me up in the morning so the three of us could drive to the airport. I couldn't sleep that night because a million things were running through my mind and causing me to panic. I was worried about meeting his family and making a good impression. I was hoping they wouldn't prejudge me like my mother did to him. I started wondering what Tristan told them about me. Then I started worrying because I still didn't buy him a Christmas present and I had no idea what to get. Sleep would not come for me that night and I knew I'd be paying for it in the morning.

As I expected, the next morning I was like the walking-dead. I was groggy and it was hard for me to perform simple tasks such as showering, brushing my teeth, getting dressed, and doing my hair. I was happy that I didn't have any *last* last-minute packing to do because Tristan and I checked and double-checked to make sure I packed everything. I didn't have time to eat because I spent so much time trying to concentrate on making myself look presentable. Putting on makeup would've been an excruciating chore, so I skipped it altogether.

Before I knew it, the doorbell rang. I sluggishly made my way to the door and when I opened it, Tristan was standing there. I peered at him beneath half-closed lids and he looked momentarily surprised. "Awww, babe. You didn't get any sleep?" All I could do was shake my head. I moved to the side to let him enter and I just stood there praying that I wouldn't fall over. Tristan went into my bedroom to get my luggage, and then he went into my hallway closet and pulled out my coat. He stopped in front of me and looked at me curiously. "You ready to go?" It seemed I was incapable of speech so I just nodded. He put on my coat for me, grabbed my luggage, and I followed him outside.

His brother Jake was in the driver's seat of his silver Nissan Maxima and he was smiling at me. He was blond like Tristan and they had the same beautiful, periwinkle blue eyes. But whereas Tristan had a boyish look to his features, Jake's were mature. Undoubtedly though, he was truly handsome. When I first met Jake I concluded that good genes must run in the Hathaway family.

Tristan headed towards the trunk of the car but he walked past me. "Bridge, get in the backseat and lay down until we got to the airport," he commanded. I didn't need to be told twice because once my head hit the soft supple leather seat cushion, I was fast asleep. I think I heard Jake say something to me but I was too exhausted to respond.

I slept during the entire plane ride. I remember Tristan whispering to me every now and then but I was too tired to remember my drowsy responses to him. I was finally fully awake when the plane landed.

We hailed a taxi, and I took the time we were traveling from the airport to their house, to freshen up and put on my makeup. I didn't want to meet his family looking like a pale zombie. I was taking in the scenery and when we drove into Brighton, I was in complete awe. It was actually a seaside city. I found that it was breathtaking in the winter and I could only imagine how wonderful it looked in the summer. I started to envision Tristan as a little boy; running around on the pier and playing at the beach. I finally understood why Brighton is sometimes referred to as 'London-by-the-sea'.

It wasn't until the taxi pulled up in front of Tristan and Jake's childhood home that I started to semi-hyperventilate. I realized that this was actually a big deal to Tristan; introducing me to his family. And I didn't want anything to go wrong. Plus, I would be staying here for over a week and I wanted to be the perfect houseguest. I didn't even get a moment to compose myself because Tristan and Jake's mother came rushing out the front door to greet us. Now I definitely saw where they got their good looks from. Their mother was stunning! She was blonde and she had sparkling blue eyes. I was tickled to see that her cheeks were dimpled like Tristan's but whereas he had one...she had two dimples. I also noticed that she had the same smile as Tristan and I realized that I instantly liked her.

Both of her sons hugged her tightly as I stood to the side to give them their intimate moment. She looked over at me while still in their embrace and said in a cheerful English accent, "Tristan, is that your Bridget? Oh my goodness." Then she came over to me and her smile was infectious. I smiled back at her and before I could speak, she embraced me just as tightly as she did her sons. She pulled away but didn't release me. Now that I saw her face close up, I noticed that Tristan had her eyes too. "It's so nice to meet you, Bridget. Tristan told me so much about you; he just goes on and on. I was so happy when he told me he was bringing you." She released me then and paused to regard me. "You look more beautiful in person than your pictures. What a lovely girl. And oh...red hair!" She smoothed my hair in a very motherly fashion and I couldn't stop smiling. I looked over at Tristan and he was smiling too. Mrs. Hathaway was affecting us all.

"Thank you," I said as I started blushing furiously. "I'm really looking forward to spending the holidays with you all. This is my first time traveling out of the country."

She continued to talk to me while her sons carried the luggage into the house. I glanced at them as they walked up the walkway and I saw their grandmother watching quietly from the front door. I heard Tristan yell, "Hiya Nanny!"

The Hathaway's Victorian home in Brighton was truly magnificent and had elaborate landscaping. Even though mostly everything was sprinkled with light snow, I could still see the beauty. Mrs. Hathaway put her arm around me as we walked up the driveway into the house.

Once I got inside, I noticed it was very spacious with a comforting old-fashioned atmosphere. I saw Tristan, Jake, and their grandmother chatting animatedly. Mrs. Hathaway turned to me and said, "I'm guessing you'll be staying in Tristan's room with him then?" Whoa! She was letting us share a room? Did that include a bed too? I honestly believed at least one of us would be claiming the couch for the duration of our visit. I shrugged in return, and she took my hand and guided me towards Tristan's bedroom.

When she opened the door, it was as I expected; there wasn't any other place for us to sleep but in one bed...together. I looked around briefly and I noticed it wasn't much different than his room in Los Angeles; except for the fact that this room was cleaner. I had to assume that his mother and grandmother had something to do with that fact. I was admiring one of Tristan's MVP soccer trophies from high school, when he came into the room with his grandmother in-tow. He gestured for me to come over and he introduced us. He was still wearing his brilliant smile when he said, "Bridge, this is my nanny."

Nanny Hathaway had a head full of white hair and it was styled in a very modern bob. I was surprised that her ivory skin wasn't as wrinkled as I expected. And I could only count maybe a handful of liver spots on her face. Perhaps it was something in the water in Brighton. Or maybe she was just a young grandmother. For some reason, I wasn't feeling as comfortable with her as I did with his mom. Maybe it was because her pale blue eyes were looking at me so intently that it reminded me of the looks he gives me sometimes. I smiled at her and said politely, "Hi, nice to meet you." I put my hand out for her to shake it and she did. That eased a little of the tension so I decided to take a risk and let some of my personality shine. "I've seen you on television." She looked at me curiously and I laughed lightly. "Tristan showed me a home video and you were in it."

She started to laugh. "Ohhhhh! Yes, yes, I remember. Tristan and those lads with the camera." She looked over at Tristan and shook her head. "Disrupting me reading and all manner of quiet in the house." She looked back and me and said, "So, you're the *one* eh? The one who captured me Tristan's heart."

What the---? His *heart*? What *has* he been telling them? Tristan didn't speak up or correct her and I started to get a little nervous as to what she meant by her comment. I didn't respond to her; I just smiled. And I think by this time my smile was frozen on my face. I looked over at Tristan for support but he was just staring at me. What the heck was going on?

After the introductions were over, Tristan showed me around the house. He told me that once he and Jake got older, Jake made the attic into his own bedroom so that allowed for him to have his own. I was so excited and honored to actually be there. I was just trying to take everything in. I was looking at the pictures on the wall of Tristan and his family, and I started to wonder about his father. He seemed to be absent from all the photographs. Tristan never spoke of his father and I never asked him why. I figured it was a private matter and he would tell me about him if he wanted to.

After he gave me the house tour, we went back into his bedroom to unpack. Mrs. Hathaway poked her head in the doorway. "Dinner will be ready soon," she announced with a smile. By the time we finished packing, a delicious aroma was permeating in the air.

Finally, she called everyone to dinner and we all sat down and got to know each other better. I was getting questions left and right; from Jake, Mrs. Hathaway, and Nanny. It was getting a little difficult to keep up. I also found it hard to understand what Nanny said most of the time because of her thick English accent. So I did what I usually do when someone speaks to me in a foreign language: smile and nod. Overall, dinner was very pleasant and I was happy to know that I would have more opportunities to enjoy sitting down to dinner with them.

I insisted on helping Mrs. Hathaway with the dishes. Tristan tried to help too but she shooed him out of the kitchen. I assumed it was because she wanted to have more girl-talk with me. After all, it's not often she gets to meet any of her youngest son's girlfriends. I was privy to find out that he had basically told her everything about me; from what grade I teach to the names of my parents. She also told me that he told her about his experience meeting my mother. I started to get embarrassed as she retold the events as they were told to her. I noticed though, that she didn't reveal any of Tristan's intimate confessions; like how he *really* felt about me. I was hoping she would explain to me what Nanny Hathaway meant when she said I captured Tristan's heart, but she didn't. And I was too afraid to ask.

We were almost done cleaning up the kitchen when I told her about my dilemma with Tristan's Christmas present. "I need to get a Christmas present for Tristan. I've been searching all month and I can't figure out what to get him. And he won't tell me what he wants; he told me to surprise him. You're his mother so you know him better than I do. Do you have any ideas?"

Kate gave me another one of her warm, motherly smiles. "Don't worry, love. I'll take you to the pier tomorrow. There are plenty of shops, so maybe you can find something for him there."

During the course of the evening I noticed that Jake had disappeared. Nanny Hathaway had settled into her room. Her door was open and I saw that she was enjoying her television. Mrs. Hathaway told me that there was bubble bath with her name on it so she went to relax in the bathtub. She and Nanny had already decorated the house with Christmas decorations before we arrived but I noticed the Christmas tree in the front room was still bare. I was standing next to it when Tristan came to stand beside me. My mind was completely lost in my foreign surroundings, that I didn't hear him approach me. When I realized it was him I asked, "When are we going to decorate the tree?"

"Probably tomorrow. We always decorate the tree on Christmas Eve." I felt him move behind me and put his arms around my waist. I covered his arms with mine and leaned back against his chest. He placed a kiss on my cheek and I felt him put his nose to my hair and inhale deeply. Then he whispered in my ear, "I'm so glad you're here, love."

I turned in his arms so that I was facing him. I put my arms around his neck and he pulled me tighter against him. I lifted one hand and ran my fingers through his blond hair. The room was dim. The only illumination was coming from the Christmas lights in the window in front of the tree and a few lit candles lined up on the mantelpiece. We gazed into each other's eyes for a moment and I saw the string of Christmas lights reflected in his clear eyes. I tilted my head up and kissed his lips. Then I whispered, "Me too."

I guess my kiss didn't satisfy his need because he leaned down and captured my mouth again. But his kiss had a clear meaning. I opened my mouth to him and his tongue met mine. We caressed each other's tongues until he captured mine and sucked on it gently. I moaned softly and I felt his hands move down to grab my butt. He pressed his pelvis against me and ground into me deeply. He was already hard. I moaned louder this time and his mouth continued to slant over mine and kiss me deeply.

I felt as if my knees would buckle. It was taking every ounce of my strength to keep myself from falling. Tristan's kisses were demanding. My hands began to rub up and down the front of his shirt. I was itching to feel his warm, bare skin so I lifted up the front of his shirt to reach my goal. I caressed his bare chest and raked my fingernails lightly over his nipples. This time he moaned softly and I felt him start to hump against me to create more friction. I truly believe this was an involuntary action from him because of his arousal. I felt his hardness poking my abdomen and as I reached down to rub him, he broke the kiss and whispered, "Let's go to my room."

He took my hand and we ran to his bedroom. When we reached our destination, he closed the door quickly and I saw him lock it. I sat down on the edge of the bed and he approached me slowly. His walk was predatory; like he was a starving lion and I was the first prey he's seen in weeks. He towered over me and I leaned back onto the bed with my elbows supporting me. His arms came down on either side of me as he leaned down to kiss me again. My arms reached up to pull him down and I let him fall on top of me.

We both scooted up the bed without breaking the kiss. I was lying with my legs spread and his body was nestled between them. Once I was in comfortable position, he broke the kiss to practically tear his shirt from his body. His bedroom was fully lit so we saw each other perfectly and clearly. I looked at up at him, and at that moment I realized what we were about to do. He knew it too because he asked tenderly, "Bridget, are you ready?"

My mouth formed the word and I was about to say it, but then I thought about the fact that I'm a guest here and this is his mother's house. I couldn't disrespect her and her warm welcome by having sex with her son in her house. I didn't feel comfortable; now wasn't the right time. I closed my eyes briefly and sighed. Tristan knew instantly what my answer was.

He removed himself from on top of me and flopped down on the bed next to me. He was lying on his back and he draped one of his arms over his eyes. I couldn't say anything because I felt horrible. I was always the one pushing him away when he tried to get sexually intimate. I knew I wanted to have sex with him but it was just that the timing was never right for me. I needed to say something to him because he wasn't speaking. He was almost motionless and the room was silent. Suddenly, he did speak and I actually jumped a little at the sound because he startled me. "You have no idea how you affect me. Every time I kiss you, I want..." He paused briefly and then continued. "I want you so fucking bad."

When I spoke next, my voice sounded big; like it was echoing in an empty room. Then I realized it was because it was so quiet you could hear a pin drop. I turned on my side to face him and said, "Tristan, I know you feel like I'm teasing you but I'm not. I know every time we kiss it's like we have to get closer. It's like our bodies aren't satisfied. Our kisses are so passionate."

He removed the arm that was draped over his eyes and they started burning into mine. I started to wonder if he held some sort of power behind them. "Can I ask you something?" I nodded. "We've been together for two months and we haven't shagged. Just tell me...what is it that you're waiting for? I thought you wanted to. When we snog, I feel like you wanna. I really don't understand now." Then all of a sudden he flipped onto his side so that he was facing me. He tilted his head to side and peered at me curiously. "Are you a virgin?" To both of our surprise, I started to laugh. Then he said, "I know I never asked you before and you never mentioned it. So I thought maybe that was the reason. Is it?"

My heart swelled at the fact that he considered my virtue to be the cause of my rejection of him. Normally, a man would never think that a woman my age could be a virgin. I smiled and moved closer to him. I kissed him on the lips again and lingered close to his face for a moment. Then I rubbed my cheek against his. I felt slight stubble on his cheek and it tickled my cheek. I looked back at his face and into his eyes. "No, I'm not a virgin. The reason we haven't slept together is..." Then I began to open up my heart and share my real fears with him. I prayed to God that I wasn't making a mistake. "I'm afraid to make love to you. And I'm afraid that you might lose interest in me once we do. I remember when you told me how quickly you used to go through women." I paused for a moment and just gazed into his eyes. My eyes were begging his to understand me. "But the biggest reason is because I want us to be in love. I don't want us to *shag*. I want us to make love." As I was speaking to him I noticed my vision became blurry. Then I realized I had tears in my eyes that were threatening to fall.

I was expecting Tristan to question my reasons but he only asked me one thing: "Do you love me?" The power behind his question was enough to make me gasp. Oh my God. I knew one of us would ask this question one day.

I had to tell him the truth but I responded in a trembling voice. "I don't know." I was afraid that wasn't the answer he was looking for and I expected him to get angry. I was scared to death as to what he would say next. I was going to hate myself if he admitted that he loved me even though I just told him that I didn't love him.

"Then I'll wait until you do."

෨

I COULDN'T SLEEP THE FIRST night staying with the Hathaways. I kept thinking about what happened between me and Tristan moments ago. I was questioning myself as to whether I did the right thing. Would Tristan's mother be upset if she knew we were having sex in her house? I mean, she didn't have a problem with us sharing the same bed. She must have known there was the possibility that we would do more than just sleep. After all, we were going to be here for over a week. I also started wondering if Tristan was really hurt by my answer when he asked me if I loved him. I could've sworn I saw a flicker of sadness and disappointment in his eyes. Maybe he didn't want to reveal it to me because he didn't want to show his true emotions.

I was lying on my back and I was wide awake. Tristan was lying on his side with his arms wrapped around me and his head was nuzzled next to mine. I was listening to his soft breathing and staring at the ceiling. The wind was blowing outside and I turned my head to look out the window. I could see the snow falling from the small space between the curtains. Suddenly, the child inside me became excited at the idea of waking up in the morning to a winter wonderland. I glanced over at the digital alarm clock on the nightstand and the glowing red digits read 2:20AM. I was restless so I decided to get up and sit in the front room near the bare Christmas tree. My mind would not let me slumber in peace despite having the warm, comforting presence of Tristan next to me.

I put on my robe and slippers, and went into the kitchen to get a glass of milk to warm in the microwave. Tristan's childhood home reminded me a little of my own childhood home in Sacramento. It was warm, cozy, and had a welcoming sense of love, family, and tradition. My own immediate family consisted only of me and my parents but we were very close-knit.

I took my glass of warm milk and walked into the front room which the Hathaways called the 'family room'. The room was dark except for the Christmas lights that were still twinkling in the window in front of the tree. The candles that were lined up on the mantelpiece had been extinguished earlier by someone. There were stockings hanging around the fireplace and I noticed for the first time that one of them had my name on it. I smiled, and when I touched it gently I felt truly welcomed. Tristan's family was being so kind and treating me as if I were part of the family. I suddenly felt upset again because my mother couldn't display those same feelings towards him.

I was sitting in an incredibly soft recliner sipping my milk and gazing out the front window when I felt a cold draft at my feet. I heard the front door close and heavy footsteps walking towards my direction. I looked up and saw a shadowy figure cross the entryway to the room. It was tall and imposing, and I squinted to try to see who disrupted my peaceful reverie. The figure stopped in mid-step and stood a few feet away from me. Then it turned and approached me. As it walked into the weak lighting, I realized that it was Tristan's brother Jake. He was wearing dark pants, a leather coat, and a wool hat. His head, shoulders, and boots were sprinkled with snow. I didn't say anything to him as I looked up from behind my glass of milk. He was speechless too until he pulled his hat off and sat in an armchair adjacent to me.

"Hey, Bridget. What are you doing up?"

I looked over at him and smiled. I wondered if he could even see my face because his face was partially hidden in shadow. "I can't sleep." Then I paused. "You know...being in a strange house and all," I lied. The tone of my voice was very motherly when I asked, "Where have you been all night mister?" I laughed softly.

Jake gave a short laugh and said, "I met up with some of my mates." He paused too and then the volume of his voice dropped. "And then I met up with one of my old girlfriends." Even though I really couldn't see his face, I could imagine his expression and knew he was grinning. It caused me to start laughing and I wondered if he waggled his eyebrows the way Tristan did whenever he said something sly. Then Jake's tone of voice changed and he sounded serious. "Are you doing alright?"

His question caught me off-guard. "Yeah, why?"

"Oh, okay. It's just you seemed a little..." He paused again for a moment but continued. "Ah well, it's probably 'cause you were so overwhelmed. But I could tell you were really nervous." Then his voice lightened again. "You looked scared shitless when you were introduced to Nanny." He laughed.

"Yeah, she was a little intimidating. But she seems really nice. She was very friendly towards me at dinner." I took another sip of my milk and then I said, "I didn't see her too much after that."

"She likes to watch her programs on the tele. Mum got her one of those DVR's so she can record all her favorites. From what I hear, she hardly ever leaves her room." I saw him shift in his chair and I noticed him take off his coat. Then it seemed like he moved closer and leaned towards me. It was then that I saw his face clearly. "I actually wanted to talk to you about Tris."

"Oh, what about him?"

He paused again and just looked at me...the same intent way that Tristan does. I was convinced that all the Hathaways had that look. After a couple seconds, he spoke again. "You know this is weird for him, right?"

I was curious now. Was Jake going to reveal any of Tristan's intimate confessions? "What do you mean? What's weird for him?"

"Bringing a girl home. Shit...having a girlfriend *period*. He's not used to this. I *still* can't believe he actually---" I thought he was going to finish his sentence but he didn't. I was listening so intently that the glass of milk in my hand was frozen in mid-air on its way to my mouth.

"He actually *what*? Actually brought me here to meet your family?" I asked urgently.

"No, I knew he would do that. I mean, he said you were his girlfriend now so I knew it was only a matter of time."

Jake still didn't answer my question and I was getting impatient. "Then what can't you believe?" The desire to know exactly what he meant was eating away at me with rapid speed. Did it have anything to do with what Nanny Hathaway said earlier about capturing Tristan's heart? Before I could stop myself, I heard myself whisper desperately, "Jake, *please* tell me."

His voice dropped again but it still had a serious tone. "You know how my bro feels about you, don't you?"

I answered truthfully when I said, "He says he wants me really bad."

"Hmmm. Yeah, I can see that." Then he paused again and I felt like getting up, shaking him, and making him tell me why he was being so cryptic. He must've been able to read my mind because the last thing he said to me before he got up and left was, "You should ask him."

I sat there in the recliner for awhile after Jake left. My glass of milk went cold and I remember hearing the grandfather clock chime four times. I turned my head slowly to look out the window and I saw that the snow was still falling. It was still dark outside but I knew the sun would be creeping through the clouds in a couple hours. I decided to climb back into bed with Tristan and turn my brain off so that I could actually get some sleep. The last thing I remember seeing before I drifted off to sleep was the glowing red digits on the alarm clock reading 4:23AM.

It was Christmas Eve. When I woke up again, the sun was shining through the space between the curtains. I carefully extracted myself from Tristan, who mumbled a few words in his sleep, and I went to put on my robe again. I left the bedroom and padded softly down the hall to the bathroom. The smell of bacon caused me to pause my steps and I passed the bathroom to take a quick peek in the kitchen to see who was cooking one of my favorite breakfast foods. I saw Nanny Hathaway with about four black cast-iron skillets on the stove. Her back was to me but I saw her mixing something in a bowl. There was a small black-and-white television on one of the counters and I saw her head turn towards it every now and then as she was mixing. I smiled inwardly at the scene and a part of me felt sad that I would eventually have to leave.

I turned and walked back towards the bathroom. I went in and brushed my teeth while I waited for the water in the shower to reach my preferred temperature. I was in the shower with my eyes closed as I let the warm water cascade over me. I was deep in-thought because I remembered that today Mrs. Hathaway was going to take me to the pier to shop for Tristan's Christmas gift. I was so deep in my reverie that I didn't hear anyone enter the bathroom...or enter the *shower*. The next thing I knew, a pair of warm, strong arms wrapped around my waist and a naked body pressed against my back. I shrieked and tried to turn in their arms but they held me still. They kissed me on the neck and I immediately knew it was Tristan. Then the realization hit me like a ton of bricks: we were in the shower together...naked! Immediately, my arms went to cover my breasts and I crossed my legs in a futile attempt to cover my pussy. I couldn't believe Tristan came into the shower. This time, I *knew* I locked the door. Oddly, my first question wasn't 'why are you here?' It was: "How did you get in?"

I heard Tristan chuckle and he said into my ear, "Mum never fixed the lock on this door. It's been broken since I used to live here." For some strange reason I started to wonder if she even knew it was broken in the first place. I felt Tristan move away from me and I turned my head towards him. He moved around my body to stand in front of me under the spraying water. Oh my God. He was wet, sexy, and totally naked! My eyes began roaming all over his nude body and I noticed he was sporting 'morning-wood'. His erection stood proud at attention and was jutting out from a patch of dark blond hair. I felt a deep flush creep up onto my face and I averted my eyes. He moved closer to me and he took my arms and pulled them away from my chest. At first I wanted to resist but then a part of me knew this moment would come eventually.

I let my arms fall to my side and looked up at him. His blond hair was darkened and plastered to his forehead. His wet lashes stood out dark against his ivory skin and the water was cascading down his perfectly chiseled torso. He was looking deep into my eyes and I saw a look cross his features that was filled with pure lust. He moved even closer to me until I felt his erection poking my belly and I gasped in surprise. He tilted his head to the side and spoke in the most seductive voice I've ever heard escape his throat. "I wanna look at you." I uncrossed my legs and stood there; wet and naked before him. His eyes raked over my body greedily. When our eyes met again, he said, "Bridget, you are *so* beautiful." Then he smirked and said, "You know I wasn't gonna let you get away with this again."

I looked at him curiously and asked, "Get away with what?"

He slipped his arms around me and closed the distance between us. My breasts were crushed against his chest and his fully-erect manhood was lying against my belly. It was hot, and hard, and I actually wanted to touch it. He leaned down towards me like he was about to kiss me and said, "Showering without me." Then he captured my lips in a deep, open-mouthed passionate kiss.

What I did next was completely spur-of-the-moment and I never would've imagined when I woke up this morning that I'd actually be doing it. But a part of me felt bad for being a 'cock-tease' so I planned to make it up to him one way or the other. Once we ended the kiss, I reached over and grabbed the soap. I lathered it thoroughly in my hands and then set it down against the shower wall. I looked into his baby blues and they actually spoke to me. I read Tristan's message loud and clear: 'Please do it'. Without taking my eyes off him, I boldly reached down and grabbed his erection. It felt like smooth, warm satin over hard steel, and it was long and thick. I began stroking it from base to tip, and when I reached the tip I would brush my thumb over the top in a swirling motion.

Tristan's breathing became labored but he didn't take his eyes off me. They had a pleading look in them and I knew he wouldn't last long. My grip on him became firmer and I continued the same stroking action. I reached down with my other hand and cupped his sac. I squeezed it gently and rolled his testicles between my fingers while I continued to stoke him faster. He started moaning and humping into my fist that was enclosed around his erection. Then suddenly, his hands reached out and he gripped my hips. His eyes closed briefly and he spoke in a strangled voice, "Please don't stop, Bridget. It feels so fucking good."

He started pulling me towards him as he backed up to lean against the wall behind the shower head. I was now standing directly under the spraying water as I continued to give my boyfriend a hand-job. He was still breathing rapidly and he started to whimper from the sexual pleasure. His body started trembling but he didn't release me or take his eyes off me. The whole act was so intimate and so intense, that the anticipation of his climax actually excited me. It wasn't long until he granted my wish. He closed his eyes again and let out a long, deep moan and his whole body shook from the force of his orgasm. The back of his head actually hit the wall, and for a moment I thought he hurt himself. I was in awe at what I seeing. I quickly looked down at his erupting cock and saw thick, white strings of semen spurt out and cover my hands while his pelvis was humping almost involuntarily. My mouth was hanging open and I stared in amazement as Tristan continued to ride his wave of ecstasy.

He was finally coming down from his orgasm as I decreased my strokes and finally released his spent manhood. His eyes were still closed and he was breathing hard. I took that moment to put my hands under the water to rinse off his seed. Then he opened his eyes and a smile lit up his face. He pushed himself up from the wall slowly and came to stand in front of me under the water. I smiled at him and laughed. "How's your head?"

Tristan laughed too and rubbed the back of his head. "It hurts a bit... but it was worth it."

After Tristan and I finished in the shower, we went back to his room to get dressed. As we were walking down the hall; he wearing nothing but a towel around his waist, and I in my robe, I saw Mrs. Hathaway coming down the stairs. And I know she saw where we *both* just came from. I was too embarrassed to make eye contact with her so I just followed Tristan into his room. While we were in the room, all shyness disappeared from me and I left myself totally open and exposed to him. We already saw each other naked so we got dressed in front of each other. After today, there was no more hiding myself from him...my body included.

Nanny Hathaway made us all a wonderful breakfast and I was honestly stuffed after eating all the food she cooked for us. Jake was still asleep so he didn't join us. While we were clearing the table, Tristan got a phone call. After he finished talking, I could tell he was excited. "That was my mate Kurt. He wants to hang out." He approached me and put his arm around my shoulder. "Do you wanna come with me?"

I smiled at him because the idea of meeting his friends from Brighton made me feel honored in some way. But before I could give him a reply, Kate intervened. "I'm taking Bridget shopping." She approached my other side and pulled me slightly towards her. "She's mine for today, son." She made it obvious that she was adamant about it so Tristan didn't argue with her...and neither did I.

Mrs. Hathaway and I headed out into the snow and she drove us down to the shopping area surrounding the pier nearby. We had a very pleasant and enjoyable ride in the car. She told me some stories about when Tristan and Jake were children which had me laughing until my cheeks hurt. I knew Tristan might be embarrassed if he knew some of the things his mother told me. As I was listening to her recall the memories, I started to understand why he was so protective of her; why he only wanted a girl who was special to him to meet her. She was really an amazing, beautiful person inside and out. I couldn't help but to express my feelings towards her so I said, "I see why Tristan loves you so much. You really are an amazing woman Mrs. Hathaway."

What she said next really topped yesterday's cryptic comment from Nanny. "For the same reasons he feels the way he does about me...he feels about you. That's why he chose you. That's why he brought you here to meet us. That's why he---" She paused again; just like Jake did last night. It was like they didn't want to tell me something. What was it? Then she quickly changed the subject. "And please don't call me Mrs. Hathaway, love. Call me Kate. One day it's going to be quite confusing for people when we're together." She looked over at me and smiled. But this smile was different, it was very...*motherly*. And I knew what she meant by her last comment...that much I was certain.

Kate and I browsed through many shops along the pier. She was being very helpful by giving me suggestions on what to buy for her son but none of them seemed to speak to my heart. We were in a small jewelry boutique looking in the glass cases when a particular piece caught my eye. I was looking in a case which contained more trendy kinds of jewelry and I saw a black leather and sterling silver ID bracelet. One look at it and I knew it would just compliment Tristan so nicely. Plus, I knew that he liked black bracelets. I looked at the price and it was within my budget but then I realized I wouldn't be able to get it engraved in time for Christmas.

Kate came over to me so we were leaning down shoulder-to-shoulder. "Do you see anything you like?"

"Actually...yes," and I pointed to the bracelet. "I'd like to get that for Tristan but the engraving probably won't be done in time."

She gave me a knowing smile and said slyly, "We'll see about that." She went over to one of the jewelers and had an animated conversation with him. She kept gesturing towards me and smiling, and by the look on the jeweler's face, he seemed to be falling for Kate's charms. She walked back over to me while the jeweler came to stand behind the glass case I was peering into. I looked up at her and she said, "Two hours."

A look of confusion appeared on my face and I repeated, "Two hours? For what?"

That's when I saw the jeweler take the bracelet out of the case. Then he spoke to me with an accent that sounded Scottish, "Miss, what inscription would you like?"

Now I knew that most places charged per letter so I had to be careful. "How much per letter?"

Before the jeweler could answer, Kate put her hand on my shoulder and said, "Don't worry about it dear. Just tell him what you want on it. What ever you want it to say." I looked over at her and she was smiling and nodding encouragingly.

I told the jeweler that I just wanted Tristan's name on it. The jeweler wrote down the name on a piece of paper and walked away with bracelet. Then I turned to Kate and asked, "Why did you say two hours? And I need to know how much the price will be with the inscription."

She was peering into another glass case as I was talking to her. Then she looked up and said, "That's how long we have to wait until the bracelet will be ready. And don't worry about the price. You'll pay what you saw listed in the case." My mouth was opening and closing like a fish out of water. What exactly did she say to the jeweler? How was this possible? I had a feeling that she could tell what I was thinking by the confused look on my face. She came over to me and put her hands on either side of my face like my own mother does sometimes. "Just look at it as sharing some of the holiday spirit, love." It was at this moment that I realized I didn't want to go back to Los Angeles. Tristan's mother was one of the nicest people I've ever met and I could honestly be content living in Brighton just so I could be near her.

Suddenly I realized that I needed to buy gifts for her, Jake, and Nanny. "Could we split up so I can check out some of the stores by myself?" I gave her a sly smile of my own when I said, "I have some other gifts to buy and you can't be present to witness me buy them."

She laughed. "Sure, love. We'll meet up in an hour, how's that?" Then she pointed to a small cafe on the other side of the pier. "I'll wait for you there."

I was browsing around a couple more shops looking for gifts for the rest of the Hathaway family. I ended up buying a lilac knit scarf with matching hat and gloves for Nanny, a collectible set of shot glasses for

Jake, and an aromatherapy bath & beauty gift basket for Kate. When I was done with my Christmas shopping, I met Kate at the cafe and we had tea and pastries while we chatted more. We were hitting it off so wonderfully that time passed quickly and soon it was time to pick up Tristan's bracelet.

We went back to the jewelry boutique to get the bracelet and when the jeweler brought it out for me to inspect, I was very impressed. The name 'Tristan' was written in a block-lettering and it didn't look rushed at all. I could imagine the bracelet complimenting Tristan so well and looking very handsome on his wrist. Inside I was beaming and I couldn't wait for him to see it. Kate was right; I only paid the price that was listed in case. They didn't charge me extra for the inscription.

When we came home, Kate brought me some wrapping paper, tags, and bows so I could wrap my presents. I went into Tristan's room to wrap them and when I was done I went into the family room. I saw Nanny taking Christmas tree decorations out of a big cardboard box and Jake was sitting on the floor unraveling tree lights. I became excited instantly because I knew we would be decorating the tree soon. I tried to help Nanny with the decorations, but Kate put a gentle hand on my arm. "Could you ring Tristan and ask him to come home?" I guess she wanted us to all decorate the tree together.

I went into the kitchen and called Tristan. When he picked up, I could hear rock music and a television in the background. "Hey baby, where are you?"

"I'm at a billiards. Why? Do you want me to come get you?"

"No, your mom wants you to come home. I think we're going to decorate the tree now."

"Brilliant!" He exclaimed excitedly. "I'll be there in a bit."

I hurried back into the family room to help the Hathaways prepare the decorations. Kate put on a holiday CD and the four of us talked and laughed together while 'Silver Bells' played in the background. By the time Tristan came home, we were ready to start decorating the tree. Jake had already put the lights on and Kate had brought out some egg nog and Christmas cookies.

Decorating the tree with Tristan and his family was a very memorable experience. I was alive with the holiday spirit and I felt like I was with my real family. Nanny had warmed up to me so quickly that I felt like I was with my own grandmother. Every now and then Tristan would show affection towards me while we stood side-by-side putting ornaments on the tree. We began to playfully throw tinsel at each other and then pick it off one another before throwing it on the tree. I caught Kate watching us with an open, approving expression on her face.

When the tree was fully decorated, Nanny approached me. "I think you should put the star on top."

I looked over at her with an expression of surprise. Her eyes were friendly and welcoming so I couldn't object. "Sure, I'll do it." Suddenly, Tristan dashed out of the room. "Where's he going?" I asked Jake who just shrugged in return. Nanny handed me the star and that's when I realized I needed help placing it on top. The tree was too tall and I was too short. And that's when Tristan came back into the room with a folding chair tucked under his arm. "Thanks, baby," I said fondly. He gave me a knowing smile and held the chair for me so I could stand on it. Everyone directed me to make sure the star was straight, and after I put it up, we all stood around the tree to admire our work.

Kate and Nanny disappeared for awhile and Tristan, Jake, and I sat around the family room drinking egg nog, talking, and munching on cookies. Then Kate and Nanny returned with presents and they started putting them under the tree. At that moment, Jake and Tristan jumped up and said they needed to get theirs. I was about to get up too but Tristan stopped me by saying, "No, don't come in the room yet! Don't come in until I'm done!" I waited awhile until he was finished and then I went into his bedroom to retrieve my hidden gifts for the Hathaways.

By early evening, we all sat down to a delightful Christmas Eve dinner. Tristan and Jake had invited some of their neighborhood friends to visit and join in celebrating the holiday. Soon after, we were all pleasantly stuffed and maybe a little tipsy from the wine that Nanny brought out during dinner. The wine flowed heavily after dinner and late into the evening. Before long, there were a lot of half-sleeping bodies lounging around the family room.

By nighttime, Tristan and Jake's friends had left and it was just me and the Hathaways. Nanny had excused herself and retired to bed and I saw Kate filling the stockings that were hanging around the fireplace. At first she didn't notice I was there but when she did, she looked at me with an affectionate smile. "I think it's time for someone to go to bed."

I smiled back at her as I stood up to exit the room. "I don't want you to see what I'm putting in your stocking." I looked around the room briefly and I saw Jake fast asleep on a sofa but I didn't exactly see where Tristan wandered off to.

It wasn't until I was about to go to bed myself, that I noticed he was already lying in bed. When I approached him, I saw that he was completely knocked out and fully dressed. I carefully removed his shoes, and then I undressed and put on my pajamas. I slipped out of the room to brush my teeth and when I returned, I climbed into bed with him and put the blankets over us. I didn't have a problem sleeping that night. I was at ease with the family and totally comfortable in my surroundings. And I was looking forward to a special Christmas with my wonderful boyfriend.

I awoke Christmas morning with someone lightly touching my face. I slowly opened one eye and I saw Tristan lying next to me with his cerulean eyes looking down at me. Then I realized what was touching me was his hands lightly caressing my face. When I opened my other eye and looked up at him, he said softly, "Merry Christmas, love." Eventually, we both got out of bed and went into the bathroom...together. I stood at the sink and brushed my teeth while Tristan used the toilet. Then we switched positions and the routine seemed all too familiar and normal. I was surprised at myself because I actually used the toilet in front of him without being shy.

We left the bathroom and went into the family room excitedly. We were both still feeling like little kids on Christmas morning. Even though we knew there was no Santa Claus, that didn't stop us from acting like there was. Nanny and Kate were already up and they were sitting in the room drinking tea. When they saw me and Tristan come in they both greeted us cheerfully. "Happy Christmas!"

Tristan was absolutely ecstatic and it was reflected in his voice. "Can we open presents now, mum? Huh? Can we?" I couldn't help but to laugh because the child inside him had fully emerged.

Kate took a sip of her tea, but I could tell she was hiding a smile behind her teacup. "Not until your brother wakes up," she said.

And just like the night before, Tristan dashed out the room and minutes later he appeared back in the room with Jake in-tow. Jake looked really sleepy and he had a major case of 'bed-head'. He looked like Tristan literally dragged him out of bed. Nanny went over to Jake and handed him a cup of tea that seemed to perk him up a bit.

We all exchanged gifts but Tristan and I waited until all the gifts were exchanged before we gave ours to each other. When the time finally arrived, it was actually a suspenseful moment and we had a fully attentive audience. We were sitting on the floor and I handed him my gift first. He smiled widely and ripped the wrapping paper off in haste. He threw the paper carelessly over his shoulder and wasted no time inspecting the box within. He quickly opened the box while I watched in anticipation. He carefully took the bracelet out and I watched his eyes as he read the inscription. "This is really wicked! I love it!" He handed the bracelet to me and said softly, "Put it on me...please?" I took the bracelet and put it on his wrist. Then he lifted his arm up to inspect it and said, "I'm never taking this off. You know that, right?"

I smiled at him in return. "I'm so glad you like it, baby." Tristan reached behind him and handed me a small box wrapped in shiny red paper with a small silver bow on top. It looked like a ring box but I didn't assume anything. Knowing Tristan, he could stuff something big into a little box. I opened the present with shaky hands and I glanced up at him. His eyes were beaming with excitement and he was smiling brightly.

When the paper was completely removed, a black suede ring box was revealed. Oh my God. I was almost afraid to open it. My hands were still trembling when suddenly, Tristan reached out to steady them. I looked up at him and he was looking intently into my eyes. I slowly opened the box and his hands fell away. I gasped and it seemed so loud because there wasn't any other sound in the room; not even the sound of anyone breathing. It was white-gold, shiny, and gleaming up at me. A Claddagh ring was tucked securely in its black satin bedding and it was calling me to possess it. I stared at it in amazement and then my vision became blurry.

Tears were forming in my eyes and before I knew it, Tristan plucked the ring out from its bed and held it up. I dropped the box and looked up at him, and a few tears trickled down my cheeks. A Claddagh ring is the traditional wedding ring of the Irish since the 17th Century but today it's worn by people all over the world as a universal symbol of love, loyalty, friendship and fidelity, and of their Irish heritage. Tristan picked up my left hand and placed the ring on my middle finger with the crown and heart facing inwards. I knew what that meant and I was speechless. My heart was pounding in my chest as I gazed at this thoughtful, beautiful, sentimental Christmas present that I just received from the man I love. The man I love. I said it...and I realized that I truly meant it. I looked up at Tristan and attempted to speak but he spoke first.

"It's a promise ring. I promise to move it to your ring finger one day."

I couldn't stop crying. It was an emotional moment and I tried to compose myself enough to speak. I would've never expected to receive a Christmas gift like this from him. And I certainly didn't expect him to explain its meaning the way he did. All I could say through my sniffling was, "Tristan...I don't know what to say."

We were looking into each other's eyes, but then he moved closer to me and pressed his lips to mine. We stayed connected to each other for a few seconds before he pulled away first. Then he simply said, "Tell me you love me."

I took a deep breath and said the words I honestly felt I should've said awhile ago but was too afraid to admit. "I love you Tristan." Right at that moment, I heard someone gasp. I doubt it was Jake because the voice was feminine so I was betting on Kate. That's when I remembered that there were other people in the room. Receiving the Claddagh ring from Tristan made me forget everything else and just acknowledge his presence.

Tristan's face seemed to relax and he looked relieved after I admitted my love for him. He cast his eyes towards the floor for a moment and he looked like he was contemplating his next words. When he finally looked up at me again, his voice was strong and he spoke with clear meaning. "Bridget, I fell in love with you the moment I met you." Then he smiled beautifully at me. "The only thing I ever wanted was for you to feel the same way about me." He only said a few words, but I was so happy to finally know that he loved me too.

Kate no longer seemed to be able to contain herself either so she rushed over to both of us and hugged us tightly. She was crying too but laughing through her tears. She looked at Tristan first and said, "Oh, my baby...in love. I never thought I'd see the day." Then she turned her attention to me with a look of motherly affection and said, "Bridget... darling, I knew when Tristan brought you here that you were very special.

The more I got to know you, the more I started to see why he loved you so much. I couldn't tell you before because it wasn't my place."

It was quiet for a mere second before I heard Nanny's dry retort. "I already told her."

Jake followed suit and said, "I *almost* told her." We all started laughing and the emotional and sentimental gift-giving ceremony at the Hathaways started to dissipate into one of much exuberance.

My first Christmas holiday with the Hathaways was one I'll always treasure and never forget. Unfortunately, December 30th came quickly and as my holiday vacation with them came to a close, Kate reminded me that I'd have plenty of opportunities to come and visit. She also said, "Nanny and I had planned to take a trip to Los Angeles, but she isn't keen on flying these days and I'm a little afraid to fly by myself."

I put a gentle hand on her arm. "That's okay. I'd rather come back to Brighton anyway. I really love it here." Kate smiled. "You and Nanny have made me feel like this is a home away from home," I admitted.

She closed some of the distance between us and embraced me. "Oh Bridget. You'll always have a home here," she said tenderly. When she pulled away from me, she kissed my cheek lightly.

After we said our goodbyes, Tristan and Jake were putting our luggage into the trunk of the taxi. Because I liked and respected Kate, I felt that I needed to reassure her of what actually happened in her house between me and Tristan. I pulled her aside to speak to her privately and said, "Kate, I don't know why I'm telling you this but I just feel like you should know." I paused and took a deep breath. "Tristan and I didn't have sex in your house." Then I thought about our sexual encounter in the shower on Christmas Eve and corrected my statement. "I mean, not in the traditional sense. Do you know what I mean?" I gave her a nervous smile and I was actually expecting her to say something along the lines of: 'You better not have sex in my house!'

And like her second-born son, she didn't cease to shock me with her words. "Bridget, I actually *expected* you to have sex. Nanny and I were wagering on how long it would be until we heard the cries of passion coming through the walls." A grin slowly crept onto her face and at that moment she reminded me all too much of Tristan.

On the plane ride home, Tristan fell asleep with his head on my shoulder. He had a look of peaceful contentment on his face as he slept.

I started to think about Christmas Day and the admissions of love that we shared with each other. My mind was made up, and I planned to make love to him as soon as we got back to L.A. And just when I thought I could stop worrying about love, sex, and true feelings…I began worrying about the future. Would Tristan be a part of it? I started to absentmindedly rub the Claddagh ring on my finger and think about its meaning in regards to the way that Tristan had placed it there. Wearing the ring on the left hand with the crown and heart facing inwards signifies that your love has been requited.

Soon my mind started wandering to a new place and the place that I envisioned involved a family of my own. I looked down at Tristan's sleeping form and kissed his forehead. He stirred momentarily and mumbled in his sleep. I gazed at this beautiful man from Brighton, England who appeared one Friday night in September and carved his way into my heart. Then suddenly, I remembered his promise to me after he placed the ring on my finger. My worries dissolved into nothingness and I couldn't stop myself from smiling; smiling at the thought of being Mrs. Hathaway.

Chapter 7

THE HATHAWAY BROTHERS AND I arrived in Los Angeles extremely jet-lagged. Because of the difference in time zones, our plane landed in the early mornings on the day before New Year's Eve. We picked up Jake's car at the airport and I asked him to take me home first. On the ride home I told Tristan that I would be visiting my parents later today so we could exchange Christmas presents. Since I didn't spend the Christmas holiday with them this year, I felt I should at least make an appearance some time shortly after. I didn't ask Tristan to come with me and he didn't volunteer. After his experience with my mother on Thanksgiving, I really couldn't blame him.

When I got home I went to my mailbox to retrieve my mountain of mail and I noticed some Christmas cards intermingled with my usual bills. I got in the house, unpacked my luggage and put on my pajamas to make myself more comfortable. I wasn't going straight to bed because I wanted to check the messages on my answering machine. I was having such an amazing time in Brighton that the thought never crossed my mind to check them. I spent about ten minutes listening to my messages; most of them from friends and co-workers wanting to send me their holiday wishes. After I shuffled through my mail to only read the Christmas cards, I decided to go to bed.

It was late morning when I woke up. Once I got out of bed, I showered and had some breakfast before I drove to my parents' house in Sacramento. It was a very emotional reunion with my mother. We ended up having a very long conversation about how I felt the last time I visited and how the way she treated Tristan affected me. In the end, she was very apologetic and understanding. She asked me to give her another chance to make amends with Tristan. I decided to take her up on her offer and I told her that I'd speak to Tristan about it to see if he would consider it. I knew he would because that's the kind of person he is.

I stayed at my parents' house well into the night. They hadn't seen me in over a month so they weren't exactly willing to let me leave so quickly. Tristan called me on my cell phone a couple times to check up on me. I repeated my mother's offer to him and as expected, he agreed to visit her again. Because it was getting so late, I decided to spend the night in my old room.

On the morning of New Year's Eve I was awakened by the ringing of my cell phone. I was still half asleep when I answered it but I heard Tristan's voice on the other end. "Bridge, are you still at your parents' house?"

I didn't speak at first because I was trying to find my voice. Finally I croaked, "Yeah." My voice was very hoarse so I tried to clear my throat.

"Oh...well, when are you coming back to L.A.?" I glanced over at the clock on the nightstand and it read: 10:20AM. This was actually quite early for Tristan to be awake and I started wondering if he had some kind of work appointment this morning.

"Um, I really don't know. I actually just woke up but I should be back some time this afternoon."

"Okay. Well, my mate Marco ringed me and said he's having a party tonight. You know, for New Year's Eve. I wanted to know if you'd come with me." His voice sounded hopeful and I don't think I could've rejected him even if I wanted to.

"Yeah sure, I'll go."

"Brilliant!"

My curiosity got the best of me again so I had to ask him, "What are you doing up at this hour? You're usually asleep."

He paused for a minute and then his voice lowered. "I've been up for hours. I couldn't sleep last night."

"Why?"

He paused again and his voice was still low but I noticed the change in tone. It was actually...*seductive*. "'Cause you weren't there." This time I had to pause. I laid there with my phone cradled to my ear and my mouth hanging open. I was thankful that he couldn't see my face because I knew I looked ridiculous. When Tristan realized I wasn't responding, he elaborated by saying, "I got so used to sleeping with you at night that when I got home I couldn't sleep. I just laid there looking up at the ceiling...thinking about you." His train of thought seemed to wander and he began talking to me as if he hadn't seen me for months. "The way you smell...the way you feel. I missed the feeling of your body lying next to mine and your soft hair tickling my face. I missed waking up to you in my arms. I took a shower this morning and I actually got pissed." He gave a short laugh. "I was pissed 'cause I was alone and you weren't there to wash my body and I couldn't wash yours." When he spoke next he sounded frustrated. "I need you so fucking bad, love. You have no idea. Please don't make me wank-off anymore."

His last statement totally shocked me because he said it so nonchalantly and without any embarrassment. For the first time since I've known him I think he shared 'too much information'. I had just woken up and Tristan was asking for too much response from my brain. All I could say to him was, "Don't worry, I won't make you wait any longer. And uh, no more wanking okay?" We both laughed. After we hung up with each other I thought about finally having sex with him. I dropped the phone and screamed excitedly into my pillow.

When I got back home in the mid-afternoon, I changed my into my gym clothes and decided to go work out. The whole time I was working out I was thinking about Tristan. I wanted to make love to him tonight and I kept trying to imagine what it would be like. I wasn't going to tell him that I wanted to; I was just going to wait for the opportune moment and go for it. It would be the first time we were going to have sex, wait scratch that...intercourse. Tristan and I had been sexually intimate but we've never gone all the way.

After I finished working out, I showered at the gym and decided to run a few errands. I needed to stock up on food because I had a suspicion that Tristan might want to stay with me for the remaining days of my holiday break. By the time I returned home again it was early evening. I came through the front door and my house phone rang. I put my groceries down and quickly glanced at the Caller ID. It was Tristan... *again*. "Babe, me and Rick will be picking you up in about two hours."

"Okay, I'll be ready."

After I hung up with Tristan, I put my groceries away and went into my bedroom. I rummaged through my closet to look for something to wear for the party. I decided to take another shower and when I was done, I got dressed and did my hair and makeup. By the time I was finished, I heard a text message alert on my cell phone. It was Tristan and he said they were almost at my apartment. I text him back saying that I would be waiting for him outside so he didn't have to come in. Then I went into the hall closet to grab my coat.

As soon as I got outside, I saw a dark blue car pull into my complex and drive towards my apartment. It was dark outside and the windows on the car were tinted so I couldn't see the car's occupants. When it finally pulled up in front of my apartment, I recognized it as Rick's Mustang. Tristan jumped out of the passenger's side and we met halfway. To my surprise, he picked me up in his arms and swung me around. I laughed with delight because I wasn't expecting this kind of dramatic greeting. Then he put me down and kissed me so passionately that I felt my knees begin to weaken. When we finally came up for air, I couldn't hold in my surprise. "What was that for?!? You kissed me like you haven't seen me in weeks!" He still had his arms around me and I smiled as I ran my fingers through his soft, blond hair.

He smiled lovingly down at me and said, "I just missed you, that's all. I haven't stopped thinking about you since we got back."

I smirked at him and replied condescendingly, "Tristan, we just got back yesterday."

He flashed a wicked smile at me this time. "I know, but do you think that matters?"

At that moment, I saw a young woman get out of the backseat behind Rick and walk around the front of the car. She stopped next to the passenger door and waved to me. I had no idea who she was but I waved back anyway. Tristan and I walked over to the car and Rick opened his door for me. When I got in the backseat, the dome light came on and I could see the mystery girl's face more clearly. Her head was turned towards me and she was smiling. She had pale white skin and long chestnut brown hair with blonde streaks. Her eyes were a stormy gray and they were darkened with heavy eyeliner. I found that she had a cold kind of beauty. A vampire was the first thing that came to mind. I said 'hello' to her and she greeted me in return. Tristan got in the backseat next to me and then Rick drove off.

Rick spoke to me first and his voice was very cheerful. "Hey Bridget, how are you doing?"

"I'm doing okay. How are you?"

"I'm alright. I can't wait to get to the party. I am *so* ready to get drunk." He paused for a mere second and then he said, "Oh! Bridget, this is my girlfriend Becca. She'll be the designated driver." He and Becca both started to laugh and then she turned around to look at me.

She smiled at me again and said, "Nice to meet you, Bridget."

"Nice to meet you too."

"Oh, and just so you know...this is the only time Rick introduces me to anyone. He only takes me out when ever he wants to get shit-faced."

I knew she was teasing him because I heard Rick say, "Heyyyyy!" She turned back around and started to laugh again.

Suddenly Tristan moved closer, put his arms around me, and leaned in to kiss me. I didn't kiss him because we had such a close audience. It was so easy to get lost in his kiss because he had such a powerful affect on me. I pushed lightly at his chest and whispered, "Tristan...not here." I glanced over towards the front seat and I saw Becca looking at us from the corner of her eye. I also saw Rick glancing back at us in the rear-view mirror.

Tristan released me, but not before I saw the dejected look on his face. He moved back to where he was sitting and turned his head to look out the window. I was confused and surprised by his reaction so I whispered his name. "Tristan?"

He was still looking out the window and he responded quietly, "I'm alright." I knew he was lying because he wouldn't look me in the eyes. Suddenly, there was tension in the car and no one was speaking. I was thankful to Rick for breaking it.

"So Bridget, how was your trip to Brighton with Tristan's family?"

It took me a minute to answer because I was still pondering my boyfriend's strange behavior. Finally, I found my voice and said, "It was lovely. Tristan's family was so nice and Brighton is absolutely beautiful. I had such a great time that I didn't want to leave. I would've liked to stay longer." As soon as I finished my last sentence, Tristan's head whipped around and he looked at me with wide eyes.

His voice was full of surprise but he sounded accusing. "Why didn't you tell me that? Why didn't you tell me you wanted to stay?"

A look of confusion appeared on my face. Surely he knew I couldn't stay longer. Did he forget that I had a job? His behavior was getting stranger by the minute. Was he really that upset that I pushed him away? I said, "Tristan, I couldn't stay longer. You know I have to go back to work." Apparently he *was* that upset because he didn't answer me. He just turned his head back around and gazed out the car window. I didn't try to speak to him again for the rest of the ride because I was too perplexed as to why he was taking my rejection so hard. Rick and Becca continued to chat in the front seat, and after awhile they seemed oblivious to the fact that they had passengers.

When we arrived at Marco's house we all got out of the car, and I went over to Tristan and put my arms around him. I smiled and his mood seemed to lighten. He gave me a peck on the lips and I looked at him with concern. "Are you okay, baby?"

This time he looked me in the eye and answered, "Yeah, I'm okay. I'm sorry, love. I just..." But he didn't finish his sentence.

We all walked to the front door and Rick rang the bell. The door opened and a tall, young man with jet black hair greeted us. Beneath his matching brows were deep, dark brown eyes that were very brooding. He was clean-shaven with nice full lips. He reminded me of someone from the Mediterranean. It wasn't long before his identity was revealed because Tristan yelled out, "Marco! Let us in you fucking cunt! And where's the beer?" I was momentarily shocked by Tristan's greeting towards his 'friend', but then I remembered that Tristan and his friends have a weird communication system between them that only other males can understand.

Marco communicated back to Tristan by saying, "Hey slut. Glad you could make it." Then he looked over at Rick and said blandly, "And I see you brought your bitch with you, huh?" Now I knew he was talking about Rick but I don't think everyone else did. In that instance, a few things happened all at once: Becca gasped, Tristan lunged at Marco, Rick held Tristan back, Marco jumped into a defensive stance, and I just stood there with my amused smile frozen in place. The entire moment was almost unreal. One minute the atmosphere was light and humorous, and the next it was like a dark cloud appeared out of no where and brought the oncoming threat of violence. In the few seconds after Tristan's attempted attack on his life, Marco quickly backpedaled and yelled, "Whoa Tris! I was talking about Rick, not your girl." Then he seemed to finally notice me and said very politely, "Hey Bridget, nice to meet you. Please come in."

He moved to the side to let us enter and I saw him pat Tristan on the back and say something to him. Tristan's demeanor relaxed and I saw him smile. It was one of the strangest things I've ever seen because the whole episode lasted less than a minute. Also, a part of me started to wonder why Tristan was so on-edge. There seemed to be no end to his abnormal behavior tonight.

When we got inside, Marco took our coats and Rick and Becca separated from me and Tristan. Tristan introduced me to a few people and then I followed him while we went to look for the food and drinks. The party itself was pretty amazing. Marco's house was huge! From the outside you'd never be able to tell but the inside looked like a mansion. There were high ceilings with strings of white lights draping across the top of the walls. There was plenty of space, and the floors were marbled and highly polished. The music was loud and there were a lot of people around just talking, drinking, and mingling. I passed one room and I saw an enormous flat-screen television on the wall. There was a long sectional couch in the room and every cushion was occupied. I assumed everyone would be gathered around the television before midnight to watch the New Year's ball drop.

All night long Tristan wouldn't let me out of his sight. It seemed like wherever he went, he wanted me right along with him. Eventually we met up with Rick and Becca again, and we were all standing around chatting when Marco approached. He continuously joked with us and he and Tristan playfully teased each other nonstop. Marco also seemed to be Tristan's sidekick. I had always thought Tristan and Rick were closer, but Tristan and Marco were two-of-a-kind. That struck me as kind of odd because moments ago Tristan tried to attack him. Naturally though, it wasn't long before I engaged in conversation with Becca and we started to ignore our boyfriends altogether.

And just when I thought Tristan's attitude had begun to normalize for the night, the following events unfolded during the party that contradicted my assumption. As the five of us continued to hang out,

Marco noticed that Tristan had finished his beer. Marco, being the wonderful host asked, "Hey Tris, you want me to get you a refill on that brewsky?"

"Nah, I'm good. I can't get drunk tonight." As soon as Tristan said this, identical looks of surprise appeared on both Marco and Rick's faces.

Marco sputtered and said, "What?!? What do you mean you can't get drunk tonight? This is my New Year's Eve party dude, and you're not gonna get fucking drunk?" He continued to stare at Tristan curiously.

Rick seemed to have similar thoughts because he moved closer to Tristan and pretended to examine him. "Who are you and what have you done with Tristan Hathaway?"

Tristan laughed and said, "I can't 'cause I have something special planned for tonight." He turned towards me and looked into my eyes. Without taking his eyes off me he continued. "And I need to be sober... my head needs to be fucking clear." I didn't say anything; I just smiled back at him.

Marco started shaking his head in disbelief and spoke directly to me. "First he falls in love, then he gets a girlfriend, and now he won't get drunk. You must be some woman, Bridget." Then he smiled charmingly, leaned closer to me and whispered, "Have you got him whipped already? You must be *really* good, Bridget."

I started to laugh and Marco joined in. As I was laughing, I glanced at Tristan and he was looking at the both of us with an expression I couldn't quite place. His jaw was set hard and his eyes narrowed slightly. Then suddenly, he reached out and gently pulled me close to him. I didn't understand the reason behind his possessive gesture and I looked up at him curiously. Surely he wasn't upset by what Marco said. He looked down at me and his face was not happy. Before I could stop myself, I rolled my eyes and looked away. My reaction was almost involuntary because of the way he was acting. What was going on with him?

I needed a moment away from Tristan, plus I needed to use the toilet. I decided to ask Marco where the bathroom was and I was pretty sure he had at least three in his house. I extracted myself from my jealous boyfriend and said, "Hey Marco, could you show me where your bathroom is?" He was talking to one of his guests before I spoke to him but when he heard me address him, he looked at me and started to speak. It was then that Tristan intervened.

"I'll show you where it is."

I looked back at Tristan with a confused expression. "Um, it's Marco's house so I'm sure---"

Tristan interrupted me. "But I know his house too. I'll show you." Before I could argue with him, he took my hand and pulled me along. I didn't resist because I figured this may be a good opportunity to talk to him and ask him why he was behaving so strangely.

The first bathroom Tristan took me to was occupied, so he took me upstairs. He approached another bathroom and knocked on the door. No one answered so he turned the doorknob. The door opened and he poked his head in. Then he looked at me and said, "This one's clear." As soon as he said that, I pushed him out of the way and entered the bathroom. I didn't get to close the door because he followed right behind me. He closed the door, locked it, and we stood there for a few seconds just looking at each other.

I wasn't ready to confront him on his attitude yet so I said, "Tristan, I need to use the bathroom." Then I tried to give him a hint that I wanted him to leave.

He didn't pick up on the hint because he didn't budge. "Go on then." And he looked at me expectedly.

I scoffed at him and said, "Uh, can you leave so I can go? I don't want you standing there."

The look he was giving me was intense and I was actually getting a little nervous. We admit our love for one another and now he starts acting like a crazy, possessive boyfriend who won't leave the bathroom when I ask. I guess he felt argumentative because he still didn't leave. "You never asked me to leave before. Why do you want me to leave now?" Then he started to approach me slowly until he was standing right in front of me looking down at me.

His presence was overpowering me and he was being awfully intimidating. But I wasn't afraid of him. I just felt like he could be unpredictable and do anything at any moment. Then I pleaded with him gently, "Please Tristan? Could you just...stand over there?" I gestured to a place behind the wall where he couldn't see me. At first he looked like he would object. Then I actually thought he was going to leave but he just walked away and stood behind the wall.

I used the toilet, and the minute I turned off the faucet after washing my hands, he came back over to me. I couldn't hold in my frustration any longer but I didn't yell at him. I spoke calmly and softly because I really didn't want to argue with him. "Tristan...baby, what's got into you tonight? Why are you acting so weird?"

His expression was blank but his question was challenging. "How am I acting weird?"

I started ticking them off on my fingers. "Uh, let's see...first you almost attack Marco, then you won't let me out of your sight, you gave Marco a death glare when we were laughing together. Oh, and let's not forget how you were acting in the car when I didn't want to kiss you." When I said the latter part of my statement I saw Tristan flinch.

He moved away from me and leaned on the opposite wall and looked up at the ceiling. He sighed heavily and I thought he was going to start speaking but he didn't. I approached him cautiously and when he looked at me, I put my arms around him and held him close. My eyes began pleading with his. "Tristan...talk to me. What's wrong? Baby, I'm not mad at you. I just want to know what's going on." I tapped his temple with my index finger and said, "What's going on up there tonight, huh?" I smiled at him to try to get him to lighten up.

He closed our embrace, and suddenly he started backing me up towards the sink until my butt touched the edge. His look was intense and for a moment he just searched my eyes. I waited in anticipation because I was very curious as to why there was such a sudden change in him. When he spoke, he had my undivided attention. "Bridget, as soon as we walked in here, every fucking bloke had their eye on you."

That wasn't the answer I was expecting so I said, "So? You're upset because other guys are looking at me?"

"It's the *way* they're looking at you. I even saw Marco checking you out when he thought I wasn't looking. I was about to rip his fucking eyes out when I saw him looking at your arse. And as far as me almost beating the shit out of him...I thought he insulted you, babe. Sometimes he can go too far."

I was honestly surprised at his reason but it still didn't explain why he became distant in the car. "What about in the car? Why were you so upset?" As I was talking to him he moved his head and started nuzzling and kissing my neck. He still had his arms around me and he pressed himself harder against me until my butt was digging into the edge of the sink. He looked back at my face and his eyes were burning with lust. He didn't answer me; he just swooped down and captured my mouth. He kissed me deeply and his tongue swirled around mine as he slanted his mouth over mine repeatedly. The kiss seemed like it would never end. Suddenly, he picked me up and sat me down on top of the sink. My legs instantly opened and he settled between them. I was amazed that he was already hard and he ground himself into me and moaned into my mouth. The whole act was so unexpected that I was momentarily stunned.

He didn't cease to amaze me because just like that...he ended the kiss and resumed speaking. "You've never rejected me before. You've always let me kiss you..." Then he started kissing my neck again and across my collarbone. In between the light kisses he said, "*Whenever* I want... *wherever* I want." My body started reacting to him; his mouth, his body, his erection, and his voice were causing my whole body to flush with heat. His pelvis started to grind into me and I felt his hardness rub my clit in just the right spot. I felt like I wasn't going to make it until midnight. I had to take him home *now*. This beautiful, slightly crazy and possessive British boy was making me very sexually aroused. His next words were spoken very seductively and I was convinced that he was a mind reader. "I'm determined to shag you. Take me home with you tonight."

I started scattering kisses all over his face and neck and in between the kisses I said, "Not *kiss* yet *kiss* we have *kiss* to wait *kiss* until *kiss* after the ball *kiss* drops." A naughty little minx inside of me decided to make herself known so I pulled up the back of shirt, put my hands in his pants and boxers, and grabbed his bare butt. I rubbed it and then I pressed his erection harder against my pussy. The sensation made us both cry out, and at that moment someone knocked on the door. Tristan swore loudly and we heard someone's muffled voice ask if they could use the bathroom.

We did end up staying until the New Year's ball dropped. Tristan and I shared a New Year's kiss and it was full of love and promise. Afterwards, he was eager to leave. We found Rick and he asked, "Rick, I need you to take us back to Bridget's flat."

Rick shook his head. "Nah man, I wanna stay. Why do you wanna leave now? The party's not over."

Tristan's expression turned hard and he stepped quickly into Rick's personal space. "You either take us *now*…or I'm taking your fucking keys, mate."

I couldn't keep the grin off my face when I saw Rick comply with his demand. Tristan was the obvious Alpha Male in his pack and as usual, he got his way. Rick actually gave his keys to Becca and she drove us back to my apartment.

It was only a few seconds after I closed the front door that Tristan was all over me. His hands were everywhere and his kisses were urgent. I won't deny that I was mirroring his actions but I knew we needed to continue our kissing and groping fest in the bedroom. It seemed like we couldn't disconnect from each other. Our mouths and arms stayed glued together as we made our way to my bedroom.

When we finally made it to my room, the air around us shifted and changed so that it was almost tangible. Somehow we ended the kiss and stood there with our eyes burning into one another. We realized that this was the moment we've both been waiting for since we first laid eyes on each other. It was an intense moment and I wanted our first time together to be special. I was excited, aroused, nervous, and scared all at once. Tristan made the first move and came close to me. He was still breathing hard from our passionate kissing. He stood before me and without taking his eyes off me, he lifted his shirt, pulled it over his head, and tossed it somewhere in the room. Then he kicked his boots off and his hands went down to unsnap his jeans.

I stopped him by placing my hands on his and I unsnapped them myself. Then with one sweep, I pulled his jeans and boxers down to his ankles. He stepped out of them and while I was still kneeling before him, I removed his socks one by one. I put my hands on him and caressed his body as I started to stand up. I let his erection brush against the front of my body and I felt him shiver slightly. Then I stood up and looked into his eyes. He slowly removed my shirt and stepped even closer to me to kiss my neck. I moved my head to the side to give him more access and he sucked on my delicate skin. I knew he was marking me…marking me as his. While he was making the hickey on my neck, his hands trailed down to my shoulders in a feather-light touch and he slipped off my bra straps. He pulled away from my neck to look into my eyes. Then his eyes traveled downwards and he pulled my bra down over my breasts.

As soon as my breasts were exposed, he bent down to take each of them into his mouth. He sucked the nipple on my left breast until it peaked and then he gave the same treatment to my right breast. Then his hands dropped to my waistline and he snapped open my jeans and began pulling them over my hips and thighs. He moved his attention from my breast and licked down my middle until he reached my belly button. He was on his knees then and he pulled my jeans down my legs as I stepped out of them.

I kicked off my boots too, and he repeated the same action I did with him by removing my socks one by one. As he was kneeling in front of me, he looked up at me and the look he gave me was filled with pure love and absolute affection. He pulled my panties down gently and when the small triangle of ginger pubic hair was exposed, he pressed his nose against my pussy and inhaled. Then he kissed it while he pulled my panties down to my ankles. I stepped out of my panties and he took that opportunity to place a hand in between my thighs. I spread my legs slightly and that was all the encouragement he needed. He brushed his fingers across the outer lips of my pussy and the sensation caused me to sigh. I knew I was already wet because when he removed my panties, I felt the air hit the moisture between my legs.

Tristan grabbed my hips which forced me to spread my legs wider. His fingers began to spread me open like a flower and his thumb gently rubbed against my clit. I knew Tristan's long fingers probably satisfied many lovers but I had no idea just how much. He inserted one of his long digits inside my slick opening and stroked the inside of my walls. Because I was so aroused, he easily inserted another finger and began a scissors-motion as his thumb continued to brush against my clit. He was pleasuring me so wonderfully that I gasped and moaned, and he took that as a sign that I wanted more.

He didn't disappoint because then he finally put his mouth on me and began licking my pussy from back to front. I started to whimper and buck against his mouth. He poked his tongue out and began flicking my clit lightly. My legs started trembling and I grabbed his hair and started running my fingers through it. I was gasping and moaning from the pleasure, and I realized that if I let him continue I would actually cum in his mouth. I said breathlessly, "Tristan...look at me." He looked up at me from between my legs and I put my hands on either side of his head to lift him up towards me. He stood up and I could see my juices glistening on his lips.

His eyes quickly filled with lust so I backed up onto the bed and laid down on it with my knees closed. He approached the bed slowly and climbed onto it at my feet. Then he put his hands on the top of my knees and spread my legs slowly. All my shyness vanished in Brighton so I didn't resist. I opened them widely and invitingly. He knelt there for a moment just staring at my open pussy that was exposed and waiting for him. He whispered, "Ohhh Bridget." Then he laid himself between my legs and the moment his warm, hard cock touched my wet, swollen pussy we both gasped in pleasure. He bent down to kiss me and I didn't recoil. I tasted myself on his lips and his tongue plunged deep into my mouth. We probably tasted every crevice in each other's mouths while we started to hump involuntarily against one another. It felt so good that we were both moaning into each other's mouths and kissing each other with even more wanting.

Eventually we ended the kiss and Tristan happened to glance over and notice the condoms on the nightstand that I placed there earlier in preparation for this moment. He rose up onto his knees and moved towards the side of the bed to retrieve them but I grabbed his hips to stop him. I was still lying on my back with my legs spread and I looked seductively into his eyes and almost purred the words: "Come here." He looked at me questioningly and tried to lie between my legs again but I said, "No, come *here*." And I crooked my index finger and beckoned him. He moved from between my legs and I said wickedly, "Bring that magnificent cock over here."

As I laid my head down on the pillow, Tristan figured out exactly what I meant. He crawled over to where my head lay and looked down at me. His knees were at the side of my head, and I turned towards him and grasped his erection. I heard him inhale sharply and he spread his legs slightly apart to give me better access.

Without hesitation, I stretched my neck and licked the pre-cum that was lingering on the tip. Then I took his throbbing manhood into my mouth. He was so big that I couldn't fit the entire length of him in my mouth so I licked up and down his shaft. When I got to the head, I sucked on it gently and darted my tongue inside the opening. I bobbed my head a little to cause more friction; all the while Tristan was moaning and gasping. I saw his legs shaking but I didn't let up. While I was stroking his erection with my hand, my mouth ventured underneath and I licked his sac and took each of his testicles into my mouth and sucked on them equally. He started whimpering and bucking gently into my fist and I increased my strokes.

Suddenly, he cried out loudly but he didn't cum. I looked up at him and he was breathing fast and his body was trembling. He yelled, "Bridget! Stop! I'm gonna..." I released him and he reached over and quickly grabbed the three-pack of condoms off the nightstand. He tore one off and held it out to me. Then he said urgently, "Put it on me. Please, love. Do it now!"

I took the condom and carefully opened the package and took the rubber out. I looked up at him again and he was holding his erection for me to place it on. I rolled it on him, and with lightning fast speed, he moved on top of me and buried himself inside me to the hilt. The sensation made me cry out his name. He fit perfectly inside me and I instinctively wrapped my legs around him. His arms were on either side of me supporting his weight and he began thrusting in a rhythm that was so pleasurable that he was actually hitting my G-spot. His pubic bone was hitting against my clit and I felt my pussy release more of its essence. Tristan must've felt it too because he moaned and starting thrusting into me faster.

I grabbed his shoulders and pulled him down so that his beautiful, tattooed body was molded on top of mine. We kissed each other deeply and continued to match each other's pace. This was the feeling I've been waiting for; to have this gorgeous boy inside me...fully and completely. We broke the kiss and held each other tightly as Tristan continued to pound into me so perfectly. His voice trembled when he said, "Hold me tight, Bridget. Don't let me go." He moaned deep in his throat as the sexual pleasure consumed him.

"Don't worry baby, I'm not letting you go," I replied breathlessly.

Our cries of passion filled my bedroom. My bed shook and rocked, and the headboard started its own rhythm as it banged itself against the wall. Tristan felt so good inside me that I wanted our love-making to last forever. I didn't care if my neighbors could hear us, I wanted the whole world to know how absolutely wonderful it was to make love to him. Suddenly, Tristan pulled himself out and lifted himself off of me. He sat down between my legs and said to me urgently, "Come here... come sit on top of me."

I didn't waste any time. I climbed onto his lap, wrapped my legs around his waist, and this time I grabbed his erection and shoved it deep inside me. We both cried out again and Tristan wrapped his arms around me so tight that my breasts were crushed against his chest. I held him as tight as I could, even though it was a little difficult because his back was sweaty. We eliminated the space between our bodies so that it looked like we were welded together.

My pelvis rocked against him while he continued to thrust inside me. Our peaks were closing in on us and we both felt it. It was like we were actually becoming one with our feelings. His cries were in sync with mine and the spectacular finale was rapidly approaching. I had my head on his shoulder and I was whimpering from the extreme pleasure while Tristan's hand reached up to cradle my head. Then he spoke directly into my ear with an urgent and breathless voice. "Look at me, love. Look at my eyes."

I removed my head from his shoulder and looked at his face. Our eyes met and locked on each other. We were breathing fast and grinding into each other until suddenly Tristan said in a strangled voice, "Bridget...I'm gonna cum. Cum with me, darlin'...right now." My body answered his immediately and before I knew it, we both yelled out in ecstasy and came together. I felt my womanly flower release its feminine nectar all over his amazing cock, and if he weren't wearing a condom I know I would've felt his too. Our bodies bucked and humped against each other rhythmically. We trembled in each other's arms and held each other tight. I feared the bed would break from under us from the force of our climax.

Never in my life have I experienced an orgasm as intense as the one I shared with Tristan. Maybe it was because our bodies were so in-tuned with each other. Maybe it was because we waited so long for this moment to happen. Or maybe it was because we were so in love.

Eventually we both started to come down and our breathing began to steady. We still didn't release each other because we were both content to just hold on and never let go. Finally, my bedroom was silent and I kept my head nuzzled in the crook of Tristan's neck and listened to his even breathing. It was strange because time seemed to stand still and we were both amazed at what had just transpired between us.

When we actually did unravel our arms and legs from each other, the only thing our bodies were capable of doing was flopping down on the bed to lay motionless. My body fell on top of his and my head rested on his lean, masculine chest. He began to run his fingers lightly up and down my back and I was surprised that he could even move his limbs. I started to laugh and it must've been contagious because he laughed too. I was so exhausted that it took an enormous amount of strength just to ask him this simple question: "Was I worth the wait?"

Tristan kissed me on the top of my head and then his fingers ceased their caress on my back. He wrapped his arms around me again and held me tightly. I was listening to his heart beat but I heard his voice rumble softly in his chest. "I would've waited forever for you. I love you, Bridget."

Chapter 8

I USED TO REALLY LOVE my car. When I graduated from high school, my parents rewarded me with one of the best gifts you can give a teenager: a new car. My car wasn't new, it was used...but I loved it. It was a 1997 Toyota Corolla and it was red; my second favorite color. When I received it from my parents, I saw it as a symbol of freedom and independence. That was long ago because lately my beloved car hasn't been anything but a symbol of headache and frustration. I've always thought Toyotas were so reliable. My father used to say that you could practically drive them into the ground before they needed to be replaced. I must have received the 'runt of the litter' because I found myself constantly taking it in for repairs.

I just left work and I was sitting in Monday afternoon's rush hour traffic blasting Shiny Toy Guns' *'You Are the One'* when my graduation present decided to take its last breath. The traffic light had just turned green when suddenly my car shook violently. I gently pressed the accelerator but the car wouldn't move. People behind me started honking at me so I pressed it harder in a futile attempt to get it to move. The engine revved loudly and it sounded like rusty metal grinding against concrete, but still no movement from the car. I started to panic and just when I thought things couldn't get any worse...they did.

The car completely shut off and stalled right in the middle of traffic. The radio and all the lights on the dashboard also shut off so I assumed that the battery had died as well. I sat there with a look of shock and bewilderment on my face. I rested my head on top of the steering wheel and wished that this was all a dream. Other motorists quickly brought me out of my reverie because they kept honking at me. And those that drove around me took a moment to tell me exactly how pissed off they were. My panic was increasing and my anger started to build so I screamed back at them from behind my still rolled-up window, "SHUT UP! JUST SHUT UP!"

After awhile I started to ignore the irate motorists and realize that I needed to call for help. Thankfully I had Triple A on my car so I used my cell phone to call for a tow truck. After I told them the location and description of my stalled vehicle, I sat quietly and waited. While sitting in the internal silence of my now inoperable Toyota, I started to worry about the cost of repairs. I was on a budget and I knew that this new catastrophe would be a major set-back in my finances. In addition to feeling angry about my car dying on me, I started to get very upset. I knew that if this repair turned out to be costly, I'd have to borrow money from someone and I hated doing that. I guess it was part of my personality but I hated having to ask for charity.

Oddly, it was at this moment that I thought of Tristan. Tomorrow was Valentine's Day and I was planning to pick up his gift today. With my plan now moot, I decided to call him and tell him what was going on in case he started to worry about my whereabouts. I dialed his number and his phone rang a couple times before he picked up.

"Hey babe, what's up?"

Because I was still highly upset and frustrated about my whole car situation, my voice was shaky when I spoke to him. "Tristan..." I actually wanted to cry but I held my tears at bay.

Tristan immediately sensed that I was upset. His voice sounded concerned with a slight tinge of urgency when he said, "Bridge, what's the matter? Are you alright?"

"Tristan, you won't believe what just happened. My car just died on me right in the middle of traffic."

"Where are you? You want me to come get you?"

"No, not yet. I just called for a tow truck. When they come, I'm going to ask them to take me to the nearest repair shop."

"Oh, okay. Are you *sure* you don't want me to come? 'Cause I will babe, I don't care."

"No, that's alright. I'll call you back later after I drop off the car. You can pick me up then." At this moment, a police car pulled up in back of me. "Tristan, I have to go. But I'll call you back sweetie...I promise." After I hung up with Tristan, I got out of the car to speak to the police. I was actually glad that I didn't ask Tristan to come because he hates the police with a passion. He admitted to me once that he and Jake both had DUI's in the past, and back in Brighton the police were basically the enemy. I felt that Tristan's extreme dislike towards the police stemmed from his problem with authority...but I didn't tell him that.

The police officer was a tall, burly man with a salt-n-pepper mustache. "So, what happened here miss?"

"Uh, my car just died...basically," I laughed. "But I just called a tow truck and they said they're on their way."

"Alright then. I'll just stay here until it gets here." He walked back to his patrol car. Then he came back with little orange traffic cones and started placing them strategically around my car.

Finally, the tow truck came and the driver hauled my little red Toyota onto his flatbed. "Where do you want me to take you?" He asked wearing an oil-stained navy jumpsuit.

"I need to take it to the nearest repair shop." While I was riding in the truck with the driver, I spotted a used car dealer on the corner. As we approached, I saw that it was also Service & Repair. "You can drop me off there," and I pointed to the dealership.

As the tow truck driver was unloading my car onto the lot, a salesman came out to greet me. He was tall and middle-aged, and he was also a fellow redhead. His brows furrowed as his eyes roamed over my inoperable vehicle. "Hmmm...I'm guessing you're in need of a repair?" He gave me a cheeky smile.

I smiled back. "Yeah, I need to get it fixed. Do you guys have time to take a look at it? I can't even move the car. Everything just shut off while I was sitting in traffic."

The tow truck driver left and the salesman said, "Sure, I'll get a couple of mechanics to move your car into the service area." He walked away and I stood there next to my car wishing that it would magically come to life so I could drive it home safely. Shortly after, I gave the mechanics my car keys and they were able to move my car. "You can have a seat in the waiting room while we take a look at your car," and he pointed to a glass door with the words: *Service Entrance.*

I was on-edge the whole time I was sitting in the waiting room. I was worrying my bottom lip between my teeth and my right knee started to bounce up and down involuntarily. I had a feeling one of the mechanics was going to bring me bad news and I would be paying a hefty price for this new repair. I was deep in-thought and when my cell phone rang, it startled me. When I answered it, I heard Tristan's voice on the other end and his voice was still laced with concern and worry.

"Babe, what's going on? Where are you now?"

"Um, I'm at a car dealer. They have a service area and they just took my car in."

"Oh. Why didn't you ring me then?" I couldn't be exactly sure, but it seemed like Tristan was getting upset too.

"Baby, I just got here. I was going to call you after I spoke to one of the mechanics about what it's going to take to fix that piece of shit."

"Okay well...let me know how much it costs."

"Tristan, I'm not letting you pay for it."

"Why not?"

I sighed heavily and my pride started to bloom inside me. "Because I don't want your money. Plus, this could be expensive. I think the battery died too."

"Bridget, I know you're too proud and everything but I wanna help you. You said it could be expensive so are you gonna be able to pay for it all by yourself?" I was silent and I knew that Tristan knew my answer. "Yeah...just let me help okay? Even if you let me pay half."

"I'll think about it," I said quietly.

This time Tristan was silent for moment. Then his voice changed to a condescending tone and he said, "You are *so* stubborn." I couldn't help but laugh inwardly because my boyfriend knew me so well.

I sat and waited a little while longer and stared at the television in the waiting room. I wasn't actually watching it, it just happened to be in my line of vision. I heard someone call my name, so I looked up and saw one of the mechanics who drove my car away approach me. He told me in 'lamens terms' what was wrong with my car. As he was speaking to me, all I could think about was how much it would cost to fix. According to him, my car had extensive damage so I knew the repairs were going to be costly...just as I feared. I was getting impatient with him because he seemed to be avoiding telling me the price. Finally I became frustrated and asked him flat-out how much the repairs would cost and when he told me, my face immediately fell. It was going to cost over $900 to drive my graduation present off this lot. I think my face turned red or I started to semi-hyperventilate because a look of concern appeared on his face and he asked, "Are you okay?" I wanted to say, 'NO I'M NOT OKAY! I DON'T HAVE THAT KIND OF MONEY!'

In the end, I told him to go ahead and fix it. In an attempt to comfort and reassure me, he said, "We already started working on it and we have the replacement parts in stock. You can pick up the car tomorrow between four and five in the afternoon."

I gave him my thanks and I walked out of the waiting room onto the lot. I grabbed my phone from my purse and called Tristan back. I told him that he could finally pick me up and where the dealer was located. He asked me again, "How much will the repairs cost?"

But I couldn't find it in myself to tell him over the phone. "I'll talk to you about it once we get back to my apartment."

Just as I was putting my cell phone back into my purse, I happened to glance to my right. A shiny ruby red convertible caught my attention and I immediately had to inspect it. I started walking towards it and as I got closer, I saw the emblem on the front: a silver Mercedes-Benz emblem. My mouth suddenly dropped because this car was hot! I began admiring it and I noticed how beautiful the color was. The top was down and it was a two-seater with dark interior and shiny silver alloy wheels. I was very appreciative of the wheels because my car had old, tacky hub-caps.

As my eyes continued to feast upon this luxurious vehicle, I looked at the back and saw dual-exhaust pipes and the badge on the car read: *SLK 280*. I let out a low whistle as I dared to look at the sticker price. The Mercedes was a 2006 and a part of me got excited to see that it was an automatic transmission because I couldn't drive a stick-shift. My eyes read down the sticker at all the car's features and when I finally saw the price, I gasped; $41,000. For some bizarre reason, my hope deflated. I honestly knew I couldn't afford the car in the first place but that didn't stop me from wishing I could. I was peeking inside the interior at the dashboard to see the mileage. I was shocked to see how low it was: only 2407 miles.

I was so enraptured by this vehicle that when the salesman approached me, he made me jump in surprise. I turned around to face him and he was smiling at me. It was the same salesman that greeted me when I brought my car here. "It's a beautiful car, isn't it?"

I smiled back at him and said, "Yeah, it is. I really like Mercedes."

"Very low mileage too. We actually got the car in today. Say, would you like to take it for a drive?"

I knew if I agreed that I would feel even worse about not being able to leave my crappy, red Toyota here and buy this majestic, ruby Mercedes. I politely declined his offer and laughed lightly. "Oh, no thanks. I'm not in the market for buying a new car right now."

The salesman looked at me skeptically because he knew as well as I did that my car was a piece of shit. He tilted his head to the side and said, "Are you *sure*? Maybe we can work out a deal."

"No, that's okay. This car is a little pricey for me anyway."

"Oh, well that's not a problem. We have plenty of other cars. You can take a look around and maybe---" We were interrupted by the loud sound of a motorbike engine. We both looked towards the sound and we saw Tristan riding towards us on his black and lime green Kawasaki motorcycle. It took a moment for the realization to hit me that *that's* what he was taking me home in. Wait scratch that...taking me home *on*. My mouth dropped again and I couldn't help but to gasp. A look of utter surprise appeared on my face and suddenly my breathing increased. I've never rode on a motorcycle before and I started to panic internally.

When I finally found my voice, I said to the salesman, "Well, that's my ride. It was nice talking to you and I'll probably see you tomorrow when I pick up my car." Strangely, he had an identical look of surprise on his face too as I quickly waved goodbye and walked over to Tristan.

For some reason I couldn't close my mouth and my feeling of surprise would not dissipate. As I approached Tristan he took his helmet off and turned the engine off. He was sitting there straddling the bike and I couldn't help but to stare openly at him. Before I could stop myself I shrieked, "Tristan!"

He started laughing. "What? What's the problem?" My eyes were wide and I was looking at his bike as if I'd never seen it before.

"I thought you'd be picking me up in a car." I honestly didn't know why I thought this because I knew he didn't have a car. I guess because I was so used to traveling in them, I didn't think of the fact that he'd arrive on his own mode of transportation.

All of a sudden, a confused look appeared on his face. "A car? What car? I don't have a car."

I sputtered and said, "Uh, I don't know...Rick's car...Jake's car?"

Tristan grinned at me and spoke to me as if I were a child. "Rick has his car and I don't know where he is. And Jake's in San Diego." Then the look of confusion reappeared on his face and he frowned slightly. And when he spoke, he actually sounded insulted. "Why, what's the problem? You don't like my bike or something?"

"It's not that, it's just..." I sighed and looked down for a moment. When I looked up at him again I spoke softly. "I've never been on a motorcycle before and I guess I'm a little nervous."

This time Tristan smiled warmly at me and his face had a look of clear understanding. "Awww, babe. Don't be afraid. I won't let anything happen to you. I won't let you fall." As soon as he said that I started to think: *Well, what if someone hits us? There's no protection on this thing.* I was still apprehensive and my eyes were roaming over his small, unsafe motorcycle when I happened to notice something pink tied down on the back. It was sitting on the part of the seat where I assumed I would be sitting. As I moved closer to look at the mysterious pink object, Tristan put the kickstand down on his bike and hopped off. Upon closer inspection, I realized that it was another helmet.

I couldn't contain my surprise when I exclaimed, "What's that?!?"

Tristan moved close to me and smiled down at me. Then he reached over his bike and untied the helmet from the seat. He picked it up and handed it to me. He continued to smile as he said, "It's for you, love. It's for whenever you ride with me." The helmet was a combination of pastel pink, white and black with a pretty magenta butterfly airbrushed on each side; it was truly feminine.

My eyes widened as I gazed at this thoughtful gift from my beautiful, caring boyfriend. I've never ridden with him before so I was curious as to when he bought the helmet. "Thank you sweetie. When did you get this?" I examined the helmet further by turning it around in my hands. It was so girly and I actually loved it!

Tristan lifted his hand to caress my cheek. The look in his sky blue eyes was full of love and I was completely lost in them. When he spoke, his voice was gentle. "The day after we met. I planned to ask you out and I didn't know if I would be picking you up. So I figured that you would need one. Since you've never ridden with me, I just kept it in case you ever wanted to."

I was momentarily shocked that he had the helmet all this time. Then it registered in my brain that the helmet was pink and I was curious as to why Tristan chose this particular color. I asked him nonchalantly, "Why did you buy me a pink one?"

He smiled charmingly down at me and he blinked slowly as if he knew I would ask. "You told me when we met that pink was your favorite color." My heart burst at the fact that he remembered my favorite color. I couldn't help but to tilt my head up and kiss him tenderly on the lips because I loved him so much.

We were getting ready to leave and I knew he could tell I was still afraid of his bike. He helped me onto the bike and as soon as I was seated safely on top of it, I quickly put my helmet on for fear that the bike would tip over and I would fall off. Tristan climbed on the bike in front of me and then he turned to look at me. "Put your arms around my waist, darlin'...and hold me tight," he said gently. He didn't need to tell me twice because I latched onto him like a leech. He smiled over his shoulder and then he turned back around and put on his helmet. He kicked the kickstand up, and as soon as he started the engine, I jumped and squeezed him tighter. He turned his head around again and yelled over the engine noise, "Don't be afraid! I won't go fast!"

He kept to his promise and didn't race through the streets like I knew he normally did. Tristan was a fearless dare-devil and I knew he pushed his bike to its limits. I kept my eyes closed the whole time and didn't loosen my grip on his waist for one second. I was absolutely terrified.

When we finally got to my apartment, it wasn't until after Tristan turned off the engine and spoke to me that I actually released him. "Babe, we're home. You can let go now." I heard him chuckle and his voice was clear. I slowly opened my eyes and I saw that he had removed his helmet. I removed mine too, and as soon as I took it off, I sighed with relief. My body was still trembling slightly from the fear of riding on it. Tristan helped me down off his bike and I knew that he noticed the state that I was in. He showed me no mercy as he started to playfully tease me. "So do you want one? How about I buy you a pink one?"

I looked at him with wide eyes and shouted, "No way!" And I shook my head vigorously.

He started to laugh and then he said, "You sure? I'll teach you how to ride it." I just looked at him with a shocked expression and he continued to laugh. "Awww, c'mon Bridge...it's fun. You liked it, didn't you? Go on, admit it."

His playfulness caused me to laugh too and I said loudly, "I was terrified, Tristan!"

We both continued to laugh and that eased most of my anxiety. He put his arm around me and we walked into my apartment. Once we got ourselves settled, we were on the sofa when he asked me about my car again. "So...what did they say?" I explained to him what was told to me by the mechanic and Tristan let out a low whistle and said, "Shit...that's really bad. And they're gonna have it fixed by tomorrow?"

"Yeah, that's what he said. He said I could pick it up between four and five in the afternoon."

Suddenly, Tristan was silent and he looked like he was deep in-thought. He looked at me for a minute and then looked away. Then it seemed like he shook himself out of his reverie and asked, "And how much is it gonna cost to fix?" I braced myself first before I answered. Tristan didn't look surprised by the expensive cost and he just nodded his head. He turned to me and tilted his head to the side. He looked at me curiously and said slowly, "And you want me to pay *half*?" He said it like he wanted a confirmation from me rather than just a plain answer.

Truthfully, I knew I couldn't even afford to pay half. I had to push my pride way down deep inside me and accept his help. I really hated doing it but I honestly didn't have a choice because the simple fact was: I needed my car. I sighed heavily and scooted closer to him on the sofa. I turned my whole body towards him and prepared myself as I asked him for money. Wait, scratch that...*a lot* of money. "Okay, here's the thing." I paused to compose my humility and then I continued. "I really can't afford to pay half so if you could pay for it...I'd pay you back. I promise."

Tristan smiled and leaned close to me. He chuckled, and his expression was one of absolute amusement. He grasped my chin gently and said, "You are so cute, you know that? Bridget, I don't want your money. You don't have to pay me back, love. I told you I wanted to help you."

"But---"

Tristan silenced me by placing his lips on mine. He kissed me firmly, and when he broke the kiss he whispered against my lips, "Just let me." His seductive spell was circling and ensnaring me, and I couldn't object. I tried to argue with him but no words would come forward onto my lips. I decided to bottle down my pride completely and just accept his help...after I kissed him thoroughly. As much frustration, sadness, disappointment, and anger that I experienced today, I really needed some loving affection. And I knew Tristan was the person who would willingly provide it to me.

After Tristan smothered me with enough affection to last me a lifetime, he actually pulled a wad of money out of his pocket and handed it to me. I was momentarily stunned by this gesture and I stared at him in amazement. I unrolled the money and started to fan through it. I realized that he gave me *a lot* more than what I needed for my car so I counted out what I needed and gave the rest back to him.

He stayed with me throughout the evening and I made him dinner. While we were eating, he paused suddenly and he looked like a light bulb just went off in his head. Then he asked me curiously, "So...who's taking you to work tomorrow?" Before I could give him an answer he said quickly, "Please let me do it!"

The thought of riding on his bike again brought an unwanted feeling of anxiety back to the surface and I started to shake my head. "Tristan---"

He interrupted me before I could object and I had a feeling that he knew I was going to. "Bridge, I know you were scared. Really, I know. But just let me take you to work in the morning and then you can have someone else bring you home. Please? I really want to. I've always thought about taking you to work." The way he started smiling at me made my heart melt and it became harder to object. Would it kill me to ride with him once more? Well...maybe. But he seemed so eager to do it and I was surprised to know that taking me to work was important to him.

Finally, I decided to take control of my fear and ride with him again. Besides, I didn't want to crush his feelings. Not to mention, he was spending over $900 to have my crappy car fixed. I sighed and spoke as if I were surrendering. "Okay, baby. You can take me to work tomorrow."

A smile instantly lit up his face. *"But...you have to be here early...like 8AM okay?"* Tristan was not a morning person and I knew this may be difficult for him to accomplish.

He didn't look perturbed when I mentioned the time of day and all of a sudden his smile disappeared. It was replaced with a very roguish expression. Tristan practically oozed natural sexiness so it wasn't difficult for him. He said slyly, "Who says I'm leaving tonight?" Then he waggled his eyebrows at me like he does whenever he says something naughty or flirtatious.

When we finished eating dinner, Tristan helped me load the dishes into the dishwasher and tidy up the kitchen. It was actually a normal routine for us because he spent most of his evenings at my apartment and I always cooked for him. I never asked him why because I really enjoyed his company and I enjoyed sharing my bed with him. I enjoyed it so much that sometimes I thought that maybe it wouldn't be so bad if he moved in. I was afraid to ask him because I feared his rejection. I could only imagine how much fun he has living in his 'bachelor pad'. I wasn't sure he wanted to make a commitment like sharing space with me on a more permanent basis. But I decided if our relationship progressed further, that maybe I would bring up the subject.

Tristan noticed that I was deep in-thought. "What are you thinking about, huh?"

Suddenly, my train of thought changed and I started thinking about his motorcycle and why he chose that instead of owning a car. I turned and looked at him curiously when I asked, "I was just wondering...why don't you have a car?"

His answer was short and sweet. "Too much responsibility."

"But you know...a car is safer than a motorcycle. And what about when it rains? Don't you get all wet?"

He started to wipe down the counter with a sponge and he wasn't looking at me when he answered. He just shrugged indifferently and said, "Eh, I'm used to it babe. I've been riding for so long...plus, it's more fun than a car." Then he said something totally unexpected that shocked me to the point where I was speechless and motionless. And to add more fuel to the fire, he stopped cleaning and looked directly into my eyes; like he wanted to make a point. "But I guess if we got married, I'd need to get a car or maybe one of those bleeding minivans. You know, for our kids."

Got *married?!?* For *our* kids?!? Tristan was the king of saying things of shock value but this was just over-the-top. We had another one of those moments; the ones where time seems to stand still and we just look at each other. I couldn't even say anything. No, scratch that...I was *afraid* to say anything.

Finally, he released me from his hypnotic spell and I said, "I'm going to call Autumn and ask her if she can pick me up from work tomorrow."

When I spoke to Autumn, she happily agreed to pick me up and I told her about my plan to get Tristan's Valentine's Day present. A few days ago, I was shopping at the mall and I saw a nice shirt that matched the color of Tristan's eyes exactly. She said that she'd take me to the mall after work so I could buy the shirt and then she'd drop me off at the dealer so I could get my car. Once we agreed to the plan, I hung up with her.

When I woke up in the morning, I was surprised that it wasn't difficult to wake Tristan. I figured that it was because he really wanted to take me to work. Part of me was truly flattered and honored, but the other part of me was fearful of sitting upon that mini rocket of his that he called a bike.

While we were in the shower together, I started to wonder if he realized that today was Valentine's Day. I was about to remind him but a sneaky side of me wanted to see if he would figure it out himself. Showering with Tristan is like the extended version of a normal shower. The reason for this is because we always end up doing something sexual. We can't just wash and get out; we have to wash, kiss, and then have some type of sex before we're satisfied with getting out. By the time we were done, we were actually running a little late.

Just like yesterday, I kept my eyes closed for most of the ride but I did sneak a peek or two just to make sure Tristan was going in the right direction. When we finally pulled up in front of the school, we attracted a lot of attention; mostly from the students. They were in awe of Tristan's cool motorcycle. When I took off my helmet, some of my students recognized me and I heard lots of "Wow! It's Miss Monahan!" and "Man, she's lucky!"

Surprisingly, this time I was able to get off the bike by myself. Tristan was also surprised because when he saw me get off, he whipped his head around to look at me. He had the bike idle while he pulled off his helmet to give me a goodbye kiss. For some odd reason, I felt like showing Tristan off a bit so I kissed him longer than was necessary. Deep inside me, I was hoping one of my co-workers would see us and notice what a gorgeous boyfriend I had. After I kissed him, a very pleased and satisfied smile stayed glued to my face as I walked up the steps to the school.

I brought my helmet with me and when I got to my desk, I proudly put it on display. As my students walked in they all stopped to look at it and some of them mentioned seeing me outside on the bike with Tristan. I was actually happy to tell them about my experience riding on it.

Since it was Valentine's Day, there came a time during the day where the students were exchanging Valentine's greetings. It wasn't until right before lunchtime that I actually received my special greeting. My students were leaving class to go to the cafeteria when I glanced at the door and noticed a delivery person standing outside. Then I noticed he had a bouquet of flowers in his hand.

After my last student left, he made eye contact with me and asked my name. I affirmed my identity, and he came into my class and told me that the flowers were for me. I couldn't contain my surprise as he placed the bouquet on my desk right next to the pink helmet Tristan bought for me. I signed a slip he had in his hand and then he left me standing there gazing affectionately at a clear glass vase containing an arrangement of two dozen pink roses. The roses were accented with Baby's Breath and the vase itself had a pretty pink bow on it. I noticed a card neatly tucked into the fragrant bouquet and I touched it gently. My eyes read over the words: *I bet you thought I'd forget, but I love you too much. Love, Tristan.* I couldn't help the tears that started to blur my vision. I was so touched that he sent me such lovely, perfect roses for our first Valentine's Day.

When classes let out, Autumn was waiting for me in front of the school and I was relieved to be traveling in a safer mode of transportation. She took me to the mall and I bought Tristan's shirt and I had them gift wrap it for me. Then she took me to the auto dealer to pick up my worthless piece of shit that I called my car.

When we got there, I didn't see my car anywhere on the lot. I retrieved Tristan's present from the backseat and then I got out of the car. I started to walk towards the service area and as I was walking I looked over to where I last saw the ruby red Mercedes; it was gone. A part of me was actually saddened by this but then my sadness quickly turned into jealousy. I was jealous because I knew that someone somewhere was lucky enough to purchase it and cruise around the city in a beautiful, expensive convertible. And here I was about to drive off in a ten-year-old, unreliable, not-worth-the-headache compact car.

When I walked into the service area, I went over to the cashier and told her what car I was picking up. She shuffled through the papers on her desk for a few seconds and then she said with a straight face, "We don't have it."

I looked at her in shock and exclaimed, "What do you mean you don't have it?!? Then where is it?!?"

"Wait one moment while I get the service manager."

I was actually fuming with anger because I just wanted my pitiful car back so I could get on with my life. I was already embarrassed that I had to use Tristan's money to pay for the repairs.

A few minutes later, a chubby middle-aged man with glasses and a comb-over came over to me and said, "Your boyfriend took the car earlier."

My emotions changed from fiery rage to utter and total confusion and it seemed like a million questions were racing through my mind at once: *Why would Tristan pick up my car? And how did he pick it up? Did someone take him here? And why did he give me the money to pay for the car if he was taking it? And why didn't he call me and tell me?* Once I had my emotions under control, I apologized to the cashier and walked out.

Autumn was still sitting in her car and she yelled out the window, "What's wrong?!?"

I walked back over to her car and got in the passenger's side. Then I turned to her with an expression of confusion. "My car is not here. Tristan took it."

Her expression matched mine. "Why would Tristan take your car?"

"I have no idea but I'm going to find out." I dialed Tristan's cell phone but he didn't pick up and I was sent to voicemail. Then I dialed his house phone and Rick answered. I think I sort of yelled unintentionally because I was frustrated and I didn't understand what was going on. When I spoke, my voice was very unfriendly. "Rick. Where's Tristan?"

He was quiet for a second before he answered. And when he spoke his voice sounded meek. "I thought he was at your house." I started to get angry again because he wasn't any help and the whole situation was getting stranger by the minute.

I replied back to him sharply, "Okay fine. Thanks." And then I hung up. I looked over at Autumn. "Rick said Tristan's at my place, so you can just take me home."

For some strange reason, she was driving abnormally slow; like she was just cruising. "Why are you driving so slow?" I asked irritably.

Without taking her eyes off the road, she replied, "To give you time to cool off, missy." Then she turned her head towards me with a stern expression. "Relax Bridge, I'm sure Tristan will explain everything." Because she was taking so long to get us to our destination, I actually started to zone out. My anger eventually dissolved and my mind started to wander. I was so deep in-thought, that I didn't realize when she finally pulled into my complex. The sun was beginning to set and I was tired and emotionally drained. I just hoped I would be able to show some excitement when I gave Tristan his Valentine's present.

Autumn pulled up in front of my apartment and I looked out the window expecting to see my red Toyota but I didn't. My eyes widened and my mouth opened in cartoon-like fashion. When she stopped the car, I slowly opened the passenger door and climbed out of the car. I took slow steps towards the space where my car should've been sitting. There was something occupying the space but it wasn't my car. It was the ruby red Mercedes Benz SLK 280. Even in the diminishing light of dusk, the car still shone. I couldn't believe what I was seeing. I approached it cautiously because I felt like if I moved too fast, the car would disappear right before my eyes. My eyes began traveling along the length of the car and when they reached the front, I noticed something on the hood. I walked slowly towards the front of the car and sitting on the hood was an enormous red bow.

Autumn came to stand next to me and when she spoke, I almost jumped ten feet into the air. Her voice was extremely cheerful. "Looks like your Toyota got an upgrade." Then she started to laugh.

As she was laughing I heard a second, more masculine voice say, "And long overdue." I turned my head towards the voice and I saw Tristan coming out of the shadows from near my front steps. It was almost like he materialized out of no where. Actually, he could've been standing there the entire time and I honestly wouldn't have noticed him because the Mercedes had my total, undivided attention. He slowly walked over to me and our eyes were locked on each other. I was looking at him like he was an angel that recently landed on Earth just for me.

Once he finally made it over to me, he put his arms around my waist and whispered in my ear, "Happy Valentine's, love." I looked up at him and this time I couldn't hold back my tears. My emotions were overflowing and I still couldn't speak. My mouth was opened to form words but I couldn't find my voice. Tristan smiled down at me and then he hugged me tightly. I held him with equal strength and I couldn't help but think of how one-of-a-kind he really is. When our eyes met again he said, "I know this is a stupid question but...do you like it?"

He was smiling so beautifully at me that I felt myself falling even more in love with him. I finally found my voice and spoke softly as to not start sobbing, "Yes, I love it. But how...I thought the roses---"

"The roses were just an introduction. This was your *real* gift."

Even though I was overwhelmed by this extremely generous and thoughtful gift, I still had a million questions. "Then why did you give me the money to pay for my car?"

Tristan started to caress my face with a feather-light touch. "I had to make you think you were getting your car back."

It was then that Autumn interrupted our sentimental exchange. Her voice was still cheerful when she said, "Tris, I think you better explain how you did it. Otherwise, Bridget is gonna be questioning you nonstop."

Tristan took a deep breath and explained, "Well, when I picked you up yesterday I saw you and that sales bloke talking next to the car. I had a suspicion that maybe you were checking it out. Then last night I saw how upset you were over the whole car thing and at that moment I decided to get you another one. So I went ahead and gave you the money to pay for the repairs. And then today...me, Autumn, and Rick went up to the dealer and I paid for your car and then bought the Benz. Rick drove your car back to our house and I drove the Benz here."

I was flabbergasted. The whole thing was almost unreal. I still wondered why he paid for my car so I asked, "Why did you pay for my car and take it if you were buying me a new one?"

"'Cause me and Rick are gonna sell it for you. And whatever money we get for it, we'll give it to you. I know you could use it. It probably won't be much but hey...it's better than nothing."

This beautiful, amazing, caring, and loving man from Brighton, England had to be really sent from heaven. Never in my life have I ever met someone as thoughtful and selfless as Tristan. At that moment I realized how much I absolutely adored him; from his strange, spontaneous possessive behavior, to his special affectionate way he can warm my soul straight to the center. There was so much I wanted to say to him as we continued to hold each other but I felt I only needed to say three words: "I love you."

"I love you too, darlin'."

Right after Tristan finished his sentence, we became magnetized and started to kiss with intense fervor that either of us couldn't resist. I was drawn to him like a moth to a flame. Our mouths mutually opened invitingly and our tongues danced around with each other. His kiss was deep and wanting, and I don't think I would've wanted it any differently. My hands reached up to stroke the soft blond hair on the nape of his neck while his hands dropped down to grasp and caress my butt. He ground himself into me and the sensation caused us both to moan. I rubbed myself against his instant hardness and moved my hands down to caress his back. Tristan's kiss was intoxicating and it wasn't long until we were both lost in it.

Suddenly, Autumn cleared her throat. Tristan tried to continue kissing me and ignore her, but I broke the kiss and looked at her questioningly with a smile on my face. "Uh, don't you wanna give something *else* to Tristan? You know..." And she held up the bag with his shirt in it. "And can we go inside 'cause I'm freezing my tits off."

When we got inside my apartment, the three of us settled into the living room and I gave Tristan his present. I had a look of excitement and anticipation on my face. And just like on Christmas, he ripped off the wrapping paper and didn't bother to look at the box inside. He quickly opened the box and smiled brightly. He gazed at the box's contents for a few seconds and then he said, "Awww, babe. This is..." He carefully took the shirt out of its box and held it up. Then he laid it on his lap and looked at me. "Bridget, love...this is a really nice shirt. Thank you."

He hugged me tightly and while I was in his embrace I replied, "You're welcome, baby. It matches your eyes so I had to get it. Happy Valentine's Day." I don't know if it was guilt but something inside myself made me point out my own shortcomings. "You know, I only got you one gift but I feel like you've given me three. Actually...you have." Suddenly, I looked down abashed because I started to compare the quantity and monetary values of the gifts we exchanged. I knew I shouldn't have, but I couldn't help it. I felt ashamed that I couldn't buy him something more expensive. I've never had anyone buy me a gift as extravagant as the one Tristan bought. I was almost prepared to reject the car because I felt it was a little *too* generous and too soon in our relationship. But I knew if I did, I would hurt his feelings.

After I spoke, the living room was dead silent. There seemed to be some leftover tears in my eyes from earlier and they finally decided to expose themselves. I hastily wiped them away but apparently not quick enough for Tristan. He moved closer to me on the sofa and when he said my name, I instantly looked up. "Bridget." His voice was soft and gentle, and it made me want to throw myself into his arms and ask him to wrap his invisible wings around me. "I wanna give you anything I can. It doesn't matter to me what it is. If you want it or need it...I wanna try to get it for you." He laughed lightly before he began to confess to me. "You know, I've never really celebrated Valentine's Day 'cause I've never been in love. And I never had a real, serious girlfriend. But today was the best Valentine's ever. Letting me take you for a ride on my bike the last couple days...that was one of the best gifts you could've given me." He looked up at the ceiling and a thoughtful expression crossed his features. "So let's see...two rides on the bike plus a shirt equals..." He put up his hand and counted on his fingers. "Hmmm...it seems to me that we're even." Then a beautiful smile graced his already beautiful face.

Some time during our moment, Autumn left the room. I actually think she left my apartment because I remember hearing the front door close very faintly. Tristan's words made me feel so much better and I smiled affectionately before I leaned in to kiss him tenderly on the lips. He gave me a loving smile in return and suddenly I remembered something of great importance. With my spirits now lifted, I stood up and took both of his hands in mine. I lifted him to his feet and said excitedly, "Hey, come on!" Then I started pulling him along as I walked towards the front door.

"Where are we going?"

I smiled over my shoulder and reached for the doorknob. "I want to take a ride in my new car!"

Chapter 9

'Love without passion is dreary; passion without love is horrific.'

~ Lord Byron

I ROLLED THE TV CART into my fourth grade classroom while my students continued chatting animatedly amongst each other. Today was Career Day at the school and my students were excited because I announced a special guest would come in and speak to them. When I told the children their guest was a Hollywood actor, I was immediately bombarded with questions as to his identity. I told them I couldn't reveal that information because it would ruin the surprise, but then they all wanted to know: 'Well, what's he been in?'

"I'll let him tell you that when he gets here," I replied to the twenty-six pairs of eyes that were looking back at me in anticipation and excitement.

When Tristan finally walked into my classroom, he had the attention of all twenty-six students. He was dressed in his usual style: a black hooded jacket, faded-blue baggy jeans, and black boots. His blond hair was perfectly tousled and he was sporting his silver earring. When he reached my desk, he took his jacket off and draped it on the back of my chair. Once his jacket was removed, it revealed a white t-shirt that only allowed the tattoo on his forearms to be visible and his black rubber necklace. I looked out at the class and all of them were staring at Tristan in amazement but it was quickly replaced by confusion. Tristan stood in front of the class, smiled brightly and greeted them all in his wonderful British accent. "Hiya kids!"

There was no response for about three seconds. Then one boy scrunched up his face and blurted out, "Who are you?" It wasn't long until a few more children followed suit with: "I've never seen you before" and "What have you been in?" Tristan looked around the class and smiled in amusement.

At that moment, I felt I needed to give my boyfriend a proper introduction. "Class, this is Tristan Hathaway. He's a Hollywood actor and he's going to speak to you today about his career. And after he's done speaking, you'll be allowed to ask him questions."

Immediately after I finished introducing Tristan, it seemed they still couldn't contain their questions because one girl asked quietly, "Are you the one who dropped Miss Monahan off at school on Valentine's Day? On the green motorcycle?"

Tristan looked over at her, but judging from the expression on his face, he wasn't caught off-guard in the least. Then he slowly turned his head to look over at me and he smirked. I smiled at him and he turned his attention back on my student and answered her with a smile of his own. "Yes, that was me." I couldn't help but notice the pride in his voice. The girl looked over at another girl sitting next to her and they both covered their mouths to stifle their giggles.

Tristan leaned against my desk as he spoke to the class about his career and how he got started in acting. I could tell he was enjoying himself because he was full of energy. I was proud of him for curbing his speech and not swearing in front of the children. Tristan had a habit of cursing a lot more than usual when he became excited. He was very charismatic when he spoke and he kept their attention. He told them about his movies and the television shows he appeared on, and he showed them video clips from his own filmography. Once he was done with his presentation, he had Q&A with the students. The friend of the girl who asked him about his motorcycle asked, "Are you Miss Monahan's boyfriend?"

He smiled again and replied, "I sure am." There was that underlying pride in his tone again when he answered.

After Q&A, I retrieved the bag I had hidden underneath my desk. Tristan had a special gift for my students, and I helped him pass out theater posters from one of his movies. When he announced to the class that he had to leave, the students and I clapped and gave him our thanks. I thought he was a perfect speaker for Career Day and he gave a bit of sound advice to the children by saying, "Don't forget kids...never give up on your dreams, stick to your goals, and always follow-through. And don't ever let anyone tell you that you can't be something. You can be anything you wanna be." Before he left, he grabbed his jacket and walked over to me. He was using my car and took me to school that morning because his bike was in the shop. He whispered, "I'll pick you up later, sweets," and then he gave me a peck on the lips.

I heard a loud barrage of "Oooooooooh!" Followed by the sound of twenty-six children laughing.

My students hurried out of class when the bell rang at three o'clock. After the last student waved to me and said goodbye, I started organizing papers on my desk and putting some of them into my briefcase. I had just put on my jacket when I heard my cell phone vibrating in my purse. I saw Tristan's picture on the LCD screen and I immediately answered. "Hey baby."

Surprisingly, his voice sounded annoyed on the other end. "Babe, I'm so sorry but I'm gonna be kinda late picking you up. I'm actually still in a meeting with my manager and the director for that supernatural film I told you about. But I promise to ring you back when I'm on my way."

"It's no problem. I'll just get some work done while I wait for you."

"Alright. I'll try to get there soon."

"Okay."

I was about to hang up when I heard him speak again. "Hey, what did the kids think of me?"

I smiled as I thought about all the questions and comments that were directed at me from the students after Tristan's departure. "They really liked you, baby. They thought you were really cool. I heard a few of the kids say that they liked your accent. The girl who asked you if you dropped me off that day said you were dreamy." I laughed lightly.

Tristan laughed too. "Brilliant! Yeah, that was really fun. And I liked seeing you in class with your students. Thanks for inviting me, love."

"Thanks for doing it. That was very sweet of you, baby."

He was quiet for a moment and then I heard him say softly, "You know I'd do anything for you."

I was quiet too as I cradled the phone against my ear. Then I replied in a soft tone as well. "I know."

After we hung up with each other, I retrieved the papers that I put in my briefcase moments ago. I sat down at my desk and decided to pass the time by grading some homework assignments. Soon I became engrossed in my work and when I looked out the window, I noticed the sky beginning to darken. I glanced at the clock on the wall and I saw that it was a little after five-thirty. I picked up my cell phone and I was about to call Tristan and ask him how much longer he would be, when it began to vibrate again. I checked the LCD screen and it was text message alert. The message was from Tristan and he was telling me that he was on his way.

As I was staring at the message, my mind started to wander and I began thinking about Tristan; his extreme attractiveness, his intense sexual prowess, his British bad-boy attitude but the loving, sensitive way he seems to cater to me. Then I started thinking about his physique and how much I loved the feeling of his gorgeous naked body on top of me; his warm, stiff erection nestled inside my pussy. At that moment, I remembered his unique smell: a smoky yet woodsy scent mixed with fabric softener and a dash of clove.

My mind flashed back and I visualized him thrusting inside me up against the wall as we showered together that morning. The memory of Tristan kissing me deeply with his tongue while the warm water cascaded over our joined bodies made my body flush with heat. Before I knew it, thoughts of my boyfriend caused me to become sexually stimulated. The crotch of my panties felt snug and slightly moist. I could feel my clit harden in response and my pussy felt swollen with arousal. All of a sudden, a naughty idea popped into my head and I text him back: **Meet me in my classroom.**

I heard Tristan's heavy footsteps coming down the deserted hallway outside my classroom. I quickly rose out of my chair and picked up an eraser. I started erasing the blackboard when I saw him enter my classroom in the corner of my eye. I looked over at him and he seemed to stop in his tracks. He looked cautiously at me before he greeted me quietly. "Hi."

I gave him a small smile and greeted him the same. "Hi."

I averted my eyes from him and resumed the task of erasing the board. I heard him approaching me slowly and then I heard him sigh. "I'm sorry, love. I know you're probably pissed at me right now."

He stood right next to me and I was immediately engulfed by his masculine scent. A warm flush passed through me unexpectedly and I swallowed thickly before I looked up at him. His expression was apologetic so I smiled again and I noticed his expression lighten. I forced myself to remain composed when I responded to him. "Actually, I'm not."

He opened his mouth slightly like he was about to speak and I purposely dropped the eraser at my feet. I kept my eyes trained on him and I saw his eyes follow the eraser as it fell to the floor almost silently. Before he had the second to look up at me, I spoke quickly in a low and seductive tone. "Could you pick that up for me?" Tristan's blue eyes met mine and he grinned as he knelt down before me to pick up the eraser. I still kept my eyes on him and I saw him pick it up with one hand. I thought he was about to stand up but instead...he stayed in a kneeling position and handed me the eraser. I accepted it from him and spoke in the same tone. "Thank you, but you are *very* tardy Mr. Hathaway."

Tristan placed both his hands on my smooth, bare legs and began a caress that started at my calves and knees. His hands traveled further north and he brought his gentle caress up to my thighs that were hidden underneath my dress. He continued to hold my gaze while he was doing this and I could feel myself getting aroused once more. Perhaps he felt the passion that was beginning to stir between us because he didn't cease his caress at my thighs. He began to slowly lift the hem of my dress and when his hands finally reached the apex of my thighs, his fingers began to tease the cotton material in the crotch of my panties. His fingertip brushed against my sensitive nub and he gave me a knowing smile. Tristan knew I was aroused and his own voice was low when he apologized again. "I'm sorry Miss Monahan."

I reached down to run my fingers through his soft, blond hair. Then I flashed him a wicked smile and almost purred the words: "Make it up to me."

Tristan didn't need to be told twice. His hands were playing along the waistband of my panties but I guess he decided they were interfering with him meeting his goal so he pulled them down to my ankles with one swipe. The next thing I knew, he quickly pulled up the hem of my dress, bunched it up at my waist with his hands, and put his mouth on my pussy. I gasped loudly and I grabbed my dress hem to relieve his hands of that unnecessary task. Besides, they could be used for doing something useful like what he started to do; using his fingers to spread me open like a flower. I felt one of his fingers rubbing my bud while another of his long digits slid into my slick opening and caressed the inside of my womanly petals. His tongue wasn't missing any of the action because it began a pleasurable motion of slowly licking my pussy from back to front. I held my dress up with one hand because my the other hand couldn't seem to detach itself from the golden strands on top of his head.

The pleasure Tristan was giving me was incredible and it wasn't long until my nether regions felt swollen again. I moaned louder and louder as I rocked my pelvis against his mouth. My voice was breathless as I expressed to my lover how he was making me feel. "Ahhhhh...oh my God, Tristan! Yes! Yes! Just like that, baby!" He started sucking on my outer petals and nibbling them gently before he would glide his tongue across. The wonderful sensation he was creating caused me to grind my pussy into his face even harder and I yelled, "Oh my God! That feels so good! Don't stop, baby...ooooohhhh...don't stop! Do it just like that!" One of his hands reached up and grasped my hip while the other hand continued the steady piston-like fingering action inside my opening. I started grunting and rocking my pelvis to match his finger thrusting. I could tell my pussy was soaked because his finger was entering me with such ease.

He started sucking on my clit and when that action combined with his fingering action took hold of my senses, I cried out loudly and came in his hot, open mouth. I reached down and grabbed his hair in a tight grip while I felt my pussy release its essence. I heard Tristan moan from between my legs and I cried out again as orgasmic tremors flowed through me. The tremors caused my body to tremble and my pelvis to hump so uncontrollably that I thought my legs would buckle from underneath me. He kept his mouth on me and continued to lap at my juices, but his hands reached up under my dress and bra to cup my bare breasts. I lifted my head towards the ceiling of the empty classroom and gasped and moaned in sheer ecstasy.

Tristan wouldn't let me ride my orgasm all the way through because he stood up suddenly, wrapped his arms around me and kissed me deeply so I could taste myself. I opened my mouth wider for him and our tongues mated fiercely. I felt his tongue stroke the roof of my mouth and across my teeth as he explored my moist cavern. I wrapped my arms around him and my hands roamed up and down his back and through his hair again. He released me momentarily and quickly took off his jacket, only to let it drop to the floor. Then he embraced me tightly and started to hump against me in an attempt to release his aching erection. I mirrored his actions and I could feel his hardness rubbing against my belly. I broke the kiss to look down at the bulge that was straining against his jeans and I heard Tristan say my name in a strangled voice. "Bridget." My cinnamon eyes met his baby blues and they conveyed to me exactly what my prince wanted me to do. We attacked each other's mouths again without reserve and I reached down to unsnap his jeans.

My hands were adept and it wasn't long until I freed Tristan's magnificent cock from its tight confines. He began sucking on my tongue while I pleasured him with long, firm strokes. I felt his pre-cum slicken his throbbing member and it actually aided in making my strokes smoother. I deliberately brushed my thumb over the top because I knew he loved when I did that to him. He rewarded me by moaning loudly and thrusting into my fist that was enclosed around him. I wanted even more sexual contact with him so I rubbed his naughty boy part against my girly ones.

Suddenly, he unsealed his lips from me because the pleasure I was giving him caused him to lift his head towards the ceiling and cry out loudly. Without taking our eyes off one another, he quickly pushed my chair out of the way and pressed me up against my desk. Even though my chair was on wheels, he pushed it so hard that it almost fell over. His expression was intense and I felt him reach down and put his hand underneath my dress again. I parted my legs and he resumed finger-fucking me with his middle finger; the longest and best finger for the task. My classroom was quiet except for the sounds of our soft panting and our random moans of sexual pleasure. My pussy was so wet from my previous orgasm that I heard the moist gushing sound as his finger penetrated me over and over. The sound aroused me even more and I think it aroused Tristan as well because we both quieted our breathing and focused on the intimate sound. He inserted a second, long digit inside my opening and started a scissors-motion which intensified the sound of my pussy being well-lubricated.

Our eyes remained fixed on one another while we masturbated each other's private parts with our hands. He fingered me quick and deep and I stroked his erection right against my outer petals. Not only were our naughty bits touching, but our hands were. I felt more of his arousal leak from the tip of his erection onto my womanly flower and at that moment, Tristan broke the connection with our eyes. The sensation seemed to overwhelm him because he closed his eyes and whispered, "Oooohhhh ssshhhhiiiit."

Masturbating one another was so intimate and intense that the feeling was almost indescribable. As we were pleasuring each other, I honestly felt that there wasn't any place that I *wouldn't* let him touch me. I loved him so much and trusted him more than anyone, that I gave him free reign over any part of my body. Tristan's actions and his words told me that he was feeling similar and that he succumbed to the realization of what we were doing to each other. I wanted him to know that I shared his feelings so I whispered back, "Yeah...you feel it, baby? Do you feel every part of my pussy?"

He opened his eyes and groaned, "Yeah. This feels sooooo fucking good." I rubbed his erection slowly between my petals and against my bud while we continued to hold each other's gaze. Tristan whispered again, "I love the way your hand feels on my cock. You make me wanna erupt all over your pretty twat." His other hand wrapped around mine; the one that was enclosed around his manhood. He guided my hand up and down his length for a brief moment while he watched me pleasure him. "Your hand is so small compared to mine. And I like your pink fingernails." He closed his eyes again and another deep moan escaped him. The sensation finally overpowered him because suddenly, he reached behind me and cleared a spot on my desk, and then lifted me onto the desk. My legs opened instantly and he settled between them. He poised himself at my entrance and said, "You have five seconds to put a fucking condom on me before I plunge my cock inside you."

I kissed his mouth hungrily before I responded. "Just do it baby, I don't care." That's all the encouragement he needed.

In the next second, Tristan plunged his raw, hard, throbbing manhood deep inside me to the hilt. We both cried out simultaneously and he grabbed my butt to pull me even closer to his body. Our mouths and bodies welded together as we made love on my desk. He grabbed my hips in an almost bruising grip as he thrusted inside me in such a forceful rhythm that it made the bottom of my desk scrape against the floor. My legs wrapped around his waist and I bucked my pelvis to meet his deep strokes. I held onto his shoulders and kissed that beautiful Brit like there was no tomorrow. In the open space of the empty classroom, the sound of our lips smacking together seemed amplified.

His t-shirt was hindering me from feeling his warm, bare skin so I lifted it up and practically tore it from his body. As soon as his shirt was removed, our lips and tongues met once more and I took delight in caressing my hands over every inch of Tristan's ivory skin that I came in contact with. We moaned into each other's mouths and came up for air every now and then as we gasped in complete rapture.

Tristan made me feel so good that all my inner thoughts and sexual feelings starting pouring out of me in a breathless voice. As he continued to pound his manhood into my womanhood, my brown eyes looked directly into his light blue ones while I confessed to him unabashedly. "I love you so much, baby. I can't even begin to tell you how much. You don't know how good you feel inside me right now. Oh my God, you have no idea. I swear…you're the best lover I've ever had in my life. I love it when you fuck me, baby…I love it. I love it when you kiss me and I love *how* you kiss me. And I love it when you lick my pussy because you do it so well. And I love touching every inch of your body. I love it when I make you feel so good that you cum really hard. I love watching you ride your orgasm because you look so beautiful to me. I love the way you smell and I love running my fingers through your hair."

Tristan held my gaze and his pubic bone began hitting up against my clit in the most pleasurable way. I threw my head back, closed my eyes and moaned in sexual satisfaction. I was still breathless when I concluded my intimate confession. "I don't want this feeling to end, baby…not ever. Oooohhhh…you can have me anytime you want." After my confession, I realized that I just opened the door wide to allow Tristan to have complete sexual power over me. It was a blatant invitation but in all truthfulness, I really didn't care. I would willingly be a prisoner of his affection and I would have absolutely no desire to be released at any time.

I know that after my bold confession, Tristan's male ego was on Cloud Nine. He confirmed my assumption because he didn't say a word; he just growled and started slamming into me even harder. When he released my hips to push me down onto the desk, I knew he was exercising the power of his newly appointed position. I laid down on my desk with my legs still spread eagle for my British prince. I was in a complete state of lust and sexual frenzy that I flailed my arms about and knocked random objects off my desk. They all seemed to hit the floor at once with a loud crash but we were too enraptured by each other to actually care. He hit my G-spot repeatedly and I cried out again and yelled, "Yes! Oh God, just like that! Straight in, baby! Pound straight into me just like that!" I arched my back off the desk in absolute bliss and gasped loudly as I tried to catch my breath. I could sense that the faster he thrusted inside me, the closer we were to approaching our shared climax.

Tristan had his arms hooked around my thighs as he pounded into me and my small breasts were bouncing up and down freely. There came a point where I opened my eyes and looked down at him, and what I saw made me thank my lucky stars that I was exactly where I was at that very moment. There was thin sheen of sweat covering his brow and chiseled torso, and his skin was lightly flushed from exertion. He looked like a lustful, tattooed angel and I wished he would span out his beautiful secret wings while he shared his body with me. His soft lips were parted slightly as he panted and when our eyes met, he began talking to me again in a dominant voice. "You like that? You like it when I fuck you like this?"

I responded in a weak and almost strangled voice. "Yes."

"You like to be fucked on your desk, don't you? I bet you fantasized about me fucking you this way, haven't you?"

"Yes," I admitted without shame.

His strokes increased and his breathing became erratic so I knew Tristan was steadily reaching his orgasmic plateau. "You want me to cum inside you? You wanna feel my cock erupt and spill my hot fucking spunk inside your twat? Tell me, Bridget! Tell me how much you want it!"

I gasped once more and sucked a huge amount of air into my lungs. When I released my breath I finally replied, "Yes, baby! Cum inside me! Please! I want it!"

Suddenly, he leaned forward over my body and quickly grabbed the top of my dress and pulled it down along with my bra. He captured one of my soft, freckled breasts into his mouth and that was all it took to send me over the edge. To my surprise, my legs opened even wider; almost involuntarily as Tristan made me cum for the second time that night. A scream unexpectedly escaped my throat as this blond Sex God in human form finally brought me to completion once again. "TRISTAN! OH MY GOD!" My butt actually lifted slightly off the desk because my pelvis bucked almost violently as more of my female essence was released from my womanly flower. I came all over his raw erection and I could feel my inner muscles clenching him; milking his cock like a steady pulse.

It was but two seconds after the first wave hit me, that I felt Tristan flood my womb with his own male essence. My beautiful boyfriend came so hard that he almost climbed on top of me to empty himself inside me. He cried out loudly in absolute passion and then he whimpered as he finally surrendered to the full sexual gratification created between us. My desk literally moved a couple feet due to Tristan's jerking motion as his orgasm ripped through his body and provided him with intense physical pleasure.

The sounds of our shared climax echoed in the classroom and probably traveled into the hallways throughout the school. I'm surprised our screams of intense passion didn't shatter any windows. If the janitor was still lingering around, I'm sure we were putting on quite an entertaining show.

As we were coming down from our mutual orgasm, I was breathing hard because I was trying to catch my breath again. My eyes were closed and I heard Tristan breathing hard as well but he seemed to be releasing curse words under his breath. I opened my eyes to look at him and his body was still nestled between my legs. His head was down and it was resting on my stomach. I saw his back and shoulders rise and fall with each deep breath he took. I reached down to stroke his hair and that's when he looked up at me and smiled. The front and sides of his hair was a darker shade of blond because it was saturated with sweat and plastered against his head. "Are you okay?" I asked with genuine concern.

He chuckled softly and nodded. His boyish voice was raspy which I attributed to the fact that we just had extremely vocal sex. And because Tristan had a British accent, he sounded even sexier. "Holy shit, babe.

That was..." He slowly straightened his posture and I felt him pull out of me and tuck himself back into his boxers.

For a short moment, I actually missed the feeling of him inside me. I laid there on top of my desk but I finally closed my legs. I finished Tristan's sentence when I said, "Intense...and wild." The passionate interlude between me and Tristan that night would probably go down in history for both of us as one of the most spectacular sexual couplings ever. I shook my head in disbelief and stared up at the florescent lights on the ceiling. I called out to the Lord one last time that night, but this time in a quiet and almost breathless voice. "Oh my God."

When I sat up, I felt Tristan press his soft lips against my forehead in a tender kiss. Then he said, "Yeah, that was fucking amazing. Definitely one for the record books." He embraced me and when he pulled away, our lips met in a slow, open-mouthed kiss. While we were kissing, I felt our mixed fluids ooze between my legs and coat the inside of my thighs.

I ended the kiss and made the mistake of looking down at my pussy because my actions caught Tristan's attention. "Damn, we're gonna have to clean you up, love." All of a sudden, he reached down between my thighs rubbed his hand over my dripping core. I couldn't help but to gasp in surprise at his boldness. Tristan wasn't remotely embarrassed or put-off and his voice was actually laced with amusement. "I think most of that is from me 'cause I gave you everything I fucking had." He laughed lightly and I laughed with him and I noticed his blue eyes were gazing at me from beneath slightly lowered lids. I could tell he was fully satiated and I knew my baby would need a nap soon. At that moment, I made the decision to drive us home because I had a feeling he'd want to snooze in the car.

After I climbed down off my desk, I said, "I'm going to the ladies' room to clean myself."

He replied, "Take your time, darlin'." He started walking around the perimeter of my desk. "I'm gonna try and put your desk right." As I looked around my desk, I realized that he did end up knocking my chair over. And the majority of the objects that were on my desk were now on the floor. Tristan bent down to pick up a broken snow globe off the floor. He started chuckling again as he looked up and showed it to me. "Look at this shit." He continued picking up random and mostly broken objects off the floor and chucking some of them into my trash bin. "This is rubbish…and this…" He looked over at me with a smile and started shaking his head. "I don't know how you're gonna explain to your kids why there's so much shit missing off your desk."

I laughed and put my hands on my hips. "I'll just tell them that I took some stuff home." We both shared another laugh as we stopped to look around at the destruction we caused in my classroom.

When I returned from the ladies room, Tristan had put my desk back in order although there were quite a few things missing from my desk. He walked over to me and put his arms around me. We held each other for a few moments and I closed my eyes and inhaled deeply. His comforting scent invaded my nostrils and I sighed in contentment. I just loved the way he smelled. "I forgive you for being late," I said quietly.

Tristan chuckled softly. "Thank you." He pulled back from me but he didn't release me from his embrace. He smoothed my hair back before he tilted his head to the side and grinned. I saw his adorable dimple on his left cheek and it actually made me smile too. "You know, you're my favorite teacher Miss Monahan. I think I love you."

I reached up to caress the side of his face and he leaned into my touch. "I love you too."

Tristan looked up at the ceiling and a thoughtful expression crossed his handsome features. I could see the faint blond stubble on his chin but that didn't stop me from tilting my head up to place a kiss there. "I think I'll leave an apple on your desk." When he looked down at me again, his expression changed to one completely roguish and he tucked a few strands of my hair behind my ear. "For making me cum harder than I've ever cum in my fucking life."

Before we left my classroom, I switched off the light and said wittily, "Well, I guess this concludes today's Sex-Ed lesson." Our laughter echoed throughout the hallway as I closed the door.

When we were walking down the main hallway to leave the school, I glanced out the window and finally realized that it was dark outside. I had my arm around Tristan's waist and his arm was around my shoulder as we walked. It was quiet except for the sound of our footsteps and I couldn't help but recall the event we both took part in moments ago. I spoke quietly when I expressed what I was thinking. "I can't believe what we just did."

Tristan snickered. "You started it this time, babe. I just came here to pick you up."

I laughed softly but I refused to accept responsibility for this daring sexual escapade. "No, you started it when you were late. If you weren't late and I wasn't sitting alone, my mind wouldn't have started to wander. Then I wouldn't have started getting horny thinking about your sexy British ass."

We reached the double doors at the front of the school and Tristan opened one of the doors for me. He laughed but his laugh was louder and it echoed throughout the hall and into the nighttime air. "In that case, I fully accept the blame for this one. If thinking about me makes you randy love, then it's totally my fault."

When we got to my car, I wasn't surprised when he handed me the keys. I knew he wanted to take a quick nap because I'm sure I wore him out and he was exhausted. We buckled our seatbelts and Tristan switched on the CD player but turned the music down low. I could still hear Arctic Monkey's *'I Bet You Look Good on the Dance Floor'* blaring through the speakers as I put the car in drive and pulled off. Tristan was quiet for a few seconds and I saw him pull his hood over his head. Then I heard his voice; it was soft and the post-sex hoarseness that it was laced with earlier had now disappeared. "Bridget...you know, you just fulfilled one of my fantasies." I turned my head briefly to look at him and his head was leaning against the window. His eyes were closed and I could see the breath from his nose beginning to fog up the glass. When he spoke again, he mumbled, "Shagging a sexy teacher on her desk." I couldn't stop the smile that appeared on my face.

As I was driving us home, I began humming along to the Arctic Monkeys song and once again my mind started to wander. I couldn't believe that I exhibited such boldness and took such a huge risk; asking Tristan to meet me in my classroom after school with the full intention of having sex with him. It was audacious, careless, and very inappropriate. Not to mention, I was breaking the rules. But I couldn't deny the unexpected yet exhilarating feeling that rushed to the surface when I first started seducing him. I felt adrenaline pumping through my veins and I honestly didn't give any thought to the possibility of getting caught. My single desire that night was to have the gorgeous blond Brit sitting next to me, deep inside me. He gave me exactly what I wanted and I realized...that I'd probably want it again.

Tristan once told me that he was addicted to me. I glanced over at him and his deep, steady breathing told me that he was completely knocked out. Even though his hood was obscuring most of his face, his profile was visible and I could see his sensual and perfect lips very clearly. I think I was becoming addicted to him too because I had a sudden urge to lean over and kiss those velvety lips. Immediately following that train of thought, came the desire to make love to him again once we got home. At that moment, I finally admitted to myself that Tristan Caleb Hathaway was my sexual drug and I was completely strung out.

Chapter 10

TRISTAN AND HIS OLDER BROTHER Jake are huge footie fans. The word 'footie' is actually short for the word 'football', which is what American soccer is called outside of the United States. Tristan invited Jake over to my apartment that evening to watch their favorite soccer team The Manchester United play against some other European team. And yes, I said that *Tristan* invited Jake over...not me. Lately, Tristan has been spending more and more time at my place rather than at his own house. Whenever he's not out of town, he spends his nights and some of his days with me. I didn't really mind because it seemed that every night we would make love. Sex with Tristan was always amazing and it never lacked in the creative department. It also warmed my heart to know that he was able to make himself so comfortable with me. I felt that it would only be a matter of time before we discussed the possibility of moving in together.

I made dinner for me and the Hathaway brothers, and after dinner the two of them settled into the living room to watch the game. They both tried to help me with the dishes but I shooed them out of the kitchen and told them to go enjoy their game. Tristan tried to coerce me into watching the game with them but I smiled and kindly reminded him that I wasn't interested in sports. He grabbed a couple beers from the fridge and then went to join Jake in the living room. I knew that watching soccer games together was one of the ways that they bonded. They were in the living room for awhile just talking as they watched television. Then the game must've started to get very intense because as I was cleaning the stove, I heard them yelling and cheering. Honestly, the sound of their brotherly bonding was very endearing to me.

I was almost finished cleaning the kitchen when Jake walked in. When I noticed him, I smiled and looked at him expectedly. He casually leaned on one of the kitchen counters and just looked back at me. I thought maybe he wanted another beer so I started to move towards the fridge. Before I could ask him, he whispered to me, "Sis, I need to talk to you." Then he whipped his head around towards the entryway to the kitchen like he wanted to make sure Tristan couldn't hear him.

Jake has been calling me 'sis' ever since he, Tristan, and I got back from visiting their family in Brighton. When he addressed me as such, I couldn't help but to smirk at him. I moved closer and whispered, "Okay, what is it?" Then I tilted my head to the side and said as an afterthought, "Do you realize that you haven't called me by my name since we got back from Brighton?" I looked up at the ceiling with a thoughtful expression and continued. "Hmmm...how many months ago was that?" Then I looked at him again and said with wide-eyes, "Five months ago!"

Jake wasn't fazed by my change of subject and he simply replied, "So you should be used to it by now. Look, I need to tell you something." I stood there waiting for him to continue so he said, "You know Tristan's birthday is tomorrow, right?" I gave him an insulted look and he quickly backpedaled by saying, "Yeah, of course you do. Anyway, we're all--" Then he whipped his head around again to make sure we weren't being heard. Once he was convinced, he continued whispering. "We're all throwing a surprise party for him tomorrow." He began to explain to me the when and where of this surprise party. Their friends were having the party at one of Tristan's favorite bar & grills; the one we went to on our first date. After Jake finished explaining the details he said almost as an afterthought himself, "Did you have anything planned for him tomorrow?"

"Yeah, I was going to take him to a movie and then out to eat, but I think the party is a much better idea."

Jake looked relieved. "Good, I'm glad to hear you say that."

Finally I realized that Jake told me about Tristan's birthday plans very last-minute and I felt that I needed to make him aware of how inconsiderate that was. When I spoke, I was still whispering but my tone was laced with sarcasm. "And I'm glad you told me this last-minute."

His face fell and he looked guilty for a quick second. Then a look of understanding appeared on his features. He pushed himself off the counter and came to stand in front of me. He put his hands on my upper arms and smiled before he said, "Oh sis, I'm sorry. You're right, I should've---" He didn't finish his sentence because something distracted him. He turned his attention towards the entryway to the kitchen. My eyes followed his line of vision and I saw Tristan was standing there... and his facial expression was not happy. Jake released me and I quickly stepped away from him. Honestly, I could understand that from Tristan's perspective, we did look a little suspicious. The air in the kitchen became tense all of a sudden and Jake tried desperately to relieve it. "Hey bro, is there a commercial or something?"

Tristan started to slowly approach us and his facial expression was one of suspicion. When he spoke, his voice was dangerously low. "Yeah."

"Oh, okay." I assumed it was quick thinking on Jake's part because he quickly moved around me and went into the fridge to get another beer. Then without looking at either of us, he walked out of the kitchen and went back into the living room. It was at that moment that I felt a very threatening vibe coming from Tristan. I tried to keep my composure as he moved even closer to me and began to occupy the space that Jake had just deserted.

I stood there frozen like a deer caught in headlights and just looked up at him. He had an intense look on his face and he began to search my eyes. Whenever Tristan did this, it felt like he was looking into my soul for the truth. It seemed like forever when he finally spoke to me. His voice was still low when he asked, "What's going on?"

I tried to maintain a straight face when I replied, "Nothing."

I guess my facial expression wasn't convincing because he looked skeptical. "Why were you and Jake whispering?"

I gave a very vague response. "Oh, we were just talking."

Tristan paused for a minute. He turned his head slightly and gave me a sidelong glance. "About what?"

"Nothing important." The minute I said it, I knew Tristan wouldn't be satisfied with my answer. I looked away from him and tried to move around him to leave but he grasped my shoulders gently to stop me. I looked back at him and his expression didn't lose any of its intensity.

"*Bridget.*" His tone of voice told me that he was demanding an answer, not asking for one.

Finally, I became exhausted by his questioning so I lied and said, "He was talking to me about a woman he met recently. He wanted my opinion on something." I knew I had to pacify him further so I wrapped my arms around his waist and looked up at him with a tender expression. I spoke softly when I said, "Baby...relax okay. He was just talking to me like a brother to a sister...that's all." Then I kissed him firmly on the lips for good measure.

Tristan seemed to relax and his arms encircled my waist. A grin slowly appeared on his face and he replied quietly, "Okay, love."

I was actually relieved that his run-in with the green-eyed monster of jealousy was finally over. I extracted myself from his embrace and said in a cheerful tone, "Now will you go back in there and watch your game. I bet you missed like five goals already." Tristan chuckled softly and then he went into the fridge to grab himself another beer. Before he left, I noticed him pause in the entryway to give me one last look.

When he was finally out of sight, I released a breath that I didn't even know I was holding. I stood there in the kitchen for a moment and braced myself on one of the counters. I couldn't believe that he would think there was something going on between me and his brother. Suddenly, a feeling floated to the surface that actually made my heart ache. I started to wonder exactly who it was that he didn't trust; was it Jake...or was it me? I was very disturbed by this so I decided to go into my bedroom and play around on the computer for awhile.

As I walked into the living room and passed the sofa that the Hathaway brothers were sitting on, it seemed like the whole scene in the kitchen replayed itself; but this time it was the opposite. Jake and Tristan were talking in hushed voices and when they noticed me come into the room they abruptly stopped talking. I didn't bother to pause my steps, I just continued walking to my bedroom like I didn't notice them. When I was halfway down the hall to my room, I turned around and tip-toed back towards the living room to eavesdrop. I pressed myself up against the wall and listened.

Jake: Tris, you need to relax bro.

Tristan: What were you two talking about?

Jake: I told you, nothing.

Tristan: It didn't seem like nothing.

Jake: What...I can't talk to Bridget without you being present? Is that it?

[Silence]

Jake: Tris, don't look at me like that, okay. This is me...Jake...your brother remember? I would never try to take Bridget away from you.

Tristan: I'd beat your fucking arse if you tried.

Jake: You know...you sound obsessed. You know that, right? Does she know how obsessed you are with her?

[Silence]

Jake: I bet if she did, she'd leave your arse.

Tristan: She wouldn't leave me...she loves me.

[Silence]

Jake: You're fucking mad!

Tristan: Bugger off.

I stood there in my hallway with a look of utter shock. My mouth had dropped and my eyes were as wide as saucers. A part of me regretted that I just eavesdropped on their conversation but the other part of me was scared of what I just heard. I turned and walked quickly to my bedroom. I shut the door and tried to distract myself by playing 'Bejeweled' on the computer.

It wasn't long until I became engrossed in the game that I heard the doorbell. At first I thought maybe I had another guest but then I remembered that I was expecting a delivery. I bought Tristan a motorcycle jacket for his birthday. I was shopping online and came across one that matched his bike and helmet perfectly. The jacket was a little expensive so I asked my parents for some extra money to purchase it. Normally I wouldn't have done that but I really wanted Tristan to have the jacket. I imagined that he would look even sexier wearing it. Tristan was already naturally sexy so I figured the whole ensemble of his bike, helmet, and jacket would just intensify it.

I dashed out of my room and ran down the hall to the front door. Out of the corner of my eye I saw that Tristan had begun to get up to answer the door. I reached the door first and quickly checked the peep-hole. Yep, it was my delivery. I opened the door and accepted my package. As I was walking back to my room I heard Tristan ask, "What's in the box?"

I didn't stop walking as I smiled and spoke over my shoulder. "Don't you worry about it. Just watch your game." Then I started laughing as I continued to make my way towards my room. Once I got to my room I put the box on my bed, closed the door and locked it. I opened the box to inspect my merchandise and I was very impressed. The jacket was so...*Tristan.* I couldn't wait for him to see it and I had a feeling he'd really like it. I had already bought a gift box, wrapping paper, and a bow so I decided to wrap the gift while I had this moment of privacy. After I finished wrapping it, I put it back in the delivery box and hid it in my closet. Then I went back to my computer to finish my game.

It was probably an hour or so later when I heard a knock on my bedroom door. It was at this moment I realized I forgot to unlock it after I finished wrapping Tristan's gift. When I opened the door, Tristan was standing there with a confused expression. "Why'd you lock the door?" Before I could answer, he came into the room and turned around to face me.

I walked towards him and stood in front of him. I replied nonchalantly, "I forgot to unlock it." Then I turned away from him and sat on the bed. It was another few minutes before either of us spoke. I decided to speak first so I asked, "So...is the game over?"

Suddenly, he walked away from me and began looking out one of the windows. "Yeah...Jake just left." He sounded disappointed. When he spoke again, his voice was quiet and he didn't turn around to face me. "Bridget, how much do you love me?"

His question caught me off-guard and I didn't answer immediately. I moved from the bed and walked over to him. He must've sensed me approach him because he finally turned around. The moment his eyes met mine, my voice caught in my throat because his baby blues were glistening with unshed tears. It was the first time I had ever seen him cry. I quickly closed the distance between us and wrapped my arms around him. I looked up into his sad eyes and I felt the immediate need to comfort him. I spoke softly to him when I said, "Tristan, I love you more than anything. What's wrong, baby?"

Tristan's arms went around me but he didn't shed his tears. I could tell he was trying to keep them at bay because he started blinking rapidly. When he answered me, his voice wavered slightly. "Would you ever leave me?"

He still didn't cease to surprise me with his questions tonight. Then I started thinking that maybe what Jake said to him earlier really struck a chord inside him. The more I got to know Tristan, the more he would openly reveal his weaknesses. One of them was jealousy, and the others were extreme sensitivity and possessiveness. And at this moment I learned of another: insecurity. I felt I needed to reassure him once more so I smiled at him and caressed his cheek. He leaned into my touch and closed his eyes. Being this close to him, I could see that his tears already wet his long lashes. "Tristan, the only way I would leave you is if you abused me or cheated on me. Why would you think I would leave you?"

He opened his eyes and looked intently into mine. A moment passed before he said, "What if someone else comes along? The truth is…you can do better than me."

"*Better* than you?!?" I was in total shock. Didn't he realize how much I absolutely loved and adored him? Why would I choose anyone else? "Sweetie, there is no one better than you…not for me. Tristan, you are the most beautiful man I've ever seen in my entire life. You love me so much and you're so good to me. Being with you is amazing and I can't imagine being with anyone else. If you want to know the *truth*…I don't think I could love anyone as much as I love you." By the time I finished my sentimental admission of feelings, my own eyes began to glisten with tears. But unlike Tristan, I couldn't hold mine at bay. He leaned down and captured my lips in a passionate, yet loving kiss. I wasn't exactly sure if I eased his fears but I was praying that I did.

The next day after work, I arrived at the bar & grill where Tristan's surprise birthday party was to take place and I saw that a lot of his friends were already there. I recognized Chad, Marco, Autumn, Jake, and Rick's girlfriend Becca. Rick was surprisingly absent but then I remembered that it was his job to take Tristan around the city and stall him until it was time to bring him to the restaurant. I also saw that Autumn brought her boyfriend Ryan. Ryan had black hair and intense brown eyes. His hair was long, but today he was sporting a ponytail. He and Autumn both had facial piercings and tattoos, and I always thought they made the perfect couple.

Marco seemed to be the one who organized the whole event and he had a section reserved specifically for the party. The section was in the back away from the entrance and that was good because Tristan couldn't see us when he came in. Our entire section had free drinks and a buffet-style food arrangement.

I was sitting down talking to Becca and Autumn, when Becca exclaimed, "And did you see the cake?!?" Her gray eyes were wide in disbelief.

I looked at her with a confused expression and smiled. "Tristan has a cake?"

"Yeah, Marco got him one."

Then Autumn chimed in. "It's tits."

My mouth dropped and I choked on a laugh. "What? What do you mean 'tits'?"

Autumn clarified by saying, "The cake...it's in the shape of a pair of tits." I couldn't help but to start laughing because that sounded exactly like something Marco would get.

It wasn't much longer until Jake had our attention and informed us that Tristan and Rick just walked in. At that moment, everyone quieted down and prepared for the big surprise. I stood up and waited, and I saw Tristan's blond head appear around the corner. As soon as he walked a few more feet to stand in the entryway, we all yelled, "SURPRISE!" Tristan was truly surprised because I saw him literally jump. A huge smile lit up his beautiful face and we yelled, "HAPPY BIRTHDAY!"

Tristan started to laugh but then he turned to Rick and said, "No wonder you had me all over the city...dragging me around and shit."

Rick smiled sheepishly and replied, "Dude, I had to stall you." Suddenly, Rick noticed me and we made eye contact. He seemed to sigh a breath of relief when he said, "Thank God *you're* here." I walked over to them and I gave Tristan a big hug. Then we kissed each other before we embraced again.

I looked over at Rick and laughed lightly. "Why'd you say that?"

"Because *this* one..." And he pointed to Tristan. "Kept asking about you all day." He started to mimic Tristan's British accent when he said, "Where the fuck is Bridget? It's my birthday and she hasn't ringed me. Why hasn't she ringed me?" He shook his head and when he spoke again his voice returned to normal. He communicated to Tristan in their own language by saying, "He was acting like a fucking pussy." Before I knew it, Tristan released me and punched Rick in the arm...*hard*. He did it so swiftly that I thought it was humanly impossible to be that fast. Rick rubbed his arm. "Owwwwww!" I knew they were teasing each other so I didn't worry about them becoming violent. Plus I knew that if Tristan really wanted to hurt him, he wouldn't have just punched him in the arm.

Everyone was having a really fun time at the party; eating, drinking, and mingling. Tristan had no problem consuming vast amounts of alcohol and I honestly didn't mind. It was his birthday and I felt that if he wanted to get drunk, I had no right to stop him. During the course of the evening, I noticed that his eyelids got heavier and his speech began to slur slightly. I stayed by his side during the party because once again... he wouldn't let me out of sight.

Strangely, I also noticed that a pretty, young woman with blonde hair and dark eyes kept watching us the entire time. Every time I looked up, she caught my eye. Her expression was neutral but her intense staring started to make me feel uncomfortable. I did my best to ignore her but something in the back of my mind told me that maybe there was more to her odd behavior.

Marco made the announcement that he had something special for the 'birthday boy'. Tristan's birthday cake was sitting on a food cart and Marco was pushing it towards the center of the party. It attracted everyone's attention and soon everyone was gathered around it with Tristan standing directly in front. I was at his side and when I looked at the cake, I couldn't help but to laugh. When everyone else caught a glimpse of it too, they joined in on the laughter.

The cake was in the shape of two large, bare breasts with two candles sticking out of the nipples. On the side of the cake there were words written in pink icing that read: ***Breast wishes on your birthday Tristan!*** Tristan smiled down at the cake and shook his head in amusement. Then Chad came over to him and placed a Burger King birthday crown on his head and said, "Here you go birthday boy!" Tristan smirked at him and it seemed that I couldn't contain my laughter. I pulled out my cell phone and took a picture of him with the crown on his head. Tristan has a great sense of humor so he smiled widely when I took it.

Marco started the chorus for '*Happy Birthday*' and eventually everyone sang loudly. While we were singing I realized that I forgot Tristan's birthday present at home. Marco's voice brought me out of my reverie when he communicated to Tristan and said, "Alright gay boy, make your wish. I know you'll probably wish for a nice stiff one."

Tristan smirked at him too and gave him the finger. He paused and looked down at the cake but suddenly, he turned to look at me. Even in the haziness of his semi-drunken state, his eyes started to burn into mine. Then he quickly looked back at the cake and blew out the candles. Marco handed him a knife to cut the cake and Tristan hesitated for a minute. He titled his head to the side and asked, "You *sure* you wanna give me that knife?" He gave Marco a false look of intimidation as if to say, 'Give it to me and I'll stab you.'

Marco retracted the knife and gave him a sidelong glance. "Hmmm... I don't know if I---"

"Give me the fucking knife, mate!" Marco started to laugh and handed Tristan the knife. As soon as he took it, he raised the knife in the air and stabbed the cake right in the middle. Then he looked over at me and asked casually, "Babe, you want a nipple?" I laughed, took the knife from him, and started carving the cake myself. Tristan went over to one of the tables and sat down...still wearing the crown on his head. Once I carved and served almost the entire cake, I heard him call my name. I looked over at him and he was slouched in his chair beckoning me to come over.

I walked over to him and he made a gesture to sit on his lap. I noticed he hadn't touched his piece of cake but he had finished yet another beer. I sat on his lap, and he straightened his posture and put his arm around me. Then he picked up his piece of cake and handed it to me. I looked at him questioningly and he spoke in a very soft, yet demanding tone. "I want you to feed me." The crown must've made him feel like a true king. I smiled at him with an amused expression and he gave me a drunken smile in return. I decided to oblige and cater to my king so I began feeding Tristan his birthday cake right in front of everyone. As I was doing this, I caught the eye of the blonde woman again and this time I noticed her expression was very unfriendly. It caught me off-guard momentarily and I quickly averted my eyes.

I continued to feed Tristan his cake but my curiosity was getting to me. I decided to question him to see if he knew why she kept staring at us all night. "Tristan, my lord?" I said as I put a forkful of cake in his mouth.

He chewed it for a second before he answered. "Hmmm?"

"Do you know that girl over there with the long blonde hair?"

Tristan looked away from me to scan the room and then he replied, "I don't see any girl with long blonde hair." I looked up and noticed he was right; she was gone. I felt relieved and I hoped that she actually left the party. Suddenly, his grip on me tightened and he leaned towards me and kissed my lips. I kissed him back and I tasted vanilla, lemon, and a hint of beer. When we broke the kiss he whispered, "I wanna open my presents now." His voice sounded very child-like and I couldn't help but to smile in amusement. I forgot that his presents were sitting on a table in the corner but I remembered again that mine wasn't there.

I had to use the bathroom so I said, "Okay baby, let me go to the ladies room and when I come back you can open your presents." He nodded and looked at me beneath half-closed lids. I got up and rushed to the bathroom because I really had to go.

When I was finished, I was about to leave the stall when I heard two female voices enter the bathroom. I peeked through the small space between the stall and the door, and saw that it was the blonde girl who was staring at me and Tristan all night and some brunette. I didn't try to hide my feet because I actually wanted them to know they weren't alone. My presence didn't seem to faze them as I listened to them have their conversation. When I heard one of them begin to speak, I peeked again so I could distinguish their voices. The blonde spoke first:

Blonde: Tristan really is a great actor...the way he's been pretending nothing happened.

Brunette: What do you mean?

Blonde: He's been avoiding me all night. He's acting like we didn't just fuck each other's brains out last weekend.

[The brunette laughed]

Blonde: I guess it's because *she's* here. I don't know what he sees in that bitch...some freckled-face, pale, redhead. I mean...seriously.

Brunette: Well, you can always try to get him alone.

Blonde: Oh yeah? How?

Brunette: Just wait until he goes to the bathroom. Then wait a few minutes and follow him in.

[The blonde laughed]

Blonde: Yeah, that might work. I mean, that would give me the perfect chance to have a quickie with him or maybe give him a birthday blow-job. Tristan does have an awesome cock.

[They both laughed]

Blonde: I still can't believe he has a *girlfriend*. I mean come on...is she that *stupid* to think that she can tame him? Duh, Tristan is a man-whore...everyone knows that.

Brunette: Yeah.

Blonde: Ugh, I'm never buying this lip gloss again. I should take it off...on Tristan's cock.

They both laughed as they left the bathroom...and I just died in the stall. I broke down and cried harder than I've ever cried before. Last weekend I was at my parents' house in Sacramento so I really don't know what Tristan was doing. I did speak to him on the phone a couple times and he just told me that he was hanging out with his friends. Was he having sex with this girl while he was having his fun? I began to sob uncontrollably. I didn't want to believe that Tristan would cheat on me after everything that's happened between us. I felt betrayed and extremely hurt. A part of me wanted to hurt him to make him feel what I was feeling but the other part of me wanted to ask him why he felt the need to have sex with someone else. Then suddenly, I realized that I still had to face him. I debated with myself on whether I should confront him now or wait until we got back to my apartment. Wait no, I didn't want him in my house. I didn't want him near me ever again.

I must've stayed in the bathroom for a long time crying because suddenly, I heard Autumn's voice calling my name. She walked up to the stall and asked, "Bridget, is that you?"

I mustered up as much strength as I could and spoke through my tears, my pain, and my heartache. "Just leave me alone!"

Autumn began to panic and her voice was laced with concern. "Bridge, what's the matter? What happened?" I didn't answer her. I got up off the toilet, hastily wiped away my tears and opened the door. When she saw my face she gasped. "Bridget, what happened?!? Tell me!" I couldn't speak to her. She tried to put a hand on my shoulder but I shrugged it off in anger. An irrational part of me began blaming her for introducing me to Tristan in the first place.

I walked past her and out of the bathroom but she followed me. As I walked, my vision was still blurred with tears and I walked with my back straight as if I was an emotionless robot. My breathing was uneven and I felt that at any minute I would collapse. I was almost back to the party and as I rounded the corner I saw the blonde girl leaning on someone. I walked a little further and when I came into the entryway to the party, I saw that she was leaning on Tristan...and they were kissing. Her blonde hair was creating a curtain around them so I couldn't see Tristan's face. I gasped loudly and covered my mouth with my hand. I heard Autumn gasp too and then swear loudly.

The blonde girl whipped her head around towards me, and that's when I met Tristan's eyes. They were wide and his mouth was hanging open in shock. A fresh new batch of tears flowed freely from my still aching eyes. I looked away from him for a split second and I saw that everyone at the party had their attention on me; me standing there humiliated and crushed. In that same second, Tristan yelled my name and tried to rush towards me. I turned on my heel and ran as fast as I could out of the bar & grill.

Even in his drunken stupor, Tristan caught up with me in the parking lot. We began to have our first argument...and probably our last. He ran in front of my path to block me and put his hands on my upper arms. I swatted his hands away and screamed, "DON'T TOUCH ME! DON'T YOU EVER TOUCH ME AGAIN!" I was trembling in anger from head to toe and I wanted to hurt him. I wanted him to feel what I was feeling.

He tried to talk to me but I kept trying to walk around his body. Everywhere I went, he blocked my path. Then he began pleading with me. "Bridget, listen to me! Please just listen to me! It's not what you think, love!"

"Don't you *dare* call me 'love'! I saw you kissing her, Tristan! I saw you!" My tears would not stop flowing and I felt like I would literally cry a river full.

"She kissed *me*! She came up to me and---"

"I don't want to hear it! I heard what she said...I heard what you did!" He tried to touch me again and I quickly jumped away from him as if his touch was fire.

"What are you on about? What did I do?"

Suddenly, I realized that we were attracting an audience. I looked over my shoulder and saw people watching our argument...one of those people was Jake. By some miracle, I was able to take control of my rage. They didn't call me a fiery redhead for nothing. When I spoke next, I didn't scream. My voice was still unfriendly and accusing but it was shaky. I took a deep breath, looked into those light blue eyes that held so much power over me and asked, "What did you do last weekend? Tell me the truth, Tristan."

When I finally calmed down, I noticed for the first time that Tristan had started to cry too. When he spoke, his voice was unlike anything I've ever heard come out of his mouth. He sounded...broken. Maybe he *was* feeling what I was feeling. "I told you...I was with my mates."

We stood there looking at each other for a moment and I actually saw my pain reflected in his face. His tears were flowing freely and his lips were trembling. I started to feel sympathy but it was quickly stomped on by the feeling of betrayal. I took another deep breath and asked quietly, "Did you...did you sleep with her?" My lips began to tremble too as I waited desperately for his answer.

When he answered me, I thought I would die. "When?" My mouth dropped and a quivering sigh escaped my lips. I moved closer to him and looked up into his eyes. I searched them and wondered why and how he could hurt me this way. I thought he truly loved me. I thought we had a special connection. He was my angel...my prince...my heart. I looked down and he began speaking to me again. "Bridget, I didn't shag her last weekend if that's what you think. But I did---"

Tristan's sentence was cut short because I started to remove the promise ring from my finger. The volume of his voice increased and he began to panic. "Bridget, what are you doing? No, no, no...don't do that! Please don't do that!" I looked up at him again with my aching, tired eyes that were still wet with tears. I took his right hand in my left hand and turned his palm up. "Bridget...*please*...don't. I'm fucking begging you. I love you...please!" And then I took my right hand and placed the ring in his palm. This time Tristan started to sob. He looked into my eyes and desperately tried to reel me in. His spell on me was broken.

I said in a quiet, small voice, "I told you...I told you the only two reasons why I would ever leave you."

His voice was barely above a whisper when he asked, "Why don't you believe me? How can you believe her over me?" I looked up at him and suddenly my anger flared inside me again. I started to think of the popular expression: '*You can't teach an old dog new tricks.*' Then I thought about what that blonde home wrecker said about Tristan in the ladies room. Maybe she was right. Maybe I was stupid. I couldn't tame Tristan because he was...

"Because you're a slut." And this time Tristan did not block my path because I left him momentarily stunned.

I saw an opportunity to get away so I ran to my car before he could stop me. I still heard him yelling and pleading with me after he finally realized that I left him standing alone. I saw in my peripheral vision that he tried to follow me but Jake held him back. I still heard him yelling my name as I peeled out of the parking lot and I know my fast little convertible made skid marks on the pavement. As I took one last glance in the rear-view mirror, I saw Tristan struggling with his brother; struggling to come after me. I was glad to get away because I think that someone called the police. I was lucky to escape when I did because I saw them coming into the parking lot just as I was leaving.

While I was driving home, my vision was still blurry from my tears of heartache and I was driving so fast that I honestly didn't care if I got into an accident. An irrational part of me was hoping that maybe death would come instantly and relieve me of my pain. I had no idea that Tristan's betrayal would hurt me so deeply. It was as if all rational and logical thought escaped me and I was functioning on pure, raw emotion. As I was racing home to bury myself in my misery, I started to realize that I was driving the car that Tristan bought me for Valentine's Day. The memory of that day hit me full-on and I almost slammed on the brakes. I started to visualize his beautiful face on that special day and how he looked down at me so lovingly. He exceeded my expectations that day and I thought of him as an angel sent just for me. The memory was like a stab in the heart so I screamed and punched the steering wheel numerous times out of hurt and anger. For a moment, I had the sudden urge to drive the car into a tree or a pole to destroy his token of love and generosity.

It was truly miraculous that I made it to my apartment in one piece. When I got out of my car, I will still shaking and trembling. I had a hard time getting my key in the door so I kicked the door out of frustration. As soon as I got inside, I slammed the front door and ran into my bedroom. I collapsed onto my bed and cried until I thought my tear ducts would dry up. My tears quickly soaked the pillow and I wished over and over that this was all a bad dream. My sobs racked my body and I breathed erratically as I succumbed to the realization that my promising relationship with my beautiful British boyfriend was over.

When I no longer had the strength to cry, all that could be heard were my hiccups that signaled the end of my intense sobbing. Soon my breathing began to even out and I closed my eyes in hopes that my tired body would fall asleep. I was emotionally drained and seeking some sort of peace from this nightmarish ordeal. Sleep would not come so easily for me that night because suddenly I heard someone banging on my front door. Immediately after the banging, I heard Tristan's voice yelling my name at the top of his lungs. I gasped and quickly sat up in bed. The banging and the yelling continued and I started to worry because he was causing such a disturbance in the neighborhood. It was almost midnight on a weekday and I knew one of my neighbors would call the authorities if I didn't intervene.

I got out of bed and ran to my front door. I wanted to yell at him from behind the closed door and tell him to leave but I knew it wasn't going to be that easy. I didn't open the door completely because I didn't want him to come in. Once I cracked the door open, Tristan immediately stopped his tirade. I looked at him and what I saw actually broke my heart even more. The outdoor light illuminated his face and I saw that it was flushed and tear-stained. His eyes were watery and bloodshot from crying, and he was breathing hard. I didn't poke my head out when I cracked the door open because I wanted as much distance from him as possible. I sighed heavily and then spoke in a shaky voice. "Tristan, I don't want to talk to you. Go home."

He moved right in front of the small space that I created between the door and the frame. When he spoke, his voice still sounded broken. "Bridget, please just let me explain. It really wasn't what you think and I *swear* I didn't cheat on you. Just here me out, love. I'm begging you... *please!*"

As I began to speak to him, it seemed that I had more tears to spare. I tried to hold them at bay but they were determined to fall. I tried to keep my voice from breaking but it was proving to be a difficult task. "Tristan, I know what I saw and I heard her tell someone that she had sex with you."

"When?!?"

"Last weekend! She said she was with you and---"

"She's a fucking liar! I didn't shag that bint last weekend!" The volume of his voice was getting louder and I instinctively shushed him. He continued defending himself but he lowered his voice slightly. "That's what I'm trying to tell you...I didn't cheat on you!"

Suddenly, I started to get angry because none of this was making any sense. "Then why would she say that, huh? Why would she say she had sex with you last weekend? It doesn't make any sense."

"Bridget, if you just let me in---"

I was still furious with him so I yelled, "I don't want you in my house! I want you to go home and leave me alone!"

"But just let me explain...*please*! Why won't you let me talk to you?" Then his voice dropped considerably and it cracked at the end of his sentence. "Do you...do you hate me?" Fresh tears trickled down his face and he put his hand in the space between the door and the frame and pushed gently. "Love...please let me in. *Please*." Tristan started to cry but he spoke through his tears. "You have no idea how much this is fucking hurting me. It hurts that you won't believe me. Why? I've never lied to you before." He started to sob and now it was seriously affecting me. My tears began to flow freely and the anger inside me was battling with my love for him. "Bridget, I need you. I would never, ever hurt you. You're a part of me...don't you know that?"

"Tristan...just go home." Then I did something that caused him to panic even more...I started to close the door slowly. He didn't remove his hand and I honestly didn't want to hurt him.

"Bridget! No! Please don't close the door on me!"

"Tristan, move your hand! I don't want to hurt you!"

"But don't you see...you *are*." He still didn't remove his hand so I took my free hand (my other hand was on the doorknob) and tried to push his hand off the side of the door. As soon as I touched him, his fingers grasped mine and held on tight. "Please let me in...I'm begging you. I just want a chance to explain everything."

I was tired, exhausted, and I really wanted to go to sleep and try to forget about everything that happened at the party. My stubbornness prevented me from letting Tristan in. Then the Fiery Redhead inside me took over the situation and she had enough arguing and crying for one night. "Tristan! I said go *home* or I swear to God you're going to lose some fingers!"

"Bridget, please just---" His sentence was cut short because suddenly Jake appeared next to him. I had no idea he was even there.

He grabbed Tristan's arm and shoulder, and spoke very sternly. "Tris, just let me talk to her for a minute." Tristan tried to struggle with him so he tightened his grip and raised his voice. "Tristan! Just go over there and let me talk to her!" Then he shoved his younger brother down the steps until he was standing on the sidewalk looking up at us. I instantly calmed down with Jake because I really had no reason to yell at him. He turned around to face me and I opened the door wider to speak to him. He spoke in a very serious tone. "Sis, just let Tristan in and talk to him."

Just when I thought I would be calm with Jake, he made my anger flare with one sentence. I raised my voice again and shouted, "What?!? Why should I?!? And why did you bring him here?!?"

Jake was surprisingly calm when he answered me. "He begged me to. I couldn't stand seeing my little brother crying like that."

I sighed heavily again. Why wouldn't the Hathaway brothers leave me in peace? Haven't I been through enough heartache for one night? Surprisingly, I was able to compose myself before I asked, "Why can't you just take him home?"

"Because he *is* home." He looked me straight in the eye and we were both silent for a moment. "He spends more time here than anywhere else."

"Jake, I don't want to talk to him."

"Don't you wanna know what happened? Don't you wanna know the truth?"

"You saw it too, didn't you? You saw him kiss her!"

As soon as I finished my last sentence, I heard Tristan yell, "She kissed *me*!"

"He's right. She kissed *him* and just at the right moment too. It was like she knew you were coming." Suddenly, Jake's expression changed and his voice turned hard. "Sis, just listen to me 'cause once I say this, I'm moving out of the way. And as soon as I do, Tris is gonna come right back up here and beg you to let him in. And if you don't, he's gonna keep begging and begging until you do. And if you close the door on him, he's gonna bang on it all night. Then one of your neighbors are gonna call the fucking pigs and they're gonna come and see him arguing with you; trying to get into your house and they're gonna try to arrest him. I know my lil' brother, ok. He'll resist and fight them, and they're gonna end up beating his arse for resisting arrest. Then I'll have to jump in and it'll be a big fucking mess. Do you want that? 'Cause I'm telling you... that's *exactly* what's gonna happen if you don't let him in. Sis, I *swear*... I've never seen him like this before. I mean, he hasn't been so completely mental since---"

Jake looked away from me for a minute and shuddered involuntarily. It was dark outside so I couldn't be sure, but his body language suggested that an unpleasant memory resurfaced for a short moment. Once he shook himself out of his reverie, he continued. "Look, this whole thing... all this shit that's happening tonight is under your control. You have the power to end this. Just...let...him...in."

After Jake spoke to me, I looked at the floor and sighed heavily as I considered his words. Deep down I knew he was right. Tristan was already here and I knew the only way he would leave would be by force. Plus, I really did want to know exactly what happened at the party. As I was deep in-thought, Tristan walked back up the steps and stood directly behind his brother. Our eyes met and his began to desperately plead with mine again. I started to visualize what would happen to him if the police came and the thought actually scared me. I still loved him and I didn't want to see him get hurt.

Jake kept to his word and moved out of the way. As soon as he did, Tristan took his place and stood right in front of me. Since I had opened the door wider when I was speaking to Jake, Tristan saw that as an opportunity to try to come inside. The door was wide enough for him to stick his arm through and softly caress my cheek with the back of hand. I was too tired to recoil from his touch and I had finally surrendered to him. I slowly began to open the door so he could enter. As he stepped over the threshold, I glanced past him and I saw Jake start to walk away towards his car.

After I closed the door, neither of us spoke as we stood there in the dark, quiet of my living room. I felt the tears on my cheeks so I wiped them away before I whispered, "Tristan, let's talk in the bedroom." Even though it was dark, he was able to find his way. He followed me into my room and I clicked on the light switch.

Once my room was illuminated, I walked towards the bed and sat down. If he was going to explain *everything*, I was ready to hear it. I looked up at him expectedly and his face was still flushed. I could see the wetness on his cheeks and my stubbornness began to fade. I started to admit to myself that I needed to give him a chance to explain. My voice was weary when I said, "So...talk. I'm listening."

He slowly walked towards where I was sitting until he was standing directly in front of me. Then he knelt down before me and looked up at me. The sight was actually heartbreaking and when he spoke, his voice was still shaky and cracking. "Bridget, I just wanna say that..." He paused and cast his eyes towards the floor. Then he took a few breaths. When he looked up at me again, his blue eyes had regained some of their fire and he was slowly smoldering me. "I love you so much. I would never hurt you. I didn't kiss that bint and I didn't shag her last weekend. What I was trying to tell you before is that I *did* shag her in the past. I didn't remember her when she sat down next to me and I think that pissed her off. Then the next thing I know...she's kissing me. As soon as she did... it was like...then you came and saw us. I didn't even get a chance to push her off me."

I spoke softly when I asked, "Did you sleep with her while we were together?"

"No! I swear I didn't. Bridget..." He moved closer to me and slowly reached out to hold my hands. I let him touch me and when he realized I wasn't recoiling from his touch, he squeezed my hands gently. "You have to believe me when I tell you this, love...I haven't had sex with anyone else since I met you."

My eyes widened and my mouth dropped after hearing this new revelation. Even though he said he was telling the truth, I found it very hard to believe and I was utterly speechless. When I finally did find the words, I said, "Tristan, you expect me to believe that *you*...the guy who admitted to being a slut...went without sex from the moment we met until the first time we made love? That was like three months!"

Suddenly, he smiled. And when he spoke again, his voice was clearer and stronger. "Yeah, I did." Then he chuckled and said, "And believe me... it wasn't easy; especially being around you. I did *a lot* of wanking."

Surprisingly, I found myself laughing lightly. I still couldn't believe he would deny himself physical pleasure because of me. I couldn't help but to ask, "Why did you do that? Before we got together, you were still free to sleep with whoever you wanted. I don't understand."

Tristan released my hands and placed his hands on my hips. Then he moved forward until my knees were resting against his stomach. I instinctively opened my legs and he settled naturally between them. He looked deep into my eyes as he searched for a way back into my heart. Once he found the path, he replied softly, "'Cause I fell in love with you. I didn't think about being with anyone else...I just wanted you."

I placed my hand on his cheek and gazed at him affectionately. I almost allowed myself to get lost in those beautiful blue eyes again but I still had more questions. His seductive spell wasn't able to ensnare me just yet so I was able to pull myself away. "So...how long ago did you sleep with her? And how did she get invited to the party?"

Tristan moved from his kneeling position to sit next to me on the bed and I completely turned my body to face him. "I don't remember exactly but I think it was some time last summer. She knew it was just a shag but she kept calling me like every day. She was basically stalking me. Eventually I got really pissed and changed my phone number." He paused again and I actually saw the wheels turning in his head. It was as if everything was becoming clearer to him. "I don't know how she found out about the party because I don't think anyone invited her. I didn't even notice she was there until she sat down next to me after you went to the loo." He paused again and then he tilted his head to the side. He looked at me curiously when he asked, "Wait, didn't you ask me who she was?"

"Yeah, because she was staring at us all night. And when I was feeding you your cake, she gave me a dirty look. What did she say to you when she sat down?"

"She asked me if I remembered her. I know I was drunk when I shagged her so I honestly didn't remember. I told her I didn't remember her and she sort of got pissy with me. She told me her name with an attitude like, 'My name is Kelly *remember?*' Then she looked back at her mate...some bird with brown hair and then she---" Tristan's eyes widened and suddenly he stood up. He turned to face me and then he yelled, "Those bitches set me up! 'Cause when she was talking to me she kept looking back at her mate. She must've been waiting for you so you would see us kiss." His voice took on a more urgent tone when he asked, "You said you heard her in the loo, right? She was talking about me and she said I fucked her last weekend?" I nodded. "She must've followed you in there...both of them! 'Cause when she came to sit next to me, she looked really happy about something. I'm telling you babe...they set me up!"

Suddenly, he knelt in front of me again and put his hands on my upper arms. He looked into my eyes and started to plead with me. "Bridge, please tell me that you believe me and that you still love me." He paused, took a deep breath, and his next words were filled heavy emotion. "And *please* tell me that you still trust me."

After everything that Tristan said he remembered about tonight, I honestly, completely and truly believed him. I gave him a genuine smile and replied tenderly, "I believe you. And baby, I still love you and I still trust you." Tristan smiled back at me and his adorable dimple made itself known on his left cheek. He reached into his front pocket and pulled out my promise ring. We looked into each others eyes for a moment, and then he slowly placed the ring back on my left middle finger with the crown and heart facing inwards. I leaned forward to kiss him and he met me halfway.

Unfortunately, the kiss ended prematurely because he pulled away first. He stood up and said, "Bridget, I need to tell you something." He paused and I looked at him expectedly to signal that he should continue. He looked down for a moment and sighed like he was dreading what he was about to say. When he looked at me again, he spoke quietly. "I meant it when I said I would never cheat on you. I wouldn't cheat because infidelity destroyed my family."

I was confused as to what he meant by that statement so I asked, "What do you mean it destroyed your family?" Tristan moved to sit next to me on the bed again and I knew he was about to confess a family secret to me.

"My father...that fucking bastard...he cheated on Mum when I was a kid." Tristan's mind began to go back in time as he retold his memory.

"Nanny had picked me and Jake up from school that day so we didn't walk home like we usually did. We were surprised when we saw one of my father's limousines in the parkway 'cause he usually worked during the day as a limo driver. We were walking up to the house, and we heard Mum and my father yelling. Me and Jake rushed in and ran to their room. What I saw...I'll never forget...for as long as I live. Mum was on the floor crying and my father was standing over her yelling...stark naked. I saw the other woman...his fucking whore...huddled in a corner with a sheet wrapped around her. When he saw me and Jake, he started yelling at us...telling us to get the fuck out. When I saw my mum crying...I don't know...I just snapped. I ran towards him and tried to attack him. I was only like ten or eleven at the time. Jake pulled me off him and that's when I heard Nanny yell. I've never heard her yell like that before. She yelled at my father and told him to leave and take his whore with him. He tried to explain but we all knew what happened. Mum caught him. She caught him shagging another woman in their bed. Nanny told him that if he didn't leave, she'd call the pigs. I ran over to Mum and held her 'cause she was still crying. Then Jake tried to tell him to leave but he wouldn't. Then they started fighting and he threw Jake down on the floor. Jake was kinda skinny back then, so he was no match for my father. While they were fighting, the whore ran out of the house. Then Nanny called the fucking pigs and soon they came to the house. Nanny wouldn't let my father take any of his clothes. Bridget, the pigs dragged him away naked...and the whole bloody neighborhood saw it."

While Tristan was telling the story, he wasn't looking at me. Instead, he was facing forward and staring out as he relived his horrible childhood memory. He looked over at me after he finished telling me about the day he witnessed his father's infidelity and his eyes were wet with unshed tears. But I knew they weren't tears of sadness, they were tears of resentment.

When he spoke to me, his voice was hard and bitter. "I'll never forgive him for what he did to Mum and neither will anyone else. That's why there are no pictures of him in Brighton. Oh, he tried to come back a couple times but every time he did, Nanny threatened to call the pigs. After awhile he stopped coming to the house. Mum got rid of all his things. She ended up divorcing him but she kept his name. She kept it for me and Jake."

When Tristan finished telling me about his father, I finally understood why he never mentioned him and I actually started to cry from sympathy. I moved closer and put my arms around him. I didn't know what to say to comfort him because it was in the past and the memory had already scarred him. While I was holding him, he said softly, "Bridget, I admit that I was a slut but I was never a fucking cheater. I would never cheat on my wife or girlfriend because I believe if you love someone, you don't hurt them by cheating on them." Then he looked into my eyes which were teary just like his and said, "I love you more than anything in the world. That's why I would *never* cheat on you." At that moment, I really believed that Tristan was my prince in shining armor...and I was lucky to have him.

As I was sitting next to my prince trying to comfort him, I remembered that I hadn't given him his birthday present. I sniffled and tried to make my voice sound cheerful. "Baby, I still have to give you your birthday present." Tristan looked over at me and smiled. The mood was slowly shifting into one of happiness so I quickly jumped off the bed to retrieve his present that was hidden in my closet. I walked back to the bed and placed the box in front of him which was wrapped in colorful wrapping paper with a big blue bow on top. His face instantly lit up with excitement and he turned his body towards me. I sat opposite him so that the present was between us. My expression was joyous and I looked at him expectedly. "Well, what are you waiting for? Open it!"

Tristan was a firm believer in getting to the point so he wasted no time in getting to the hidden surprise inside. My eyes widened with excitement and anticipation as he opened the gift box and pushed the tissue paper to the side. We both saw a glimpse of green and black and then suddenly he gasped. He slowly pulled the jacket out of the box and held it up in front of him to admire it. Then he placed it on his lap and ran his hand across the new, smooth leather. His blue eyes sparkled with surprise and happiness and he started to laugh. He looked at me and when he spoke, his voice was filled with joy. "Babe, I love this!" He jumped up off the bed, unzipped the jacket, and quickly put it on. He looked down at himself to admire it again before he quickly walked over to the full-length mirror on my closet door.

I walked over and stood next to him. I couldn't help but to smile as I watched him enjoy his birthday present. "This jacket is wicked! I can't believe it! Thank you so much!" He turned his body a couple times as he admired himself in the mirror. Then he turned to face me and posed for my amusement. I couldn't help but to start laughing. He gave me a roguish look, which came so natural to him, and asked, "How do I look in it?"

I moved close to him and adjusted the jacket even though it fit him perfectly. Then I put my arms around him, looked into his eyes and said, "You look perfect." Tristan slid his arms around my waist and held me tight against his body. We gazed into each other's eyes for a moment and I realized that his seductive spell finally captured me. I whispered against his lips, "Happy birthday, baby."

Tristan gently rubbed his nose against mine and whispered back to me, "It is *now*."

I've always heard people say that make-up sex is the best sex you can have. Since making love to Tristan was always incredible, I wasn't quite sure if the sex that night was the best. But it was definitely on my list of most spectacular nights ever. We both went through so much crying, anguish, heartache, and hurt that we needed the release like we needed to breathe. We kissed each other with equal fervor as our hands rubbed and caressed all over each other's bodies. I couldn't stop the moan that escaped my throat as I felt the passion begin to stir between us once more. We both decided that each of us was wearing too much clothing so we hastily stripped down to our birthday suits. I appreciated the fact that he was careful enough not to toss his new jacket on the floor. He seemed determine to take me as swiftly as possible so he backed me up towards the bed and I pulled him down on top of me. I spread my legs invitingly for him and he began to rock his pelvis against me. I felt every inch of him harden and rub against my clit in the most delicious way. His mouth captured mine in a deep, open-mouth kiss while he grabbed both my arms and lifted them above my head. He held them there by grasping both of my small wrists in one of his large hands.

He unsealed his mouth from mine and I was spellbound by his blue gaze. I raised my pelvis to match his rhythm and I moaned louder but he silenced me by kissing me deeply again. His tongue caressed mine and then I sucked on it before he returned the favor. I reached down to stroke his erection and he moaned into my mouth. Then he broke the kiss to whisper against my lips, "Put me inside you." I felt that his pre-cum had already slickened his manhood and I knew I was already wet from arousal. I was about to guide him inside me when I remembered that we needed to use a condom.

I whispered, "Tristan, you need a rubber."

He surprised me by replying softly, "Why, love? I haven't been wearing them lately." I was shocked that he actually remembered. "Bridget, I *swear* to you...I don't have anything. Please trust me."

I smirked at him as I reminded him of *another* consequence of unprotected sex. "What if I get pregnant? I'm not on The Pill, you know."

Tristan didn't look disturbed by my admission. I was actually surprised when he gave me a knowing look as if he already knew this information. He ran his fingers through my hair and whispered, "I'm not going anywhere, babe. I promise." At that moment, I read something else in his eyes...a message. He started to rub himself against me again and I made a decision that could possibly affect both of our lives dramatically. Without hesitation, I boldly reached down and put his raw erection inside me. I lifted my hips to take him in even deeper and when I felt him bury himself all the way to the hilt, I cried out in absolute bliss. He began thrusting inside me and it wasn't long before he set a rhythm that made me whimper from the intense sexual pleasure. We held each other tightly as our bodies began the synchronized motion of our love-making.

The pleasure that Tristan was giving me was almost indescribable. He started to pound into me faster and I knew my bed would need to be replaced very soon. Our cries of passion were reverberating off the bedroom walls. I gasped in surprise and he smiled devilishly before flipped us over. I straddled him so I could ride my British ivory stallion into a sexual frenzy. Tristan grabbed my hands and entwined our fingers. He held them against his chest and looked me in the eye while we made love. I leaned down to kiss him and then I slowly outlined his sensual lips with my tongue. He started to buck faster and harder and I felt him drive himself inside me even deeper. I met him stroke for stroke as I let him completely possess me sexually. He released my hands so he could reach up and squeeze and knead my soft, freckled breasts. Our bodies being joined and Tristan's hands cupping my breasts sent a feeling sheer bliss through every nerve ending. I closed my eyes and lifted my long auburn hair off my shoulders as I rode him freely with just my hips.

We wanted to ride the wave of ecstasy together as we always did. The end was near because I could feel myself approaching the edge of my sexual plateau. My beautiful prince sat up and wrapped his strong, tattooed arms around me in a tight embrace to eliminate any space between us. I felt my breasts crushed against his masculine, toned chest and I imagined being encircled by Tristan's invisible wings. His unique scent surrounded me and I open my eyes and they were met by a light blue heat that was glazed over in pure lust. He kissed me greedily as he continued to grind his hips into mine and slide his erection in and out of me with perfect ease. I started to feel that tingling sensation deep inside my belly. I kissed him again and then I said urgently, "I want to feel you, Tristan. Cum inside me! Do it, baby!" He started to pound into me harder and faster and that's when I went over the edge. My climax rippled through me and I cried out his name. "TRISTAN!" I felt my pussy release its essence and my body trembled as I concluded that Tristan... magnificent Sex God...was the best lover I've ever had.

It wasn't but a second later that my prince followed me into ecstasy. Tristan's orgasm made him call out my name and it never sounded so good to my ears. "BRIDGET!" His body jerked and his pelvis bucked against me as he jumped over the edge to meet me. I felt him spill his warm seed like an erupting volcano and he held onto me tightly as he filled me completely. I actually felt every part of his body tremble from his intense climax. As the little orgasmic tremors that rocked his body began to subside, he buried his face in the crook of my neck. He kissed it and then I felt the pressure as he sucked on my delicate skin to mark me. Our intense coupling released his primal nature because then I heard his muffled voice say, "You're mine."

Eventually, our bodies began to relax and Tristan's strong, tattooed arms enclosed my body in a warm and comforting embrace. As we were lying in bed, our minds still in a cloudy post-coital haze, I couldn't help but to think about what kind of man Tristan would be if he *hadn't* witnessed his father's infidelity. Would he be as loyal to me as he was now? Would he have disregarded my feelings and had an affair like some of my ex-boyfriends had done? An unexpected feeling floated to the surface of my consciousness and it frightened me because I realized how scared I was to actually lose him. I would've never taken him back if he admitted to cheating on me or if I truly didn't believe him. But I'll admit that I felt intense love and a powerful connection to him. Tristan told me that I was a part of him and I honestly felt that he was a part of me too.

It wasn't long until Tristan fell asleep. I had my head on his chest and I was listening to his heartbeat and his steady breathing. When I kissed his chest and squeezed his body tighter, he stirred and mumbled in his sleep. I smiled inwardly because I was so accustomed to his sleeping habits. It wasn't long before I drifted off to sleep and forgot my doubts about his loyalty. I made up my mind that I trusted him fully and completely.

The next morning I was making breakfast as I was getting ready for work and I heard the doorbell. It was early in the morning so I wasn't expecting any guests. I went to the front door and peeked out of the peep-hole, and I saw Autumn and her boyfriend Ryan standing there. I opened the door to greet them but I was momentarily shocked. I stood there staring at them with wide-eyes because they both looked exhausted. Autumn's bleach-blonde hair was in some sort of 'bed-head' state and she wasn't wearing any lip gloss. Her eyeliner and mascara were smeared giving her a raccoon appearance.

Ryan didn't look any better; his ponytail was falling out of its band and he had dark circles and bags under his eyes. I guess they noticed my surprised expression because Autumn said blandly, "Yeah...we know we look like shit. Can we come in?" I moved to the side to allow them to enter and that's when I noticed Autumn's clothes. Her shirt was ripped severely like it got caught on something. They both walked over to the sofa and sat down. I went over to join them and I saw Ryan lean his head back and close his eyes. I honestly thought he would fall asleep at any minute. I sat next to Autumn and she asked urgently, "Where's Tristan? Is he here?"

"Yeah, he's here. He's still asleep."

She seemed to sigh a breath of relief. "Oh good. So you two made up then?" I smiled at her and nodded. "Awesome! Then it wasn't all for nothing."

I looked at her with a confused expression and asked, "Huh? What do you mean?" Now that I was looking at her face close up, I noticed faint red scratches on her face. I took in her full appearance and concluded that she must have gotten into a fight. The realization hit me hard. "Hey, what happened to you? Why do you have scratches on your face?" I reached out and gingerly touched her face.

Autumn suddenly perked up and exclaimed, "I beat the shit out of that fucking cunt! I wasn't gonna let her get away with that." Right at that moment, I was convinced she was Tristan's long-lost sister. I couldn't believe that she fought the blonde home wrecker. Wait, correction: *Kelly* the blonde home wrecker. Autumn seemed excited so I let her continue. "As soon as Tristan ran after you, I got all in her face and I was like, 'What the fuck are you doing? Who are you and how'd you get in?' Then the bitch had the nerve to tell me to 'fuck off'. So I kicked her ass. Her brunette friend bailed on her so she had no help. You should've seen Marco...dude was cheering me on!" Autumn started laughing and she playfully hit Ryan on the chest to wake him up. He actually *did* fall asleep. "I kicked her ass, didn't I babe? I mean, she scratched me and tore up my shirt like a little bitch but she got it worse."

Ryan opened his tired eyes and replied sleepily, "Yeah...you fucked her up real good."

Autumn turned back around towards me and smiled. "Someone called the cops though. And they arrested me and shit...but you know... my baby bailed me out this morning."

"It took me all night to get up your bail money."

My best friend seemed very pleased with herself and I couldn't help but to look at her in amusement. "Autumn, I can't believe you did that."

"Bridge, I wasn't gonna let her get away with what she did. She was the one who made you cry in the bathroom, wasn't she?" I cast my eyes down at my lap as my mind flashed back to last night's memory of hearing that Tristan cheated on me. "I knew she had something to do with it. What did she say?"

Honestly, I didn't want to relive the memory but I figured that Autumn had a right to know. After all, she was involved too. "She was telling her friend a lie about sleeping with Tristan last weekend. At first I believed her...that's why I was so upset. But Tristan explained everything to me last night and I believe him."

She looked away from me and seemed to be deep in-thought. When she spoke, it was like she was talking to herself. "I knew something was up." Then she shook herself out of her reverie and said, "When you were walking back to the party...after you stormed out of the bathroom...I was walking behind you. I saw her 'partner-in-crime' poke her head around the corner as you were coming."

Suddenly, clarity came to me full circle and I finally understood exactly what happened last night. My mind quickly flashed back again and I saw all of last night's events like an instant replay. But this time I put together Autumn and Tristan's perspectives, and I saw how Kelly's lie manifested into something that almost ruined my relationship with Tristan. It was at that moment that I was sorry I didn't get a few good punches in on Kelly myself.

I made Ryan and Autumn breakfast, and the three of us ate and chatted for a short while. Autumn told me that Rick had brought Tristan's presents back to the house, so I made a reminder to call Rick when I got home. It wasn't long after we ate, that my jailbird best friend and her weary boyfriend left my apartment.

I was putting the breakfast dishes in the dishwasher when Tristan walked into the kitchen. His blue eyes were puffy from just waking up and his blond hair was like a little bird's nest on top his head. He was naked as the day he was born, but he wasn't sporting his usual 'morning-wood' and a part of me was actually disappointed by that. As I looked at him, my heart swelled at how this was such a familiar sight and I loved seeing him like this every morning. He came over to me and kissed my forehead before he greeted me. "Mornin' babe. Is Autumn here? I heard her big mouth."

I laughed and said, "No, she and Ryan just left." I was about to continue putting away the dishes when I remembered that he hadn't heard the latest news. "Hey, you won't believe this..." Then I paused and corrected my statement. "Wait, you probably will. Autumn beat up Kelly last night after you left." Then as an afterthought I said, "Oh, and your birthday presents are at Rick's." I caught myself after I said my last statement and I realized that Jake was right. My apartment *did* become more of a home to Tristan than the house he shared with Rick.

The top half of Tristan's body had disappeared into the fridge as he grabbed a carton of orange juice. I took that moment to admire his perfect ass that was graced with two dimples on either side. When he registered what I had just told him, a smile slowly crept onto his face. He stood at the counter to pour his juice and he started to chuckle. Then he looked over at me and said, "Yeah, that sounds like Autumn." He drank his juice to the bottom of the glass and then turned to face me. His facial expression changed to one more serious and his voice was hard. "But I'll tell you something, babe. I'm glad Autumn beat her arse 'cause if she didn't...I would've made sure that bitch paid for what she did. She almost made me lose you."

My eyes roamed over his entire naked body as he walked over to me and put his arms around my waist. I instinctively wrapped my arms around his neck to close the distance between us. He leaned down to kiss me and I tasted minty toothpaste and the tangy orange juice on his lips. Then he whispered, "And I can't lose you...not ever." I smiled warmly at him and he gave me a wicked smile in return. "So, do you have time for a quickie before work? You know that always puts a smile on your face and a strut in your walk." He waggled his eyebrows at me and I couldn't help but to laugh.

I looked up at the ceiling with a thoughtful expression as I considered his offer. Then I looked into his eyes and said with equal brazenness, "I don't think I can have a good morning unless you take me up against this counter right now." My naughty words made Tristan groan and he ground his pelvis into me. The sensation made me gasp and his eyes burned through to my soul before he captured my mouth in one of his possessive, yet passionate kisses. Even though we were just going to have a quickie, I knew I would be late for work. It was then...as he was thrusting inside me so deep that I thought I would cry from the pleasure...that I decided that Tristan was mine too. And I was never going to let anyone try to take him away from me again.

Chapter 11

EVER SINCE THE FIRST TIME Tristan and I made love, it had become one of our favorite activities. I've never been a very sexual person but he awakened a part of me that yearned to be taken over the edge and into ecstasy whenever possible. It was so strange to me how both of our sex drives could easily go into hyper-speed. I guess because he's a very sexual person, it was only natural that he introduce me to the idea that making love could really be fulfilling.

As Tristan was coming down from his orgasm after taking me on top of the kitchen counter, I happened to glance over at the microwave and see the time. I had about thirty minutes to get to work without being late. His breathing began to steady but he was in no rush to release his possessive hold on me. He began scattering light kisses up and down my neck, and across my jaw line. Sometimes he could be so sexually intoxicating. Even though our minds were still clouded by lust, I had to remind him that I needed to go to work. "Mmmmm...baby, please stop. You know I have to go to work." He started kissing my lips and I knew if I gave into temptation, it wouldn't take us long to get aroused again. A part of me wanted to call in sick and go back to bed with my British prince, but my guilty conscience reminded me that I already used enough false sick days to stay home with my Sex God of a boyfriend.

Tristan decided to exercise is mind-reading ability because he said, "You don't want me to stop." Then he whispered, "Call in sick, babe."

His seductive kisses continued and I tried to speak between them. "Sweetie, I can't. *kiss* I've already used *kiss* a lot of them. I really *kiss* have to *kiss* go. Tristan *kiss* please..." For some reason, I happened to look down at the place where our bodies were joined and his eyes followed. When our eyes met again, his blue gaze was intense and lust was slowly filling his beautiful orbs. He started to move inside me again and I quickly held his body still. "Baby, no I can't!" I was still amazed by his ability to get aroused again so quickly after having sex.

He ceased his movement, tilted his head to the side, and flashed me a wicked smile. His voice was soft and seductive when he said, "You *sure* you don't fancy another go?" He kissed me deeply and his warm tongue swept through my mouth as a moan escaped me unexpectedly. When we broke the kiss, my eyes ventured towards the microwave again and I saw that more time had passed by.

"Mmmmm...baby, I can't. I really want to but I have to go now." He released me reluctantly and it took every ounce of strength I had to unwrap my legs from around his waist. I also noticed he took longer than necessary to pull himself out of me. I could tell by his extremely relaxed demeanor that he was fully satiated and I had no doubts that once I left the apartment he would go back to sleep.

I carefully climbed down off the counter because my legs felt like jelly and I wasn't completely confident that I wouldn't collapse. He gave me a sly smile and he looked mighty proud of himself as he watched me struggle to walk. I had to go to the bathroom because I had to clean myself and make myself presentable to teach children. As I was walking, I noticed that he caused yet another run in my stockings. I laughed inwardly because it seemed that every time we had quickies in the morning, some article of clothing on me always got destroyed. By the time I finished cleaning myself, changing my stockings, and fixing my hair, I had ten minutes to get to school. I dashed out of the house but not before catching a glimpse of a naked Tristan laid out on the sofa. I yelled, "See you later, babe!" before I closed the front door.

On my way to school, I called the principal to tell him I was running late and his tone of voice suggested that he was not happy with this information. Because I was so late getting to school, the faculty parking lot was full. I parked on a side-street and something caught my attention as I walked around to the front of the school. A young woman in her early to mid twenties was helping her child out of their minivan. The child looked like she was pre-school or kindergarten age. I watched them intently as I continued walking and as I got closer and turned towards the front steps, I could see that she also had an infant in a car seat.

For some reason I halted my steps and stood watching the woman with her child. I assumed the little girl was hers because of the uncanny resemblance. Suddenly, I started to wonder about the children's father and a million questions went through my mind: *Is he still with the mother? Are they married or just dating? Does he work while she stays home with the kids? Is she a single mother? Is he out of town a lot and she raises the kids by herself?* I finally shook myself out of my reverie when I realized the young woman was smiling at me. I smiled back and then I turned to walk up the front steps into the school.

As I was walking to my class, I immediately started thinking about Tristan and our recent unprotected sex that could result in a child of our own. Tristan was just starting out in his acting career and I felt that he had the potential to become very successful. Every week he was meeting with casting directors, receiving scripts, and traveling out of town on business. His manager definitely kept him busy and it was truly miraculous that he actually had his nights free to spend with me. I started to imagine if we did have a child together, how involved would he be in raising that child? I knew that the busier he got, the less time he would spend at home. I didn't want to raise a child by myself and I didn't want to be a single mother. Plus, I knew I wasn't financially ready but I've never discussed Tristan's financial situation with him. He was able to afford buying me a $41,000 car and I wondered how much of his savings that actually amounted to.

Although I loved Tristan, I discovered another one of his weaknesses was impulsiveness. I could honestly say that it became one of my weaknesses as well. But I realized that a relationship between two impulsive people could prove disastrous. I had to be the more responsible one or else both our lives could be headed in a direction that neither of us were completely ready for.

Last night I read a message in Tristan's eyes. That message was a clear affirmation that he was aware of the consequences of my decision to have unprotected sex with him. At that moment, I fully comprehended the message and I halted my steps yet again. Tristan wanted a baby. But the real question was...did I? And did I truly believe that he was ready to become a father? And why would a man his age want a child already? I reminded myself to ask him about that tonight. We've been in a relationship for almost eight months and although we both pledged to stay with each other, I realized that nothing is guaranteed. I reached the door to my classroom and I made another decision as I put my hand on the doorknob to enter. I decided to go on birth control and try to prevent a pregnancy from happening now.

During my lunch break I called my gynecologist, Dr. Boykin, and made an appointment. The relationship I have with her started when I was sixteen and over the past nine years I came to know her like an aunt. So when I begged her to squeeze me into her schedule that afternoon, she happily agreed to see me.

I went to her office immediately after school. After waiting a few minutes in one of the exam rooms, she greeted with a friendly smile and a hug. Dr. Boykin was around my mother's age and her thick sable hair brushed against her shoulders. "So, what brings you here today, Bridget?"

She stood in front of me wearing a white lab coat with a lilac shirt underneath. I looked into her brown eyes that were a shade darker than mine and said, "I need to start taking birth control." I couldn't meet her eyes when I confessed, "I recently had unprotected sex and I don't want to get pregnant. Is there anything you can do to prevent it from happening?" At that moment, Dr. Boykin became my Savior. She offered to give me Emergency Contraception Pills and I gladly accepted. Since I've never had many lovers or had unprotected sex, I wasn't very informed about the types of birth control that were available.

She did give a warning though. "ECP's are not always one-hundred percent effective, so make sure you don't miss your next period. If you do, I expect to see you back here."

My next period was due in two weeks and I knew I would be anxious as I counted down the days. She also drew my blood to test me for HIV and any STD's. I did believe Tristan when he said he was disease-free, but Dr. Boykin insisted, and deep down I knew I should.

When I got home I decided that I needed to have a talk with Tristan and tell him about my decision to go on birth control. I also wanted to tell him that we needed to continue using condoms just to be extra safe. I wasn't sure how he'd react to the news because I noticed how much he enjoyed not using them. As the evening passed, I actually started to get nervous about telling him because I was hoping it wouldn't lead to an argument.

It was almost 9PM when I heard the doorbell. I knew it was Tristan so I quickly ran to answer the door. Once I let him in, we greeted each other with our customary 'hello' kiss. He still had his arms around my waist when he smiled and asked, "So babe, when do you think I could get a key?"

There were some nights where he didn't come to my apartment until very late at night. This caused me to have to get up in the middle of night to let him in. It seemed that he refused to sleep at the house that he shared with Rick. I started to wonder if he ever went back there at all because a lot of his clothes had found their way into my closet. I decided to test my assumption so I said, "You know Tristan...if it's ever really late, you could always go to your house and sleep."

He gave me a confused look. "Why would I wanna do that?" Then his expression changed and a sly grin crept onto his face. "You know I can't sleep without you, love."

I smiled in response to his words and I couldn't help but to feel flattered. "Believe me, I'm not complaining because I like sleeping with you too. But what about the expenses at the house? I'm assuming you and Rick split everything 50/50? Do you still give him your half even though you hardly stay there?"

He shrugged and replied simply, "Yeah."

This time it was my turn to look confused. "Why? Why not just stay there? That way you won't be paying for nothing. I just don't understand because you eat here, shower here, and sleep here." I gave him a knowing smile before I said, "You stay with me whenever you're not out of town. Plus, I noticed more and more of your clothes appearing in my closet."

Tristan raised an eyebrow and asked, "Why don't I just move out?" His question caught me off-guard momentarily and he took that opportunity to shock me even further. His expression turned serious and he looked intently into my eyes. "Let me move in with you." I knew by the tone of his voice that he wasn't really *asking*.

I was surprised that I didn't hesitate before I answered. "Okay." I had to be under his spell again because I was lost in his eyes. Sometimes I wondered about Tristan and how he was able to manipulate me with his baby blues. When I finally came to, I said, "I'll make you a copy of my key."

Suddenly, a dazzling smile lit up his face. "Brilliant! How about tomorrow? Can I move in then?"

I was utterly amazed that he wanted to move in so quickly. After I thought about it, I decided that the weekend would be more ideal because that way I could help with the moving. "Um, what about this weekend? Saturday would be better for me because I'll be here and I could help out."

Tristan looked confused for a second, but the expression quickly vanished. It was replaced with a thoughtful look. He looked up at the ceiling and his mind seemed to be far away. "Yeah, that would be better. Rick's little brother is coming on Saturday."

"Great, then he can help too!"

He didn't look at me and it seemed like he was still talking to himself. "Actually, he'll be moving in."

I couldn't help but to look confused myself. "Oh, you guys were getting another roommate?"

When he finally did look at me, another sly smile appeared on his face. "No. I already told Rick I was moving out and he's been looking for another roommate. His bro called him just in time and told him that he needed a place. I guess it worked out for the both of them." As Tristan was telling me this, my eyes widened and my jaw dropped because it finally registered in my brain that he planned to move in with me before he asked me.

He rendered me speechless for a moment because there was just no end to his ability to shock me. It was then that I remembered that I had something important to discuss with him before we got side-tracked with talk of finally moving in together. "Baby, I need to talk to you about something."

His expression changed to one of concern and he asked, "Is everything alright?"

"Yeah, we just need to talk." I pulled myself out of his embrace and he followed me over to the sofa. He sat down next to me and I turned my body to face him. He was looking at me intently and I felt that I needed to get to the point. I took a deep breath and said, "Tristan, I started The Pill today. I saw my doctor after school and she started me on it." Then for some reason, I couldn't look him in the eye when I spoke my next words. "And she gave me something to make sure I don't get pregnant now. You know, because we haven't used any protection." I chanced a glance at his face and he actually looked confused. I was shocked that he didn't have an immediate reply so I continued. "And we need to start using condoms again."

My last sentence finally triggered a response from him. "Wait...why? I mean, I thought..." He paused and looked down for a moment. When he looked at me again his expression was still one of confusion. "So, you don't wanna get pregnant?"

He asked the question so nonchalantly that I was temporarily speechless, if not a bit shocked. I guess my earlier assumption was correct. He *did* want a baby. I couldn't help but to ask, "Tristan, do *you* want a baby?"

The smile that appeared on his face was so genuine and so lovely that I already knew his answer before he spoke. "Yeah, I wouldn't mind if we had one. We plan on getting married one day, right? I thought that's what you wanted. I thought that's why you didn't make me wear protection."

The expression of utter shock would not disappear from my face. I couldn't believe that this twenty-four year old man wanted a baby. We weren't married and we weren't even living together...not officially. Suddenly my brain showed me a mental calendar and I calculated that we haven't even been together a year. Tristan's impulsiveness was reaching new heights right before my eyes. "But Tristan, you're so young. I mean, we're both young but..." I was honestly at a loss for words and I shook my head in disbelief. Part of me was actually flattered that he wanted a child already, but I couldn't help but to feel that he really didn't know what he would be getting into. I wasn't sure that he realized what a big responsibility having a child was. At that moment, I felt I needed to remind him. "Do you realize what a big responsibility having a kid is? You won't even own a car because it's too much responsibility. Do you think you could handle a child? And don't you think it's kind of early in our relationship?"

Surprisingly, the smile on Tristan's face remained and he replied casually, "Yeah I know it's a big responsibility. And babe, I told you I'm not going anywhere. Whether we have the baby now or later, it doesn't matter to me. And I don't think we're too young. Mum had Jake when she was twenty-three. And I would be raising the baby with you and I think you'd be a great mum." Then his smile widened and he added, "And I'm not the only one who thinks so."

I was stunned by his entire reasoning but I was especially curious about his last statement. "Who else thinks so?"

His answer was short and sweet. "Mum." My jaw dropped yet again. Tristan's mother told him that I would be a good mother? I know he noticed my shocked expression and the fact that I wasn't responding so he decided to elaborate. "She told me that I chose the perfect woman to be the mother of my children." Then he gave a short laugh and added, "She said she wants little blond and redheaded grandkids running around the house." There was a little sparkle in his eyes and I had a sneaking suspicion that he was imagining the scene.

I had no idea that Kate shared her desire to be a grandmother with Tristan. Surely, I thought she would've expressed those feelings to Jake because he's the older son. My inner thoughts continued to find their way out of my mouth. "But shouldn't she have said that stuff to Jake? I mean, he's older and he would be more likely to have kids right now."

"But Jake's not in a serious relationship...I am. Plus, we're in love and she knows I wanna marry you."

"But Tristan, most guys your age aren't thinking about having kids. As a matter of fact, most of them try to avoid impregnating women."

As the king of saying things of shock value, Tristan proved to me why he still reigned. He paused for a moment and looked deep into my eyes. I didn't even notice that he moved closer to me until I noticed the blond stubble on his chin and the fact that the irises of his eyes were a pure sky blue. "Bridget, I'm not like most guys." I couldn't argue with him on that point because he was definitely one-of-a-kind. "And I can only imagine you as the mother of my kids."

In the back of my mind, a question started to brew. It was so great and I was so curious, that I had to ask him. I hoped I wasn't overstepping the boundary of personal information but the desire to know started to slowly eat away at me. When I could no longer contain the urge, my voice lowered to the point where I sounded timid and I asked him. "Have you ever gotten anyone pregnant? I mean, have any of the girls you've slept with ever had an abortion?"

I heard Tristan swallow hard and I knew my question caught him off-guard. His face actually flushed slightly and I wondered if he was going to tell me the truth or tell me it was none of my business. I was hoping for the former. He looked away from me for a moment and I knew he was debating on whether he should tell me. I had a feeling the answer was affirmative because he was hesitating to answer. Finally, he turned to look at me and his expression was serious. "Yes." He didn't elaborate and I didn't ask him to divulge any further details. I also couldn't hide the disappointment in my face before I looked away from him. I mentally kicked myself for asking him the question in the first place, knowing I would be disappointed if the answer was 'yes'. He must've sensed my true feelings because he said my name softly. "Bridget." I turned to look at him and he frowned slightly. He searched my eyes and then took both of my hands in his. He spoke in a very low voice and it sounded like he was pleading with me. "Please don't judge me."

His words actually stopped my heart for a moment. My expression changed to one of complete warmth and affection as I placed my palm on his cheek. I looked tenderly into his eyes and said, "Sweetheart, I'm not judging you. I swear I'm not. I *do* want to have your children...believe me I really do. I could just imagine how beautiful they'd be. But I think we should wait, sweetie. We have plenty of time to have them and I think that you should concentrate on your career right now. You know I fully support you and I'll always be here for you. I was thinking about this today before I went to the doctor, and I think it's best if we don't rush things. Honestly, I wasn't thinking when I let you inside me without protection. I guess I was just..." I sighed because my pride wouldn't allow me to admit that I was irresponsible and careless. "Baby, when I'm ready to have kids...I'll let you know." I smiled adoringly at him and moved my other hand to run my fingers through his soft blond hair that I loved so much. "Because I can only imagine *you* as the father of my children."

Tristan slowly began to close the distance between us as he leaned forward to kiss me. Right before our lips connected, he whispered, "I think I love you too much." I finally surrendered to his spell and let him 'snog' me senseless. It was clear to anyone who ever witnessed us together that Tristan and I were undeniably in love.

When we finally detached our mouths and bodies from each other, I heated some dinner for Tristan. We sat at the dining room table while he ate his dinner and I finished grading homework assignments.

After dinner we were both really tired so we decided to go to bed. Our nighttime shower lasted longer than necessary because we had to fool around like we always do. We didn't have intercourse because of the absence of condoms in the bathroom. After the first time we made love, Tristan and I agreed to keep condoms in easy-to-get-to places all over the apartment. This was because our sex drives were so high; we would make love in any room at any given time.

It wasn't until we were in the bedroom and I was sitting at my vanity brushing my hair, that I realized they were missing. Tristan was in bed, and he was lying naked on his stomach. It was customary for both of us to sleep nude because of our bedtime activities. I paused my brushstrokes and looked over at him. "Where are the condoms that were in the shower?"

The look on Tristan's face was one of absolute adoration. He was facing me with his head cradled on his crossed arms. His eyes were a clear, cool blue and he was just gazing at me with his lips slightly apart as he watched me brush my hair. My voice seemed to bring him out of his trance and I was actually upset that his expression changed to one of acknowledgment. At that moment, I would've paid money to know exactly what he was thinking before I spoke to him. Before he answered, he smiled and chuckled lightly. "I threw them out," he replied very nonchalantly.

A look of confusion naturally appeared on my face. "Why'd you do that?"

"I thought we didn't need them anymore."

"So you threw them *all* out?"

He blinked slowly and replied, "Yep." Wow, he really was serious about the whole 'baby' thing to actually get rid of the only means of contraception we had. I guess he realized the consequences of his actions because then he said, "I'll buy some tomorrow."

Once I finished brushing my hair, I climbed into bed with my prince but I decided to tease him as punishment for his carelessness with the condoms. I sighed dramatically and said, "Oh well, I guess we won't be having sex tonight." I turned on my side away from him and feigned sleep, but he put his hand on my shoulder and gently pulled me so that I was lying on my back.

He leaned over me until there was probably an inch between us and his eyes began to smolder me with hot blue flames. He tilted his head to the side in a way that made him look completely roguish, and he spoke softly but sternly. "Oh yes we are."

He was being so dominant with me that it was beginning to turn me on. I lifted an eyebrow and smirked at him. "Oh really?"

Suddenly, he pulled the comforter off us with one swipe. A wicked smile appeared on his face and he said, "*Oral* sex." Then he laid down on his back and pulled me on top of him. I looked down at him questioningly and he said in the same dominant voice, "You're facing the wrong way." A look of comprehension appeared on my face and I gasped. Then the naughty little minx inside me became excited so I gave him a wicked smile in return before I proceeded to reposition my body into the '69' position.

I can honestly say that Tristan was the first man to get me to perform that sexual position. It's definitely not for the shy or easily-embarrassed, so I was never bold enough to attempt it with past boyfriends. But because I was so comfortable with him and trusted him completely, I had no problem with presenting myself to him in that manner. I found that it was actually very pleasurable and because of the extreme intimacy of the position itself, I expressed my desire to do it more often. For all that I lacked in sexual experience, Tristan more than made up for it and I was truly grateful.

The weekend brought the beginnings of June and Tristan left early Saturday morning to help Rick move his brother into his former residence. By afternoon, Tristan was back home and I was dressed for moving. I put my hair up in a messy ponytail, and I wore an old pair of jeans and an old faded t-shirt. He was in the kitchen on the phone with Rick and I assumed he was coordinating the moving plan with him. After I finished putting on a pair of beat-up Nike sneakers, I met him in the living room.

He was standing there with an expression like he was waiting to tell me something. I was feeling excited and cheerful at the thought of him staying with me permanently. I know my cheery mood was reflected in my voice when I asked, "So, is everything set? Are we ready to go?"

He smiled down at me and put his hands on my upper arms. "Um, babe. You don't have to come with me. I only have a few things to bring."

My smile disappeared and was replaced with a look of confusion. "Huh? What do you mean?"

I heard a car horn honking outside and I assumed that it was Rick. Tristan pecked my lips and quickly said, "Just stay here, love. Wait for us to come back." He opened the front door but looked back at me one last time. I was speechless and still confused, so I guess he felt the need to ease my confusion. "You can help us bring my stuff in, okay?" Before I could respond, he closed the door behind him. I rushed over to the window and I saw him get into a black Ford F150 pickup truck with two men. One of them I recognized as Rick but the driver was unfamiliar.

It was probably an hour and a half before I heard the doorbell. I was sitting in the living room watching TV and I quickly got up to answer the door. When I opened it, I saw Tristan, Rick, and the mystery driver holding dresser drawers. I moved out of the way so they could enter and as Rick passed me, he said, "Bridge, this is my brother Chris."

As soon as I set my eyes on Chris, I could tell he and Rick were related. He was attractive and he had the same dark curly hair and matching eyes just like his brother. In contrast to his older brother, Chris had a youthful face but like Rick, he had a very athletic physique. He was the third one to come through the door and he smiled and greeted me as he passed. "Hi, Bridget." The three of them disappeared down the hall and I saw them turn towards the bedroom. Then a few seconds later, Rick and Chris walked out with Tristan in-tow.

I stopped Tristan and asked, "Do you guys need help?"

"Ummm...not really. But I guess you can carry a bag."

I really didn't understand what was going on. I knew Tristan was moving in but what exactly was he moving *in*? "Tristan, what did you bring?"

He smiled widely and started counting off the items on his fingers, "A dresser, my laptop, my luggage, a few bags of clothes, a box of shoes, and another box with just my personal shit."

My jaw dropped suddenly and I asked, "That's *it*? That's all you're bringing? I don't get it. What about---"

As we were talking, Rick and Chris continued to carry Tristan's belongings into the apartment. On one of their trips back out the front door, Rick stopped and interrupted us. He communicated to Tristan in their own language by saying, "Hey dickhead, let's get a move on it. I still gotta help Chris get settled in." Before Tristan could communicate back, I turned and walked out the front door because I had to see for myself what he was moving in.

I walked over to the pickup truck and looked in the back, and I saw that Tristan was right. There were a couple of big, black garbage bags and a large cardboard box left sitting there.

The guys came back outside and grabbed the remaining items. I stood there empty-handed until Tristan came over and handed me one of the garbage bags. He smiled at me and asked in a very polite tone, "Would you carry this in for me, love?" I smiled back at him and the two of us walked back into *our* apartment.

Once everything was moved in, Rick and Chris left me and Tristan in the bedroom. We were putting the drawers into his dresser when Tristan asked, "So, where are we gonna put this?"

I briefly looked around the room and saw that there would be ample space next to my chest if we moved it over a few feet. "We can put it next to mine. We just need to move it a little."

After we moved my chest, his dresser was able to fit snugly next to it. We were standing there looking at them when I heard him chuckle. I looked over at him and he remarked, "My dresser looks like pure shit next to yours." Then he started to laugh. "It looks like I took it out of a scrap yard or something." Tristan's dresser was made of dark oak but the wood looked severely weathered. There were also a couple knobs missing from some of the drawers and one of the drawers would not close completely. My chest on the other hand, was made of birch wood with a snow-white finish. It was a six-drawer chest and it had elegant vines and flowers carved into the top and bottom. The drawers had faux crystal knobs with gold accents and the chest itself was significantly taller than Tristan's dresser.

I couldn't help but to notice the drastic difference between them and I started laughing too. "Hey, I don't care what it looks like. As long as it serves its purpose, right? But don't worry, we'll replace it because I have a feeling it's outlasted its usage."

We put some of his clothes into the drawers and then we moved on to the closet. I made extra space in my closet for Tristan when I first noticed more and more of his clothes being left behind. We were both quiet as we stood side-by-side hanging his clothes on the closet rack. My mind started to wander and I started thinking about the fact that he didn't bring many belongings. "Tristan, how come you hardly have any stuff? And what are you going to do about the rest of the stuff you left at the house?"

Tristan continued to pull his clothes out of the garbage bags and hang them up. "When I first came to The States, I didn't have much. And I guess over the years I didn't really acquire much. Just the necessities, you know. And I told Chris he could have my bed. Of course, he brought his own mattress." He chuckled after the latter part of his sentence. "And if you remember, I really didn't have that much in my room anyway. What you saw was mostly just clothes and other rubbish. All the other furniture in the house is really Rick's 'cause most of that shit was there when I moved in, except for the gaming setup. I put a lot of my money into that. But hey…" He shrugged nonchalantly. "He can have it. I don't really give a shit." I was smiling as I listened to him talk and I was honestly surprised at how humble he lived.

Suddenly, Tristan dropped one of his shirts he was about to hang and he turned to face me. I stopped hanging his clothes too so I could give him my attention. He moved closer to me and put his arms around my waist to embrace me. "You know babe, this is only temporary. Eventually, I would like to get us a bigger place."

Tristan's thoughtfulness was warming me to the core. "Really?"

He smiled down at me and said, "Yeah, like a big house with a yard. You know, so we can have barbecues."

I laughed and said, "You know how to barbecue?"

"No, do you?"

"No, but my dad has been grilling for years. I'm sure it can't be that hard and we can always teach each other."

Tristan placed a tender kiss on my forehead before he replied, "Good, 'cause what kinda bloke would I be if I can't barbecue? I just hope I don't singe my bleeding eyebrows off." I couldn't help but to laugh as I imagined him firing up a grill for the first time. Suddenly, his expression changed and his playfulness seemed to disappear. When he spoke to me, his voice was soft but there was an unmistaken serious undertone. "Bridge, now that you let me in...I won't ever leave you." His look was intense and he slowly leaned his head closer to mine as he began to descend onto my lips. "Love, I promise you'll never be alone." He reached his destination and sealed his promise by capturing my mouth in a passionate, yet loving kiss.

A few weeks later, I was relieved and overjoyed when my period came on time. I was confident that I wasn't pregnant but I took a home pregnancy test just to be sure. When it proved to be negative, I told Tristan and he seemed to display false enthusiasm. I had a feeling that deep down, he really wanted a baby but I really didn't know *why*. Dr. Boykin also called me to inform me that my STD test was negative. I still had to wait a couple more weeks for my HIV test but I was confident that it would be negative too. I trusted Tristan and I knew he would tell me if he had a virus as serious as HIV. I was so happy to officially share my place with him and it was a comforting feeling to know that I wouldn't be alone anymore. He had become my best friend in addition to being my lover and I couldn't imagine being without him.

Following my feelings of joy and contentment, came the unexpected feelings of worry and uncertainty. I was afraid of these new feelings because I didn't want to need Tristan. It was one thing to want someone but a completely different thing to *need* someone. Neediness can lead to obsession or possessiveness; both of which could be detrimental and unhealthy in a relationship. Then I started thinking about Tristan and the feelings that he's expressed towards me. I knew he loved and cared for me immensely but I couldn't help but to recall his comment about 'loving me too much'. He had already revealed to me that he was possessive but was it at a level where I should be concerned for myself? He also told me on a few occasions that he needed me but did he mean it in the literal sense? I remembered when I overheard Jake express his opinion that Tristan was obsessed with me. Was there any validity to his opinion and did Jake see a side of Tristan that I didn't see? People always say that love has a way of making you blind to the truth. I started to fear for my relationship with Tristan because I realized we may be in trouble. And the *truth* was...I didn't know what to do about it.

Chapter 12

'Love is composed of a single soul inhabiting two bodies.'

~ Aristotle

I REMEMBER ONE DAY I was talking to Jake and I asked him, "If I didn't know Tristan, how would you describe him?" I figured because Jake was closer to Tristan than anyone and he would be brutally honest, that he'd be the best person to ask. Of course, Tristan was present during my questioning but that didn't deter Jake from expressing is honest opinion. After taking a minute to process his thoughts, he told me that Tristan was like a storm. Not any storm in particular like a tropical storm or a winter storm; just a storm. He described his younger brother as the calm before it, the unpredictability during it, and the aftermath concluding it. When I asked him to elaborate and explain, he said, "Tristan comes across as a gentle soul, but you'd never think he could totally flip your world upside down until you don't even know which way is up. When you get to know him, he'll surprise you because he's unpredictable and wild. He affects the people he comes in contact with; even after he leaves you. He's the type of person that you'll always remember."

One Friday night in early June, I was awakened by the feeling of someone gently shaking my body and calling my name. I slowly opened one eye and I immediately felt Tristan's presence surrounding me. The digital alarm clock was on my side of the bed so when I opened my eye, I saw the clock's red digits glaring back at me and they read: 2:54AM.

I knew Tristan was leaning over me because I heard his voice above me. He whispered in the dark, "Babe, wake up. I need to ask you something."

"Can't it wait until morning?"

"Bridge...*please*. I need to ask you *now*."

His voice sounded urgent so I turned over to lie on my back. I spoke softly but I wasn't whispering. "What is it?"

He paused for a moment and then he said, "You remember a couple weeks ago when you asked me if I ever got anyone pregnant? If any birds I've been with ever had an abortion?"

I perked up because I wasn't expecting him to bring up that particular subject. "Yeah, I remember."

The bedroom was almost pitch black and I couldn't even see my hand in front of my face. The only light in the room was the neon glow from the alarm clock. He paused again and when he spoke, his voice sounded closer. "Why'd you ask me that?"

This time I paused. Deep down I didn't want to talk about it but Tristan seemed determined to bring up the subject again. At first, I was reluctant to answer and I wanted to answer his question with a question of my own: 'Why are you bringing this up now?' But I was too tired to play '20 Questions' with him and I wanted to know where this conversation was going. I answered truthfully when I replied, "I asked you because I wanted to know if you ever discussed having children with any woman besides me."

This time I knew he was closer because his scent engulfed my senses. "Bridget, I've never wanted to have a baby with anyone; not until I met you." His statement made me smile but I knew he couldn't see my face. "I would never wanna raise a kid with anyone I didn't love, and I've never been in love so..." He paused again but he had my undivided attention. "I'll admit that I made mistakes in the past." He gave a short laugh and continued. "Like *a lot* of fucking mistakes, but I don't think having a baby with you would be a mistake." Suddenly, he lowered his voice and it was gentle. "Tell me again why you don't want one."

Far away in the back of my mind, I had a feeling he would ask me that question again. Then I remembered that I really wanted to know *why* he wanted a baby. "Tristan, I do want one but---"

April Bostic

He interrupted me before I could finish. "But why don't you want one *now*? Why do we need to wait? Bridge, I wanna marry you...you know that. What, do you think we can't afford to take care of a baby?"

I sighed heavily because I couldn't believe we were having this conversation at three o'clock in the morning. "Tristan, I don't know about your financial situation but I know I can't afford a baby right now. Plus, I told you that you should concentrate on your career."

"Shouldn't that be my decision? What I wanna concentrate on? And Bridge, I know I may not look like it...but I *do* have money."

His last statement was a really big eye-opener. It was so big, that it made me sit up in bed. My sudden movement must have startled him because I felt his body shift. I was totally confused by his persistence with the whole 'baby' subject. I needed to know where his deep desire for a child was coming from. "Tristan, why do you want a baby so badly? Why do we have to have one now? What's the rush?"

Even though the room was very dark, I could see the outline of his body. I felt the mattress move and his body shift again. When he spoke this time, his voice sounded muffled and I knew that he laid down and turned away from me. He actually sounded upset when he said, "You have no idea how I feel about you."

I moved my body until I was lying against his. I used my hand to feel his body position and I confirmed that it was turned away from me. I snuggled up against his back and put my arms around him so that we were spooning. He didn't answer my question so I pleaded with him gently by asking, "Tristan, what's wrong? Why are you so upset about this?" For a minute, a part of me became annoyed because I felt like he was being overdramatic. But the other part of me remembered that Tristan is very sensitive. I've never been with a man as emotionally sensitive as Tristan and it took me awhile to understand him. Eventually I realized that I needed to be more patient with him when dealing with his feelings. "Baby, listen to me okay? You can talk to me. Whatever you're feeling...you can tell me. I love you and I promise I won't ever judge you." My voice took on a more stern tone as I finished by saying, "No more secrets, Tristan."

It was probably a full minute before he spoke, but when he did...it actually gave me a chill. "What if it's bad?"

208

I hesitated for a moment because his question caught me off-guard. Once I composed myself, I tried to make my voice sound understanding. "I don't care if it's bad, you can tell me. Tristan, you told me that I was a part of you. Well, you're a part of me too and I want you to be able to tell me anything. Tell me how you feel about me."

He still didn't turn around to face me and I had a sudden urge to see his facial expression. I wanted to jump up and turn on the light but I felt that if I let go of him, I would lose the moment and he wouldn't open up to me. His tone of voice still sounded upset and he still spoke quietly. "If you knew how I really feel...you'd leave me. That's why I can't tell you."

"Tristan---"

"Please go to sleep, Bridget. Forget I asked about the baby. I won't bring it up again. But just promise me that if you do get pregnant...you won't get an abortion."

The stubbornness inside me wanted to demand that he tell me, but I was too tired and too confused to deal with his up-and-down emotions that night. I did feel that I needed to reassure him about the abortion because I would never consider that option if I accidentally got pregnant. I placed a gentle kiss on his shoulder blade before I whispered, "I promise." He covered my arms with his and I felt slightly relieved. I did go back to sleep but I knew that Tristan was lying. He would bring up the baby again.

Saturday morning I was in the kitchen looking for something to make us for breakfast, when he casually walked in and headed for the refrigerator. When I looked at him, I did a double-take because he actually looked *awake*. In the mornings, Tristan has a fresh 'I-just-woke-up' look about him. He's usually naked, his eyes have a post-sleep puffiness to them and his hair is messy. But that morning, his hair was still messy but he had on boxers and his face was completely alert and aware. He actually looked like he'd been up for awhile. I couldn't contain my curiosity so I asked, "Did you just wake up?"

He opened the refrigerator and stood motionless in front of it like whatever food he desired would magically pop out. He quickly glanced at me before he turned his gaze back onto the refrigerator. "No, I woke up when you did."

His response struck me as odd because I woke up thirty minutes ago. "Oh, so you were just lying in bed?" He didn't look at me, he just nodded.

At that moment, I realized that he was still upset about last night. But why? He's the one who ended the conversation when I was completely willing to hear him out. I walked over to him and put my hand on his arm. This gesture garnered his attention and he turned his head to look down at me. "Tristan, I want you to talk to me. I don't want us to start our weekend with all this..." I paused and looked around the kitchen as I searched for my word. "Tension." I moved in closer and embraced him. I silently prayed that he would open up to me so I looked pleadingly into his baby blues and said, "Last night you said I have no idea how you feel about me. And if I did know, I'd leave you. Why did you say that?"

"'Cause you would."

"What do you mean? Why would I leave you?" As an afterthought I added, "It's okay to tell me."

He looked away from me for a moment and sighed. When he looked back at me, his expression turned serious. He searched my eyes like he was trying to see if it really *was* okay to tell me. When he spoke, I was actually shocked to hear that his voice was shaky. "Bridget, I..." He took a deep breath and then I saw the muscle in his jaw twitch. I tried to plead with my eyes for him to confess. I say 'confess' because I had a feeling that was what he was about to do. When he continued speaking, it was like he was pouring his heart out to me...and his soul. "You're not gonna like what I say, but this is how I feel. I don't like sharing you. Sometimes I get pissed when you hang out with your mates without me. I hate it when other blokes look at you 'cause I know they want you. I know they'd like to take you away from me. I know you love me but I still think you could do better than me." He gave a short pause and I was shocked to the point that I was speechless. I just stood in his arms and listened to him continue his confession. "Bridget, when I used to meet women, all I wanted was a shag. You know how much I like sex and I told you that I was a bit of a slut. If I thought they were fit or whatever...and we hit it off...I only wanted one thing. And after we shagged, we went our separate ways 'cause I wasn't interested in more than that."

Tristan removed himself from our embrace and leaned against one of the counters. "The truth is, you're not the first of Autumn's friends that she introduced me to. But you're the first one that I didn't feel the need to just shag and be done with. I bet you didn't know this but, I saw you when you first came into her flat the night we met. I saw you before you saw me. You don't see it love, but you have this presence about you when you walk into a room. It's like..." He put his hands on the countertop to brace himself and he took another deep breath. His voice was still shaky as he spoke and his gaze was slowly piercing through me. "You are *so* beautiful to me. When I first saw your picture, I wanted you immediately. And when I met you, I knew that sex wouldn't be enough for me. I had to have you...every part of you."

Suddenly, his voice lowered and I thought at any moment it would break. "When I fell in love with you...I fell hard. I've never felt like this about anyone...*ever*. You make me feel *so* good. And it's not just the sex... it's everything. The way you touch me, the way you look at me, the way you talk to me...the way you treat me. And when we make love, it's like... the best fucking feeling in the world. I can't get enough of you. I don't..." And that's when I saw them; tears started to fill his beautiful blue eyes. I thought they would fall at any moment but he began blinking rapidly to keep them at bay. His voice finally broke when he admitted, "I don't know what I would do if you ever left me. I think I'd fucking die."

I guess the admission was too powerful because the tears began to trickle down his cheeks. He spoke through his tears and through the sound of my heart breaking at the sight of how vulnerable he was. "I know that's fucked up, believe me I know. I shouldn't be *saying* this shit. I shouldn't be *feeling* this shit. But I..." He paused to try to compose himself but he was failing. "I can't help it...I just can't." Tristan moved so quickly that before I knew it, he put his hands on either side of head and looked deep into my eyes as he begged me. "Tell me how to stop. Tell me how to stop loving you this way."

It wasn't until I realized he was expecting me to respond, that I felt my own tears on my own cheeks. I was so stunned by everything he told me and I honestly didn't have an answer for him. How do you tell someone to stop loving you a certain way? But what really scared me was his admission that he didn't think he could live without me. I had no idea that I affected him that way and his confession caused me to feel deep sympathy for him. I didn't think of myself as all too special. I was just ordinary; the girl-next-door type. I was a twenty-four year old redheaded schoolteacher from Sacramento, California. But evidently, to Tristan I was someone very special and someone he couldn't live without.

I knew that I had to calm him down but I also had to make him understand how dangerous it was to fixate on someone. To my own surprise, my own voice cracked when I said, "Baby, I don't know how to tell you to stop but you can't revolve your world around me. And I'm not saying I will, but if I ever left you...you should still get on with your life. It scares me that you think you'd die without me."

He sniffled and replied, "I'm sorry love, I don't wanna scare you. But that's just how I feel. You asked me...you wanted to know the truth. You said 'no more secrets Tristan'. And I don't think I *could* get on with my life if you left me. I love having you in my life and if you weren't there..." He paused again, and the look he gave me almost stopped my heart. "I *need* your love Bridget. And if you took it away...then I would fucking kill myself." His voice was losing its strength once again and his tear-filled gaze pierced through me when he finished with, "I would rather die than live with the pain I would feel from not being with you."

"Tristan, you can't---"

"But that's the truth! And I don't know how to stop feeling this way! I don't wanna feel this way Bridget, but I can't stop!"

Tristan's confession was scaring the hell out of me. My heart was thumping so hard that I could hear the pulsing and the blood whooshing in my ears. The sound was almost deafening. For the next few moments, neither of us spoke. We just looked into each other's eyes like we were trying to communicate telepathically. It was almost like all the words had been said and true understanding lay behind our eyes. The silence was broken because I said the first resolution that came to my mind. "Maybe you need help."

It wasn't until after I said it that I found out it was the wrong thing to say to him. His expression changed and he looked insulted, confused, and surprised all at once. Then he released me, walked away and kept his back to me. His voice sounded resentful when he asked, "You think I need therapy?"

At first I was afraid that he'd be angry with my answer, but then I realized that he really did have a problem. I wasn't going to renege on my opinion so I replied, "Yes, I do. If you know you shouldn't feel this way and you want to know how to stop, maybe you need professional help."

He finally turned around to face me and his expression was one of suspicion. His eyes narrowed slightly and his voice turned hard. "You think I should talk to some fucking stranger about my deepest feelings for you?" Then for the first time in our relationship, Tristan actually raised his voice at me and we weren't even having an argument. "It's no one's business! I shouldn't have even told *you*!" His jaw was set hard again and I just stared at him with wide-eyes. He glared at me for a second before he walked away and out of the kitchen.

I stood there looking after him and I was frozen in place because I couldn't believe he reacted that way. First he asked me to help him and then when I gave him a suggestion, he got angry. Suddenly, my own anger flared inside me because of his overreaction. The Fiery Redhead was about to go and give him a piece of her mind but the phone rang. Because I was still mad at Tristan, I answered the phone in an unfriendly voice. I didn't even bother to look at the Caller ID, I just grabbed the receiver and yelled, "Yeah?!?"

"Hi Bridget, it's Amy." Amy's voice sounded very meek and suddenly I felt bad.

When I spoke again, my voice was apologetic. "Oh. Um, sorry." I didn't recognize the voice or the name so I said, "Uh, Amy *who*?"

She laughed lightly and replied, "It's *Amy* silly. You know from high school...senior year...Mr. Fields' English class. Does that ring a bell? Remember we went double to the prom?"

As she was talking, the memory came back to me and I saw her face clearly in my mind. My voice was suddenly very cheery and as bright as sunshine. "Oh yeah! Hi, Amy! What a surprise! How are you?" Amy moved to Sacramento during my senior year in high school and we became fast friends. We shared a couple classes together and we both went to the prom together with our boyfriends. After high school, she attended a semester at the same college I attended, but her parents moved away again and she transferred to another school that was closer to her new home. We saw each other two years prior to her calling me and we had exchanged numbers. Since then, I hadn't spoken to her in over a year.

"I'm doing okay. I'm still living in Houston. How are things in Los Angeles?"

I lied and said, "Oh, everything is great here." I felt like adding: 'Except I think my boyfriend is psycho and he's obsessed with me.'

"Good, good. Look, I called you because I wanted to tell you that I just flew into L.A. last night. I'll only be in town for the weekend because I'm attending my brother's art exhibit this afternoon. But I was wondering if you wanted to hang out and catch up."

Amy was definitely my savior today because she gave me the perfect outlet to escape Tristan's drama. I thought that having a female to talk to just might be the release I needed. I would've talked to Autumn about his behavior but deep down I had a feeling she was biased when it came to him. He was like her brother and I felt that maybe she would be too quick to take his side. "Sure Amy, I think that's a great idea!" Just as I finished my sentence, I happened to glance towards the entryway to the kitchen and I saw Tristan standing there. He was looking at me with a neutral expression and he was fully dressed. His hair wasn't wet so I knew he didn't take a shower. Then I started wondering how long he had been standing there. I averted my eyes from him when I heard Amy speak again.

"Say Bridge, would you want to go to the exhibit with me this afternoon? That is, if you're free. I do have an extra pass."

I cast my eyes back on Tristan and replied, "Yeah, I'm free. And I'd love to go." His expression changed then and he stared at me intently. I averted by eyes again as I took down her address and told her that I'd pick her up in a couple hours. She was staying with her brother across town and I knew the location, so it wouldn't take me long to get there. After I hung up with her, I was actually excited because I decided to plan a 'Girl's Night Out'. I figured we would attend the art exhibit and then have dinner and drinks later that night. I haven't had a Girl's Night in so long and I felt it was overdue.

I was still angry with Tristan so I decided to be spiteful and only make breakfast for myself. He didn't speak to me as he watched me make pancakes for myself and then walk out into the dining room, but he did follow me.

As soon as I sat down, he sat in the chair adjacent to me and asked, "Who was that you were talking to?"

Without looking at him I replied shortly, "My friend Amy." Then I stabbed my pancake with my fork.

"Oh, and you're gonna hang out with her today?"

I chewed my food for a few seconds and then I took a sip of my orange juice before I answered him. "Yes."

Tristan's voice got quiet when he replied, "Oh. Where are you going?" I didn't reply and the dining room was silent for a few minutes. The only sound was my fork against the plate as I continued to stab at my pancakes. I chanced a glance at Tristan and he was staring at me, but the look on his face was filled with sadness and dejection. For a moment, I was going to stop ignoring him but my stubbornness wouldn't allow me. I cast my eyes back down at my plate and that's when he finally broke the silence. "I'm sorry, love. I'm sorry I yelled at you."

I looked up at him and when I spoke, my voice was friendlier. "Tristan, I was just trying to help you. I mean, you asked me how to help you, didn't you?"

He looked down abashed and murmured quietly, "Yeah."

"Do you have something against therapy?"

He looked up at me and just like the changing of the tides, his expression turned intense. His voice also started to have an edge to it. "I don't like talking to people about what goes on in my head; especially not some fucking stranger."

"But Tristan, maybe someone can help you understand why you feel this way about me."

"Oh, I understand why. I told you, remember? I told you why I love you so much. The problem is...how do I stop?"

"No, the problem is that you think you can't live without me. That's not healthy Tristan...that's dangerous!"

"I know that! Don't you think I know that?!?" He put his elbow on the table and covered his eyes with his hand. I noticed that his hand and arm were trembling and I realized how hard he was struggling with his emotions. When he spoke again, his voice was soft but shaky and I could tell he was getting more upset with each word. "No one can help me Bridget." He paused for a moment and then he said quietly, almost under his breath, "Bugger this."

Suddenly, he got up from the table and walked away and out of the dining room. Then I heard the front door slam and a minute later I heard the loud sound of his motorcycle engine. I heard Tristan as he rode away and I sat there in shock because I had never seen that side of him before. My nerves were frazzled and I was on-edge. I needed an escape so I decided to call Amy and ask her if I could come over. She happily agreed, so after I finished eating my breakfast, I showered and got dressed. It was probably an hour later by the time I rang the doorbell at her brother's apartment.

When she opened the door she hugged me tightly and said, "Bridget! Oh my God! It's so good to see you again!" I was so happy to see her and I hugged her just as tightly.

When I pulled away from her, I noticed that she had lost a considerable amount of weight since the last time I saw her. Amy has always been overweight since I've known her, but now she looked like a completely different person. "Wow, look at you! You look gorgeous!" Amy had shoulder-length, straight black hair and warm chocolate eyes. She still had a cherub face but it was noticeably thinner. She had perfect white teeth and near flawless ivory skin. She was about a couple inches taller than my 5'4" and she was absolutely adorable.

"Thanks Bridge! My ex-boyfriend convinced me to join the gym with him about a year ago and I just got hooked. The pounds started to drop and I just didn't stop!" We both laughed before she continued. "Wow, look at you. You still look the same...still as beautiful as ever." We embraced again and she moved to the side to let me enter. Once we were both inside, we chatted for awhile but then we decided to leave because the art exhibit opened at 1PM. As we were walking out, she was following me to my car and when she realized what we would be driving in she exclaimed, "This is your car?!?"

I beamed at her and replied, "Yep. It was a Valentine's Day gift from my boyfriend." Amy had a look of surprise and disbelief on her face as she walked around the perimeter of my car to admire it.

She stopped for a moment and said, "Wow, you are *so* lucky. None of my boyfriends would ever buy me a car like this. This is *so* nice. Your boyfriend must be some guy."

I replied sardonically, "You have no idea."

Amy and I had a great time at the art exhibit. I never really been that interested in art but I saw plenty of pieces that I would've liked to display in my apartment. As the two of us were spending the day together, I couldn't help but to think about Tristan and how he left this morning. He hadn't called me and I couldn't help but wonder where he was. It was then that I realized my anger towards him had disappeared. My anger was replaced with regret and I wished we could start the morning over so we could avoid his emotional breakdown.

After the exhibit, we had a light lunch and then we cruised around Los Angeles while I told her about my plans to take her out that night. She told me that she didn't really have anything spectacular to wear, so I took her shopping so she could buy something flirty and sexy to show off her 'assets'. By the time we got to my apartment to change clothes, it was evening and Tristan still wasn't home. I'll admit that a part of me was actually saddened because I hadn't spoken to him since that morning.

Amy was browsing through my closet when she said, "Bridge, I want to meet some hot L.A. guys. You have to take me out somewhere so I can meet some. I just got out of a relationship a couple months ago and I'm ready to start dating again. I mean, I don't even care about the long-distance thing. I just want to hook up with someone." She giggled and it reminded me of how we used to have girl-talk back in high school.

"Sure, I think I know a spot. But I have to warn you…even though L.A. doesn't lack in men, it definitely lacks in the quality of them."

Amy gave me a sly smile before she replied, "Then I guess you got one of the good ones, huh?" While we were out, I briefly filled her in on my relationship with Tristan. I basically told her how we met and how we dated shortly before officially becoming a couple. I showed her a picture of him on my cell phone and her jaw dropped. She commented on how gorgeous he was and I actually felt pride because Tristan was without a doubt, the best-looking boyfriend I've ever had.

As the evening wore on, we took turns showering before getting dressed to go out. We both took a considerable amount of time doing our hair and makeup, and overall we had fun just being 'girly'. I was taking Amy to a very exclusive nightclub so I wanted to look my best. Summer was almost here so it was warm enough for me to wear my favorite little black dress. The dress had spaghetti straps and the top of the dress was a black clingy material that accentuated my upper body. The material below the waist was black satin that flowed when I walked and the hem was probably three inches above the knee. It was definitely a sexy little number. I wore a pair of black strappy shoes with a 1 1/2 inch heel, and my ensemble was complete with a white gold tennis bracelet, diamond stud earrings, and a thin white gold chain with diamond circle pendant.

Amy was looking just as stunning, if not more because she was wearing a silk, strapless turquoise dress with the matching shoes. She was also wearing the prettiest dangle heart earrings and I begged her to tell me where she got them. By the time we were finished, we looked like a couple of Hollywood starlets and I knew we would fit right in with the club crowd.

It wasn't until Tristan came home right before we were leaving, that I knew our night would take a turn for the worse. Inside I was praying that he was in better spirits but when I saw the look on his face when he saw my appearance, I knew I was kidding myself. Amy and I were standing in the living room doing a last-minute check of our purses' contents when he walked in. When he saw me, he stopped in his tracks. His eyes widened, his lips parted and he looked like he was about to speak but I spoke first to make polite introductions. "Tristan, this is my friend Amy." I heard Amy say 'hello' but Tristan didn't respond to her. I looked over at Amy and she was just looking at me in confusion. I looked back at Tristan and his eyes seemed to be fixed on me. My voice sounded unsure when I said, "Yeah...um, we're going out so---"

Suddenly, he came out of his trance because he interrupted me by asking, "Where are you going?" Surprisingly, his voice was neutral like he was asking me what was for dinner.

I smiled and said, "I'm taking her out to meet some guys." I laughed. "Yeah, she's back on the market so we're going to a club to---"

This time his voice had a tinge of surprise. "You're going out to meet blokes?"

"Actually, I'm taking *Amy* out to meet blokes."

Tristan gave me the once-over and when our eyes met, his expression was not happy. "Dressed like that?" I scoffed at him and rolled my eyes and that's when he finally spoke to Amy. He looked at her and said politely, "Hullo Amy. Would you excuse us for a second?" Then he gently took my arm and pulled me towards the bedroom. While we were walking, my anger caused by his possessiveness started to grow.

By the time we reached the bedroom and he closed the door, I was ready to unleash it. Unfortunately, Tristan got his words in first and I was surprised when he didn't raise his voice. He was actually relaxed but I knew it was only the calm before the storm. "Why are you taking her out to meet blokes? She can't find a boyfriend on her own?"

I looked at him in disbelief. Then I remembered what he said earlier about not liking me to go out with my friends without him. I decided that he was just going to have to get used to it. "First of all, she asked me to take her out to see what L.A. has to offer. I wanted to object because L.A. is not known for its quality of men. But anyway, what difference does it make *where* we're going and *why* we're going?"

"I was just asking, Bridget. I mean, she's a pretty girl. I don't see why she needs your help." I didn't provide him with a reply, I just walked away from him but I didn't get very far because he reached out and grabbed my hand. "Why are you wearing that dress?"

"Tristan, I don't feel like getting into this right now. We have to go."

Suddenly, he let go of my hand and moved around my body to block the door. He looked into my eyes for a moment before he said, "You're wearing my favorite dress." Then he stepped closer to me until he was standing right in front of me. He leaned his head down towards me and sniffed. "And you're wearing the perfume I bought you." The perfume in question was *Lolita Lempicka*; another of Tristan's favorites on me. He tilted his head to the side to regard me and I was actually frozen because I wasn't sure what was going to happen next. When he spoke again, his voice was soft but accusing. "You sure *you're* not looking to meet some blokes too?"

His possessiveness had caused me to reach my breaking point and I snapped. "What?!? Tristan, I can't believe---"

"You know what, Bridget? I don't wanna argue with you." He turned around, opened the door, and stood to the side to let me pass. His voice was hard when he commanded me. "Just go."

I put a hand on my hip and said defiantly, "No, I'm not going anywhere!" Then I moved towards him and pushed him out the way so I could close the door again. "I'm not leaving until we get this out in the open because I'm tired of this shit!" I slammed the door and rounded on him.

"Bridget, I hate arguing with you and I don't wanna do it."

"Then tell me what your problem is Mr. Hathaway! I can't dress up and go out with my friend without the third degree from you? And then you accuse me of going out to meet guys? Where the hell do you get off?"

Tristan still didn't raise his voice and I was honestly surprised because the Fiery Redhead was in full force. "I'm sorry, okay? I just don't understand why you need to get all dressed up."

Although he didn't yell, that didn't stop me from releasing my frustration onto him. "Because I want to! Because we're going to an exclusive club and I want to look nice! Why do you have a problem with that?!?"

I guess he could no longer contain his temper because he finally raised his voice and shouted, "'Cause the fucking vultures will be all over you!" He took a deep breath, closed his eyes, and pinched the bridge of his nose. Then he lowered his voice but I could tell he was trying to control his anger. "You know what...just go. I don't give a shit."

I honestly could've stayed there all night and yelled at him. I just wanted to make him see how irrational and immature he was being. But I remembered that Amy was here and she was waiting for me to show her a good time. I didn't want to disappoint her so I said sharply, "Fine." Then I walked towards the door, yanked it open, and walked out. I tried to compose myself by the time I got to the living room and met Amy.

When I approached her, she looked at me cautiously. "Is everything alright, Bridge?"

I sighed. "Yeah, Tristan is just playing possessive boyfriend again." Then my voice hardened when I said, "But he'll get over it."

"Oh, did you still want to go out?"

Tristan walked past us on his way to the kitchen but he paused his steps momentarily to look at me before he continued on his way. As soon as he disappeared from my line of vision, my voice suddenly turned cheerful and I spoke a little louder than necessary. "Of course I want to go out. Let's go!"

When Amy and I got to the club, we danced, ate, had a few drinks, and I helped her scope out potential mates. I did get approached quite frequently and I was grateful that Tristan wasn't there. I knew there would've been a few confrontations that would've escalated into violence because most of the men that approached me had clearly been drinking. It didn't take long for Amy to strike up a conversation with one guy and soon she left me in our booth to dance and flirt the night away with her new boy toy.

I sat alone while the bass in the club music thumped under my feet, and the strobe lights danced on the walls and floor. Every now and then, a guy would approach me and try to spark up a conversation, and each time I politely lied and told him I was with a date. Some of them were persistent, so the Fiery Redhead had to let them know I wasn't remotely interested. I was about to get myself another drink when Amy came back without her boy toy. When she sat down, she was breathless and her face was flushed. "L.A. is so much fun! Wow, I think I really need to consider moving here. It's so much more fun than Houston."

I laughed and said, "Yeah, it's fun...if you're into that kind of entertainment. So, where's your new man?"

"I sort of left him on the dance floor. I didn't want to leave you alone for too long. Besides, I already got his digits." She pulled a napkin out of her purse and waved it. I was so happy that she hooked up with someone. I just hoped he would turn out to be as good a guy as Tristan. Just when I started thinking about him, my cell phone rang; it was him. Suddenly, my anger returned because I remembered how he accused me of trying to meet guys so I didn't answer the phone. As we sat and chatted above the loud music, he called a couple more times and I still didn't answer.

Amy heard my phone ringing and asked, "Why don't you just talk to him?"

"Because I'm pissed at him right now and he needs to learn that I won't always forgive him so easily when he acts immature."

Then Amy began to ask questions and I found myself confiding in her. I didn't mean to, but Tristan had caused a lot of confusion and frustration to build up inside me. I felt that if I didn't release it, I would eventually snap and probably say things to him that I would regret later. "Is he always like that whenever you go out?"

"Only when I go out without him."

"Why do you stay with him if he's so possessive?"

"I guess because I let it slide and he doesn't get violent about it."

"But you know Bridget, it could lead to violence. A lot of times, that's how it starts. It's subtle at first and then it manifests into physical or verbal abuse."

The thought of Tristan becoming abusive struck a nerve inside me and I didn't like the cold feeling I got when I thought about it. "Tristan would never abuse me."

"How well do you know him? You said you guys have been together for eight months? That's not long enough to *really* know a person." All of a sudden, Amy became my therapist. "I'm assuming you told him how his jealousy and possessiveness makes you feel?" I nodded. "And did he tell you that he'll stop or that he'll try to change?"

"He says he doesn't know how to stop."

"That's not good, Bridge."

"I told him that he should get professional help."

While Amy was talking to me, she was calm and she spoke softly. But I found myself beginning to panic as she continued to make me aware of the problems in my relationship. "And what did he say when you told him that?"

I looked down and replied quietly, "He said he doesn't like talking to strangers about his feelings."

She sighed and said, "So he's not willing to get help for his problem." Amy wasn't asking, she was stating a fact and I confirmed her statement by shaking my head. Then she asked the question that I was dreading ever since we started on the topic of Tristan. "Why don't you just break up with him? Find someone who doesn't have jealous and possessive tendencies; someone more secure."

Suddenly, the dam broke and my voice cracked. I was on the verge of tears when I finally admitted to Amy what my real fear was. "I can't break up with him! If I do, I think he'd---"

Amy's voice took on a more urgent tone. "What? He'd what? Hurt you?"

"No...hurt *himself.*" Tears started to fall and my eyes started to burn so I knew my mascara had run into my eyes. Amy handed me a napkin and I dabbed at my eyes. When I looked at the napkin I saw the black smudges.

Her voice was soft, but stern when she finally confirmed what I was truly feeling. "Bridget, he's making you feel trapped. You won't leave him because you fear what he'll do to himself. If he won't get help, and he won't change...you *have* to get out."

The thought of what Tristan would do if I left him chilled me to the core. When I spoke next, it was out of total fear. "But what if I did leave him and then he killed himself?" I let out a shaky sigh. "Amy, I don't think I could live with myself. I think I'd..." Oh my God. Suddenly I realized that I actually shared Tristan's feelings and he and I were truly one. It was at that moment that I realized...he couldn't live without me and I couldn't live without him. I really would *die* if anything ever happened to him. I honestly wouldn't want to live if he was gone from this earth. The realization hit me full-on and I actually gasped because the truth of the matter was: I was just as fucked up as he was.

Amy's voice brought me out of my reverie. "Are you okay?"

After my epiphany, I had a sudden urge to talk to Tristan and tell him how I was feeling. I fumbled in my purse for my cell phone and I said, "Yes, I just..." I flipped my phone open and pressed the number stored for Tristan's cell phone. "I just need to talk to Tristan."

His phone rang a couple times and when he picked up, his voice sounded quiet and detached. "What is it, Bridget?"

"Tristan, I need to talk to you."

Suddenly, his voice was laced with concern. "Is everything alright?"

"Yeah. Just...please be home soon. We really need to talk."

"I *am* home."

"What? But it's Saturday night and I thought you'd be with your friends or something. What are you doing home?"

There was silence on his end for a few seconds. I heard him sigh before he responded somberly, "Bridget, I'm not in the mood to go out."

At first I wasn't going to ask him my next question, but my curiosity got the better of me. "Are you home because you're waiting for me?"

"Yes," he responded flatly. To this day, Tristan's honesty still amazes me.

"Alright then. I'll be there in a few." Then I snapped my phone shut. I started to get up from the booth when I realized I had brought Amy with me. "Oh, do you mind if I leave now? I really need to talk to Tristan. It's kind of important." I pulled some money out of my purse and handed it to her. "I'm really sorry about this, Amy. Here's some cab fare so you can get home."

She looked confused when she asked, "Is everything okay? What's going on?"

I smiled and said, "Yeah, I think everything will be fine. I just realized something, that's all." Then I paused and put my hand on top of hers. "But I do want to thank you because you really opened my eyes."

She laughed lightly. "You're welcome." Then she gave me a side-long glance and said, "But I have a feeling you're still not going to break up with him, are you?"

Before I walked away I sighed and smiled slightly. "No, I'm not. Because honestly, I don't think I want to. I love him."

When I got back to my apartment, I saw Tristan in the living room watching TV. He looked over at me as I closed the door and then he stood up when he saw me approach him. As I approached him, I saw a few beer bottles scattered atop the coffee table and I knew he'd been drinking. The closer I got to him, the stronger the smell of beer. When I looked at his face, he looked so different to me. His expression was filled with misery and he seemed lost. Before I could speak, he closed the distance between us and embraced me tightly. We stood there for a few moments just holding each other when all of a sudden I felt his body trembling. He sobbed once and it was at that moment I knew he was crying.

I rubbed his back soothingly to try to calm him and I whispered words of comfort in his ear. Then I ran my fingers through his soft blond hair and that's when he whispered in a shaky voice, "I'm so fucking sorry, love." My fingers ceased their movement in his hair and I gently pushed his head up so that I could look at his face. When I saw it, my heart broke and my own tears started to blur my vision. His voice was broken as he continued to apologize. "Bridget, I'll try to change for you. I will. I'd do anything for you. I don't want you to be angry with me 'cause I hate arguing with you." He paused to try to compose himself before he continued. "I'm trying, love. I'm trying to be the boyfriend that you want but it's not easy for me 'cause…" He sniffled and hastily wiped the tears from his bloodshot eyes. "I really don't know how. I'm just going on what I feel." His gaze began to pierce through me. "Please don't give up on me, Bridget," he pleaded desperately; his lips still quivering. Then he pulled out of our embrace and turned away from me. He yelled, "Fuck! I'm always crying in front of you like some kinda fucking pussy! What the hell is *wrong* with me?!?"

I gave him a sad smile and when I spoke, my own voice was laced with heavy emotion. "Tristan, you can cry in front of me. Don't *ever* be afraid to show me your emotions. I know having a relationship isn't easy for you and I know you're trying. No one ever said they were easy." I sighed.

"Look, I'm not mad at you anymore because I think I understand now. I think I understand how you feel."

He turned to face me and he sniffled again. A look of mild confusion appeared on his face and he asked, "You do?"

I approached him and reached out to caress his cheek. Then I kissed him firmly on the lips before I said, "Well, I don't understand the possessive or jealousy thing, but I understand when you said you don't think you could live without me. Because honestly…I don't think I could live without you either."

"But you said that's dangerous. You said it's not healthy for our relationship."

"Yeah, I know. But just like you…I can't help feeling this way. I think I love *you* too much."

He gently took my head in his hands and looked intently into my eyes. I was lost in his beautiful cerulean eyes and I honestly didn't want to be found. When he spoke this time, his voice was stronger. "Bridget, I'll try my best not to be such an arsehole when you go out without me. I can't promise I won't be jealous when other blokes look at you 'cause… well, I know what they're thinking. I used to think the same thing." He was quiet for a moment and we just gazed into each other's eyes. I honestly believed that our souls communicated whenever we did this. Suddenly, he spoke again and his voice softened. "Do you wanna know why I want a baby so badly?" My eyes widened slightly as I prepared myself for his new confession. "It's 'cause if we had one…we'd be bonded forever. We'd be bonded through our child. So even if you stopped loving me one day, I would still have a part of you. And if you broke up with me, I would still see you 'cause the child would keep us connected."

I was so touched and so happy to finally know why he wanted to give me his child. I was nearly breathless as I replied, "Ohhhhh Tristan." He wrapped his strong, tattooed arms around me and looked down at me with a semi-drunk smile. I slowly wiped the tears from his cheeks and he leaned into my touch and briefly closed his eyes. I ran my fingers through his hair and then I caressed his handsome face. "Don't worry sweetie, it'll happen. I promise. And how many times do I have to tell you that I won't leave you? Tristan, I'll never stop loving you. You'll always be my prince."

He kissed the palm of my hand and the gesture was so tender and loving. When he spoke, his voice was soft and sweet. "And you'll always be my princess." I brushed my fingers across his sensual lips before I tilted my head up to lose myself in this beautiful English boy. Tristan's love rained down on me and I was caught in a storm that I didn't need any shelter from.

Chapter 13

It was late-afternoon on the Friday before my birthday and I was on summer vacation. I was sitting on top of one of the kitchen counters at Autumn's apartment while she was doing some last-minute checks on the guest list. The guest list in question was the one for my upcoming birthday party. She was shuffling through invitations and hastily scribbling away on a notepad in front of her. As she was leaning on the counter heavily engrossed in her task, I could hear her mumbling to herself as she continued to check off names on the list. She paused her pen strokes for a moment to look up at me and smile. "Bridget, I'm telling you, everyone is gonna be there tomorrow. People have been RSVP'ing like crazy."

I was watching her with wide-eyed amusement but I really didn't understand why she insisted on making a fuss for my 25th birthday. I hopped off the counter to get a closer look at the guest list. I picked up the notepad and as my eyes scanned down the page, I realized that I didn't know most of the people on the list. Without taking my eyes off the list I couldn't help but to comment. "But Autumn, I don't know that many people. I have no idea who most of these people are." I paused and read one of the names on the list. "Joey Bennett? Who's that?"

Suddenly, she snatched the notepad out of my hand and continued her task. "Don't you worry your pretty little red head about it. Look, when I throw a party, everyone wants to come. Besides, it's your 25th birthday and it should be special." Then she looked up at me and smiled again. "I'm *so* glad my parents are out of town so I could use their beach house.

When people saw that it's a beach party with free food and drinks...and I'm the hostess...everyone wanted to come."

I laughed and replied, "Hey, I'm not complaining. I appreciate you throwing me a party but there's only one person I care about showing up."

She looked up at me and we both shared a knowing smile. "Oh, you know Tristan's gonna be there. That boy is crazy in love with you. If I told him that you went to the moon, he'd be looking for the first rocket ship he could find." I felt my face flush and I looked down in embarrassment. "You think I don't know how much he's in love with you? Did I ever tell you *exactly* what happened after you guys met?" I shook my head. Autumn started to recall the memory of that night in September when Tristan and I first met and I found myself going back in time with her.

It was almost 5AM and everyone had left Autumn's apartment except Tristan. Autumn was in the kitchen cleaning up and he walked in with a dreamy expression on his face. When she saw the expression on his face, she laughed and asked, "What are you so happy about?"

"I think I'm in love with your mate."

"Who? Bridget?"

He sounded almost breathless when he said, "Yeah...Bridget."

Autumn continued cleaning and throwing away empty bottles and cans. "Of course you are. I knew you'd like her. I mean, you were already practically drooling over her pictures on MySpace."

"Aut, you don't understand. She's like..." Tristan paused and looked up at the ceiling with a thoughtful expression. "Everything I want. She's so fucking beautiful and sexy. I love her hair and her cute little freckles. As soon as I met her I just wanted---"

"To fuck her brains out?" She laughed. "I saw how you were staring at her."

Tristan looked at her intently. "You have no idea. I wanted to kiss her so fucking bad. But seriously, I think I want her. And not just a shag...I wanna get to know her."

"Tris, you wanted her when you first saw her on my top friends remember? Remember you were asking me, 'Who's that bird...the redhead?' I knew you were attracted to her. Plus, the dream I told you about really freaked me out 'cause it was just too much of a coincidence."

"Well, I told her about your dream and she asked me if I believed it."

Autumn's eyes widened and her voice had a tinge of surprise. "You did? What did you say? And what did she say?"

He smiled brightly and replied, "I told her that I believed you; that I needed to meet her. And she believes that she needed to meet me too." *He paused and said almost as an afterthought,* "Oh, I sent her a friend request."

"Really? Did you send her a message or leave a comment on her board?"

Tristan looked down abashed. "No."

"Why not?"

"'Cause I didn't know what to say."

"Well, did she ever talk to you?"

"Aut, she has like over a thousand friends. I don't think she even remembers me. When I saw her on your friend space, I clicked on her profile and saw that it was private. I wanted to see her pictures so I sent her a request. She accepted me like the next day."

Autumn looked at Tristan with a confused expression. "So let me get this straight. You friended her just so you could see her pictures?" *She laughed.*

Tristan smiled widely. "I'm glad I did though, 'cause the ones of her in the bikini..." *Another dreamy expression crossed his face and he was breathless once more.* "Holy shit." *He lowered his voice and said,* "You know, don't tell her this but I saved some of them on my computer."

She laughed again. "Oh my God, Tris! You're a stalker!"

"Yeah, I think I am. I check her profile like every day. And sometimes..." *He paused to grab an unopened beer bottle from her. As he twisted off the cap he continued.* "I read some of the comments these blokes leave her..." *He paused again to take a sip.* "And I wish I could delete their arses."

Autumn's eyes widened in surprise. "Whoa. That's some psycho shit right there, Tris."

Tristan continued to drink his beer. "Yeah, I know. I can't help it. You know I'm fucked in the head. I barely even know her and already I feel like she's mine." *Suddenly, his voice turned serious and he spoke quietly again.* "Do you think she fancied me? I mean, do you think I'm her type?"

She put her hand on his arm and gave him a reassuring smile. "Tristan, trust me...she's your soul mate."

I had no idea that was how Tristan and I became friends on MySpace but Autumn's story finally solved the mystery. I also had no idea that Tristan was so interested in me before I met him in person. I started to realize that he really *did* know more about me than I knew about him because I honestly didn't remember accepting his friend request. Tristan also didn't comment much on Autumn's board so I didn't notice him then either. It was only after we got to know each other personally, that we communicated on MySpace.

When I got home after visiting with Autumn, I was checking the messages on the answering machine when I heard the doorbell. Tristan wasn't home and I was secretly hoping it wasn't one of his friends. He seemed to know half of Los Angeles and there were always people showing up on our doorstep unexpected. Before I answered the door, I checked the peep-hole and I saw Jake standing there. I'm always delighted whenever he stops by so when I opened the door to greet him, I had a huge smile on my face. "Hi Jake! What a surprise!"

I opened the door wide enough for him to enter but strangely, he didn't come in immediately. He just stood outside smiling at me. Then his expression turned curious and he asked, "Is my little bro home?"

"Uh, no he's not. His manager has him running all over L.A. today so I think he's pretty busy. I don't know when he's coming home." This time I gave him a reassuring smile and said, "But you can still come in."

He still hesitated but eventually his feet moved and he stepped over the threshold. When I closed the door behind him, he said, "You know, Tristan might get pissed if he knew we were alone. You know he's paranoid."

I walked over to Jake and stood in front of him. "What? He doesn't trust us together when he's not around?"

He put a hand on my shoulder and said, "I don't think he trusts any bloke alone with you."

I walked towards the sofa and he followed me. "Well, he's just going to have to get over that. I mean, you're his brother for God's sake. What does he think...we're going to have an affair behind his back or something?"

"I think he fears losing you."

"But I've told him so many times that I'm not leaving him."

"It doesn't matter. He doesn't feel secure enough that he can keep you."

"Why? Where does his insecurity come from? I don't understand because he's so attractive and popular and---"

A Rose to the Fallen

"That doesn't mean a thing. Tristan has never been the type of person to think highly of himself." Suddenly, Jake's voice lowered and he said, "If you wanna know the truth...he thinks you're too good for him."

"What? Why would he think that?" I asked in a voice full of surprise.

"Sis, I remember the time when he told me that he first met you. He ringed me early in the morning and I could tell even then that he was really in love with you. And the way he spoke about you, it was like... he put you up on this pedestal." Just like Autumn had done earlier, Jake began to recall the memory and I found myself going back in time with him during his phone conversation with Tristan.

Jake: Tris, do you know what time it is? Why the hell are you waking me up?

Tristan: Bro, I have to talk to you. You won't believe what happened to me tonight.

Jake: *sigh* And this can't wait until later when I'm awake?

Tristan: No. Look...[pause] I think I'm in love.

Jake: [pause] She was that good, huh?

Tristan: No, you fucking twat. I'm serious. I met Bridget tonight.

Jake: Bridget?

Tristan: You know, the redhead bird. The one I showed you on MySpace.

Jake: Oh, you mean the one you're stalking?

Tristan: Jake, listen to me okay. I'm serious. I met her and I'm in love with her.

Jake: Wait, you just met her tonight and already you love her? What the fuck?

Tristan: I can't explain it; I just am. I know I am.

Jake: How do you know it's not just infatuation? There's a difference, you know.

Tristan: I know that, alright. It's love, I know it. I've never felt this way about anyone before. When I met her it was like...I wanted her.

Jake: Yeah, you usually do. You wanna shag them.

Tristan: No, I don't just wanna shag this girl. I...want...her. Seriously. She's perfect. And bro, if you saw her...[pause] she's absolutely beautiful.

Jake: Wait, this is the same bird with the bikini? The one you have on your computer?

Tristan: Yes, cunt. The same one.

Jake: I thought you were afraid to talk to her? You said that you didn't think you were her type. She's a 'good girl', remember?

Tristan: Yeah I know, but Autumn introduced us 'cause she thought Bridget would like me.

Jake: Well, does she?

Tristan: I think so. But what if she thinks I'm a...you know.

Jake: A complete nutter?

Tristan: Shut the fuck up okay. I don't think she smokes and she doesn't really drink. She's a fourth grade teacher for Christ sake. And what if she finds out about my sexual habits?

Jake: Maybe you should just be honest with her. Tell her up-front what you're about.

Tristan: No! Then she definitely won't like me and I want her to like me.

Jake: Tris, listen to me 'cause I'm gonna say this and then I'm hanging up so I can go back to sleep. If you tell her what you're about and let her get to know the real you...and she still likes you...then she's The One. If not, then cut your losses and move on 'cause you could do better.

Tristan: But Jake, that's the thing. I don't think I can do better. She's everything I've ever dreamed of. [pause] If you laugh, I'm gonna stab you in the fucking throat. [pause] Deep inside...like in my heart...I've always wanted someone like her. The more I talked to her and spent time with her...the more I wanted her. I fell in love with her the moment I met her. It was like...just seeing her pics made me like her. But then I met her in person and I fell in love with her. And honestly, I want a good girl. I need one.

*Jake: *sigh* Then go after her. Just fuck everything and do it. 'Cause you know you'll never forgive yourself if you don't and some other bloke gets her first.*

Tristan: Yeah, you're right, bro. 'Cause I'd probably wanna beat the shit out of anyone who touches her.

Jake: Oi, where'd that come from? Since when are you the jealous sort?

Tristan: I told you...I'm in love with her.

*Jake: I guess you are 'cause I've never heard you talk like that. Alright you knob, I'm going back to sleep. *CLICK**

Jake's entire memory shocked me to the core. I had no idea that Tristan had confessed his true feelings to Autumn *and* Jake so quickly. I also had no idea that Tristan felt that I was too good for him. The truth was…I thought he was out of *my* league. He was an up-and-coming actor, extremely good-looking, very popular, and I knew he could probably get any woman he wanted. I always thought of myself as ordinary so I actually never believed someone like him would be interested in someone like me. We did have some things in common but it seemed like we were from different worlds. I was happy to know that it was Jake who actually convinced Tristan to be honest with me. I always appreciated Tristan's honesty and I'll be forever grateful to Jake for giving his younger brother such sound advice.

My birthday party started in the early evening on Saturday. When Tristan and I arrived at Autumn's parents' beach house in Malibu, I was totally amazed at the elaborate detail she put into the festivities. The party itself was taking place in the back of the house on the beach and when we walked around the side of the house towards the party, I was shocked at how many people were there. The first thing I noticed when we walked onto the beach was a giant white banner with hand-drawn balloons strung up in the air with magenta words which read: *Happy 25th Birthday Bridget!* It wasn't dark yet so I could see colorful balloons strung high on wooden poles that were streaming above our heads.

I could see a couple of tables with food and a few more tables with a punch bowl and next to the table were giant barrels filled with ice and drinks. I saw someone grilling food on the barbecue and the aroma that was permeating in the air was mouthwatering. There were tables with umbrellas and chairs in a section over by the food and some people were sitting down eating, drinking, and chatting. The music was loud and I saw that she had actually hired a DJ. I saw a bonfire a few feet away but it wasn't lit yet. There was also a volley ball net and lounge chairs where people could relax and soak up the remaining rays of the day's sunshine.

Tristan and I walked hand-in-hand and he spoke to gain my attention. "Babe, look over there! Look at all those presents!" I turned my head towards where he was pointing and I saw a long table covered with presents and gift bags. My mouth dropped and my eyes widened in surprise because I couldn't believe that so many people thought to give me a birthday gift. I probably didn't know the majority of them. I guess because they were invited to a birthday party for Autumn's friend, a lot of people felt that they should get me something.

I was so overwhelmed that I was almost speechless. Once I was able to speak I replied, "Oh my God, Tristan. I can't believe this. This is almost unreal."

He laughed and said, "Autumn sure knows how to throw a party."

It wasn't long until people I actually knew came over to me and wished me a happy birthday. I received hugs and birthday wishes from Autumn, Rick, Becca, Ryan, Jake, Marco, and even Amy. I was so happy that she was able to make it and we giggled like schoolgirls at how amazing the party was. Everyone ate, drank, played volleyball, danced and partied even after sunset and I noticed that someone had lit the bonfire. Tristan and I stayed glued to each other like Siamese twins. I found that I wasn't annoyed that he wanted to stay with me because I really enjoyed having him around me on my special day.

We were standing by the bonfire and he had his arms around me while I was leaning back against his chest, when we heard the music stop. Then we heard Autumn's voice on the microphone say, "Okay birthday girl, it's time for your cake!" We turned towards her voice and then we followed her line of vision to see that a giant cake was being transported over near the food area. People started gathering around the cake as Tristan and I walked over. When I got closer I noticed that it was a huge, rectangular white cake with pink flowers and piping. There were two candles on the cake, one was a '2' and the other a '5'. The words on the cake read: **Happy Birthday Bridget**. I was in such awe at how beautiful the cake was that I didn't notice Autumn approach me and kiss me on the cheek. "Happy birthday, Bridge."

I looked at her with teary eyes and smiled. "Thanks Autumn." Then I felt Tristan put his arm around my shoulder and kiss my other cheek. I looked up at him and his beautiful blue eyes were sparkling in the firelight.

Soon Autumn started singing '*Happy Birthday*' and everyone joined in. Once everyone stopped singing, Tristan whispered in my ear, "Make a wish." I closed my eyes and wished to stay with him forever. Then I blew out the candles.

Autumn handed me a knife and after I cut the first piece, I looked up and saw...my parents! They were both smiling at me and I couldn't contain my surprise. "Mom...Dad?!?" I handed the knife to Autumn and she continued to carve and serve my birthday cake. I walked over to my parents and hugged them. "What are you doing here?"

My mother smiled and said, "We got an invitation from your friend Autumn. We would've been here sooner but your father had an emergency at the hospital. You know we wouldn't miss your birthday."

I looked up at my father and he smiled. "Happy birthday, sweetheart. We left your gift over by the other thousands of presents." He laughed. "I had no idea you had so many friends."

I smiled back and replied dryly, "Neither did I." It was at that moment that I felt Tristan come to stand by my side.

Suddenly, my mother spoke again and her voice was very apologetic. "Oh Tristan, I am *so* sorry." She moved closer to him and put her hands on his upper arms. "I wasn't very nice to you when you visited us on Thanksgiving and I never got a chance to apologize. I shouldn't have treated you that way and I hope you can forgive me. You're important to my daughter and I shouldn't have prejudged you. I hope you can give me another chance to make it up to you." My mother didn't try to hide the tears that were welling up in her green eyes.

Tristan, being the type of human being he was, embraced my mother and said, "It's okay Mrs. Monahan. I have no hard feelings...honestly." My father approached him with a smile and patted him on the back.

Tristan released my mother and she sniffled. "Thank you, Tristan." Then she hastily wiped the tears from her eyes. "I would've really liked to meet your mother. Bridget told me what a wonderful woman she is."

He looked down at my mother and said cryptically, "Mum has a fear of flying but I have a feeling you'll be meeting her soon." Then he turned to me and stared intently into my eyes. I just looked at him in confusion and a smile slowly crept onto his face.

We all went back to get some cake and the four of us plus Amy, sat down at one of the tables to eat and talk. All through dessert, I kept glancing over at the table of presents. Tristan could tell I was anxious because he leaned towards me and asked, "You wanna open your presents now, don't you?" I nodded excitedly and I ate my cake quickly before I jumped up to walk towards my birthday presents.

Tristan, Amy, and my parents followed me over to the long table, and I gazed in wonder at the amount of presents I had to open. Autumn and

Jake quickly came over and it wasn't long until more people started to gather around. It probably took me a half hour to open all my gifts and as I got to the last one, I realized that none of them were from Tristan. The last gift I opened was a Hooters t-shirt from some guy named Dave Woods and I tried to hide my disappointment of not receiving my boyfriend's gift. While Amy and Autumn were browsing through my opened gifts in utter amazement, Tristan whispered to me, "Will you take a walk with me by the water?"

I looked up at him and smiled widely. "Sure baby, I'd love to." He took my hand and guided me towards the shore. It was late, so it was getting chilly and I couldn't help but to shiver slightly. I had on a sleeveless top and I could feel the goose bumps prickling on my arms. Tristan must've noticed because he unzipped his hoodie and put it on me while he was left wearing a black t-shirt. I snuggled into his hoodie because it smelled like him and his scent always comforts me. He kissed me on my forehead before he took my hand again and we continued our walk. The area by the shore was pretty deserted and the only light was coming from the moon hanging high above us and the faint lights from the party in the background.

It didn't take us long to stroll away from the festivities. We slowly walked hand-in-hand in silence while we listened to the ocean waves crash softly against the beach. Suddenly, Tristan broke the silence. "So, are you enjoying your birthday?"

"I sure am." He paused his steps and stood in front of me. He looked down at me and smiled. Then he put his hands on either side of my face and I leaned into his warm hands. I closed my eyes in contentment and he kissed each of my eyelids. The gesture was so tender and loving that a small sigh escaped my lips. When I opened my eyes, I was about to kiss him when I noticed something on his inner left wrist that I'd never seen before. I took his left hand and moved his wrist close to my face so I could get a better look. As I ran my fingers across the area, I noticed that it was a tattoo. "Baby, what's this? A new tatt? You didn't tell me that you got a new one." I looked up at him and there was a ghost of a smile on his face.

He spoke softly when he asked, "Did you read it?"

I stared at the tattoo but because it was dark, I couldn't make out the words. "Uh, I can't really tell what it says."

Tristan pulled out his cell phone and flipped it open. The phone's backlight illuminated the space between us and he held it up next to his wrist. "Read it now."

My eyes scanned the tattoo; it was a four-letter word written in black, Old English text. I turned his wrist so I could read it properly and I spoke slowly. "It says...*Brìd*." I looked up at him in confusion and at that moment, Tristan communicated to me through his eyes. Understanding finally struck me and I gasped. My eyes widened and I exclaimed, "Tristan! You put my name in Irish on your wrist?!? Why would you do that?!?"

His answer was simple. "Because I love you."

"But baby, a tattoo is permanent and there's no guarantee that we'll stay together."

His voice took on a lighter tone. "Do you plan on leaving me? 'Cause I plan on staying with you until I die."

"No, but---"

He silenced me when he cupped my face in his hands again and looked into my eyes. "Then I didn't make a mistake. Bridget, I love you and I wanted your name on my body."

"I love you too, Tristan."

For the next few seconds we just gazed in each other's eyes under the moonlight. I was slowly falling under his seductive spell but he spoke before I could be fully enraptured. "You know babe, Autumn was right. You *are* my soul mate." Then he said something that rendered me completely speechless and motionless. "Will you marry me?" He paused and smiled beautifully down at me. "This time I'm really asking, love."

I hesitated for a moment; not because I wasn't sure what I would say, but because I couldn't believe that he asked me; right here...on the beach...in the dark...on my birthday. I couldn't help the tears that started to blur my vision as I looked upon his handsome, angelic face. The moonlight turned his hair a lighter shade so that it was almost white blond. His eyes were dark but I could see his long lashes casting shadows on the top of his perfect cheekbones. He really looked like a fallen angel and I honestly wouldn't have been surprised if wings suddenly sprouted from behind him and fanned out high and wide before my eyes. I spoke softly and I almost choked on my answer. "Yes."

Tristan released me and slowly put his hand in his front pocket. He pulled out a dark ring box and slowly opened it. He held the open box in front of me and I gazed in wonder at the sparkling ring that was staring up at me. He plucked the ring out of its bed and gently placed it on my left ring finger. I held my hand up to my face to admire it and suddenly the light from his cell phone illuminated the ring so I could see just how beautiful it actually was. In the center was a pink gemstone in the shape of a heart. The main heart was surrounded by another heart that was made up of a row of little diamonds. The diamonds traveled in two rows down the side of the ring that split the band before the band came together in the back in what looked like solid white gold. I felt the tears trickling down my cheeks in happiness and Tristan's voice broke the spell that the ring had cast upon my eyes.

"It's a pink sapphire. I know you love pink so..."

I looked up at my British prince and smiled. My voice was still soft when I said, "Tristan, it's beautiful...and perfect. I love it." I wiggled my fingers on my left hand and said, "Now I have *two* of your rings."

He stepped closer, and wrapped his arms around my waist to embrace me. Then he whispered, "One for my heart...and one for my soul. Happy birthday, Bridget." He leaned down to capture my mouth in a passionate kiss. I opened my mouth invitingly and his warm tongue twirled around mine before it brushed up against the roof of my mouth. I put my arms around his neck and moaned softly into his mouth. He slanted his mouth over mine repeatedly before catching my bottom lip and sucking on it gently. He released it, only to nip at it lightly before he ran his tongue across my lip to soothe the bite. He trailed open-mouth kisses along my jaw line and down my neck, and I tilted my head to give him all the access he needed. When he found the delicate spot behind my ear, he sucked gently until he made his mark.

My hands reached up into his soft hair and I ran my fingers through it as another small sigh escaped me. Then I put my hands under his t-shirt and rubbed his bare skin. Tristan's mouth found its way back to mine and his tongue continued to plunder inside. He had his hands on either side of my head as he kissed me possessively and moved his pelvis to grind himself into me. I responded by grabbing his butt and pressing myself harder into his already growing erection. The kiss intensified and we moaned louder as we continued our assault on each other's mouths.

I honestly thought he would pull me down towards the sand and we'd make love on the beach. It was too easy to get lost in each other. Suddenly, my brain remembered something very important.

I broke the kiss and whispered breathlessly, "Baby, I think we have to make an announcement."

Tristan was breathing hard too and I could see his breath against the chilly nighttime air. "Yeah, you're right." Then he chuckled. "This should be interesting."

We started to walk back to the party and when we arrived, we made our way towards the DJ booth because there was a microphone. Tristan said something to the DJ and he turned off the music and handed me the mic. I tapped on it to make sure it was still working and I cleared my throat. "Um, can I have everyone's attention please?" When I looked out I actually started to get nervous because everyone...even my parents...was looking at me intently and expectedly. A nervous smile appeared on my face and I said, "Um, I just want to say thank you to everyone who came to my party. And thank you to anyone who was thoughtful enough to give me a birthday present. I really didn't expect all this and the shock still hasn't worn off." I laughed lightly and I heard some other people laugh. "Um, this truly is the best birthday I've ever had. But really, I say this because something very special has happened tonight." I paused and looked over at Tristan. He was smiling at me and for some reason my voice caught in my throat.

He must've sensed my hesitation to continue speaking so he took the mic from me and said, "I asked Bridget to marry me." The moment after he made the announcement, you could've heard a pin drop.

Something inside me awakened and I quickly took the mic from him and added, "And I said 'yes'." There was another two seconds of silence before I heard the thunderous sound of applause and cheering. Before I knew what was happening, people started to gather around the DJ booth to congratulate us on our engagement.

The first person I heard was Autumn and her voice was high-pitched and she was crying. "Oh my God, Bridge! I knew this day would come. I knew you guys would get engaged." Then she rushed towards me and hugged me tightly. "I'm so happy for you. Oh my God, you have no idea." She released me and I saw that her tears had caused her heavy eye makeup to run. She gave me a kind smile before she sniffled and asked,

"Let me see your ring." I showed it to her and she gasped. She held my left hand and stared at the ring with her mouth agape. "Holy shit dude! This is so...so...*you!*" Then she hugged me again but after she released me, she went over to hug Tristan.

Amy came over to me and hugged me. Then we did a little girly dance which consisted of jumping up and down because we were both excited. "Bridget, this is amazing! I would've never thought you were going to get engaged on your birthday." She paused to look at me and smile. "Well...let's see it." I honestly would not get tired of showing off my ring. Her reaction was similar to Autumn's because she gasped and her eyes widened in surprise. She grabbed my hand and gazed at the ring in wonder. "This is *so* beautiful! Wow! What is that pink stone?"

"It's a pink sapphire," I said proudly.

"Oh...my...God! Tristan really has good taste. It's so perfect for you." I smiled at her before we hugged each other again.

I caught eye contact with Marco and he yelled out, "I hope you know you're marrying a psycho Brit!" Then he laughed which caused me to shake my head and smile.

Chad approached me with a big grin on his face. I hugged him and when he released me he said, "I can't believe Tris isn't gonna be a bachelor anymore. You are an *amazing* woman Bridget." Then he peered at me curiously. "How the hell did you tame him?"

I laughed. "If I tell you Chad, then I'd have to kill you." A wide smile broke out on Chad's face. As an afterthought, I said seriously, "But trust me...I didn't *tame* Tristan. It's in his heart to be wild...to be free."

Rick came over to me and gave me a hesitant hug. "Congratulations Bridget." Then he paused and looked at me with a crooked smile. "You know, I always thought you and Jake made more sense." His comment made me look at him quizzically. "You know, 'cause he's kinda normal and you're normal. But I guess Tristan would need you more. He needs someone like you." I smiled warmly at him because that was honestly the nicest thing Rick had ever said to me.

I gave him my thanks and it wasn't but a few seconds later that Jake approached me. I was a little nervous because I had a feeling that he heard what Rick said. He confirmed my assumption because he leaned down towards me and said in a low voice, "Rick doesn't know me very well. I am *far* from normal." We smiled at each other and then we embraced tightly.

When he released me, I said fondly, "Now I'll really be your sister."

"Bridget..." I looked at him with wide-eyes because that was the first time since we returned from Brighton that he called me by my name. "You became my sister when you told my brother that you loved him. I knew at that moment that he'd wanna marry you."

At that moment I realized how lucky Tristan was to have a brother like Jake. Something sisterly inside me wished for him to experience this same kind of happiness so I said, "You know Jake, this could be you. If you find the right girl...you could settle down too."

He cast his eyes towards the sand but not before I caught the shy smile that appeared on his face. "I don't know, sis. I don't know if there's a 'Bridget' out there for me." He paused and spoke softly when he said, "I think you're kinda...one-of-a-kind." All of a sudden he gave me an intense look which made my face flush with heat.

I was temporarily caught off-guard and before I could reply, my mother and father came over to me and Jake walked away. I was feeling apprehensive because I wasn't sure how my mother was going to react to the engagement. She actually surprised me because she hugged me tightly and spoke in a trembling voice. "Congratulations sweetheart."

She released me from her embrace and I looked at her skeptically. "Mom, are you *really* happy for me?"

"Of course I am, dear. I know how much you love Tristan. And honestly, he really does seem like a very nice boy." Then she paused and gave my new fiancé a side-long glance. "Not to mention...I know the two of you will give me some beautiful grandchildren." She winked at me and I laughed in surprise. "I guess he was right. I *will* be meeting his mother soon." Her last statement caused me to pause and cast my eyes skywards. I thought back to Tristan's earlier statement and I wondered how long he had been planning to propose to me. My father brought me out of my reverie when he congratulated me and I hugged him in return.

Tristan came over to us and my father immediately shook his hand. "I hope you know you're getting a very special woman, Tristan. She's our only child."

Tristan's voice was strong and clear. "Yes, I know Dr. Monahan. And don't worry...I'll take good care of her." Tristan looked over at me and our eyes met. "I promise." Then my mother hugged him before they both left me and Tristan standing alone. We walked away from the crowd as the DJ started the music again. We stood by the bonfire to get warm but this time we faced each other and held each other close.

We shared a loving kiss before I asked, "So are you ready to be married to me?"

Tristan smiled and replied in his boyish voice laced with a British accent, "Of course I am. Bridget, you're everything I've ever wanted in a woman and I love you more than anything in the world." He paused for a moment and tilted his head to the side. "Are you ready to be Mrs. Hathaway?"

I reached up to caress his face and I felt the slight stubble on his cheeks. I was struck with the sudden urge to give him a nice shave and I reminded myself to ask him if he would let me later tonight. I looked affectionately into his baby blues and I spoke directly from my heart. "I would be honored."

Chapter 14

Late afternoon, on the Sunday after my birthday, I had decided to do some grocery shopping. Before I left the house, Tristan had given me his shopping list as a reminder to stock up on some of his favorite snacks: shortbread 'biscuits', cookies-n-cream ice cream, BBQ flavored 'crisps', and the big frozen pretzels that you have to heat up in the toaster oven. After the first time Tristan accompanied me on my grocery shopping trip, I decided that it would be best if I continued that activity on my own. He had a habit of filling our shopping cart with any and every little thing his heart desired. This always resulted in us spending a lot more money on groceries than was absolutely necessary. That day while I was in the store, I got a text message from him saying that Jake was visiting and requested that I make my 'delicious fried chicken' for dinner. Tristan asked me if I could pick up the ingredients and of course I happily agreed. It seemed that the only time Jake had a home-cooked meal was when he visited with us.

Little did I know that something terrible would be awaiting me when I got home. I was greeted by a scene that I honestly never want to see again. As soon as I opened the front door, a commotion to my left startled me and caused me to freeze on the spot. I saw Jake and Tristan on the floor in the living room...where my coffee table used to be...and they were fighting. I dropped my grocery bags and I didn't even close the door because I ran over to them to try to break up the fight. Tristan was on top of Jake punching on his body while Jake was making a futile attempt to push his little brother off him. All kinds of expletives were coming out of Tristan's mouth as I tried to pull him off his brother. I grabbed a hold of Tristan's waist and screamed, "TRISTAN! TRISTAN! GET OFF HIM!"

He was in an absolute rage and suddenly, one of his arms hit me really hard across my shoulder and upper arm and I flew back against one of the end tables. I hit my head on the edge of the table and a sharp pain shot through the back of my head. The lamp on top of the end table started to wobble from the impact and I thought that it was going to fall on top of me at any minute. In that exact second, Tristan realized that he hit me and he jumped off his brother and ran over to me. He quickly steadied the lamp before he turned his attention on me. I closed my eyes and started rubbing the back of my head when I heard him say, "Babe! Oh my God, I'm so fucking sorry! I didn't mean to hit you! Are you okay?!?" He lifted me up into a sitting position and I opened my eyes. When I looked at him, I saw his baby blues looking back at me with deep concern. His eyes scanned over my body and when he saw me holding the back of my head he said, "Oh shit, you hurt your head. Does it hurt really bad? Let me see it, love. Oh fuck, I'm *so* sorry Bridget."

I groaned while I continued to rub my head. I pulled my hand away to check for any blood and when I didn't see any I said, "I'm okay, I'm okay."

"Really? Let me see your head."

"Tristan, I'm fine...really." I tried to stand up but my legs were a little shaky, so he helped me get back on my feet. As soon as I was standing I raised my voice again. "What the hell is going on?!? Why are you two fighting?!?" I looked over at Jake and he was standing next to my broken coffee table. His face was red and he was breathing hard.

He didn't answer me but Tristan was quick to explain the situation. "My brother's a back-stabbing cunt! Tell her what you said you fucking wanker! Go on, tell her!"

I continued looking at Jake and I asked calmly, "Jake, what's going on?"

Jake gave a short laugh and shook his head. "He's completely mental."

"He wants you Bridget! My own brother wants my fiancé! Tell her what you said to me you arsehole!"

Jake still spoke in a calm voice. "Sis, he's blowing things out of proportion."

"No I'm not you fucking shit!" Tristan started to charge towards him again and it took every ounce of my strength to hold him back. He continued yelling as I tried to restrain him. "Tell her what you said Jake! Tell her how you wanna take her away from me!"

I knew that I wouldn't be able to get a hold of the situation until Tristan calmed down. I put my arms around his waist and squeezed him. Then I yelled to get his attention. "Tristan! Tristan! Listen to me!" Then I released him and began pushing him towards the armchair. "Please! Just sit down and let me talk to Jake!" When he reached the chair he was still glaring daggers at Jake and I knew I still hadn't garnered his full attention. "Tristan, baby...look at me." I reached up and put my hands on either side of his head and tilted his head down towards me. When our eyes met, I spoke sternly. "Tristan, listen to me. Just let me talk to Jake and find out what's going on okay? Please just sit here. *Please.*"

He complied and sat in the chair. Then he turned his eyes away from me to glare at his brother again. "Fine, I'll sit here. But ask him what he said to me!"

I took a deep breath and turned away from Tristan to slowly walk over to Jake. I stood a few feet in front of him and spoke calmly again. "Jake, please tell me what's going on. What did you say to make Tristan so angry?"

I guess Tristan still couldn't contain his anger because he yelled out, "Tell her you fucking cunt!" I quickly turned to face Tristan and I saw that he had stood up.

"Tristan, please sit down! You're making me nervous." He glanced at me before he returned his burning glare upon his brother and then he sat back down.

When I turned back towards Jake, I stepped closer to him and pleaded, "Jake, please just tell me what the hell is going on. I've never seen you two like this before. What happened to cause you to start fighting? Just tell me...*please.*" Because I was so close to him, I could see that his bottom lip was bleeding and every now and then he would suck his lip into his mouth.

He hesitated for a minute and just looked into my eyes. As soon as he opened his mouth to speak, he had my undivided attention. "We were talking about your engagement and I asked him if he was really ready to be married. He told me that he was and how much he loves you and everything. Then he said that he wanted to have a baby with you but you said that you weren't ready. When he told me that, I was like...what the fuck? Are you mad? You want a *baby*? I told him that I don't think he's ready to be a father and he got pissy about that. Then I asked him if he was ready for all this. You know, for a wife and family because I know he has a hard time keeping his prick in his trousers. I reminded him that it wasn't too long ago that he was whoring himself all over L.A."

Tristan interrupted and yelled, "Jake, you're a fucking slut too!"

Jake yelled back, "I'm no where near as bad as you were!"

"Bollocks!" I turned towards Tristan and he looked at me. "I learned everything I know from him!"

I yelled back at Tristan in frustration, "Tristan, please be quiet!" Then I turned back towards Jake and sighed.

Jake continued to speak to me calmly. "So then I told him that if he gets you pregnant and he doesn't do right by you that I would help you raise the baby. He got *really* pissed about that and we had words. So I yelled at him and said if he fucks up the good thing he has going with you...if he cheats on you or doesn't treat you the way you should be treated...that I would step in and show you how a *real* Hathaway treats a woman." My eyes widened and my mouth dropped. "And that's when he punched me. Then I hit him back and we started fighting. He's the one that pushed me on the bloody table."

It took me a few seconds to find my voice because I couldn't believe what Jake said to his own brother. Jake must've really been trying to provoke him or something because those were definitely words that would trigger Tristan's violent side. When I finally found my voice, I spoke softly and asked, "Why did you say that, Jake? You knew that would upset him."

I guess Tristan decided that he had stayed quiet long enough because he continued to unleash his rage. "'Cause he wants you, that why! He's a two-faced back-stabber! He wants to take you away from me 'cause he can't find his own woman! I knew it! I knew he wanted you!" Tristan got up from the chair and I felt him approach me from behind. I was still looking up at Jake in confusion, but I was glad that I was standing between the two Hathaway brothers to keep them from pummeling each other again.

Jake still didn't answer my question so I asked again but in a more stern voice. "Jake, why did you say that?"

Tristan spoke up again. "'Cause he has feelings for you!"

My voice turned soft again when I asked, "Jake, is that true? Do you have feelings for me that are..." I paused so I could swallow the nervous lump in my throat. "More than a sister?"

Jake hesitated again and averted his eyes from me. "Look, if he can't---"

I interrupted him and spoke in a stern voice again. "Just answer the question."

The tension in the room was so thick, it was almost suffocating. It was one of the most uncomfortable situations I'd ever been in and deep inside me, I wished my body was somewhere else. Jake looked into my eyes and I saw and heard him swallow hard. It seemed like forever before he spoke but when he did, it was like everything I built up about him as my brother came crashing down on me. "I think you're a great girl, Bridget. You're beautiful, smart, and you're amazing to put up with Tristan. And if you weren't with my brother...who knows what would've happened with us. But I won't deny that I'm attracted to you."

Tristan made a move from behind me and I ducked my head instinctively to avoid getting hit. "YOU FUCKING---"

Due to quick thinking on my part, I spun around and grabbed him before he could attack his brother again. I was honestly surprised I was able to restrain him because he actually moved very quickly. When I grabbed him, I threw him off-balance and he almost fell over. He was able to maintain his balance and when I realized he wasn't going to move, I released him but I stayed in between the two brothers. Jake didn't budge an inch from his position. It was almost like he was ready to take whatever Tristan was going to dish out. He yelled back at Tristan, "She asked me a question dickhead! I'm just being honest!"

Tristan continued to yell over my head. "Yeah, like you were so *honest* when I first asked you how you felt about her, right?!? I'm paranoid, yeah?!? I knew you liked Bridget! You're a fucking liar, Jake! A *fucking* liar!" The situation was escalating towards violence again and I was afraid to have more of my furniture destroyed. There were a few seconds of silence and then I heard Tristan speak again, but this time his voice was low and...deadly. "Get out." I looked up at Tristan's face and his jaw was set hard and he was staring venomously at Jake. His face was twisted in anger and his blue eyes were blazing with fire. Then he yelled louder and it actually startled me. "I SAID GET OUT JAKE!"

My eyes were wide and I quickly turned to see Jake walk away and out of the still-opened door. Tristan moved around my body and slammed the front door after him. Then he banged his fist on the door a couple times in anger before he rested his forehead against it. I was temporarily frozen in place and I stared at him as he took a few deep breaths to try to calm himself. It wasn't until I saw his body trembling that I actually moved and approached him. I stood next to him and I saw that he had started to cry. When he spoke, his voice sounded broken. "I can't believe my own brother wants my fiancé. I can't believe he wants to take you away from me. Why does he have to like *you*? Out of all the girls in the fucking world."

When I reached out to touch him, I said his name softly but he avoided my touch and walked around me to sit on the sofa. He sat down, and leaned forward with his elbows on his knees. He put his head in his hands, and I rushed over and sat next to him. I began to rub his back soothingly and I saw a few tears fall from his eyes and land on the carpet. When he spoke again, his voice was quiet and weary. "I knew it, Bridge. I knew he liked you." Tristan lifted his head and leaned back with his head against the sofa. He didn't look at me when he sniffled and said, "When we were in Brighton, I had a feeling he was starting to like you. You were talking to him more and he was really getting to know you. I saw how he would look at you sometimes. I brought it up to him once and he denied it. He said I was being paranoid." Then Tristan turned his head to look at me and his face was flushed and tear-stained. He shook his head and whispered, "He's a fucking liar."

I scooted closer to Tristan and wiped the tears from his cheeks. I spoke softly when I said, "Tristan, he shouldn't have said what he said. I don't condone that at all but you can't get mad at him for his feelings." Tristan jerked his head and he looked like he was about to interrupt me but I continued. "Baby, listen to me. Even though he has feelings for me, he's never acted on them. Not once has he ever been indecent to me or tried to come on to me. He's never even tried to put the thought into my head that I should cheat on you with him. It's one thing to have inappropriate feelings for someone but a totally different thing to actually act on them."

"But babe, he wants you. He wants to take you away from me. You heard him!"

"Tristan, I heard him say that if you didn't treat me right or if you cheated on me, that he'd try to take me."

He sighed. "But still..."

"I know, he shouldn't have said that. But Tristan, he's your brother. You can't fight your brother over me."

Tristan looked at me intently and his voice turned hard. "But I would. If he touched you Bridget, I swear to God I would hurt him."

"I honestly don't think he would try anything while we're still together. I mean, don't you think if he really wanted to...he would've done it already? I think he does respect our relationship but he was---"

Tristan raised his voice and he looked affronted. "Are you taking his side?!? Didn't you hear what he said?!?"

His tone of voice caused me to raise my voice. "Yes I did! But I'm trying to make you understand..." I sighed heavily and closed my eyes briefly to try to calm myself. Seeing Tristan fight with his brother had my nerves totally frazzled. Once I composed myself, my voice was softer. "Look, you're brothers. You shouldn't let a woman come between you."

"We usually don't. You're the first."

I looked at him with wide-eyes and neither of us spoke for a few seconds. Then I mumbled quietly to myself, "Great, that makes me feel so much better."

Sometimes I wonder why I bothered mumbling because Tristan always hears what I say...and that time was no exception. "You have no idea how you affect blokes, do you?"

I wasn't sure what he meant by that statement so I became defensive and I leaned away from him. "So this is *my* fault now?!?"

His eyes widened in surprise and he quickly reached out to put his hands on my shoulders. He quickly backpedaled by saying, "No, no, this isn't your fault, babe. I'm just saying that I understand why he's attracted to you 'cause most blokes are."

I scoffed. "No they're not. I may be beautiful in your eyes, but most guys are not---"

He smirked and spoke sardonically. "Oh, so that's why whenever we go out I have to hold myself back from ripping some fucking bloke's eyes out for gawking at you."

As Tristan was talking, something in my mind decided to turn the tables on him and I thought: *Two can play this game.* "And what about you mister tall, gorgeous, blond hair, blue eyes, tattooed Brit? I know American women just fawn all over you, don't they? I bet your accent makes their panties wet, doesn't it? You could probably get them to do anything you want. Don't think that I don't see how girls look at *your* sexy ass." I guess he couldn't handle a dose of his own medicine because he looked away from me and I could tell that my words made him uncomfortable. "Yeah, don't talk about how I affect men okay? Because I can talk about how you affect women. But see, I'm not the jealous type."

Without looking at me, Tristan continued to speak in a sarcastic tone. "Well, good for you. But I can't fucking help it."

All of a sudden, a question started to brew in the back of mind and I was anxious to ask it. Before I could stop myself I blurted out, "Have you always been the jealous type?"

He turned to look at me and said, "Bridget, I've never had a serious girlfriend so why would I get jealous?"

My own tone of voice was sarcastic when I said, "Oh I don't know. What about the girls you slept with? Did you get jealous if they slept with someone else?"

Tristan's expression turned to one of confusion. Then he chuckled and started shaking his head. He leaned over and grasped my chin gently and shook my head lightly. "You're so innocent, you know that? I guess you don't know how the game is played, huh?" Then as an afterthought, he said, "Well, I guess you wouldn't. You weren't a slut like me." He paused and then he said, "Anyway, once I shagged a bird, I just moved on. I didn't really care who she shagged after me. Honestly, why would I? It was just sex...nothing more. I didn't develop any feelings for them."

My mind was desperately searching for some kind of explanation for Tristan's jealousy that didn't have to do with me. Then I remembered something he told me on our first date. "Well, what about when you were in school? You said you had girlfriends in school, right? Were you jealous if other boys looked at them or tried to talk to them?"

A thoughtful expression appeared on his face as he took a moment to think about my question. Then he replied slowly, "I can't really remember." He looked at me again and said, "But I don't think so 'cause my feelings for them were no where near what I feel for you." I couldn't hide my disappointment because I was really hoping that I wasn't the sole reason for his jealous tendencies. I would've felt a lot better if I had known that Tristan had always been like this. Then I wouldn't feel like he really needed to change. I made the decision to marry him even though he's a jealous person, so did I really have the right to ask him to change now? And if I did, would he even be able to? He told me in the past that he didn't think he could. His jealousy caused him to physically fight with his brother and I couldn't help but wonder what other problems it would cause once we got married.

My mind started to drift back to the fight a few moments ago and I finally decided that the whole situation was going to be resolved and we were all going to put it behind us. I hated seeing Tristan and Jake fight because I considered them my family and their animosity towards each other was breaking my heart. When I spoke to Tristan again, my voice was stern and absolute. "Look Tristan, Jake is going to apologize for what he said and then you two are going to make up." Tristan tried to speak but I put my hand up to stop him. "I don't want you fighting and hating each other. You're brothers! I only wish I had a brother or a sister. You don't know how lucky you are. Listen, let's give it a couple days to let the both of you cool off. Then I'll ask him if he'll come over so we can talk about this like adults. But he *will* apologize because he was wrong to say that to you."

Tristan nodded and agreed quietly. "Alright. And babe, I'm sorry I broke your coffee table. I'll buy you another one." I glanced over at the remains of my coffee table and I noticed that not only was it completely destroyed but the Hathaway brothers destroyed my decorative seashells I had displayed on top. I reached over to pick up one of the shattered shell pieces and I turned it over in my hand. I really loved those shells. I heard Tristan say in a soft voice, "I'm sorry about the shells too. I'll try to replace them."

I threw the remnant of shell back onto the pile of garbage and said dismissively, "Don't worry about it. I'm just glad neither of you were severely hurt." I kissed him firmly on the lips to comfort and reassure him and then I got up and grabbed the grocery bags I had dropped by the door. I took them into the kitchen and I started to wonder if I should make the fried chicken. I decided against it and I made me and Tristan spaghetti for dinner that night.

Tristan's fight with Jake seemed to affect him for the rest of evening. He was somber and distant, and he barely spoke to me. It wasn't until we were sitting down in the dining room having dinner that he finally spoke. And of course, he brought up the subject of Jake. "Bridget, do you think my brother is attractive?"

His question caught me off-guard and I had a spaghetti noodle halfway up to my mouth when he asked his question. I slurped the noodle into my mouth and chewed my food for a few seconds as I contemplated an answer that wouldn't cause him to react aggressively. After a moment of thought, I decided to just be honest. "Um, yeah I think he's handsome."

"Would you ever go out with him?" I looked at him questioningly and he rephrased his question. "I mean, say for instance that we did break up. Would you date him?"

This time I didn't hesitate because the answer was easy. "No, I wouldn't."

"Why not?"

"Because I don't think it's right. If I'm in a serious relationship with you and then we break up, I wouldn't go and date your brother. I'm not like that." At that moment I realized that I had the perfect solution to ease Tristan's fears. "Baby, what Jake said...about taking me if you didn't treat me right...it would *never* happen. I would never be with him."

"What if we had a baby and then he tried to step in?"

"He wouldn't replace you as the father. You'd always be the baby's father regardless if we were together or not." Then I smiled and tried to emphasize my point by saying, "What Jake said would...never...happen. Trust me. I'm not interested in Jake; never have been...never will be."

My reassurance was a success because Tristan perked up and his tone of voice lightened. "Then will you tell him that? Tell him what you just said."

"Sure, I'll tell him. Just as long as you forgive him when he apologizes." All of a sudden my mind flashed back to what I saw when I came home and I added, "And as long as you two go back to being loving brothers and put this behind us. Because I hate this, Tristan. I hate seeing you two fight. I'm so used to you guys joking around and insulting each other... *playfully.* I was so scared when I saw you fighting. You're both my family and I hate seeing my family beat up each other."

He reached over and put his hand on top of mine. He smiled slightly and said, "Alright babe. I'll hear him out. And if he apologizes, I'll let it go."

I was skeptical about his quickness to forgive, so I narrowed my eyes and gave him a side-long glance. "Do you promise? You promise that after this is over, you won't bring it up again?"

He chuckled and replied, "Yes, I promise. Believe me, I don't wanna think about this shit ever again. But now that you said you'd never wanna be with him...I actually feel better now."

The next morning after we ate breakfast, I started to feel a sudden urge to speak to Jake and resolve the riff that had been built between him and Tristan. Even though I told Tristan that I'd give them a couple days to cool off, I was too anxious to have the Hathaway brothers back together again. We were loading the breakfast dishes into the dishwasher when I asked, "Could you call Jake and ask him if he'll come over after work today? I know I told you to give it a couple days but I just want this to be over with."

He replied irritably, "Bridge, I really don't wanna talk to him right now."

"Okay then, can you give me his cell number so I can call him?"

Tristan sighed and then he started to walk towards the bedroom. I followed him and when we got there, he took his cell phone off the nightstand and handed it to me. I searched through his phone book and when I found Jake's cell phone number, I dialed it. Tristan sat on the bed and watched me as I waited for Jake to answer. Jake's phone rang a couple times before he picked up and he must've thought it was Tristan because his voice sounded annoyed. "What the fuck do you want?"

I paused for a second before I said, "Uh...Jake, it's me...Bridget."

He paused too before he replied quietly, "Oh, sorry. Hi."

"Hi. Look Jake, I want you to come over after work today. I want you to apologize to Tristan for what you said to him. You know you were wrong to say what you said."

"But I meant it."

"That doesn't mean you should've said it." I sighed. "Jake, have you ever heard the expression: Some things are better left unsaid?"

Jake was silent for a few seconds. I heard him sigh and I knew that he knew I was right. He confirmed my assumption because he said, "Yeah, you're right. I shouldn't have said it."

"So will you come by after work today so we can resolve this once and for all? Because honestly Jake, I can't stand this. I can stand knowing that you and Tristan are fighting and that you're angry with each other. I do love both of you, you know." In the corner of my eye, I saw Tristan shift from his position on the bed.

Jake was silent again. When he spoke, his voice was so quiet that I could hardly hear him. "You love me?"

"Like a brother," I added quickly. I glanced at Tristan to check his facial expression. He seemed relaxed so I averted my eyes again.

"Oh." He sighed again. The pause on his end was longer this time and I assumed it was because he really needed to think about if he wanted to come over. After a few seconds, he finally spoke. "Alright then, I'll come by later."

"Great! I'll see you then!" Then I hung up.

It was probably around 7PM when I heard the doorbell. I had a feeling it was Jake but I checked the peep-hole anyway. I saw the familiar head of blond hair so I quickly opened the door wide enough for him to enter. When I saw his face, he looked depressed and he wouldn't make eye contact with me. He walked past me to stand in the living room and I closed the door and slowly walked to stand in front of him. He had his hands in his pockets, he was looking down at his shoes and he wasn't speaking. I had a feeling this whole apology thing was going to be emotional for him so I reached out to take his arm. The gesture caused him to whip his head up and he finally looked me in the eye. I gave him a small smile and then I guided him over to the sofa.

Just as we sat down, Tristan walked out of the hall and approached us. I looked up at him and I could tell he was angry. His jaw was set hard and his eyes were narrowed slightly. He came to stand next to me and he crossed his arms and looked down his nose at his brother. The tension returned in the living room and it was another few seconds before anyone spoke. I had a feeling Jake needed to be coerced into his apology so I turned my body towards him and spoke softly. "Jake, don't you have something to say to your little brother?"

Jake looked over at me and then up at Tristan and then back at me again. He nodded and then he looked back up at Tristan. "I'm sorry bro. I'm sorry about what I said to you yesterday. I shouldn't have said it." Then he put his head down.

"You're damn right you shouldn't have said that shit," Tristan said sharply. I looked up at Tristan and spoke to him through my eyes. I wanted him to know that we were trying to resolve this maturely; not start another fight or argument. He must've understood because he sighed and spoke softer. "You really hurt me, Jake."

"I'm sorry."

"Why'd you say it? You know I'd never cheat on Bridget and I'd never hurt her. Why would you even think that I would fuck up what I have with her? Do you think I'm daft or something? You know how I feel about her."

"I know you love her, alright. I just..." Jake paused and took a deep breath. I had a strong feeling he was about to unveil his true feelings. He confirmed my assumption because he said, "I guess I said it 'cause I was jealous." He paused again and I looked at him with wide-eyes because I wasn't expecting him to admit that. "If you wanna know the truth... I envy you and I wish I had the kind of relationship that you have. Do you know how hard it is to find someone who will really accept you for who you are and truly love you? You really lucked out when you met her, you know that? And regardless of what you may think bro, I'm not a slut like you were. Yeah, I may shag different birds but I'm actually looking for something. Every time I meet a woman, I'm hoping that maybe...just maybe...she's The One. I see what you have going with Bridget and I wish I could find someone like her."

Tristan scoffed. "Are you shitting me? Since when do we have the same taste in birds?"

"I guess since she came along."

At that moment, both Hathaway brothers looked at me and I felt like running away and hiding. I was feeling very uncomfortable and I had to think quickly to take the focus off me. I couldn't believe that Jake liked me this way and I honestly would never look at him the same way again. Every time I would look at him, I would know that he secretly desired me. Deep inside, I wished he had never confessed his true feelings. I tried to switch the subject so I stood up and said, "Okay, now I want you two to make up."

Tristan cocked his head to the side and grinned. "Not until you tell Jake what you told me yesterday. Go on, tell him."

I sat back down and turned to face Jake again. He looked at me expectedly and I sighed and said, "Jake, listen. I think you're very handsome and you're a really good guy and all, but..." I paused and prayed that I wasn't crushing his feelings too badly. "I would never be with you if Tristan and I broke up. You would never be able to have me because I'm just not interested in you that way."

Jake smirked at me before he looked up at Tristan. Then he nodded and started chewing on his bottom lip. "Hmmm...that's interesting. Well, I'm glad you told me that." I was about to speak again but he spoke first. "But let me ask you something."

"Okay."

"What if I met you first?"

Tristan spoke up and asked, "Jake, what the fuck are you doing?" But his tone of voice made his question sound more like a warning than an actual question.

Without taking his eyes off me, Jake put his hand up. "Just let me ask her a question, okay? Bridget, what if you didn't know Tristan and we met first and I asked you out. Would you have gone out with me?"

I hesitated for a moment and then I looked up at Tristan. He was looking at me intently and I started to get nervous. I was about to lie to Jake but I figured since everyone was being honest today, I may as well keep the honesty going. "Um, yeah I probably would."

Jake paused for a second, looked away from me, and started to scratch his chin. "Hmmm..." Then he looked back at me and asked, "And then what if you met Tristan?" I looked at him questioningly because I really didn't understand the question. He sensed my confusion so he rephrased his question. "Alright, we went out and then...I don't know...I introduced you to Tris. What would you do?"

I thought about his question for a moment and then I looked up at Tristan again. Strangely, this time he was grinning at me and his cute dimple made itself known on his cheek. I smiled back at him and then I looked at Jake and he was looking at me expectedly. Then I looked back at

Tristan and I said slowly, "I would..." It was at that moment that I really wanted to renege on my decision to be honest. I made the decision to answer truthfully, so I put my head down and admitted, "I would want to go out with Tristan." Then I started laughing. I looked at Jake and said, "I'm sorry Jake, I'm sorry." Jake was grinning at me and it caused me to laugh harder. I paused to look at Tristan again and he was beaming at me in appreciation. I fell back against the sofa and covered my face with my hands as I continued to laugh. I heard Tristan start to laugh too and I found that I couldn't stop.

I guess my laughing was contagious because Jake laughed lightly and said, "Yeah, that's what I thought you'd say."

I finally stopped laughing and I put my hand on Jake's arm and looked at him intently. I spoke seriously when I said, "But listen Jake, if we were already in a relationship and *then* I met Tristan...I wouldn't want to go out with him. I would stay loyal to you." Jake smiled and nodded. Then I playfully hit him on the arm and said, "*Now* will you two make up?" I looked up at Tristan and he was looking at Jake with a warm expression and I knew he had forgiven him.

Jake stood up slowly and faced his little brother. He grinned and then he reached his arms out. They embraced for a couple seconds and then I jumped up to hug them both. They each put one arm around me and I closed my eyes to bask in the love of the wonderful, beautiful Hathaway brothers. It was quiet for a moment until all of a sudden Jake broke the love *and* the silence when he said, "So Bridget, how about you make me some of your delicious fried chicken? I'm really starving." The three of us started chuckling and I knew I had my two favorite men back together again.

Since Tristan and Jake were back on good terms with each other, I decided to grant Jake's request that evening and make him my fried chicken. During dinner, the three of us relaxed in a comfortable atmosphere of just talking, laughing, and Tristan and Jake resumed their brotherly teasing. At one point during the meal, Jake asked, "So have you two decided when you're getting married?"

His question caught me off-guard for a moment and I paused right before I was about to take a bite out of a drumstick. Tristan had just proposed to me a couple days ago and we hadn't really discussed any details regarding the wedding. We were still feeling the hurt over him and Jake's fight so we didn't do much talking on the marital subject. Jake's question caused me to realize this and I replied, "Actually, we haven't talked about any details. We don't know when we're getting married or even where we want the wedding to take place."

Tristan joined our conversation and remarked, "Whatever you want, babe. I'll leave it up to you."

Jake looked at me and smiled. "Well, you just tell me where and when, and I'll be there."

It wasn't long after we all finished eating, that Jake decided to leave. Later that evening, I decided to go into the bathroom and draw myself a bubble bath. Tristan was lounging on the living room sofa with his laptop on his stomach when I approached him. He was typing away on the keyboard but he looked up at me when he noticed I was standing beside him. When our eyes finally met, I informed him casually, "Hey baby, I just wanted to tell you that I'm going to have a bath now."

He didn't respond to me at first; he just looked at me. I was about to walk away, when suddenly he smirked and tilted his head to the side. "*You're* having a bath?"

I looked at him in confusion and repeated my statement. "Yeah, I'm going to have a bath."

The smirk fell from his face and he moved the laptop from his body to sit up. Then he looked up at me and repeated his question. But this time, his expression was more serious. "*You're* having a bath?"

We were both silent for a moment as I tried to figure out why he repeated his question. His eyes started to burn into mine and I wondered if maybe Tristan really *was* a telepath. Just as I was about to laugh out loud at the idea, comprehension finally struck me. I smiled widely as I corrected my statement. "I mean, *we're* having a bath. The tub should be almost full by now."

When Tristan smiled back at me, I knew that's what he wanted me to say. He stood up so that he was right in front of me and he reached out to lightly caress my cheek with the back of his hand.

He followed me into the bathroom and he started to get undressed as I turned off the water. Once we were both undressed, we got in with Tristan leaning back against the tub and me sitting between his legs with my back to him. He grabbed the sponge and started to wash my back. We were silent for a few moments as I enjoyed the comforting feeling of my fiancé washing me so lovingly. When he spoke, his voice was soft. "You know, I love baths. I love taking a bath with you more than taking a shower."

I turned my head slightly to look at him as he moved the sponge to massage my shoulders. "You do?"

"Yeah, it's so much more relaxing." He paused his movements with the sponge to say, "Let me wet your hair, love." I nodded and he dipped the sponge into the water and began squeezing the water on top of my head. Once he was satisfied that my hair was fully saturated, I saw him pick up the bottle of shampoo.

As Tristan began to gently massage the shampoo into my hair, I started to think back on Jake's question about the wedding. I figured now was a good time to discuss it so I said, "So baby, when did you want to get married?"

"It doesn't matter to me. 'Cause you know if it were just up to me, we'd get married tomorrow."

"Well, since wedding preparation takes time...I'm thinking that maybe we could get married in August. I'd like to get married before I go back to school."

"Sounds good to me."

"But where?" I paused as I pondered the ideal place for me and Tristan to exchange our vows. Suddenly, I was struck with an idea but I wasn't sure if it was possible or even affordable. "You know, it's too bad we can't get married in Brighton. I would've loved to get married on the beach there."

"Why can't we?"

My eyes widened and I turned my body completely so that I could face him. Tristan paused his actions in my hair and grinned at me. "But how would we fly everyone out there? And how many people are we inviting anyway? Are we having a big wedding or a small wedding?"

Before he answered me, he squeezed the sponge over the top of his head. His hair was pretty soaked after just one douse, so he took a couple handfuls of soapy suds from my hair and started transferring it onto his hair. Once his hair was equally soapy, he took one of my hands and placed it on top of his head. I knew he wanted me to wash his hair so I smiled in return and complied. As I was massaging his scalp with my fingertips, he finally responded. "I think we should have a small wedding.

You know, just close family and friends. And I could pay to have your parents flown out to Brighton...that's not a problem. Who else did you wanna invite?"

"Well, since you said just close family and friends...I guess I'd want my parents there and Autumn as my maid of honor. Because you know, if it wasn't for her...we would've never met."

"Yeah, you're right. And I know just the place where we could get married."

"We'd have to find a hotel for Autumn and my parents."

Tristan looked at me in confusion. I stopped washing his hair when I decided that it was cleaned thoroughly. I was about to start squeezing the sponge over his head when suddenly, he dipped down and submerged himself under the water. When he resurfaced, he smoothed his hair back and continued. "They don't need to stay at a hotel; we can all stay at Mum's."

Now it was my turn to look confused. "How would we manage that?"

Tristan smiled. "Trust me, there's room for everyone. Plus, I think it would be really nice to have everyone together. You know, I haven't told them that we're engaged."

"Why don't you call them tomorrow and tell them?"

"I'd rather tell them in person. Fly out with me, love. Let's tell Mum and Nanny together. And I can show you the place where we should get married. I think you'll like it."

The following morning, I called my parents and told them about our plans for the wedding. They both agreed to let Tristan pay for their plane tickets, but I was surprised when my mother didn't object to staying at Kate's. I was also surprised when my father said, "Bridget, listen to me, sweetheart. I want to pay for the wedding." I tried to object but I couldn't get a word in. "Look, money is no object. You're my only child and you're still my little girl. I'm your father and I want my daughter to have the wedding that she wants."

At this point I was so thankful for his generous offer that I started sniffling. Once I composed myself, I said, "Tristan and I are flying out to Brighton in the evening and if the wedding coordinator needs a deposit to get things moving, I'll give it to her. But I'll let you pay for the balance, Daddy, if it makes you happy."

"Yes, it will make me happy, darling."

My mother took the phone from my father because I heard her ask, "When are you getting your wedding dress, honey?"

"Umm...I don't know, Mom. But you can take me shopping for one. I'll let you and Dad know the date once I know when the coordinator can book our wedding."

"Well, we're both going to need at least a week's notice, but other than that...we can fly out for the wedding anytime."

Once I got off the phone with my parents, I called Autumn and filled her in on all the details. When I told her that I wanted her to be my Maid of Honor she started crying hysterically. Once I was able to calm her down, she said, "I'm so excited, Bridge. I think it's so cool that you and Tris decided to get married in Brighton. I've never been there before so I'm really looking forward to going." She also spoke similar words that Jake spoke, but the only other thing she wanted to know was, "Just tell me what color my dress should be."

"Don't worry, Aut. When I go shopping for my dress, we'll get yours too."

While Tristan and I were packing our luggage, I briefed him on the conversations I had with Autumn and my parents. Then he said, "I called mum and Nanny and told them we were coming but I didn't tell them why. They didn't really ask because they were just thrilled that we were coming to visit again." It's been six months since I've seen them and a part of me felt bad that we didn't take the trip sooner.

That night, we boarded a plane to England and when we arrived in Brighton it was around 9AM. We hailed a taxi and drove to Tristan's childhood home once again. But this time, the scenery was completely different. We had the windows rolled down and as we drove by the beach I could smell the salty sea air. I heard the seagulls in the early morning sun and I looked up at the blue sky above us that was filled with wispy white clouds. Since it was summertime, the city sometimes referred to as 'London-by-the-sea' was at its most beautiful. I saw a few people already bustling about on the boardwalk and I could see a tall roller coaster in the distance at The Funfair on Brighton Pier. I immediately became filled with childlike excitement and I looked over at Tristan with a huge smile on my face. He must've read my mind again because he smiled back and said, "Don't worry, love...we'll go to the fair before we leave."

Kate must've sensed our arrival because when the taxi finally pulled up in front of the house, she came rushing out to greet us. She was wearing a pale yellow dressing robe with white slippers, and her blonde hair was pulled up in a bun. She was smiling brightly as she approached us and I couldn't contain my happiness. I met her halfway and hugged her first, while Tristan was helping the cab driver take our luggage out of the trunk. I embraced her tightly because I was so elated to see her again. I didn't want to let her go as the memory of my last visit with her filled me completely. She held me just as tightly and spoke in her wonderful English accent. "Ohhh, it's so good to see you, love. I've missed you so much." When we pulled away from each other, we both had tears in our eyes.

I sniffled and smiled at her before I replied, "I've missed you too." She smoothed my hair in her usual motherly fashion and that's when Tristan approached us.

"Hiya Mum," he said as he reached out to embrace the woman who birthed him.

They embraced for a few moments and when they pulled away from each other, Kate spoke again. "Ohhh, my baby...back to visit us again." Then her expression changed to one more serious but she playfully hit Tristan on the arm. "Took you bloody long enough. How dare you keep Bridget away from us for this long."

Tristan smiled and rubbed his arm as if it really hurt. "I'm sorry, Mum." He laughed and it caused Kate's expression to lighten once again.

Kate helped us with our luggage and the three of us walked into the house. She helped us bring the luggage into Tristan's old room but on our way, I saw Nanny in the kitchen making breakfast. Her back was to us and she was dressed in a flowery dressing robe with dark blue slippers. The smell wafting from the kitchen was absolutely delectable and ironically, my stomach rumbled. I began to look forward to Nanny's cooking after suffering the taste of airplane cuisine. I stopped at the entryway to the kitchen and exclaimed cheerfully, "Hi Nanny, we're back!"

She was watching the little black-and-white 'tele' that was on one of the counters before she turned her head at the sound of my voice. When she saw me and Tristan, she immediately dropped the spatula in her hand and quickly walked over to us. Her expression was full of joy and she beamed at us. "Bridget! Tristan! Oh my heavens!" I dropped my suitcases so I could hug her and she began to laugh gleefully. "I'm so happy to see you!" When she released me, Tristan hugged her as I looked on in utter delight. Eventually, she went back into the kitchen to continue cooking breakfast while Kate, Tristan, and I brought the luggage into his bedroom.

Before Kate left the two of us in the room, she informed us that breakfast would be ready soon. Tristan and I took that time to unpack and when we were almost done, he asked, "So, do you want to tell them or do you want me to do it?"

My mind was already made up when he first told me that they didn't know. "They're your family so you should tell them."

Nanny treated us to a very delicious breakfast and I savored every morsel. If I was absolutely truthful, I would admit that I preferred Nanny's cooking over my own mother's...but I would never tell my mother that. After breakfast was when Tristan finally decided to break the news of our engagement. The four of us were in the kitchen cleaning up when he handed his mother a plate and said, "Mum, I have to tell you something."

She didn't look at him as she placed the plate in the sink that was beginning to fill with soapy dish water. "What is it, love?"

Tristan paused and looked at me. I nodded in encouragement and he announced, "Me and Bridget are engaged."

It was a full two seconds before Kate or Nanny realized what Tristan had just said. But when they did, they exclaimed in unison. "What?!?"

"We're gonna get married...here...in Brighton."

I actually braced myself for their reaction because I knew it would be emotional. Kate didn't disappoint because she gasped and then her hand flew up to cover her mouth. I watched her intently as she looked at Tristan and then at me. Right at that moment, her blue eyes... identical to her son's...filled with tears of happiness. It didn't take long for the tears to fall and she dabbed at her eyes. "You proposed to her?" Almost as an afterthought, she rephrased her question. "I mean you proposed *officially?*" We both nodded. "Oh my goodness!" Her laugh was one of pure joy and she closed the distance between her and Tristan and embraced him. Then suddenly, she started crying again but she spoke through her tears. "I can't believe my baby is going to get married. But I knew this day would come...I knew it. When you told me how much you loved Bridget, I knew you'd want to make her your wife."

Suddenly, she released him and gestured for me to come over. "Come here, Bridget." I quickly walked over and she hugged me in return. "I'm so happy for both of you. I always knew you were perfect for my Tristan. I can't wait to have you as my daughter-in-law." She pulled away from me but didn't release me. Then she sniffled before she added, "Although, I already consider you my daughter-in-law. I tell all my girlfriends that you are." She laughed lightly and waved her hand dismissively when she said, "The actual ceremony is just legal rubbish." She smiled warmly at me and I couldn't help but to blush at her confession.

Nanny came over to us and when I looked at her, I saw she had tears in her eyes as well. She hugged Tristan since Kate still had me in her embrace. "Now you remember what I told you."

"Yes, Nanny," Tristan answered.

I had no idea what they were talking about but I figured it was something private between the two of them. When Kate finally released me, she asked, "So where are you two getting married? And when is the wedding?"

Tristan spoke first. "I'm taking Bridget to Due South today to see if she'd like to get married there. I figured that would be a good place since she wants to get married on the beach. We don't know when yet. We have to talk to a planner or whatever you call them to see when they can book us. And Mum, since it'll be just us, Jake, Autumn, and Bridget's parents... could we all stay here? I thought it would be nice if we're all together."

Kate agreed immediately. "Of course! We'll make room. And you want to get married on the beach? Oh, that's wonderful! And Due South is superb!"

It was at that moment that Nanny approached me. I leaned down to hug her and she whispered in my ear, "You be patient with me Tristan. He may be a grown man but his heart is still innocent to love. Take special care of it."

An overwhelming feeling flowed through me when I heard her words and it took no more than a mere second to fully comprehend her meaning. Tristan *was* innocent to love because he'd never experienced it before he met me...and Nanny knew it. I've reminded myself countless times to be patient with him because he really didn't know how to have a serious relationship; it was new to him. He once told me that he's just going on what he feels. And what he feels is extreme and intense love for me and I had to know how to handle it if I was to be his wife.

A little while later, Kate gave Tristan her car keys so we could drive over to Due South. As we were about to leave, I asked him to wait for me in the car because I needed to get something out of one of my suitcases. I wasn't being honest because the truth was that I needed to speak to Kate about purchasing a wedding ring for him. He went ahead to the car and when he was out of sight, I ran upstairs.

Kate was in the hall closet putting laundry away when I approached. When she noticed me she smiled and asked, "Is everything alright dear? Aren't you leaving now?"

"Yes, but I was wondering if you'd help me with getting Tristan's ring."

"Sure, I'd love to help you. We can go back to the little boutique where you got his bracelet. Maybe you can find something you like there."

"Great!"

"How does tomorrow sound? Right after breakfast?"

"That's perfect! Thank you Kate!" I gave her a quick hug before I dashed back downstairs to meet Tristan in the car.

It was still strange for me getting in on the left side of the car but not sitting behind the wheel. I remembered back to when I first did it; Kate drove me to the pier the last time I visited. I initially tried to get in the car on the right side...the passenger side in America, until Kate reminded me that it's the opposite over there. It was also a little strange seeing Tristan drive on the left side of the road. I was so used to seeing him drive my car...on the right side of the road. But he did it so naturally; like he never forgot how. I asked him how he was still able to do it without crashing and he replied, "It's just like riding a bike, babe. I'll teach you how to do it." I started to visualize the catastrophe I'd cause if I attempted it, and I politely declined his offer. It was at that moment that I realized I could never drive in England.

When Tristan informed me that we arrived at Due South, I learned that it was actually a restaurant slash venue on Brighton Beach. It was nestled between Brighton's piers in a Victorian archway. They could perform the wedding ceremony for you on the beach and you could have your reception in one of their dining rooms with beachside views. When we got out of the car, I immediately liked the surroundings. We were practically right on the beach and Tristan told me that they have private dining for more intimate, smaller weddings. We walked inside and I was even more impressed; I could see the beach as soon as I stepped inside. I couldn't help but to remark, "This is perfect."

"I had a feeling this is what you were looking for." As we were walking towards the receptionist at the front desk, he put his arm around my shoulder and whispered in my ear, "But we're getting a hotel suite after the wedding...just the two of us. I can't have our families hear me shag you rotten on our wedding night." I smiled and looked at him with wide-eyes. There was a sly smile gracing his features and he waggled his eyebrows at me. I laughed lightly because he was being naughty and when we approached the receptionist, Tristan said, "Hullo. Um, we'd like to speak to someone about planning a wedding."

The receptionist was a young woman; probably in her late-teens if I had to take a guess. She smiled brightly at Tristan and asked in a very polite and professional tone, "Do you have an appointment?" At that moment, I started wondering if he actually made one.

He paused for a quick second and looked at me. I looked at him expectedly as if to say: 'You knew you had to make an appointment right?' I guess he didn't because he replied, "Uh, no we don't." The receptionist gave a small sigh and Tristan instantly turned on the charm. He leaned closer to her and softened his voice. "But we traveled here from The States 'cause we really wanna get married here. Is there anyone who could talk to us now?" He smiled his beautiful smile at her and his cute dimple made an appearance on his cheek. His charms started to work like magic because the receptionist's lips parted, her eyes widened slightly, and a sort of dreamy expression crossed her face. Tristan finally won her over by looking intently into her eyes and saying, "*Please*, is there anything you can do?"

For a minute, I started to feel invisible because she didn't glance at me once since we came over to her. Then all of a sudden, he released her from his spell and she picked up the phone and dialed someone. She chatted with them for a few minutes and then she hung up. She looked back up at just Tristan and said, "The Bookings Manager will be right with you. You can have a seat over there." And she gestured to an area which looked like a small waiting room.

Finally, I got frustrated with her ignoring me and I spoke loudly. "Thank you!" I felt like adding: 'Inconsiderate bitch.'

She tore her eyes away from Tristan and looked at me. Then she gave me a small smile and replied politely, "You're welcome." I had a sneaking suspicion that I really wasn't. Tristan gave her his thanks and then we walked over to the waiting area to sit down.

It was only about five minutes before a middle-aged woman by the name of Ms. Colby approached us and introduced herself. After shaking our hands, she guided us into an office to discuss our wedding plans. The whole ordeal took about an hour and surprisingly, Tristan did most of the talking. The only thing I gave my opinion on was the table decorations, the menu, and the cake. But Tristan was able to get us a private room, a DJ, and a photographer. Ms. Colby was able to book us for August 31st and she asked if that worked with our schedules. I was about to tell her that it was fine, but then I remembered that I had to go back to school the following week and that wouldn't leave any time for our honeymoon. I immediately realized I had to bring that to Tristan's attention. "Baby, if the wedding is the last week in August, then we won't be able to go on our honeymoon. I start school the following week and they won't let me take that much time off so early in the new year."

Tristan looked concerned and he cast his eyes down as he processed what I just said. Then he looked up at Ms. Colby and tried to turn the charm on her. He leaned forward and put his arms on her desk. Then he asked in a soft voice, "Is there any way you could book us earlier?" Then I noticed him tilt his head to the side and smile at her. Oh God, please let it work on her too.

She looked at her computer screen and typed on her keyboard for a few seconds. Then she shook her head and said, "Sorry, no. Even without the private room...that's the soonest we could fit you in."

I heard Tristan swear under his breath. He sighed and looked over at me. He still spoke softly when he asked me, "What do you wanna do, babe?"

I gave him a sad smile and replied quietly, "I really like this place. It's perfect."

Tristan turned in his chair to face me and took both my hands in his. He moved close to me and looked into my eyes before he spoke. "Darlin'...listen. We can get married here and then as soon as you can get time off...we'll go on our honeymoon; anywhere you wanna go. I don't care if I'm filming...we'll go." He gave me a peck on the lips and finished with, "I promise."

I smiled while I secretly wondered why all men couldn't be like him. Then I nodded and replied, "Okay, let's do it."

Tristan turned back to Ms. Colby with another brilliant smile and gave her two words: "Book us." I gave her my credit card for the deposit and after we left Due South, Tristan kept to his other promise and took me to The Funfair on Brighton Pier.

We had so much fun there; going on most of the rides, eating hotdogs and we shared cotton candy and an ice cream cone. It was the first time we had ever been to an amusement park together and we both turned into children as we got lost in the thrills and excitement. He even won me a big pink teddy bear that he carried on his shoulders as we walked around the fair together. We met some of his neighborhood friends there and when he proudly introduced me as his fiancé, I couldn't help but to feel honored. None of his friends could believe he was getting married and they were all completely shocked. One of them commented that I must be very special to be able to capture Tristan's heart. It seemed a lot of people in Tristan's life felt that way about me.

We practically spent the whole day at the fair and by the time we returned home, it was late and Kate and Nanny were already asleep. I remembered back to what Kate said about me and Tristan having sex in her house, so I didn't object when he asked if I wanted to. We did make love but for some reason...Tristan could not be quiet. Even though he was thrusting inside me so pleasurably, I managed to exhibit some self-control and not make any loud noises. Unfortunately, the same could not be said for him.

At first I was on top, riding him into a sexual frenzy as I put my hand over his mouth to muffle his cries of passion. There came a point where the pleasure became too intense for him, so he sat up and kissed me fiercely before we wordlessly switched positions. He laid his naked body completely on top of mine and held me in a tight embrace as he started to pound me deep into the mattress. His head was in the crook of my neck and I could feel his warm breath as he panted rapidly. He started moaning louder so I shushed him and whispered, "Baby, be quiet."

I heard his muffled voice say, "I can't, love...I can't...oh shit, oh shit..." I had a feeling he was about to cum because I knew I was. I felt a tingling sensation deep in my belly and the first wave of pleasure hit me. I went over the edge but I quickly smothered my cry by biting down hard on my knuckles. I held Tristan with my free arm and my body trembled as orgasmic tremors rippled through me.

All of a sudden, his body tensed and he held me so tight that I couldn't move. He yelled my name out loud and I quickly shushed him again even though I knew it was too late. Unless Kate and Nanny were extremely heavy sleepers, I had a feeling he already woke them up. He put his face into the pillow and yelled again as he joined me in orgasmic bliss. I heard a long moan come from his throat and he continued to hump against me as he emptied his seed inside the rubber. When he finally relaxed, he took his head out of the pillow and started laughing. I laughed too and then he said, "There's no fucking way I can be quiet when you feel this damn good."

In between my chuckling I managed to say, "Hey, I did it."

Tristan lifted himself onto his elbows so he could look down at me. He tilted his head to the side and peered at me curiously. "Babe, I know you came. Why didn't you say anything?"

I laughed harder, but quietly. I decided to lay on the sarcasm when I responded, "Don't you see...that was the beauty of it. You didn't *hear* me. And I didn't wake up the other people in the house. You should try it some time." The both of us continued to laugh before we exhausted ourselves even more and fell into a peaceful slumber.

The next morning was very odd because Tristan and I woke up before Nanny and Kate. Since I was up before them, I decided to cook breakfast. Tristan was sitting at the kitchen table drinking juice and reading the newspaper and the whole scene seemed so domestic to me. I glanced at him when he wasn't looking and I smiled lovingly. How I looked forward to so many more mornings like this with him. The sausage and eggs were done, and I was waiting for the last pieces of toast to pop up when Kate walked into the kitchen. She halted her steps momentarily to look at me and smile, and I smiled in return. Then I remembered what happened between me and Tristan last night, and I flushed in embarrassment before I turned away.

The next events that happened were so humorous to me, that I wished I actually lived with both of them. I heard Kate say, "You couldn't be quiet, could you boy? I heard you all the way upstairs. And I bet if your brother was here, he would've heard you all the way up in the bloody attic. I bet even Jesus himself heard you up in heaven." I chuckled softly but I kept my back turned because I was still too embarrassed to look at her. I stood at the stove and made two plates for me and Tristan as I continued listening.

Tristan replied to his mother, "I'm sorry Mum, but you don't understand. It just feels so fucking good that---"

As soon as I heard Tristan swear, I quickly turned around. He didn't get to finish his sentence because his mother rushed over and hit him on the back of the head before she yelled, "Oi! What did I tell you about that mouth, Tristan Caleb?!?"

I couldn't help but to laugh. She looked over at me and I felt the sudden need to side with her. I snitched on my foul-mouth prince when I said, "Kate, Tristan has a filthy mouth."

"Yeah, I know he has a filthy mouth. I've told him about those kinds of words in my house." She hit him on the back of the head again and spoke in a stern voice. "Didn't I?"

Tristan smiled and rubbed the back of his head. "Yeah. Sorry Mum." Kate shook her head and walked over to the stove to make herself a plate. When she approached, I started to walk over to the kitchen table to sit down and eat with Tristan.

She remarked, "Thank you so much for making breakfast, Bridget. That was very sweet of you."

"You're welcome."

As soon as I put Tristan's plate in front of him and sat down, he leaned towards me and spoke in a dominant, low voice. "You love my filthy fucking mouth, don't you?" Before I could respond, he kissed me deeply and plunged his tongue into my mouth. I tasted the tangy orange juice and I broke the kiss as soon as I saw Kate turn around. I wasn't exactly sure but I had a feeling she saw us.

She confirmed my assumption because she said, "You're not going to do that while we eat, are you?" She laughed lightly and shook her head.

Then she sat down next to me and sighed as she put strawberry jam on her toast. "You two love-birds..."

It wasn't long until Nanny joined us in the kitchen. She greeted us all with a "Good morning." She really didn't say much else and I was hoping she wouldn't comment on Tristan's inability to have sex quietly. Kate didn't mention it again and I thought I would be spared any further embarrassment. I guess it wasn't meant to be, because as soon as Nanny sat down next to Tristan and poured herself a cup of tea, she looked at me and spoke casually. "Ever thought of putting a muzzle on him dear? That way he won't wake up the whole bloody neighborhood." Kate started to laugh and Tristan grinned with a mouthful of toast, but I flushed beet red and put my head down.

I felt Kate pat me on the back and she tried to comfort me by saying, "Oh we're only teasing, love. You're a beautiful girl and we know Tristan can't help himself." If that was meant to be comforting, it wasn't working. I was further embarrassed and I felt like hiding under the table. I started to wonder if they would find it terribly rude if I continued eating my breakfast under there.

Later that morning, Kate drove me to the pier again and we went to the little jewelry boutique where I bought Tristan's Christmas gift. When we walked in the store, the jeweler who sold me Tristan's bracelet recognized us immediately. He came over to us, smiled, and spoke in his Scottish accent. "Why hullo there. Nice to see you again."

I smiled at him and replied, "Hi. Nice to see you too."

"What can I help you with today?"

"I'm looking for a men's wedding band."

As soon as I told him what I wanted, his expression changed. It was actually warmer...if that was possible. His smile widened and he gave me sidelong glance. "Did your gentleman friend love the bracelet so much that he eventually proposed?" He gave a short laugh. Before I could answer, he walked away and stood behind one of the glass cases.

Kate and I followed him and stood on the other side. He pulled out one of the trays that contained a variety of men's wedding bands. Kate and I leaned over it as we briefly looked at the qualities of each ring. Then suddenly, one of them caught my eye and I actually gasped. Before I could stop myself, I plucked the ring out so I could get a better look. Upon closer inspection, I realized it was actually a Claddagh ring.

I couldn't contain my surprise. "Kate! Look at this one! It's a Claddagh ring!" The ring was actually a 7mm band with the Irish Claddagh and a Celtic symbol engraved around the length of the band.

She took the ring from me to inspect it herself. "Yes, this one's beautiful."

I tore my eyes away from the sparkly ring to ask the jeweler, "Is this white gold?"

He grinned at me and replied, "No miss, that's platinum."

Kate let out a low whistle and handed me the ring back. Under normal circumstances, I would've asked about the price. But because it was a wedding ring for the man I love...I didn't care. "I'll take it." I had already measured Tristan's ring finger before we left, so I told the jeweler what size I needed. Imagine my utter surprise when he told me the ring was already the exact size I needed. The Fates were definitely with me that morning.

He took the ring away to have it cleaned and when he returned with it, he put it in a beautiful, white suede ring box with royal blue satin bedding. I handed him my credit card and when he rang up the purchase, I couldn't help but to look at the price as it flashed up on the cash register: £920. The first thought that entered my mind when I saw that was: *Tristan is worth so much more.*

That night was our last in Brighton before we would return for the wedding because Tristan got an email from his manager saying that he had some casting appointments lined up for him. We made love again and just like the night before...Tristan could not be quiet. I gave up my attempts at trying to silence his pleasure because I realized it was futile. Besides, Nanny and Kate were already aware of how loud he was when we made love. Once we were both satiated, I was lying on his chest listening to his heart beat when he said softly, "I'm gonna need your ring, love...the promise ring. I need to have it resized so I can put it on your ring finger. Remember I promised you that?"

I smiled as my mind flashed back to last Christmas when Tristan made his promise. "Of course I remember." Then I started thinking about the ring that was already occupying my left ring finger...my engagement ring. How would Tristan fit the promise ring on my finger with the engagement ring? "Um, baby?"

"Hmmm?" He replied as he began running his fingers gently through my hair. His bedroom was dim and there was only one light on; the lamp on the nightstand.

"The promise ring won't really fit properly with the engagement ring. It's kind of---"

"Bugger! I forgot about that." Tristan was silent for a moment before he continued speaking. "Maybe I should get you a different ring as your wedding ring. One that will match with---"

"No! Tristan, you've given me enough rings." I paused as I thought of a solution. Once I decided on one, I sat up and said, "Look, this is what I'm going to do." I took my engagement ring off my left ring finger and put it on my right ring finger.

Tristan gave me a confused look. "Why are you doing that? Are you supposed to do that?"

I smiled warmly at him before I leaned down to kiss him. I spoke softly when I said, "It doesn't matter what finger it's on...I know its meaning. The only ring that really matters is this one." And I pointed to the white-gold Claddagh ring still snuggled on my left middle finger. Then I took it off slowly and placed it on the nightstand. "You do what you need to do with it and then you put it back where it belongs." I reached over and turned off the light, and then I laid back down with my head on Tristan's chest. His beating heart provided me with the lullaby I needed to have a goodnight sleep.

He wrapped his arms around me and kissed the top of my head. Then I heard him whisper in the dark, "I can't wait to make you my wife."

I heard myself whisper back before I drifted off into a place of sheer contentment and peace, "Soon my love...soon."

Chapter 15

A FEW DAYS AFTER WE returned to Los Angeles, I made a lunch date with my mother and Autumn so we could go shopping for my wedding dress and Autumn's Maid of Honor dress. My mother insisted on taking us to this ridiculously expensive bridal shop in Beverly Hills. Autumn and I didn't argue because she also insisted on purchasing our dresses. Autumn couldn't pick out her dress until I decided on what I wanted and I was actually having a hard time deciding. I think part of the problem was that my mother kept showing me all these white dresses. But deep down, I didn't want to wear white; I wanted to wear my favorite color on my special day: pink. When I told her that, she gave me a confused look. "Why do you want to wear pink on your wedding day sweetheart?"

"Because it's *my* wedding Mom and I want to wear my favorite color."

She sighed. "Very well."

The three of us plus the saleswoman, who was assisting us, spent another couple hours going through pink dresses. I tried a few of them on, but I didn't like the way any of them fit on me. Just as I was about to give up and ask my mother to take us somewhere else, something caught my attention in the corner of my eye. Over where the cashier's counter was, there was a dress hanging up on the wall. It was covered in plastic but I saw that it was pink.

I quickly left Autumn and my mother and walked over to the counter to get a better look at the dress. I asked the cashier about it and she said it was a return that they just received a few minutes ago. She took it off the wall and carefully removed the plastic. It looked like it hadn't been worn; the tags were still on it and it had that new garment smell. Did I mention it was absolutely breathtaking? It was an *Atelier Aimée* and it was a one-piece floor-length strapless dress. The material was one-hundred percent Organza with pale pink top layers and white layers nestled delicately underneath. It was light and airy; the perfect summer wedding dress. There was also a string of feminine pink, silk roses that accented the pink layer of the dress. When my mother and Autumn came over to me and saw the dress, they both gasped.

Autumn replied, "Whoa! Bridge, that dress is hot! You should get it."

I grabbed one of the tags to check the size and I was thrilled when it was exactly my size. The Fates were with me again after all. I heard my mother's voice to the side of me say, "Well, try it on honey." I didn't need to be told twice. I took the dress and went back into the fitting room to try it on.

When I came out wearing it, both of their mouths dropped. "That's beautiful Bridget," my mother said breathlessly. She stood up and walked over to me to admire it.

I went over to one of the full-length mirrors and the saleswoman said, "Oh, that one compliments you perfectly. It's a very nice choice."

Autumn had a similar response. "Yep, that's the one. That's definitely you." She laughed. "Oh my God, you look so girly!"

I couldn't help but to twirl around in the dress. It was the first time in my life that I'd worn a dress like that. My senior prom dress was no where near as beautiful as this *Atelier Aimée*. I turned to my mother and smiled widely as I announced, "Mom, I want this one." She smiled and seemed to sigh a breath of relief.

Suddenly, Autumn came over to us with a one-piece, chiffon knee-length dress with a draped V-neck bodice. The pink was a similar shade to my dress. "I'll take this one Mrs. Monahan!" She said brightly.

I was utterly amazed at how fast she chose a dress. "Aut, how'd you come to a decision so quickly?"

She replied sarcastically, "Bridge, I saw this dress like two hours ago. As soon as you said you wanted pink...which I had a feeling you did...I decided I liked this one."

After we decided on the dresses, the saleswoman helped us pick out shoes. In addition to my shoes and the lacy light blue garter belt (to be my 'something blue') that Autumn insisted on, I chose a lovely silk flower headpiece that contained roses that matched the string of roses on my dress. Autumn also pointed to a small bouquet for me to carry as I walked to the wedding arch. The flowers were fresh and would need to be ordered in advance. "What's the point if the wedding is going to be so small?" I asked her. "I don't think I need a bouquet."

Autumn's hazel eyes widened and she scoffed in disbelief. She answered me simply when she said, "'Cause that's what the bride does. She throws the bouquet."

As the cashier rang up our purchase I couldn't help but to notice the total. My eyes practically popped out of their sockets and I swiftly looked over at my mother. She didn't bat an eyelash when she handed the cashier her Platinum Visa.

After we left the shop, we grabbed a bite to eat before we took Autumn home. My mother took me back to my apartment next but she told me she couldn't stay. Before I got out of the car she said to me, "Honey, I just want you to know how happy I am. I really had a wonderful time today...despite spending almost four hours in a bridal shop." She laughed lightly before she continued. "But it was worth it. It's not often I get to spend this kind of quality time with you anymore. I know you have your friends and your students and now Tristan takes up much of your life." She paused. "I understand...really I do. You're in love and I can see how much you enjoy being with each other. I just want to say..." It was then that her voice wavered slightly. "I'll always be here for you and I fully support your decision to marry Tristan. I want you to know that you don't need to be skeptical of my truthfulness when it comes to the way I feel about him. I really do like him and I think you're good for each other. When I look back on it now...I don't know why I acted that way towards him when he first visited us. Maybe...deep down...I knew he'd be the one to take you away from us and I was...afraid." I noticed the tears in her eyes and she daintily tried to wipe them away.

I leaned over to hug my mother after her heartfelt confession. My own vision was blurry when I replied, "Thanks Mom, that means a lot to me. And don't worry, Tristan's not taking me away from you and Dad.

We'll try to visit more often...I promise. And I can't thank you enough for buying my dress...and Autumn's dress...everything."

"That's what mothers are for sweetheart. One day I hope you'll experience the phenomenal thing called motherhood."

I laughed. "Whoa, slow down Mom. Let me get married first...then we'll talk about kids. I already heard enough about it from Tristan." Oops, I didn't mean to let that one slip.

My mother's green eyes widened in surprise. "Tristan wants children?!? Already?!?"

"Yeah, he does."

"And *you* don't?"

"I do...just not right now."

She shook her head in disbelief. "Wow, that's unusual. I mean, for a man his age to want a child. Usually, it's the other way around and the woman wants the child."

"Yeah, well Tristan is...unusual." I gave her a quick kiss before I took my packages out of the trunk and headed towards my front door. Once I was inside, she drove away.

I walked into the bedroom to hang up my wedding dress. It's a good thing it was covered in white paper so Tristan couldn't see it. A few moments later, he walked in. I found his presence strange because I didn't see his bike outside, so I immediately asked him about it. "Where's your bike? I didn't see it outside." It was at that moment that I actually got a good look at him. He was limping slightly and he had red scratches on the right side of his face; they weren't deep but they were noticeable. I was immediately filled with worry and I rushed over to him and put my arms around him. My voice was laced with heavy concern when I asked, "Baby, what happened to you?!?" He also had a cut on his bottom lip and a black-and-blue bruise under his right eye which was slightly swollen. He didn't answer me right away and I started to get scared. "Tristan, what happened?!? Are you alright sweetie?"

He tried to smile slightly but I saw him wince. I ran my fingers through his blond hair and then I lightly brushed one of my fingers over the cut on his lip. It was then that he finally answered me. "I got into an accident. Some fucking bastard came out of no where and knocked me off my bike. It's completely totaled. After he hit me, he peeled off. It was a goddamn hit-and-run." As he was talking, I couldn't help but to kiss him in every place I could see that he was hurt.

"Oh my God! When did this happen?!?" I started to move us towards the bathroom so I could try to clean him up.

"This afternoon. The ambulance came and took me to the bloody hospital. I told them I was fine but they wouldn't listen to me."

"Why didn't you call me?!?"

"Because love, you were out with your mum and I didn't wanna bother you with that shit. It was bollocks...really. I'm fine. As soon as they took me to the hospital, I checked myself out." I closed the toilet lid and made him sit down on it as I opened the medicine cabinet. I put some Peroxide on a cotton ball and dabbed at his cut lip. Tristan grabbed my hand to stop me and he said softly, "Bridget, I'm fine. Please don't fuss over me."

I couldn't stop the tears that started to form in my eyes as I looked at my prince's bruised face. All of a sudden I started to hate the fucking bastard who knocked my love off his motorcycle. How dare anyone hurt my Tristan. I don't know where the feeling came from but I started to feel extremely protective over him. I bent down and kissed his hurt lip again. To my surprise, Tristan added pressure to the kiss and a moan escaped him. When we broke the kiss, I smiled at him as I caressed his still-beautiful face. "But I like fussing over you." Then I sat on his lap and continued to dab the cotton ball on all his cuts and bruises. When I spoke again, my voice took on a more seductive tone. "Just tell your princess where it hurts so I can kiss it and make it all better."

Even though Tristan had just been involved in an accident, that didn't prevent him from standing up and lifting me into his arms. He growled, "You know you make me fucking randy when you talk like that." Then he kissed me deeply as he quickly walked back to the bedroom with me still in his arms. When we got to the bedroom, he deposited me onto the bed before he lifted his t-shirt over his body. "There's one place that really hurts right now. It's just aching to be kissed, love." He reached down to unsnap his jeans and they fell to the floor.

I smiled up at him and spoke in an innocent voice. "But baby, you're hurt."

"Yeah, I'm in a shitload of pain. I need a lot of kisses, princess." Then he pulled his boxers down with one swipe.

As soon as Tristan's black cotton boxers hit the floor, he wasted no time crawling onto the bed and covering me with his naked body. He laid between my legs and embraced me tightly as he continued to kiss me with an urgent need. I wrapped my arms around him and my hands began roaming up and down his back, and across his broad shoulders. I felt him begin to grind his pelvis into me and the sensation caused him to moan softly into my mouth. He felt so good on top of me, that I grabbed his bare butt and rubbed myself against him to create more friction. He moaned louder and I actually felt the vibration in my own body. Finally, I unsealed my lips from his and whispered, "Tell me where it hurts."

He trailed feather-light kisses down my neck and nibbled my earlobe before he found my mouth again. Then he kissed me deeply once more before he replied softly, "You know where it hurts." And he emphasized his statement by grinding himself into me again.

I smiled against his lips before I pushed him onto his back so I could keep my promise to kiss the hurt away. He fell back easily and he laid still and obedient before me while he awaited his princess' seductive touch. I sat next to his body and smiled wickedly down at him as I raked my fingernails lightly down his chest and over his peaked nipples. My soft caress traveled south and he arched his back almost instinctively as my fingers crossed over the flat plane of his stomach. Without taking my eyes off his Adonis form, I took my index finger and traced his 'treasure trail' from his belly button all the way down to the thick blond patch surrounding his throbbing erection that was standing proud at attention. He shivered slightly as I took it gently into my palm and stroked it once from base to tip. When I brushed my thumb over the top, a clear drop of pre-cum beaded on the tip to make me fully aware of how aroused he was. He arched his back off the bed again and moaned as he begged me. "Bridget...*please.*" I tore my eyes away from his manhood to look at his face and he was gazing at me under half-closed lids. His lips were slightly parted and I heard his breath coming out in soft pants.

I decided not to tease my prince any further, so I bent down and kissed the top of his erection. I heard him inhale sharply and I peppered kisses up and down his shaft. I cupped his sac with my other hand and squeezed it gently. Then I placed a few light kisses there as to not neglect it from my affection. Tristan began to moan louder and thrust gently into my fist that was enclosed around him. Suddenly, he spoke again but this time his voice was strong and his tone was dominant. "Put me in your mouth."

I looked at his face again and his expression was intense. He reached his hand out to smooth my hair before I felt him gently nudge my head down towards his aching hardness. Being his princess, I had to comply with my prince so I moved from my sitting position to lie on my stomach. I wanted to be absolutely comfortable if I was going to have Tristan under my own feminine spell. Because he was so blessed, I couldn't fit the entire length of him into my mouth, so I improvised and put as much of him as I could in my mouth without gagging. I alternated between sucking firmly and stroking in a rhythm that had this British boy whimpering and moaning in sexual ecstasy. He continued to stroke my hair as I pleasured him. I bobbed my head as I sucked him, and it wasn't long before his legs began to tremble.

His hands moved from my hair and I saw him quickly grab the comforter in a tight grip. I already knew how my baby liked it best, so I quickened my pace and made sure to swirl my tongue over the top. Tristan responded immediately and his breathing increased rapidly while his legs continued to writhe against the bed. Then I did his favorite thing; I darted my tongue inside the opening and he rewarded me by crying out sharply. I began sucking him harder, and he said these last words before he finally succumbed to my attentions. "Bridget! Oh shit, I'm gonna cum, babe. Right now...right fucking now!"

I had already decided I was going to let him release into my mouth, so I relaxed my throat in preparation for what was about to happen next. I cupped his sac again and I felt his testicles draw up towards his body which signaled the beginning stage of his orgasm. Suddenly, his entire body became as taught as a bow string and he yelled my name before he flooded my mouth with his warm seed. I noticed that his toes curled and I knew at that moment I had complete sexual power over him. His body trembled as he rode his wave of pleasure and his pelvis bucked almost involuntarily. Tristan arched his back once more and a long deep moan came from his throat, followed by a heavy sigh of gratification.

When he finally stopped erupting, I suckled him gently until I felt his entire body relax. I released him with a 'pop' and then I rubbed soothing circles over his stomach with my hand. When I looked at him, his eyes were closed and a smile of contentment graced his bruised but still lovely face. I spoke in an equally soothing voice when I asked, "Does it feel better now, my prince?"

Either my actions tickled him, my words amused him, or both because he chuckled softly. Without opening his eyes, he replied, "Much better. Thank you, princess."

I sat up and licked my lips before I remarked, "Mmmm...you've been drinking a lot of that pineapple juice, huh?" Tristan opened his eyes and looked at me. "You taste sweet, baby."

A rare, shy smile appeared on his face. "Um...yeah. Thanks babe."

I laughed and moved my body so I could lie next to him. I ran my fingers through his hair and lightly caressed the right side of his face where the angry red scratches stood out noticeable against his beautiful ivory skin. Then I abruptly changed the subject. "I think we should write our own vows. What do you think?"

Tristan stretched his sinewy form like a giant feline, and then he put his hands behind his head. "Yeah, that's a good idea."

"But you have to memorize them. You can't stand up there and read from a scrap of paper."

He chuckled again and replied, "I know that, babe. I'm an actor remember? I have to memorize scripts. Plus, do you think I wanna look like a fucking idiot on our wedding day? What would I look like standing up there trying to wing it?"

I laughed lightly to cover up the fact that I made a foolish assumption about him. At that a moment, I noticed something that I hadn't seen before. I was actually surprised because it was right in front of my face (well, not *right* in front) the whole time I was giving Tristan a blow-job. A nasty horizontal gash had made a home on his right knee. It was about four inches long and it was deep. I started to realize that was probably what was causing him to limp. I couldn't contain my shock when I saw it. "Tristan! Look at your knee!"

He looked taken back for a second; probably because I raised my voice. "What? Oh yeah. It's nothing, don't worry about it."

"It's nothing, huh?" I touched it gingerly with my finger and as soon as I did, his leg jerked and he quickly sucked some air between his teeth. "Yeah right." I prodded around the cut but I avoided touching it directly again because I didn't want to cause my fiancé anymore pain. My voice was laced with concern when I said, "You should have that looked at. Did you put anything on it? What if it gets infected?"

Tristan sat up and looked down at his knee. Then he reached down and acted like he was inspecting it. "It's not that bad. I'll put some ice on it."

I moved back up towards his face and put my hands on either side of his head. My eyes scanned over his face and I noticed the swelling around his eye went down considerably but it was still bruised. He seemed to heal quickly and I said, "Well, at least your eye looks better." My mind started to think back on his accident, and I realized he hadn't divulged all the details. I was curious to know, so I asked, "Did you see the car that hit you? Did you catch the plates?"

Strangely, Tristan averted his eyes from me and laid back down. He didn't look at me when he answered. "No, it all happened so fast."

"When they hit you, were you on the freeway? Did you get knocked into traffic or something?"

He paused momentarily before he answered me. "No, I got side-swiped and lost control of my bike. I fell off on the side of the road...into some grass and bushes. And then my helmet came off." Well that would explain him surviving with only minor cuts and bruises.

"Are you going to pursue this with the cops? I mean, it was a hit-and-run after all." It wasn't until after I asked the question, that I realized it was a *stupid* question. I knew Tristan would never talk to the police.

And sure enough, he gave me a look as if to say: *'Are you fucking kidding me?'* I was actually surprised that he didn't say it out loud. I was also surprised by what came out of his mouth instead. "Bridget, just forget about it alright."

I couldn't contain my surprise or my confusion. Someone hit him, totaled his bike, drove away, and he wanted to forget about it? That just didn't make any sense to me. "What do you mean forget about it? Tristan---"

He interrupted me before I could finish. "Just...forget it. Please? Some bastard just got away with it. I don't really care that much."

Something was definitely up. No normal person would just forget about an accident like that so quickly. "Tristan, they totaled your bike. You know...that hot little green and black mini-rocket you loved so much? Don't you care about that? What are you going to do about your bike?"

He shrugged and replied simply, "I'm gonna get another one." The idea of Tristan getting another bike didn't sit well with me. I couldn't help but to visualize him getting into another accident and next time not walking away with just cuts and bruises. Those motorcycles offered no protection what-so-ever and I really wasn't ready to take another chance with him. I decided that he needed to know how I felt about his decision. I shook my head and just as I was about to give him my opinion, he quickly spoke again. "I know what you're gonna say. You don't want me to get another bike. You want me to get a car, don't you?"

Earlier in our relationship, his statement would've shocked me. But Tristan was so good at reading my mind, that it didn't faze me. "But baby, they're safer."

"Bridge, I could get hurt driving a car too. Some arsehole can hit me and drive off just the same. Or I could get hit just walking down the bloody street. I like motorcycles, babe. I enjoy riding them." I tried to speak again but he continued. "I'm not gonna let one accident stop me from riding."

Tristan seemed to have already made up his mind and I knew I couldn't win this argument. The only thing I could do was make him aware of my concern for his safety. If he wanted to take another chance and test his luck, I wouldn't be able to stop him. "Okay Tristan. You go ahead and get another bike. Please try to be careful, okay? I just want you to be safe."

He sat up and kissed me on the cheek before he put his arms around me. "Alright, love. I'll try."

When he released me from his embrace, I hopped off the bed. He looked at me questioningly and I said lightly, "Well, get dressed. It's not too late, so we can still go and check out some new bikes." Tristan smiled in return and I couldn't help but to notice how slowly he got out of bed. Even though he wouldn't admit it, I could tell he was still in pain. I was about to change my mind and tell him that we'll go another day but I knew he really wanted to go. I also knew he loved bikes, although I was strongly opposed to him traveling on one. Then I remembered that in relationship you have to support one another...even if you don't share the other's enjoyment.

Before we left to go to the motorcycle dealer, I went back into the bedroom to get something I thought Tristan would want. When I approached him, he was standing in front of the mirror in the living room and he was prodding at his bruised right eye. I casually handed him a pair of sunglasses. He took them from me and a confused expression appeared on his face. "What are these for?" It was actually an honest question because in reality it wasn't remotely sunny outside. But I was surprised to know that he *really* didn't know why I gave them to him.

"I thought you'd want to cover your eye."

The confused expression remained on his face. "Why would I wanna do that?"

His question caught me off-guard and it took me a few seconds to answer. My eyes scanned his face and before I could stop myself, I laughed and said jokingly, "Because...baby, you look like someone just beat your ass." I continued to laugh but I noticed Tristan wasn't laughing. As a matter of fact, he wasn't even smiling.

When he spoke, his voice was hard and it wiped the smile right off my face. "I don't fucking care if people see my face like this." He tilted his head to the side to regard me for a moment, and I was frozen in place because he seemed to be scrutinizing me. When he spoke again, he lowered his voice. "Do you think I'm vain?"

"Uh...no," I replied in a small voice.

"Then why do you think I wanna cover my face?"

"Ummm...I just thought you wouldn't want people to see."

"*Why?* Why wouldn't I want them to see?"

I did believe that Tristan cared about his looks but I didn't think he was conceited or 'vain' as he put it. I answered truthfully when I said, "I thought you'd be feeling self-conscious. You know, that people are staring at you wondering what happened to your face."

My answer seemed to satisfy him because his expression lightened. "Oh." When he said that tiny little word, I sighed in relief. And just when I thought we were back to an understanding, Tristan said something that really shocked me. "Babe, when I was growing up in Brighton...my face looked like this every other week."

Now it was my turn to look confused. "Why?"

"'Cause I was always getting into fights. I was a really angry kid." He sighed and slowly walked away from me.

I walked over to him and stood in front of him again because I wasn't letting him end this conversation that easily. "Why were you an angry kid?"

It was a few seconds before he spoke and for a moment, he just looked into my eyes. Then he said, "I was angry about my father...that fucking bastard. And Mum was depressed for a long time 'cause of him. That really affected me. And my fucking teachers...and the pigs who were always harassing me and my mates. I just..." He looked away from me and shook his head. For a moment, it looked like he was briefly reliving the memories that caused him pain. "I just took my frustration out on other people. The smallest thing would set me off. After awhile, people really started to tread carefully around me."

After Tristan's confession, I realized that my fiancé had anger issues. If he was no longer suffering from them, I wasn't quite sure because the only time I'd seen him physically fight was when he fought his older brother in my living room. Before I could respond, he walked away again towards the front door. He turned his head to look at me and asked, "You ready to go?" Without actually saying the words, I knew he was telling me that the conversation was over. I saw him put the sunglasses on the side table before we left.

When we got to the motorcycle dealer, I was following him while he browsed the different bikes that were displayed on the lot. I noticed that his main concern seemed to be the speed because he kept saying, "I wonder how fast this one goes" before he checked the sticker on each one. It didn't take him long to make a decision because one bike in particular caught his eye and he made a bee-line towards it. He inspected it for a few seconds before he said cheerfully, "This one, babe! I want this one!"

I smiled because I saw that it was basically the same color as his old one. "The same color *again*? You don't have to get the same color." The bike Tristan picked out was lime green and black. It said 'Kawasaki' on the top and 'Ninja' on the side in black letters. It had two fat, black rubber tires covering black and silver wheels. I'll admit that it was actually hotter than his previous bike.

He smiled back at me. "Yes I do. It has to match my jacket." The jacket he was referring to was the lime green, black, and white motorcycle jacket I gave him for his birthday. "Besides, this is the same bike I had before...just the newer model."

I happened to glance at the shiny all-black one sitting next to the bike he chose. "What about a black one? You know, since that's your favorite color."

Tristan's mind seemed to be made up. "Nope. I want this one."

"Okay, well let's---"

My sentence was cut short because a male voice interrupted our conversation. "Tris?!? Oh no way!" I turned my head and I saw a young man come jogging towards us from inside the showroom. He was tall and slightly tanned with spiky blond hair. When he reached us, he had a wide smile on his face and he looked completely surprised. "Dude, what are you doing here? I thought you'd still be in the hospital." He laughed and when I looked up at him, I realized that I'd never seen him before. This mystery guy must've sensed my gaze on him because he looked over at me and put his hand out for me to shake. "Hi, I'm Dane."

I smiled back and shook his hand. "Nice to meet you. I'm Bridget." Dane had very dark eyebrows which told me that he probably bleached his hair. He had cocoa brown eyes and kissable, naturally pink lips. He was sporting a silver stud in his left ear and he was really cute. He reminded me of a skater-boy. I averted my eyes from him because I didn't want Tristan to catch me staring at his friend. Instead, I looked over at Tristan and strangely, he seemed to be trying to ignore Dane.

Dane walked closer to him and when he spoke, he still sounded amazed. "Don't tell me you're shopping for another bike already? You've got to be the only person I've ever met who---"

Tristan finally looked at him. But when he did, his expression was angry. He said loudly, "Shut the fuck up, mate!" I was so shocked by Tristan's unwarranted response that my mouth dropped. Not only was I shocked, but I was totally confused. Why was he acting like this towards him? Dane didn't seem fazed by Tristan's outburst but he immediately stopped talking. I heard him chuckle and he looked over at me with a huge grin on his face. Either Dane was just a strange kind of guy or something fishy was going on. I heard Tristan sigh and when he spoke again, he still sounded annoyed with him. "What the fuck are you doing here?"

Dane replied casually, "I'm picking up a part for my bike. I got this new exhaust and I think it's gonna help me whip your ass next time." While Dane was talking, Tristan quickly grabbed my arm and started pulling me away towards the showroom. It was almost like he couldn't stand to be in Dane's presence. Dane didn't pick up on the hint because he started following us. "I swear dude, we thought you were dead."

As soon as he made that statement, it sparked something in my brain and I stopped in my tracks. To my surprise, Tristan still tried to pull me along but I held my ground. I yanked my arm out of his grasp and moved towards Dane. I asked with wide-eyes, "You saw the accident?"

He was still grinning when he replied, "Yeah, I did."

I heard Tristan's voice again and it sounded like he was speaking through clenched teeth. "Dane...*shut up*." I whipped my head towards him and he was looking at Dane intently. Actually, it looked like he was trying to communicate to him through his eyes. When he noticed me looking at him, he averted his eyes from Dane to cast them on me. Then he quickly looked away. Tristan didn't look away fast enough because the look in his eyes told me that he was hiding something. At that moment... I was determined to find out what it was.

I turned back towards Dane and asked in an urgent voice, "Did you see the car that hit him?"

The grin that was on Dane's face disappeared and it was replaced by a look of confusion. "What car?"

My mouth dropped and I whipped my head around to look at Tristan again. He looked at me before he glared at Dane through narrowed-eyes. Then he sucked his cheeks in slightly and started walking towards him in a threatening manner. "What the fuck, mate? I told you not to mention it in front of Bridget, didn't I?"

Dane still looked confused when he answered him. "I don't remember you saying that."

"You know I did! Don't play like you're fucking daft alright!"

Dane laughed and I actually thought he was crazy because Tristan looked like he was about to kill him. It was but a few seconds into their exchange that I realized my earlier assumption was correct: Tristan was hiding something. Tristan had his back to me so I walked over to him and turned his body to face me. I looked into his eyes and spoke in a stern voice. "What's going on, Tristan? You told me that you got hit by a car. Did you lie to me?" Deep inside me, a little flame was starting to grow. I was slowly beginning to get angry because I didn't appreciate being lied to. The fact that Tristan didn't provide me with an immediate answer ignited the flame and the Fiery Redhead emerged. "Tristan, answer me!"

I heard Dane say, "Whoa, I think I'm gonna---"

I looked over at Dane and I saw him slowly backing away from us. He didn't finish his sentence because I quickly rushed over to him and grabbed his arm to stop him from leaving. He looked at me in shock and he probably thought I was crazy. I didn't care and I spoke to him in the same tone of voice I used on Tristan. "Oh no you don't! You're not going anywhere. You're going to stay right here. You saw what really happened?" He nodded. "Good, then you can stay here and make sure Tristan tells me the truth." Dane's eyes widened but he didn't disobey me; he stayed glued to the spot.

I rounded on Tristan and stood right in front of him. He was looking into my eyes and chewing on his bottom lip. I noticed that he irritated the cut on his lip and it started to redden. He actually looked nervous but I was too angry to care how he was feeling. I wanted to find out what really happened and why he felt the need to lie about it. I sighed and closed my eyes briefly in an attempt to control my temper. When I spoke again, my voice was calmer. "Tristan, what really happened to you?" He averted his eyes from me and that simple dismissive gesture caused me to yell again. "Tristan! I swear to God you better start talking or I'm leaving you!"

Suddenly, Tristan's eyes met mine and I saw the color drain from his face. His eyes widened, his lips parted slightly and then I saw him swallow hard. When he spoke, I was surprised that his voice was shaky. "What do you mean you're *leaving* me?"

"I mean I'm getting in my car, I'm driving home and I'm leaving you here!"

Strangely, his demeanor relaxed and he actually sounded relieved when he said, "Oh." He licked his lips briefly and then he took a deep breath. The longer he hesitated to explain, the angrier I got. A few seconds ticked by and I got fed up because he still wasn't speaking. I huffed loudly and turned on my heel to walk away towards my car. After I took a few steps, was when he finally admitted the truth. "I didn't get hit by a car!"

I turned back towards him and spoke loudly. "Then what happened?!?"

He took another deep breath. "The truth is...I *did* fall off my bike, but..." He paused. "A car didn't knock me off. I was racing and I lost control 'cause I wasn't paying attention."

I couldn't contain the utter shock I felt from that simple explanation. "You were racing?" I already knew Tristan raced on his bike but why didn't he tell me that in the first place? Why did he create the story about the hit-and-run? I still felt like he wasn't telling me the whole story. "Why didn't you tell me that? I know you race through the streets like a crazed maniac."

"No, I wasn't racing through the streets. I was *racing*. You know, like in an actual motorcycle race." I was still confused by his explanation so he explained further. "Me and some of my mates...sometimes we ride down to the valley and there's this place...it's deserted. And we race there. I didn't tell you 'cause I thought you'd get angry. I thought you'd try to tell me to stop doing it or give me an ultimatum or some shit. And you know I hate arguing with you, so I thought it would be better if you didn't know."

Right after Tristan finished talking, a salesman finally decided to come outside and greet us. Unfortunately, his timing was extremely bad. He approached us and spoke in a cheerful voice. "Hello folks! How can I---"

I was in no mood to talk to him so I put my hand up and said, "I'm sorry, but we're busy right now."

He laughed nervously. "Okay...well, I'll just be inside if you need any help." And then he scurried away.

I walked over to Tristan and looked into his eyes again. Before I could speak, he said softly, "I'm sorry, love. I'm sorry I lied to you."

"Tristan, I still don't understand why you lied."

"What if I came in the room with my face all fucked up like this and told you that I totaled my bike 'cause I was racing? And that I wanted to buy another bike so I could continue to race? That wouldn't have caused an argument between us? You would've been completely okay with that?"

"No, of course not."

"That's why I didn't tell you. I didn't wanna argue with you about it. Remember earlier Bridget, you tried to argue with me about getting another bike." He walked away from me and I noticed for the first time that Dane had left. Tristan started slowly walking past a row of motorcycles and lightly touching each one as he passed.

I walked over to him and when he saw me approach, he turned around to face me. I spoke gently when I said, "Baby, it's normal for couples to argue sometimes. We're not always going to agree on *everything*. But you still shouldn't have lied to me. You should've just told me the truth."

"But I hate arguing with you. That's what I'm trying to tell you. And I'm sorry but I'll avoid it if I can. The last thing I want is for you to be pissed at me. Then you start ignoring me and shit. You have no idea how that makes me feel." After the latter part of his statement, I saw his eyes become glassy. He started blinking rapidly and then he walked away from me again. His voice was shaky when he asked, "Can we just get this bike please?"

I sighed. "So you're still going to race? You're going to buy this brand new bike and race it?"

He didn't look at me when he answered. "Yes."

Even though Tristan said he didn't want to argue with me, I couldn't help but to voice my concern. "But Tristan, what if you break your neck? What if---" At that moment, Tristan turned and looked intently into my eyes and it caused me to stop speaking. I was doing exactly what he was trying to avoid in the first place. I sighed again and cast my eyes skyward. I didn't understand why he couldn't see how he was putting himself in unnecessary danger. He wasn't exactly a professional motorcyclist. He was being so ruthless and I actually felt helpless to stop him. In the end, I realized there was only one thing for me to do: stay true to my word and support the man I love. I walked over to the lime green and black motorcycle that he had chosen to continue his deadly obsession and said defeated, "Okay baby, let's get your bike."

And just when I thought the drama would end once we returned home, I was in for yet another intriguing conversation. We had just finished eating the McDonald's that I picked up on our way home (Tristan followed me home on his new bike) when I started thinking about the fact that he kept his racing a secret. Until today, I had believed that he was always completely honest with me. The realization that he wasn't, caused me to feel uneasy and I couldn't help but to wonder what other secrets he was hiding.

Tristan was sitting on the sofa looking over the paperwork for his recent purchase, when I sat down next to him and asked, "So, are there any other secrets I should know before we get married?" I looked at him expectedly and he just stared at me with a piece of paper in his hand. Then he smirked and dropped the paper onto the coffee table. He looked away from me and started scratching his head so I tried to press him by saying, "Well, is there?"

He turned his head to look at me and the smirk disappeared. His expression was serious when he asked, "What do you wanna know, Bridget? I've told you that I've been arrested before."

"Have you ever done drugs?"

He let out a breath through his nose and said sarcastically, "What do you think?" I didn't reply; I just looked at him. "Of course I have. But I was never a fucking druggie, if that's what you think."

"Are you bisexual?" This time he laughed out loud. "Look, I know you've had a promiscuous past, but I just want to know if it ever involved men." There was a ghost of a smile on his face as he continued to just look at me. "Well? Have you ever been really drunk and just...I don't know..."

He looked away from me again and suddenly, his voice turned hard. "I don't label myself *anything*."

That was probably the next to last thing I would've expected him to say (the last thing I expected was 'yes'). He still didn't look at me so I rephrased my question to get a more accurate answer. "Have you ever been with a guy?" This time he looked at me but he just stared into my eyes. It was actually unnerving because I felt like he really wanted to say something but something else was preventing him. I tilted my head to the side and pressed him by saying, "So you're still not going to answer?"

He averted his eyes from me yet again and stared ahead of him. It was a full minute before he spoke and I just sat there and watched him. I was actually anticipating his answer but he didn't give me one. Instead, he spoke softly and continued to stare into space. "Bridget, there's some things I can't tell you 'cause I don't wanna see the look on your face when you hear it." When he finally turned to look at me, it felt like his eyes were piercing into me. "I don't wanna see your eyes judging me or have you thinking: 'he's really fucked up.' Believe it or not, I care about your opinion of me." He looked away again and began rubbing the back of his neck. I had a feeling he was doing that because he was uncomfortable.

I scooted closer to him and took one of his hands in both of mine. He still wouldn't look at me, so I kissed him on the cheek and tried to reassure him by saying, "Baby, I told you I would never judge you. And we shouldn't keep secrets from each other."

All of a sudden, Tristan's demeanor changed and his voice was clipped. "Your life has been so fucking easy."

His statement caught me off-guard and I leaned away from him. "What? No it hasn't!"

He took his hand out of my grasp and when he spoke again, he actually sounded resentful. "You've been so sheltered and spoiled your whole life. Your parents gave you everything. And you're so innocent."

His tone of voice caused me to immediately get defensive and his assumption shocked me to the core. I couldn't help but to wonder where his words were coming from. Was this how he really felt about me all along? Was he just now letting me know his honest opinion of *me?* "Tristan, I'm not---"

He interrupted me by asking, "What's the craziest shit you've ever done in your life?"

I scoffed and shook my head in disbelief. In all truthfulness, I've never really been the crazy sort. I've always been level-headed and kept two feet firmly planted on the ground. I spoke softly when I admitted, "Actually, my life has been pretty tame." Then as an afterthought I said, "Until I met you."

Suddenly, Tristan stood up and I had a feeling we were going to go through another emotional and dramatic episode, so I braced myself for it. He didn't disappoint because the next thing out of his mouth was, "You have no idea the things I've done or the things I've seen. I may be young, but I've been around."

Something in the back of mind remembered how much of a Mama's Boy he was, so I felt I needed to make him aware that I knew that. "Tristan, I've seen how your mom and Nanny treat you. They coddle you."

"They *try* to. But for a long time, they couldn't reach me 'cause I was fucking wild." All of a sudden, his facial expression changed. I'm telling you, this boy could change moods faster than my dad could change a tire…and he was pretty quick. Tristan looked very upset and he confirmed my assumption because when he spoke, his voice was trembling. "Bridget, I'm not the type of person that you think I am. I know that you like how I look on the outside, but inside…" He paused briefly. "There are parts of me that are ugly and parts that you won't understand." He knelt down in front of me and took my hands in his. Then he looked up at me and his periwinkle eyes began to burn into my chocolate ones. "Do you still wanna marry me? Do you still want me, knowing that there are things I couldn't bear to tell you…things I don't think I ever could?"

It was already too late by the time I realized that my vision was blurry. How was Tristan always able to affect me like this? I felt the urgent need to comfort him because I could tell he was in emotional pain and I knew he was still in physical pain. I laid my palm on his warm cheek and looked into his eyes with all the love I could muster. My own voice was laced with heavy emotion when I told him what I felt his heart needed to know. "Baby, listen to me. There is nothing…and I mean *nothing*…that you can't tell me. If you can't confide in me…your soul mate…then who can you confide in? I think you're beautiful inside and out, and you have a wonderful heart. I don't care if the things you've done in your past are bad. I just want you to know that you don't have to keep secrets from me." My tears were determined to fall so I didn't hold them back. "Tristan… love…that's all I was trying to make you understand earlier. That's all." I guess my words affected him because as I looked at my future husband's face, I saw that he allowed his tears to fall too. I leaned forward and kissed him gently on the lips and that's when I felt his tears intermingle with mine. When I pulled away, I whispered, "I would never tell any of your secrets for as long as I live."

Tristan looked down for a moment and then to my surprise, he quickly stood up again with his eyes ablaze. It was the strangest thing, but it seemed like all the sentimentalism that he displayed towards me just moments ago went right out the window. He turned around and yelled, "FUCK!" And he actually startled me. When he spoke his next words, his tone was angry but his voice was still on the verge of breaking. He faced me again and said, "Bridget, I'm so fucking tired of crying! And I'm tired of feeling all this emotional shit!" He may have been tired of crying but he was actually speaking through his tears. I was in total shock at how out-of-control he was and for a moment, I didn't even recognize him as the man I knew. It was almost like a different person emerged and this new Tristan was disgusted and fed up with the 'sensitive Tristan'. He hastily wiped the tears from his eyes as if they repulsed him. When he spoke again, his tone was still laced with bitterness but his voice was stronger. "You know, it was easier when I just being a slut. I didn't give a shit about anything and I shagged whoever the fuck I wanted."

Tristan was one of the most unpredictable and complicated men I've ever known. A question reached the surface of my consciousness and I wondered if maybe he was bipolar. After everything I said to him, I honestly didn't understand his outburst. I thought I had comforted and reassured him when I told him that he didn't have to be afraid to tell me anything. Did he not believe me? My mind came back to the present and to the comment he just made. I loved Tristan with all my heart and every ounce of my being, but I'll be damned if I stay with someone who doesn't really want to be with me. I wasn't a stupid woman and I was fully capable of 'reading between the lines' when it came to men. And it sure sounded like he was second-guessing his decision to be with me. If he'd rather go back to his old life, I wasn't going to stand in his way.

My voice turned hard and it seemed as if my tears had dried up on their own. "You can always go back to being a slut. No one's stopping you." Then I stood up and walked towards him. My expression was serious and my voice was absolute. "But just know this...I won't stick around. It's your choice. Tell me right now...is this the life you want...to be married to me?" And just when I was trying to keep my composure, I let my emotions overpower me again. I loved this crazy, beautiful, British boy so much that it was sickening. But I felt that I had to give him one last chance...one last chance to tell me if this was the life he wanted. And if not...well, I just prayed that my heart would mend. "Tell me now..." My voice finally cracked at the end and I wish I had been stronger. "Or let me go, Tristan."

Tristan's face was no longer angry, it was filled with sadness. In that single moment, he conveyed his feelings to me through his eyes...as he so often did, because I finally understood the reason behind his emotional breakdown tonight. Something in my chest tightened when I looked into his watery baby blues and it was almost like I was feeling his conflict. And that's exactly what it was; he was conflicted. For someone who's never been in love and has no idea what love can make you do, or how it can make you feel...I couldn't help but to feel deep sympathy for him. But what could I do to ensure he never felt this way again? How could I protect his heart? Nanny Hathaway told me to take special care of it. But a part of me started to wonder if I really could. Suddenly, my tears flowed freely as I desperately waited to hear my fate with him.

He walked away from me and stood next to the front window. He pulled the curtain aside to gaze out of the glass and I heard him sigh softly. I wrapped my arms around myself as if I was cold and I looked down at my feet. At that moment, I wished Tristan could hear my thoughts. Maybe he did, because then he finally spoke. "Nanny told me one day... about some people who go through their whole lives in heartache and they don't know why. They try to fill it with success, money, drugs, sex but nothing soothes the hurt. They even try to have relationships with other people but they never work out. The reason those people feel that way is because they're actually one half of a single soul. And until they find their other half, they'll never be happy. But if they're lucky enough to find the other half of their soul...they'll be happy and they'll feel love for the rest of their life. But the love they feel is so intense and so powerful, that sometimes it's scary. When the two people come together and become one soul...what they feel for each other is actually love in its purest form. They may feel like they can't live without the other person. And the reality is...they can't...not really."

I was still looking down at my feet as I listened to him tell Nanny's story. I guess that's why I didn't notice when he moved from the window to stand directly in front of me. I felt him take his finger and lift my chin so our eyes would meet. There was wetness on his cheeks and his eyes were still watery. He wiped the remaining tears from my cheeks but neglected to wipe his own. Then he continued to speak. "Once I told Nanny that I didn't understand my feelings for you. I told her that they scared me and that I didn't understand why I loved you so much. And this is what she told me, Bridget." Tristan began to run his fingers through my hair and gently caress my face as he spoke. "She told me not to be afraid and that there was nothing wrong with me. She told me that I found my other half and I won't have to sleep around anymore trying to stop the ache in my heart. And she was right. That's why I fell in love with you when I first met you. I didn't understand how it was possible 'cause I never believed in love at first sight. Not until Nanny told me what I had found."

Tristan smiled and slipped his arms around my waist to pull me close to him. I don't know why, but I needed to be in his arms like I needed air in my lungs. I wasted no time in closing our embrace and I heard myself start to sob in relief. He leaned his head down to kiss me firmly on the lips. When we ended the kiss, my prince continued to wipe my tears as he continued to reveal his feelings. "My father...before he became a cheating bastard...told me that a man will go through many flowers in his lifetime; probably even more weeds. But there is only one rose. And you know a rose has thorns so you won't get to it so easily. But when you do get your rose, you hold onto it...you never let it go." Tristan looked intently into my eyes and I knew at that moment that he wanted to stay with me. "You're my rose Bridget...my pretty red rose." He kissed me again and then he whispered, "That's why I'll never let you go. I wanna marry you and I wanna be with you for the rest of my life, 'cause I won't be able to truly live unless I'm with you. You make me happy."

I smiled slightly and sniffled. "Do I really make you happy? I seem to make you more upset than happy."

He put his hands on either side of my head and continued to look into my eyes...into *our* soul. "Bridget, I've never been happier in my whole life and I *swear* that's the truth. I would never wanna go back to my old life...not after feeling how wonderful this life is with you." I reached up to wipe his tears, even though most of them had already dried on his cheeks. My fingers must've aggravated a scratch, a bruise or something because I saw him flinch. Tristan looked down for a moment and when he met my eyes again, he had a sheepish expression on his face. He spoke so softly that it was almost a whisper. "Babe?"

"Hmmm?"

"My leg hurts...and the right side of my face hurts."

I laughed lightly and shook my head. After everything we went through that night, he finally admitted he was really in pain. I was about to say something out loud to that effect but I realized it actually took him a lot of 'bollocks' to admit it. I guess crying in front of me was no longer a display of weakness, but admitting to being in physical pain was. There was just no end to his inexplicable and sometimes bizarre personality. But I loved and accepted him exactly the way he was. And I wouldn't want him any other way. Besides, I was going to spend the rest of my life with this blond, sexy and wild Brit. In my heart, I wanted to be the tigress to his tiger...the Bonnie to his Clyde...the other half to his soul.

Chapter 16

WHEN TRISTAN AND I ARRIVED at Autumn's party which was taking place at a gay nightclub in West Hollywood, there was a long line of people outside waiting to get in. When he first told me where the party was, I was totally confused because Autumn was straight. But then I remembered that she has a lot of gay friends and the club was one of her favorites. She's the type of person who doesn't care what kind of club it is...as long as she can get drunk and have a good time. Tristan took my hand and we walked right up to one of the bouncers who were standing at the front door. Without saying a word, he flashed him our invitations to Autumn's party and the bouncer let us pass without a second glance.

Inside the club, the bass in the music was thumping something fierce and the tempo was fast-paced. It was dark except for the strobe lights and the bright spotlights above the cage dancers. I stared in amazement at a couple of sexy half-naked men dancing sensually in two steel cages suspended above the dance floor. I tore my eyes away from the cage dancers because Tristan took my hand again and started guiding me through the crowd. I couldn't help but notice all the men around me. Some of the men actually looked like women to which I was even more surprised. Tristan turned his head towards me and yelled over the music, "I think I see them over there!" He pointed and I followed with my eyes. I saw Autumn's unmistaken bleach-blonde head sitting in a section of tables with about ten other people. She was drinking and laughing, and I found myself eager to be included in the fun.

At one point during the night, I dragged Tristan onto the dance floor with me. We were dancing with each other and having a great time when out of the corner of my eye, someone caught my attention. I tried not to stare but it was almost like I was enraptured by him. He was tall with a lean physique and his hair was blond like Tristan's but slightly longer. I noticed his eyes were a dark shade of blue, and they were big and almond-shaped. He had pouty, naturally pink lips and my female brain began to think about how sensual they were. His face seemed very young; like he was in his early twenties. He was wearing a black short-sleeve shirt which clung to his torso very nicely and a pair of black relaxed-fit jeans. I also noticed he was sporting a couple of black necklaces; one of which had a big cowry shell as a pendant.

Oh, did I mention that he was beautiful? Now don't get me wrong... Tristan was without a doubt, the most beautiful man I've ever seen but this dancer came in at a close second. I found myself almost spellbound as I watched him become a willing slave to the rhythm of the club music. I couldn't tell if he was dancing alone because another guy was dancing in back of him very closely but he seemed oblivious. I was grateful that Tristan was dancing behind *me* and didn't notice that I was transfixed by this other boy.

I turned my body to face Tristan but my eyes kept finding their way over to this mystery guy. I looked back and forth between the two of them before finally resting my eyes on Tristan. He pulled me close to his body so we could dance more intimately and when my eyes settled upon his velvety soft lips, a vision flashed in my mind: it was Tristan and the blond boy; stark naked and sprawled out on my bed in a tangle of arms and legs. Their heads were close together because they were in the midst of a deep and passionate kiss. The imagery my brain produced caused my girly parts to become aroused. I won't deny that the idea of Tristan with another beautiful boy peaked my curiosity.

All of a sudden, I was brought back to reality but I found myself under the gaze of both Tristan and this other boy. I started to feel extremely warm and my heart began to race. It also didn't help that Tristan started to grind his hips against my pelvis and I could feel his hard steel beneath the fabric of his pants. An unexpected desire floated to the surface of my consciousness and I was trying desperately to dismiss it. With thoughts of Tristan in the heat of passion with this other boy, his seductive blue eyes on me, and the feeling of Tristan's body against mine...I could hardly catch my breath. I felt so overwhelmed that I decided it would be best to remove myself from the dance floor. I grabbed Tristan's arm and spoke in an urgent voice, "Baby, I think I need to sit down for a minute."

He quickly took my hand and guided me back towards our table. I sat there while I tried to compose myself and Tristan sat next to me with a look of concern. He asked me how I was feeling and I replied half-truthfully, "I'm fine. I just needed to catch my breath." It wasn't long until my boy-on-boy thoughts disappeared but little did I know that it would be very short-lived. For awhile, I just sat there with the rest of Autumn's party; laughing and drinking. Then I happened to glance towards the bar and I saw the fair-haired beauty again. He was standing there sipping his drink and looking out at the club scene. He was trying to be nonchalant about it but I noticed his gaze kept settling upon our group. Tristan was smoking a cigarette while he drank and socialized. I always said that he made smoking look sexy and tonight was no exception.

Suddenly, my secret desire bloomed within me again but this time I was powerless to stop it. Immediately following that feeling, came a rush of bravery and determination. I looked over at the mystery boy who seemed interested in us and our eyes met again. I flashed him a wide smile and he looked momentarily startled. Then a crooked, sexy grin slowly crept onto his face. Right at that moment, he gave me the encouragement I needed to try and fulfill my sexual fantasy. I had to discuss it with my fiancé first, so I leaned closer to Tristan and whispered in his ear, "I need to talk to you in private for a minute."

He turned to look at me and a grin appeared on his own handsome face. One of our past sexual trysts took place in the ladies room at a L.A. nightclub and I guess Tristan was under the impression that I was extending a second invitation. He whispered back brazenly, "*Do you now? You want me to shag you rotten in the loo again? Are you feeling randy, love?*" He waggled his eyebrows at me and I felt him put his hand on my bare thigh under the table. It started to slowly make its way under my skirt in a gentle caress and I felt a couple of his long fingers creep between my legs and inch towards the crotch of my panties.

I smiled as I stilled his naughty hand with my own. "No, lover-boy. I need to talk to you about something."

I took his hand; the one that now a mere centimeter away from reaching its goal and guided him towards a part of the club that was away from the loud music. We stood up against a wall and faced each other as I confessed my secret fantasy. The first step is always persuasion so I looked into his baby blues and trailed my fingers down the side of his face in a feather-light touch. My fingers followed a path across his curved lips and over his strong chin. I tried to make my voice soft and sweet when I began. "Baby, there's something I want you to do for me."

He stepped even closer to me and reached out to caress my cheek with the back of his hand. His own voice was soft when he replied, "I'll do anything for you, love. Just name it."

I paused before I dropped the bomb on my unsuspecting fiancé. "I saw this really cute guy out there and I want to see if he'd come home with us." I returned one of his signature gestures by waggling my eyebrows at him.

Tristan's eyes widened in shock but the look was quickly replaced by confusion. "Wait...what?" Suddenly, his expression turned serious and he put his hands on my shoulders. "Bridget, I love you...you know that. More than anything in the world---"

"I know, baby." I reached up and cupped his face in my hands. "I love you too."

"But I'm not letting another bloke shag you. I'm not sharing you. So there's no way in hell that I'm doing a threesome. Call me a selfish bastard...I don't care. I'm sorry love, but that's where I draw the line."

Oh how I was looking forward to Tristan's reaction when I dropped my second bomb on him. First I smiled deviously because he had absolutely no idea what I was really asking. Then I lowered my voice and laced it with a seductive tone as I finally elaborated on my fantasy. "Baby, I don't want to shag him." His look of confusion appeared once more and I laughed inwardly. "I want *you* to shag him...and I want to watch." His expression of utter shock had returned so I felt I needed to explain. "Look, we're getting married in two weeks and I want to get this urge out of my system before then. Plus, it's my fantasy to see you with another guy and you said you'd do anything for me."

As I was explaining to Tristan what I wanted him to do for me, he started chuckling and shaking his head in amusement. The volume of his voice increased until his chuckle turned into a full-on outburst of laughter. His voice was loud when he asked, "Are you fucking serious?!?"

His laughter was contagious and I found myself laughing with him. "Yes, I'm serious! I want to watch you enjoy yourself with another guy."

After his laughter died down, a smile remained on his face. He looked into my eyes for a moment before he gave me his answer. "Alright, if the bloke is down for it...then I'll shag him for you. Just point him out."

In my excitement at Tristan agreeing to fulfill my fantasy, I squealed in delight and tilted my head up to kiss him firmly on the lips. Then I took his hand and my feet moved quickly as I guided him back towards the bar where I last saw the pretty blond boy. He was still standing in the same spot but he was talking to another guy. I rudely pointed at him and said excitedly, "That's him! The one standing over there by the bar with the black shirt."

I looked up at Tristan to see his reaction and he seemed to be studying him. Then he said humorously, "He's a good-looking bloke...in that poofy sort of way."

I laughed and replied, "You're *pretty* yourself Mr. Hathaway."

Tristan suddenly looked affronted. "Oh no I'm not!"

Either Tristan was in denial or he really didn't know what the word 'pretty' meant when applied to a male. At that moment, I felt I needed to make him aware of himself. "Oh yeah? Well, what about that time you told me you got passed over for a role because the director said to your face that you were too *pretty?*" He was speechless immediately after I refreshed his memory and I felt mighty smug. "Yeah. See, I'm not the only one who thinks so." I was still feeling courageous too so I looked over at the Blond and said, "I'm going over there to try and proposition him." I looked up at Tristan to see his reaction again and I was surprised to see that he was looking at him too.

Without taking his eyes off him, Tristan nodded and gave me the go-ahead. "Okay. If you need me, I'll be over at our table." As I started to walk away towards the bar I heard him yell, "And don't think I didn't notice he's blond like me!" I turned my head around and smiled sheepishly while Tristan wore a smug expression of his own. I immediately thought to myself: *'Touché Mr. Hathaway.'*

Unfortunately, my courage began to diminish the closer I got to the bar. I couldn't believe what I was about to do. And just when I started having second thoughts, I found myself standing right in front of Tristan's potential bedmate. He looked over at me and now that I saw his face close up, I realized he was just as pretty as Tristan. He smiled and for some reason I couldn't speak. I just looked up at him with wide-eyes and my mouth slightly agape. He looked over at the guy he was talking to and shrugged in confusion. Then they started laughing but when he laughed, it sounded boyish. And when he spoke, the voice that came out of his mouth was exactly the same. "Hi."

I mentally smacked my forehead before I finally opened my mouth to begin to tell him what I desired from him. "Hi. Um...I was wondering..." I paused and laughed lightly out of pure nervousness. Then I started fidgeting. "I was wondering...uh...if I could...like...talk to you for a minute." I was so relieved when I finished my sentence because it was actually excruciating for me. I noticed my palms were sweating so I quickly wiped them on my skirt.

"Yeah, sure." His voice was light and airy with a tinge of amusement. He was probably amused by the fact that a girl approached him in a gay club.

"Um, I kind of wanted to talk to you alone. I mean, if that's alright with your..." I looked over at the guy he was talking to moments ago because I wasn't sure if he was his boyfriend, his date, or someone he was trying to hook up with.

To my relief, the guy shrugged indifferently and replied, "Hey, fine by me." He looked over at the Blond and said, "Talk to you later." And then he walked away.

Pretty Boy was looking at me expectedly and I found myself enraptured by him yet again. He had very kissable lips and I imagined them sealed to Tristan's soft lips. I mentally slapped myself again and reminded myself that I was here on 'official business'. I felt I needed to introduce myself so I said, "Um, I'm Bridget by the way." I smiled and tried to make it seem genuine even though I was scared shitless.

He smiled again and I noticed he had perfectly straight, white teeth. "Nice to meet you, Bridget. I'm Justin."

Right at that moment, I remembered how Tristan is always one to get to the point. I decided to take a page from his book so I said, "Look, this may sound crazy and I want you to know that I've never done this before but..." I paused and took a deep breath. Then I attempted to proposition a total stranger into having sex with my fiancé. "I wanted to know if I could take you home with me and my fiancé."

Justin's reaction really didn't surprise me because I would've reacted the same way if I was in his shoes. His eyes widened and his mouth dropped in sheer disbelief. Then it sounded like he was choking on a laugh. "Excuse me? You want me to have sex with you and your fiancé?"

I shook my head quickly and put my hands up in defense. "No! Not with me...with *him*." I was suddenly filled with embarrassment so I cast my eyes downward as I disclosed the last part of my request. "And I'd just be watching." I looked up to see his reaction and he was just staring at me in complete shock.

And just like the changing of the tides, the look of shock disappeared and he seemed to be scrutinizing me with his eyes. He tilted his head to the side and the gesture reminded me all too much of Tristan. Then he asked, "Is your fiancé the guy you were dancing with?"

"Yes, his name is Tristan." As soon as I said that, it looked like the wheels were turning in Justin's head and I was hoping that I wasn't far from closing the deal. I figured he would need another visual of Tristan so I quickly pointed towards Autumn's party and yelled, "Actually, he's over there!"

Justin craned his neck to look over at our table and then he looked back at me with me grin. "Yeah, I noticed you dancing together. I have to admit, you're both pretty hot."

His compliment caused me to laugh again and it also seemed to ease some my anxiety. I decided to return the compliment so I mustered up some audacity and said, "Well, if the way you dance is any indication of way you move in the bedroom then I'm *definitely* talking to the right guy." I put some icing on the cake by ending the compliment with a wink. It worked like a charm because a shy smile graced his handsome features and he rewarded me with a rosy blush. I couldn't help but notice how young he looked and my curiosity got the better of me. "Say, how old are you?"

"Twenty-one," he replied casually.

"Oh. So...do you think you'd be interested?" Because I was inexperienced at propositioning people and I had no idea what I was doing, I almost foiled the deal by saying, "I could pay you if you want." By the reaction on Justin's face, I knew I just insulted him. I quickly backpedaled and said, "Wait, I mean...I didn't mean that! Oh shit." I put my head down, closed my eyes and covered them with my hand. Then I took another deep breath and tried to speak respectfully. "I really didn't mean to say that. I'm sorry." I chanced a glance at him from between my fingers and I saw that his brow was knitted tightly together. I felt bad for insinuating that he was a 'rent-boy' so I continued to apologize. "You're not a prostitute, Justin and I didn't mean to make it seem like I was trying to buy you. I'm really sorry; I don't know what I'm doing."

I sighed and started looking around the club as I tried to think of what to say to salvage the deal. I spoke quietly and honestly when I admitted, "I just think you're really attractive and I'd like very much to watch you have sex with my fiancé. You're both beautiful and it's actually my fantasy to see two beautiful men together."

I waited in anticipation as Justin processed my offer in his head. He surprised the hell out of me when he said casually, "Sure, I'll do it."

When he finally gave me his consent, I released a breath that I didn't even know I was holding. Then I smiled widely and exclaimed, "Great! Thank you Justin!" I was so happy that I almost hugged him. But instead, I took his hand to guide him towards our table and introduce him to the other blond boy he'd be sleeping with tonight.

I attempted to pull him along but I noticed that he wouldn't budge. I released his hand and turned back around to face him. I could tell he was feeling apprehensive because he averted his eyes from me and started looking down at his feet. I approached him slowly and he looked up at me and spoke very softly. "Bridget, you should know...I've never done this before either." My eyes widened because I thought he was telling me that he was a virgin to homosexual sex. He must've noticed my expression because he quickly added, "No, I mean...I've never had anyone ask me if they could take me home to have sex with their..." He paused just to look at me and I truly saw the youthfulness in his eyes.

I took his hand again and smiled warmly. I had a sudden urge to caress his lovely face but I didn't think he'd appreciate that and I wasn't sure if Tristan was watching us. I tried to reassure him by saying, "Justin, it's okay sweetie. I understand if you don't really want to do this. I mean... you don't even know me."

"I wanna do it...really, I do. I just want you to know that this is new for me." He let go of my hand and put his hands in his front pockets which made him look even more boyish. "Tristan is cool with this? I take it he's bi, right?"

That question still remained a mystery to me so I answered truthfully when I said, "Uh, I don't know for sure if he's bi but...yeah, he's cool with this. He knows it's my fantasy and he wants to fulfill it for me."

All of a sudden, a smile lit up Justin's beautiful face and this time he took *my* hand. "Well, since you seem like such a nice girl and your fiancé is totally hot...I wanna fulfill your fantasy too."

I took Justin over to Autumn's party and introduced him to everyone. I've never seen Tristan act shy before and it actually touched my heart. When Justin said hello to him, Tristan greeted him the same but quickly averted his eyes. I sat on one side of Tristan and asked Autumn's friend to move down a seat so Justin could sit on his other side. Tristan really wouldn't talk to him so I communicated to Justin with my eyes and jerked my head towards Tristan. I was asking Justin if he'd try to engage in conversation with him. He quickly picked up on the hint and it wasn't long until he was able to get Tristan to talk to him. I made eye contact with him again and gestured with my hands for him to move closer. I was relieved when he did and Tristan didn't try to recoil from him.

When they both reached for the plate of nachos at the same time and their hands touched, I almost squealed out loud in joy. And the fact that neither of them tried to pull their hand away, made me giddy in my chair. I sat there with an approving smile on my face as I watched the two boys warm up to each other and I found myself even more anxious to take Justin home with us.

When Tristan and I announced that we were leaving and taking Justin with us, I made the mistake of making eye contact with Autumn. She smirked and gave me a knowing look before she batted her eyelashes innocently. Did she know what the three of us were about to do? Just as we were walking away, I heard her yell, "Have fun!" I whipped my head around to look at her with wide-eyes and she just winked at me. Yep, she knew.

Because my car is a two-seater, Justin had to follow us home in his own car. Once we got back to our apartment, we immediately went into the bedroom. It was quiet for a moment as the three of us just looked at each other. I was thankful to Tristan for being the one to break the silence. "So babe, do you wanna direct us or do you want us to do whatever we want?"

"Uh, do whatever you want." I sat down on the bed and smiled up at both of them. "I'll just enjoy the show." The suspense was actually killing me. For a minute, a part of me felt like I wasn't really there. I wasn't really about to witness Tristan have sex with another guy; it was all a dream. But when I saw Tristan move in close and slip his arms around Justin's waist...I knew it was for real.

They were exactly the same height and I watched as Tristan embraced him but not too tightly. Justin put his arms around Tristan and that's when it happened: they kissed each other on the mouth. Before I could stop myself, I blurted out in total shock, "Oh my God!" I heard Tristan chuckle and then he looked over at me with a smile. "I'm sorry, I'm sorry." I did the zipper motion against my lips to indicate that I would remain quiet.

Justin started to laugh too but he was quickly silenced when Tristan placed his mouth on his again. They had just begun but it was honestly one of the sexiest things I've ever seen. Tristan kissed him deeply, slowly and deliberately. I saw him take one of Justin's plump lips into his mouth and suck on it gently. I actually envied Tristan at that moment because I secretly desired Justin's pouty lips. Their mouths slanted over each other's repeatedly and I could hear soft moans escaping their throats. They both had boyish voices so it was hard to distinguish between them. And because the room was so quiet, I could hear their lips smacking.

I scooted along the edge of the bed until I was sitting right next to where they were making out. The bedroom was fully illuminated so I could see their tongues twirling around and darting back and forth into each other's mouths. Justin reached up and ran his fingers through Tristan's hair and I noticed Tristan pull him closer to his body. His embrace tightened and his hands began to roam up and down Justin's back. I kept chanting in my head: '*Take off your clothes*' and they must've heard me because they began to slowly undress one another. Every now and then as an article of clothing would drop to the floor, their mouths would find each other and they'd resume their passionate kissing. It wasn't long until they were both completely naked and at that point, I was completely in awe.

Once their clothing was removed, I realized that they were so similar in physical appearance that it was scary. Their vanilla skin tones were basically the same and they both had dark blond pubic hair. The only real difference between them was that Tristan's physique was more muscular and his arms were graced with tattoos whereas Justin's weren't. They embraced each other again and their kissing became more intense; as did the moaning. I looked down and I saw their erections...practically the same color and size...rubbing together and suddenly my breathing increased. I covered my mouth with my hand to keep from yelling out in surprise again.

Suddenly, Justin reached down and grasped Tristan's erection and I felt a lump catch in my throat. I stared with wide-eyes as I watched this youth pleasure my fiancé in a way that only I did. He continued to deep-kiss Tristan as he stroked his hardness in a firm grip from base to tip. Before I could stop myself, I whispered to Justin, "Brush your thumb over the top...my prince likes that."

Justin followed my instruction immediately and his actions elicited a deep moan from Tristan. Justin started to increase his pace and Tristan broke the kiss and groaned in pleasure, "Ohhhh fuuuck." He closed his eyes and I noticed his breathing become labored. I looked down at what was enclosed around Justin's fist and I noticed Tristan's erection was leaking with arousal. Justin's hand was glistening with it and I was shocked once more when I saw him take some of Tristan's essence and glide it over his own aching hardness. Tristan has always been the perceptive type, so it didn't take him long to reach down and grasp Justin's weeping erection and repeat the same motion that was being done to him.

For the next minute, I watched in sheer fascination as these gorgeous boys masturbated one another while they kissed fiercely. I found myself getting so turned on that I could feel my clit harden. I swallowed thickly and squashed down the desire to reach out and touch the beautiful display in front of me. I reminded myself that I wanted to be an observer in this homo-erotic sexscapade and I was determined to let the two boys enjoy themselves.

Tristan pulled away first and they were both breathing hard. His azure eyes connected with Justin's indigo and I noticed their manhoods were both coated with their arousal and standing proud against the dark blond of their groins. I couldn't help but smile inwardly when I saw that my baby was slightly bigger. Tristan moved towards the bed and I quickly scooted out of the way. I sat Indian-style at the foot of our queen-size bed and watched him lay down on his back to present himself, and Justin crawl up the bed on his hands and knees like a lithe feline. They seemed to have some sort of wordless communication between them because Justin knew exactly what Tristan wanted. He placed a kiss on Tristan's lips before he moved down to lay himself between his legs.

Now, I've heard of people 'deep-throating' before but I've never been able to do it myself. But when I saw Justin take the entire length of Tristan's swollen member into his mouth...I realized he was better skilled at oral sex than I was. He sucked him slowly but firmly and I saw Tristan reach out and grab the comforter in a tight grip. Justin cupped his sac with one hand and squeezed it gently while his hand stroked Tristan's rigid shaft and his plump lips traveled up and down its length. Tristan whimpered in wanton passion and began to lift his hips slightly off the bed to match his rhythm. I looked over at his face and I could tell he was taking great pleasure in receiving a blow-job from another boy. I felt flushed with heat, and the crotch of my panties felt snug and slightly damp. I was so aroused, that the womanly flower between my legs was already oozing its nectar.

Tristan released his grip on the comforter to thread his fingers through Justin's wheat-colored hair that was so similar to his own. At that moment, I realized how gentle Tristan was being with this boy. Not once did I see him try to dominate him or display any rough behavior towards him. It actually warmed my heart and I gazed adoringly at the beautiful Brit who was fulfilling my fantasy right before my very eyes. It wasn't until I turned my attention back on Justin and saw him dart his tongue into the sensitive opening on the tip of Tristan's penis, that I heard him cry out loudly in extreme pleasure. I smiled because I knew that was my prince's favorite thing. All of a sudden, he reached down to grab Justin's head and he spoke in an urgent and breathless voice, "Stop! I don't wanna cum yet."

Then Justin did something I'd never seen before; he quickly enclosed his thumb and index finger around the base of Tristan's erection and squeezed. Then he looked up at Tristan and asked, "Are you okay now?" Tristan took a few breaths to recover from almost reaching his climax, before he nodded and sat up. Justin lifted himself from his position on the bed and their lips met again briefly.

They switched positions but Tristan sat between Justin's legs and spread them slowly. Justin didn't resist and he actually opened his legs wide to invite Tristan to do whatever he wanted. Their eyes met and Tristan pulled his body towards him to allow Justin's legs to rest on his hips. Tristan took advantage of the position because he began to stroke Justin's erection up and down in a quick but firm grip. Justin moaned and closed his eyes as he enjoyed the sensation. The entire scene was so arousing, that I found myself fighting the sudden urge to turn their coupling into a threesome.

While Tristan continued to pleasure him, he looked over at me and asked, "Babe, could you get a condom off the nightstand please?" As soon as he said that, I saw Justin's eyes snap open. I reached over towards the nightstand and took a condom out of a small, shallow glass bowl. I took the liberty of opening it myself and then he commanded me gently, "Give it to Justin." I smiled and handed the condom to Justin and he looked over at Tristan for further instruction. Tristan told him exactly what to do. "Now put it on me." Tristan always likes for me to put the condom on him before we make love, so I figured it was only right that Justin assume the duty. After Justin rolled the condom on him, Tristan kissed him in thanks before he laid back down. This time I saw Justin grab the comforter but I also noticed his eyes widen slightly. He seemed afraid and I was about to alert Tristan but I wasn't exactly sure that's what he was feeling.

Tristan took some of Justin's arousal and smeared it over his puckered entrance to lubricate him. As soon as Tristan tried to penetrate him, Justin confirmed my assumption. He quickly sucked some air between his teeth and I saw his knuckles turn white as he held onto the comforter in an almost death-like grip. Tristan heard the sound and looked up at him with concern. "Are you alright, mate? You're really tight."

Justin's eyes were squeezed shut but he slowly opened them and looked down at Tristan. His lips were a thin line and he nodded his head before he replied quietly, "Yeah, I'm okay."

Tristan looked at him skeptically and tried to penetrate him again. I moved closer and saw that he only got the head inside before Justin groaned in pain. His reaction caused Tristan to cease his actions once more. "Justin, am I hurting you? Tell me the truth."

He didn't answer right away; he just looked back and forth between me and Tristan and we were looking back at him with identical looks of concern. Then he cast his eyes towards the ceiling and sighed. His voice was quiet when he admitted, "It's just...I haven't done this in a long time."

Right after Justin's admittance, I saw Tristan slide the condom off and toss it on the bed. He replied to Justin in an equally soft voice, "Then I won't shag you, mate." The next thing I knew, Tristan put his left middle finger in his mouth and sucked on it for a couple seconds. When he pulled it out, it was covered thoroughly in saliva. I had no idea what he was about to do but it wasn't long until the mystery was revealed. Although he didn't put his erection inside Justin, he didn't hesitate to put his finger inside him. He prodded and poked at Justin's opening for a moment and then he gently slid his long, thin finger inside but just up to the second knuckle. I quickly assessed Justin's reaction and when I saw that his eyes were closed but there wasn't an expression of pain on his face, I assumed he was okay.

I turned my attention back on Tristan and I saw him turn his finger upwards and make some sort of fingering motion inside him. It wasn't until I heard Justin cry out loudly for the first time, that I realized Tristan was doing something extremely pleasurable. The sound of Justin's voice startled me but I was actually glad to hear him being so vocal. Tristan didn't let up on the fingering action and he used his right hand to resume stroking Justin's erection. Justin was moaning louder and louder, while his legs began to tremble. I looked at his face and his expression was one of absolute bliss. I couldn't help but wonder what Tristan was doing to him. All of sudden, Justin started to express exactly what he was feeling. "Ahhhhhh...that feels sooooo good."

Tristan began to talk back to him and I found myself enjoying the sexy, dirty boy-talk. "You like that, huh? You like it when I wank you off? You feel my finger inside your tight little hole?"

"Yeah. Please don't stop."

"Don't worry, I'm not gonna stop. I'm not gonna stop until I see you erupt all over my fucking hand."

Justin released a deep throaty moan and I noticed him begin to wrap his long legs around Tristan's waist. "Right there...ohhhhhh...just like that. You're hitting it right there. Ahhhh...jerk me faster!"

Tristan complied immediately and sped up the pace. "Like this? Is this the way you like it?"

"Ohhhhhh yeah. It feels soooo good."

Justin started whimpering and breathing fast and I started getting really turned on. I stared in complete wonder at what the two boys were doing in front of me and I whispered to myself in disbelief. "Oh my God."

Tristan kept his word and continued jerking and fingering his new boy-toy at a rapid pace. But when he said, "Are you gonna cum for me? Cum for me, Justin. Give it to me." Justin reached the edge of his sexual plateau and it was all over.

Justin cried out in passion, and right at that moment, Tristan pulled his finger out and Justin sat up with lightening fast speed and wrapped his arms around him. I sat there staring with wide-eyes because I realized the finale was steadily approaching. To my extreme surprise, Tristan quickly grabbed both of their rock-hard erections in his large hand and masturbated them together. Justin kept him in a tight embrace that made them look like they were welded together. Their mouths seemed almost magnetized because the kissing was intense and almost bruising. Tristan stroked their manhoods faster and faster and they moaned into each other's mouths in absolute pleasure. Both of their masculine ivory bodies were now glistening with sweat and their pelvises were bucking at a pace that was frenzied and almost desperate. They were completely lost in each other and the whole act was so passionate that I could actually feel their sexual energy engulfing me.

I lifted myself onto my knees and moved right next to them to watch the magnificent spectacle from a front row seat. I was captivated when my fiancé brought them both to sexual completion. One, two, three more strokes were all it took to send the blond angels into sheer orgasmic ecstasy. When they came, they unsealed their lips from one another and cried out to the heavens that created them. The tattooed angel tried desperately to hold onto their almost identical male parts as they finally erupted on each other...together. Thick spurts of creamy white flowed all over the tattooed angel's hand and covered both of their throbbing members. The younger angel whimpered as his orgasm ripped through his beautiful body and the tattooed angel comforted him by quickly embracing him with both of his strong arms. They gasped, they moaned, they trembled, and they held onto each other as wave after wave of physical pleasure washed over them. I was surprised to see both of them squirt even more of their divine essence all over each other's flat stomachs as they rode the rest of their shared orgasm. The angels' cries of passion filled the bedroom tonight and will forever be burned into my memory.

Soon they started to come down from their climax and the only sound in the room was their heavy breathing. Tristan released Justin from his embrace and Justin fell back onto the bed and tried to catch his breath. Tristan was still sitting on the bed but his head was down and I watched as his shoulders and chest rose and fell with each deep breath. A few seconds later, he flopped down onto the bed next to Justin to lie on his back. I knelt there for a moment and just looked at them in astonishment. They were both pleasantly flushed from exertion and truly resembled a pair of lustful angels.

I laid down next to Tristan and I put my arms around his body and kissed his chest lovingly. He embraced me and I wished he would wrap his secret wings around me. When I looked up at his face, he was looking down at me with a grin on his face and I could tell he was fully satiated. He kissed the top of my head and spoke in a raspy, sexy voice. "How was that, love? Did you enjoy the show? Did we fulfill your fantasy?"

"Yes! Baby, that was amazing!" I sat up and looked over at Justin and he was looking back at me with a lazy, yet satisfied smile on his face. "Justin...thank you, sweetie."

Justin's voice was laced with post-sex hoarseness too and he sounded breathless when he replied, "Anytime, Bridget...anytime." He laughed softly which caused me and Tristan to start laughing with him.

I looked back and forth between them and smiled widely. Then I shook my head in disbelief. "Wow, I can't believe it. That was so much more than I expected. Not to mention, it was the hottest thing I've ever seen in my life! What was that you were doing to Justin that drove him crazy?"

Tristan grinned mischievously. When he replied, his voice took on a British upper-class accent. "That was called 'massaging the prostate', darling."

Justin started laughing again. "That's like the most intense pleasure you can give to a guy."

My eyes widened with intrigue after receiving this new information and I slowly turned my head to look at Tristan. Our eyes met and I smiled deviously because I planned on trying that technique on him. And judging from the look on his face...he knew it too. I leaned down to kiss my fiancé properly and then I murmured against his lips, "Thank you, baby."

Tristan pecked my lips once more and replied, "You're welcome, love. I told you I'd do anything for you. Since it was your fantasy...I wanted it to be good. And I wanted you to remember it always."

"It was beyond good and I'll always remember it," Justin remarked. Tristan and I laughed again.

I looked into Tristan's eyes, which reminded me so much of the sky on a clear summer day, and spoke from my heart. "Tristan, I will always remember this night for as long as I live. No one has ever fulfilled any of my sexual fantasies. You're the first and you made it very special for me." Then I looked over at Justin and agreed with him. "And yeah, it was beyond good." I looked back and forth between them again and I was suddenly filled with gratitude. "Both of you are absolutely beautiful and what you allowed me to see tonight was better than I could've ever dreamed. The way you were so tender with each other..." I paused and put my hand to my chest because the boys truly rendered me speechless.

I laid down next to Tristan because I just wanted to hold my baby and let him sleep peacefully in my arms, but it seemed that he had more energy to spare. "Babe, if you take your clothes off...I'll take care of you next. You know I only need a few minutes to recharge."

I knew Tristan was exhausted and he really did bring me pleasure even if he never touched me. But I didn't want tonight to be about me; I wanted it to be about him. I had no intention of being involved because I wanted to watch the love of my life enjoy himself with another beautiful male of my choice. That was my desire...my fantasy. I considered Tristan's offer and decided that I was content without having sex with him. I looked up at my soon-to-be-husband and smiled warmly. I reached up to smooth the hair back from his sweaty brow and then I leaned over and repeated the action on Justin. Then I sat up and quickly stripped down to my undies and I noticed both of the boys were watching me intently.

They both wore identical expressions of surprise when they realized I wasn't getting completely naked.

I hopped off the bed to turn off the wall light. Then I climbed back into bed and laid on the other side of Tristan so that he was still in the middle. When I started pulling back the comforter, I felt both of them shift on the mattress so we could get under the covers. "Let's just go to sleep boys," I said quietly once we were all snuggled in. "And sweetheart, I've already been satisfied tonight and I have absolutely no complaints. You and Justin have made me a very happy woman."

I put my arms around my love once more and laid my head on his warm, bare chest. Tristan held me in his strong, tattooed arms and I closed my eyes to allow his wonderful heart to lull me to sleep. Suddenly... in the darkness of the bedroom...I heard a boyish voice speak. It wasn't laced with a British accent so I knew it was Justin. "You know Tristan, when I first saw you...I thought you would totally dominate me."

"Tristan only dominates me," I interjected with a laugh.

Justin laughed softly before he continued speaking to Tristan. "When I saw your tatts and I saw you smoking and drinking beer...I started thinking, 'Yep, he's a top.' Then when I heard you talk and how much you swear...I was like, 'Oh man, he's a British bad-boy.' I thought once I went home with you guys, you would be pulling my hair and pushing me around."

Tristan's voice sounded surprise when he asked, "Do I really come across like that?"

"Yeah, you do. But you know what?" Justin paused. "You were really nice to me. And I just wanna say...thanks."

I kissed Tristan's chest again and said, "Awww, baby" in the darkness.

Now I couldn't be sure, but I was willing to bet that Justin's gratitude made Tristan feel awkward because his response was, "Eh, you're welcome, mate. Now can we *please* go to sleep? I'm fucking exhausted."

The next morning I woke up first. After I carefully extracted myself from Tristan's embrace, I was pleasantly surprised to see Justin's head resting on his shoulder. I smiled at the scene before me and combed my fingers lightly through Justin's hair. Then I repeated the same action on my beloved. With their heads so close together in the morning sunlight, I could really see how the color of their hair was very similar. As I gazed at the two blond angels slumbering next to each other in bed, I realized that they looked even more beautiful.

I climbed out of the bed and put on my robe and slippers. After I brushed my teeth, I went into the kitchen to make the three of us some breakfast. I was almost done frying the bacon, when the tattooed angel walked into the kitchen. He was still naked as the day he was born, his light blue eyes were adorably puffy from sleep, and his golden hair was ruffled which gave him a 'bed-head' appearance. He placed a soft kiss on my forehead and greeted me in his boyish voice that was laced with a sexy British accent. "Mornin', love." He sniffed the air and a smile graced his lovely, Nordic features. "It sure smells good in here."

I smiled in appreciation. "Good morning, baby." Then I asked out of curiosity, "Where's Justin?"

He was pouring himself a cup of coffee when he replied, "The poor lad's still asleep. I think I wore him out last night." He chuckled softly.

All of a sudden, my thoughts began to wander again. I started to recall last night's events and I remembered how comfortable he was with Justin. It was almost like the whole homosexual experience wasn't new to him. Then I started wondering if maybe he was just acting. Maybe that's why he put on such a good show. A peculiar question started to brew in my mind and I wondered how he knew about massaging the prostate. Did a woman do that to him in the past or was it another man? Then I remembered that he never answered my question about being bisexual and I never brought up the subject again. I figured now was as good a time as any to get a final confirmation. He came near me to swipe an already-cooked strip of bacon from the plate next to the stove. Before he walked away, I looked up at him and said, "So, last night...you seemed as if you've done that before."

He held my gaze for a few seconds while he slowly chewed the bacon in his mouth. Then he averted his eyes from me and walked away. I had to know this time. I wasn't going to let him keep the secret from me any longer. His back was to me and I spoke softly as I desperately tried to get him to admit the truth. "I won't judge you, sweetheart. Not ever...not for anything. I mean, how could I after what you did for me last night?"

He turned around to face me and he tilted his head to the side to regard me for a moment. Then he slowly walked back over to me and like always, I couldn't keep my eyes from roaming all over his nude Adonis form. His voice was low and his tone was serious when he asked, "You swear?"

"Try me. Look in my eyes, Tristan. You'll know if I'm judging you."

He licked his lips briefly and I saw him swallow hard as his azure eyes began to search mine like he's done so many times before. What he saw behind them must've made him feel secure because finally he said, "Maybe I have." My first and only reaction was to smile because I was just happy to know the truth at last. He actually looked relieved and he smiled back at me which caused his cute dimple to make an appearance on his left cheek.

As we gazed into each other's eyes for that brief moment, I began to appreciate all the different facets of Tristan's personality. And I'll admit that deep down inside me...I had a feeling he was bisexual all along. Tristan is very carefree so he's always struck me as the kind of person who would see past gender and just see another *person* who he's attracted to. He said he doesn't label himself anything so maybe my assumption about him was correct. And maybe that's why he was so comfortable being sexually intimate with Justin. I decided not to press him any further because I knew that was the best admission I was going to get out of him. I really didn't have a choice because he seemed to be telling me without saying the actual words, that the subject regarding his bisexuality was closed. He shifted his eyes back to the plate of bacon and said, "So babe, is breakfast ready yet? You know your prince is hungry."

Chapter 17

Our ten and a half-hour nonstop flight from Los Angeles landed, the six of us in England shortly before noon on the day before the wedding. Jake was able to rent a van to accommodate us and the vast amount of luggage we all had. The wedding was on a Friday and we were only staying in Brighton for the weekend. We planned to catch a flight back to The States on Sunday morning because the majority of us had to return to work that week. As we started to drive towards Brighton, Autumn and my mother were in absolute awe. I couldn't stop smiling as I listened to them say repeatedly, "Ooh, look at that!" and "Wow, this place is amazing!"

Jake pulled into the driveway of his and Tristan's childhood home and as soon as we all got out of the van, my mother said to Tristan in an almost breathless voice, "Tristan, you have such a beautiful home."

Tristan smiled and replied, "Thanks Mrs. Monahan." It was at that moment that Kate came out of the front door to greet us.

She had a bright smile on her face and she looked like she was trying to contain her happiness. I was surprised when she headed straight towards me and said, "Oh, you're all here!" She gave me a tight hug and I embraced her just the same. When she pulled away from me, she smoothed my hair and asked, "So...are you excited?"

I smiled as I looked at her beautiful face. "Yeah, I am. But I'm also a little nervous. I can't believe I'm going to be Tristan's wife tomorrow."

She embraced me again and patted me on the back. "Don't be nervous, love. You were meant to be together. And you're going to have your family right there with you."

When she released me, my parents came over to us. I was so elated to finally introduce them to Kate that I was practically beaming. "Mom, Dad...this is Tristan's mom Kate. Kate, this is my mother Sharon and my father Brad."

Kate, being the kind of woman she is, hugged my mother first and said, "It's so nice to finally meet you, Sharon. I'm so happy that our children are getting married."

"Nice to finally meet you too," my mother said with genuine happiness.

When she released my mother, she looked at her with a warm smile. "Bridget is such a beautiful girl. Whenever she comes to visit us, I don't want her to leave. I absolutely adore her." Then she looked at me with motherly affection and I couldn't stop the tears that began to cloud my vision. "She's very special to us." She looked back at my mother and said, "Well, now I see where Bridget gets her lovely red hair." I started to feel very lucky that I was about to acquire such a wonderful mother-in-law.

My mother smiled at the compliment and replied, "And I see where Tristan gets his good looks." She laughed lightly. "I'm also excited about the wedding. My husband and I have really been looking forward to the day where our Bridget would find that someone special to settle down with. And you have a very lovely son, Kate. Ever since Bridget has been with Tristan...I've never seen her happier." Both Kate and my mother looked at me with loving expressions and I couldn't help but to smile shyly.

Kate put her hand out to my father. "Nice to meet you, Brad."

My father shook Kate's hand and replied, "Likewise. And thank you for letting us stay in your home, Kate. We're really looking forward to getting to know the family. And I agree with Sharon one-hundred percent. Tristan is a good man; the kind you hope your daughter would choose for a husband. Oh, and I must say...you have a lovely home."

"Thank you, thank you. Let me help you with your bags." Just as Kate started to walk towards the van, she noticed Autumn and said cheerfully, "Is this the infamous Autumn?" She laughed as Autumn smiled widely.

Tristan was taking a suitcase out of van when he turned his head and smiled. "Yeah that's her, Mum."

Kate walked over to Autumn and embraced her. "I was wondering when I'd get to meet the daughter I never had. Tristan told me you're the sister I *should've* given him."

Autumn laughed and didn't hesitate to let her personality shine through. "Hey, you can always adopt me. I wouldn't mind moving to England." Kate laughed in amusement. Jake came over and hugged his mother and it wasn't long until Tristan followed suit. We all helped with the luggage and walked up to the house together.

When we got inside, Kate turned to my parents and said, "I've set you up in my room upstairs."

A concerned look appeared on my mother's face. "Oh Kate, we don't want to put you out. Really, it's no problem for me and Brad to stay at a hotel."

Kate shook her head. "Nonsense. I don't mind...not in the least. Tristan said he'd like us all to be together and I agree wholeheartedly. I'll be sleeping with Nanny. And Autumn..." She turned her heads towards Autumn. "We'll set you up on the sofa-bed if that's alright with you?"

Autumn shrugged and replied nonchalantly, "Yeah, that's fine with me."

"But you can put your things in Tristan's room." Kate headed upstairs and my parents followed her. I saw Jake follow behind them and I assumed it was because his room was in the attic.

Tristan, Autumn, and I started to walk towards Tristan's bedroom when I started thinking about Nanny's whereabouts. While we were walking down the hallway which led to his room, I thought out loud, "Where's Nanny?" Just as we were passing the door to the first-floor bathroom, the door opened and Nanny appeared. My voice was full of surprise and I exclaimed, "Nanny!" We must've startled her because she looked momentarily shocked.

"Oh my! You're all here?" She clapped her hands together and laughed in delight. "How wonderful!"

Tristan spoke and said, "Nanny, this is Autumn."

Autumn smiled brightly. "Hi Nanny."

"Oh hullo dear. Nice to finally meet you. I've heard a lot of stories about you." She smiled and her eyes crinkled in happiness.

Autumn looked over at Tristan with wide-eyes and said, "Oh no. Dude, what did you tell your grandmother about me?"

Tristan laughed and then he turned to continue walking to his room. He didn't turn his head when replied loudly, "I have no idea what Nanny's talking about!"

"Well dears, I'm going to busy meself in the kitchen. I'll make you all a nice lunch, yeah?" The mention of Nanny's cooking actually made my mouth water. "I can't wait to meet your parents, Bridget. Where are they?"

"Oh, they're upstairs with Kate."

"Well, I'm sure you'll introduce me." She smiled and patted me on the shoulder before she started walking towards the kitchen.

Once Autumn and I entered Tristan's room, we began unpacking. I unzipped my wedding dress that was still covered in white paper and looked over at Tristan with a smile. "Hmmm...I don't think I can leave this in here. I don't want you peeking." Then as an afterthought, I said, "You know we can't see each other while we get dressed for the wedding, right?"

Tristan gave me a knowing smile. "I know that, babe. We'll get ready at the hotel but in separate rooms." He held up his bag that contained his tuxedo and said, "Although...I'm hanging this up in here. I know you won't peek."

Autumn chimed in with a confused expression. "What hotel?"

"I booked me and Bridge a hotel suite for after the wedding. You know, so we can shag like fucking rabbits in private." After he spoke to Autumn, he looked over at me and waggled his eyebrows.

Even though I knew Autumn was used to the way Tristan spoke because she spoke the same way...his lewd comment caused me to flush in embarrassment. Then I started thinking that even though we would be alone in our suite, Tristan would definitely make the other guests aware of his presence when we made love.

After he hung up his tuxedo that was still in its bag, he went to sit on the bed. That's when Autumn approached him and remarked, "Tris, your mom is fucking hot. Did she ever model or anything?"

To both me and Autumn's surprise, Tristan smiled and replied casually, "Yeah, she used to back in the day."

Autumn and I looked at each other. Then I said to her, "*Now* do you see why my baby is so damn sexy? It's in his genes!" I looked over at Tristan and he was grinning in appreciation.

She laughed lightly. "Yeah, I do. I mean, I've seen her picture before but seeing her in person..." She shook her head in amazement. "I swear... if I had a mom like that, all my guy friends would wanna sleep with her."

Tristan chuckled. "Believe me, I've had some mates tell me that they would shag my mum." Autumn and I both shared identical expressions of utter shock. "But after they picked themselves up off the fucking ground, they never said that shit again." Autumn and I both laughed because we could definitely imagine Tristan punching his friend for making a suggestive comment about his mother.

Then Autumn said something that totally changed the mood in the room. "I know you hate your dad and everything but do you have any pictures of him around here?" She started turning her head as her eyes scanned his bedroom.

His voice turned hard when he replied, "No. And you won't find any in the rest of the house either." At that moment, Autumn knew the conversation was closed.

I guess she felt guilty for bringing up the subject of Tristan's father because she started looking down at her feet. Tristan got up from his spot on the bed and approached her. His voice was gentle and he put his hand on her shoulder. "Hey, do you wanna go outside and have a fag?" She looked up at him and nodded. He turned to me and asked, "Babe, do you wanna come outside with us?"

"No, that's okay. You guys go ahead. I'm going upstairs to hang my dress in your mom's room." Tristan nodded and then he and Autumn walked out to go have their cigarette. I put a few more of my clothes in the closet that needed to be hung and then I walked out of the room with my dress. I decided that it would be safe from prying eyes upstairs in Kate's closet.

When I made it to the top of the stairwell, I happened to glance to my right and I saw the door at the end of the hallway which led to Jake's room. I don't know why I wanted to go up there but something inside me wanted to talk to him. Ever since he confessed his true feelings for me, our relationship wasn't as comfortable as it once was. I noticed his conversations with me started to get shorter and shorter, and he would visit me and Tristan less and less. Deep inside, I was hurt by that because I had such a wonderful friendship with him prior to his confession. After the first time I visited their family, Jake had become the big brother I never had.

Before I knew it, my feet started moving towards the door to his attic bedroom and it was but a few seconds later that my hand was on the doorknob. I turned it slowly and when I realized it wasn't locked, I opened the door. I slowly walked up the steps and when I reached the top, I called out his name softly.

"Over here." I almost jumped out of my skin. I turned my head towards the sound of his voice and I saw him standing against the far wall on the other side of his bed. I slowly approached him as my eyes took in unfamiliar surroundings. When I spent the Christmas holidays with the Hathaways, I only saw Jake's room once. And that was when Tristan and I were up there and Jake showed me the CD's he had of some British rock bands. As I got closer to him, I noticed his suitcases on the bed and assumed he was still unpacking. They were empty so I figured he had just finished. He moved around his bed to stand next to me and then he looked down at me with a curious expression. His voice was quiet when he asked, "What are you doing up here?"

I laid my dress down on his bed and replied flippantly, "Oh, I just wanted to come up here and say 'hi.'" Then I smiled when I said, "You know, I may not see you for the rest of the day. The last time I was here with you, you seemed to always disappear like a thief in the night." He chuckled before he made himself a spot on the bed. I sat next to him and continued to playfully tease him. "I know when your old girlfriends hear that you're back in town, they're going to want to hook up with you. I know the ladies can't resist your Hathaway charm."

He smiled warmly at me until all of a sudden, he turned his head and the room was quiet for a few moments. I was about to break the silence when he spoke first. "Bridget, I just want you to know that I *am* happy you're marrying my little bro. I know things have been kinda weird between us and I know it's my fault. I'm really sorry about how I've been avoiding you."

"It's okay, Jake. But you should know that I really miss you sometimes."

He smiled again and then he said, "The other day, I was thinking about that little comment Rick made at your birthday party...when he said that Tristan would need you more. And I realized that he was right." Jake stood up and started closing the opened suitcases on his bed. "Me and Tris...we're completely different blokes. He's a lot more sensitive than I am and he needs constant reassurance and attention. And the fact that you understand him and you're patient with him...it told me that he really *did* need someone like you. He needs you more than I would if I were your boyfriend." He walked back over to me and smiled down at me. "But I still wanna be your brother." Then his expression changed to one more serious and his smile disappeared. "And I promise I won't *ever* cross that line."

I stood up and took one of his hands in both of mine. I smiled and reassured him by saying, "I know, Jake...I know. I still trust you. And I'd like very much if you'd still be my brother." He smiled back at me and I knew we were back to being brother and sister once more.

After my short visit with Jake, I went back downstairs to put my wedding dress in Kate's closet. When I got to her room, she and my parents were sitting comfortably while they laughed and talked. I hesitated before I entered because I enjoyed seeing them get along and I didn't want to disrupt the scene. Kate happened to glance in my direction and when she saw me, she exclaimed, "Oh Bridget! I was just having a very nice conversation with your parents." She must've noticed my dress in my arms because then she said, "What's that you've got there?"

"This is my dress. I wanted to keep it up here so Tristan wouldn't try to peek at it." I laughed lightly.

Kate smiled and then she moved from where she was sitting. "Oh, well I'm sure I have some room in here for your dress." She walked over to her closet and I followed her. I had no idea that when she opened the closet doors, they would lead to a huge walk-in closet which had ample space for my wedding dress. I hung my dress up and gave her my thanks before I walked over to my parents.

"Tristan's grandmother is downstairs. She's making us all lunch but I'd like to introduce you."

"Sure, sweetheart. We'd love to meet her," my mother replied.

When we all got downstairs, I had my parents follow me into the kitchen so I could introduce them to Nanny. Nanny was so delighted to meet them, and the feeling seemed to be mutual.

Once Nanny finished making lunch, everyone gathered in the dining room to eat. Tristan and I sat next to each other, and every now and then we would smile at each other. We did this because we both saw how our future in-laws were getting along so well. Jake and my father started their own conversation on the side about soccer, Kate and my mother chatted animatedly, while Nanny engaged Autumn in polite conversation. Tristan leaned over towards me and whispered in my ear, "See, I told you this would be a good idea to have everyone together." I responded by giving him a kiss on the lips because I couldn't agree with him more.

During our meal, Kate asked if everyone would like to take a drive to the pier after lunch. Everyone agreed except Jake who replied, "I can't, Mum. My mate rang me and I'm gonna meet up with them." Then he turned to look at me and winked. I took a sip of my iced tea to hide the knowing smile on my face.

After lunch, everyone minus Jake piled up in the rental van and Kate drove us down to the pier. Once we got there, Autumn and my mother seemed unable to contain their joy. Seeing my mother this happy touched a special place inside me. I knew at that moment that my family and Tristan's family was a perfect match. We all had a wonderful time and Kate seemed to be the tour guide for Autumn and my parents. Tristan and I fell behind after awhile and we slowly walked hand-in-hand and talked about tomorrow's big day.

I couldn't help but wonder if Tristan was sharing my anxiety about the wedding, so I asked, "Are you nervous about tomorrow, baby?"

To my surprise, he replied, "No, not at all, love. I'm really looking forward to getting married to you. Are *you* nervous?"

"Yeah, a little bit," I admitted.

"Why?"

"I don't know. I guess because I can't believe it's actually going to happen."

Tristan let go of my hand and put his arm around my waist as we continued to walk. He pulled me closer and I put my arm around his waist and leaned my head against him. His masculine, comforting scent mixed with the sea air, put me in a complete state of contentment. He spoke softly when he said, "You wanna know something? One night, after we had already met...I started to fantasize about marrying you. And if you wanna know the truth, I would've proposed *a lot* sooner but I was too afraid to ask you. We were just starting our relationship and I knew you would think I was rushing things. But honestly, I really *was* ready to marry you. I would've jumped at the chance if you'd let me."

Tristan's words caused me to pause my steps. I extracted myself from him and looked into his eyes. I was speechless for a moment because I couldn't believe what he had just confessed to me. He looked back at me and I saw a smile slowly appear on his face. He reached out and ran his fingers through my hair. At that moment, I found my voice. "You would've married me sooner?"

"Definitely. Or if at any moment, you asked me to marry you...I would've said 'yes'." My eyes widened in response to Tristan's words. I couldn't help but to smile lovingly up at this beautiful Brit who I'd be marrying in less than twenty-four hours. I pulled him close to me and kissed him and I honestly didn't care if people were watching.

We left the pier and headed over to Due South to meet with the wedding coordinator and receive our instructions for tomorrow. We also needed to inspect the setup for the actual wedding on the beach and the reception in the private dining room to make sure everything was satisfactory. Since Jake was the only missing party, Tristan said he would fill him in on his 'best man' duties for tomorrow. When Tristan and I saw the wedding cake, we were both pleasantly surprised and a bit shocked. It was the perfect beach wedding cake; it was a three-layer cake with an ivory colored frosting. Each layer was adorned with edible sugar seashells, starfish, and coral. There was also edible white sugar pearls strategically placed on each layer of the cake. I couldn't help but to laugh after I heard Tristan's comment. "This looks too beautiful to eat. We should just take it back home and put it in a glass case."

By the time we returned home, it was early evening. I was in the Hathaway family room with my parents and Autumn, when Tristan came in and approached my father. "Hey Dad, there's a footie match coming on the tele. You wanna catch it with me?"

My father, who had been pretty subdued during the day, perked up immediately and replied, "Sure, that sounds great!"

They both left the room and a wide smile appeared on my face because I noticed for the first time that Tristan called my father 'Dad'. I was so touched because he seemed to say it so casually and without any prior thought. I actually started getting misty-eyed and Autumn came over to me with a concerned look on her face. "You alright, Bridge?"

I nodded. "Yeah, I'm fine. I'm just happy, that's all."

Later that evening, Kate went into the kitchen to start dinner and to my surprise...my mother joined her. It wasn't long until they struck up another conversation and soon they started cooking dinner *together*. Autumn and I went outside to the back patio and we were sitting on a wicker patio sofa chatting when Tristan poked his head out the back door. "Babe, guess what?"

I turned my head towards him and I was surprised when I saw his facial expression. He actually looked...giddy. "What?"

"I just tried to go in the kitchen, and my mum and your mum both told me to get out. So you know what that means right?" I shook my head. "They're gonna have a mother-to-mother talk." It took me a moment to fully comprehend but when I did, I gasped and my hand flew up to cover my mouth. Tristan started nodding excitedly and laughed. "Yeah." Then he disappeared back inside.

My eyes were wide and I continued to stare into space in complete shock. You knew your mothers really liked each other if they wanted to be alone so they could 'talk'. Autumn's voice brought me out of my reverie. "So that's *good* news then?" Then she started laughing.

I laughed with her, when suddenly I started to remember why all of this was happening in the first place; falling in love with Tristan, him and I getting engaged and now married, meeting his wonderful family and then his family taking so quickly to my family. It was all because of Autumn. If she would've never called me that Thursday night last September and begged me to meet Tristan, I would've never met him and none of this would be happening. My life wouldn't be where it is today and I felt like I owed her so much. At that moment, I realized that I had to tell her exactly how thankful I was to her.

Once our laughter died down, I turned my body to face her and I said, "You know Aut, none of this would be happening if it weren't for you. If you never would've introduced me to Tristan, we would've never fallen in love and we wouldn't be getting married tomorrow. That one phone call you made to me actually changed my life. I feel like I owe you so much..." I paused because tears started to blur my vision. I tried to compose myself before I continued speaking. "You're the one who brought Tristan into my life and I've never been happier." I sniffled. "And I just want to say...thank you."

Autumn's own exotic hazel eyes were glassy when she smiled back at me. She sniffled too before she playfully hit me on the knee. "Aww, Bridge. You don't have to thank me. You know, it's strange but I think I'm connected to you guys somehow. I mean, why else would Tristan mention you in the dream if you weren't meant to be together? And the strange thing is, first I had the dream and the child version of him is telling me that he needs you. Then the next day he tells me that he saw you on my top friend space and how beautiful you were. I guess someone, somewhere decided to use me to make the connection between you."

After Autumn finished talking, I realized my mouth was hanging open and my eyes were wide. I couldn't help but wonder if her dream was more than just a coincidence. "You know, even when Tristan was running around being a man-whore with all these chicks, I knew there was some other reason he was doing it besides the need to satisfy his lust. It was almost like..." She paused and cast her eyes skyward as she thought of her next words. "He was using sex to fill something else he was missing. But I don't know what. A couple times when he was drunk, he told me that his heart aches for something but he didn't know why or what it was aching for."

When Autumn said her next words, I felt a chill run straight through me to the bone. "Maybe it was aching 'cause he needed you." She laughed again. "Who knows? All I do know is that ever since he met you, I've never seen him so happy."

I leaned over to hug Autumn; my second best friend (Tristan was my *best* friend) and she met me halfway. I don't know if she'll ever truly understand what an important instrument she played in helping my heart find its true love.

Jake didn't return for dinner and I wasn't really surprised. Once again, the atmosphere in the dining room was extremely pleasant. As I looked around the table at our families, a part of me wished I could enjoy more dinners like this. It was truly a comforting and joyous feeling. In the back of mind, I started planning the next Christmas holiday and I thought of asking Kate and Nanny to fly out to Sacramento. I figured it would be nice if they visited my childhood home and became the guests instead of the hostesses for once.

Late in the evening, Jake finally returned home and we all discussed the plans for tomorrow to make sure everyone was on the same page. Tristan, Jake, Autumn, and I would leave in the morning and get ready at the hotel suite while the parents got ready at the house. Then the parents would meet us at the hotel and since it was assumed Tristan would be ready first...he, Jake, Autumn, and Nanny would then leave for Due South. Once I was ready, I would leave the hotel with my parents, and Kate would drive us to Due South for the wedding. Tristan also mentioned that we could have breakfast at the hotel.

That night after I helped Autumn get settled into the sofa-bed, I went into Tristan's bedroom and my eyes fell upon a very inviting scene. The room was dim and Tristan was lying in bed completely naked with a sexy grin on his face. As tempting as my fiancé looked sprawled out on his full-size bed, I had to turn down his offer. I laughed lightly and said, "You better put some boxers on mister. We're not doing any of *that* tonight."

Suddenly, his expression turned to one of confusion and then he frowned. "What? You mean we're not gonna---"

I whispered harshly, "Are you crazy?!? My parents are upstairs Mr. I-Don't-Know-How-To-Have-Sex-Quietly!"

He scooted to the edge of the bed as I bent down to pull my pajamas out of my suitcase. His voice sounded hopeful when he asked, "But what if I put my head in the pillow?"

I whipped my head up to look at him with wide-eyes. "No! I don't want to take the chance of you accidentally taking your head *out* of the pillow." Tristan looked down in disappointment so I went over to him and caressed the side of his face. My voice was soft and my tone was apologetic when I said, "I'm sorry, baby. You're going to have to go without sex tonight. But just remember that tomorrow night you can shag me rotten."

Tristan lifted his head and grinned at me. Then he scooted back up the bed and got under the covers. "I'm not putting on any bleeding boxers though. Your cute little bum is gonna feel every inch of how fucking bad I want you tonight."

After I changed into my pajamas, I grabbed my toothbrush. I was halfway to the door when I looked back at him and smiled. "You can make me feel it all you want. I just don't want to feel any poke-poke because you're not getting any." Then I turned to open the door and walked out to the bathroom.

When I returned to Tristan's bedroom, I turned off the light and climbed into bed with him. He wrapped his arms around me so that we were in a spooning position and then he kept to his word: I felt his arousal against my butt. He rubbed himself against me once and then I heard him groan in the darkness. "Fuuuuuck, this sucks babe."

If I admitted the truth, his discomfort was partially my fault. I spoiled him sexually; whenever my beautiful Sex God wanted my body... I gave it to him. I was a *willing* love slave. I did feel bad so I whispered an apology. "I'm sorry, baby."

He paused for a moment and then he said quietly, "You know I'm addicted to you. I don't think I can sleep without having a mind-blowing orgasm first."

"I know it's difficult but just try to think of something to take your mind off me."

Tristan laughed out loud. "You're lying in my arms and you don't want me to think about you? We're getting married in a few hours and you don't want me to think about you?" He continued to laugh but he lowered his voice.

I laughed quietly. "Yeah, you're right." I paused as I tried to think of a solution to ease his sexual frustration. I turned onto my back and that caused him to release his hold on me. Then I said, "Lay your head on my chest, sweetie." I felt him shift on the bed and he put his arms around me again. When I felt the weight of his head on my breasts, I whispered, "Listen to my heart. Just relax, close your eyes and listen to it." I ran my fingers gently through his hair to aid in soothing him.

Neither of us spoke for the rest of the night. After awhile, the sound of Tristan's deep steady breathing told me that he'd fallen asleep. It wasn't long until I drifted off into a peaceful slumber myself, with thoughts of Tristan in his wedding tuxedo looking the part of a true prince.

The next morning was our wedding day. The actual ceremony was to start in the early afternoon, so Tristan, Jake, Autumn, and I had to be at the suite early enough to give us time to get ready. Tristan and I were in his bedroom and we had just finished getting dressed in our casual clothes, when he came over to me and put his arms around my waist. I closed our embrace as I put my arms around his neck. He held me close and kissed me firmly on the lips before he said softly, "You know, I'm really looking forward to you being Mrs. Hathaway."

I smiled. "Me too, baby."

"If someone would've told me this time last year, that I'd be getting married the following year...I would've said they were fucking mad."

"Who would've guessed that the two of us would marry each other?"

Tristan moved his hands and gently put them on either side of my head. He looked deep into our soul as he spoke. "It was fate, love. That's what I believe. I stopped questioning why we met, a long time ago." He paused for a second and then he tilted his head to the side to regard me. "I may sound like a complete nutter but I believe we were born for each other. Why else would we be two halves of one soul?" Before I could respond, my soon-to-be-husband leaned down and captured my mouth in a proper kiss. We almost ended up on the bed until my brain remembered that we had two other people waiting for us so we could drive to the hotel.

After Tristan, Jake, Autumn, and I retrieved our luggage which contained the things we needed for the wedding, we headed over to the hotel. Tristan was driving Kate's car and when we pulled up to the valet in front, Jake exclaimed, "Bloody hell! This is where you booked your suite?!?"

Tristan turned his head around and replied casually, "Yeah, why?" Jake didn't respond; he just shook his head in disbelief.

I turned towards Jake and asked curiously, "Why, what's the---" I didn't get to finish my sentence because one of the valet opened my door. Tristan popped the trunk and I saw a couple of bellhops take our luggage out. I also saw him give the car key to the valet and before I knew it, the valet drove the car away.

As the four of us started walking into the lobby was when I finally understood Jake's reaction. The hotel was *very* 'posh'. It made the Waldorf Astoria in New York City look like a Holiday Inn. My eyes practically popped out of my head as I stared in shock and amazement...and that was just from seeing the lobby.

I heard Autumn exclaim to my left, "Holy shit dude! I've never seen an indoor fountain so fucking big in my life!" As soon as Tristan checked in, the bellhops took our luggage to our suite. Then the four of us headed to the dining hall for breakfast.

I didn't have much of an appetite because I was so nervous about the wedding. I didn't want anything to go wrong and I began to recite our wedding vows in my head so I wouldn't forget them. Tristan must've sensed my anxiety because he reached over and put his hand on top of mine. I looked over at him and there was a loving smile on his face. He spoke gently when he said, "Don't worry, love. Everything will be fine... you'll see. You have nothing to worry about. Bridget, we're gonna be *married*." He gave me a pointed look and his azure eyes were intense. I entwined our fingers and gave his a tight squeeze.

Tristan, my other half, was able to ease my fears and I replied, "You're right, baby." Suddenly, I started to feel very hungry. "Hey, will you pass me the croissants?"

After breakfast, we headed over to the elevators to go up to the hotel suite and get ready for wedding. The suite was on the top floor and when the elevator doors opened and we stepped out into the hall, Jake let out a low whistle. When we finally made it to the door to the suite, Tristan opened the door and I swear...Autumn, Jake, and I were practically frozen on the spot. Tristan may as well have opened up the pearly gates of heaven because I think a warm golden glow was emitted from the suite when the door opened. Nobody moved for about two seconds and Jake finally broke the silence when he asked, "Bro, how much did you pay for this room?"

Tristan turned to him and smiled. "Wouldn't *you* like to know."

When we finally moved to go inside, the four of us walked around the room in amazement. It wasn't like anything I expected and I couldn't believe Tristan spent so much money for one night. Either his impulsiveness was skyrocketing or he really, really loved me. It was like a huge apartment or penthouse suite and I was in total shock. Suddenly, I heard Autumn yell from somewhere, "HOLY SHIT! CHECK OUT THIS BATHROOM!" Tristan, Jake, and I followed her voice and we found her in a huge marble and mirrored bathroom. She was sitting in the empty bathtub...wait scratch that, empty *jacuzzi*.

Tristan put his arm around my shoulder and said excitedly, "Me and you, doll. We're getting in there tonight!" Then he got in next to Autumn and I realized you could probably fit ten other people in there with them. With his arms stretched wide, he exclaimed, "Babe, look at all this room! Oh shit, can you imagine?" He waggled his eyebrows at me and I shook my head in absolute amazement.

Then I heard Jake yell from another room, "THAT'S NOTHING! LOOK AT THIS BED!" The three of us ran to where we heard his voice and when we entered the bedroom, I saw a huge California King-size bed in the middle of the room with what looked like black silk sheets.

Tristan wasted no time and he ran and jumped on the bed. I figured for all the money he spent on this suite, why shouldn't he put his boots all over it? He smiled widely and looked at me. "Bridge, come here. Get on here."

I climbed on the bed and laid down on it. When I realized how comfortable and spacious it was, I knew we'd have a spectacular wedding night. Tristan moved next to me and leaned over me. I laughed lightly and stretched my arms over my head. "This is really, really nice baby."

He spoke softly and it almost seemed like he forgot we had company. "Yeah, I know." Then he licked his lips and said seductively, "You have *no* idea what I'm gonna do to you tonight." Then he leaned down and kissed me deeply. A quiet moan escaped my throat as he swept his tongue through my mouth and then twirled it around mine in a gentle caress. I reached up to grasp the soft hair on the nape of his neck and I felt his hand brush the side of my breast. I was almost lost in Tristan's passionate kiss until I pulled away to look down towards the foot of the bed. I was actually relieved when I saw that no one was standing there. Tristan brought my eyes back to his when he whispered, "Kiss me again." I smiled and tilted my head up to meet his sensual lips once more. After all, I saw no harm in allowing my prince to indulge himself for a little while longer.

As we agreed yesterday, Tristan and I got dressed in separate rooms. Autumn and I were in the bedroom getting dressed, and Tristan and Jake were in another room. We did our hair and makeup first. I decided to leave my hair down in loose curls and I didn't go heavy on the makeup. Underneath my dress, I wore a pair of white lacy panties that had a satin crotch. I never worn them before but I bought them from Victoria's

Secret awhile back. So they did qualify for my 'something old'. I didn't need a strapless bra because one was built into the bust of the dress. I put on the lacy light blue garter belt and then Autumn helped me put on my dress.

A little while later, I heard a knock on the bedroom door. Autumn went to answer it and my parents walked in. When my mother saw me, she gasped loudly. "Oh my goodness! Sweetheart, you look lovely!"

I smiled widely. "Thank you, Mom."

My father remarked, "Yes, you look absolutely gorgeous, honey."

"Thanks Daddy."

My mother came over to me and said, "Darling, I wanted to give you these." And she took a pair of white pearl-drop earrings from her purse. Her voice wavered slightly when she spoke again. "These are for your 'something borrowed'."

I took the earrings from my mother and my own voice was laced with heavy emotion. "Ohhh Mommy. Thank you so much." We embraced each other before she put the earrings in my ears. Now I had my 'something borrowed', my wedding dress that was my 'something new', my panties that were my 'something old', and my garter belt that was my 'something blue'. I felt complete...except for my Claddagh ring that Tristan had yet to place back where it belonged.

Autumn and my mother continued to help me get ready, when all of a sudden we heard the one person that was occupying my thoughts. Tristan's voice was on the other side of the door. "Bridget? I won't come in love, but I just wanna say..."

I rushed over to the door so I could speak to him from the other side. "I'm here, baby."

He took a deep breath and then he continued. "I just wanna say that I love you and..." He paused again. "I'll see on the beach, darlin'."

I smiled and placed my hand gently on the door as if I could feel his presence through the expensive wood. "I love you too. I'll see you under the arch."

I heard my mother say, "Tristan looks so handsome, sweetheart." She laughed lightly. "I almost didn't recognize him. I think you'll be very pleased when you see how nice your fiancé looks."

"I can't wait," I replied. Autumn was helping me with my rose hairpiece when we heard another knock on the door.

"It's Kate and Nanny," I heard Kate say from the other side of the door. My father let them in and when they came in, their reactions were similar to my mother's.

Kate gasped and quickly covered her mouth with her hand. Then she spoke in a breathless voice. "Bridget, you look stunning! Oh my...I can't believe how beautiful that dress is." She came over to me and put her hands on my bare shoulders. I could see the genuine affection in her eyes when she said, "You look just like a princess." I couldn't help but to smile in response to her compliment.

"Thank you, Kate."

Nanny came over to me and gave me a gentle hug. "I don't want to wrinkle your pretty dress dear." When she pulled away from me, she smiled and leaned up to kiss me on the cheek. "You look very pretty. I can't wait to see the look on me Tristan's face when he sees you." She chuckled softly. Then she sighed and a wistful look came across her features. "I wish me Charles was here to see this day."

Autumn announced, "Well, I'm going downstairs to meet Jake and Tristan. Are you coming Nanny?"

"Yes dear, I'm ready."

Autumn turned to me and smiled. "Well, it's almost time, Bridge."

"Yeah," I said nervously.

"It'll be great, you'll see. Tristan's gonna be your husband!" She laughed. "Sexy, British Tristan!" I laughed too and she paused to regard me for a moment. "You really do look beautiful."

She kissed me on the cheek and I couldn't help but to blush. "Thanks Aut."

"I'll see you on the beach girlie! I'll be right next to you so don't be nervous." Then she gave me another warm smile before she turned to head out the door with Nanny.

Kate approached me and briefly put her hands on either side of my face in her usual motherly fashion. "Ohhhh Bridget, I just wanted to tell you..." She paused and that's when I saw the tears in her eyes.

"Oh no, Kate. Please don't cry. If you cry, you're going to make me cry and I don't want to mess up my makeup."

She laughed lightly. "I'm sorry, love. I can't help it. I just wanted to tell you how happy I am that you and Tristan are getting married."

Suddenly, I heard my mother's voice say softly, "Let's go Bradley. I think The Groom's mother would like a few words with The Bride." I looked over at my mother and she smiled with teary eyes. My father smiled too and he gave me a small wave before they both left me and Kate alone in the bedroom.

Kate gave me another one of her very motherly smiles. Her voice was laced with heavy emotion but it was strong. "Bridget, for a long time... Tristan was very unhappy. I think part of the reason was because his father and I got a divorce and I went through a bout of depression for awhile after we separated. I could tell Tristan was very affected by it and I tried to help him through it but it was difficult because I was having a hard time coping myself. For awhile, I felt helpless because I couldn't help my son. Tristan's always been very sensitive and I knew when he acted out, it was out of hurt and anger. I couldn't help him and his teachers couldn't reach him. Not even Nanny, who he was always close to, could get him to really open up and express his feelings."

She moved to sit on the bed and I sat next to her. She turned towards me and took both my hands in hers. "When Tristan moved away to The States, I knew why he was leaving; he needed an escape. And I really couldn't blame him. But I noticed afterwards that he wasn't so angry. Whenever I spoke to him on the phone or he came to visit, I noticed a complete change in him for the better. But you know, even though he was in better spirits once he settled in Los Angeles, I knew he still wasn't completely happy. I've known him since he was born and I could tell he was still missing something in his life. He would tell me how he was taking his acting seriously and concentrating on making a career for himself. But I knew that even his acting career wasn't filling the emptiness."

Kate tilted her head to the side and suddenly, her expression seemed to change. It was lighter and more open; like she just discovered something new. "It wasn't until he ringed me one afternoon and told me that he met a fourth grade teacher with beautiful red hair named 'Bridget'. I was surprised because his voice was unlike anything I've ever heard from him. He was so excited. Even more excited than when he told me he got his first role on the tele. Or the time he told me he finally got a role in a major film. I knew this 'Bridget' was someone very special. Then he surprised me even further because he told me that he was in love for the first time. He was in love with you."

Kate stood up and took my hands. She gently pulled me to my feet and I looked into her blue eyes which were identical to Tristan's. She gave me a kiss on the cheek and then she lightly touched the flowers in my hair. "That's why I know you're perfect for my son. You were able to make him feel like no one else could. You were able to reach inside him and touch a place in his heart that he held guarded for so long." She paused and I really felt the weight of her words hit me. "You opened him up, love."

I could feel my tears on the verge of falling but I held them at bay with all the strength I could muster. Autumn and I worked hard to get my makeup right and I wasn't going to let my tears ruin our hard work. My voice had lost some of its strength when I said, "Thank you, Kate. You have no idea what that means to me."

"No, thank *you* Bridget...for giving me my son back." She sniffled and then her expression turned serious. "Now, I want you to tell me if there's ever a time where Tristan doesn't do right by you. I've given him a long talk about what's expected of him and how to be a good husband and father. And he promised to abide by my words."

I laughed lightly and replied, "Don't worry, I will."

Kate took a deep breath and straightened her posture. She looked intently into my eyes and said softly, "Well, are you ready?"

I inhaled deeply and released my breath slowly from my mouth. Then I nodded and my voice was strong when I answered, "Yes, I'm ready."

Chapter 18

AFTER KATE AND I HAD our emotional pre-wedding talk, I made sure to pick up my bouquet before we left to meet my parents outside. The four of us left the hotel and headed over to Due South. Once we got there, we walked inside the lobby and started heading towards the two glass doors which led to the actual ceremony on the beach. Kate turned to me and smiled. She didn't say anything to me but I could see in her eyes that she was wishing me luck. She gave me another kiss on the cheek before she left me and my parents to take her seat behind Tristan and Jake.

The closer we walked to the two glass doors that led to the wedding, the more nervous I started to get. My body started to tremble slightly and that's when my mother embraced me. I guess she could sense my anxiety because she rubbed my back soothingly and whispered, "Don't worry, sweetheart. You have nothing to be nervous about. You're about to marry the man you love." Then she pulled away from me and smiled lovingly. "And your father and I will be right there with you; sitting right behind you. This is a very special day, honey. Be happy...be ecstatic! But don't be nervous."

My mother's words seemed to ease some of my anxiety because I no longer felt like I would tip over. I smiled back and replied, "You're right, Mom. I'm about to marry Tristan and I shouldn't be nervous about that."

She gently put her hands on either side of my face. "That's my girl." She gave me one last smile before she quickly walked away from me and my father to take her seat.

My father and I were slowly walking arm-in-arm and it was but a few seconds later that we reached the glass doors. Suddenly, two men in all-white tuxedos smiled at us from the other side of the doors and opened them for us. A warm, gentle sea breeze caressed my face and I felt it blow through my hair. I could smell the salty sea air mixed with my strawberry-scented shampoo. I looked out onto the beach and I could see the white wedding arch standing tall against the horizon with white ribbons blowing in the wind. And that's when I saw Tristan in the distance. My heart started to race and I inhaled sharply. I couldn't see him clearly but I knew it was him. He was wearing black and I could see Jake standing next to him; also wearing black. On Tristan's left, I saw Autumn standing alone in her pink dress; her bleach-blonde hair bright in the sunshine.

Immediately after I noticed Autumn, I realized there were a lot more people sitting in white chairs behind them besides my mother, Kate, and Nanny. I was under the impression that our wedding would be very intimate but it seemed that more people had showed up to join me and Tristan in our nuptials. I assumed they were Tristan's family and friends and I found myself very anxious to meet them. I glanced to the right of the guests and I saw a raised platform with a few people sitting on chairs with instruments. My eyes widened in surprise because I realized that we had a small orchestra. I was expecting to see someone with an organ playing *'Here Comes the Bride'* as I walked down the aisle.

We were still standing in front of the opened doors when I heard my father's voice. "Are you ready, sweetheart?"

I turned to look up at him and I saw his face smiling down at me. His eyes were sparkling and I saw the crinkles in the corner of his eyes which told me that he was truly happy. It actually warmed my heart to know that I could have my father give me away on my wedding day. I smiled back at him and took another deep breath to ease the butterflies still fluttering around in my stomach. "Yes, I'm ready Daddy." He nodded and then we walked through the glass doors.

As soon as we stepped foot onto the sand, I saw tall wooden poles decorated with white flowers and ribbons. There was a clear, open path from the glass doors to the wedding arch and my father and I continued to slowly walk arm-in-arm while I held my bouquet with my left hand close to my bosom. The closer we got the guests in the back row, the louder I could hear the orchestra playing. The classical music was absolutely lovely to my ears and I realized they weren't playing the typical '*Here Comes the Bride*'; they were playing '*Jesu, Joy of Man's Desiring*' by Bach.

The serene Brighton beach before me and the music put me in calmer spirits and I smiled warmly as I walked with my father. While I was walking I kept thinking: *I can't believe this is happening. I'm actually getting married to the most beautiful man I've ever met.* Once we reached the back row, I looked around at the guests and I saw lots of smiling faces turned in my direction. When we made it to the front row, I looked down and saw Kate and Nanny sitting to my right and they were smiling too. Kate's blue eyes were glistening with unshed tears. My mother was sitting to my left behind Autumn. She was also smiling and I saw tears of joy in her eyes as she dabbed at them with a white tissue. Autumn was smiling widely and she quickly gave me a 'thumbs-up'.

I looked across from Autumn and I saw Tristan standing to my right and he was looking at me in mild amazement. His light blue eyes were wide and his lips were slightly parted. My smile widened as I walked closer to my soon-to-be-husband and stood to face him; still holding my small bouquet of flowers. My father released my arm and stood in back of me; adjacent to Tristan.

The orchestra stopped playing and Tristan continued to gaze at me in wonder while he gave me the once-over. When his eyes met mine again, he smiled warmly at me. His beautiful smile combined with his tuxedo made him look more handsome than I've ever seen him and I couldn't help but to admire him for a moment. His tuxedo jacket and trousers were soft-black but his shirt, vest, and tie were a pure creamy white. He also had a matching white scarf peeking out from his front jacket pocket. His blond hair was combed neatly and I noticed he was still sporting his silver hoop earring in his left ear. Even though this was our wedding, I knew Tristan wouldn't lose his inner style completely. In all honesty, he looked like a true English prince and I needed him to know how handsome he looked. Before I could speak, I saw him open his mouth to speak first. For a moment, no words came forth and he just continued to gaze into my eyes. Then he spoke in a quiet voice, "Bridget... you look absolutely breathtaking."

I smiled back at him and his sweet compliment caused me to blush. I was filled with heavy emotion because I couldn't believe this gorgeous

Brit who I met last fall was standing here before me; ready to take me as his wife. "Thank you, baby," I responded in a soft voice. "You look..." I was almost speechless. I've never seen Tristan dressed so formal and I was almost at a loss for words. My mother was right; I was *very* pleased. Finally, I found my voice and I finished my sentence. "So handsome, Tristan." He grinned at me in appreciation. "Just like an English prince."

"Thank you, love," he replied. He gave me a roguish look when he said, "But I must say...*you're* the one who looks like royalty on this beach."

I couldn't stop another blush from creeping up onto my face even if I wanted to. I happened to glance over Tristan's shoulder and I saw Jake smiling at me. He looked very sophisticated as well and I couldn't help but to think the two Hathaway brothers together made a very attractive package. I smiled at Jake and gave him a small wave. He gave me a nod in return that was almost a bow, before he turned his head to face the... sea captain?!?

I finally noticed the older gentleman standing patiently in front of me and Tristan. He was not a priest, or a reverend, or even a minister; he was a real sea captain! I could tell by the way he was dressed; in a navy and white formal coat with a gold stitched anchor on the breast. Then my brain remembered that Brighton is a seaside city and I was sure that plenty of boats and ships come in and out of the harbor. Why shouldn't Tristan and I get married on the beach by a sea captain? I couldn't help but to think how fitting it was. The sea captain was smiling down at us from under his full white mustache. I heard a charming Irish accent come from his mouth when he spoke. "You look lovely dear."

"Thank you," I replied kindly.

"Are you two ready?"

Tristan and I looked at each other and we shared a smile. Then we turned towards the captain and nodded.

And that's when the ceremony began.

The sea captain's voice was clear and strong as he spoke the opening words of the ceremony. "We have come here in celebration of the joining together of Tristan Caleb and Bridget Raegan. The law of life is love unto all beings. Without love, life is nothing. Without love, death has no redemption. If we learn no more in life, let it be this: marriage is a bond to be entered into only after considerable thought and reflection. As with any aspect of life, it has its cycles, its ups and its downs, its trials and its triumphs. With full understanding of this, Tristan and Bridget have come here today to be joined as one in marriage."

The captain turned towards me and continued to speak. "Others would ask at this time, who gives Bridget in marriage? But as a woman is not property to be bought and sold, given and taken, I ask simply if she comes of her own will and if she has her family's blessing. Bridget, is it true that you come of your own free will and accord?"

Surprisingly, my voice was strong when I answered. "Yes, it is true."

The captain responded, "With whom do you come and whose blessings accompany you?"

And that's when I heard my father's voice behind me. "She comes with me, her father, and with all of her family's blessings." I turned slightly to look at him and he was looking down at me with such pride. I couldn't help but to smile at him and I found myself blinking rapidly to keep my tears at bay. He smiled back at me, and for the first time, I saw his eyes...the same color as mine...glistening with tears of happiness. He moved to take a seat next to my mother and that's when I heard the captain's voice again.

"Tristan and Bridget, please join hands." Tristan and I turned to face each other, and Autumn moved closer to me so she could take my bouquet. Then Tristan reached out and grasped both of my hands in his warm ones. Once our hands were joined, the captain continued. "Let the strength of your wills bind you together. Let the power of love and desire make you happy and the strength of your dedication make you inseparable. Be close, but not too close. Possess one another, yet be understanding. Have patience with one another, for storms will come but they will pass quickly. Be free in giving affection and warmth. Have no fear and let not the ways of the unenlightened give you unease, for you are never alone."

The captain turned to me again. "Bridget, I do not have the right to bind you to Tristan, only you have this right. If it is your wish, say so at this time."

I smiled and replied, "It is my wish."

He turned to Tristan and said, "Tristan, if it be your wish for Bridget to be bound to you, place the ring on her finger." Tristan let go of my hands and I saw Jake hand him a shiny ring. Tristan and I looked into each other's eyes for a moment and then he grinned. He gently took my left hand in his right, and placed my white-gold Claddagh promise ring on my finger with his left hand. The heart and crown were still facing inwards but this time he placed it where he promised to last Christmas: on my left ring finger. After he placed my wedding ring on my finger, the captain said to him, "Please recite your vows to Bridget."

In the back of my mind, I was praying that Tristan memorized our vows word-for-word. A part of me felt guilty for doubting him but I couldn't help it. I was honestly shocked when he looked directly into my eyes and spoke in a strong, confident voice without a single pause. He held my hands in a firm grip as he swore his heart to me forever. "I, Tristan, take you, Bridget, in marriage. To be my beloved. To walk, run, and dance this new path together. To love, care and share. To let the winds dance between us. Let the fires burn within us and the waters flow through us on our sacred journey together. I promise to love you wholly and completely, without restraint, in sickness and in health, in plenty and in poverty, in life and beyond, where we shall meet and love again. I promise to stand by you and uplift you, so that through our union we can accomplish more than we could alone. I promise to be a faithful mate and to unfailingly share and support your hopes, dreams and goals. I promise to respect you always as I respect myself, for you are my best friend. With this ring may a new life begin. With this ring I thee wed. From now until I take my last breath, I give you my heart and share with you my soul. To you Bridget, this is my solemn vow."

I felt a couple tears fall from my eyes and I was powerless to stop them. Tristan was holding my hands so I couldn't wipe them away. I was hoping that the warm sea breeze would dry them on my cheeks. Since the moment I met Tristan, he had always been so in-tuned with me. He must've known what I was thinking because he released one of my hands to gently wipe the tears from my cheeks. He smiled knowingly and at that moment, I was absolutely convinced I found my other half in the gorgeous blond angel looking back at me.

The captain turned to Tristan and spoke similar words he spoke to me. "Tristan, I do not have the right to bind you to Bridget, only you have this right. If it is your wish, say so at this time."

Tristan replied in a strong voice, "It is my wish."

The captain then turned to me and said, "Bridget, if it is your wish for Tristan to be bound to you, place the ring on his finger."

I felt Autumn move close to me and she presented Tristan's open ring box to me. I carefully removed his platinum Claddagh wedding band from its royal blue satin bedding and presented it to Tristan. He held his left hand out for me and I grasped it in my left hand. I placed the ring on his left ring finger with the crown and heart facing inwards using my right hand. As soon as Tristan saw what I had just placed on his finger, he gasped and whipped his head up to look at me. His eyes were wide and a look of surprise crossed his beautiful features. I guess he realized that he'd have to speak quickly before the captain continued because he said softly, "You got me a Claddagh ring too?" I smiled and nodded, and he looked back down at his ring in amazement. When our eyes met again, he was smiling even brighter than the sun shining down on us. "Thank you, darlin'. I love it."

I heard the captain's voice again as me addressed me once more. "Please recite your vows to Tristan." I took a deep breath and repeated the same words to Tristan that he spoke to me earlier. I looked directly into his eyes as I spoke in a clear and confident voice. I was speaking directly from my heart and I knew that Tristan realized that.

We both turned to face the captain once more and he looked down at us for a moment before speaking. Then he also took a deep breath and addressed us both. "You have chosen and vowed to walk the same path and embark upon a quest together. As you embark upon this quest, do so with joy and love in your hearts. But remember always...you cannot be true to one another unless you are true to yourself." He smiled warmly and paused. Then he addressed everyone at the wedding when he announced, "And now by the power vested in me, I pronounce you husband and wife for all lifetimes. You may kiss your bride."

Tristan and I turned to face each other, and my new husband didn't waste any time kissing his bride. He put his hands on either side of my face and kissed me gently at first. Then he slanted his soft, sensual lips over mine once...and then twice...before he deepened the kiss. When he unsealed his lips from mine, he whispered against my mouth, "I love you Mrs. Hathaway."

I pecked his lips once more before I whispered back, "I love you too Mr. Hathaway."

We embraced each other and that's when I heard the sound of many people clapping.

Before I knew what was happening, Tristan released me and Autumn came over and hugged me tightly. "This is so awesome, Bridge! Congratulations!" We pulled away from each other and she handed me my flower bouquet.

"Thanks, Aut."

My mother and father came over to me and Tristan and congratulated us. Jake approached me slowly and for a moment, he hesitated. So I smiled and moved closer to him and that's when he reached out to hug me. I held him tightly and when we pulled away from each other, I tilted my head up and kissed him on his smooth cheek. He smiled back at me before he looked down shyly.

Kate and Nanny also approached and congratulated me and Tristan. Kate embraced me tightly and when she pulled away from me, she touched the flowers in my hair and smiled. I saw that she still had tears in her eyes as she looked at me with motherly affection. "Welcome to the family, love." Then as an afterthought she said, "I mean, *officially*."

"Thank you, Kate." I hugged her again and as I held her, I began to feel like I wanted to say something to her that I should've said earlier. My voice trembled but I spoke from my heart. "I mean...*Mom*."

She pulled away to look at me and her light blue eyes were still teary but they were widened in surprise. Then she smiled again and I saw fresh tears trickle down her beautiful face. I think I rendered her speechless because she couldn't finish her sentence. "Ohhh Bridget, I..." She sniffled and laughed lightly.

I just smiled and replied, "You don't have to say anything."

More people started to approach me and Tristan, and it wasn't long until Kate was introducing me to more of Tristan's family. I met some of his aunts, uncles, and cousins. Some of the relatives were actually from Tristan's father's side which I was pleasantly surprised by. I was so overwhelmed but extremely honored to meet every last one of them.

After awhile, Tristan approached me and told me that the photographer wanted to take photos of just the two of us. We excused ourselves from our families and walked over towards the shore where the photographer was waiting. I bent down to remove my shoes and I heard Tristan's genuine laughter. "Babe, what are you doing?!?"

I was feeling absolutely elated and free so I replied with a smile, "I don't care! I'm walking barefoot!" Once I removed my shoes, I lifted the hem of my wedding gown while Tristan took my other hand and we ran across the beach. The photographer took our pictures by the ocean and I was anxious to see how they would come out.

We returned to our guests and mingled for a little while longer. Autumn approached me and smiled but I noticed this time her smile was mischievous. "What? Why are you looking at me like that? You're up to no good, aren't you?"

She didn't provide a response, she just turned away from me and announced loudly, "Hey everyone! The bride is gonna throw the bouquet! All you single ladies gather 'round!" Then she started laughing. Autumn was definitely able to get all the single women's attention because it wasn't long until a small group gathered in front of us. They looked at me eagerly and Autumn moved away from me to take her place in the crowd. Then she yelled over at me, "Well, turn around and throw it!" The other women started laughing and cheering me on.

With a wide smile, I said, "Okay, here it goes." I turned around and yelled, "Ready?!?" Then I tossed the bouquet over my head. I quickly turned back around and I saw the bouquet bouncing from one hand to another; all the while the women were laughing.

Finally, I heard Autumn exclaim, "Alright Kate!" A space opened up in the crowd, and I saw Tristan's mother standing there holding my flower bouquet. Our eyes met and we smiled at each other.

After I threw the bouquet, Tristan didn't waste any time fulfilling his part of the Groom's tradition. He approached me with a sly smile and whispered seductively, "It's time for me to remove that bothersome garter belt from your person, love."

I became giddy with anticipation and I couldn't keep the smile off my face. Autumn didn't have to make the announcement to all the gentlemen at the ceremony, because Tristan did the honors himself. The men gathered quickly in front of us but I couldn't keep my focus on them because Tristan kneeled slowly before me. Now his smile only played at the corners of his sensual mouth, but I could tell by his affectionate gaze that he was really looking forward to this moment. He gently lifted my right leg and his nimble fingers glided the soft material of my dress up my calf and further north past my knees. He was careful not to expose too much of my bare thigh because then he broke the connection with our eyes and his face disappeared under my dress where only he could see the rest of my smooth, milky skin.

I shivered under his touch when I felt his warm lips place a kiss to my inner thigh before his teeth began to gently pull the lacy blue garter belt from its snug home. My fingers combed lightly through his golden locks as he took his time removing it. The other men made sounds of impatience. "Oh come on, Tris! Stop teasing us, mate!" I heard someone call out.

When I finally felt him slip the garter belt down to my ankle, he yanked it off quickly and without warning, tossed it casually into the sea of men waiting with anxious faces. To my surprise, he tossed it *over* the crowd and I laughed out loud. Tristan may as well have thrown a bone to a pack of hungry dogs, the way they all chased after it. I wasn't that surprised when I saw that Jake was the victor. He twirled my garter belt around his index finger with an expression of smug satisfaction. I secretly knew that he would be more determined than anyone else to claim some small piece of me.

The entire wedding party gathered inside of Due South for the reception in our private dining hall. Tristan and I were still walking hand-in-hand but when we got inside the room, he let go of my hand. "Babe, you don't know how lucky you are that you can wear that dress. I'm in this hot tuxedo..." He paused and lowered his voice. "Sweating my fucking bollocks off." He removed his jacket and put it on the back of a dining chair.

I laughed lightly and moved closer to help him get more comfortable. I helped him unbutton his vest and take it off. "That's right sweetie, you get comfortable." I took his vest from him and he began to loosen his tie.

When he was finally free of his formal confines, he sighed in contentment. "Ahhh, that's *much* better."

Everyone sat at a long dining table with elegant decorations while we were served delicious appetizers and a main course by waiters in black-and-white tuxedos. During the meal, Jake stood up and garnered everyone's attention for a toast to the bride and groom. After dinner they brought out our wedding cake and as I expected, I heard plenty of 'ooh's' and 'ahh's'. Tristan and I stood in front of the cake and he put his hand on top of mine as I cut into the first piece. I took the piece of cake in my hand and smiled up at him. "Here baby, take a bite." And I put the cake close to his mouth.

He grinned before he narrowed his eyes slightly and began looking at me skeptically. "Are you gonna smash that in my face?"

My eyes widened and a mock expression of confusion appeared on my face. I replied innocently, "Huh? What are you talking about, sweetheart?" I heard some people start laughing. Then I smiled again and tried to coerce him further. "Just take a bite. I'm sure it's delicious." As soon as Tristan moved his mouth closer to the cake and attempted to take a bite, I smashed as much of it as I could into his mouth. Some of the cake actually made it into his mouth, but the rest of it landed around his mouth and on his nose and chin.

He took it all in fun because he started chewing and commented with a mouth full of wedding cake, "Mmmm...you're right love, this cake is delicious." Before I had time to react, he quickly grabbed a chunk off the cake itself and smashed it into my mouth. "Here, try some." At first I couldn't speak because my mouth was full but that didn't stop me from laughing. As I was chewing my food, Tristan started taking icing and cake off my face with his fingers and eating it. He kept commenting on how good it was and that caused me to laugh harder. Tristan joined in on the laughter and soon everyone else did too. A waitress actually carved and served the cake and I told her to make sure Tristan gets the piece with his handprint.

I noticed the DJ in the room when we first walked in but he didn't play any music. That is, until after dessert. He got on the microphone and announced, "Could I have everyone's attention please?" Tristan and I were still sitting at the table but I was sitting on his lap. We all looked over at him and he spoke again in his wonderful English accent. "I would like everyone to gather 'round please. This first dance is for...the Bride and Groom."

I gasped and whipped my head around to look at Tristan with wide-eyes. I spoke in a hushed but urgent voice when I said, "Oh no! Baby, I didn't pick a song!"

Tristan's expression remained calm and a smile slowly crept onto his face. His voice was soft when he replied, "Don't worry, love. I picked one." The music started to play and he took my hand as I rose off his lap. He guided me to the area where there was enough room to dance and put his arms around my waist. He held me close, and I continued looking at him in surprise until I heard the opening lyrics of Savage Garden's *'I Knew I Loved You'*. Then I smiled lovingly and put my arms around his neck as we slowly danced to the perfect love song for our wedding. As the song continued to play, I laid my head on Tristan's shoulder and let the melody fill me completely.

~*'I knew I loved you before I met you. I think I dreamed you into life'*~

The lyrics definitely mirrored what was in my heart, and how I felt about the beautiful man I was dancing with.

~*'I knew I loved you before I met you. I have been waiting all my life.'*~

I closed my eyes and swayed to the music with my husband. Our bodies were already in-sync with each other, so slow-dancing with one other was effortless; it was natural. Soon, the final lyrics played before the music began to fade.

~*'I am complete now that I found you.'*~

As the rest of the afternoon wore on, Tristan and I shared a few more dances. He also danced with his mother and my mother, and I danced with my father and Jake. The DJ was playing Muse's *'Starlight'* and Tristan was twirling me around on the dance floor when I happened to see Kate in the corner of my eye talking to someone I didn't recognize. Tristan dipped me once and when he pulled me back up, he put his arms around me. As he was turning us around, I remarked casually, "Baby, why is your mom talking to a chauffeur? Do you think there's a limo outside for us?" I smiled widely in excitement.

Tristan glanced around the room until his eyes settled on his mother and the chauffeur. I was looking at his face while we danced, when all of a sudden, I felt a tightening in my chest. It actually felt like the whole joyous mood had been abruptly crushed by an enormous weight. I couldn't understand it but immediately following the uncomfortable feeling, I saw Tristan's face turn red and he set his jaw hard. His breathing became erratic and I was suddenly filled with worry. I wasn't exactly sure what was going on so I asked cautiously, "Baby, what's the matter? Are you okay?" He didn't answer me, nor did he look at me. His eyes seemed to be fixed on a particular spot.

I turned my head towards where I saw Kate and the chauffeur, and I saw him standing motionless like a statue and he was looking straight at us. Actually, it seemed like he was looking directly at Tristan. I whipped my head towards Tristan again and he was staring daggers at this tall man. His facial expression slowly twisted into anger and the muscle in his jaw twitched. At that moment, I felt a very threatening vibe coming from him. A dark storm was settling right above our heads and it was about to start a down-pour. I tried to take control before something bad happened so I spoke in an urgent voice and tried to get his attention. "Tristan! What's the matter? What's wrong? Please talk to me!"

He finally looked away from the man and turned his head to the side away from me. He started breathing rapidly and that's when I felt his entire body start trembling. When he opened his mouth to speak, his voice was dripping with venom and he sounded like he was trying to contain his rage. "That's my *father.*"

I gasped out loud and whipped my head back towards the chauffeur... wait scratch that, his father. He was still standing there watching us, and Kate was standing next to him and she also had her eyes fixed on us. Something inside me told me that some major drama was about to unfold. Just as I slowly turned my head to look at Tristan again, he released me suddenly. I spoke calmly and carefully because he looked like a wild tiger that was just released from its cage. "Tristan..."

And just like that, he ignored me completely and made a bee-line towards his father. I couldn't help but notice the aggressive way he was approaching him and I prayed that a fight wouldn't break out. Just at the moment, the music stopped and everyone was quiet...except Tristan. As he was charging towards his father, he yelled, "WHAT THE FUCK ARE YOU DOING HERE?!?" I ran after him and I was relieved when he didn't attack his father. Actually, he couldn't attack because Jake blocked his path and was holding him back. Tristan continued to unleash his rage and struggle with his brother and for the first time, I was truly afraid to try and intervene. "WHY ARE YOU HERE?!? WHAT DO YOU WANT?!?"

When I reached them, I was able to get a good look at his father. He was tall and I could tell he was over six-feet. He had a lean but muscular build and it was obvious that both of his sons took after his stature and physique. He had taken off his chauffeur hat which revealed sandy blond hair that was slightly graying, and well-trimmed side burns. He had azure eyes too and now I couldn't tell if Tristan and Jake got their eye color from their mother or their father. He was clean-shaven and *very* attractive. Even though this was a tense moment, I couldn't help but to feel relieved to finally see where the other half of Tristan's sexy genes came from. Surprisingly, his father's expression was calm and I couldn't help but notice the look in his eyes. He actually looked sad. And the more Tristan yelled at him, the more hurt he look. "I WANT YOU TO LEAVE! DO YOU HEAR ME?!? YOU'RE RUINING MY WEDDING!"

Tristan's father tried to speak but Kate spoke first. She approached Tristan without fear or hesitation and began pleading with him. I had never heard her voice like this, and it actually broke my heart. "Tristan, darling...please calm down. I invited him."

All of a sudden, Tristan stopped struggling with Jake and he swiftly turned his head to look at his mother. His face fell and his mouth opened slightly in shock. He pushed Jake off him and slowly walked over to stand in front of his mother. Tristan looked down at her in disbelief and started shaking his head. When he spoke, his voice was low but shaky. "What?" He paused and took a breath. "You..." He paused again and started looking at Kate as if he didn't know her. "*You* invited him? How could you, Mum? How could you invite him to my wedding?" And just like the changing of the tides, Tristan's mood shifted into anger once more and he yelled at his mother. "HOW COULD YOU DO THIS TO ME?!? ON MY WEDDING DAY! WHY MUM?!? WHY?!?"

Kate moved closer to him and reached out to touch him but he recoiled from her. I saw the tears begin to fill her eyes as she tried to reason with her son. "Darling, listen to me." She took a deep breath to try and compose herself and then she spoke again. "I've forgiven him."

Tristan's eyes widened again and he exclaimed in disbelief, "What?!? What do you mean you've forgiven him?!? Did you forget what he did, Mum?!? Did you forget how he destroyed us?!? He destroyed our fucking family!" Right at that moment, I believe Tristan's horrible childhood memories came back to haunt him and his emotions overpowered him once again. He began to cry but he spoke through his tears of anger and sadness. "How many nights did I have to stay up with you, Mum?!? How many?!? How many times did I have to listen to you cry?!?" He paused and closed his eyes tightly and pinched the bridge of his nose. I wanted to go over to him and embrace him but I was too afraid; too afraid that he'd recoil from me too. Then he opened his eyes and shouted, "'CAUSE

OF THIS FUCKING BASTARD!" And he pointed directly in his father's face. His father didn't budge or speak; he just put his head down in shame.

The fact that Tristan was cursing didn't faze Kate and she didn't bother to reprimand his foul mouth. She just looked up into her son's eyes and replied quietly. "I haven't forgotten, love. And I'll never forget. But I've learned to forgive, darling. And I was hoping that you would too."

It was then that I finally heard his father's voice. It was a deep baritone and also laced with an English accent. "Son, I know you're angry and you have every right to be."

"Don't fucking talk to me you goddamn cheater! You have no idea how much you hurt Mum! How much you hurt all of us!"

"That's where you're wrong, son. I know exactly what I did. And for that I'm truly sorry and I have been for a very long time."

Tristan finally lowered his voice but it wasn't any friendlier. "I want you to leave. I don't want you here, do you understand me? You're not welcome."

His father nodded and turned to walk away and I saw Kate begin to follow after him. That's when I finally found the bravery and strength to try and save Tristan's family...my other family. I blurted out, "No, wait Mr. Hathaway!" He stopped in his tracks and turned back around at the sound of my voice. I cautiously moved closer to Tristan and put my arms around his waist. He didn't respond or look at me so I said softly, "Baby, maybe you should hear your father out."

Suddenly, without looking at me, because he was still glaring daggers at his father, he snapped at me and said, "Stay out of this Bridget!"

The Fiery Redhead emerged immediately and I snapped back, "No, I won't stay out of this! I'm your wife now, remember?!?"

Tristan extracted himself from my embrace and his voice was full of contempt when he said, "You know what? Bugger this, I'm leaving."

He started to walk towards the door to the room while his mother called after him. I quickly began following him to try and get him to stop. Once he reached the door, he yanked it open. Tristan was really fast because he was already halfway down the long hallway when I reached him and ran in front of his path. He tried to walk around me but I blocked his path. Then I began to desperately plead with him. "Tristan! Please just listen to me, okay? *Please!*"

He put his hands on my upper arms and looked into my eyes. I stared back at him and I could see the hurt reflected in his baby blues. "Just let me go, Bridget. I wanna get the fuck out of here."

"I know, baby. I know you want to leave. But just let me talk to you first, okay? Just hear me out and if you don't like what I say, then you can leave, alright?"

Tristan released his gentle grip and stood in front of me. Then he moved over to the opposite wall and leaned against it. He took a deep breath and cast his eyes up towards the ceiling. I moved in front of him and put my arms around him again. He looked down at me and I could tell that he was on the verge of breaking down. I wondered if that might be just what he needed to understand and see clearly. Once I made up my mind that I was going to try, I treaded carefully because I wanted to try to get through to him. My voice was gentle and calm when I spoke. "Tristan...love...I know you're hurting right now. Believe me, I know. I can feel it, sweetie. I can feel your pain. But just hear what I have to say... *please.*" I paused and looked deep into his eyes to try to connect with him. "Your mother...the one who your father hurt the most...has forgiven him. She's forgiven him, baby. And she's asking you to forgive him too."

He shook his head. "I can't, Bridge. I can't. You don't know how much he hurt me."

"Yes, I do. You've told me how much he hurt you. And today, you've *shown* me how much he's hurt you. But baby, if your mother can forgive him...so can you." I tilted my head up and kissed my husband because I could feel his composure slipping. "Tristan, sweetheart, I know what kind of person you are. You're a good person." He started shaking his head again. "Yes, you are. You're a *wonderful* person and you have an unbelievable heart." His lips started trembling and I could see the tears welling up in his eyes. I was close to reaching that place in his heart; the place that was reserved for his love for his father. "And you're a better man than your father." I threaded my fingers through his hair because I knew my affection calmed him. "Your mother knows that too and she knows you have it in you to forgive. I know you love her, Tristan. And I know you'd do anything for her. Try to forgive him. Do it for your mother." The tears he was holding at bay finally started to trickle down his cheeks. He blinked rapidly but that just caused more tears to fall. His lips trembled more violently and he started sniffling.

Now was the time; the time to get him to open that door in his heart...open it up and let his father back in. I reached up and laid my hands on his chest and continued looking into his watery eyes. I paused for a moment and just looked at him and he returned my gaze with an extreme intensity. "Baby, let me ask you something, okay? And I want you to promise me that you'll answer truthfully. Will you do that?" He sniffled again and nodded. "Before he cheated, was he a good father? Was he a good father to you and Jake?"

Tristan looked up at the ceiling again and I saw more tears leak from his blue eyes. He didn't answer immediately but instead, he took a shaky breath and slowly released it from his mouth. Then he looked down at me and murmured quietly, "Yes."

When I spoke again, my voice was so soft that it was almost a whisper. "Deep inside you, in your heart..." And I placed my warm hand over his beating heart. I paused one last time because I was finally going to ask him the question I've wanted to ask him ever since he told me about his father. "Do you miss your father?" I also braced myself for his reaction.

Tristan inhaled quickly and that's when it happened...he finally broke down. Blood rushed to his face, his lips began trembling violently again, and he continued to look deep into my eyes. His voice was strangled when he finally admitted the truth. "Yes." All of a sudden, he sobbed once and then he quickly wrapped his arms around me. He held me tightly and I immediately held him as tight as I could. My new husband began crying harder than I've ever heard him cry before. He held onto me as all the years of hurt, anger, sadness, and pain came rushing to the surface and then poured out of him until it was overflowing. I was Tristan's anchor at that very moment and if I dared to let him go, he would drown in anguish. His sobs racked his entire body and I began rubbing his back and stroking his hair as I desperately tried to ease his pain. But I knew that he needed this pain, he needed to feel this so he would be able to let his father back into his life. I didn't cry with him because I knew that he needed me to be the strong one. After all, I was his other half; if he was vulnerable, then I had to be impervious.

When Tristan finally calmed down and I heard the slight hiccups which signaled the end of his intense sobbing, he released me and I began to wipe his tears away. His face was completely flushed and his eyes were bloodshot. He took a couple deep breaths and I kept stroking his hair and face to help him relax. Once I believed he would be able to function, I said, "Let's go talk to your dad." He took one more deep breath and nodded.

Just as I was about to walk away from him, he pulled me back close to his body and leaned down to kiss me. I kissed him back and tried to convey as much love as I could through the kiss. Tristan let me know that he received it because he deepened the kiss and moaned softly into my mouth. When we ended the kiss, he held me in his arms again and said quietly, "What would I do without you?"

I brushed the stray tears I saw lingering on his long, darkened lashes. Then I smiled at my prince and replied, "I'm your other half remember? When you're hurting, I'll be strong for you. I'll be your strength."

We looked into each other's eyes and Tristan's next words actually made my heart ache for him. His voice was soft but it was also desperate. "Promise you won't ever leave me."

I sealed my promise with another tender kiss. "I promise, sweetheart."

We walked back towards the dining hall and I was actually relieved that someone closed the door. We went inside and I saw Mr. Hathaway, Jake, Nanny, and Kate sitting at the dining table talking to my parents. Jake saw us first and when he did, he alerted his company and they all turned their heads towards us. My parents remained sitting at the table because they were probably trying to stay out of it. Jake also remained seated and I saw him speaking in hushed voices with my mother.

Kate and Mr. Hathaway walked over to us and I noticed that he kept his distance. I noticed Tristan was quiet so I looked over at him and he had his arms crossed and he was looking down at the floor. He started digging the toe of his shoe into the carpet and biting his bottom lip. At that moment, I knew this would be a difficult reunion. Kate approached us and looked over at me with a sad smile. She mouthed: "Thank you" before she looked over at her youngest son. She said his name softly and he finally looked up at her. She approached him slowly and then she reached her arms out to him. I was surprised when Tristan didn't hesitate. He closed the distance between them and embraced her.

His father moved closer and that's when Tristan released his mother from his embrace. His father began speaking calmly to him but you could hear the underlying caution in his voice. "I saw you get married, Tristan. I watched in the distance. It was a very beautiful ceremony." Tristan didn't respond or even look at him so Mr. Hathaway turned to me and said, "And you have a lovely bride. I see you found your rose." As soon as he said that, Tristan briefly looked up at him.

His father stepped closer to me and finally introduced himself. "Hullo Bridget, I'm William. But you can call me Will." And he put his hand out for me to shake.

I shook his hand and smiled warmly. "Hello, nice to finally meet you." I decided to try to lighten the mood so I added, "What if I just call you 'Dad'?"

It worked like a charm because both of Tristan's parents laughed. Will dashed a brilliant smile when he replied, "If you wish." That seemed to put him in better spirits because then he said, "I bet you're wondering why I'm dressed like this? I haven't dressed like this in years, but today was a very special occasion."

To all of our surprise, Tristan finally spoke up. He looked at his father and a confused expression appeared on his face. "What are you talking about Dad?" I was even more surprised because one, his tone of voice wasn't clipped in any way. And two, he actually called his father 'Dad'.

Apparently Will was surprised as well because he seemed to perk up. "Well, if you're both ready to leave...I would ask that you follow me outside." My eyes widened in surprise and I quickly looked over at Tristan with a smile. He still looked confused but he did follow me, Will, and Kate outside.

As we were walking, I noticed Jake, Nanny, Autumn, my parents, and a few other of Tristan's family members following behind. We walked out the front doors of Due South, and sitting in front of the building was a beautiful classic convertible. It was gleaming in the sunlight and the paint was a soft buttercream color. The word *Excalibur* was in silver and it was displayed regally on the side of the car. My parents were standing a few feet to my left and I heard my father let out a low whistle. Then I heard him say quietly to my mother, "That's a Rolls-Royce, honey."

I couldn't contain my excitement and I exclaimed to Will, "Is this yours?!?" I approached the car so I could admire it closely.

Will laughed in delight. "Oh no, this is a special order rental. When Kate told me that Tristan was getting married, I put a rush on the order."

I was still busy admiring the car but I glanced up and saw Kate say to Tristan, "Your father owns a car and limo service in London."

Tristan looked unimpressed but that didn't stop Will from correcting her. "Actually, I own *three*." Kate smiled at him and apologized for her mistake, but not before I saw Will smile at her first.

When I saw the 'Just Married' sign on the back of the convertible, I exclaimed again but this time to Tristan. "Baby, come look at this! It says 'just married' on the back!" I looked over at Tristan, and he was still standing in front of the building on the sidewalk. He was looking at the car with a neutral expression and he wasn't remotely excited. Nor did he move an inch when I asked him to come take a closer look. I approached him and began to quietly plead with him again. "Tristan, please get in the car. Don't you want to ride in it? Look how nice it is. Your father seemed to go through a lot of trouble to get it for us. *Please*, won't you get in? I'd really like to ride in it, not to mention...I'd like to speak more with your father." Tristan didn't say anything. I tried to search his eyes but he averted them from me.

Since I wasn't able to persuade him, I sighed and turn back towards the car. Will was standing next to it and he was looking at me expectedly. But when he noticed the expression on Tristan's face, his face fell. I attempted to lift his spirits, so I walked up to him and gave him a friendly smile. "I'd like to ride in it, Dad."

He smiled back at me but I could tell it didn't reach his eyes. He opened the door for me and gave a slight bow. "After you madam." I stepped into the car and he closed the door behind me. I looked over at Tristan and he was staring directly at me. Behind his eyes, I saw a conflict building inside him and I knew he was debating with himself. That's when Will approached him and began trying to reach his son.

"Tristan, I know you're angry with me. You probably still hate me and I understand, son. Really, I do. But I wanted you to know how sorry I am for the things I did. I'm sorry that I hurt you all so badly. I was a real shit, I know that. But I wanted to see your wedding. I haven't seen you in twelve years and I wanted to see my youngest son get married. Mum told me how much you love Bridget, so I knew I'd never see you get married again." He laughed lightly and I actually saw a flicker of something other than animosity in Tristan's face. I saw Will hesitate for a split second and then I saw him touch Tristan for the first time. He put his hand on Tristan's arm and when he didn't react negatively, I knew Will was able to reach him. Will realized it too because it seemed as if renewed confidence flowed through him and his voice was stronger. "I'm just asking you to give me another chance. But I'll understand if you don't. And you don't *have* to ride in the car with me, Tristan. I'll give you the keys and you and Bridget can go and keep the car for as long as you want. It's your choice. But I want you to know that I really wanted to do this for you."

Will reached into his pocket and pulled out the car keys and dangled them in front of Tristan. Tristan looked at him and sighed, and then he turned his head away. I saw him look over at Kate and she had a hopeful expression on her face. He turned to look at me and I nodded encouragingly. Then he averted his eyes from me to look at his father again. I couldn't see his father's expression but I had a feeling he looked remorseful.

All of a sudden, I saw Tristan give his father a small grin. Then he looked back at me and said, "Move over, Bridge." I squealed in delight and quickly scooted over to make room for my husband. Tristan got in next to me and I hugged him tightly before I kissed him.

"I'm proud of you, baby." He smiled back at me and I knew he was in slightly better spirits.

We waved goodbye to everyone and Will got in the driver's seat. That's when I heard Kate say to him, "Be careful, Will. Don't drive too fast."

He put on his chauffeur hat and turned his head to look at her. "Yes, darling."

Will drove us around Brighton and Hove, and the neighboring towns. As we were driving, other motorists would honk and wave at us. I felt so pretty in my wedding gown that I waved back as if I was royalty. Tristan just looked at me in amusement while he occasionally waved back at people. I remarked to him excitedly, "I feel like Princess Di."

His eyes widened in horror and he replied, "Please don't say that, love. You remember she died in a car crash driven by her chauffeur."

I apologized because I actually felt guilty for saying such a foolish comment, but that's who I truly felt like.

I knew the riff between Tristan and Will wasn't completely filled just because Tristan accepted his father's offer to drive us around. That would be too naive for anyone to think. It wasn't long until my assumption was confirmed because Tristan started asking his father questions from the backseat. "So, do you still live in Brighton?"

His father looked at him in the rear-view mirror as he answered him. "No, I live in London."

"How long have you lived there?"

"Almost ten years."

"Do you have any other kids?"

Tristan's question seemed to catch his father off-guard. Will quickly recovered because he replied, "No, I don't. You and Jake are all I have."

For the next few minutes, Tristan was silent and I engaged in polite conversation with Will. While I was speaking to him, Tristan had his head turned and he was looking out at his surroundings. When he spoke again, he asked a very interesting question. "Are you seeing Mum?"

His father didn't answer for a couple seconds. But when he finally did, his voice was quiet. "Yes, but we're taking things slow. She still doesn't trust me and I can't say that I blame her."

Tristan didn't seem perturbed by this new information and he asked casually, "How long have you been seeing each other?"

"Almost six months. We didn't tell you and Jake because we knew you were both still angry with me." Will stopped speaking for a minute and then he asked curiously, "How did you know?"

"You slipped up and called Mum 'darling' before we left."

"Oh." He chuckled softly before he added, "You've always been very perceptive, son."

Tristan paused for a moment and then he asked quietly, "Why'd you cheat on her?" I had a feeling that was the one question he wanted to ask from the very beginning. I'll admit that I was also waiting in anticipation for Will's explanation.

To my surprise, Will didn't hesitate to answer this question. "Because I was thinking with my prick. Excuse my language, Bridget. But that's the truth, son. Mum and I were going through rough times. I'm sure you remember. We were arguing a lot. Then one day, I was picking this woman up from a hotel and we struck up a conversation. She was very flirtatious towards me and I didn't put up any resistance. If you want to know the truth, a part of me was looking for an escape from what I was going through back at home with your mum. And this stranger, who I had just met, presented the opportunity and I jumped at it. I don't know what I was thinking when I took her back to our house. I guess there was the excitement of it all. I didn't think about how it would hurt you all if you found out. Honestly Tristan...I deserved to get caught. I was a complete bastard and I deserved everything I got. And if I was in your position, I wouldn't have forgiven me either."

After Will finished telling Tristan the one thing he was probably wondering since he was a little boy, Tristan nodded and seemed to accept his reason. Suddenly, Tristan reached over and grabbed my hand. I looked up at him and he was staring at me intently. He gave my hand a tight squeeze before he started rubbing the back of it with his thumb. Then he turned his head towards his father again. "Dad?"

I actually saw Will perk up when Tristan addressed him as such. "Yes, Tristan?"

Tristan paused again and looked down at his lap. He looked like he was deep in-thought or contemplating his next words. I saw him take a deep breath and then he spoke to his father again. "I want you to make me a promise. Make a promise to your youngest son on his wedding day."

Will's voice was soft when he replied, "*Anything*, son."

When Tristan spoke again, I was surprised to hear that he actually sounded like he was about to cry. "Promise that you'll never hurt Mum again."

Will responded immediately. "I promise."

Tristan released a breath and looked over at me. When I saw that his eyes were filled with unshed tears, I immediately became strong for him. He turned back to his father and said the one thing that Will probably wanted to hear ever since he lost his family. "Then I forgive you."

Will was quiet in the front seat for a minute. Then I heard him reply in a trembling voice. "Thank you." It was but a couple seconds after he spoke that I saw him wipe the tears from his eyes.

Tristan looked over at me again and I smiled proudly at him. Then I leaned over and kissed him with all the love and affection I could display with his father in such close proximity. I knew when we ended the kiss that I had left Tristan unsatisfied. He turned towards his father again and asked, "Dad, do you think you could drop me and Bridget off at our hotel?" Then he looked at me again and a sexy smile appeared on his face and he waggled his eyebrows.

When we got to our hotel suite, I saw Tristan put a 'Do Not Disturb' sign on the door. I laughed inwardly because I knew no one would disturb us. But I knew he would disturb our guests when started making love because he was incapable of being quiet. I took his hand and guided him into the bedroom. I lit a few candles that were in the room and after I finished lighting the last one, Tristan came up behind me and put his arms around my waist. What he started was one of the most intense, passionate, and extreme couplings we ever had. He leaned his head down right next to mine and whispered *very* dirty words in my ear, "Bridget, I'm gonna fuck you harder than you've ever been fucked in your life. You're gonna beg me to stop. But I have to tell you love, I'm not gonna stop." Then he nipped my earlobe and I quickly sucked some air between my teeth before I moaned softly. "So don't ask me to."

He turned me in his arms and swooped down to capture my lips in a deep and almost bruising kiss. I felt his warm tongue plunge deep into my mouth and he crushed me close against his body. I wrapped my arms around him and moaned into his mouth. I felt his erection poking my belly and we both ground into each other to intensify the feeling. Then he released my mouth and ran his tongue slowly across both my lips.

I found myself tilting my head up towards him for more, but he bent his head down next to mine and continued whispering brazenly in my ear. "I'm not wearing any protection tonight. I don't want a single fucking thing between my cock and your pussy. And when I'm done with you, my spunk is gonna be dripping down your creamy thighs. You're not gonna be able to walk straight and you're gonna beg me to fill you even more."

Tristan's vulgar words caused my breathing to increase and I could feel my lacy white panties becoming moist with arousal. I moaned deeply and said his name in a breathless voice. He moved his head to look at my face and even though the bedroom was dim, I could still see the beautiful blue of his eyes. I pulled him close to me and continued to speak in a breathless voice. "I want you to take me. I want you to do whatever you want to me. Give it to me like you've never given it to me before. I want it...I *need* it. I don't want to be a good girl anymore."

Tristan released a growl from deep in his throat as he grabbed me and began backing me up towards the nearest wall. He slammed me up against it and attacked my mouth again. My hands flew up into his hair and my fingers tangled themselves in the soft blond strands. After all the emotions we both experienced that night, we needed each other's bodies like we needed to breathe. Suddenly, Tristan released his possessive hold on my body and commanded me in a dominant voice, "Take off the dress."

I didn't need to be told twice. I kicked off my shoes and I quickly turned my back to him and said urgently, "Unzip me, sweetie. Hurry!" I felt Tristan's agile fingers unzip my dress in one swipe. He wouldn't let me turn around because he quickly pulled the dress down but was careful not to be too rough with it. Once I stepped out of it, he picked it up and tossed it on a nearby armchair. He still wouldn't let me turn around because he covered me with his body and pressed me up against the wall. I felt him reach down and rip my panties completely off. They were made of a fragile material so they put up no resistance.

He continued to be dominant towards me and he whispered in my ear, "Don't fucking move." I complied with my prince and I heard him remove his clothing. I was still breathing rapidly because I was desperate for him to take me; I was actually aching for him. Within a few seconds, I felt him cover me with his body again...but this time he was completely naked. His name escaped my throat in a deep moan when I felt him rub his warm, hard erection between my crack. Then he bent down and sucked on my neck. I tilted my head to the side to give him more access because I knew he was marking me. He ground his hips into me and I started gasping and writhing against him to create even more friction. He released his mouth from my delicate skin and I heard him growl in my ear, "You're mine, Bridget. You'll always be mine."

That's when I felt him enter my pussy deeply from behind. I cried out loudly even though my face was pressed against the wall. Tristan took both my hands and spread them on the wall in front of us. Then he covered my hands with his and began to pound into me...hard. I felt his warm breath on the side of my neck and I moved my head to the side to find his mouth. We kissed each other feverously while he continued thrusting inside me harder and deeper.

Then he hit my G-spot and I screamed, "YES! YES! AHHHHH!" The next thing I knew, he pulled out of me and turned me around to face him. I didn't realize our feet were moving until I found myself being pressed up against the glass on the balcony door. In less than three seconds, he plunged his raw manhood deep inside me again all the way to the hilt. We both cried out together and he hooked one of my legs around his waist. He took my body forcefully and I could feel my bare ass against the cool glass. His tall, strong body pinned me there as he drove into me hard, over and over. At first I had my arms around his neck but then he grabbed both of my wrists and held my arms above my head. There was practically no space between our bodies as Tristan filled me completely. And every time he would slam into me, my body would bang against the glass. I cried out in ecstasy, "Oh you feel so good, Tristan! I love your cock, baby! I fucking love it!"

Tristan smothered my cries of passion by kissing me deeply while he pleasured me beyond words. My arms were still above my head but he quickly grabbed my hands, entwined our fingers, and held them there against the glass. My husband wasn't relinquishing his dominant position any time soon and he continued to seduce me until I thought I couldn't take it any longer. Either that or the glass would break.

After awhile I couldn't hold myself up with my one leg. He must've sensed it because he lifted me completely off the carpet while he was still inside me. Both of my legs instinctively wrapped around his waist and he carried me over to the California King-size bed in the middle of the room. We were still connected when he fell on top of me and began pounding me deep into the soft, extremely comfortable mattress.

All of a sudden, he pulled himself out of me again and commanded me sternly. "Come here, Bridget. Up against the headboard. Now!" We both moved towards the top of the bed and I turned around to face the headboard. I put my hands out to brace myself and Tristan wasted no time in continuing our love making. He grabbed my hips and the harder he fucked me, the louder I cried out. It seemed like I was the one who was disturbing our neighbors, and in the back of my mind I was hoping that our walls were sound-proof.

It wasn't long until I felt the tingling sensation in my belly and I knew my orgasm was within close reach. I yelled out to my husband, "Baby, I'm close! Oh God, oh God! Please! I'm going to cum!" My body started to tremble but to my complete surprise, Tristan pulled himself out of me yet again.

"No you're not. You're not cumming yet." He turned me around and pulled me close to his body and continued kissing me intensely. I ran my fingers through his hair and I felt that it was partially wet from him sweating. My hands moved down and I grabbed his shoulders, and that's when he pushed me down on the bed and spread my legs wide.

I laughed in surprise before I licked my lips and purred seductively, "Fuck me hard, baby. I'm a naughty girl now. I deserve it hard." For a minute, he didn't move an inch and his blue eyes began to burn into mine. The expression on his face was intense and he didn't say a word. Then he looked down at my exposed pussy, grabbed both of my thighs and plunged his erection deep inside me again. I screamed out loud as he started to fuck me without mercy.

My head was thrashing back and forth against the pillow. I grabbed the bed sheets as if I was holding on for dear life and I arched my back off the bed in absolute ecstasy. I couldn't help but wonder if Tristan was possessed by some sexy, lustful incubus or Sex God because the way he was pleasuring me was incredible. I thought he was going to split me in half but it felt so damn good and I didn't want it to end. And just when I thought it couldn't get any better, he started saying things to me in his sexy British accent that made me want to literally cry from the extreme pleasure. His strokes were deep and as he spoke his sentences, he would slam into me. "Who do you belong to? Say it, Bridget! Who do you belong to?"

I almost forgot how to form words, but I quickly answered the best I could even though my voice was strangled. "Ahhhh...you...you! I belong to you!"

"And whose cock do you love more than any other?"

"Yours!"

"And who fucks you like you've never been fucked in your whole life?"

I was trying to catch my breath and answer him at the same time. I guess I didn't answer quickly enough because he started pounding into me harder. His pubic bone was hitting against my clit so perfectly that I felt my pussy release more of its essence. "You! You fuck me the best, baby!"

"And what's my fucking name?"

"Tristan!"

He released his grip on my thighs and I knew I'd see his red fingerprints against my pale, white skin. Tristan laid down and covered my naked body with his and captured my mouth again. We held each other so tight that we were becoming welded together. He didn't let up for a second and we continued to match each other's pace. When we finally broke the kiss to come up for air, he looked directly into my eyes and asked in a breathless voice of his own, "And what am I? What am I, Bridget?"

"Tristan...I can't...ahhhhh! Oh my God, I can't baby! Please! Please, I have to cum now!"

"WHAT AM I BRIDGET?!? SAY IT!"

"YOU'RE MY FUCKING PRINCE!" I screamed at the top of my lungs. I came so hard that I thought my half of our soul was going to rip itself from my body. My back arched off the bed again and a long moan escaped my throat. Tristan yelled loudly too as he joined me in our intense orgasm. I felt him spill his warm seed deep inside my womb and I actually starting crying from the pleasure. It was the first time I ever cried and I honestly couldn't help it. He made me feel so good and I loved him so much, that I didn't know any other way to express what I was feeling. Tristan didn't dare remove himself from on top of me and we just embraced tightly while our bodies trembled and our pelvises continued to meet and hump against each other. When he finally pulled back to look at my face, he smiled down at me and kissed my lips before he wiped my tears away. I couldn't help but wonder what seeing my tears did to his male ego.

We were both breathless but Tristan managed to speak first. As he spoke, he smoothed the hair back from my sweaty brow. "Bridget, I love you so much. You have no idea how much." He kissed my forehead and I felt how soft his lips were against my damp skin. "I don't think there are words to describe how I really feel about you."

I looked adoringly up at him and he was flushed from exertion and there was a thin sheen of sweat covering every inch of his ivory skin. He

April Bostic

was still panting softly and for a quick second, my mind flashed back
to the first time we made love and he looked exactly this way. From the
moment I met Tristan, I believed he was the epitome of male beauty. And
after he shared his body with me and expressed his love physically, he
was even more beautiful. His azure eyes began to search mine, but this
time I knew he wasn't actually searching for something behind my eyes;
he was conveying his feelings.

The emotions I experienced after our coupling and the thoughts of
my new husband almost caused me to choke on my words but I forced
myself to remain composed. "Baby, that was…" I closed my eyes briefly
and sighed softly as I tried to express exactly how Tristan made me feel.
"The best sex I've ever had in my life. You're amazing. No, *more* than
amazing." I laughed lightly and repeated his earlier statement because I
felt that 'amazing' didn't do Tristan's love-making justice. "I don't think
there are words to describe how you make me feel." I tilted my head up
and rubbed my nose gently against his. Then I whispered, "I love you too,
baby. More than you know."

Once we both had enough strength to detach from one another, we
laid naked and sweaty atop the black silk sheets and made pillow-talk.
I was lying on my side in the middle of the bed and Tristan was lying in
back of me. I wasn't really surprised that both our voices were laced with
post-sex hoarseness. Tristan was running his fingers through my hair
that was fanned out on the bed when I said, "Baby, I know we're going
back to L.A. soon but there's one more thing I want before we leave."

"What's that, sweets?"

I smiled, and even though Tristan couldn't see it, I know he *heard* it
in my voice. "A tatt."

I felt him shift behind me and he leaned over me. I turned on my
back to look up at him and this time he could see my smile. He was
looking down at me in shock when he replied, "You want a tatt? Are you
serious?"

"Yep, I want one to match yours. You know, the one you have of my
name. I want your name on the inside of my right wrist and I want the
same lettering too."

Tristan gave me a side-long glance. "Are you *sure?* You know it may
be painful for you. Do you think you could handle it?"

I tilted my head up and kissed my beautiful British husband. He smiled lovingly down at me and brushed his fingers across my lips. "Of course I can handle it. I'll have you right next to me. And if I get scared, you'll be strong for me. Won't you?"

Tristan leaned closer to me and spoke in a soft but raspy voice. "That's right, love. I'll be strong for you; just like you were for me." He bent down to kiss me again and then he said, "Tomorrow I'll take you to the place where I got one of mine done. My mate works there and I trust him to do yours."

I reached up and gently caressed his handsome face. "That sounds good to me," I said as I stretched my limbs. That's when I realized my pussy was actually sore. I couldn't stop myself from laughing.

"What's so funny?"

"You wore me out baby, and I don't think I can walk."

Tristan laughed too. Suddenly, he moved and climbed off the bed. "I think I can help you with that." He reached over and pulled me towards the edge of the bed. Then he lifted me in his arms and I laughed in absolute joy. "Remember I said we're getting in the jacuzzi? The warm bubbling water should make you feel all better." He leaned his head towards me and kissed me deeply and I could feel the passion engulfing us once more. "And if not...well, then I'll just take care of you personally." He waggled his eyebrows which caused me to start laughing again.

The next day I got my first tattoo, and it was painful just like Tristan said it would be. But he was right next to me and he held my left hand the entire time. He was strong for me that day and after awhile I forgot about the pain. As we were flying back to Los Angeles, I couldn't help but to think about how I was no longer Bridget Monahan. I was now Bridget *Hathaway*. I wasn't Tristan's girlfriend or his fiancé. I was his wife. I began thinking about writing my new name on the blackboard when I started the new school year and the idea actually made me feel giddy. Tristan must've noticed the smile on my face because he asked, "What are you thinking about?"

I answered him simply. "Being Mrs. Hathaway."

Chapter 19

'Maybe the wildest dreams are but the needful preludes of the truth.'

~ Alfred, Lord Tennyson

IT WAS LATE SPRING THE following year and we were on our way to the Los Angeles premiere of Tristan's new vampire film. I was standing in the living room checking the contents of my purse when I called out to him. "Tristan, come on baby! We don't want to be late!" A limousine was supposed to pick us up and take us to the premiere but for some reason, Tristan rejected the idea and insisted on driving us there in my car.

After a few seconds, he came jogging into the living room. When he reached me, he started straightening his shirt collar. "How do I look, babe?" My British husband looked good enough to eat. He was wearing his Valentine's gift from last year: a sky blue, button-down, shirt with the sleeves rolled up to his elbows so he could display his lovely tatts. The color of his shirt was the exact shade of his eyes and I remembered choosing the shirt for him just for that reason. The top button of his shirt was undone because he decided to go tieless for this event. I could see a small expanse of ivory skin that was exposed. Tristan was never one to tuck in his shirts, so it hung over a pair of casual black pants with black shoes that completed his ensemble. He was also not a man to go without accessories, so he was wearing his black leather ID bracelet on his left wrist, a couple of rubber black bracelets on his right, and a small silver hoop in his left ear.

Once I finished admiring him, I reached up and smoothed a few stray blond hairs that were sticking up awkwardly on top of his head. When I was satisfied that his hair looked perfectly tousled, I smiled and remarked, "Tristan, you look like walking-sex."

He grinned widely in appreciation. "Thanks, love." Then he gave me the once-over and licked his lips. His look was definitely predatory when he said, "So do you." Suddenly, his blue gaze turned intense and I saw pure lust cross his beautiful Nordic features. At that moment, I knew he was thinking naughty thoughts.

I won't deny that I was thinking along the same lines but I've come to accept the fact that it's *my* responsibility to make sure we didn't get lost in each other. Once Tristan ensnared me in his seductive spell and became aroused, it was hard to stop him. Not only that, but it was even harder to resist him. And it didn't matter if we had some place to be; he would make us late so he could finish what we started.

Before we became side-tracked by devouring each other with our eyes, I broke the spell that Tristan was beginning to cast on me and took his hand. "Let's go lover-boy." We headed outside and got into my ruby red Mercedes Benz convertible.

While Tristan was driving us to the premiere, I couldn't help but notice he was going in the wrong direction. I turned to him with a look of confusion. "Tristan, where are you going? The premiere is in the other direction."

He quickly glanced at me before he turned his eyes back on the road. "I'm just taking the long way."

"But baby, we're going to be late."

He didn't look at me but I saw a smile appear on his face. "Hey, there's nothing wrong with being fashionably late."

I chuckled and shook my head. "Whatever you say. This is *your* movie."

When Tristan finally stopped the car, he pulled over on a side-street in a suburban neighborhood in Hollywood. My eyes scanned my surroundings and an expression of confusion appeared on my face. "Why are we stopped? What's going on?" He turned the engine off and unbuckled his seatbelt. When he turned to face me, he was grinning. I looked at him questioningly but his facial expression remained the same. Then I saw his eyes quickly dart to something behind me. "What?" He

jerked his head in the same direction so I turned my head to the right and I saw a house. "What? The house?"

"Do you like it?"

I was still confused so I turned back to face him. "Yeah, it's really nice. Why?"

Suddenly, he raised his right arm and smacked the top of my headrest with his hand. His voice was filled with absolute joy when he replied, "Good! 'Cause it's gonna be ours!"

It took a couple seconds for me to comprehend what he was saying. But when I finally understood, my eyes widened in complete surprise. "What?!? What do you mean it's going to be ours?!?"

Tristan laughed and his blue eyes were sparkling with happiness. He quickly opened his door and got out of the car. Once he closed his door, he turned to me and asked, "Well, don't you wanna see it?"

I was still in shock, but I managed to open my door and get out of the car. By the time I stood up, Tristan came around to my side and closed my door. Then he took my hand and we walked up to the gate. I saw him pull out some keys from his pocket and use one of them to open the gate. As I looked at the front of the house, I realized it was a turn-key gated English Tudor. The gate was a few feet long and it stretched along the front of the house. I saw that the entrance to the driveway which leads to the garage was operated by an automated gate. Once Tristan opened the gate, he took my hand again and we walked up the sidewalk to the front door. The landscaping was very attractive and the gray shutters gave the house a very 'country' feel. I happened to look up and I saw a small terrace connected to one of the second-story windows that was decorated with flowers.

He opened the front door and when we walked in, I was immediately in awe. I looked around and I took in the polished hardwood floors and the high ceiling. The smell of the fresh off-white paint filled my nostrils and I noticed the long wooden staircase. I heard Tristan's voice say, "This is the living room, babe. And look, we have a fireplace!" I walked over to where he was standing and admired our new fireplace. Before I could respond, he took my hand again and pulled me into a different room. "We have three bedrooms and three loos. We also have a den that you can make into your office. You know, so you can work on your school stuff in your own private room. There's a laundry room with a washer and dryer down in the basement and look love, this is your new kitchen!"

He let go of my hand and I looked around my new kitchen in amazement. I was nearly breathless when I responded, "Oh my God, Tristan. This is my kitchen? This is *my* kitchen." I glided my hands across the smooth counter-tops. I looked inside a few of the cherrywood cabinets and the stainless-steel refrigerator. I was inspecting the vintage, but mint-condition stove that had a griddle and two ovens and the dishwasher while Tristan continued describing all the house amenities.

He pointed and said, "That's our dining room over there and it has stained-glass windows and a chandelier!" Then he pointed in a different direction and said, "And that's uh..." He paused and tapped his finger against his chin as he thought. "What did the realtor bloke say? Oh yeah, that's a breakfast nook!" I walked into each room to look around and Tristan came to stand beside me.

We went downstairs to the finished basement and he was chock full of ideas about what we could do with it. I was admiring our new washer and dryer when he took my hand again and said excitedly, "Oh yeah, I have to show you this! C'mon!" He pulled me along again and we went back upstairs, then up the wooden staircase and entered what looked like the master bedroom. Tristan confirmed my assumption because he said, "This is gonna be our room, babe." Then he took me into another room which happened to be a bathroom. "And this is the master loo. But check this out." He stood next to the bathtub and smiled widely.

Once I looked at the tub, I gasped. Then I said with wide-eyes, "Clawfoot tubs?!? Oh my God! I've always loved these!"

Tristan continued to smile. "Yep, and over here..." He moved to stand next to the glass shower doors which led to a large hexagon-shaped marble shower. "Look how more spacious the shower is." And then he waggled his eyebrows at me. I laughed in delight as I moved to inspect our new shower. Suddenly, it seemed like he was struck with an idea. "Oh yeah! Babe, you have to see this!"

He took my hand again and I followed him back downstairs and out the French doors in the kitchen which led to the back of the house. He put his arms out wide and announced, "This is the backyard!" We were actually standing on a patio and I looked around in surprise. Tristan bounded off the patio steps and stood in the grass. I went over to him and he exclaimed happily, "Now we can barbecue!" We both laughed. "Your dad gave me a few pointers." He moved over to another area of the yard and said, "I'm gonna set up the grill right over here." I looked at him with pure affection because I was so glad to see him so enthusiastic. Then he pointed across the yard and said, "Back there...those are our fruit trees! And we have *two* fountains, babe!"

As I was admiring the stone fountains, I couldn't help but wonder about the price of house. "Um...how much is this place?"

Tristan replied casually, "A little under a mil." My eyes widened in shock. Then he spoke in a condescending tone. "Babe, it's Hollywood. I was lucky to find a house this nice for that price. I already gave the bank a down-payment but we still need to sign some more papers for the mortgage."

As Tristan was explaining, I couldn't help but wonder where he got the money for a house this expensive. I thought out loud when I asked, "Where'd you get the money for the down-payment?"

Strangely, Tristan looked away from me when he answered. "When I told Mum and Dad that I wanted to buy us a house, Dad offered to help me with the financial aspect. He said he'd give us anything we needed. He actually gave me most of the down-payment and I put in the rest."

I was honestly shocked but I was also extremely thankful. That was a very thoughtful, not to mention generous thing for Will to do. I started to wonder if that was his way of trying to build on him and Tristan's relationship. Ever since Tristan forgave him on our wedding day last year, Will made a constant effort to reach out and support Tristan in any way that he could. And I truly respected Will for not allowing the long distance between them to stop him from having a relationship with his youngest son.

Because Tristan averted his eyes from me when he admitted that his father helped him purchase the house, I knew he was feeling ashamed. I wanted to reassure him that it was okay to accept his father's help, so I approached him and encircled my arms around his waist. I spoke in a gentle voice when I said, "That was very thoughtful of Dad. When you speak to him again, please thank him for me."

That seemed to make Tristan feel better because he smiled and kissed my forehead. "Yeah, I'll tell him."

We walked around the full length of the backyard when Tristan remarked casually, "Eventually, I'd like to put in a pool."

My mouth dropped. I've never had a pool before and I laughed in delight. "A pool?!? Baby, that would be awesome!"

Tristan beamed. "Yeah, I know. Can you say 'pool party'?" We both laughed.

We approached the garage and Tristan began to resume his role as the realtor. "This is a two-car garage. I was specifically looking for one 'cause I figured I'd have to get a car eventually." Then he mumbled, "Or a bloody minivan." I laughed. "You know, for our kids."

"Oh, you mean when we *decide* to have kids?"

"Yeah," he replied quietly. "We have an automatic garage door opener and for added security...the gate to the parkway has an automated gate." Tristan pointed to a window above my head and I followed with my eyes. "Did you notice the terrace with the flowers? Only our bedroom has them. When I saw them, I thought that maybe you'd like them." While I was admiring the terrace from below, he came up behind me and put his arms around my waist. He held me close and I covered his tattooed arms with mine. Then he kissed the side of my neck and his lips traveled upwards to my jaw and then my cheek. His voice was low when he asked, "So what do you think?"

I couldn't help but to smile widely in genuine happiness. This was the last thing I would've expected to see when we left the house that afternoon. "I think..." I turned in his arms to face him and I put my arms around him and kissed his velvety lips. "I love this house. Thank you so much, sweetheart."

Tristan leaned down and captured my lips again because my kiss didn't satisfy his need. He slanted his mouth over mine a couple times and moved his hands to either side of my head so he could kiss me deeply. He gently nibbled my bottom lip and lightly ran his tongue across it before we ended the kiss. Then he put his arms around me again and smiled. "I'm so glad you love the house. I wanted to keep my promise to you, love. I told you that I would get us a bigger place." Tristan looked up at the sky and I found myself just gazing at him adoringly. "And who knows, maybe when I make it big...we can sell this place and get a huge fucking mansion." He looked down at me and began to gently rock me back and forth in his arms.

I reached up and caressed his cheek and then I brushed my fingers softly across his lips. "We don't need a mansion, sweetie. This house is perfect for the two of us."

"And our kids," he added.

I sighed and then I looked down in defeat. "Yes, *and* our kids."

As Tristan and I walked back through the house to leave out the front door, he had his arm around my shoulder. He leaned his head down and spoke in a low voice close to my ear. "You know when we move in, we're gonna 'christen' every room in this house."

I laughed lightly as I wrapped my arm around my beautiful husband's waist. My voice took on a more seductive tone when I replied, "I'm looking forward to it."

When we got back in the car, I turned my head to look at the house one last time. I was filled with hope when I turned to look at Tristan. I smiled warmly and looked lovingly into his baby blues when I said, "It's going to be perfect. I just know it."

My handsome soul mate smiled back at me and caressed my cheek with the back of his hand. His voice was soft and sweet when he replied, "We'll make it perfect, love...'cause it'll be our home."

ᔕ

WE MOVED INTO OUR NEW home about a month later. I was awakened in the middle of the night by Tristan gently shaking my body. I slowly opened my eyes and I became aware that he was talking to me. His voice was more of a mumble because he was still half-asleep. "Babe, please answer the phone...it keeps ringing." At first I didn't hear anything. I took a moment to concentrate and I heard the phone ringing faintly from downstairs in the kitchen. I was still very sleepy so I slowly got out of bed and padded barefoot down to the kitchen to answer the phone.

When I picked up the receiver, it took me a few seconds to answer because I had to find my voice. My throat was hoarse from sleep, so my voice sounded more like a croak. "Hello?"

"Bridge?!?" It was Autumn...and she sounded frantic. "Oh my God! I'm so glad you answered. I was hoping you would pick up. I'm so sorry to wake you."

My eyes were closed when I first picked up the receiver. But when I heard the urgent tone in her voice, my eyes immediately opened. "What's the matter, Aut?"

I heard her take a deep breath. "Bridge, please don't think I'm crazy, alright? But this is just like too fucking weird, okay? I just had another one of those dreams and it freaked me out. But what's even freakier is that I haven't had a dream like this since the one about little Tristan telling me that he needed the red hair girl."

As soon as Autumn explained the reason for her call, I immediately perked up. "Well, are you going to tell me what this one was about?"

There was silence on her end for a few seconds. Then I heard her take a shaky breath. "Okay..." She paused again. "Oh my God, Bridge. I'm sorry but this dream was like so real. When I woke up, I didn't even realize where I was."

I could tell she was really panicking so I tried to get her to calm down. I spoke slowly when I said, "Autumn, just relax okay? Just take a few more deep breaths and calm down. When you're ready to talk, just open your mouth and tell me about the dream."

She paused again and I could hear her breathing hard on the other end. Deep inside me, I started to panic because I was worried that it was more of a nightmare. When she finally spoke, she had my undivided attention.

"I was walking on a beach. It was a warm sunny day and there were other people around doing...you know...whatever. Then all of a sudden, this soccer ball bounces across my path. I see it stop, so I go over and pick it up. Then this little girl with wavy blonde hair...she had to be like three or four years old... comes running after the ball. She's wearing a purple and pink bathing suit with Tinkerbell on the front. When she sees that I'm holding it, she says, 'bugger' and I notice she has a British accent. I smile and look down at her and I see that she has pretty blue eyes. She approaches me cautiously at first and then it's like...I don't know...like she finally recognizes me. Her expression changes and she smiles at me. She walks over to me with her hands out like she wants me to give her the ball. I kneel down to her level and hand it to her and she looks at it for a minute. Then she looks up at me and says, 'Thanks Auntie Autumn.' But she doesn't say my name right...it's like she can't pronounce it. So after she says my name, I'm looking at her in total shock 'cause how does she know who I am? And just when I'm about to ask her how she knows me...I hear

Tristan's voice. I look around and I can't see him but I hear his voice as clear as day. He yells, 'Katie! Bring the ball back, love!' I'm still looking around in confusion, right. Then all of a sudden, the little girl...I guess she's Katie...waves at me and says, 'Bye!' Then she runs away towards the sound of his voice. I look in the direction that she's running and I still don't see Tristan. I tried to follow her but then something happened...like everything went black.

And that's when I woke up."

For a moment, I was a little annoyed that Autumn woke me up at... I glanced at the clock on the wall...two o'clock in the morning, to tell me this dream. I didn't see what was so 'freaky' about it. At that moment, I felt that I needed to tell her my opinion. "Aut, what's so weird about that? I don't understand why you're so freaked out."

Instead of answering my question, she was silent for a moment. Then suddenly, I heard her voice but it was so low that I could barely hear her. "Are you pregnant?"

Her question caught me off-guard and I sputtered. "What?" This time I paused because I couldn't believe she asked me that. I needed to reassure her so I replied, "Aut, you know I'm on The Pill."

"But you and Tris stopped using condoms right?"

"Uh...yeah," I replied quietly.

"You know Bridge, The Pill isn't always one-hundred percent effective." We were both silent and then I heard her sigh. "Just do me a favor and let me know if you miss your next period, okay?" My eyes widened and I was about to respond to her but she continued. "Remember I told you that I think I'm connected to you and Tristan?"

"Yeah?"

"I'm telling you Bridge, these dreams are just too weird for me. I never have dreams with kids in them...*ever*. This is the second time in my life that I've had one. You already know about the first time. And both dreams involved you and Tristan." She paused and I heard her take another deep breath. "When I woke up from this dream, I didn't even realize I was in my bed. I thought I was still at the beach looking for Tristan and the little girl."

"Wait, how do you know this dream involves me? And how can you be sure that Katie is me and Tristan's daughter? Did Tristan ever tell you that he liked the name 'Katie'?"

"Bridge, it was so obvious. She looked just like the both of you. And Tristan has never talked to me about kids' names."

In all truthfulness, Autumn's dream started to freak me out too. Why was she having these types of dreams? And was she *really* connected to me and Tristan? All of a sudden, I started feeling overwhelmed and uncomfortable. I didn't understand what was going on and I was too exhausted to try. Tristan and I 'christened' our house that night and I was completely worn out. I heaved a heavy sigh and said, "Hey, do you think we could talk about this later? I'm really tired right now."

Suddenly, her tone of voice seemed to lighten. "Sure! I'm so sorry, Bridge. I know I woke you up and I probably woke Tristan up too. Okay, well...I'll talk to you later." Before I could respond, I heard her hang up. I stood motionless with the receiver to my ear for a few seconds until I heard the annoying beeping sound coming from the phone which told me that I needed to hang up.

I was still pondering Autumn's recent dream as I walked back upstairs to the bedroom. I tried to put it out of my mind as I entered our still darkened room and crawled back into bed with Tristan. I scooted close to his warm, naked body and I put my arms around him. I laid my head on his chest in hopes that his beating heart would help lull me back to sleep. I felt him embrace me and kiss the top of my head. Then I heard him mumble sleepily, "Who was that?"

I whispered, "That was Autumn."

"Is everything alright?"

"Yeah. She just..." I paused and squeezed my eyes shut in an attempt to stomp down on my feeling of uneasiness. "She had a dream that she met our future child and it freaked her out."

This time Tristan didn't respond immediately. When he didn't respond after the next few minutes, I assumed he fell back to sleep. As much as I tried not to, I laid there thinking about Autumn's dream. Then I started wondering if maybe I was pregnant or about to become pregnant. I closed my eyes again and tried to block out her voice and the imagery that her dream created in my mind.

Eventually, my body relaxed completely and I began drifting off into another peaceful slumber with Tristan's comforting scent surrounding me. Suddenly, his embrace tightened and I heard his quiet voice in the darkness. "You know babe, if we have a little girl..." He paused for a short moment. "We should name her after Mum." He paused again and then I heard him mumble, "But we'll call her Katie."

And that's when my eyes shot open.

After his baby name request, I noticed that Tristan fell back to sleep with ease. At least one of us was able to, because the unexplainable coincidence between Autumn's dream and his comment, left me wide awake for hours. For awhile, I kept wondering what the deal was with Autumn. Why was she having these dreams that involved me and Tristan, and more importantly...how? How was she able to predict our futures through dreams? So far, her predictions have been limited to our love lives and our children. But what else would her dreams predict? Would she know if one of us was going to die? For a minute I started to think that maybe she was a true psychic. I usually roll my eyes whenever I see any of those psychic reader commercials on television. I'll admit that I'm a skeptic and I don't really believe there are mystical powers at work beyond human awareness. Was she the one person who was finally going to make me a believer?

A few times during the course of our relationship, Tristan spoke to me about fate. He believes he was destined to meet me as we're two halves of a single soul. Maybe I was supposed to meet Autumn on MySpace because she was the bridge that would connect me to Tristan. Everything was all so confusing and as hard as I tried, I couldn't make any sense of it. That's when another old memory resurfaced and I remembered one day when Tristan told me that some things in life just defy all logic. At this point, I found myself agreeing with him completely.

As I lay in Tristan's comforting embrace with my head on his warm bare chest, I succumbed to the realization that it was hopeless to try and get a good night's sleep. Even the sound of his wonderful heartbeat wasn't enough to lull me back to sleep and make me forget about the strange, yet scary coincidence between him and Autumn. I slowly removed myself from his embrace and my movement caused him to stir slightly in his sleep. Thankfully, I couldn't decipher Katie's name again in his quiet mumbling. I got out of bed and put on my robe and slippers. Then I opened the hope chest at the foot of the bed and pulled out a cozy blanket.

I decided to go outside in hopes that the cool, crisp summer air might help to clear my head a bit and alleviate my restlessness. I went downstairs and walked through the kitchen, then out the French doors to the back patio. I sat on a wicker patio sofa and turned my body to lay with my feet propped up onto the cushions. I tilted my head up to gaze at the bright stars that were clearly visible against the infinite blackness of the night sky. For some strange reason I singled out a lone star. I closed my eyes and wished quietly to myself, *Please...someone just tell me what's going on.* The naive part of me hoped that a little voice would answer me right away inside my head and the mystery of Autumn's dreams would be revealed. Then I could sigh a breath of relief and go back to bed with the satisfying feeling of complete understanding. But that was not to be, and there was no voice that would help me solve the mystery. I laid outside in the backyard for hours. I ended up watching the sunrise with a blanket wrapped around me and perplexity still clouding my mind.

It wasn't until the first rays of the sun hit me that I began a whole other train of thought. I started to wonder about the question Autumn posed to me: was I pregnant? Is that why she had the dream about Katie? Because Katie had already made her way into this world? Right at that moment, I untangled myself from the blanket and hurried back into the kitchen. I had Dr. Boykin's home number on speed dial so I immediately called her. I was like a niece to her so I knew she wouldn't mind too much if I awakened her so early in the morning. Besides, it was an urgent matter and it could be life-changing. I needed to know for sure before I made myself crazy with worry. I needed to know at least part of the answer to the riddle. To my relief, Dr. Boykin wasn't all that upset and she told me to come into her office when she first opened at 9AM.

My current state of anxiety prevented me from trying to catch even a couple hours of sleep, so I decided to start a pot of coffee and make breakfast. After I ate, I put Tristan's plate in the oven to keep it warm. I took a long shower and when I returned to the bedroom to get my clothes, I saw him moving around in the bed. I was putting on my undies when I heard him speak in a voice still thick with sleep. "Where are you going, babe?"

I glanced at him briefly while I continued to get dressed. "I'm going to see Dr. Boykin."

Tristan sat up and rubbed at his eyes. "What's the matter? Something must be wrong if you have to see her this early in the morning." He stretched his sinewy form and yawned like a giant cat. "What time is it anyway?"

"It's a little after eight." I figured since he was awake now, I may as well share with him the reason why I missed a whole night's sleep. "Baby, I have to tell you something, okay?" I walked over to the bed and sat next to him. He was sitting up against the headboard and looking back at me through sleepy eyes. "I didn't tell you all the details about Autumn's dream. In her dream, she heard you call our child 'Katie'." That garnered a reaction from him because his lips parted and I noticed his eyes widen slightly. "We had a daughter, Tristan. And when I asked her if you ever mentioned that name to her, she said no." There was a look of total shock on his face and I felt like telling him that I knew exactly how he felt. "So when you told me that you wanted to name our daughter Katie, I just..." I cast my eyes down and shook my head. "I guess it just freaked me out. I didn't get any sleep because I was up all night thinking about her dream; thinking about *why* she had the dream and *how?* What's the connection between her and us? And when she asked me if I was pregnant---"

"Wait, hold on a second." Tristan closed his eyes briefly and sighed. Then he started scratching his head while he wore an expression of confusion. "She had a dream that she met our future kid? And then she heard me call her 'Katie'?" I nodded. His expression changed to one of mild amazement and he repeated my earlier actions by shaking his head. The volume of his voice lowered when he asked, "How did she know I wanted to name our daughter that?"

"That's the thing...she *didn't* know. She just heard you say the name in her dream. But what I don't get is...why would she hear you say that particular name? Of all the girls' names in the world? And then like a few minutes later you mumble in your sleep that if we have a little girl you want to name her 'Katie'. That's just too weird."

"Tell me about it." Neither of us spoke for the next couple seconds; we just looked at each other. "You know Bridge, when you told me about her dream...I was awake. I heard everything you said. That's why I mentioned naming the baby after Mum 'cause I believed you were pregnant." Tristan's expression softened and he took both of my hands in his. "Look, if Aut's first dream is any indication, then she had this dream for a reason and it's probably true." He looked into my eyes and right at that moment I knew he truly believed our baby was growing inside me.

I couldn't help but to sigh heavily because I hated when I couldn't make sense of something. I thought out loud when I said, "I still don't understand why she's having these dreams and how she's doing it."

"Maybe she's psychic. Anything's possible, love. I definitely wouldn't rule it out."

"Baby, you know I don't believe in that stuff."

Tristan smirked. "Obviously you do if you're gonna see your doctor to find out if you're pregnant."

His comment shut me up immediately. I'll admit that I was curious but I wasn't a believer yet. I got up from the bed and continued getting dressed. "Well, I just have to know, Tristan. I have to find out if there's any truth to her dream."

I sat down at my vanity to do my hair when he came to stand next to me. "I'm going with you." I looked up at him in surprise but I was actually relieved that I wouldn't have to go through this alone. "I wanna know too, babe. I wanna know if there really is a little Katie inside you." He leaned down to kiss the top of my head before he walked away towards the bathroom.

We were sitting in Dr. Boykin's office and I was filled with anxiety once again. She had just given me an examination and a pregnancy test and we were waiting for the results. My right knee kept bouncing up and down involuntarily and I was worrying my bottom lip between my teeth. All I could think about were the test results; yes or no? Positive or negative? I thought that maybe I'll be able to tell the answer right away by the expression on the doctor's face when she comes back into the office. Unless she puts on a poker face. Then I'm doomed to find out the answer when she's ready to reveal it. I started thinking that if it's positive, how would I handle being pregnant and becoming a mother in nine months? I also couldn't help but to think about Tristan's reaction and if he was ready to be father.

I was actually zoning out for a minute but Tristan brought me back to the present when he put his hand on my knee to stop the bouncing. I turned to look at him and he smiled slightly and put his arm around me to comfort me. He spoke softly when he said, "Don't worry, love. If you're pregnant then we'll just start our family a little earlier than planned, that's all. Everything's gonna be okay. We're in this together, remember?"

He pulled me closer to his body and I couldn't help but nuzzle my face into his cotton t-shirt and breathe his familiar scent.

When the door opened, I was immediately alert and I lifted my head up from Tristan's chest. I looked at Dr. Boykin's face and her expression gave nothing away. She was holding a single piece of paper in her hand as she walked over to her desk and sat behind it. Her expression still didn't change as she slid the paper across the surface of her desk over to me and Tristan. I looked down at the paper but I was so nervous that I couldn't reach for it. Thankfully, Tristan picked up the paper instead. I turned to look at him and I watched his eyes dart back and forth across as he read it. If I wasn't so close to him, I wouldn't have noticed the subtle change in his breathing pattern. Right at that moment, my face flushed with heat and my ears felt hot because I knew the results just by his mild reaction. I swallowed hard and just as I was attempting to speak, Tristan turned his attention to me. His cerulean eyes bore into my toffee ones for a couple seconds and a smile played at the corner of his lips. "We're pregnant, love."

The smile broke free and at the same time, I heard Dr. Boykin's kind voice. "Congratulations."

Tristan handed the paper to me and I took it from him carefully as if it were fine china. He put his arm around me again and kissed my cheek. I heard him whisper in my ear, "I love you."

I finally found my voice and responded in turn, "I love you too." My eyes scanned the paper until they rested on a little box in the bottom right-hand corner. In the middle of the box was one word: *positive*. I tried to share Tristan's genuine happiness but the reality of the situation was all too shocking for me. According to the paper I was twenty-four days long. My last period was not exactly on schedule but sometimes it's off by a couple days so I didn't think anything of it this time. Before I knew it, my breathing increased and I whispered, "Oh my God."

That's when I heard Dr. Boykin speak again. "I take it this wasn't planned?"

Tristan answered her because I was still in a state of shock. "We planned on having kids, just..." He paused and I continued to stare at the word 'positive'. I felt his eyes on me so I looked over at him with wide-eyes. "Not yet," he finished in a quiet voice.

We listened to Dr. Boykin tell us about prenatal care and all the precautions I'll have to take now that I was carrying a little life inside me. She was also telling me about the changes that will occur to my body over the next few months. I couldn't really speak because the realization that I was pregnant didn't fully register yet but I heard Tristan say that he'll come with me to every doctor's visit. As I watched him listen intently to Dr. Boykin, I could tell he was truly happy about the results. He was smiling and he even laughed a couple times when she mentioned mood swings and the possibility of strange food cravings.

I, on the other hand, was too pissed off at my birth control for failing me. I started regretting the decision to allow Tristan to stop using condoms. One night while we were in the midst of our passionate love-making, he expressed his desire to take the condom off because he said the sex felt so much better without it. Of course I agreed with him because sex was a lot more enjoyable when I could feel his raw, stiff erection nestled deep inside my pussy. The next day, they were all in the trash and I never opened another condom packet for him again. I guess the condoms were actually preventing me from getting pregnant because my birth control alone did not protect me. Damn Tristan's super sperm.

It wasn't until we were driving home in silence, that my mostly unresponsive mood began to affect my husband. "You're not excited about this, are you?" Tristan was driving us back home and I was staring out the window. I kept repeating in my head: *I can't believe I'm pregnant.* When I didn't answer him, he started to get really upset. "Bridge, I know you weren't ready for this but it happened, okay? We have to deal with this." I still didn't respond. "Say something! Anything! *Please.* You're making me feel like you don't want the baby." I turned to look at him and he glanced at me. His brows were knitted tightly together and his expression was filled with worry.

I sighed as I tried to think of what to say to reassure him. I did want the baby but that didn't mean I was ready for it. I couldn't believe my whole life was about to change...again. And so quickly too. Tristan and I haven't even been married a year. "Tristan, I do want the baby, I'm just---"

"I know you're not ready. I know, Bridget. But sometimes things happen when you don't expect them to. And sometimes things happen that you don't want to happen. But you just have to deal with what life throws at you. Trust me, I've learned from experience." All of a sudden, his tone of voice changed. It was like whatever he was thinking about lightened his mood. I was watching him as he spoke and I noticed he was wearing a wistful expression. "But you know what? Sometimes it turns out to be really good in the end and you realize all the shit you went through was totally worth it."

I decided to pick his brain. "Oh yeah? Like what?"

Tristan smiled. "Like being with you. I never expected to fall in love with you. And I never expected you to stay with me. There were so many times when I thought you would leave; that I was just too fucked in the head for you to put any effort into trying to understand me; that you'd finally realize that you could find someone better; someone who isn't the jealous type." We stopped at a red light, and he took the opportunity to turn and look at me. "But you didn't. You stuck with me, Bridget. You ended up marrying me and now you're having my baby. It doesn't get any better than that...not for me." He leaned across the seat and kissed me. His lips were so soft and his intoxicating masculine scent invaded my nostrils. I put my hand on his cheek as he deepened the kiss and I felt his warm tongue plunder inside my mouth. It wasn't until someone honked at us that we realized the light changed.

Knowing Tristan the way I do, I knew I still had to reassure him that I wanted the baby. "Tristan, I'm not angry or upset. I want to have the baby. It's just that this is extremely life-changing. Not to mention... having a baby is expensive. My body is going to change and I need time to take everything in, that's all." All of a sudden my own words caused me to panic and a million questions ran through my mind: *Would we be able to afford having a baby? How much were diapers nowadays anyway? Who would take care of the baby once I was done with maternity leave and Tristan was working? Would we hire a nanny?* My voice took on a more edgy tone because of my current state. "I'm sorry if I'm not ecstatic about it like you are. I mean, you're the one who wanted a baby before we even got engaged. This is something you've wanted for a long time. I didn't want to have kids until later on."

"Later on? Like how much later?"

"I don't know...just later. When we're both---"

"What? When we're in our thirties or something?" His tone of voice suggested that he didn't like the idea one bit.

But it sounded like a good idea to me. "Yeah, what's wrong with that? Or at least until we've been married for awhile."

"Babe, I don't wanna be some fifty-year-old bloke trying to keep up with my kid playing footie. Besides, Mum says that having kids is for the young."

Trying to get Tristan to understand my feelings was becoming taxing so I sighed again. "I have a lot to think about, okay? I'll be more enthusiastic once I've had some time to let everything sink in." I turned my head to look out the window again as a signal to Tristan that I didn't feel like talking about it anymore.

He respected my wishes but he said this last thing to me before we remained silent for the rest of the drive home. "You worry too much." Sometimes my husband was too perceptive because I really *was* doing more worrying than actual thinking.

When we got home, Tristan was on the phone for at least an hour because he called most of his friends and family to spread the baby news. I was lounging on the living room sofa reading one of the many pamphlets that Dr. Boykin gave us when he approached me. I looked up at him and his expression was one of absolute joy. "Dad is thrilled about being a granddad and Mum said she's telling everyone she knows that she's gonna be a nana." He laughed lightly. "And Nanny actually started crying." I couldn't help but smile as I thought about how Tristan's family must be feeling. I know that Kate expressed to Tristan numerous times her desire to be a grandmother. "They wanted to speak to you but I told them you weren't feeling very *enthusiastic* right now." I immediately felt bad because they wanted to tell me how happy they were but I couldn't share their happiness. Why couldn't I feel happiness too? "Hey, aren't you gonna tell your parents? And what about Autumn? I didn't ring her 'cause I thought you'd wanna tell her how her dream was right...*again*."

The mention of Autumn's name caused an unexpected feeling of animosity towards her. I immediately wanted to talk to her just so I could tell her that I never wanted to hear another one of her freaky dreams again. I also wanted to confront her about why she's having the dreams and how. I put on a false smile and almost gritted my teeth as I replied, "I'll tell my parents the news later. But you're right, I should call

Autumn." What I needed to say to her required her physical presence so I added, "As a matter of fact, I'll ask her if she can come over."

Tristan started to walk away but he spoke over his shoulder. "Oh, Jake's coming over later and we're gonna check out some minivans."

A look of confusion naturally appeared on my face. Our baby was only an embryo right now and he wanted to look at minivans already? "Don't you think it's a little early for that?"

He answered me from in the kitchen. "I just wanna take a look at them so I'll get used to the horror of driving one."

I called Autumn and asked her to come over but I kept my voice neutral. I didn't give her any specific details or reasons as to why I wanted her to come over.

When she rang the doorbell about a half-hour later, she was her usual chipper self. "Hey Bridge, what's up?"

Only one of us was feeling chipper so I responded blandly. "Hey Aut. I just need to talk to you." I closed the front door and turned to walk towards the sofa. She followed me and we sat down and faced each other. She looked at me expectedly so I got right to the point. "It'll please you to know that I found out I'm pregnant." Her eyes widened and she gasped loudly before she covered her mouth with her hand. "Yeah. Tristan and I went to see my doctor and she confirmed it."

She removed her hand from her mouth and continued to look at me in shock. "Holy shit!"

"I'll also have you know that I didn't sleep at all last night after you told me about your dream. I was so freaked out that I had to know for sure if I was pregnant."

Her face fell and her voice was quiet when she said, "I'm sorry, sweetie. I didn't mean to freak you out. I just wanted to tell you about it 'cause it freaked *me* out. But congrats on the baby. I'm really happy for you and Tris. I can't wait to be an aunt." She smiled slightly but I couldn't return the gesture. Then she laughed but it sounded like a nervous laugh. "If you have a girl, I think I may have to open my own psychic reading business."

That comment broke the camel's back and I snapped at her. "Aut, what the hell is going on? Why are you having these dreams? How are you connected to me and Tristan?" I guess she didn't expect that type of reaction because her expression turned to mild shock and she started blinking rapidly. I also noticed that she started tapping her fingers against her knee. Either she was stalling or she was purposely avoiding my questions. And the longer she was taking to answer, the more impatient I was getting. I leaned closer to her and whispered harshly because I didn't want Tristan to come over and interrupt us. "Did you know that after I got off the phone with you, Tristan said if we have a daughter that he wanted to name her 'Katie'? Then the next day I find out I'm pregnant!" Her eyes widened even more than before. "Can you explain that to me? Because I'm at a total loss. I don't understand any of this and I don't like when things don't make any sense. I swear, if we end up having a girl... I'm *really* going to freak out!"

She finally responded to me but she spoke quietly. "I don't know, Bridge. But it all started after we became close friends. One day I put you on my top friends space and that night I had the dream about little Tristan. Then the next day he tells me that he's attracted to you and he starts asking me all these questions about you. That's all I can tell you."

I sighed heavily and shook my head in frustration. Then another question started to brew in the back of mind. Once it reached the front, I asked it out loud. "Have you ever had these strange dreams before that involved other people?"

"No, but..." She paused and I saw her swallow hard. She actually looked nervous. "I told my mom about both of my dreams and she told me that my grandmother had a similar experience when she was around my age. I think she was a little younger than me though. She was very close to her older sister and one night she had a dream that her sister died in an accident. The next day was Thanksgiving but her sister never showed up. They found out that her train arrived so they were trying to figure out what happened to her. She was a college student. Anyway, come to find out...her sister *was* killed. She was shot during a robbery at a drug store a few miles from their house."

Autumn paused again because she probably noticed I was looking at her with wide-eyes. "You know Bridge, after my mom told me that story...I started thinking that maybe I inherited some kinda ability from my family. And maybe I'm having these dreams 'cause you and Tris are the only people I've ever really been close to. I'm not close to my brother or my sister or my parents. I have a lot of friends but you and Tris are my besties."

After she told me her grandmother's story and called me one of her 'besties', I started to feel bad for taking my frustration out on her. When I learned of Autumn's first dream, I chalked it up to just coincidence. But now...I wasn't so sure. I was still feeling confused and angry and I just wanted all of this unexplained phenomena to end. I took a deep breath, closed my eyes and tried to calm down. When I felt that I could keep my temper under control, I spoke calmly. "Look Aut, I'm telling you right now...for the record...I don't want to hear about any more of your dreams. Don't even tell Tristan because he'll just tell me."

What she said next oddly sent my temper ablaze again. "Then who do I tell if not my besties?"

"I don't care! I just don't want to hear them anymore! You tell me this dream and now I'm fucking pregnant! I'm not ready to be pregnant!" Saying that last statement out loud actually felt good; like a weight was lifted off my chest.

Unfortunately, my outburst attracted Tristan's attention and he came jogging into the living room. He looked back and forth between me and Autumn and he wore an expression of concern. "What the fuck is going on? Babe, why are you yelling?" I didn't respond because once again I was trying to put my temper in check. For a minute I started wondering if I was already experiencing mood swings.

Autumn stood up and looked down at me with a lukewarm gaze. "You know what, Bridge? That's fine. I won't tell you anymore of my cracked out dreams. And news flash hun, you would've found out regardless if I told you about my dream or not. It was just meant to happen."

"Oh God, please don't start with all that fate shit, Autumn," I said exasperated.

Tristan chimed in, "You don't believe in fate? What about us?"

I felt like they were both teaming up on me so I went into defensive mode. Before I could get a word in, Autumn spoke up again. "Did it ever occur to you missy, that the only reason I had the dream in the first place was *because* you were preggers?"

She was not putting this one on me. "What about all the 'Katie' stuff? How do you explain that, huh?"

"I don't know, Bridge. I told you I don't know!"

Tristan was watching our exchange silently but I guess seeing his wife argue with her best friend was too much for him. Especially since

Autumn was his friend too. He raised his voice and Autumn and I immediately stopped yelling. "ALRIGHT ENOUGH!" He turned to look at me and his expression was intense. I started to get a little nervous because I thought he was going to give me an earful, but instead he sat on the sofa next to me and held my hands. His voice was surprisingly soft when he said, "Babe, you're pregnant. You shouldn't get yourself all worked up like this. Listen to me okay...just listen. At this point, Autumn's dream really doesn't matter. It's not important right now. It really isn't. The only thing that's important is that we're gonna have a baby. That's all we should focus on. The baby's already here. How or why it happened doesn't matter."

He scooted closer to me and began looking into my eyes. "Why can't you just be happy? Why can't you be happy knowing that our love created a new life?" He gently placed his hand on my belly. "Our baby's in there... growing. It's a part of me and a part of you. You don't have to worry, Bridget 'cause I'll be raising Katie with you. You're not gonna go through this alone. I'm your husband remember? I swore my heart to you and I swore to stay with you until I take my last breath." He leaned in closer to me and whispered, "Do you remember?" I nodded and he placed a soft kiss to my lips. When he pulled away from me, the air made contact with the wetness on my cheeks and I realized I was crying. Tristan cupped my face and began to slowly wipe my tears away with his thumbs. "I know this is a life-changing event and it's a life-long commitment too. You never stop being a parent. I thought I would be scared of being a father but I'm not. You shouldn't be scared either darlin', 'cause I'm gonna be with you every step of the way."

I sniffled and managed to crack a sad smile. "I *am* happy, Tristan." He raised a skeptical eyebrow at me. "I am, I'm just..." I paused to take a breath. "You were right about me. I *do* worry too much. I'm sorry but I can't help it. I may teach children but they're not my own. At the end of the day, they go home to their parents. And I've never had to raise one from birth."

Tristan put his hands on my shoulders and continued to look into my eyes as he spoke. "It's gonna be okay, Bridget. You'll be a wonderful mum. I know the kinda woman you are. I mean, just the way you care for *me*..." He tilted his head to the side and gave me loving smile and I couldn't help but to smile in return. "Whatever comes our way, we'll get through it." He held me close to him and I relished being in his strong protective arms. I don't care what anyone says...Tristan was my own angel, and I was going to give birth to an angel's child. "Me and you, doll. I have faith in us."

"So do I," I heard Autumn say softly. Being in Tristan's embrace made me forget she was still there.

Tristan turned to look at her and then he got up off the sofa. He approached her slowly and shook his finger at her as if she was a naughty child. "And you...don't tell my wife anymore of your dreams, okay? She obviously can't handle that creepy shit. Look, just tell us if it's bad. Like, if you have a dream that one of us dies."

As soon as he said that, Autumn and I both gasped. "Baby, don't say that!"

"You fucking jinx!" Autumn yelled.

Tristan shrugged as he looked back and forth between me and Autumn. "What? What did I say?" Strangely, Autumn went over to Tristan and started brushing invisible things off his body. He looked at her in confusion but he started chuckling. "What the fuck are doing, Aut?"

After she finished brushing absolutely nothing off his body, she hit him on the arm playfully. "Don't say shit like that, Tris! I just told Bridget that my grandmother had a dream where she predicted her sister's death. And the next day her sister really died."

Tristan's eyes widened in shock and he turned on the spot. "That's it I'm leaving. I think I hear Jake's car outside anyway." He headed straight for the front door and Autumn and I both watched it close after he disappeared behind it.

Autumn turned to look at me and I asked quietly, "Is Jake really out there or is Tristan just standing outside?"

She walked over to one of the front windows and looked out. "Yeah, his car just pulled off."

"I didn't hear any car. I'm telling you Aut, Tristan has dog hearing. Did you know I can't even mumble around him because he always hears what I say?" We both laughed and I realized that I wasn't even angry anymore.

I don't think Autumn was either because she moved to sit next to me again. She picked up one of the pamphlets and flipped through it.

Something must've grossed her out because she shrieked. "Ewwwwww!" Then she dropped it back onto the coffee table as if it had caught on fire.

"What is it?"

She scrunched up her nose like she smelled something foul. "It was a picture of how wide your pussy will stretch once you give birth. Shit, I feel for you Bridge...I really do."

I smiled but responded sarcastically. "Gee, thanks." We were both silent for a moment but I felt that I owed Autumn a huge apology. "I'm sorry, Aut. I'm sorry I yelled at you."

She gave a short laugh. "You called me over here just to let me have it, didn't you?"

I smiled sheepishly this time. "Yeah, I did actually. I was really mad at you. And for no good reason either. I guess I was just looking for someone to blame because my damn birth control didn't work. I was just being stupid. But you know what, Tristan's right. The dream doesn't matter anymore. I have more important things to worry about."

"No you don't. You heard what your hubby said. No worrying. Just be happy."

I called my parents to tell them the good news. I say 'good' because I finally forced myself be happy about my pregnancy. I started imagining the baby coming out looking just like Tristan. He really is a beautiful man so I know the baby he's given me will be beautiful too. My parents were both excited and my mother told me she wanted to take me shopping for baby stuff this weekend. I told her I'd take a reign check until I'm a little farther along. I didn't tell my mother about Autumn's dream because as far as I was concerned, it was over. Plus, I knew she would just question me nonstop and I didn't have any answers myself. Even though I wasn't going to dwell on the dream, I still wanted to know that last piece of the riddle: was the baby growing inside me little Katie? Tristan seemed convinced we were having a girl because I caught him referring to the baby as 'Katie' in our earlier conversations.

When Tristan returned home, he and Jake brought back Thai food for lunch. Autumn was still hanging out with me at home so the four of us settled into the dining room to eat. They all had beers with their meal, but Tristan politely poured Sprite soda into my glass. As he poured my drink he chuckled and said, "Just pretend this is *Smirnoff Ice*." That was one of my favorite malt beverages.

Lunch was filled with playful banter that usually took place whenever the four of us were together. Autumn asked Tristan about the minivans to which he replied, "We checked out this fully loaded Chrysler Town & Country..." He let out a low whistle. "I never knew a minivan could be so advanced. I'm telling you Bridget, it was really high-tech. But I just couldn't bring myself to consider it. I got in it and..." He shook his head. "I can't drive a bloody minivan. It's just not gonna happen." I was about to reply but he exclaimed quickly, "But! I was thinking, since safety should be our biggest concern..." I actually gaped at him because this is the same man that rides a very *unsafe* motorcycle. "Volvos are usually rated pretty high in safety tests so maybe we should get one of them. I think I can deal with driving one." He grinned before he took a bite of his fried wonton. "What do you think, babe?"

I think I can deal with driving a Volvo too, so I replied agreeably, "That sounds good to me."

"I figured since we're gonna have more kids, we should get a wagon or---"

I had to interject my husband right there before he got carried away with this whole baby making business. "Wait...excuse me? So you already have this all planned out, huh?"

Tristan nibbled on some tiny vegetable and he didn't meet my eyes as he spoke. "Yep, I'm gonna knock you up at least once more. Maybe twice." His eyes darted over to me and he grinned wickedly. Then he waggled his eyebrows because he knew he was being naughty. I gasped at his audacity and threw some of my own tiny vegetables at him which caused him to laugh heartily.

Because Tristan spoke so highly of Volvos, I asked him to take me to see them. After lunch, we all hopped in Jake's car and drove to the nearest dealership. Tristan was right; I was very impressed with their safety features and we both particularly liked the V50 wagon. And it definitely screamed 'family mobile'. Right then, agreed to purchase it when we were ready. I told him I would trade in my convertible because if we were starting a family, it wasn't really practical.

That night after we made love, we laid naked and sweaty atop the cotton sheets on our king-size bed. I was right where I wanted to be; in my lover's embrace. We were both fully satiated but we made pillow-talk as we gently caressed each other's bodies. I was laying with my head on his chest because I loved listening to his heartbeat. It reminded me that the gorgeous blond Brit lying completely naked in my arms was full of youthful life and he was all mine. I felt Tristan press his soft lips to my forehead and his hand rest against my flat belly. He spoke in a raspy voice that was laced with a sexy British accent. "I can't wait to see your belly all swollen with my baby. Just thinking about that shit turns me on. And I can't wait to see how beautiful she is. I hope she has red hair like you." I found Tristan's last comment ironic because I was hoping the baby would be blond like him.

I intended to kiss my beloved's chest but I found a sensitive nipple instead. I flicked my tongue out to gently lick one of his many erogenous zones. He moaned softly as I spoke back to him. "*She?* You really think we're having a girl?"

"I believe Aut's dream. Are you really okay with naming our daughter after Mum?"

"Yeah, I don't mind. You know how much I love your mom."

"If the dream is wrong and we have a boy...you can name him whatever you want."

"Ooohhh, really? Anything I want?"

"Yeah, just don't name him after me. I hate my fucking name and I don't want my son to suffer with the name 'Tristan'."

This was the first time Tristan ever expressed dislike for his name so I couldn't help but to look at him in disbelief. "What?!? Baby, I *love* your name!"

"And I love it when you say it. Especially when we're fucking and you scream it at the top of your lungs. But you're the only person who makes it sound good. Bridge, if you love me...promise me you won't make our son a junior."

I pursed my lips and pouted a little as I tried to figure out a way to persuade Tristan to let me name a son after him. If we had a little boy, that's exactly what I intended to do. Now, if we had a second son in the future, then I'd actually have to do some thinking about boy names. "Hey, what if we call him 'TJ' for short? That's pretty cool...TJ."

Tristan ceased his gentle caress on my back and he didn't answer immediately so I knew he was thinking about it. When he finally did speak, I was elated by his response. "Alright, then I guess it's not so bad." All of a sudden, the mood in our bedroom changed because he turned serious. His azure eyes began to pierce through me when he said quietly, "I wanna tell you a secret." I looked at him with intrigue and he continued to stare directly into my eyes when he said, "Every time I'd cum inside you, Bridget...I would secretly wish that you'd get pregnant." I gasped in surprise and he smiled devilishly. "This is my second wish in a row that came true."

I was curious so I asked, "What was your first wish?"

Tristan kissed me softly and when he unsealed his lips from mine, he answered me in a sweet whisper. "To be happy."

Chapter 20

Some mornings Tristan and I would just lie in bed for awhile; not sleeping or making love, but just talking. It was one of those mornings the day after we found out we were going to be parents. We were naked and sprawled out on the huge plane of the bed; atop the soft down comforter and the cool cotton sheets. We were both lying on our sides facing each other; just making morning conversation like we so often did.

"So, tell me where this confidence comes from where you don't mind being naked in front of people."

Tristan chuckled softly. "I don't know, babe. I guess 'cause I'm not ashamed of my body, I don't care if people see me naked. Nudity's just not a big deal for me. You know, it kills me when I see you get out of bed and put on your robe and slippers. I just watch you like, 'Why won't she just walk around naked?' I've never seen you walk around the house naked. You know, you shouldn't be embarrassed in front of me, love."

"I'm not embarrassed, it's just---"

And just in that split second, Tristan turned on the intensity. He had a peculiar way of changing the mood between us with just one look. "Bridget, I've seen every part of you. You've spread your legs wide for me and there's nothing I haven't seen. The same goes for me; you've seen every part of me."

"I guess it's just a habit. Ever since I was younger...it's like routine: get out of bed, put on my robe and slippers. But I can totally understand *you* walking around naked. I mean, if I looked like you...I probably wouldn't be shy either." My hungry eyes traveled the length of Tristan's beautiful Adonis form until they rested on the magnificent treasure nestled between his legs. "Besides, you should be proud that you're so... *blessed*. Why not show it off?" I gave him a sexy grin and he laughed. "It just used to amaze me whenever I came over to your house and I'd see you walking around naked like it was nothing. I guess Rick was used to it though, huh?"

"Yeah, he didn't care. Well, when I first moved in, he did. But I told him real quick that he was gonna have to get used to seeing my arse 'cause being naked in the house was just something I did; just like with my smoking. I mean, I would cover up if we had company; except if it was Jake, Marco, or Autumn." My eyes widened at the mention of Autumn's name and Tristan noticed.

I guess he thought he slipped up and shared too much information because he averted his eyes from me and I saw him swallow hard in nervousness. His voice was low when he said, "I guess I should tell you that me and Aut shagged in the past. Did she ever tell you that?" The secret was finally revealed. I remember asking Autumn if she was ever sexually involved with Tristan in the past but she never did answer me directly. Leave it to Tristan to finally tell me the whole truth.

To my own surprise, I wasn't upset about this new revelation at all. "No, she didn't tell me but I did ask her one day. She never admitted it though. But you know what? I kind of figured that you guys slept together at some point. I mean, you two are really close and your personalities are so similar. I knew you probably clicked immediately when you first met." As I was talking about him and Autumn, a curious question popped into my head and I wondered why I never asked him a long time ago. "Hey, why didn't you ever claim *her* as your girlfriend?"

"Can you really picture me and Aut as a serious couple? I mean... *really*? We'd probably do more arguing than anything else." All of a sudden, his expression turned serious and I was being smoldered by the hot blue flames from his beautiful orbs. "She never understood me the way you do. I mean...deep inside. She's a good listener and all...like whenever I needed someone to talk to and Jake wasn't around. But she just didn't understand that emotional part of me; but you understand. Honestly, I don't think me and her would've lasted a week. We're better off just being mates."

Because my words let Tristan know that I was okay with the sexual history between him and Autumn, he quickly changed the subject and brought it back to his nudity. "But I looked at it like this: if I pay half the bills, I should be able to walk around naked in my own fucking house."

"Were you like that when you lived at home?"

"I've always been free about my body. When I was a kid, sometimes I would run out of the house naked and Mum or Dad would have to chase after me. I think all the neighbors saw my little boy bits at least once." I started laughing because I imagined the scene in my head. Then strangely, I started imagining our own child doing the same thing and Tristan chasing after them. He must've sensed my train of thought because the next thing he said was very cryptic. "I think we should have like 'naked time' for our kids. If they feel like being naked in the house, I don't think we should discourage them. We should teach them that they shouldn't be ashamed of their bodies. What do you think?"

What I was thinking was that all this talk about nudity was causing me to focus more on Tristan's naked body lying a few inches from me. My eyes started to roam over his sexy form again and I smiled wickedly as I began to slowly crawl towards him. "I think..." I laid down next to him and molded my body to his. I put my arms around him, hooked one of my legs over his, and rubbed my moist center against his thigh. I moaned in satisfaction and then I kissed his soft sensual lips. "I like when *we* have naked time.

He chuckled softly as he encircled his arms around me. "Let me ask you something, love."

I darted my tongue out so I could taste the smooth skin in the hollow of his neck. "Hmmm?"

"Where do you draw the line sexually? Like, what's the limit of what you won't do? I know we've done some nasty, freaky shit but I never asked you what your limit is."

I smiled against his neck as I thought of my answer. "Ummm---"

"Like, I told you that I won't do any threesomes. I draw the line when it comes to sharing you with someone else."

"What if I shared *you* with someone else? You know like...what if when we brought Justin home...I joined in but I didn't touch him and he didn't touch me?"

Tristan seemed to already have his answer because he replied immediately. "No fucking way."

"But we wouldn't be touching each other. Besides, Justin is gay so--"

"Babe, he was watching you when you stripped down to your knickers; just like I was. He's not gay...he's totally bi. I'm telling you, he thought he was gonna have more work to do. And gay or not, when everyone's randy...the lust you feel just takes over and you'll grab anyone."

As Tristan was talking, I thought I figured out a loophole in his "no threesome" rule. "What about me, you, and another *woman?*"

"Nope."

I gasped in disbelief. "Are you serious!?! That's like every guy's fantasy to have two girls at the same time."

"Been there...done that. Bridget, I'm a selfish bastard when it comes to you and I don't want anyone else touching you; not even another bird. I remember that time when Aut was drunk and she kissed you on the mouth. I almost smacked the piss out of her." Tristan started laughing so I knew he was only half-joking.

Right at that moment I finally realized something we've never done sexually. "Oh, I know! I won't let you stick it in my butt. I don't do anal. That's an exit only!"

He chuckled again. "Oh yeah, that's right. We've never done that."

"And we won't either. I think you have enough 'holes' to stick your cock in, don't you?"

Tristan started laughing again. Then he leaned down and murmured against my lips, "But I let you stick your finger in mine." He pressed his lips to mine. "Mmmm...do you remember that, love? Remember what you did to me?" I felt Tristan spring to life and slowly rub his hardness against my lower abdomen.

The sensation caused me to purr in sheer delight. "Mmmm...yes, I remember. I was massaging your prostate though and that's the only way I could get to it."

Tristan rolled our bodies over until he was on top of me once again. He looked down at me and smoothed my hair away from my forehead as he spoke. "Remember how hard I came? I screamed your name, Bridget." He spoke his next words very slowly. "You...made...me... fucking...*scream.*" His mouth connected to mine and our tongues mated fiercely. He entwined his fingers into my long, auburn strands and I felt him gently tug my hair so my head would tilt back at his command. He kissed me deeper so we could taste every crevice in each other's mouth. His hips ground into mine and I felt his erection poking me hard; like it was demanding entrance into my warm sheath. It felt like steel but hot and throbbing with masculine power. When he unsealed his lips from mine, he switched our positions again so I was lying on top of him. His long legs wrapped around my waist in an obvious possessive position, and once again I was in my angel's embrace. "I love you so much, Bridget," he whispered softly into my ear.

I murmured against his neck, "I love you too, baby." Then I happened to glance at the alarm clock on the nightstand and I realized that I was almost late for my dentist's appointment. "Oh shit!" I tried to extract myself from Tristan's cocoon-like embrace but he wouldn't let me go. "Tristan, I have to get up! I have to go!"

"Huh? Where? Where do you have to be?" He rubbed his naughty bits against mine and it took every ounce of my strength not to react to him. "Except here with me. Let's just stay in bed all day and shag like fucking rabbits." He started kissing my neck and I knew that's all it would take for him to ensnare me in his sexual spell. "I'll let you take a break so we can eat and use the loo." He chuckled softly but I kept telling myself, *Whatever you do...don't look into his baby blues or else he'll trap you.* I never met a man who could manipulate me into doing anything so easily.

"As much as I'd love to spend all day in bed with your gorgeous British ass, I have to see my dentist in like thirty minutes."

He moved his head to look at me and I tried not to hold his gaze. "Bridge, you have perfect teeth. Why do you need to go to the dentist?"

I couldn't help but to laugh because his comment really didn't make any sense. "Well, if you'd like my teeth to stay this way...I have to go to the dentist." I reached between our bodies to tickle his ribs and he laughed sharply. I saw my opportunity to escape and I took it. I lifted myself off his body and climbed off the side of the bed. I only made it to the door to our master bathroom before I found myself being held by the waist.

Tristan spoke into my ear and his warm breath tickled my neck. "Wait, wait. Before you go...can you make me something to eat?"

I turned in his arms to face him and then I lifted a haughty eyebrow. "There's some pop-tarts in the---"

He gave me a pleading look. "Bridge...*please?*" Then he started peppering kisses on my cheeks and across my jaw line. "Please, please... can you make me some pancakes?"

I sighed dramatically even though I had already decided I would cook for him. "Tristan, you know...all you have to do is add water to the pancake mix and---"

Tristan ceased his heated kisses upon my face and looked at me. "Bridget, you know I can't cook for shit. I'll burn our fucking house down if you let me near the stove. I can't even boil water, babe." I couldn't help but to laugh because he really *was* helpless in the kitchen. Right at that moment, my husband turned on the charm and I was the one who was helpless; helpless to resist him. His voice was soft and sweet as he continued to beg me for food. "*Please* can you make me some pancakes, darlin'? I love you so much." He kissed me on the lips and I melted instantly.

"Okay Tristan, I'll make you some pancakes."

He gave me a tight squeeze and held me for a few seconds. "Thanks, love!" He finally released me with a peck on the lips and once I was in the bathroom, he poked his head in the doorway. "With bananas too?"

I looked over at him and put a hand on my hip. Then I sighed defeated. "Yes, with bananas." He flashed me a wide smile and his adorable dimple made an appearance for my pleasure.

After I showered and got dressed, I went into the kitchen to make banana pancakes for me and Tristan. I called to him from the kitchen to tell him that breakfast was ready. Within a few seconds, I saw him enter the kitchen still naked and I couldn't help but notice the excitement on his face. Were my pancakes that good? "Babe, guess what? I just spoke to Jake...he got the promotion."

"Really?!?"

"Yeah, and he's having a get-together tonight at his to celebrate."

"That's great! I'm so happy for him!"

"Do you know what he said? 'First order of business bro, I'm getting rid of the Maxima.'" Tristan laughed.

Over breakfast, Tristan filled me in on all the details behind his older brother's promotion. Jake worked for a Fortune 100 bank and he was promoted to Senior Relationships Manager in the Global Information Technology department. The promotion was a big deal because over the last few years, Jake has been working hard to build a career for himself. Along with his new position came a corner office with a view, lots of traveling opportunities and a highly generous salary.

When I came back from my dentist appointment, Jake paid a visit to me and Tristan to show off his newly purchased, silver BMW 650i convertible. Tristan was so impressed with it that he actually snatched the keys from his brother and pulled me along with him so we could take the bimmer for a spin. We didn't actually take it for a 'spin' because he stopped at a couple of his friends' houses to show off his *brother's* new car.

Not only was Jake my brother-in-law, he was like my real brother. We've been close ever since I spent Christmas in Brighton, England with the Hathaways in 2006. Part of me hoped that Jake would find that someone special because he really was a great guy. I always characterized him as the strong, silent type. He was handsome and he had the patience of a saint. That's why I always thought he'd make a good husband and father one day. But I guess when you have a younger brother like Tristan; you have to have almost infinite patience.

Tristan told me that Jake had a tough time growing up in Brighton; as did he. But unlike Tristan, Jake handled his problems a lot more maturely than his little brother. He had his share of run-in's with the authorities in both The U.K. and The States but he didn't get into as much trouble as Tristan did. Jake was usually the one bailing Tristan out or giving him a good talking-to or ass-kicking if the situation called for it. I guess with the absence of their father during most of their adolescence, Jake felt the need to step in and fill the role of father-figure for Tristan even though he's only three years his senior. Tristan also told me that when he could no longer bear living in Brighton, they moved to The States together. Tristan looked up to his older brother his whole life and I was honored to be friends with the man who helped my husband become the person he is today.

In the evening, Tristan and I were getting ready to go to Jake's promotion get-together. We were sharing the master bathroom; I was straightening my hair to change my usual waves, and Tristan was shirtless and standing over one of the sinks giving himself a quick shave. I was almost done with the last chunk of my hair when I casually asked, "So does Jake have a girlfriend yet? Or is he still sowing his wild oats? I was just wondering if he'll be introducing me to a special lady tonight. Usually when we're out with him on social occasions, there's always some random 'bird' on his arm." It's only natural when living with a Brit, to pick up on a lot of British words and phrases. Before you even realize you're doing it, you start incorporating their words into your own American vocabulary.

Tristan splashed some water on this face and wiped the remaining shaving cream off his jaw and chin. Once he was done cleaning himself, I noticed he was just looking at me in the mirror. He was smirking and I saw a glint of something akin to mischief in his eyes. "Yeah...*Lauren*. He met her at the gym."

My eyes widened in surprise and I put my straightening iron down on the counter. "Really?!? So, they're *serious*?" Tristan started chuckling and I looked at him in confusion because I didn't understand what he found so humorous. It wasn't long until his chuckling turned into genuine laughter. "What's so funny?"

"I can't take it anymore! I can't hold it in, I'm sorry. He told me not to tell you, but I have to. It's just too fucking hilarious to me!" He paused to take a breath and to try and compose himself. "His new girlfriend looks just like you, Bridget." Tristan couldn't keep his composure or contain his laughter.

I, on the other hand, continued to look at him with a confused look on my face. "What do you mean she looks like me?"

Tristan moved closer to me and I turned to face him so we were no longer talking to each other in the mirror. "She's a redhead like you, almost the same size and height as you...she even has freckles. He brought her into this pub a few nights ago to introduce her to his mates. You know it's a big deal for us Hathaway brothers to do shit like that. Anyway, I was there and I noticed right away that she looked like you. Rick was there too and he leaned over towards me and whispered something like, 'I didn't know Bridget had a sister.' I tried not to laugh but I couldn't help it. Rick was laughing too but Jake was kinda pissed at me 'cause he gave me this look. And to answer your other question, they're pretty serious. She moved in with him a few days ago but they've only been seeing each other for a little over a month." Tristan turned his attention back to the mirror and ran a hand through his blond locks. "And he said *I* rushed things with you? Heh! What a fucking hypocrite."

Out of everything Tristan just said, all I could think about was the fact that Jake didn't want me to know. We were like brother and sister so why didn't he want me to know about the new woman in his life? He's been with her for over a month and I was just finding out about her now? Jake was keeping me in the dark but I didn't understand why. And I was truly surprised that he would let someone move in with him after only knowing them a month. I didn't know Jake to be so impulsive; that was his younger brother's forte. I couldn't help but to ask, "Why didn't he want you to tell me about her?"

Tristan turned to look at me. "Probably 'cause you'd think he was pathetic for choosing a woman who's almost the splitting image of the woman he can't have." I had a strong feeling that was how *he* really felt about Jake.

I remember that Jake had a crush on me in the past and Tristan knew it too which is probably why he found the whole thing hilarious. I wasn't exactly sure if Jake still liked me in more than a sisterly way but after hearing this new girlfriend development, I was really starting to wonder. "But I was going to meet her eventually, right? I mean, he wasn't planning on hiding her from me forever, was he?"

"All he said was, 'Don't tell Bridget about Lauren. I wanna introduce them myself.'" Tristan smirked again. "So much for me keeping his secret."

Even though Tristan found Jake's new girlfriend humorous, I could tell he was bothered by the fact that Jake chose someone who resembled me; especially knowing that Jake had feelings for me in the past. Maybe that's why he revealed his brother's secret. Tristan was masking his disapproval with humor but he wasn't fooling me. I was his other half and I knew him too well. I decided to test my theory so I put a hand on my hip and smirked back at him. "You don't have a problem with the fact that your brother chose a woman who looks like me?"

As expected, my question hit a nerve with him and his jovial mood disappeared. "I don't have a problem with it. But he's seriously underestimating my intelligence if he thinks that I can't see the real reason why he's with her."

"Tristan, maybe he really likes her."

"Yeah, I know he does... 'cause she looks like *you*. Bridget, I know he still fancies you." For the next few seconds, neither of us said anything; we just looked at each other.

I didn't want our conversation to sway towards Jake's hidden feelings for me because the last time we went down that road, Tristan and Jake resorted to fisticuffs. "So, aside from her looking like me, what's she like?"

"She's really nice. I talked to her for a bit and she and Jake seem like a good match. I mean, she's a year younger than me but hey..." He shrugged nonchalantly. "I just couldn't get over how much she looked like you. But I still think you're more beautiful." Tristan tilted his head to the side and his eyes raked up and down my body. "Way more beautiful...and sexier." My husband was still able to make me blush with his compliments. Tristan loves whenever I blush for him so he smiled roguishly before he leaned down to kiss me on the lips. Then he walked out of the bathroom. Within a few seconds I heard him yell from the bedroom, "Hurry up, babe! I wanna get there before all the food's gone!"

On the ride over to Jake's apartment, all I could think about was Lauren and Jake. I was anxious to meet her and anxious to ask Jake about his reasons for keeping Lauren a secret from me. This was also the first time since I've known Jake that he's claimed someone as his girlfriend. The type of women he involved himself with in the past were all different; so I had no way of determining exactly what his type was. That was the main reason why I never tried to hook him up with anyone. If he chose Lauren to be his girlfriend and she looked like me...I concluded that I must be his type. I'll admit that didn't sit too well with me because I was hoping that Jake's desire for me would've faded away long ago. If he's still harboring feelings towards me after all this time, that tells me that maybe what he feels is more than just a crush. And since I'm Tristan's wife now, that didn't look too good for Jake at all. Tristan was borderline obsessed with me. Wait, no...he *is* obsessed with me. He's also the jealous type; not a good combination for any guy who wants something that Tristan has.

The scene at Jake's top-floor, loft apartment in Los Angeles certainly didn't qualify as a 'get-together'. Get-togethers consist of a few people; usually no more than ten. There were a lot more than ten people having a grand 'ol time. Since Jake was a smoker like Tristan, the air in his apartment was a bit smoky. I was trying to see through the haze to see if I could catch a glimpse of Jake's new lady. He answered the door when we rang the bell, and I was expecting her to be within close distance; but she wasn't. I wanted to just blurt out 'Where's Lauren?' but then I remembered that I wasn't supposed to know about her.

I was still scanning the crowd for redheads when Tristan put his arm around my waist and spoke in my ear, "Come up on the roof with me, love. You shouldn't be around all this smoke." Being pregnant was still new to me and sometimes I forget there are things I have to be more conscious of. I nodded, and Tristan guided me through the apartment to take me up on the roof where some of the other partygoers were congregating and enjoying the clean breathable air. It was summertime and the night temperature was perfect for being outdoors.

Jake didn't come up to join us and I found myself getting impatient because I thought he would've introduced me to Lauren by now. I decided to vent a little to my husband. "Why hasn't Jake introduced me to Lauren yet? Why's he hiding her from me?"

"I don't know but I didn't see her inside. Maybe she had other plans." I deflated inwardly because I was really looking forward to meeting her. With my hope now crushed and my bladder full, I decided to use the bathroom. I told Tristan I would be right back and I told him exactly where he could find me should I be gone too long. Because he usually requested that I stay by his side during all social functions, I had to tell him that.

I ran-walked down to the bathroom and silently prayed that it would be unoccupied. And just when I reached the bathroom door and raised my fist to knock...it opened and another redhead with brown eyes and freckles almost ran into me. She flashed me a smile before she murmured quietly, "Oh sorry." Then she moved around my body to leave. I stared after her with wide-eyes and my mouth slightly open because I had a sneaking suspicion that was Lauren. My very first impression of her was: *Wow, she's really pretty. They think she looks like me?* Right at that moment, nature called me back to the present and I rushed into the bathroom.

When I finished, I washed my hands quickly and dashed out of the bathroom. I made my way through the party and tried desperately to locate the redhead again. Ah-ha! There she was; standing over by the tank which contained Jake's huge, scary albino python. She was talking to her new boyfriend...my brother-in-law. Oh, Jake was going to introduce us right *now*.

As I was walking towards them, Jake looked over at me. We made eye contact and I noticed his expression change; he actually looked nervous. Too bad, he should've told me about Lauren sooner. I walked right up to them and stood there until both he and Lauren acknowledged my presence. She turned around because her back was to me. Our eyes met and she must've realized I was the girl she almost ran into moments ago. "Oh, hello again."

I smiled brightly and held out my hand for her to shake. "Hi. I'm Bridget, nice to meet you." Screw Jake and his late introductions.

She smiled in return and shook my hand. "Hi Bridget, I'm Lauren." Yes you are. Now that I could get a good look at her, I concluded that she was a lot more beautiful than me. I made a mental reminder to have Tristan's eyes checked. But I did notice some very uncanny similarities between me and her. Our hair was the same shade of red and hers was even long and wavy just like mine. We shared the same eye color and I can honestly say that we were pretty equal as far as freckles. She was probably a few inches taller than me and we were both wearing heels. But her feminine frame was more on the waif side because I definitely had more hips and butt than she did. I could tell she was young, and I smiled inwardly at the fact that we were both members of the *Itty Bitty Titty Committee*. I'll admit, I was totally amazed by how similar we looked. But if Tristan thinks Jake picked her as a consolation to me; he was kidding himself. Lauren was hot!

Jake finally opened his mouth. "Lauren, this is my sister-in-law." I was still smiling but when I looked up at Jake, I made sure my eyes said something else: 'I'll talk to you later mister.'

Lauren's eyes widened and her mouth formed a tiny 'o'. Then her head began to nod. "Ohhhh...Bridget. Yeah, Tristan told me about you. I met your husband a few nights ago at a bar that Jake took me to. Wow, it's nice to finally meet you. Tristan just went on and on about you." She laughed and it was a carefree and girly kind of sound. Her youthfulness really shined through.

I was about to reply but I heard Tristan's voice say my name over the loud rock music. "Bridget! What are you doing in here?!? All this fucking smoke! Are you mad, woman?!?" He came over to me and grasped my arm. "Come back outside, love. C'mon." Then he seemed to notice Lauren because he said, "Oh hey Lauren, nice to see you again." He gave her a wide smile and I saw his cute little dimple on his left cheek.

"Hey Tristan, nice to see you too."

Tristan started to pull me along so I smiled at Lauren and said wittily, "Well, I have to go! Me caveman husband wants him wife away from bad smoke."

We were walking away when I heard her laugh and say, "Bridget, wait! Hold on a sec!" I stopped in my tracks and my sudden movement caused Tristan to stop too. She turned to Jake and said, "Let's go outside with them. It *is* kind of smoky in here." I yelled in triumph...in my head. Now I could really talk to her and see what kind of person she was. Jake nodded in agreement and they both followed me and Tristan up to the roof.

I sat with Lauren and tried to get as much information on her as I could without being too nosy. Like a real sister, I wanted to make sure that I approved of my brother's girlfriend. I think she was feeling comfortable around me because she didn't seem to mind opening up to me. I was friendly towards her but I also took on the role of Interviewer. "So Lauren, tell me about yourself," I said as I smiled and turned my body to face her. I crossed my legs and clasped my hands on top of my knees.

Her bow-shaped lips twitched in amusement before she gave a short laugh. "Well, Bridget..." She spoke in a tone that suggested she was aware I was interviewing her. "I recently moved to Cali from Washington State because I got a job offer doing web design."

"Oh, I see. Do you have any siblings?"

"Yeah, I have a younger sister Jenna who's still in college but she still lives with the 'rents in Washington."

"Did *you* go to college?"

She gave me a toothy smile. "Sure did. I graduated from WSU." She impressed me even further when she said, "But I'm taking online courses towards my Master's degree." Kudos to Jake for choosing a woman who had ambition just like he did.

As Lauren and I got to know each other, I realized that she was someone I wouldn't mind hanging out with. She didn't seem as wild as Autumn, so I felt comfortable that I would be able to keep up with her. I found that she was very bubbly; she actually reminded me of Autumn in that regard but without the foul mouth. She was very sweet and I found myself taking to her almost immediately. I could honestly see why Jake would like her personality regardless of the fact that he thought she looked like me. And I'll admit that people may mistake us for sisters. If Lauren really *was* my younger sister, I was convinced that she would definitely be known as The Pretty One.

While Lauren and I continued our girl-talk, Jake came to stand beside her. I watched her lean into him and put her arm around him. Jake put his arm across her shoulders and bent down to place a tender kiss on her forehead. Their open affection reminded me of me and Tristan and I couldn't help but to smile approvingly. I asked her casually, "So...how do you like Jake's new car?"

She shrugged nonchalantly and crinkled up her nose in obvious distaste. "Eh, it's alright. It's a bit too flashy for my taste, though. But you know...as long as he likes it." She looked up at Jake and they smiled warmly at each other. I was bursting at the seams with the urge to say 'Awwww!' I thought they were just so cute together.

Jake's party lasted well into the night but soon the guest count started to dwindle. After the last remaining partygoer left, it was almost three o'clock in the morning. I was in the kitchen helping Jake and Lauren clean up when I noticed that Tristan was absent. "Where's my husband? Why isn't he helping us clean up?"

Jake gave a short laugh. "That lazy blither fell asleep."

"He fell asleep?!?"

Lauren added, "I saw him knocked out on the couch."

I walked into the living room and low and behold, Tristan was conked out. I heard Jake yell from the kitchen, "He probably fell asleep so he wouldn't have to help me clean up!" Tristan let out a loud, drawling snore and right at that moment, I knew he was feigning sleep.

I approached his seemingly sleeping body and looked down at him. I shook my head at his nerve and then I hit him on the leg. I whispered harshly, "Wake up Tristan! I know you're not sleeping!" His snoring abruptly cut off and he opened one sleepy eye to look up at me. With my hands on my hips, I pursed my lips and narrowed my eyes at him because I knew he was faking. A small grin appeared on his face before he shut his one eye and rolled over with his back to me. I huffed loudly and turned on my heel to march back into the kitchen.

I picked up another trash bag and said to Jake, "He's not really sleeping; he's faking it."

Jake looked at me curiously. "How do you know?"

"Because Tristan doesn't snore when he sleeps. I walked in there and he was snoring like a freight train. He only wants you to *think* he's sleeping." Lauren started laughing.

After about fifteen minutes, Tristan sauntered into the kitchen. I figured his conscience finally got to him and he was going to help us, but instead he came over to me and grasped my arm. "C'mon babe, I'm really tired. I wanna go home."

Jake looked at him and his eyebrows shot up towards his hair line. "You're not gonna help me clean up?!?"

"Bro, I'm not gonna be hanging around here all fucking night. Do you know what time it is? You better call a maid service."

I gaped at him in disbelief. "Tristan, I want to stay and help Jake clean up."

Jake cut in, "You know what Bridge? It's alright. Me and Lauren will clean this shit up tomorrow. It's no big deal."

I was very surprised by Tristan's behavior so I thought a little punishment was in order. I played on Tristan's jealousy when I leaned into Jake's personal space and laid my hand on his arm. "Jake, call me on my cell if you need any help tomorrow. I'll be happy to come over and help you guys clean up."

Jake could tell what I was doing and I guess he decided to punish his little brother too. He looked into my eyes and smiled charmingly. His voice was sickeningly sweet when he replied, "Oh, I *definitely* will." He averted his eyes from me to look over my head and I knew he was staring Tristan down.

I wanted to see Tristan's reaction so I turned to look at him. My punishment had the desired effect because his face didn't look happy at all. He opened his mouth to retort something back to Jake but I quickly raised my index finger and mouthed the words: "Don't you start."

Before we left the apartment, Lauren and I exchanged numbers because I told her that we should hang out some time. Truth be told, I didn't have that many close friends. But I figured since we got along so well, it couldn't hurt to try and build a friendship with her; especially if she was dating my brother-in-law. When Tristan and I got to my car,

I was surprised when he opened my door for me. Chivalry wasn't dead with him but I knew he was being extra polite because I was upset with him earlier. During our ride home, I didn't give him the silent treatment because I felt he'd been punished enough. "You know Tristan, I really like Lauren. I think she's good for Jake."

"Yeah, she is."

"Oh, and if you think your brother *settled* for her because he can't have me, you're sadly mistaken. She's so much prettier than I am and I think you need to get your eyes checked."

Tristan busted out laughing and the sound actually startled me. "Are you fucking kidding me?!?" He started laughing harder. "Why do you think she's prettier than you? I'm sorry love, but I have to completely disagree. She's *not* prettier than you. And he *did* settle 'cause there's no woman on earth that can compare to you; especially your heart." I couldn't really argue with Tristan because I was sitting on Cloud Nine from his compliments.

The next day Tristan had a couple of auditions lined up so I was doing some unpacking alone. I was working in the den slash my new office, when I heard the doorbell. I jogged towards the front door and checked the peep-hole. I saw a familiar head of blond hair so I opened the door and greeted my brother-in-law with a wide smile. "Hi Jake! Come on in!" He smiled back at me and stepped over the threshold. "Hey, why didn't you call me to help you guys clean up? My offer was really genuine you know."

He chuckled and replied, "Yeah, I know. But me and Lauren took care of it ourselves. Besides, I know you have enough work to do around here." At the mention of Lauren's name, I realized that I never did get a chance to ask him why he kept their relationship from me. "I just came by to drop this off to my little bro. I saw his mate Dane at the gym today and he told me that Tris would probably wanna read this." He handed me a slightly curled magazine and my eyes scanned over the cover with the bold words *Motorcyclist*.

Since the magazine was already curled, I didn't feel too bad about rolling it up. I tapped it against my palm and gave Jake a hard look. We were both silent for a moment and I was hoping he would pick up on what I was trying to convey to him through my eyes. When he didn't speak first, I decided to try and coax him. "So...are you going to start talking or are you going to make the Fiery Redhead beat it out of you?" I started hitting the rolled-up magazine against my palm harder in a threatening manner.

I saw Jake swallow hard as his light blue gaze pierced into me. I couldn't wait for his response any longer so I blurted out, "Why didn't you tell me about Lauren, Jake?!? Why'd you keep her a secret?!? Don't get mad at Tristan but he told me that you've been seeing each other for over a month! A month, Jake! You didn't say *anything* to me! And she moved in with you too?!? Don't you think I would've wanted to know that you had a *girlfriend*?!? I would've invited you guys over for dinner..." I shook my head at him in disappointment and sighed heavily. "I can't believe you." I walked away from him towards the living room and I was hoping he would follow me.

I sat down on the living room sofa and crossed my arms over my chest. I narrowed my eyes at him because I was really upset with him. I watched as he approached me cautiously; he knew he was in hot water. His voice was low compared to how mine was when I unloaded on him seconds ago. "I know. You're right...I should've told you but..." He sighed and then he sat next to me. "I thought you were gonna poke fun. You know, 'cause she looks like you and you know how I feel about you."

"What?!? First of all, please give me some credit, Jake. I'd like to think of myself as a little more mature than Tristan. I wouldn't have made fun of you or her." My voice softened suddenly because I realized what he just confessed to me. "And Jake, if you're only with Lauren because you think she looks like me...that's not fair to her. You can't compare her to me because we're different people."

I was looking at him as I spoke but I noticed he wouldn't meet my eyes. He must've been truly ashamed of himself. "I know, Bridget. I know. But you just don't understand. When I look at her, I see you. That's what attracted me. And it just makes me feel like...I don't know...I can just pretend she's you." My eyes widened to the size of saucers. He turned to look at me and the look he was giving me was beginning to make me feel very uncomfortable. This was not the Jake I was used to. "I can't get over you. I tried...and I can't."

He got up from the sofa and turned to face me. "Look, she has no idea that I have feelings for you. I just treat her the way I would treat you and she's none the wiser." I couldn't help but gape at his audacity and nerve. What Jake was doing to Lauren was deceitful and I was very surprised at him. "I don't expect you to understand. But I didn't tell you about her 'cause I was afraid that you'd see what I was really doing with her. I know you're a very intelligent woman, Bridget."

"I would've met her eventually so what difference did it make when you introduced us?" I stood up to face him and I looked into his eyes to try and make him see reason. "Jake, you have to get over me. You *have* to or else your relationship with Lauren isn't going to last. You can't keep pretending she's me forever. You have to give her a chance and see *Lauren* for the person she is. She deserves that; she's a really wonderful girl. In the short time that I spent with her last night, I instantly liked her."

What Jake said next actually made my face flush with heat. "That's the same way I felt about you when I first met you." We were both silent and we shared a look. "I'm just sorry that Tristan got to you first. But hey...it's alright now. I've got my *own* Bridget." I gaped at him again and he held my gaze with an intensity that I was very unfamiliar with. "Look, I have to go. Tell my brother that I stopped by." Then he turned on the spot and let himself out.

Tristan and I agreed not to keep secrets from each other, but after the front door closed, the only thing that went through my mind was: *I am definitely not telling Tristan about this conversation.* Even though Jake didn't ask me to, I decided to keep his confession a secret because I wanted to protect him from my angel's wrath.

Chapter 21

ONE OF THE THINGS I love about being an elementary school teacher is summer vacations. An added benefit to teaching America's young future leaders is that I get ten weeks of time off to do whatever my little heart desires. Last summer was definitely the best summer vacation to date because it was the first summer that I spent almost every day with Tristan. The beginning of the season began with a special party for my 25th birthday which included a much unexpected marriage proposal on the beach. As the season came to a close, I bonded my soul to Tristan's through marriage in the beautiful city sometimes referred to as 'London-by-the-sea' Brighton, England.

The beginning of this summer, we moved into our new house in Hollywood. We were lucky enough to completely finish unpacking a couple days before the July 4th holiday. We still didn't furnish the basement yet because Tristan finally came to a decision to turn it into a rec room; complete with a bar and a big screen television. I heard him talking to Jake on the phone the other day about purchasing a pool table. He was also adamant about putting a swimming pool in the backyard so we were just beginning to shop around for contractors. But as far as the rest of the house, it was slowly but surely becoming a home.

Even though I was on summer vacation, Tristan was still working... sort of. His manager was continuously sending him on casting auditions but to his misfortune, he hadn't been able to land anything solid. After his latest film wrapped up production, he was having a hard time finding another gig. He really preferred working on films but he told me that he'd return to television if he was offered a decent role. He also expressed to me that he felt like he was being type-cast as some bad-boy, rebel, or street kid. He was getting tired of auditioning for the same kinds of roles. He wanted to branch out and try something different; "flex my acting chops" he once said.

Today I was doing some cleaning and reorganizing if I felt that something should be moved. Because I was pregnant, I didn't move anything too heavy. Once I was done, I folded up the last of the cardboard boxes that we used for moving and I tied them up. I was carrying them outside to place in the front of the house for trash, when I saw Tristan pull into the driveway on his motorcycle. Although, I wouldn't exactly say that he *pulled* in. He was going pretty fast and for a moment I thought he would actually crash into the garage door. His bike fell short a few feet from the door and I heard the tires screech as he slammed on the brakes. Something told me that he was either really excited about something or really pissed off. From the moment he turned off the engine and hopped off his bike, I knew his mood was leaning more towards the latter. There was just something in his body language that suggested that he was highly agitated.

I didn't realize just how much until I saw him throw his helmet down on the ground and yell, "FUCK!" The helmet bounced off the concrete driveway and I saw the visor and another piece of something pop off and land in the grass nearby. The helmet rolled slightly before it came to a complete stop next to the garage door. He didn't stop there because he walked over to the helmet and kicked it like it was a football. It flew across the yard and ricocheted off the fence only to land back on the ground again.

I wanted to stop him before he kicked his helmet until there was nothing left of it, so I ran over to try and intervene. "Tristan...baby, what's the matter?" He started walking towards it again to continue taking his frustration out on it. Luckily he didn't and he paused at the sound of my voice. He turned around to face me and when I finally reached him, his expression told me that he was *royally* pissed off. "What happened? Why are you so upset?"

Everything about his disposition told me he was on the verge of snapping. I needed to tread carefully with him when his temper was ablaze like this. I should know because we were very similar in that respect whenever we got really angry. His voice was loud and completely on-edge. "Babe, you won't believe the shit I've been through today. I'm telling you...these fucking auditions are pissing me off!" He growled and then he grabbed his hair in frustration. Then he turned around and yelled into the sky.

I approached him cautiously and spoke softly because he started pacing like a wild tiger in a cage; a very *angry* tiger. "Tristan, just calm down, sweetheart. Take a couple breaths and tell me what happened."

His blue eyes were fierce and blazing but he paused and I saw him attempt to compose himself. "Okay...so I had like three auditions today, right?" I nodded. "So the first one...I get there and when I go inside...some bint tells me that casting's been closed; they already picked someone. So I'm all like, 'Well why didn't anyone ring me?' So she says, 'Oh, well I thought Anthony would've told you.' That fucker didn't tell me anything! I just wasted my fucking time...got up early and shit for nothing! I'm telling you babe, I'm like this close from firing his arse. It's not like he's getting me the good roles anyway. It's all the same shit! Anyway, so now I have like an hour to kill until my next appointment. I stop by Rick's for awhile and then I go to my next one. I waited for over *three* fucking hours before I got called. And do you know what they said as soon as I walked in?"

"No, what?"

"You're not tall enough." He chuckled but there was absolutely no humor in his voice. "Do you believe that shit?" He spoke his next words as if he were explaining to a child. "Now it says right on my stats sheet that I'm five-eleven." Then he raised his voice again. "How fucking tall do they think five-eleven is?!?"

I decided to take a chance and touch the irate tiger so I put my arms around him and tried to console him. "Baby, some of those directors are just assholes. They don't really care if they waste your time. All they care about is getting the role filled."

Tristan laughed this time but once again...there was no humorous undertone. "Oh, but wait. The last one is the best one. Get this...I actually got to *read* for this part. I had to use my Yank accent and since the character is supposed to be Southern, I had to put a twang in it. I thought it was pretty good but apparently those bastards didn't think so. Do you know what one of the directors said? I was reading the lines and he goes, 'Uh, I can still hear your British accent.' Babe, you said it yourself that my Yank accent is flawless, right?"

Tristan's American accent was so authentic that sometimes I'd forget he's really a Brit. "Yeah it is, baby. He was probably just being a prick. Either that, or he doesn't know what Southerners sound like."

"Yeah, it was total bollocks! I know he's bullshitting me right so I read the lines again...the *exact* same way and then he says, 'Ah, that's much better.' Fucking lying bastard! Get your hearing checked! I could tell they didn't want me anyway 'cause they kinda rushed me out." Tristan sighed heavily and shook his head. "I'm sick of Hollywood, babe. I haven't really built up my res but already I'm sick of it. And I'm sick of auditioning for the same goddamn roles over and over. I think I'll just stick to Indie films."

I really didn't know a lot about the whole casting process for films except from what Tristan explained to me; that it was grueling and nerve-racking. But I can understand how he could get tired of auditioning for the same roles. It doesn't give an actor the opportunity to master their craft if they're pigeon-holed into one type of character of all time. I also sympathized with him because he's come home frustrated many a days and told me how he couldn't understand why he wasn't getting any offers. Today was just the day that he finally reached his boiling point.

While I had Tristan in my arms, I could feel that his entire body was tense so I embraced him tighter and tried rubbing his back to soothe him. When he laid his head on my shoulder, I knew he was accepting my comfort. I softened my voice as I continued to console him. "Sweetie, don't worry. You'll find something. And you'll see; the perfect role will come up and it'll be made just for you." I laughed lightly. "Hey, it'll probably be the one to launch your career. Just don't give up, baby." I kissed his cheek because I really did feel bad for him.

All of a sudden, Tristan pulled away from me and the look in his eyes was raw and unmistakable self-doubt. He confirmed my assessment because he asked me quietly, "Bridget, do you think I can act?" He frowned slightly and I saw his eyebrows knit tightly together in worry. "Tell me the truth...the *honest* truth. Please, love. Your opinion means more to me than anyone's." Tristan feeling insecure about his acting abilities was not new to me. I remembered back to when I first saw his last three films; where he took on serious roles. He asked me to critique his performance but I really couldn't say anything negative because I thought he was absolutely brilliant.

I smiled and reached up to thread my fingers through his soft blond hair. My fingers trailed down his cheek and traveled along his jaw line. I looked into his baby blues and tried to convey to him what I truly felt in my heart. "Tristan, I think you're an *amazing* actor. You're the best in my eyes. You have a lot of potential and I can tell that you take your job seriously. I only see good things for you in the future if you just stick with it. And don't worry, there will be other casting directors that will see what I see in you. And they'll give you your shot. You'll shine brightly and all those other directors that passed you over in the past will be kicking themselves and saying, 'Why didn't I hire that kid?' When they turn you down, they don't even realize that they're turning down a star." He smiled at me and it actually lit up his beautiful face even more than the sunshine that was beaming down on us. I finally felt his body relax in my arms and I knew at that moment that I lifted his spirits. And if Tristan was happy...then I was happy.

He leaned down to kiss me and he lingered close to my face before he rubbed his nose against mine. "Thanks, love. That means a lot to me coming from you."

I smiled warmly. "Hey, it's the truth...the *honest* truth." We embraced each other again and this time I felt Tristan hold me closer against his body. "You know I'll always be your cheerleader, Tristan."

Tristan laughed softly. "I love you, Bridget."

"I love you too." We still had our arms around each other as we started to walk back to the house. That's when a piece of his helmet came into my line of vision. "Hey, what about your helmet? I think you destroyed it."

He waved his hand dismissively. "Eh, fuck it. I'll get another one."

Once we were inside, Tristan went into the living room to watch television. His broken helmet was still on my mind so I went back outside to gather up the remaining pieces of it. It was lying against the garage door and when I picked it up, I could really see the extent of the damage that Tristan caused. There was a long crack on the side and it was scratched up pretty bad. The visor was also missing and there was now a hole in the part where your mouth goes. I decided that it couldn't be salvaged so I ended up throwing it in the trash. When I came back in, I was sparked with one of my brilliant ideas. I sat down next to him and gave him a wide smile. He looked over at me and I said cheerfully, "You know what we should do? We should go somewhere; just leave Cali for awhile. Tell Anthony that you're taking a break. And when you're ready...then you can come back and deal with the bullshit again. What do you say?"

He seemed to like my idea because he grinned. "Yeah, that's a good idea. I really do need to get away from Cali for awhile. But where should we go, babe?"

I cast my eyes towards the ceiling and tapped a finger against my chin as I thought. "Ummm..." Right at that moment, Tristan's cell phone rang.

He looked down at the LCD screen on his phone, and then he looked back up at me with a wide grin. "It's Seth." I turned my attention to the television while he had his phone conversation. The name 'Seth' sounded familiar but I couldn't put a face to the name. Tristan had so many friends that it was impossible to keep track. After he finished talking, he snapped his phone shut. I could tell he was excited because he leaned towards me with a smile. "You wanna get away from Cali?" He paused. "We're going to New York."

"City?" It wasn't until after the word left my mouth that I felt sort of stupid. But it was an honest question. For all I know, he could've meant upstate New York.

Tristan chuckled at my stupidity. "Yes darlin'...New York *City*. We're staying with my mate Seth 'cause he has a guest room in his flat. He told me his plans for the 4th and I told him that we'd come to celebrate too. You know...drinks, partying...probably catch some fireworks later. Besides, being on the other side of the country sounds pretty good right about now."

I scooted closer to Tristan and hugged him. "Oooh! That sounds fun! I haven't been to New York City since I was a kid and my parents took me to Rockefeller Center. Oh wait, and I think I saw '*Cats*' there too."

"Oh shit, that reminds me...I have to try and book our flights." Tristan reached for his laptop that was sitting on the coffee table and then he settled it onto his lap. I snuggled close to him and looked over his shoulder as he went online to book our plane tickets. "Ah...here we go. Here's one that leaves L.A.X. tomorrow. If we take it, we can be in New

York by...three in the afternoon." Tristan looked at me for my approval. "What do you think? We can take a cab over to Seth's flat."

I smiled widely and kissed him on the cheek because I always love going on trips with him. "Sounds perfect, sweetie. Book us!" As Tristan started typing away on his laptop to book our plane tickets, I remembered that we needed to start packing. "While you take care of that, I'm going to start packing." I started to get up from the sofa, but he reached out to grab my hand.

"Wait, wait. Hold on a second." He quickly typed on the keyboard for a few more seconds while simultaneously clicking the touchpad. Then he pushed his laptop to the side onto one of the sofa cushions. "Come here for a minute, love." He grinned at me but I could tell he had something naughty on his mind; I could just feel it. So I wasn't surprised when he pulled me onto his lap and made me straddle him. He kissed me on the lips and wrapped his arms around me. "Mmmmm...don't go yet."

I gazed lovingly into his baby blues and ran my fingers through his hair. My voice was soft as I spoke to him. "Why, what's wrong baby?"

Tristan began scattering light kisses down my neck and across my collar bone. In between his kisses, he said, "You know I've had a really shitty day. I just..." But he didn't finish his sentence. It was almost like something distracted him. He paused to reach out and take some of my long hair into his hand. He spread the strands out on his palm and just looked at it like he was admiring the color. I couldn't help but to smile as I watched him. Then to my delight, he put my hair to his nose, closed his eyes and inhaled deeply. He sighed with an air of contentment and then he smiled. "I love your hair." He looked into my eyes briefly and I caressed his face and traced his shapely brows before I leaned my head down to press my lips to his.

As I threaded my fingers through his golden locks, I couldn't help but to gaze at him adoringly. In all truthfulness, I did that a lot because I found Tristan to be so pleasing to the eye. I believed that if the Greek Gods really existed in our time, Tristan would be one mortal that would spark major jealousy among the deities. My imagination began to run wild and I imagined them inviting him atop Mount Olympus so they could all bask in his masculine beauty. My mind was still clouded by thoughts of the Gods as I continued to caress the planes of his face as if to burn them into memory. I spoke from deep inside my heart when I said, "You are *so* beautiful, Tristan." I rubbed my cheek against his like a house cat and inhaled deeply to take in the unique scent that was just Tristan.

While still in each other's embrace, he whispered back, "*You're* beautiful, Bridget. I'm so lucky to have you." He held me tighter and I returned the gesture with equal strength.

I had to disagree with Tristan on that point because I felt that I was the lucky one. I was given a very precious gift; something that no one has ever been given…and I wasn't talking about the baby inside me. "Tristan…*I'm* the lucky one. You gave me your heart; brand new…right out of the box. You've never given your heart to anyone before, but…" I moved my head closer and kissed the tip of his nose. "You gave it to me." Tristan met my eyes with an intensity that told me that what I was saying really touched him. "And me…" I laughed softly. "I gave you my heart with band-aids on it. It was broken and then mended…and then broken again…and then mended again." I sighed. "Mine has scratches, chips and dents. It's not new but it's still good." I kissed his lips again. "It's been so used that it could break easily. All I ask is that you be careful with it." I couldn't stop the unshed tears from blurring my vision because I really did speak the truth about my heart. I trusted him and I believed that he would never hurt me. He always kept his promises to me and he promised to love me until death do us part. I'll admit that I pray every day that he'll keep to his word.

Tristan tilted his head to the side to regard me. A smile graced his lovely, angelic features and his fingers traced the outline of my lips. Then he grasped my chin gently in his hand as he spoke to me. "Bridget, my heart's not new, darlin'. It only looks new but it's really just…refurbished." He laughed lightly. "It's been hurt many times in my life; not by love… by other things…bad things. And the truth is…my heart is more fragile than yours. I don't think you even know the power you have over me. You have the power to destroy me. Do you know why?" Tristan's words frightened me a little and I shook my head. "'Cause I can't live without you and I need your love like I need to breathe." Then he whispered softly, "I promise I won't break your heart. Just keep loving me and I'll make it like new again."

We shared a smile and Tristan sealed another one of his promises with a sweet kiss. I really didn't want to remove myself from his lap but

I remembered that we still had to pack for our trip to New York. "Baby, you know...we still have to pack."

Tristan chuckled. "Oh shit, you're right." His voice softened when he said, "But thank you, princess. You made your prince feel so much better."

The next day we boarded our flight from Los Angeles to New York City in the late morning. I was excited to stay with Tristan's friend Seth and celebrate the July 4th holiday. And not just because Tristan told me that he lived in Central Park West; a very upscale section of Manhattan. We actually arrived in the city on July 3rd and when our plane landed, we hailed a taxi to Seth's residence. We pulled up to this very nice high-rise apartment with a friendly doorman that greeted us on our way in. Tristan and I walked up to the front desk and told them who we were here to see. Within a few seconds, we were granted permission to go up to his apartment and we walked towards the elevators. During our elevator ride, I started trying to imagine Seth's face in my mind. When I couldn't, I realized it was because I've never met him before. I decided to ask Tristan just to see if perhaps he could refresh my memory. "Baby, have I ever met Seth before?"

"No, you haven't. But you've seen him before."

I turned to look at Tristan with an expression of confusion. "Where? Is he one of your friends on your MySpace profile?"

"Yeah, he is."

I tried hard to remember Seth's face but I was drawing a complete blank. When the elevator doors opened, we stepped out and walked towards Seth's apartment. We were standing right outside his door and I could hear music playing inside. It sounded like rock blended with ska, and it reminded me of the music those eccentric artists listen to. Tristan rang the bell and after a few seconds, we were greeted by a nice-looking young man with messy brown hair and bright blue eyes. He had a five o'clock shadow and he smiled widely as he greeted us. "Dude, you made it!" When he hugged Tristan I could tell that he was really glad to see him. Once the boys finished greeting each other, Seth turned to face me and Tristan introduced us.

"Seth, this is my wife Bridget."

"Hey Bridget, nice to meet you...*finally*." He put his hand out for me to shake.

I shook his hand and greeted him in return. "Nice to meet you too."

He looked over at Tristan. "I still haven't forgiven Tris for not inviting me to your wedding." He laughed. "That was like a once in a lifetime thing for this guy." He put his arm around Tristan's shoulder in a real 'buddy-buddy' kind of way. "I mean...Tris getting married?!? I didn't want to miss that!" He stepped away from Tristan and shrugged. "But ah well...he sent me some very nice wedding pictures." All of a sudden, it was like a light bulb went off in Seth's head. "Oh! And enough with you guys standing outside in the hall...come on in." Tristan grabbed his luggage and I attempted to grab mine but Seth grabbed them instead. I smiled at him in thanks and he replied, "Please...I insist." I couldn't argue with him if he was going to be chivalrous.

Once we were inside, I was in awe at how nice his apartment was. It had a modern-artsy kind of feel but very casual. He was also extremely neat because I couldn't see one thing out of place in his whole apartment as he gave me the 'grand tour'. He showed us to our room and I was delighted to see a roomy, queen-size bed in the middle. I just hoped that Tristan wouldn't want to 'shag' in it. The last thing I wanted was for Seth to hear us in the heat of passion. He'd most likely hear Tristan because he was incapable of having sex quietly.

Seth left me and Tristan alone in the room for a minute and that's when Tristan came up behind me and whispered in my ear. His tone was soft, yet dominant and I knew to take anything he said seriously. "I know what you're thinking." He kissed the side of my neck. "We're Seth's guests and you don't wanna be rude by having sex in his flat." My eyes widened at his intuitiveness. He licked the shell of my ear and nibbled my earlobe. Then he nipped at it and I quickly sucked some air between my teeth. I also couldn't stop the soft moan that escaped my throat. "Don't even *think* about denying me, Bridget. We're gonna be here for three days and we're shagging..." He sucked on the pale skin of my neck briefly before he released his mouth to speak again. "every..." He found my skin once more. "fucking..." This time I felt his tongue lave at the exact same spot; right behind my ear. He knew where my erogenous zones were and I felt my knees getting weak. "night." Before I could respond, I felt him move away from me and I actually felt cold. Tristan was such a tease when he wanted to be.

I turned around to face him and I saw him unzipping one of his bags to start unpacking. I swallowed thickly because I was still trying to recover from his sexual spell that he wove around me moments ago. When I finally found my voice, I put my hands on my hips and tried to display some ounce of confidence. "For your information, I wasn't thinking that at all," I lied.

Tristan looked up at me and raised a superior eyebrow. "Yes you were." He looked intently into my eyes and rendered me speechless. Damn the power behind his baby blues.

While we were unpacking, Seth came back into the room. The three of us chatted and laughed for awhile when all of a sudden, a woman called his name from another room. "Will you guys excuse me for just a second?" He stepped out of the room and a few minutes later, I heard him and the woman arguing. Tristan and I looked at each other in confusion. He started walking out of the bedroom to investigate and I followed behind him.

We saw Seth and a slender, dark-haired young woman standing in his living room having a heated argument. They abruptly stopped because she looked over at us. I saw that her eyes were dark too, and her face was very pretty. She looked to me like she was maybe Brazilian or Latina. Seth noticed they were attracting an audience and he walked away from her, towards us. That simple dismissive action set her off and she started speaking to him rapidly in some language that was not English. Seth turned his head towards her and spoke in a stern voice, "Just give me a minute, alright?!?" He sighed as he continued walking towards us. Once he reached us, he put his arms out and started shaking his head. "I'm sorry, I was going to go out on the town with you guys tonight...you know, have some drinks. Me and Tris really need to catch up. But Bianca---"

Right at that moment, the young woman walked over to us and I noticed immediately that she had a very imposing presence. It was almost like she demanded to be noticed. "Seth, aren't you going to introduce me to your friends?" Her accent was very exotic and it went right along with her looks.

He was still facing us and I saw him roll his eyes in irritation. Then he turned to her and spoke in a calm voice. "Bianca, this is my friend

Tristan and his wife Bridget. They're here from Cali and they're going to be staying with us for a few days."

She smiled and greeted us both with a friendly, "Hi, nice to meet you." Then, just like the changing of the tides, she looked at Seth with her eyes ablaze. "You didn't tell me they were staying here. Why didn't you tell me that?"

Seth put on a false smile and he sounded like he was speaking through clenched teeth. "I did, sweetie. Remember I told you that we were having guests for the July 4th holiday?"

She put a hand on her hip and it was obvious that she was giving him major attitude. "Yeah but you didn't say that they were *staying*. I thought they were like, you know...stopping by."

I didn't want them to get into a fight on me and Tristan's account, so I decided to step in to try and remedy the situation. "Look, it's okay... really. Tristan and I can stay at a hotel." I looked over at Tristan for confirmation. "Can't we, baby?"

Tristan agreed right away because he could see that Bianca was pissed off. "Yeah, it's no problem."

Bianca immediately dismissed the idea. I found that contradictory because she obviously had a problem with our presence. "No, you guys can stay. I just wish that *somebody* would've told me first." And she whipped her head towards Seth again.

Seth sighed heavily. "I *did* tell you."

"No you didn't!"

"Yes...I *did*."

"I swear Seth..." Then she started going off on him in her own language and she completely lost me. I found it kind of funny that Seth just stood there and took it. And he actually seemed to understand what she was saying because he responded back to her in English.

While they were arguing, I found myself looking on in amusement. Tristan and I didn't argue that often so when other couples did it, I found it interesting. Tristan interrupted the domestic show I was watching because he leaned down towards me and whispered, "Let's get out of here for awhile." I looked up at him and nodded in agreement. Then he grasped my arm and carefully guided us around the bodies of the still-arguing Bianca and Seth. Once we reached the door, he yelled out, "We're just gonna go out for awhile! We'll be back later! You two kids just... yeah." Seth looked over at us and nodded in acknowledgement.

I've never seen Tristan rush us out of a door so quickly in my life. Even when we were on the other side of the door, I could still hear them yelling at each other inside the apartment. Tristan seemed to sigh a breath of relief. "Babe, I am so glad to be out of there. Seth told me that Bianca was hot-blooded...but damn! She practically tore him a new arsehole...right in front of us!" Tristan started laughing.

We started walking hand-in-hand down the hallway towards the elevators, and their voices began to fade. That's when I asked casually, "What language was she speaking? That didn't sound like Spanish to me."

"She's Brazilian, so I think that was Portuguese."

While we were in the elevator, Tristan briefed me on Bianca and Seth's relationship. Basically they were the break up and make up type of couple. They constantly did that but more often than not, they were usually together. He also informed me that Seth was multi-lingual and he knew Portuguese fluently.

Once we left the apartment, Tristan expressed that he was starving and he knew this great Irish pub and restaurant that he wanted to take me to. He took me to Connolly's Pub & Restaurant on West 54th Street in Manhattan, and I can honestly say that it was a lot different than the Irish pubs I've been to in California. Connolly's just seemed to be more authentic. Tristan had a Guinness beer along with his bangers and mash; a traditional Irish meal which consists of sausage and mashed potatoes with an onion gravy. I had a Diet Coke along with the shepherd's pie because Tristan told me it's the best I'll ever have just short of having it in Ireland. He was absolutely right because it was delicious!

We dined for awhile because we also enjoyed the live entertainment. It was nice to just relax in a pleasant atmosphere, away from Hollywood. I noticed that during our stay in New York, Tristan completely forgot about his troubles with his casting auditions. We didn't talk about them at all during our evening together and I was truly glad about that. The last thing I wanted was for our little vacation to be ruined by unhappy thoughts.

When we finally decided to leave the restaurant, we walked out onto the street and into the night air. I had no idea that time had passed so quickly. But it usually does whenever I'm having fun with Tristan. We stood in front of the restaurant for awhile because Tristan wanted to have a cigarette. He made me stand a few feet away from him because he didn't want me near the smoke. Passersby must have thought we looked pretty strange talking to each other from that far a distance. Once he was done with his cigarette, he flicked it away and we took a short stroll down the street with our arms around each other. "So, do you think it's safe to go back there?"

I laughed lightly. "I don't know, but we can try." Tristan took out his cell phone and called Seth to tell him we were coming back. I heard Tristan ask him if the coast was clear and when he turned to me and nodded, I knew the tropical storm known as Bianca had either left or calmed down. We hailed a taxi to head back to Seth's apartment, but I noticed that Tristan was having trouble communicating with the driver. I attributed it to the fact that he barely spoke English. Something inside me wanted to suggest that we just get the next one but when Tristan gestured for me to get in, I took the risk.

While we were in the taxi, we ran into heavy traffic because of an accident. Tristan tried to tell the driver to take another street but I don't think the driver understood. He made a few wrong turns to Tristan's discontent and when he finally got fed up, he told the driver to let us out. As soon as I stepped out of the taxi, I found myself in unfamiliar surroundings. "Baby, where are we?" Tristan paid the driver...actually he threw the money at him and then he came over to me.

He sighed heavily and looked around in confusion. "Well, there's Central Park." And he pointed at the park.

"But this isn't where Seth lives. Are we on the wrong side?"

Tristan was quiet for a minute, and I watched his face as his eyes darted around the area. "Yeah, we are. He's actually on the other side." He pointed at the park again. "West...through the park."

I was watching the taxies drive by and I was about to suggest that we hail another one, when Tristan moved right in front of me; blocking my view. I looked up at him questioningly and I was surprised to see that he was smiling. "Let's take a walk."

I pointed at the street. "But the taxies---"

He took my hand and placed a tender kiss on my palm. "It's a beautiful night, Bridget. Let's just walk through the park." He gave me a hopeful look and I looked at him with worry.

"But it's dark. What if we get robbed?"

Right after my question, Tristan's expression turned serious. His voice was low and he looked intently into my eyes when he said, "Bridget, I would die first before I let anyone hurt you." I gave him a small smile and let him take my hand and guide us through Central Park.

While we were walking hand-in-hand once again, I noticed that there were other people around so I didn't feel too nervous. Don't get me wrong, I was still nervous but not as much as I was when he first suggested that we walk. I guess my inner thoughts were showing on my face because Tristan looked over at me and asked, "Are you okay, babe? You look a little nervous." Tristan is so perceptive and has always been able to read my face like an open book so I wasn't that surprised by his question.

I responded sarcastically because I really was nervous. "Uh, yeah. I mean, it's dark and we're walking in Central Park. Some crazy person can just come out of no where and rob us." I started looking around the park and I noticed we were alone now. "Or worse." I instinctively squeezed his hand tighter. Tristan let go of my hand and I panicked for a millisecond before he put his arm around my shoulder.

"Don't be nervous, love. I'll protect you." I felt him kiss my forehead and the feeling of his soft lips against my skin actually eased my fears slightly; just slightly because I doubt Tristan could defend me against a gun. Maybe a knife but I wasn't sure about a gun. And just when I thought we might make it to the other side safely, it started to rain. He put his arms out wide as the raindrops fell against his open palms. "Oh shit! No fucking way! Just our luck, right?!?" But Tristan's voice wasn't angry or annoyed; it was actually joyous because he laughed out loud. "C'mon babe, let's run!"

"Tristan!" I laughed in surprise because he grabbed my hand again and started pulling me along as he ran in the rain. It started to down-pour and the momentum of our running caused the rain to pelt me in the face. Not to mention, I could feel the water seeping through my white sleeveless shirt and my denim shorts. "We're getting soaked!" He turned to look at me and we slowed down the pace. Then all of a sudden he changed directions. "Where are we going?!?" We were going into a lighted underpass apparently.

We finally stopped running and I leaned against the stone wall to catch my breath; all the while I was dripping wet from head to toe. To make matters worse, my skin broke out in goose bumps and I started shivering. It was quiet in the underpass except for the sound of the summer rain pouring down on the bridge above us. I could also hear Tristan breathing but he wasn't panting like I was moments ago. I knew I looked like a wet dog and I remarked sardonically, "This is just great." I sighed and shook my head.

Tristan didn't say anything as he slowly walked towards me. It wasn't until he was standing directly in front of me, looking down on me, that I saw the unmistakable lust in his light blue eyes. His voice was low when he asked, "You're cold, aren't you?"

I smirked at him and gave a sarcastic reply. "Did my shivering give me away?"

He smirked back and then he turned on the intensity in his eyes and they began to smolder me. He moved closer and I could feel the heat radiating off his body; it actually provided me some momentary comfort. "No."

To my surprise, he reached out and cupped my breasts through my shirt. He brushed his thumbs over my peaked nipples and I knew at that moment exactly why he asked his question. My *nipples* gave me away. He held my gaze as he started gently squeezing and kneading my breasts. Then he reached under my shirt that was plastered to my skin and put his surprisingly warm hands under my bra; directly on my bare breasts. I gasped once and he swallowed it by capturing my mouth with his. He pressed me up against the wall and dug one of his hands into my wet hair to grasp a few strands. He kissed me deeply with his tongue while he continued to tease one of my nipples and grind his hips into mine. We were both soaked to the bone and dripping water on each other. We moaned into each other's mouths but because of where we were, our moans were loud and they reverberated off the walls in the underpass. Tristan began to harden and I rubbed myself against him in return. I reached down to grab his butt and press his body closer to mine. He moaned louder and then he broke the kiss to gasp in pleasure. My hands shot up into his wet, blond hair and I tangled the strands in my fists. He started kissing my neck while his hands roamed across my breasts and down my flat stomach.

He was definitely warming me up because I was aroused to the point of feeling flushed. I started to hump against him because the ache between my legs was becoming more prominent. Tristan reached down and unsnapped my shorts. He shoved his hand inside my panties to reach my swollen, aching core. He rubbed me in just the right spot and he made sure to brush over my clit repeatedly. I cried out in absolute pleasure. "Tristan! Oh my God! Yes! Yes!" I grunted and began to buck against his hand. "Deeper! Finger me, baby!" He inserted a couple long digits inside my opening and fingered me quick and deep; exactly how I like it. I gasped again as I reached down to try and free his cock from its confines. It only took me a few seconds but once I had it in my grasp, I stroked him firmly from base to tip. He moaned again and started thrusting into my fist.

His voice was breathless as he expressed his pleasure. "Wank me faster, Bridget! Yeah...just like that." I sped up the pace and I noticed that he did too. A few more seconds and neither of us would be able to stand it any longer. Tristan wanted exactly what I did so he pulled my shorts and panties down my hips and I spread my legs as far as I could. He looked me in the eye and kissed me deeply again. Then he said, "Put me inside you. Don't worry if anyone sees us 'cause I don't fucking care. I just want you, Bridget."

The underpass was illuminated with a golden light. It wasn't very bright but I could see tiny water droplets on his long, darkened lashes. The color of his eyes stood out even more in this strange light; they were a crystal clear blue like the ocean in The Caribbean. And I found myself mesmerized. His gaze pierced through me and my prince entranced me with his soft but dominant tone. "Make love to me." His erection was still in my hand but I felt him put his hand over mine and guide himself inside me. I cried out softly as my warm sheath enveloped the entire length of his hardness.

He made love to me up against the wall with deep, hard strokes. He cradled the back of my head with his hand to make sure I didn't bang it against the stone wall. Our cries of passion were loud and echoed throughout the small space beneath the bridge. Sinful lust engulfed us both and I don't think we would've stopped even if the police approached us. Go ahead and arrest us for indecent exposure and lewd acts. Tristan and I were undoubtedly in love and we expressed it whenever the mood struck.

I wasn't cold anymore. Tristan's body filled me with warmth that was so hot that I felt it all the way to my toes. We came together in ecstasy and we held each other like there was no one else in the world but us. I was so used to the sound of our voices when we shared our orgasm together. It was like our own personal song; a song which sung of two halves of one soul; bonded together by pure love and expressed through blissful passion.

Once we both caught our breath again, we remained in a wet embrace. I heard Tristan whisper in my ear and his warm breath actually felt good against my skin. "Are you still scared?"

I kissed the side of his neck and held him tighter against me. "No, I'm not scared. I have you with me. And I'm definitely not cold anymore." I laughed lightly. Tristan pulled back, but he kept himself still nestled inside. He looked at me but the dim light caused part of his face to be hidden in shadow. I trailed my fingers down his smooth cheek and across his soft lips. "But you know, if we don't change out of these wet clothes, we're both going to get sick."

The golden light in the underpass still allowed me to see his lovely smile. "Then we'll both just stay in bed together and share our germs. Trust me, I wouldn't mind spending all day in bed with you." He waggled his eyebrows at me and I couldn't help but to laugh. The sound echoed throughout the underpass along with the sound of the steady rain overhead.

The next night after we enjoyed a 4th of July barbecue on the terrace of one of Tristan and Seth's friends' penthouse apartments, we enjoyed fireworks overlooking the Hudson River. Tristan had me in his protective embrace as we stood together and watched the bright lights fill up the sky and the loud cracking sound boom in our ears. Being in New York City again was memorable and watching the fireworks show was absolutely spectacular. But making love to my beautiful British husband in the rain in Central Park will always be in my heart forever. As I gazed adoringly into his eyes, I saw the fireworks reflected in them. Tristan looked down at me and even though the lights lit up his eyes, I saw nothing but pure affection behind them. And I realized that all of our interludes of passion were more than just sex between us. They were part of our own storybook romance. Since the moment I met Tristan, he gave me the chance to experience what true love felt like...with my very own prince charming.

Chapter 22

WHOEVER THOUGHT OF THE EXPRESSION *'Time flies'* was truly a bona fide genius. My summer vacation was quickly coming to an end and before this week was over, I would be starting a new school year and teaching another class filled with fresh faces. But even though the summer was almost over, I was still in very high spirits. I was feeling absolutely elated today because it was Sunday, August 31, 2008 and Tristan and I were celebrating the one-year anniversary of the day we exchanged vows on the beach in Brighton, England. In the days prior to our anniversary, we were trying to figure out how we wanted to celebrate the day we bonded our hearts and souls to each other for all eternity. We put so much money into our new house this summer that by the time our anniversary date was approaching, we were actually strapped for cash. So we both agreed that because we were limited in our finances, we shouldn't celebrate by doing anything or going anywhere extravagant. We finally settled on having a little end-of-the-summer barbecue in the backyard and inviting some of our close friends.

I found it strange that it was actually the first barbecue we had at our house all summer. I remember when Tristan first bought the grill over a month ago. We were in Lowe's and he was so excited about buying one. Unfortunately, his enthusiasm seemed to wear off quickly. For the next month and a half, it just sat in the backyard; he never fired it up once. But he told me that today he was finally ready to put it to use. At first I was skeptical about his grilling skills because the boy honestly could not boil water. He reassured me that he knew what he was doing because he remembered the Grilling 101 course my father gave him a few months ago during a barbecue at their house. So I put my confidence in him and gave him the green light to be The Man of the Grill today. But truthfully, having an anniversary barbecue with close friends was sort of bittersweet and I thought it would be a perfect ending to another amazing summer with Tristan.

I was pleasantly surprised when Tristan woke up early and went in the backyard to set up for the barbecue all by himself. I knew he had to be careful because now there was limited space outside because the contractors started digging up the ground in preparation for our new in ground swimming pool. He was still out there when I finished getting dressed and went into the kitchen. I was pulling out the family-size bags of potato chips and pretzels from one of the cabinets when I heard the doorbell. I had to assume it was our first guests of the day. I ran to the front door and I wasn't really surprised when I checked the peep-hole and saw Autumn and Ryan standing there. I figured Autumn would show up early to offer assistance with the barbecue. I opened the door and I noticed she was holding a large red bowl topped with aluminum foil and Ryan was holding a platter covered in plastic-wrap. Upon closer inspection, I realized the platter contained about a couple dozen devilled eggs.

A few nights ago, I assigned Tristan the responsibility of putting together the guest list and contacting each person. I felt that it made more sense for him to do it because he has more friends than I do. After he contacted all the people on the list, he informed me that he told everyone he invited that they each had to bring something for the barbecue. He said, "I told them don't worry about buying us an anniversary gift; just bring food." At first I gaped at him in utter shock because of his audacity but he wasn't fazed by my reaction and he responded with, "Hey, we don't have the money to cater a whole fucking barbecue. So we need all the help we can get." So yesterday, I contributed my part and went to the grocery store. I picked up some paper plates, plastic cups and utensils, chips, pretzels, and a few cases of soda. I also made potato salad last night that was still chilling in the refrigerator.

I smiled and greeted Autumn and Ryan in a cheerful voice. "Hi guys, glad you could make it. You know you're early right?" I moved to the side to let them enter.

As expected, Autumn smiled and replied, "Yeah, I know. But I thought you may need some help setting up." I closed the door and they followed me into the kitchen.

She sat the large bowl on one of the counters on the center island and my curiosity caused me to ask, "What's in the bowl?"

She pulled back the foil for my inspection. "I made a salad. By the time I remembered that I had to bring something, I only had time to make a salad and some devilled eggs."

I leaned over the counter to take a peek inside the bowl and my eyes feasted upon a very delicious looking tossed salad. I was internally grateful to her because I was hoping at least someone would bring a green salad. I looked up at her and grinned in appreciation. "It looks good to me." Then I picked up the bowl and carried it over to the refrigerator. Autumn put the devilled eggs inside the refrigerator too, and that's when I heard the doorbell again. "Wow, more guests already? I'll be right back."

I dashed towards the front door, and when I opened it again I saw Jake and his girlfriend Lauren standing there. "Hi Bridget! Happy anniversary!" Lauren said gleefully. She gave me a wide toothy smile and I couldn't help but to smile back at her.

"Thanks Lauren." I saw that she was holding a cake of some sort. I looked over at Jake and I wasn't surprised at all by what he brought. He was holding two cases of beer in his arms.

He flashed me a grin and then he said, "I got some ice in the car. Do you have a cooler for me to put this in?"

"Uh, yeah. Just follow me." Once we were all inside, I closed the door and had them follow me into the kitchen. When I got there, I noticed that Autumn and Ryan had disappeared and I assumed they went out to the backyard to help Tristan.

I was pulling out a couple of coolers from the pantry closet when Jake asked about his little brother's whereabouts. "Where's Tris?"

"He's out back setting up. Although, I think he should be almost done by now."

He nodded and that's when Lauren said, "Jake, let me have the keys so I can get the ice out of the trunk." Jake dug in his front pocket for a quick second and then he handed her the car keys. Once Lauren was out of sight, I was putting the coolers on the counter when I felt his eyes on me. It was quiet in the kitchen and for some strange reason, I was feeling uncomfortable being alone with him. I was also afraid to make eye contact with him because I knew he possessed the same ability as Tristan: to pierce his gaze into me. So you can imagine the sheer relief I felt when I heard Tristan and Autumn's voice within close distance.

A few seconds later, they entered the kitchen with Ryan in-tow. When I looked at Tristan, his blond hair was wind-blown and I could see that his cheeks were slightly flushed. I concluded that he must have been working hard outside. He leaned on one of the counters and gave me an affectionate smile that caused his cute little dimple to appear on his left cheek. "I'm all done outside, babe. Damn, I wish that blasted hole wasn't there. I would've had so much more room."

I laughed flippantly and replied, "*You're* the one who wanted a pool. You didn't fall in, did you?"

Tristan smirked at me before he gave a dry laugh. Then he turned to Jake and said, "I need you to go to the store with me. I have to get the hamburgers and hot-dogs."

Autumn asked curiously, "What else are you grilling?"

Tristan whipped his head to look at her and his expression was blank. "Uh...that's it."

She looked at him with wide-eyes and exclaimed, "That's it?!? You're not grilling any chicken or vegetables? Ryan made these shrimp skewer---"

He cut her sentence short and responded sharply, "I don't know how to grill that shit, okay."

Autumn didn't seem affected by Tristan's tone of voice because she turned her head towards her boyfriend and smiled warmly. "Ryan does. He even grilled some yummy portabella mushrooms." I looked at Ryan and he was grinning, and I could tell he was basking in Autumn's adoration.

Tristan turned his attention from her and said dryly, "Yeah, well good for Ryan." I was trying not to smile at Tristan's coarse reply but I was amused by the fact that he was having a run-in with the green-eyed monster of jealousy. I wondered if he was feeling some kind of machismo grilling competition with Ryan. I was honestly surprised when he came over to me and stood with his back to Ryan and Autumn. Then he asked me quietly, "Is it alright if we just have hamburgers and hot-dogs?" A worried look crossed his features for the briefest of moments but it didn't go unnoticed by me.

I smiled just as warmly as Autumn did towards Ryan and I laid my hand on his smooth cheek. I looked into his clear azure eyes and replied softly, "That's fine, baby." I decided to pacify him further by saying, "You know I love hamburgers and hot-dogs. And I can't *wait* to taste your barbecue." I gave him a peck on the lips and a bright smile lit up his beautiful face.

I seemed to boost his confidence because his tone of voice turned cheery. "And you'll get the first hamburger and the first hot-dog." He walked over to Jake and gave him a pat on the back and then he started walking out of the kitchen. "Let's go." Jake immediately got up from the stool he was sitting on and followed his younger brother.

I finally noticed Lauren was back and once again I was curious about what she brought to the barbecue. Her cake was covered and was sitting on the island counter. "Hey Lauren, what kind of cake is this?" I carefully took the cover off and she moved closer to me and smiled.

"It's a coconut cake. I made it myself." I nodded and wore a thoughtful expression as I admired the two-layer round cake with white frosting and coconut shavings. I detected a tinge of worry in her voice when she asked, "Is coconut okay? Do you like coconut?"

I smiled kindly at her and softened my voice as I reassured her. "Yeah, I do."

Her face relaxed for a split second but it was quickly replaced with uncertainty once again. "Does Tristan?"

I smirked at her and replied, "Tristan likes cake and this is a cake. So he'll eat it…trust me." She smiled again and this time I could tell she was relieved.

All of a sudden, I heard a male voice call out, "Hello?!? Anyone here?!?" I looked up and I saw Tristan's friend Dane walking towards the kitchen. He stopped in the entryway and smiled from ear-to-ear when he saw all of us. "Oh there you are. I ran into Tris on his way out and he told me to just come in." Dane was holding a large cardboard box that was hiding most of his body. I found it kind of funny that I could only see his head as he was talking.

I walked over to him and asked, "What's in the box?"

"Oh, Tris told me I was in charge of the music. He said to bring a stereo and some CD's so...here it is. I also got some chips and salsa in the car 'cause he told me to bring food too." I couldn't help but to laugh because so far, everyone was following Tristan's instructions. Ryan came over and helped Dane with the box after I told him he could set up in the backyard. I followed them outside because I wanted to see the results of Tristan's hard work.

When I walked outside, I noticed that in addition to our patio set that included a large round table, umbrella, and four cushioned chairs, Tristan set up a long table that seated ten. Actually, he put two rectangular tables together and placed the chairs around. He also had a small table next to the grill and a couple more tables for what I assumed would be for the food. He also had some lounge chairs set up. Crystal clear water was flowing and cascading from both of our beautiful stone fountains and I could honestly say that the entire backyard scene was very appealing; regardless of the fact there was a huge gaping hole in the ground. I thought Tristan did a wonderful job and I could imagine how the scene would look once everyone was here enjoying the barbecue.

While Dane and Ryan set up the music, Autumn, Lauren, and I sat outside and had girl-talk for awhile. Soon there was techno music filling the backyard and the barbecue was slowly but surely coming alive. Tristan and Jake came back from the store and they were both carrying grocery bags. They put the bags on the table and of course I had to come over and inspect. Tristan started pulling the groceries from the bags as he spoke to me. "I got hamburgers, hot-dogs, rolls, cheese, ketchup, mustard, barbecue sauce, and a bag of charcoal." I looked over at Jake and he was setting up the coolers with the ice, beer and sodas. I turned my attention back on Tristan because he asked, "Is that good, babe? Did I forget anything?"

I was inspecting the pack of hamburgers before I smiled and answered reassuringly, "Nope, I think that's everything." Tristan looked relieved and he smiled back at me. It wasn't long until the girls and I went back inside to bring out the food and the other barbecue necessities. Dane went back to his car and grabbed the chips and salsa, and he put it with the rest of the food that was set out. I noticed that Ryan was standing next to Tristan by the grill and it seemed to me like Ryan was helping him. And judging from the light expression on Tristan's face, he had no qualms accepting his help.

Suddenly, I heard a male voice yell out, "Tris is barbecuing?!? Holy shit!" There was immediate laughter and I looked towards the voice and I saw Rick, Becca, and Rick's younger brother Chris entering the backyard from the side of the house.

I started laughing too and that's when I heard Tristan retort, "Yeah, that means you better be nice to me or else I'm gonna burn your fucking burgers!" Rick walked over to Tristan and I saw the both of them laughing together. He patted Tristan on the back and I quickly went over to greet our newest guests. Chris and Becca were standing together and they were both holding platters of something.

Chris gave me a smile that lit up his youthful brown eyes, "Happy anniversary, Bridget."

I smiled in return. "Thanks, Chris. I wasn't expecting to see you here."

"Yeah, Tristan said I could come if I brought some food." At that moment, he presented the platter in his hands. "So I got brownies." He laughed lightly as I took them from him.

"Wow, thank you." My eyes widened and I was practically salivating at the mouth as I stared at the large plate piled high with chocolate brownies covered with chopped nuts.

Becca spoke next and her voice was gleeful. "We just came from the supermarket." I looked over at her and she made a point of showing me what she brought. "I saw this shrimp ring and I just had to get it." Becca's platter contained a ring of at least fifty already-cooked and peeled shrimp on a bed of greens surrounding a small bowl of what looked like cocktail sauce. I happened to glance back at Rick and I noticed a case of beer sitting next to his feet as he chatted away with Tristan. Before I could stop myself, I chuckled softly and shook my head because I wasn't surprised that he brought beer. I knew that Tristan would be happy because his motto has always been: 'The more alcohol…the better.'

It wasn't long until the smell of barbecue was permeating in the air. I walked over to Tristan and I was actually giddy to see him engrossed in his role as The Man of the Grill. The hamburgers and hot-dogs were sizzling nicely on the rack while the charcoal crackled and burned slowly underneath. Every now and then, he would brush the meat with barbecue sauce and flip and turn almost like a pro. I was so proud of him that I put my arms around him and tilted my head up to give him a loving kiss. I smiled affectionately and spoke tenderly when I said, "I'm so proud of you, baby. I think you're doing a great job." Deep down, I knew Tristan needed to hear that because he was always seeking my approval and reassurance.

He slipped his free arm around my waist and held me close. "Thanks, babe. I appreciate that."

My eyes became transfixed on the meat and I said, "I can't wait to taste it. I'm telling you, those burgers are making my mouth water. I bet they taste fantastic." I was telling the honest truth because the aroma alone was making my stomach rumble.

Tristan laughed lightly and then he released me and said, "Remember I promised that you'd get the first ones?" I smiled and nodded as he moved away from the grill to grab a paper plate from one of the tables. I watched him put a hamburger and a hot-dog roll on the plate and then come back over to me. He handed me the plate and asked, "You want cheese on your burger?"

The smile was glued to my face and I bounced up and down on the balls of my feet in excitement. "Yes please!"

Tristan continued to laugh as he opened a package of processed cheese and slapped it on one of the burgers. Within seconds, the cheese was melted to a yellow gooey perfection and he took the cheeseburger off the grill and put it on my roll. Then he used the tongs to grab a hot-dog and he gave that to me too. He grinned and there was a look of anticipation on his face when he said, "Okay, now take a bite and tell me what you think." He kept his eyes trained on me as I took a bite of the cheeseburger first. In my eagerness to please him, I forgot that it was scorching hot. I immediately fanned my open mouth to cool off my scalded tongue. A look of shock appeared on Tristan's face before he started laughing again. In between his chuckles he asked with genuine concern, "Are you alright, love? You know it's hot. I just took it off the grill." He continued to laugh as I tried to chew and fan my mouth at the same time.

I spoke with my burnt mouth full of food, "Yeah...it's good...it tastes really good." When I was finally able to close my mouth and chew, I grinned and gave him a thumbs up. I made a sound of satisfaction after I took another bite and walked away to enjoy the first taste of my husband's barbecue.

Tristan continued to grill and it wasn't long after I sat down with my food that a line began to form next to him for some hamburgers and hot-dogs. I was sitting at the long table eating when I heard a familiar voice call my name. I looked up and I saw Amy walking towards me. She was smiling brightly and I immediately jumped up to greet her. When I reached her, I stopped short because her appearance caught me by complete surprise. I couldn't help but to notice the drastic physical change in her since I last saw her at my 25th birthday party. Amy was thin the last time I saw her but now she was even thinner than me! I gaped at her and exclaimed loudly, "Oh my God! Amy, look at you!" She looked great and I couldn't tear my eyes away from her.

My mind flashed back for a moment and I remembered when we were in high school and she was always so self-conscience because she was overweight. I had a feeling she didn't worry about that anymore. She was wearing a pale yellow sleeveless top and a cute denim skirt which showed off her lean, tanned legs. Her hair was also longer; it was now waist-length and I found myself feeling kind of jealous because she was so attractive. Oddly, I started feeling self-conscience about myself because I knew it wouldn't be long until my belly was swollen with Tristan's baby.

"Happy anniversary, Bridget!"

"Thanks, Amy! Oh my God, I can't get over how great you look."

"Thanks. I've just been working out and eating healthy."

My eyes continued to roam up and down her body in amazement. "Wow," I said breathlessly.

I finally noticed she was carrying something when she tried to hand it to me. "I brought fruit salad." There was also a wrapped present sitting on top of the bowl of fruit salad. "Oh, and that's for you...for your anniversary." She winked at me and I immediately started wondering what was inside.

I took the covered bowl with the box on top from her. "Thanks."

She laughed casually, "You have to eat healthy, Bridge."

For some strange reason, my train of thought changed and I started wondering how she got invited. I know I didn't invite her since I wasn't in charge of the guest list. Tristan was in charge but Amy wasn't one of his friends. So how did he call her and how did he get her number? My inner thoughts found their way out of my mouth when I asked, "Did Tristan call and invite you?"

She shook her head. "No, I got your message on MySpace." Then she scrunched up her face in confusion. "Don't you remember?"

I shared an identical look of confusion with her. "I didn't send you a message."

"Yes you did." When she continued speaking, it was like she was quoting me. "You said you really wanted me to come to your anniversary barbecue and you'd appreciate it if I brought some food." She laughed again and I immediately looked over at Tristan. Then I remembered…he knew my old MySpace password. He must've logged in as me at some point and contacted Amy to invite her. My feeling of confusion was quickly replaced by a feeling of adoration for Tristan because he was thoughtful enough to invite one of my closest friends instead of just inviting all of his friends.

I felt that Amy deserved the truth so I said, "Oh, I know what happened, Amy. Tristan logged into my MySpace and he invited you. You see, I put him in charge of the guest list." A look of understanding came over Amy's face and her mouth formed a tiny 'o'. "But I'm glad he did because I'm so happy to see you."

She smiled fondly at me when she said, "Me too, Bridge." She followed me while I put her fruit salad with the rest of the food. I carried her gift box over to the table I was sitting at and put it in the middle. Once my arms were free, I gave her a huge welcoming hug. Then I walked back over to Tristan and put my arms around him from behind.

"Mmmm…what's this for?" He asked in a low voice. He turned his head slightly to look at me.

I held him tighter and tilted my head up to place a kiss on the back of his neck. I spoke quietly when I replied, "Thank you for inviting Amy, sweetie. That was very thoughtful of you."

"You're welcome, love. I knew you'd probably wanna see her."

"Yeah, I did."

I heard Amy's voice again but this time she yelled, "Hi Tristan!" I looked over at her and she was waving excitedly.

I looked at Tristan's face and he was gaping at her in shock. "Amy?!? Oh shit! You're disappearing!" Amy started giggling and I couldn't stop myself from laughing at his comment. I walked back over to Amy and I noticed there were two cards on top of her present. I picked them up and I saw that one was from Jake and Lauren, and the other was from Autumn and Ryan.

As the day wore on, I was filled with such joy to see everyone getting along and having a good time. I was pleasantly surprised when Tristan's friend Tyler strolled into the backyard holding a cardboard box filled with bottles. He was dressed in a white t-shirt that clung to his toned muscular torso and a pair of khaki board shorts that seemed extra baggy. Some of his chin-length dirty-blond hair was hidden underneath a black bandana. He spoke loudly as he made his presence known. "Man, I love the smell of barbecue in the summer." He garnered everyone's attention; especially Tristan who quickly walked towards him.

It was evident that Tristan was extremely happy because I could hear it in his voice. "You made it!"

"Hell yeah I did! I missed your wedding, man. I wasn't gonna miss this too." He put the box on the ground and he and Tristan gave each other very brotherly hugs. I walked over to them because I was curious as to what was in the box. Tyler looked over at me with his topaz eyes and smiled roguishly. "Hey Bridget. How you doing?"

"Hi Ty, nice to see you again."

"Yeah, likewise." He gave me a hug and when he released me, he said, "Happy anniversary."

"Thanks." I cast my eyes towards the box that Tyler brought and I noticed it contained an assortment of hard liquor. I put a hand on my hip and sighed. "Oh my God. Ty, what is this?" He gave me a sly grin as I bent down and pulled a bottle of Absolut Vodka from the box.

Tristan exclaimed loudly, "Now *that's* what I'm talking about!" Tyler's box of liquor began to draw attention because more people started gathering around.

I heard Autumn say excitedly, "Bridge, I'm gonna get that cranberry and orange juice out of your fridge. We're gonna have some real fucking drinks!" Before I could say anything, she dashed towards the back door.

Tristan yelled out, "And get that lime juice too!"

I heard Chris say, "I have a taste for a Rum & Coke right about now." He leaned down to peer into the box. "I see that rum in there, Ty." He laughed and picked up the bottle. "I have to tell you, you're The Man." Tyler laughed too and he picked up the box and brought it over to the long table. Everyone else followed him like lambs to the slaughter. He started pulling the bottles out and many hands started picking up each of them to check the labels.

Rick had a bottle of gin in his hand when he said, "I am *so* getting drunk tonight."

Becca retorted, "Then I guess it's a good thing I'm here."

I laughed. "Oh yeah, you're the designated driver, right?" Becca nodded to confirm my statement and then she laughed along with me. Autumn came back outside with a variety of juices and it wasn't long until everyone except me was drinking some kind of alcoholic beverage from a plastic cup. I felt really left out, and I'll admit that the temptation and peer-pressure to join in was overwhelming. But I remembered that I was carrying someone very precious inside me so I could afford to feel left out for a few more months.

Tristan finally joined us at the table to eat after I ordered him away from the grill. "Baby, we have enough hamburgers and hot-dogs now. Come over here and eat." When I saw him take the last of the meat off the grill, put it in a foil pan, and close the grill lid...I knew he was done with his grilling duties for the day.

Everyone was sitting down; eating, drinking, and chatting while the music continued to blast into the late afternoon. I was sitting at the long table in between Amy and Lauren, when Tristan came up behind me and said rudely, "Uh, can someone move over so I can sit next to my wife?" Lauren got up immediately and made herself a comfortable seat on Jake's lap. Jake was sitting at the head of the table; leaning back casually in his chair and sipping a can of beer. Once Tristan took Lauren's place and sat down next to me, he was sitting adjacent to his brother. Different conversations were going on all at once but there was one particular private subject that had only been spoken in the past between a select few: namely me, Tristan, and Jake. But today, someone who I least expected took notice of the subject and changed the entire mood at the barbecue.

When Lauren got up, her action caught Chris' attention. He was sitting directly across from me and I noticed his head move back and forth between me and Lauren. His eyes rested on me and he asked innocently, "Are you two sisters?" He looked back at Lauren again. Right at that moment, Rick and Tristan both started laughing and it wasn't the first time they shared a laugh regarding the resemblance between me and Lauren. I looked over at Jake to see his reaction and he was looking down at the table with an unreadable expression.

I turned my attention back to Chris and answered in a friendly tone. "No, we're not."

His eyes widened in surprised. "You're not?!? But you look alike." I noticed the volume of the other conversations at the table begin to quiet down a bit. "Are you cousins?"

Tristan chimed in and I could tell that Chris' questions were amusing him. "They're not related at all, mate."

Chris sputtered. "But...but..." Then he started shaking his head in disbelief. "Wow." He took a sip of his drink and I could still see his eyes darting back and forth. He leaned on the table towards me and grinned. "So, Bridget you're with Tristan..." He turned to look at Lauren again. "And Lauren you're with...Jake?"

Lauren's voice was chipper when she responded. "I sure am." She put her arms around Jake and pecked him on the lips in a display of open affection.

Chris looked between Tristan and Jake and asked another innocent question: "So, you two like the same kind of woman?" And that's when I suddenly felt real tension in the air. But I only felt it on my right side; where Tristan and Jake were sitting. At this point, Chris' innocent conversation attracted everyone's attention. Neither Tristan nor Jake responded to Chris at first and I looked over at Tristan who just stared intently into my eyes. I glanced at Jake and Lauren, and she didn't look affected by the conversation. The same couldn't be said for Jake because he was staring at Tristan with an intense look. I think he knew that his little brother was going to say something that would cause even more tension.

And to my disappointment...he did. "I had my woman first," Tristan said in a hard voice. To add more fuel to the fire in this unsettled rivalry between the Hathaway brothers, he said it while he was returning Jake's look with equal intensity. And I know *everyone* noticed.

When I saw Lauren's joyous expression change to one of sadness and confusion, I knew that I had to take hold of the situation. I really liked her and I didn't want her to get upset over something she was totally clueless about. Not to mention, it was something that was immature and ridiculous between Tristan and Jake. I was disappointed in both of them because I thought they would've been mature enough to finally put it to rest. I put a hand on top of Tristan's to garner his attention. It worked because he finally turned his attention away from his older brother. I made sure my voice was soft and sweet when I said, "Baby, there's a present in our bedroom closet. Can you go up there and get it? I have a nice surprise for you." I smiled at him while I trailed a finger gently down the side of his cheek. Tristan's expression softened like butter and I knew I was able to take his mind off Jake momentarily. After he got up from the table and went inside the house, I announced, "When Tristan gets back, I'm going to open these." And I touched one of the cards in the middle of the table.

That's when Amy remarked enthusiastically, "Ooh! Open mine first."

Tristan came back outside with the present and I stood up to meet him. Amy cleared a spot on the table and he put it down. I watched in anticipation as he ripped the wrapping paper off with haste.

I heard Autumn say in a sing-song voice, "I already know what it is." Then she laughed.

Once all the wrapping paper was removed, Tristan opened the unlabeled box inside. Once he opened it, he gasped in surprise and pulled out a tray of personalized billiard balls. The balls were clear except for a strip of color in the middle. They were each numbered but they had a special personal touch: the Gemini symbol with the initials TCH in white cursive. I could see the sheer happiness on Tristan's face as he took a couple of the balls out to examine them. "Babe, these are wicked! I can't believe it!" Tyler came over and reached out to inspect one of the balls too.

"Yeah man, these are awesome. We need to crack these babies like right now." He laughed lightly.

I put my arms around Tristan and kissed his cheek. "They're for your new pool table. Happy anniversary, baby."

Tristan put his arms around me and held me close. My kiss on the cheek didn't satisfy his need and he didn't hesitate to kiss me properly in front of everyone. When he unsealed his lips from mine, he said, "I love them darlin', but the pool table is *ours*."

I smirked. "You know I can't play."

"With me as your teacher…you will soon enough. Since we have our own table, we'll have plenty of time for practice. Just wait, before you know it…we're gonna be a husband and wife hustling duo."

I heard laughter and then Tyler's retort, "He ain't lying, Bridge. Tris is a killer on the tables."

All of a sudden, something distracted Tristan because he averted his eyes from me and looked over my head. "Well, well, well," he drawled. "If it isn't M&M." Then he said loudly, "You're late!"

I turned my head and I saw Marco and his new girlfriend Michelle walking towards us. Since both of their names started with the letter 'M', Tristan nicknamed the couple 'M&M'. Marco was carrying a huge watermelon in his arms and he communicated to Tristan in their own language by saying, "Hey, fuck you. I showed up, didn't I? And look…I brought food for His Majesty."

Michelle giggled at her boyfriend's vulgar yet witty response. She was blonde, slender, and tanned but it was a healthy golden complexion. Her aqua blue eyes squinted in happiness when she saw Tristan. "Hey Triscuit! Happy anniversary!" My lips began to twitch, and soon a smile broke free on my face because of the way she greeted him. I guess Tristan had a nickname too. She smiled brilliantly and laughed, and I could see what Tristan was talking about when he told me that she was from Beverly Hills. She was drop-dead gorgeous and she looked like a model.

Tristan released me to greet our latest guests, and as he approached them, he greeted Michelle first with a friendly, "Thanks Michelle. It's nice to see you." Then he communicated back to Marco by saying, "Oi, you late cunt! Are you gonna cut that big fucker?"

Marco gave him a false look of intimidation and communicated once again. "Yeah, give me a knife and I'll cut it. Then I'll cut your fucking throat. How about that?"

Some people started laughing at their exchange and I heard Chris say in an almost dreamy voice, "I love watermelon."

The boys' playful banter continued and it caused me to sigh in exasperation. Finally, I interrupted them by saying, "Tristan, bring that watermelon in the house please, so I can cut it." Tristan took the giant melon from his friend and I saw him act like he was going to bash it over Marco's head. Marco actually flinched and ducked his head which caused Tristan to bust out laughing.

I was inside the house for awhile because the watermelon was so big and it took awhile to cut into slices. After I was done, I went back outside and served it on a large cookie sheet. As soon as I placed it on the table, many hands reached in at once to grab a huge slice. Michelle came to stand next to me and I couldn't help but to scrutinize her beauty from the corner of my jealous eye. I always felt that Autumn and Tristan were like brother and sister but seeing Michelle up close, I realized she really *looked* like she could be Tristan's sister.

While everyone was enjoying the juicy but messy fruit, I started opening the anniversary gifts on the table. I complied with Amy's request and opened hers first. I gasped in surprised and blushed furiously as I pulled a lacy, pink teddy from the Victoria's Secret gift box. I heard a few "Ooooh's" coming from around the table.

Dane commented first. "Yeah man!" Then he grabbed Tristan's shoulder and laughed.

Michelle commented next. "Oooh, I like that Bridget." She reached out to touch it gently. "And Victoria's Secret too?" She looked over at Amy with a smile. "Nice choice, Amy."

Amy beamed. "Thanks Michelle." Then she looked at me with a naughty grin. "I thought you and Tristan might enjoy that."

In less than a second after her comment, I realized that she just opened the door wide for one of Tristan's lewd comments. And the fact that he consumed a lot of alcohol today, I knew he wasn't going to exercise any tact. I whipped my head towards him just as he was about to comment and I quickly covered his mouth. I was relieved when his comment ended up as a mumble against my hand.

The next gift I opened was from Autumn and Ryan, and it was two certificates to a couples spa & resort in Southern California. After Tristan and I gave them our thanks, I opened Jake and Lauren's card. I gasped in total surprise when my eyes rested on the two first-class plane tickets to Ireland tucked inside the card. I've never been to my Homeland but I've always wanted to go. I exclaimed in utter shock, "Jake! Lauren! I can't...I can't believe this." I was truly speechless.

Lauren smiled kindly. "You guys have fun now." I gave her and Jake big hugs in thanks because that was the last thing I expected to receive from them. I was also happy to see Tristan actually show affection towards Jake when he thanked him. At that moment, I knew the silent animosity between them had finally dissipated.

I turned towards Tristan and looked tenderly into his eyes. "Do you have something for me, sweetheart?"

He returned my gaze and I saw his expression soften once again. He spoke quietly when he said, "I do, but I don't wanna give it to you yet." He gave me a sly grin and for some reason I thought my gift was something sexual.

"But I can get that anytime I want."

Tristan laughed. "*Now* whose mind is in the gutter? It's not *that*, babe."

Once everyone was pleasantly fed and most of our guests were enjoying a nice alcohol-induced buzz, Tristan stood up from the table with a plastic cup in his hand that contained the alcoholic beverage of his choice. There were random conversations going on but he demanded everyone's attention in his usual, unconventional way, "Oi, you lot...shut the fuck up for a minute. I have something to say to my wife." Everyone quieted down and looked over at him expectedly. I grinned and I know my eyes were probably twinkling in amusement. But inside, I was anxious to know what he wanted to say and I was bursting with anticipation. He returned my grin with a handsome smile while he held his cup like he was making a toast...which is exactly what he did. His expression was warm and open, and his voice was gentle as his baby blues met my eyes. "Bridget...darlin'..." He paused and looked down at the table for a moment. Then I saw him take a breath before he continued speaking. "After I say this, please don't say anything, love. I just want you to listen to what I have to say and keep it locked in your heart, okay?"

I nodded and responded quietly, "Okay, baby."

"You remember that night I told you that I wished to be happy...and my wish came true?" To comply with his request, I answered silently with a nod. "It came true the night I met you. And since I've been with you, you've made me feel like the luckiest person in the world. I've never really been a sentimental kinda bloke, but when I'm with you...I can't help but to shower you with all the love and affection I have to give, and tell you how wonderful you make me feel. Sometimes I wonder…who out there loved me enough to send me the other half of my soul? Bridget, you've shown me a love and a life that I never thought I would have. That's why I hope and pray every day that our marriage lasts forever; even after we've both flown away from this earth." Since I was sitting close to him, I could see the unshed tears glistening in his periwinkle eyes. And I know he saw how his beautiful speech affected my heart when tears trickled down my cheeks. He leaned down and kissed me tenderly on the lips and when he stood up, his voice was almost a whisper when he concluded his toast by saying simply, "I love you."

I broke my silence to respond in kind. "I love you too, baby."

He held up his cup and I heard Autumn's quiet voice. "Cheers." A second later there were 'cheer's' all around the table as everyone touched their plastic cups together. Afterwards, I took a sip of my soda and then I smiled adoringly at my special blond angel looking down at me.

It wasn't long before the sky began to darken and strangely, that's when Tristan went inside the house. All of a sudden, little white lights; like Christmas lights, came on and illuminated the entire backyard but not too brightly. I saw that they were draped along the entire length of fence. Tristan came back outside and I looked at him in surprise. We shared a look and I exclaimed, "Tristan! You did this?!?"

He grinned and he looked mighty proud of himself when he answered me. "I sure did."

Soon our guests began to migrate. Most people still remained in the backyard but I noticed Jake, Autumn, Ryan, and Lauren started hanging out in the front of the house. I was sitting with Tristan and some of our other friends just chatting and munching on chips when Jake came jogging towards us. And judging by the look on his face, whatever he had to say required immediate attention. He approached Tristan and said in a serious tone, "Bro, you have to come out front. There's this car that keeps circling the block. It's kinda suspicious 'cause it doesn't have any plates and the windows are blacked out. I can't see who it is. And it slows down in front of the house each time it comes around." I could detect the humor in his voice when he said, "Have you made any enemies recently? Are we gonna have to ring the old crew from Brighton?"

In contrast to Jake, Tristan's expression was void of all humor and he stood up swiftly. Jake's report on the activity taking place in the front of the house sparked everyone's interest because we all followed as he led the way.

All fourteen of us stood on the front yard like a gang and waited in anticipation for this suspicious car. I stood right next to Tristan and I could tell he was tense. His jaw was set hard and I watched his eyes dart back and forth as he looked down both sides of the street. Within a few minutes, I saw a black sports car drive slowly up the street with no headlights on. I heard Tristan say in a voice that was barely above a whisper, "Who the fuck is that?"

When it stopped right in front of the house, everyone froze like deer caught in headlights. But our collectively frozen state lasted only a couple seconds because Chris made a move first. In an obvious display of bravado, he started walking threateningly towards the street. He yelled, "What the hell do you want?!?"

Luckily, the naive youth only got to take a few steps before his older brother yanked him by the shirt and yelled at him. "What the fuck are you doing?!?" Rick dragged him back to where we were all grouped together. "Have you ever heard of a drive-by? Are you trying to get us all shot up?"

I heard Tristan's quiet voice again. "If they wanted to shoot us, they would've done it by now." Right at that moment I felt a horrible chill run up my spine. Who was this person or persons in that car and what did they want?

The car didn't move for a couple minutes but then it slowly drove away. I started to feel uneasy and scared, and I wanted the car to go away for good. I didn't want to feel this way on my anniversary so I said determinedly, "I'm calling the cops." I started to walk towards the front door when Tristan grabbed my hand.

"No! Don't call the fucking pigs. I don't want them here ruining our anniversary."

I rounded on him and my voice cracked out of total fear. "Tristan, that *car* is ruining our anniversary and I want it to go away!" I could feel myself beginning to tremble and panic at the idea of the car coming back around. Tristan held me close and tried to comfort me. I buried my face into his t-shirt and even though it smelled like charcoal, I could still smell his unique scent very faintly.

I heard his voice in his chest. "Dane, let's get in your car and see if we can find out who it is." I immediately jerked my head up to look at him with wide-eyes.

Then I heard Rick say, "But the windows are tinted, how are you gonna see inside?"

Tristan answered him quickly. "Maybe we can corner them and get them to come *outside*."

Tristan's plan had danger written all over it so I shook my head vigorously. "Tristan! No! They'll see you in the car!"

He replied calmly, "Dane's windows are blacked out too so they won't see us. And if they decide to start racing us, I know his suped up RX-8 will have no problem catching them."

Dane exclaimed happily, "You're damn right it won't!"

Right after Dane's comment, Ryan pointed to the street and said, "Look, here they come *again*. What do they want?"

Tristan released me suddenly and yelled out to the car in frustration, "What the fuck?!?" Then he turned to me with his blue eyes ablaze. His voice was hard when he said, "You want the car to go away? I'll make it go away." Then he moved towards Dane and said in an urgent tone, "Wait until they pass and then let's go."

Tyler chimed in and asked Dane, "Hey, you got room for me in the back seat?"

Dane smiled. "Yeah dude."

He smiled back. "Good, 'cause I'm in." It was at that moment, I realized that Dane, Tristan, and Tyler were actually getting hyped up about this.

And just like before, the car stopped in front of the house for a couple minutes before it drove away again. As soon as it drove down the street and was out of sight, Tristan clapped Dane on the back. "Now! Let's go!" Tristan ran with Dane right behind him, followed by Tyler.

I yelled out to Tristan in an attempt to get him to stop this foolishness. "Tristan! Stop! This is crazy!" But the boys didn't stop until they reached Dane's blue and yellow Mazda RX-8 parked on the street. I saw the three of them get in quickly and the headlights come on. Within a couple seconds, they were turned off.

That's when I heard Marco's dry remark. "Your *husband's* crazy. I told you that you were marrying a psycho Brit."

For the next few minutes some people in our little group chatted quietly amongst each other. I was frozen on the spot just staring at Dane's car and knowing that the three of them were sitting there waiting to basically ambush this mysterious driver. My nerves were frazzled, I was fidgeting my hands, and worrying my bottom lip between my teeth. Inside I was praying that the black sports car would not come back around. My prayer went unanswered because once again…the car crept slowly up the street again. For some odd reason, this time it didn't stop in front of the house like it did before; it just kept going. Once it was out of my sight, I saw Dane's car with the headlights still off, follow the black car down the street. And right at that moment, I started to cry.

My tears flowed freely because I was so afraid that something bad was going to happen to Tristan; that it was the last time I was going to see him alive and he wasn't going to come back. Didn't he know how much I needed him? Who would be a father to our baby and help me raise it? I didn't want to live without his love and affection because he was the other half of my soul; he completed me. But Tristan was ruthless and fearless and he didn't even realize how bad I was affected by his rash decision. His hatred towards the police made him stubborn and that's why he didn't want them involved. But I'd rather have them involved than have Tristan take the matter into his own hands. Who knew what kind of person or persons were inside that mysterious car. Maybe they were actually waiting for someone to follow them so they could lead them somewhere dangerous. Maybe they were circling the block to try and coax one of us into taking the bait. My beloved took the bait and I was more scared than I'd ever been in my entire life.

Tristan's name escaped my lips as I continued to cry. I felt like the black sports car was terrorizing me silently. Suddenly, I felt Amy holding me in her arms. She tried to calm and comfort me but I began sobbing uncontrollably. The idea of losing Tristan scared me to death and before I knew it, my knees met the ground because I collapsed. Some of my other friends gathered around me to lift me up and that's when Autumn decided to give me a pep-talk. Once I was standing again, she put her hands on my shoulders and looked me in the eye with a serious expression. "Bridge, listen to me, okay. Nobody fucks with Tristan Hathaway. And nobody fucks with the people Tristan loves and cares about. He saw that you were getting scared and he didn't hesitate to go after that crazy fuck driving that crappy Eclipse. He knows as well as I do that if the driver decides to fuck with them, their car doesn't stand a chance against Dane's car. And Tristan's not gonna let them get away with this shit...trust me. Don't worry, okay?"

Through my sobbing I managed to say, "But...what...if...Tristan... doesn't...come...back?"

She scoffed. "Oh, he's coming back. Don't you worry about that. Tristan doesn't play around and he can be just as fucking crazy and psycho as the next man."

Marco interjected. "Amen sister!"

I heard a chuckle from Jake but Autumn continued speaking to me in a firm voice. "You're the love of his whole existence and he'll protect you from anyone on this earth." She gave me a small smile and wiped the tears from my face. Then her voice softened when she said, "Trust me, sweetie. Your hubby will be back."

And he was...about an hour later. But by this time, I moved to the sofa in the living room and I was lying down with all of the women surrounding me. All the guys were still outside in the front of the house like they were standing guard. Suddenly, the front door opened and the first person I saw was the only person I really wanted to see...my British prince. I sat up quickly and he reached me before I could even stand up. He held me in a tight embrace and I immediately started crying again...but this time in relief. Tristan spoke soft comforting words in my ear as he rubbed my back soothingly. "It's alright, love. Everything's alright. I don't think they'll be back."

I pulled away to look at him with my face still tear-stained. "What happened Tristan? Tell me *exactly* what happened and don't you dare leave anything out."

Tristan attracted a thirteen-person audience because everyone was waiting to hear the details; even Dane and Tyler were waiting for a recap. Dane had a huge grin on his face and was kind of bouncy like he was still hyped up. Tristan took a deep breath and when he spoke, I could sense that he was amused by the whole ordeal. "Well, we weren't following them for long before they caught our scent. They were about to turn the corner to probably come back around again, when they realized they were being followed. Then they sped up but of course we kept up with them. A few times they tried to dodge us but they couldn't shake us."

Tyler interrupted. "Not with this crazy motherfucker behind the wheel!" And he put his arm around Dane's shoulder.

Tristan gave a short laugh before he continued. "Babe, we ended up on the fucking freeway! We pulled up right next to them and they tried to side-swipe us!"

My eyes widened and I gasped in surprise, and that's when Dane blurted out, "There was no way in hell I was letting them fuck up my new paint job!"

Tristan continued. "We swerved out of the way but we kept tailing them. Then I realized we weren't gonna get them to stop unless we made them crash. I had a good mind to tell Dane to try it but then I thought: 'I don't want that shit on my conscience right now.' We ended up just letting them go." Tristan ran a hand through his blond hair and sighed. Then I noticed his expression turn to one more serious. "Bridget, I'm telling you…the next time I see that car…" He shook his head swiftly. "I'm not gonna be fucking around with them."

After Tristan's last comment, the living room was dead quiet. All I could hear was my own breathing because my mouth was still hanging open in shock. Tristan was still looking into my eyes with a heated intensity and I held his gaze just the same. Then I admitted in a quiet voice, "I was so scared, Tristan. I was scared you weren't going to come back to me. I'm not ready to lose you, baby." A few more tears leaked from my eyes and I began to sob softly.

Tristan placed tender kisses on my face and I relished his warm affection. When he kissed my forehead, his nose lingered against my hairline. Then I heard him inhale like he was breathing me in. He embraced me again and whispered, "I'm not gonna leave you like that, love. If I die…it's gonna be in your arms. We're gonna die together just like in '*The Notebook*', remember?" He pulled away from me and cupped my face in his hands. Then he gently brushed my tears away with his thumbs. His voice was soft when he said, "Hey, come out back with me. I wanna give you your present now."

Tristan helped me to stand and then we put our arms around each other and walked through the house to the backyard. Our entire party followed us and once we were outside, he released me and I saw him whisper something to Dane. Dane went over to his stereo and started rummaging through his CD's. Tristan was standing still patiently; just looking at me with a grin on his face. I didn't dare move because I was anxiously awaiting my anniversary present. And then...the music began to play. I didn't recognize the song at first but then I realized it was one of Tristan's favorite songs: Coldplay's '*X&Y*'. He reached his arms out and beckoned to me. "Dance with me, love." I didn't hesitate for a second and I quickly closed the distance between us and entered my angel's embrace once again.

We slow-danced together on the grass with the little white lights twinkling in the background. We were in our own little world because I had completely forgotten that we had guests. I laid my head on his chest and listened to his lively heartbeat. I found myself sighing in relief because it was beating fiercely and it reminded me that he was in my arms; still alive and breathing. I felt him shift and take my hand, and I instinctively knew that he wanted to turn me. I obliged and as soon as my back was to him, he released me suddenly. Before I could turn back around, he slipped something across the front of my neck. The sensation tickled for just a moment but it was warm and it brushed me like a gentle caress. I lifted my long hair off my neck and shoulders to allow him to clasp the necklace. I looked down at my chest and I saw a silvery pendant in the shape of a heart; it was glimmering and just resting quietly against my skin. I touched the pendant and that's when I felt Tristan take my other hand and turn me around again.

Once I was facing him, he embraced me again and held me close. I looked into his beautiful cerulean eyes and smiled lovingly. He spoke softly when he said, "I know you can't really see it right now, but it says '*Mo Anam Cara*'." My eyes widened immediately and I lifted the pendant again to take another look. Unfortunately, Tristan was right because in the dim light I couldn't make out the words.

But that didn't stop me from asking, "What does that mean?"

"It's Irish Gaelic for 'my soul mate'." I looked upon my soul mate's handsome face and he smiled beautifully down at me. Then he moved his head and whispered in my ear, "Happy anniversary Mrs. Hathaway." A moment later, Tristan's mouth descended upon mine. As soon as our lips melted together, I savored his kiss and I let myself get completely lost in it. Even though today was one of the most frightening days of my life, it was also one of the most special. And I felt so lucky and so honored to have taken this lovely British boy's last name...exactly one year ago today.

Chapter 23

'To be trusted is a greater compliment than to be loved.'

~ George MacDonald

It's been three weeks since my whole traumatic experience with Tristan and the mysterious black sports car. I'll admit that after it happened, we would look outside every night just to make sure it didn't creep back up the street again. Tristan said he couldn't think of anyone in particular that would stalk us and I couldn't think of anyone either. We felt assured in regards to the security of the house itself because we invested in a top-of-the-line security system. To my relief, the car didn't come around after that night but I couldn't stop wondering who it was and why they decided to terrorize us. I was also relieved because I didn't want Tristan turning into some kind of vigilante. I remember listening to him as he laid out his plan on what he was going to do the next time he saw the car. He was so animated about it and he actually had a Plan A and Plan B; both completely reckless and totally insane. Maybe Marco was right and Tristan really *was* a psycho Brit.

When I expressed my concern about his plan; which was basically a deadly game of 'Cat & Mouse' combined with a ruthless game of 'Chicken', his response actually frightened me. He looked me in the eye and said, "But they'll know I'm not fucking around this time. I told you babe, I'll protect you from anyone and I'll die first before I let anyone hurt you." Didn't he realize that his death would hurt me most of all? I guess he was serious about finding out the identity of the crazy asshole that raced him and his friends and almost knocked them off the freeway. I really do thank God for Dane's quick reflexes and his semi-professional car racing skills. I hate to think of what would've happened if Dane hadn't swerved out of the way in time. In the end though, Tristan believed it was just some stupid kids who decided to fuck around with people for fun. If that's true, then I really regret not involving the police because those 'stupid kids' almost cost Tristan and his friends their lives.

Now that school was back in session, I was so busy that I didn't have time to worry about what happened on our anniversary. Not to mention, I was almost four months along so continuing a healthy pregnancy occupied a lot of my thoughts. Plus, the unfurnished nursery and the unfinished swimming pool were still on my list of things to worry about. We couldn't decide whether to go unisex with the nursery in case we had a boy or put our faith in Autumn's dream and turn it into a little princess room. So because of our extreme indecisiveness, the nursery was void of any decoration or furnishing except for some plain white window blinds. The construction for the pool was on schedule but it would still be awhile before it was completely finished. In the meantime, we had to deal with the fact that our backyard looked like someone was testing grenades.

It was Thursday night and I just got home late due to an after-school faculty meeting. The grandfather clock told me it was 8PM when I opened the front door and stepped into the foyer. The first floor was quiet but I could hear Tristan and his friends down in the basement. Deftones' *'Hole in the Earth'* was blasting through the floor and I could feel the vibrations under my feet. And even though the music was loud, I could still hear the cracking of the billiard balls and gunshots from one of his videogames. I don't know how many friends he had down there, but I was positive that they were all being thoroughly entertained. As I walked past the basement door, the distinct aroma of pizza invaded my nostrils. The smell actually made my stomach rumble because I was practically starving. I was also tired, so I was grateful there was pizza and I wouldn't have to cook. With Tristan and his 'mates' around, I just hoped there was still some left.

I walked into the kitchen and sat on a stool to take my shoes off because my feet were killing me. As took a moment to rub them, I noticed a little notepad on one of the island counters. I immediately recognized the handwriting as Tristan's and my eyes read a short simple message: *Babe, don't cook anything. There's pizza downstairs. Love, Tristan.* I couldn't stop the smile that appeared on my face as I began thinking about how thoughtful and caring he is. I tore the note off the pad and chucked it into the trash bin.

All of a sudden, my thought pattern changed like the channels on a television because I started thinking about the fact that he's probably been home for hours having fun. Meanwhile, I was at school dealing with nine-year-olds and trying to schmooze the principal with my ideas for our new tutoring program. I'll admit that sometimes I envied Tristan's profession. Even though he was going on casting auditions without landing any roles, his agency still paid him. And he always had his nights free to do whatever he wanted. There were times when he would bring home a script and go over it for hours on end but it was rare. Me, on the other hand, I never had a free weeknight except for Fridays. Since tonight was not Friday night, that meant I had work to do. And as soon as I went downstairs, I planned to tell Tristan & Co. to keep it down so I can work peacefully in my newly furnished office.

Another rumble from my stomach brought me out of my reverie and I hopped off the stool to go claim a couple slices of pizza. I was walking out of the kitchen when I heard my cell phone vibrating inside my purse that was sitting on the counter. I was about to ignore it because satisfying my hunger was my main priority but something told me to just answer it. I fumbled inside my purse and when I retrieved my phone, I saw a name on the LCD screen that belonged to a person I hadn't seen in over a year. And for some strange reason, seeing the name brought back one single memory which caused my face to flush with heat. My hands began to tremble and I knew it wasn't because the phone was vibrating. When I finally built up the courage to answer, my voice betrayed me and I ended up answering in a meek voice. "Hello?"

There was a slight pause on the other end and I was surprised when the boyish voice that responded was shaky and quiet. "Bridget?"

I paused too because I was wondering why Justin was calling me. "Yeah?"

He paused again and then I heard a soft sigh. Then it sounded like he was breathing erratically. "Please help me."

His voice cracked and I heard him sniffle, so I immediately became concerned. "Justin, what's wrong?"

He was quiet for a couple seconds but when he continued speaking, I realized that he was actually crying. "I need your help. *Please*. Can I come over? Where are you?" I could sense the panic in his voice and it was causing me to panic too.

"Justin, tell me what's going on. Why do you need my help?"

Another pause and more sniffling. When he spoke again, I could barely make out what he was saying in between his sobbing. "I got...beat up...badly."

I gasped in shock. "Oh my God! Justin---"

"You're the first person I thought to call for help. I went to your apartment but they told me you didn't live there anymore. Please Bridget, I need you to help me."

My mouth was hanging open in disbelief and my own breathing was becoming erratic. The thought of Justin battered and bruised really scared me. "Did you call the cops?"

When he answered me, his voice broke and he sounded very child-like. "No...I'm afraid."

I took a deep breath because I was trying to calm my nerves and regulate my breathing. Then I realized I had to try and calm him down as well. "Okay sweetie...where are you now? Do you want me to come get you?"

"I'm about a block from your old apartment. I don't wanna leave my car. If you tell me where you live, I'll come over. Are you really far? Please tell me that you're not far away." He started crying again and I could feel tears pricking at the back of my eyes. "Bridget...please...I'm bleeding really badly."

His plea started to really affect me and I before I knew it, my vision started getting blurry. All I could think about was the last time I saw him. Justin was tall, blond and blue-eyed just like Tristan and he was almost as beautiful. I remember his angelic, youthful face. And I remember that it was not only his beauty that caught my attention, it was the way his body moved on the dance floor. But what I remembered the most was that he and Tristan became the first people to ever fulfill my sexual fantasy. I chose him for my beloved and the boys were sexually intimate with each other right before my very eyes. And to bring an end to that amazing night, I slept in the bed with two sinful fallen angels. The whole experience with Tristan and Justin will forever be burned into my memory.

Once I composed myself enough to speak, I gave Justin directions to our house. I heard him release a shaky sigh when he realized I wasn't that far from him. "Thanks Bridget, I'll be there soon."

"Justin, tell me what happened."

The last thing I heard from him before he hung up was, "I'll tell you everything when I get there."

I was pacing in the living room and biting my fingernails as I anxiously awaited his arrival. My hunger was now forgotten because all I could think about was his frantic phone call. What happened to cause someone to beat up a person as nice and sweet as Justin? I couldn't stop wondering how bad his injuries were. The fact that he said he was bleeding really badly put me in a complete state of panic. I also couldn't help wondering why he wouldn't go to the police. I really hoped he didn't have the same hang-up with the police that Tristan did.

Speaking of Tristan, he was still downstairs with his friends and I was actually nervous about getting him involved. He tended to be very impulsive and I had a feeling he'd try to avenge Justin by going after the person that beat him up. Even though Tristan admitted to me that he's calmed down considerably since he's been with me, I knew the British bad-boy inside of him was always looking for a reason to get into a fight.

Soon I stopped my pacing and just stared intently out the front window. I was praying that Justin would find the house without any problems. The last thing I wanted was for him to bleed to death because he got lost. Twenty minutes passed by when I recognized his black Toyota Scion tC pull up in front of the house and park on the street. I immediately rushed out the front door without even closing it.

I must've sprinted from the living room to the street because I reached him within a few seconds. Since it was dark outside, I couldn't really see him until he stumbled out of his car and the street lamps revealed to me the actual state he was in. He was dressed in dark clothing and I rushed over to him because I could see that he was unsteady on his feet. I was truly amazed that he was able to drive. He was hunched over and his head was down so I couldn't see his face, but I put my arms around him to keep him upright. I felt him latch onto me for support and that's when I finally heard his boyish voice again. "Bridget..." He started crying again and I felt him bury his head in the crook of my neck.

I immediately felt sympathy and I held him in a tight embrace and tried to comfort him. "Shhhh...it's alright sweetie. I'm here now and I'm going to help you." A rush of motherly protection came over me and I felt the instinctive need to take care of him. Even though I was afraid of what I was going to see, I had to look at his face. I released him from my embrace so I could lift his head. He was sniffling and as I lifted his head, my only reaction was to gasp in shock. The street lamp gave me a glimpse of the real brutality that was done to Justin's handsome features. My eyes scanned his tear-stained face in the dim light and I could see that one of his eyes was completely swollen shut. At that moment, I realized that he drove here using the vision of only one eye. There was a bruise on his right cheek and as my fingers began to gingerly caress his face, I could see and feel blood. It was trickling down the side of his face from his hairline, and it smeared around his nose and the side of his mouth. I was cupping his face in my hands and he looked intently into my eyes. His lip was trembling and I noticed it was bloody too. We held each other's gaze and for that brief moment; even in the semi-darkness, I could see the pain and raw fear etched in his face.

In that next second, he clutched me again and began to sob softly. And I finally broke down and cried with him. Even though I only spent one night with Justin over a year ago, I still felt a deep affection for him. He was young and it was obvious that what happened to him was very traumatic. Deep inside my heart, I saw him as another beautiful angel just like Tristan. But this angel came to me for help.

Justin leaned on me for support as we walked back to the house. As soon as we got inside, I finally closed the front door and guided him into the kitchen. He sat down on a stool very slowly while I still supported his weight. The lighting in the kitchen was bright and I could see that his black shirt was stained with blood. His head was down and his blond fringe covered his eyes and most of his face like a veil. I could hear him breathing but it was uneven. I stepped closer to him and whispered his name. When he lifted his head again, I couldn't stop the fresh tears from welling up in my eyes. I covered my mouth with my hand as my wide eyes took in every detail of his assault. How could someone do this to him?

What heartless, vicious human being...wait scratch that...*animal* could beat him to a bloody pulp and just leave him? He was holding the right side of his rib cage and taking slow but shaky breaths. I was thinking the worse; like maybe he had broken ribs. And judging from his face, I wondered what else was broken or fractured. I was about to suggest that he let me take him to a hospital but first I wanted to know what asshole did this to him. "Justin, what happened to you? Who beat you up?"

His voice was quiet and trembling when he finally told me what happened to him tonight. "I was at this club...it's a gay club but not the one I met you at. I ran into this guy I used to know from school...Pete. After we talked for awhile, he told me that he always had a crush on me. He asked me back to his place and I went with him." Justin paused and then he began looking down at the floor as he spoke. "When we got to his house, we were making out and stuff...and then his brother Johnny came home. I don't think Pete was expecting him. Johnny caught us in the middle of it and I could tell he was drunk. He was really pissed off and he started..." Justin paused once again and I could see that retelling the story was upsetting him. I started rubbing his back in hopes that it would soothe him.

Our moment was interrupted because Tristan walked into the kitchen. "Babe, I had a feeling you were home. Did you get my---" His sentence fell short when he took in the scene before him. "What the fuck?" Time seemed to stand still as his azure eyes widened in shock and they fell upon Justin's battered form sitting at the island counter. I stood there frozen like a deer caught in headlights because I wasn't exactly sure how Tristan was going to react. I looked at Justin and he was just looking down at the floor. Tristan's expression changed quickly from shock to concern and he made cautious steps towards us. His voice was low when he asked Justin, "What happened to you, mate?"

Justin responded quietly, "I got beat up."

Tristan finally reached him and began scanning his body with his eyes. Then I watched as him gently lifted Justin's head and cupped his face in his hands. He wore a clear expression of worry as he turned Justin's head from side-to-side. "Who beat you up?" Justin didn't answer him and I saw him cast his eyes towards the floor. Tristan's hands dropped down to his shoulders and I watched his eyes as they continued to scan Justin's face. Then he gave him an intense look and asked in a hard, serious tone, "Who did this to you?" Tristan looked over at me and his face was twisted in anger. "Bridget, what the fuck is going on?"

Justin's voice was on the verge of breaking as he finally brought Tristan up to speed with what happened to him. Then he continued with his story. "Johnny was with a friend and when he saw what his brother was doing...I guess he just snapped. First he yelled at Pete like, 'What the fuck are you doing you little faggot? My brother's a fucking queer?!?' Then he started hitting him and I tried to get him to stop. The next thing I know his friend...I don't know who he was...grabs me and knocks me down on the floor. He started saying, 'Two little fags, Johnny. I think we're gonna have to teach them a lesson.' Then they both started laughing. Johnny turned his attention on me and kicked me when I was trying to get up."

Tristan interjected and I could sense a dangerous undertone in his voice. "He kicked you?"

"Yeah." I looked over at Tristan and I saw him swallow hard. His brows were knitted tightly together and I could feel a threatening vibe emanating off him. It was obvious that Justin's recount of the events was rapidly darkening Tristan's mood. "I fell back down and Johnny kicked me a couple more times. Then he got on top of me and started punching me in the face. I covered my face but then he started punching my body. He pulled me up by the hair and threw me onto their coffee table. It broke from under me and that's when he started choking me and saying, 'You trying to turn my little brother into a faggot like you? I'll fucking kill you, you goddamn pillow-biter!' His friend was restraining Pete 'cause he was trying to tell his brother to leave me alone. But he wouldn't...he kept his hands around my neck and kept squeezing." At this point, Justin began to cry again. "I thought I was gonna die. Finally, Pete got loose and pulled his brother off me. I was choking and crying. I was so scared."

I started crying too and I put my arms around him. I looked up at Tristan and I actually saw tears in his eyes that he was trying to keep at bay. Right at that moment, I knew that the intimacy shared between him and Justin truly affected his feelings towards the younger blond. "Pete begged Johnny to let me go 'cause he kept saying he was gonna kill me."

I couldn't help but to ask, "Why didn't you go straight to the police? You really should report this asshole. I mean, he tried to kill you Justin."

Justin sniffled a couple times before he answered me. "Because... Johnny said if I went to the cops that he'd kill me and my grandmother. I've known both of them since we were in high school so he knows where I live."

Tristan chimed in again and I could detect the anger in his voice. "Fuck the pigs. I'll take care of that homophobic bastard right now." He reached over to grab the little notepad off the island counter and made a point of slamming it down in front of Justin. "I want you to write down anything you can about this arsehole. I wanna know what he looks like and where I can find him."

My earlier assumption proved correct because Tristan was ready to avenge Justin. I didn't want Tristan getting into trouble so I tried to intervene. "Tristan---"

I guess Tristan knew I was going to object so he didn't hesitate to interrupt me. "No Bridget! That wanker isn't getting away with this shit!" He gestured towards Justin. "Look at what he did to him!" I immediately shut my mouth, and I guess Justin was too afraid to argue with him because he complied instantly and started scribbling away on the notepad. Tristan leaned over him and added, "And put your mobile number on there too in case I have to ask you something."

About a second later, I heard Dane's voice coming towards us. "Tris, how long does it take to grab some more beer?" When he entered the kitchen, he approached us but stopped short when he saw Justin. "Whoa! Dude, what the hell happened to you?" Justin glanced up at him for a second but quickly averted his eyes.

That's when I saw Rick and Marco saunter into the kitchen. Dane stood in front of Justin with a look of mild curiosity and disbelief while Marco casually remarked, "So, what's going on? Why's there blood on the floor?" His comment caused everyone to look down at the floor. I noticed that Justin had trailed little droplets of blood on the linoleum. There were a few more next to the stool he was sitting on and I realized that I had to get him cleaned up.

I looked up and I saw Rick trying to get a peek of Justin's face. Justin was still looking down at the floor and his fringe hid his face from view. He was probably feeling like he was on display. Rick asked quietly, "Who's this?"

I responded in the same tone. "This is Justin...our friend."

I was about to ask Justin to follow me into the bathroom so I could tend to his wounds when I heard Tristan's voice again. But this time he sounded excited with a tinge of determination. "Let's go mates. We got some business to take care of tonight."

Dane was equally excited when he responded. "Oh yeah? What's the plan?"

Tristan was on his way out of the kitchen but he turned his head and smirked at his blond spiky-haired friend. "We're gonna kick somebody's arse."

When I realized that Tristan was serious and was recruiting his friends yet again, I tried to step in and make him see reason. "Tristan, not again okay. I know there's some other way we can handle this."

And just like the last time, I was powerless to stop him and he just ignored me. He looked over at Rick and said, "Wait for me, alright. I'll be right back."

"Tristan!" I stomped my foot like a child but he was already out of sight. I heard his heavy footsteps as he dashed up the stairs.

Within a few minutes he came back downstairs and jogged into the kitchen. Rick, Marco, and Dane just stood there like the Three Stooges awaiting further instruction from Tristan; their fearless leader. He went over to the island counter and tore off Justin's notes from the little pad. I guess the reality of what Tristan was going to do finally hit Justin because he tried to deter Tristan from seeking revenge on his behalf. "Tristan... man, you don't have to do this."

Tristan stepped close to him and I was surprised when he took Justin's face into his hands again. His voice was stern when he said, "Did you look in the mirror, mate? Have you seen your face?" He released Justin and stepped away but this time his voice was low and deadly. "I'm gonna make that fucking cunt look ten times worse. Trust me, he's not getting away with this shit; not if I have anything to do with it."

Tristan led the way and his three soldiers followed after him. I followed behind them as well, because I was going to try once more to persuade him to listen to my idea. I didn't really have an idea that didn't involve the police but I didn't want Tristan out there fighting like some street kid. I was already going to tend to Justin's wounds, I didn't want to have to tend to his too; and possibly three of his friends. I tried to plead with him but they had already made their way out the door and were walking towards Marco's black Hummer that was parked in the driveway. In my frustration, I yelled out to Tristan, "Fine! Go and fight like an animal, Tristan! But don't call me if you get arrested because I'm not bailing you out!"

Marco turned his head towards me and grinned. "Yes you will."

Dane started laughing at Marco's retort so I yelled at him too. "This isn't funny Dane!" I watched the four of them pull out of the driveway and drive off into the night. Strangely, I wasn't feeling afraid for Tristan's safety as much as I was feeling anger because of another one of his impulsive decisions. I'll admit that it warmed me a tiny bit that he wanted to avenge Justin but I felt there was a better way of doing it than resorting to violence. But then again, this was Tristan I was talking about and he would always be a British bad-boy at heart.

I was still angry at them so I slammed the door and marched back into the kitchen. As soon as my eyes fell upon Justin again, my whole mood switched back to motherly protector. I approached him again and spoke gently when I said, "Come on sweetie. Let's get you cleaned up, okay?" He nodded and as he tried to get off the stool I noticed him wince and grab his right side again. I let him lean on me for support and we walked slowly to the first-floor bathroom.

I made him sit on the toilet lid as I dabbed at his cuts and bruises with peroxide. He winced a few times in pain so I gently blew on his open cuts. Justin kept his eye on me the entire time, and I'll admit that being alone and this close to him brought an unexpected feeling to the surface of my consciousness. I don't know why but maybe it was because seeing his sad indigo eye staring up at me really pulled at my heartstrings. I put some band-aids on his cuts and tried my best to wash the blood out of his golden hair. Once all the blood was pretty much gone from his face and hair, I could finally see the Justin I remember beneath the surface.

When I happened to look down and see that he was still clutching his ribs, I realized that I hadn't seen the extent of the damage done to him. I also remembered that he had dried blood on his shirt. "Justin, could you take your shirt off? It has blood on it and I'd like to clean it for you."

He tried to lift his shirt with shaky hands but he was having obvious difficulty. I assisted him with removing it and I gasped in shock once again when I saw the bruises covering his torso. Some of the bruises were an angry red and some were a deep purple. I also saw the handprints around his neck from when Johnny tried to squeeze the life out of him. I couldn't believe what I was seeing and before I could stop myself, I started crying again. "Oh my God, Justin." I looked into his eye since his other one was still swollen and he was looking back at me with a tear-filled gaze. I reached out to touch him but I couldn't bring myself to because he looked so fragile. I was looking in absolute horror at the utter cruelty that was done to him just because of his sexual orientation. Once I composed myself, I asked quietly, "You should let me take you to the hospital. I mean, you could have broken ribs or internal bleeding."

Justin started shaking his head. "I don't wanna go to the hospital. I hate hospitals." All of a sudden he put his head down again like he was ashamed.

"Why sweetie?"

I heard him take a shaky breath. When he looked up at me, my heart broke from the sight of how vulnerable he was. "My mom wasted away in a hospital. She had cancer and I would visit her almost every day even though I was so scared. I went anyway 'cause you know...she was my mom." I saw a few tears leak from his eyes but he spoke through his painful memory. "I would throw up every time I would leave 'cause I just..." He reached up to wipe the tears from his eyes. "I couldn't stand seeing her like that. I was with her when she took her last breath and something weird happened." He paused and his voice was barely above a whisper when he said, "I think I scared her." He started shaking his head again as he pleaded with me. "Please Bridget...don't take me to the hospital."

After his confession, I replied gently, "I'm going to get you one of Tristan's t-shirts. I'll be right back."

I turned around to walk out of the bathroom but he called my name quietly. I froze on the spot not because he said my name but because the way he said it reminded me of someone else. Sometimes when Tristan's voice is low, I can't detect his British accent. He and Justin have similar boyish voices and in this instant...they sounded exactly alike. I turned around to face him and he was just looking at me. His expression was full of hurt and he looked in desperate need of comfort.

Before I knew it, I approached him and let my eyes scan his still-beautiful face. I threaded my fingers through his soft blond strands and at that moment, he returned the affection. He reached up and brushed his hand across my cheek in a gentle caress. I found myself being pulled closer to him; not by his arms but by some invisible force. He opened his legs almost invitingly and I stood in between them. My other hand found its way into his hair too and I relished the fact that his hair felt like Tristan's. There were so many similarities between them. All of a sudden, my mind flashed back and I remembered the night they fulfilled my sexual fantasy and I saw the two of them naked. Their lean, ivory bodies almost had the same physique and how they were the same height.

My mind flashed back to the present and I remembered again that Justin was hurting and he needed someone. He had been beaten and traumatized, and I was the first person he thought to call for help. Not another friend or an ex-boyfriend; not even Tristan...but *me*. I felt honored that he chose me and I couldn't help but to gaze adoringly at him. He smiled up at me and my eyes darted to his plump, sensual lips. I remembered that I envied Tristan when he kissed those pouty lips over and over again. I wanted to kiss them too. I wanted to know what they felt like between my own lips. I was also feeling deep sympathy and compassion for him, and I wanted to hold and cradle him and make the hurt go away. Justin didn't deserve what happened to him and I wanted to help him. After all, he chose me. The temptation proved to be too much and it didn't help that he encouraged me by tilting his head up towards me. His hand that was on my cheek brushed across my lips and I wanted his lips to follow the same path...just once. All rational and logical thought eluded me, and I finally submitted to the other blond angel and gave into temptation like Eve and the apple.

My lips connected to Justin's and I tried to convey as much comfort through the kiss as I could. We only moved our lips slightly but I actually felt the warmth all the way down to my toes. His pouty lips felt exactly like I thought they would; soft and full like little pillows. I sucked his bottom lip into my mouth very gently and a moan escaped both of us at the same time. Mmmm...his kiss felt so nice and I admitted to myself that I wouldn't mind getting lost in it for a little while. Actually, it wasn't that different from Tristan's kiss. Tristan! As soon as my husband's name entered my mind, it came with a mental slap across the face and I pulled away. The realization of what I just did caused me to stumble back a few feet and clap my hand over my mouth in shock. Oh my God! I just kissed another man...willingly.

Justin was looking back at me in surprise and he said quickly, "It's okay, Bridget. It was nothing; just a comfort kiss."

I know my eyes were wide and I started shaking my head vigorously. "Oh my God, I can't believe what I just did. I shouldn't have kissed you like that." Then I started apologizing. "I'm so sorry, Justin."

He chuckled softly. "Hey, I kissed you back so it's my fault too." I quickly turned my back to him and started biting my nails nervously. I couldn't believe what I just did. I crossed the line and there was no going back now. I felt Justin approach me from behind. His voice was soft when he said, "You don't have to mention it to Tristan. I'm not gonna say anything."

I turned around to face him again and continued looking at him in worry. Then I admitted in a quiet voice, "I just...I couldn't help it. I can't believe I gave into temptation so easily. What kind of wife am I?" Tears welled up in my eyes and I felt extremely guilty because the truth of the matter was...I just cheated on my husband. I moved around Justin's body to sit on the toilet lid because I felt myself on the verge of collapsing. It was a good thing I was sitting down because the realization that I cheated on Tristan with the man he was out defending, hit me like a ton of bricks. I broke the trust in our marriage and I didn't think I could feel any more horrible until Justin's cell phone rang. It startled both of us and he quickly unclipped the phone from his belt and flipped it open.

"Hello?" Justin paused for a minute and looked at me. Then he said, "Hold on, let me put you on speaker." He pressed a button on his phone and said to me, "It's Tristan."

My eyes widened and then I heard Tristan's muffled voice coming through the phone. "We found Johnny and I'm gonna cure his homophobia right now." Justin and I shared an identical look of surprise.

Immediately following my feeling of surprise came sheer panic because I realized Tristan was really about to fight someone. "No! I want you to come back home right now Tristan! Do you hear me?!?"

Tristan didn't respond right away and I waited in silent fear for his response. When he finally spoke again, I noticed his voice sounded detached. "Sorry love...you're breaking up. I can't hear you." I heard a click and right then I knew he just hung up on me. I just stared at Justin's phone because I couldn't believe Tristan would disregard me so nonchalantly.

Justin's voice brought me out of my reverie when he said humorously, "Tristan is kinda crazy, isn't he?"

I couldn't help but to smile wearily. "That's an understatement."

I gave him one of Tristan's t-shirts and some Vicodin for his discomfort, and then the two of us settled into the living room. He was holding an ice pack on his swollen eye and we sat down together on the sofa. I was taken by surprise when he laid down with his head on my lap. I gave into temptation once again and threaded my fingers through his hair. I also leaned down to place a tender kiss on his cheek. I didn't feel too guilty about giving him affection since it wasn't any worse than the lip-lock we shared earlier. It didn't take long for the pain medication to kick in and soon he was napping on my lap like a giant house cat.

But about forty-five minutes later, Justin sat up quickly as if someone had doused him with cold water. I was amazed by his swift movement because I thought he was in pain and he was obviously fast asleep a moment ago. I stared at him with wide-eyes, but he sat as still as a statue just facing forward. I wondered what was wrong with him and why he awakened so suddenly. I was about to ask him, but then I heard the front door open and the voices of Tristan & Co. approaching us. I gasped in disbelief. Did Justin hear them coming? Because I didn't.

That's when I realized the scene Tristan could've walked in on. I was grateful to Justin in that instant because I wasn't sure how Tristan would react seeing us in that position. Then I started thinking about the kiss we shared and I prayed that he wouldn't find out. I even reminded myself not to hold Tristan's gaze because I was afraid he'd find out the truth behind my eyes. He had power behind his baby blues and I've learned never to underestimate him. Tristan and his friends entered the living room and I could see that Rick and Dane were still hyped up, Marco looked alert and Tristan wore a serious expression. He sat down next to Justin and said, "Johnny won't ever touch you again."

In my relief that he was finally home, I exclaimed loudly, "Tristan, what happened?!?" At that moment, I realized that Tristan's face didn't have any cuts and bruises. I found that strange and for a minute I thought maybe he actually talked out his problem with Johnny. I was kidding myself because as my eyes continued to scan his body for damage, I finally noticed the knuckles on his left hand were red and swollen. I exclaimed once more which brought it to everyone's attention. "Look at your hand!" Tristan briefly glanced at his knuckles before meeting my eyes. I stood up swiftly and put my hands on my hips. "I'm getting you some ice and you're going to put it on those swollen knuckles of yours Mr. Hathaway." I gave him a stern look before I turned on my heel and walked out of the living room to go to the kitchen.

Since Justin was using the only ice pack we had, I returned with a bag of frozen corn and slapped it none too lightly on Tristan's injured hand. He winced and looked up at me questioningly but I just narrowed my eyes at him. It served him right for disobeying me and going out into the night to play hero for Justin. Tristan obeyed me this time and he kept the bag on his knuckles. Dane's bouncy movement caught my attention and I guess he couldn't contain his excitement any longer because he said to Tristan, "Dude, tell them what went down." Dane looked at me and grinned like the Cheshire Cat. "Bridget, wait until you hear this shit. Your man is a force to be reckoned with, I'll tell ya."

Marco remarked in a sing-song voice, "Psychooo," and he did the crazy gesture with his index finger next to his temple.

Dane patted Tristan on the back and exclaimed happily, "Tris kicked his ass so bad that I think he went crying home to mommy." He laughed heartily. "Actually, I think the dude pissed himself because I saw the stain on the front of his pants." Dane continued to laugh and Tristan beamed in appreciation. But when Tristan looked at me and my expression revealed that I was not amused, the smile dropped from his face.

He sighed before he began to recall the events of his adventure. "We found Johnny and his mate at a Seven-Eleven down the street from his house. They hung around in front for awhile but we just sat in the truck and waited for the opportune moment. Then I realized that the stupid fucks actually walked to the store and they had no car. Once they decided to leave, we followed them until I told Marco to chase them into an alley. We high-beamed the shit out of them and revved the engine to scare them a bit. They started running but we cornered them in a dead-end. Me and Dane jumped out the truck and to make a long story short...I fucked Johnny up real good. He can't fight for shit and he tired quickly because he's such an out-of-shape porker. Dane took care of his mate with ease but after a few punches, he turned pussy and told us he was sorry."

I was gaping at Tristan and shaking my head in disbelief. I noticed Rick was kind of quiet so I turned my head towards him and crossed my arms over my chest. I asked in a very haughty tone, "And what was your role in all this mister?"

Rick gave me a toothy smile. "I was the look-out." I almost cracked a grin because he actually sounded proud of the role Tristan probably assigned to him.

I turned my attention back on Tristan again. "Did the cops come?"

This time Tristan smiled. "Hell yeah they did."

Marco chimed in. "We heard them coming."

I whipped my heads towards him and lifted a curious eyebrow. "So what did you do?"

Tristan laughed. "We fucking ran! Marco was the getaway driver and he sped off like he was in the Indy 500." His three soldiers joined in on the laughter and I even saw Justin smiling. I guess I was the only one who wasn't amused. Maybe because I was the only mature person in the living room. Or maybe because I was a female and didn't understand all this macho bravado bullshit. I knew that Tristan could sense my current mood which is probably why he turned his attention back to Justin.

His voice was surprisingly soft when he said, "Look mate, Johnny's not gonna go to the fucking pigs and he's not gonna go after you or your family. When I stepped to him, I told him exactly why I was gonna kick his arse. At first he wasn't listening to me and he called you a name that I won't repeat. So I just knocked a few of his fucking teeth out for him. He knows now that if he goes to the pigs about me, you'll go to them about what he did to you." Tristan actually had the nerve to smirk. "So, we came to this sort of...*understanding*...if you know what I mean." Then he put his hand on Justin's shoulder.

Justin nodded. "Thanks for defending me, Tris," he said with a crooked grin.

Tristan smiled. "No problem, mate." As I looked at the two of them sitting next to each other, I thought about my secret kiss with Justin and

I felt horrible again. My husband had no idea that Justin's gratitude was masking a betrayal that he probably couldn't imagine.

That night before I went to bed, I set Justin up in the guest room. It wasn't much of a room yet but it did have a twin-size bed. I was still feeling guilty about kissing him so I didn't invite him into our bed like I did the last time. Plus, I wasn't sure if Tristan would be okay with it. As I tucked Justin in in a very motherly fashion, I noticed his socked feet sticking out at the foot of the bed. "Justin, are you comfortable? Would you rather sleep on the sofa? It's actually longer than this bed."

He replied softly, "No, I'm more comfortable up here with you guys."

Unfortunately, I wasn't comfortable having him so close to us because I couldn't keep my mind off him as I made love to my husband that night. I tried to focus on Tristan but it was proving to be very difficult. I couldn't really enjoy myself and I was feeling self-conscience that Justin could hear us. Actually, I know he heard Tristan because I was the only one being quiet. When I finally succumbed to the realization that I couldn't focus on my husband, I did something I've never done before with Tristan: I faked an orgasm so our love-making would end quickly. Tristan usually followed right after me and tonight was no exception. But he is also very perceptive and I couldn't help but wonder if he realized what I did. I tried to make it seem as real as possible so he wouldn't be able to tell the difference. If he did know I faked it, he didn't say anything. As he was coming down from his real moment of intense sexual ecstasy, he kissed my forehead and then he held me in his tattooed arms. As soon as I knew he was fast asleep, I cried myself to sleep silently because I've never felt more deceitful than I felt that night.

I was awakened in the middle of the night by the feeling of someone poking me in the shoulder. I slowly opened my eyes and I saw a tall, shadowy figure standing above me next to the bed. Before I could speak, I heard Justin's quiet voice in the darkness. "Bridget, can I talk to you?"

I rubbed at my eyes and my voice was thick with sleep. "Are you having pain, sweetie?"

He hesitated for a couple seconds before he replied, "Um, yeah. I can't sleep." I carefully extracted myself from Tristan's embrace and he stirred in his sleep and mumbled a few words. I was naked so I put on my robe and he followed me into the master bathroom. I stood there while he took a couple more pain pills and then chucked the paper cup into the trash bin. I gave him a friendly smile and I was about to walk out of the bathroom when he called my name again. I turned around to face him and soon as our eyes met he said, "I wanna tell you something."

I stood there for a moment but then I realized the bathroom door was wide open. The last thing I wanted was for Tristan to hear us so I put up my hand and said very quietly, "Okay, wait a minute." Then I closed the door. As I tip-toed back towards him, I gave him an important warning. "Speak very quietly because Tristan has dog hearing," I said jokingly.

Justin looked at me with a confused expression, but he followed my instruction and spoke just above a whisper. "But he's asleep."

His statement caused me to remember the incident on the sofa before Tristan and his friends arrived. "Yeah, so were you, remember?" I paused and looked into his eyes. He held my gaze but he didn't say anything. I could feel my anxiety rising to the surface when I asked, "Do you have really good hearing too?"

"Yes," he said softly without hesitation. I started to feel even more nervous and I swallowed thickly. Justin and Tristan were just too much alike. It was almost like they were twins except they weren't the same age. Neither of us spoke for the next few seconds. Then suddenly, his expression turned serious. That's when I noticed the swelling in his eye went down considerably because now I could see two big almond-shaped indigo eyes looking back at me. He stepped closer to me and I was filled with the sudden urge to hold him in my arms again. "I just wanted to tell you that the night you guys took me home with you...I was hoping..." He averted his eyes and looked down at the floor. "I wanted to sleep with you too, Bridget. I was hoping you would join in and we'd have a threesome." He finally met my eyes again and a part of me wondered what the hell I was I thinking when I asked this *boy* to make love to my husband last year at Autumn's birthday party. "I actually noticed you on the dance floor." He smirked which caused a crooked grin to appear on his face. "Don't you remember me checking you out?"

I remember very distinctly but I thought he was checking out Tristan. My inner thoughts found their way out of mouth when I said, "I thought you were checking out Tristan."

He laughed quietly. "I was...but I was also looking at *you*."

His statement was confusing me so I finally decided to get confirmation on a question that was perplexing me for some time now. "I thought you were gay."

He moved even closer to me and at that moment, I realized Justin had his own unique scent. He smelled like the beach; a light, fresh outdoorsy scent but with a hint of salt water and a musky undertone. It was unlike anything I've ever smelled and I don't think I'll ever forget it. He continued to look affectionately into my eyes as he smiled and shook his head. "No, I'm bi...just like Tristan." My eyes widened in surprise because yet another similarity between them was just revealed. All of a sudden, he reached out to brush my cheek again. "I know nothing will ever happen between us but I just wanted you to know that."

I started to wonder where in the world this blond boy came from and if it was from the same place that Tristan came from. I found myself mesmerized by him just like the night I first saw him on the dance floor. Before I knew what was happening, his head started moving closer to mine and I realized he was going to kiss me again. But this time, I was able to pull myself away. He might have been able to entrance me but he couldn't weave a seductive spell around me like Tristan could. Tristan was my soul mate and he was a master at seducing me. I quickly stepped back from Justin and shook my head. "I can't."

He actually looked surprised by my reaction but he recovered quickly and apologized. "I'm sorry, Bridget." Then he surprised *me* when he asked, "Can I sleep in the bed with you?"

He looked hopeful, but my eyes widened again as I tried desperately to make a quick decision. Then I remembered the last time he slept with us. "Sure, as long as Tristan's in the middle."

His face fell instantly and he averted his eyes yet again. "Oh. That's okay then...I'll just go back to my room."

I wasn't expecting that type of response and I started wondering if he *really* liked me more than a friend. He turned to walk out of the bathroom when something inside me decided to provide him with an explanation. "It's just..." He turned back around at the sound of my voice. I sighed before I revealed one of Tristan's faults. "Tristan's the jealous type." I closed the distance between us and looked into his pretty dark blue eyes. "That's why we didn't have a threesome that night and that's why you can't sleep next to me."

Justin tilted his head to the side and the gesture reminded me of Tristan. "Doesn't it bother you that he's a jealous person?"

I waved my hand dismissively. "Yeah, but I'm used to it."

He gave me the first intense look I've ever received from him when he said, "I'm not like that." He also rendered me speechless. I wondered if Justin knew I was making mental notes of his and Tristan's similarities, and if he wanted to point out a difference between them. He smiled charmingly and I found that he still looked beautiful despite his current state. He leaned down to give me a kiss on the cheek and I actually felt the heat lingering on my skin from his lips. He started to walk towards the closed door but he turned his head towards me and spoke in his boyish voice that was absent of a British accent, "Thanks for everything. Goodnight Bridget." He left me standing there in a daze after he walked out of the bathroom.

I climbed back into bed with Tristan but once again, all I could think about was Justin. But this time, my thoughts weren't filled with guilt...they were filled with desire. I secretly desired Justin in our bed. I wanted to be the one to sleep in the middle of two gorgeous blond angels and have both of them wrap their invisible wings around me. I wanted to smell both of their unique masculine scents surrounding me and feel both of their male hardness against my female body. My lust was suddenly accompanied by another sinful emotion: greed. It was a much unexpected feeling and I tried to squash it down but I couldn't fight it, nor could I deny it. Tristan truly satisfied my need for love, sex, affection, attention, and all the other things wives look for from their husbands. But for some reason...this American boy that was born and raised in California like me...came into my life and I wanted more. I wanted to know what it would feel like to receive Justin's love and adoration, in addition to Tristan's. I finally drifted off to sleep that night but I had a very naughty dream; a dream that both Tristan and Justin were making love to me...and sharing me equally.

Chapter 24

THE NEXT MORNING WAS FRIDAY and I woke up early to get ready for another school day. Tristan was still fast asleep but he had a grin on his face as he slept peacefully. I chuckled softly because I wondered what he was dreaming about. All of a sudden, his fight entered my mind and I was relieved when I picked up his left hand and saw that the swelling had finally gone down. I put on my robe and slippers and went into the master bathroom. As I was brushing my teeth, I had the sudden urge to check on Justin. I walked down the hall to the guest room and when I opened the door, I was slightly distressed that he wasn't in bed. I checked the second-floor bathroom but the door was wide open and it was unoccupied.

I went downstairs and when I reached the bottom of the stairwell, I called out his name. No answer. It wasn't until I went to check in the kitchen, that the little notepad on the island counter caught my attention. There was writing on the top but it wasn't there last night after Tristan took Justin's notes on the homophobic and evil Johnny. I picked up the notepad and my eyes read a new message:

Bridget, I went to the hospital. Please don't worry. I didn't wanna wake you. Thanks for taking in a wounded animal last night. ☺ *I'll bring Tristan's shirt back. I promise. --Justin.*

I couldn't stop the grin from appearing on my face as I looked at his hand-drawn smiley face. Then my eyes read over the message again but this time I saw something I didn't notice before. Right above Justin's name was the letter 'L' but it was scratched out. I carefully tore the note off the pad and folded it neatly into a tiny square. Then I tucked it into the pocket of my robe.

After I tucked Justin's note into my robe pocket, I remembered that I still had to get ready for school. I went back upstairs to take a quick shower and then I grabbed my towel and padded barefoot back into the bedroom to get dressed. I tried to be quiet as I pulled my undies out of the top drawer of my wooden chest but I still managed to wake Tristan. He tossed and turned in the bed a couple times before I saw him finally sit up. He ran a hand through his messy blond hair and then he rubbed at his sleepy eyes. As he was giving his sinewy form a good morning stretch, my voice was apologetic when I said, "Baby, you don't have to get up now. It's really early. I didn't mean to wake you." I was still wrapped in my towel when I walked over to him and stood next to the bed. I smoothed his hair lovingly even though it did nothing for his current bed-head state and I kissed the top of his head. "Go back to sleep, sweetheart."

He made a sound of contentment at my affection towards him and he slipped his arms around my waist. I was pulled closer to him and I felt his hand glide across my slightly-bulging belly in an obvious protective gesture. His voice was raspy from sleep when he responded. "Mmmm... it's alright, love. I can't sleep anymore." He released me and pulled back the comforter which revealed his gorgeous, nude body that I took delight in ravishing quite frequently. When he got out of bed, he stood in front of me and put his nose to my wet, freshly-shampooed hair. He inhaled deeply and he made another sound of contentment before he said, "I actually wanted to talk to you before you went to work."

Suddenly, I was filled with anxiety. I began worrying if he knew I faked my orgasm last night or if he heard me crying. I think I accidentally sniffled once but I did it so quietly that I know he couldn't have heard it. I made sure he was sound asleep; breathing deeply and evenly when I decided to turn on the silent waterworks. He walked away from me towards the bathroom and I resumed getting dressed.

I was in a bra and panties when I heard the toilet flush and saw him reappear in the bedroom. I was buttoning my blouse when he came to stand right in front of me again. To my surprise, he put his hands on top of mine to cease any further buttoning action. I just stood there; half-dressed and almost frozen with my blouse undone. I looked up at him and he leveled his blue gaze on me with an unreadable expression.

I quickly averted my eyes because I was afraid to hold his gaze; afraid he would look inside me and see my true feelings and the betrayal I committed last night. Sometimes the power behind Tristan's baby blues perplexed me. The power was actually his intensity and his eyes were the key to his keen intuitiveness towards me.

Because I was trying to avoid looking directly in his eyes, I settled my gaze on his sensual lips instead. Then I saw them open because he asked in a gentle tone, "So, how's Justin? Is he still asleep?"

"Actually he left some time during the night...or the morning. I guess he was in a lot of pain because he went to the hospital."

"He went to the hospital by himself?"

My mind wandered for a moment and I thought of the little note tucked in my robe pocket. "Yeah, apparently." After a couple seconds, I brought myself back to the present.

Tristan didn't seem to notice that I zoned out and if he did, he didn't say anything. I actually thought he was going to ask me how I knew Justin went to the hospital but he didn't say anything about that either. He seemed relaxed about Justin's whereabouts because he said almost dismissively, "Eh, he'll be alright." And that's when it happened; he looked inside me. He must have looked because he asked cryptically, "Is everything alright, babe? Is there anything you wanna talk about?" I tried not to gape at him because once again, it was like he knew the truth but was waiting for me to admit to it. Maybe it was just the guilt I was feeling but for a split second, I actually wanted to pour my heart out and get all my secrets off my chest. I wanted to confess to everything I did last night but the logical part of my brain yelled at me and told me to shut the hell up. The last thing I wanted to do was to cause major drama early on a Friday morning.

So I put on my best poker face and continued to lie. I answered casually, "Yeah, everything's fine. Why?" Before he could reply, I turned away to grab my pants off the bed. I didn't reach my goal because he quickly grabbed my hand. I guess my answer wasn't believable. Once I was facing him again, he put his arms around me and held me close.

"Bridget, I know you were pissed at me last night. I'm sorry if I acted..." He averted his eyes from my face and began looking around the room with an expression of contemplation. Then he looked back at me and continued. "Like I was fucking mad. I know it seemed like I was ignoring you when you were trying to reason with me. But you don't understand. I was just so..." He paused again and let out a soft sigh. Then he started shaking his head. "I saw what happened to Justin and I just snapped. When I went upstairs to get more beer for my mates, that was the last thing I expected to see. And when he told us what happened, I got so pissed that all I could think about was giving Johnny what he had coming to him. I didn't want him to get away with what he did to Justin."

I gave him a reassuring smile. "It's alright Tristan. I understand. I really do. I mean, if it was Autumn...I'd probably react the same way. I'd want to hurt whoever hurt her."

Tristan laughed lightly. "Love, you're pregnant so you're not fighting anyone. You just leave that to me."

All of a sudden, his light expression vanished from his face and his voice turned hard. "I wanted to just kill that bastard. And I'm telling you babe, I almost did. While I was beating the piss out of him, I was in a rage and I swear I could've killed him."

My eyes widened at his confession. My voice sounded frightful mixed with sheer disbelief. "Tristan..."

"Dane had to pull me off him. He said it was 'cause the pigs were coming but I know he did it 'cause he saw that I went completely mad. He knew that if he didn't step in, I was gonna kill that fat piece of shit." His voice was low when he admitted, "And he would've deserved it. He tried to kill Justin and he probably would've done it if his bro didn't step in. Justin was lucky that Pete saved him. And so was Johnny...he was lucky that Dane saved his sorry arse 'cause I wasn't gonna show him any mercy." Right after Tristan's statement, a strange visualization entered my mind and I pictured Tristan not as an Angel of Mercy but a ruthless Archangel. I was actually glad I wasn't there to see him fight because I didn't want that kind of horrific memory for the rest of my life.

"I'm so sorry if I made you worry. You know how much I love you and I didn't mean to hurt you. You're pregnant and I know you don't need to deal with all this stress right now." Right at that moment, I felt extreme guilt float to the surface once again and I was filled with the urge to confess. He placed a tender kiss to my lips. After he unsealed his lips from mine, I licked my lips and I tasted minty yet fruity toothpaste.

I smiled warmly at him and reassured him by saying, "It's okay, baby. I'm not mad at you."

He began to gently rock me back and forth in his arms. His voice was gentle again when he replied, "I thought that's why you were crying last night...'cause you were still upset with me." My eyes widened to the size of saucers and the action didn't go unnoticed by Tristan because he raised a knowing eyebrow and smirked. "You didn't know I heard you last night, did you?" Oh my God. Right at that moment, I wondered what else he heard; like maybe me and Justin's conversation in the bathroom. My mind began scrambling for an explanation but he didn't let up on his bizarre ability at expert perception. "You were trying to be quiet about it, weren't you?" He chuckled softly but my mouth was opening and closing like a fish out of water. I guess he found my expression amusing because he laughed lightly.

I began sputtering in disbelief, "But...how..." Unfortunately no words would come forth as I continued to stare up at him in confusion and mild amazement. How the hell did he hear me crying? Did he hear that one barely audible sniffle that I made? Finally, I was able to form a complete sentence but it came out a little louder than I intended. "How did you hear me crying last night?!?"

Tristan averted his eyes from me and he lowered his voice when he answered. "I don't know...I just did." When our eyes met again he said, "But I didn't say anything 'cause I knew you were trying to be quiet about it. So I figured you didn't want me to know you were crying."

"But that's what I don't understand. I was *quiet*. I hardly made any noise."

Tristan gave me an intense look but I couldn't stop gaping at him in shock and disbelief. "I still heard you, Bridget." For a minute I wondered if he truly had above-average human hearing. I always joked about him having dog hearing but now I found myself actually believing it. Strangely, time seemed to stand still for a moment after he spoke and the air felt funny. I felt like something odd was shifting around us. I began looking around the room as if that something was tangible and I could actually see it. Tristan garnered my attention because he tried to rationalize the situation by saying, "Maybe I just sensed that you were upset. You know we're connected to each other. We share a bond." Bond or not, I couldn't make any sense of his ability because it was just plain creepy. I wasn't going to bring up the Justin conversation in the bathroom in case there was that small possibility he didn't hear it. And I definitely wasn't telling on myself in regards to my fake orgasm. I could just imagine his reaction after learning that tidbit of information. But Tristan wasn't letting me off the hook so easily because then he asked the most dreaded question: "Why were you crying?"

I looked up at him again but quickly averted my eyes in fear that he'd see the truth behind them. For the next couple seconds, I was trying to think of a lie to convince him everything was alright. So first I gave a dramatic sigh and then I answered with, "I guess seeing Justin beat up and then you going out to fight...and the whole mysterious black car incident a few weeks ago. Everything hit me all at once and it was too overwhelming for me. Plus, you know my emotions are out-of-whack because I'm pregnant. I think I cry too easily. You remember that stupid commercial that made me cry?" I looked at Tristan's face again and he was looking back at me with a worried expression. Even though he looked worried, he also looked like he believed my explanation. But I knew I had to further convince him that I was fine even though I really wasn't. I reached up to caress the side of his face and he leaned into my touch almost instinctively. My voice was soft when I said, "Don't worry baby, I'm okay."

Tristan tilted his head to the side to regard me. He tried to hold my gaze but I kept darting my eyes to every place except back into his. "Has anyone ever told you that you're a bad liar? I know you're not okay, love."

I tried to persuade him further as I continued getting dressed. "Really Tristan...I'm fine." He didn't argue with me but I knew he still didn't believe me.

When I came home from school, Tristan's bike wasn't in the driveway so I assumed he was either working or hanging out with his 'mates'. Before I could even get out of the car, Jake's silver BMW pulled up right next to me. He turned off the engine and for the next couple seconds, we just looked at each other. I decided to break the gaze first and I got out of my car. He mirrored my actions and we met each other halfway and stood in front of his car. I quickly gave him the once-over and judging by the way he was dressed, he was either coming from the gym or going to it. He grinned at me once our eyes met again. "Hey, Bridge." I noticed over the past few months, Jake hasn't called me 'sis' as much as he used to. I couldn't help but to attribute that to our current strained relationship.

I smiled back at him and greeted him the same. "Hey, Jake." Then I decided to make small-talk. "Did you just get back from the gym?"

After my question, he looked down at himself like he didn't realize what he was wearing. Then he looked back up at me with a friendly expression. "No, I'm here to pick up Tris for footie. We're having a late game today." Every week, Tristan and Jake met up with some of their friends to play soccer. They usually played on the weekend but I guess today was a change in their usual plans.

My brain realized again that Tristan's bike wasn't in the driveway so I decided to inform Jake. "Tristan's not here."

Jake looked away from me and his expression made him look guilty about something. His body language confirmed my assumption because he stuck his hands in the side pockets of his sweatpants and he looked fidgety. He didn't meet my eyes when he finally admitted, "Actually, I was hoping to catch you by the time you came home 'cause I needed to talk to you."

My eyes widened in surprise. "About what?"

His voice was low when he replied, "I spoke to Tris earlier today and he told me about what happened last night." I wanted to ask: 'Which part?' When I didn't respond, he said, "He told me he fought some bloke that beat up your mate." I didn't know what to say so I just continued to look at him. Then I realized that Jake referred to Justin as *my* friend and not Tristan's as well. "At first, I couldn't believe it; not that he got into a fight, but that your mate...what's his name?"

"Justin." I decided to correct Jake's assumption about Justin so I added, "And he's Tristan's friend too."

That revelation must've been new to Jake because it made his eyebrows shoot up towards his hairline. "Really? I didn't know that."

"Yeah, we met Justin at one of Autumn's parties last year." I caught myself before I disclosed any further details on Tristan and Justin's 'friendship' because I wasn't sure if Jake knew about what they did that night. Then I started wondering if Jake even knew his little brother was bisexual.

"Oh, well I guess that explains it then. 'Cause I was wondering why he would defend one of your mates...and a bloke too. I didn't know Tris was alright with you having mates that have a 'Y' chromosome."

For some reason, I felt the latter part of his statement was a cheap shot at me because he knows I tolerate Tristan's jealous tendencies. I didn't react to his statement but I did start wondering if Tristan told him the whole story. "You know why Tristan beat up Johnny, right?"

"Yeah, 'cause Johnny is a homophobe and he beat up Justin 'cause he's queer." Jake started rubbing the stubble on his chin and he gave me an odd look. "It's strange that I've never heard of this 'Justin' fellow before today. That's why I didn't know he was Tristan's mate too."

I felt like Jake was trying to get some information or confession out of me but I wasn't sure what he wanted to know. I was getting a little nervous because he started to pierce his light blue gaze into me like Tristan does whenever he's turning on the intensity in his eyes. Before I even gave Jake the opportunity to try and press me for whatever he wanted me to say, I turned away from him and started walking towards the front door. He followed right behind me and he kept following me until I reached the kitchen. I put my purse and briefcase on the counter and went into the refrigerator for a cold bottle of water. As I twisted off the cap, I asked casually to make more polite small-talk, "So, how's Lauren doing? I haven't heard from her in a few days."

Jake took a seat on one of the stools at the island counter. He didn't answer me right away and he started tapping his fingers against the counter-top. Without looking up at me, he answered in a quiet voice. "We broke up."

I almost choked on my water. "What?!? What do you mean you broke up?!? Why, Jake?!?" Deep inside me, I was praying their break-up didn't have anything to do with me. I remembered I predicted that their relationship would be short-lived when I found out the real reason why he was with her. But I decided to be optimistic and give Jake the benefit of the doubt. I put my trust in him and I believed he would give Lauren a chance.

To my complete surprise, he started laughing. "It's kinda funny, actually. I always hoped it would never happen like that...but it did."

I put my water bottle on the counter and narrowed my eyes at him. My voice was hard when I asked, "What happened, Jake?"

His laughter quieted down until it was a soft chuckle. A smile played at the corners of his mouth when he admitted, "I accidentally said your name while we were shagging." I gaped at him in utter shock and he had the audacity to smile at me like it was funny.

The next thing I knew, my feet moved quickly and I went over to him and started hitting him. And as I abused him, I yelled, "Jake, you idiot! You stupid, stupid, stupid!" He tried to shield himself from my attack but I just kept hitting him until I felt satisfied.

When I finally exhausted myself, he looked up at me with wide-eyes. Then he tried to apologize. "I'm sorry, alright?"

"Don't apologize to me! Apologize to Lauren! I can't believe you, Jake!" I had some energy left to spare so I hit him a couple more times. "How could you be so stupid?!?" I took a couple breaths to try to control my temper and compose myself. I started thinking about Lauren's feelings and how hurt she must've been. Then I started wondering how he explained his 'slip-up' in bed. They're making love and he says *my* name? How did she react to that? What did she think about me? I began thinking the worse and I wondered if she thought he was having an affair with me. The idea alone made me feel completely uneasy. Lauren and I were friends and I didn't want her to think that I would betray her too. "Jake, what did Lauren say when you said my name?"

He shrugged nonchalantly. "She asked me why I said it."

I narrowed my eyes at him in suspicion. "And what did you say?"

"I lied and said that I spoke to you earlier that day and you were just on my mind." Jake got off the stool and walked over to me. He must've been feeling mighty bold to stand that close to me because I was on the verge of unloading my anger on him again. "I told her I was sorry and that I didn't mean to say it. Then she got up and I asked her what she was doing and she said she wanted to know if I was telling the truth. She went for her cell phone...I guess she was gonna ring you...and I stopped her. That's when she knew I was lying. She asked me if I was cheating on her with you and I said 'no'. Then she asked me if I had feelings for you." I gave him an expected look to signal that he should continue but he just looked at me. How dare he cut off his recount of the events at that moment.

I yelled impatiently, "And?!?"

Finally, he finished with, "And I said 'yes'."

I grabbed my open water bottle off the counter and hit him with it. I didn't regret it one bit when some water splashed on him. I had a good mind to pour the entire bottle over his stupid blond head. I poked him in the chest and my voice was stern when I said, "Listen to me, Jake. You're going to apologize to Lauren again and you're going to get her back. Get on your damn knees and beg for her forgiveness." He opened his mouth to speak but I didn't let him get a word in while I was berating him. "She was good for you and good *to* you."

"But I can't 'cause she moved out and went to live with her parents in Washington."

That was a lame excuse so I yelled at him again. "So take your ass up to Washington!" I took another deep breath. "Look Jake, I know you were happy with her." Surprisingly, my voice softened as I tried to make him see reason. "She was The One...your rose. And just like your father said...you never let it go. I know she loves you Jake...she told me herself." I stepped closer to him and looked into his eyes that were the same color as Tristan's. "Do you love her?"

Jake held my gaze for a moment and I noticed he was hesitating to answer me. But when he did, his voice was quiet. "Yeah, I do love her."

I hit him again to knock more sense into him. "Then go after her!" I grabbed him by the upper arms to hold him in place and I tried to do what the Hathaway brothers do: turn on my own intensity and pierce my brown eyes into his dense, male skull. "Whatever it takes Jake. Humble yourself and beg your rose to come back to you." I think my fiery redhead intensity worked because he nodded in compliance.

I released him and then something strange happened. He looked like he was going to move away from me, but then decided against it. His six-foot frame was looking over my head towards the entryway to the kitchen. My back was to the entryway so I couldn't see what he was looking at...but I had a pretty good idea. There's only one person that could make him freeze on the spot like that. I slowly turned around and I saw Tristan standing there. His fists were balled up at his sides and he was staring daggers at Jake. The tension that crept into the room was slowly surrounding me and I wanted to prevent it from suffocating me like it did the last time I was in a similar predicament. I had to act quickly so first, I took a few steps away from Jake towards Tristan but I stayed in between them. I knew Tristan wouldn't knock down his pregnant wife to charge towards his older brother. Then I spoke calmly and gently to Tristan. "Hi baby. Did you just come in?"

He still didn't look at me and his voice was dangerously low. "No, I've been home."

His comment caused a look of confusion to appear on my face. "Oh. I didn't see your bike in the driveway."

Tristan took a couple steps towards me. He glanced at me briefly before he set his flaming blue gaze back on his brother. "It's in the garage."

My mouth formed a tiny 'o' and I nodded. Then I asked cautiously, "So, how long have you been standing there?"

He finally reached me and he stood right in front of me. Tristan almost gritted his teeth when he replied, "Long enough." I almost jumped back because I could feel a threatening vibe radiating off his body.

Jake finally spoke up and his voice sounded amused when he asked, "And what did you hear?"

Tristan growled back, "Everything."

My eyes widened in shock again and at that moment, I reached out and put my hand on his chest. "Tristan...baby...calm down, okay. Don't do anything rash...*please*. I don't want any fighting in this house!"

I heard Jake's calm reply, "I'm not afraid of him. I used to help Mum change his nappies."

To my complete surprise, Tristan didn't react to Jake's retort. He just stood there and spoke to Jake in the same calm tone of voice. "I don't know whether to kill you or tell you that I agree with Bridget that you should get Lauren back." The difference between Jake's calm demeanor and Tristan's was that I knew Tristan was actually trying to control his anger. I knew he was royally pissed off because then he said, "You're lucky Bridget is standing between us 'cause she's the only thing preventing me from beating your arse."

Jake gave a dry laugh and I think it set Tristan's temper off because he gently pushed me aside. His actions caught me off-guard and by the time I regained my position, it was already too late. To my relief, Tristan didn't attack; he just stepped into Jake's personal space and gave him a hard look. His voice was dripping with venom when he delivered his warning. "That's strike two with you and my wife. One more and I'm not letting you off the hook. Next time, not even Bridget will be able to stop me 'cause then...you won't be my brother anymore." Tristan looked like he was about to hit him but Jake didn't budge an inch. I was the one who was frozen on the spot and I braced myself for Round Two between the Hathaway brothers. The fight never came because Tristan lowered his voice and said, "Do we understand each other...*bro?*"

Jake gave him a curt nod and then Tristan stepped away from him. Tristan's back was to him when he blurted out, "I'm sorry, Tristan. I know I broke your trust but I'll do whatever it takes to build it up again."

Tristan heaved a heavy sigh and then he turned around to face his older brother. He sucked his cheeks in and crossed his arms over his chest. He narrowed his eyes slightly and he looked at him skeptically. "What you *should* do is get yourself a fucking plane ticket and fly your arse to Washington."

Jake put his head down and mumbled quietly, "Yeah, you're right."

At that moment, I thawed myself from my semi-frozen state and approached Jake. Then I started pushing him out of the kitchen. "I want you to go in my office, go on the computer, and book your flight. And call your *mates* and tell them you're not playing *footie* today. Do you hear me, Jacob William Hathaway?"

Jake chuckled. "Yes ma'am, I hear you."

Once he started walking by himself towards my office, I said, "I don't want Lauren hating me because you're so damn stupid." He laughed again before I saw him disappear from my line of vision. I started walking back towards the kitchen to deal with Tristan but I saw him making his way up the stairs. I put my hand on the banister and called up to him. "Where are you going?"

He stopped to turn and look down at me. "I'm gonna change and then I'm gonna play footie. I'm fucking pissed right now." He finished speaking in a sarcastic tone. "What was that my teachers used to tell me? Oh yeah. I need an outlet to vent my frustration." He turned away from me and I quickly ran up the stairs to catch him. He paused his steps when he realized I was right behind him.

We faced each other on the same step and I could see in his face that he was really upset. He was smoldering me with an intense look but I also read a message behind his eyes and I comprehended immediately. He wanted my comfort so I closed the distance between us by putting my arms around him. I tilted my head up to kiss his soft lips and I was grateful that he didn't recoil from me. As I kissed him, I was thinking of how I could make him feel better. At first I was going to resort to sex but something in the mature part of my brain thought to do something that would be more supportive. Once I reluctantly unsealed my lips from his, I whispered against his mouth, "I'm going with you." I smiled at him and I saw his expression lighten right before my eyes. I giggled playfully. "It's the princess' duty to be a cheerleader for her prince." He smiled widely and I felt his mood shifting. The dark cloud that was over both of our heads moments ago was slowly drifting away. I ran up the stairs ahead of him and I heard his rapid footsteps behind me.

When we got to the bedroom, Tristan changed into this athletic-wear and I changed into a comfortable t-shirt and a pair of jeans. After I finished changing clothes, I grabbed my sneakers and I was on my way out the door when I spoke over my shoulder. "I'm going downstairs to pack your bag, okay baby? Water, towel, and your energy bars, right?"

Tristan was lacing up his own sneakers when he looked up at me. "Yeah, that's good."

By the time I packed his little sports bag and we headed out the door, Jake had already left. Tristan and I drove to the field where his friends were already gathered together for their evening soccer game. I recognized Rick and Chris, and they were both surprised to see me. It wasn't often that I watched Tristan play soccer because the truth is, I wasn't into sports and I found the game to be boring. When I told them why I was there, they laughed and Rick playfully teased us. We took it all in fun but Tristan ended any further banter from Rick when he said, "You're just jealous 'cause your woman isn't here cheering you on." Rick didn't have any comeback for that truthful statement.

Since I was Tristan's cheerleader, I stood on the side lines mostly yelling and cheering. There were other people watching the game and they just looked at me like I was crazy. Even some of the players gave me strange looks as they ran past me. But I didn't pay them any mind because I had one single job to do: support and cheer for my husband. Tristan just smiled and every time he looked over at me, he would either wave or wink at me. Some people that were sitting on the bleachers behind me would laugh whenever I would try to play referee in Tristan's favor.

At one point in the game, an opposing player wearing a purple shirt stole the ball from Tristan as he was kicking it down the field towards his opponent's goal. I yelled out in typical soccer hooligan fashion that I learned from my British husband, "Hey, you in the purple shirt! You suck!"

The guy kicked the ball to his teammate and looked over at me in confusion. Then he pointed to himself. "Who, me?"

"Yeah you! You're a wanker!" He shook his head like he couldn't believe what I just said, and then he resumed his game. I heard Tristan's boyish voice boom with laughter. I looked over at him and he was almost doubled-over. I just smiled widely and clapped in encouragement. "Let's go Tristan! Score that goal!"

During Tristan's team's first time-out, he jogged over to me. I reached down to get his sports bag at my feet and I pulled out a bottle of water. He took it from me in thanks and gulped it down like he was dying of thirst. "You want one of these now?" I held out one of his energy bars.

After he got his fill of water, he shook his head. "Nah, I don't need it right now." He handed the bottle back to me and gave me a peck on the lips. "Thanks, love." Then he copped a feel on my butt before he jogged back onto the field. I gasped loudly in surprise and he looked back at me with a wicked grin.

The game went on even after the sky darkened and the lights came on and illuminated the field. I was getting tired of standing so I sat on the bleachers to continue my cheerleading for Tristan. Then something bizarre happened. When I was first watching Tristan play, I noticed how fast he could run. Now I actually got a glimpse of how quick his reflexes were. A player on the opposing team stole the ball from him, but I noticed he was able to do it because Tristan's attention was on something else. But just as the other guy stole the ball, Tristan made a series of lightning-fast moves with his feet and stole it right back. Then someone else tried to steal it but he ran faster and faster down the field; all the while doing some defensive foot work. The other players soon fell behind and when Tristan reached the opponent's goal...he hesitated for a mere second. There was no one around him except the goalie that was facing him.

The next thing happened so quickly, that if you blinked you would miss it. He faked the goalie left but moved his feet so quickly that he went right and kicked the soccer ball directly into the net. In my astonishment, I stood up and said out loud to no one in particular, "Did you see that?"

Tristan's teammates ran over to him and congratulated him, and one of the people playing referee said the game was over. I assumed Tristan's team won because the other team looked pissed off.

Because the game was over, Tristan came jogging towards me again. When he reached me, he had a huge smile on his face but it wavered slightly when he saw my shocked expression. "You alright, Bridge? Did you see my goal?" All I could do was nod slowly. He slipped his arms around my waist and when he kissed me, I seemed to snap out of it. "Thanks for being my cheerleader, babe. You were great and you really helped me out there."

I finally found my voice and replied simply, "You're welcome, baby."

He released me and grabbed his sports bag that was sitting at my feet. "You know what? I'm fucking starving." He put his arm around my shoulder and we started walking off the field.

He said something else but I wasn't listening because I was still thinking about what I just saw on the field. How was he able to move that fast? I wanted to see his ability up-close-and-personal so I was struck with an idea. I pulled away from him and stood in front of his path. I smiled and put my hands out; palm-side-up. "Do you know this game? Put your hands on top of mine."

Tristan smirked and dropped the bag to the ground. "Yeah, I know it. I put my hands on yours and you try to slap my hand before I pull it away. It's a game of reflexes, right?" I nodded. Tristan humored me and put his hands on top of mine. He kept his eyes on me while he grinned in amusement. I met his eyes but I noticed every time I tried to slap his hand, he would move it away. I couldn't slap it...not even once. I decided to try and focus so I averted my eyes from him and rested them on our hands. I tried faking him out a couple times to make him think I was going to move my hand and slap his but his hands never moved. It was like he wasn't falling for my trick.

I looked up at him in amazement. "How are you able to do this?" I still continued to try and slap his hand but my hands were just meeting the air. He pulled them away with ease and he did it without breaking his gaze on me.

Then I felt a chill run through me when he said, "I know you, Bridget." My eyes widened in shock and I switched our hand positions so he had to try to slap mine. Nothing changed between us as I focused on our hands because he was able to slap my hand every time I tried to move it away.

"Seriously, Tristan. How are you able to do this? You're not even looking at my hands."

I slowly lifted my head to meet his eyes and his gaze was intense; it was piercing through me. There was an eerie quietness surrounding us and all I could hear was his hands hitting mine repeatedly. *SLAP* *SLAP* *SLAP* I was convinced that he knew exactly when I was going to move my hand because he never missed. But how did he do it? He confirmed my assumption because he said, "I can sense when you move. Even before you do it...I just know you're gonna do it. I can feel it." *SLAP* *SLAP* *SLAP* *SLAP* I sighed heavily as I became frustrated with not being able to win this hand-slapping game. I switched our hand positions again and moved my hands rapidly to try to slap one of his. But each time I kept meeting the air. "I told you...we're connected." I tried faking him out again but I couldn't fool him. I felt him move closer to me and I got a whiff of his intoxicating scent but it was mixed with the musky smell of sweat. His voice lowered and I felt another chill run through me. "I'm the other half of you, Bridget."

I dropped my hands and gasped in fright because right at that moment, I knew there was something different about the man standing in front of me. And deep inside, way down in the core of my soul...I was truly afraid to find out what. As if being pulled by an invisible force, I took a cautious step back from him. If I was being honest with myself, I'd admit that I did it out of fear and uncertainty. That's when I felt a cool breeze and goose bumps prickled on my skin. Tristan broke our intense gaze and bent down to pick up his sports bag.

All of a sudden, it was like someone else was talking to me. It was still his voice but the extreme intensity that laced his voice earlier had completely disappeared. "So, are you gonna take me to that deli? I really want another one of those cheese steaks." He grinned and I saw his cute little dimple on his left cheek. Whatever just happened between us seemed to pass and I forced myself to smile. Is that what he was saying before; that he wanted a cheese steak?

We drove across town to the Italian deli that I believed had the best cheese steaks on the West Coast. Because it was a beautiful night, Tristan and I sat outside at one of the tables and ate our food. While we ate, we made pleasant conversation with our usual playful teasing of one another. Then he switched the subject to Jake and I was surprised when I didn't hear any animosity or sadness in his voice. I mean, they just had a falling-out but he no longer seemed affected. "You know babe, I don't trust Jake anymore." He took another big bite of his cheese steak and I could tell he was enjoying it. I just looked at him with a worried expression. I wasn't going to ask him why he didn't trust his brother because I already knew the answer. "I know now that he's in love with you. If he's had feelings for you all this time...it's not just a crush anymore...it's love." He dipped some of his French fries in the ketchup and munched on them. "I feel sorry for Lauren 'cause he doesn't really love her. And I feel sorry for Jake 'cause until he gets over you...he'll never be happy." Tristan stole a couple French fries from my plate when he noticed his fry count dwindling. "I *do* want my brother to be happy."

I replied, "Tristan, Lauren makes him happy." But even I was beginning to doubt my belief.

Tristan wasn't convinced and he raised a skeptical eyebrow. "If you say so." He dipped another French fry but this time he grinned and held it up to my mouth. I ate it graciously and darted my tongue out to lick the remaining ketchup off his fingers. His grin widened and his eyes sparkled with adoration before he continued eating. "But you know what, Bridget," he said with a mouth full of cheese steak. To my relief, he chewed and swallowed before he resumed talking. "I still trust you. I'll always trust you." I wasn't expecting him to say that and my hand froze as I was going to take a sip of my drink. Oh God...not now. I didn't want my guilt to return already but Tristan didn't show me any mercy. "I know you'd never hurt me. You wouldn't break your promise to me 'cause we always keep our promises to each other."

I smiled warmly at my trusting and unsuspecting husband as I finally took a sip of my soda. Even though I was smiling on the outside, the guilt from my betrayal was rapidly eating away at my insides; particularly my heart and my half of our shared soul. It would only be a matter of time before Tristan felt it too...if he didn't already.

When we returned home, Tristan headed upstairs because I teased him by saying, "Go upstairs and take a shower Mister Stinky." I went back into the kitchen to put the remaining contents of his sports bag in the refrigerator and I saw the light blinking on the answering machine. I decided to check our messages but that's when he came up behind me and put his arms around my waist. "Fuck a shower, I wanna take a bath with you." Then he scattered kisses on my cheek, across my jaw line and down my neck.

His kisses and the idea of taking a warm bath with him made me feel giddy. I reached up to run my fingers through his soft hair as he continued to smother me with loving affection. "Okay, baby. Go run the water. I just want to check our messages first."

He disappeared like a ghost and dashed out of the kitchen. A second later, I heard his footsteps as he ran up the stairs in haste. Before I could even press the 'PLAY' button on the answering machine, my cell phone rang. I retrieved it from my front pocket and I saw that it was Jake. I picked up immediately. "Jake? Where are you?"

"I'm in Washington. I'm telling you, this job does have its perks. I caught a really good flight and it didn't take me long to get here."

I was feeling impatient so I said, "Yeah, yeah. So what happened with Lauren?"

He paused and I started getting nervous. I also dreaded the worst: that Lauren told him to go to hell. "We talked and...we made up. She's coming back home with me."

I released a breath I didn't even know I was holding. "Thank God. I was going to kill you if she didn't take you back. I mean, forget about Tristan's threat. I was going to *kill* you, Jake." He laughed on the other end but I was being dead serious. "So, how did you get her back?"

"Well, I did what you said and I got down on my knees and begged her. At first she wouldn't talk to me and her dad threatened to kick my arse if I didn't get off their property. But I stood my ground and told him I flew all the way to Washington for his daughter. And I wasn't leaving until she heard what I had to say. Finally, she came to the door and I told her how much I loved her and how I missed her after she left. I told her I didn't think about you at all 'cause all I could think about was her. I told her it was actually a good thing that she left me 'cause I never would've realized how much I needed her in my life." He paused for a moment before he continued. "But I think what really did it was when I told her about finding my rose and never letting it go. When I told her she was my rose...she started crying. I asked her if she'd give me another chance and take me back... and she said 'yes'."

"I'm glad, Jake. I'm glad you're back together."

"Oh, and she said she doesn't hate you."

I laughed in relief. "Thanks." I thought back to what Jake said to get Lauren back and I couldn't help but wonder if he was being sincere to her. He already deceived her once so I was skeptical of his truthfulness towards her. My tone turned serious when I said, "But let me ask you something. Did you mean what you said to her?" There was silence on his end for a couple seconds.

Then I finally heard his baritone voice that was laced with a British accent. "Yeah, I meant it, Bridget; every word. And you were right. Look, I'm not a needy kinda bloke like Tristan but I do like having Lauren around. And she really is good for me and she was always good to me. She didn't deserve what I did and I promise you...and her...that I'll treat her the way she ought to be treated."

I cradled the phone to my ear because I felt pride in my brother-in-law. It was like Jake was finally growing up and being a mature boyfriend. "Good, I'm glad to hear that."

"Well, I have to go. I just wanted to ring you and tell you what happened. If Tris ever forgives me...maybe I'll see you."

"Jake, he already forgave you."

"Maybe. But he doesn't trust me anymore. And you know...that's important to me. It's important to him too." God, could Jake sense my betrayal as well? What was with these Hathaway brothers? "I just have to think of what to do to gain it back; if it's even possible. 'Cause you know...sometimes when you lose someone's trust...you can't get it back." All of a sudden, I swallowed hard and I could feel myself breaking out in a nervous sweat. Jake's words really hit me and they made me realize the parallel between me and him. The way he felt about Lauren and the way I felt about Justin. He saw me in her which attracted him and I saw Tristan in Justin which attracted me. He broke Tristan's trust and if Tristan ever finds out what I did...so would I. Oh my God. What was I going to do? How would I tell my husband the truth? I didn't want to lose his trust especially when he told me he could always trust me. I wanted to cry but I heard Jake's voice again. "Goodnight Bridget."

My voice cracked because of my current state of emotions. "Goodnight." Then I hung up before my emotions overpowered me. I had to pull it together quickly because I heard Tristan come into the kitchen. My back was to him but I could hear his footsteps.

"The bath is ready."

I tried to compose myself before I faced him. I dug deep down and tried my hardest to mask my true feelings. Once my mask was in place, I turned around and smiled brightly. "Great!" Then I started walking towards him.

Tristan tilted his head to regard me and he put his hands on my shoulders as I tried to walk past him. "Bridge, you okay?"

"Huh?" I waved my hand dismissively and laughed lightly. "Yeah, I'm fine." Lying to him was becoming exhausting. I decided to switch the subject to take the focus off me. "I was just talking to Jake and he told me that Lauren took him back." Tristan gave a small grin but he didn't say anything. "Yeah." I nodded. "He flew all the way to Washington and got her back."

He finally responded. "Only because you told him to."

I scoffed. "No! Because he loves her, Tristan."

All of a sudden, he started walking circles around me. "He doesn't love her, Bridget. You can't love two people." He stopped in front of me. "'Cause the reality is...you don't *really* love anyone. You can't cut your heart in two and share it. You only give it to one person. And the one that has your whole heart...is the one that you truly love." I couldn't meet his eyes as he was talking to me because I felt like he knew the truth. And one glance into my eyes at this very moment would reveal all my secrets. I was scared to death when I felt his finger lift my chin and make me look into his eyes. I began to pray silently: *'Please God, please don't let him find out what I did; at least not until I'm ready for him to know. I'm so sorry for what I've done and I'm not ready to break his heart.'*

To my relief, he didn't see the truth because he said, "You know, the night that I met you...at Autumn's flat...Jake was supposed to go with me. I didn't know I was meeting you until I got there and she told me that she invited you. But that night, Jake had a change of plans and decided to go to some pub and meet one of his mates that came into city." A slow grin crept onto Tristan's face and his eyes glinted almost evilly. It distorted his face and made him look devious. "I bet he kicks himself every fucking day for not going with me that night. Who knows what would've happened if we both met you at the same time. Who knows which brother you would've chosen at the end of the night." The grin fell from his face like it melted off. "I might not be standing here with you...it could be *him*."

Right at that moment, I started shaking my head. "No, Tristan. I would've picked you...without a doubt. I already told you that I'm more attracted to you."

He gave me a sidelong glance. "Are you *sure*? Jake's more articulate and sophisticated than me. He's smarter than me, he's older, and more mature. He's not the jealous type and he's not fucked in the head like I am."

I sighed in exasperation. "Why do you keep saying that? You're not fucked in the head. Everyone has their flaws...their issues...their weaknesses." I cast my eyes towards the floor again and spoke quietly as I thought of my marital infidelity. "Even *me*."

I felt Tristan put his arms around me again. His voice was tender when he said, "Hey, I'm not trying to upset you. I'm just telling you how I feel. You know, you made me feel so good today. Jake pissed me off to the point where I just wanted to..." He paused and shook his head. "But you made me feel so much better. You always know what to say to make me feel better. And you always know the exact way I wanna be touched when I'm upset. When I was playing footie, I didn't think about him once. That's another reason why I love you so much." He kissed my lips and I molded my body against my soul mate's. "And that's how I know you love me, sweets. I don't doubt your love...not for a second. Besides, you've never given me a reason to." I could feel my tears threatening to fall as he expressed his trust in me once again.

He released me and put his arm around my shoulder. "C'mon, let's take a bath." We started walking out of the kitchen together. "I'm really dirty...and smelly. Your prince needs his princess to wash every part of his body; especially one part that needs your special attention." I looked up at him and he waggled his eyebrows. I couldn't help but to smile because I loved it when he was being naughty. Regardless of Tristan's faults and mistakes, I loved him wholeheartedly. And I prayed he would still love me regardless of mine.

Chapter 25

'Nothing weighs on us so heavily as a secret.'

~ Jean de La Fontaine

THE END OF SEPTEMBER WAS rapidly approaching and it was now Saturday; the beginning of the last weekend of the month. I was lounging in the living room watching television when I heard the doorbell. When I answered the door, I was utterly shocked to see Justin standing there. He gave me a beautiful smile and his indigo eyes sparkled in happiness. I was caught off-guard for a moment because he looked completely different than the last time he came to our house; all battered, bloody and bruised. Because of my current state of shock, it took me a second to find my voice. "Justin! Oh my God, what are doing here? I got your note and I thought you'd still be in the hospital." A look of worry appeared on my face as I thought back to the night I took him in. "Actually, I was hoping you were going to call me because I wanted to visit you." I noticed he had a bandage on the bridge of his nose and the black-and-blue bruise on his right cheek had disappeared. And his once-swollen eye was back to normal. You couldn't tell someone had beaten him up two days ago and I wondered if he was a fast healer like Tristan.

He was holding Tristan's black t-shirt and he presented it to me. "I just came by to drop off Tristan's shirt," he said in his boyish voice. I took it from him and then he said, "I was actually feeling better after you gave me the Vicodin so I just went home."

I opened the door wider and moved to the side to let him enter. Once he stepped over the threshold and stood in the foyer with me, I found myself standing very close to him. I inhaled deeply as I took in his unique scent. All of a sudden, I had the urge to put my arms around him and be engulfed by the essence of Justin. The feeling was so unexpected that I had to take a couple steps back and give myself some distance before I did something I would regret later. In an attempt to ignore the temptation to hold him, I tried to distract myself with casual conversation. "So, you *didn't* go to the hospital?"

Justin was standing with his hands in his front pockets and he just looked at me for a couple seconds before he spoke. I wondered if he noticed how I abruptly distanced myself from him. If he did, he didn't mention it. Instead he replied, "No, I didn't need to. I was about to go, but as I was driving...I wasn't having any pain. My ribs didn't even hurt anymore. So I just decided to go back home. And I'm glad I didn't go to the hospital 'cause I told you how much I hate them." He chuckled and he seemed to be in better spirits. I caught myself reaching out to touch him and I swiftly pulled my hand back. Justin met my eyes and he gave me a curious look. Then he asked quietly, "Is Tristan home?"

I was surprised when I answered him in a low voice as well. "No, he's not home." He nodded and I noticed him take a step closer to me. I was tempted to take a step back but I knew he would realize what I was doing. My voice lightened when I elaborated on Tristan's whereabouts. "He's out with his friends somewhere." I smiled, and then suddenly, he reached out to touch a few strands of my hair. I watched him slowly rub the strands between his fingers almost absentmindedly.

He held my gaze and moved even closer to me, and I found myself breathing him in again. A fuzzy haze was clouding my head and I tried to keep my composure as he continued speaking to me in a quiet tone. "You know, Bridget...I'll be getting my own place soon. For the last month, I've been looking for an apartment." He smiled affectionately and his question sounded genuinely innocent when he asked, "Do you know of any places around here for rent?" I obviously misread him completely because then I felt him tuck my hair behind my ear. Right at that moment, I knew he was flirting with me.

My eyes widened in surprise and I felt flushed from head to toe. I took a couple steps back from him again and he quickly pulled his hand away as if I had burned him. Then he cast his eyes towards the floor and spoke just above a whisper. "Maybe I should go."

"Yeah," I murmured back. I could feel something beginning to stir between us again and I knew if he didn't leave, it could prove disastrous; especially for me. I already crossed the line with him once and I was afraid of what would happen if we were alone together for too long. Then I began to realize that I was trying to distance myself to protect *him* from *me*. The realization came as a shock and my eyes looked everywhere but at Justin because the truth of the matter was...I didn't trust myself around him.

I finally met his eyes because I felt him touch my shoulder. He gave me a sad smile but then he turned away from me. Right before he reached for the door handle to let himself out, I called his name. "Justin!" He turned quickly and I stood in front of him a little closer than I should have. I needed to know the answer to this question before he left. I took a deep breath and I fidgeted my hands nervously. I was having trouble meeting his eyes because I was unsure if I should even know the answer. But I was filled with curiosity so I asked him timidly, "If me and Tristan... you know, if we weren't together---"

I didn't get to finish my sentence because Justin already knew what I was asking. He gave me another beautiful smile and brushed my cheek with the back of his hand in a tender caress. "Definitely; without a doubt. It would be me and you, Red."

I couldn't help but to smile back at him because the idea of being with him was a nice but unrealistic thought. He opened the door but he looked back at me one last time and said, "I'll see ya." But right at that moment, I knew he wouldn't, because I made up my mind that I was never going to see him again. If I wanted my marriage to last with Tristan, I knew I had to finalize this difficult decision. Justin tempted me way too much and every time I would see him...I would desire him.

I closed the door behind him and leaned all my weight against it as I closed the Justin Chapter in the book of my life. I did feel some regret because he really was a sweet and beautiful boy. It wasn't long until I could feel the tears pricking at the back of my eyes. I blinked rapidly to keep them at bay because suddenly I became angry with myself for wanting two men. Then I started to think of all the women who would love to trade places with me and have a husband like Tristan. Not to mention, the ones who would love to take him away from me. I can't count the number of times I watched women ogle him in bars and clubs; waiting for me to leave his side so they could flaunt their asses around him like bitches in heat. Then I started thinking about all the women who would love to experience the kind of love I have and to spend the rest of their life with their true soul mate. Once I realized how truly blessed I was to have Tristan, I decided not to shed a tear for Justin.

I started walking back to my office and I was still holding Tristan's t-shirt when another curious thought entered my mind which caused me to pause my steps. As I put the shirt to my nose, I wondered which gorgeous blond angel it would smell like: Justin or Tristan? I closed my eyes, inhaled deeply, and made a sound of contentment. My mind shifted to visions of a sandy beach during the summer and the smell of salty sea water. I saw a shirtless blond surfer boy running on the sand and carrying a yellow and white surfboard. He was wearing a necklace with a big cowry shell pendant that bounced as he ran towards the sea. The waves were calling to him; beckoning to him like a lover. I saw him dive like a professional swimmer and his lean, tanned body disappear into the crystal clear, blue water. A toothy smile appeared on my face when I realized the shirt still smelled like the younger angel.

Tristan's voice interrupted my reverie when he asked, "What are you doing?"

I didn't even hear him come in. I was standing in the living room with my back to him. I quickly turned around to face him and strangely, I felt embarrassed for smelling the shirt so I tried to hide it behind my back. And because I was taken by surprise, I started stuttering while I tried to explain. "I...uh...I was..."

He approached me slowly and he had a look of suspicion on his face. "What's behind your back?" Before I knew it, he was standing right in front of me but I noticed him lean his body from side-to-side to see what I was hiding. I revealed the shirt and held it out to him but he didn't take it.

He just continued to look at me with suspicion so I decided to provide him with an explanation. "This is your shirt. Justin was borrowing it and he just brought it back."

"I know. I saw him as I was coming in." For a minute, I thought Tristan would find out what happened between us so I averted my eyes from him. That's when he asked, "Why were you smelling the shirt?"

My eyes widened because I had no idea that he saw what I was doing. His keen perception was forever baffling me but I scrambled for a response. I answered truthfully when I said, "I was just seeing if it still smelled like you."

He tilted his head to the side and then he crossed his arms over his chest. His voice was low and it was still full of suspicion. "Like me...or like Justin?"

I gaped at him and exclaimed loudly, "What?!?"

Tristan started walking circles around me again and he was actually making me nervous. "You know, he wants to shag you." I whipped my head around to look at him with wide-eyes and I was grateful that he stopped walking because his movements were making me dizzy. "Yeah, I just spoke to him outside and he admitted it." I immediately started wondering what else he admitted; like maybe a certain comfort kiss that he and I shared. All of a sudden, I found myself going back in time with him to his conversation with Justin moments ago.

Justin was walking towards his car that was parked in the driveway when something caught his attention and made him pause his steps. A car pulled up in front of the house and a few seconds later, Tristan emerged. He jogged towards him and exclaimed happily, "Hey Justin, how you doin', mate?"

Justin smiled. "I'm fine. I was just dropping off your shirt that Bridget let me borrow."

Tristan nodded and then he placed his hand on Justin's shoulder. "I'm glad you're alright. And it's nice to see your face is back to normal. I see you're a quick healer like me."

"Yeah, I feel a lot better."

"Well, it was good seeing you but I have to---"

Tristan was about to walk away but Justin called after him. "Wait, Tristan!"

"Yeah?"

For a moment, Justin didn't meet his eyes. But when he did, he spoke nervously. "I wanted to ask you something." Tristan gave him an expected look. "I was wondering...you know...when I'm feeling better...if we could have some fun again." He smiled slightly.

Tristan's brows knitted together in confusion. "You mean you wanna shag again?"

Justin stepped closer to him and spoke quietly. "Yeah, but maybe Bridget could join in next time."

He gave Tristan a hopeful look but Tristan gave him a hard look and his voice was dangerously low. "You wanna shag my wife?"

His reaction caught Justin off-guard but he quickly backpedaled. "I was thinking more along the lines of a threesome."

Tristan responded coarsely, "No fucking way." Now a look of confusion appeared on Justin's face but before he could speak, Tristan continued. "The only cock that's gonna touch Bridget...is mine."

"But Tris, me and you---"

"That was different, mate. The only reason I messed around with you is 'cause Bridget wanted me to. It was her fantasy to watch me with another bloke. Make no mistake about my intentions, alright? I only did it for her."

A look of understanding came over Justin but it was quickly replaced with a thoughtful expression. "But what if she wants to sleep with both of us? A lot of women have a fantasy about being with two guys at the same time. And I think it would be fun if we had a threesome, don't you?"

"I don't do threesomes. Bridget knows that." He shook his head. "Just forget about it, mate. 'Cause it ain't gonna happen."

Justin couldn't hide the disappointment in his face or the sound of defeat from his voice. "Okay. Well, I just thought I'd ask." He walked away towards his car but looked back at Tristan. "I'll see you around."

Tristan was already at the front door when he turned his head and answered back, "Maybe."

My husband was giving me an intense look after he finished telling me about his conversation with Justin. I decided to try and throw him off the scent by playing naive. "I didn't know he wanted to sleep with me."

Unfortunately, I was fooling him. "You didn't know that?" I shook my head. "Hmmm...then what were you two whispering about in the loo the other night?"

Right at that moment, I gasped in sheer disbelief. How the hell did he hear me and Justin in the bathroom? He was asleep. I even made sure of it. Something was *definitely* going on with Tristan and even though I was afraid to find out what it was, I needed to know for my own sanity and peace of mind. Before I knew it, I started trembling in fear at his bizarre intuitiveness and I covered my mouth with my hand. For the next few seconds, I just stared at him with wide-eyes like I didn't even know him. While I was silent, Tristan took the opportunity to shock me even further. "I guess you didn't know I heard that either?"

"Tristan...how..." I just shook my head while I tried to control the fear inside me. Then I asked quietly, "What's with you?"

He cocked his head to the side but he still wouldn't turn down the intensity in his eyes. He responded calmly, "What's with *me?*" Then it was like he was finally releasing some pent up frustration because he yelled, "What's with *you?!?*"

Even though he raised his voice at me, I tried not to react. I was still playing naive as I kept my meek tone of voice. "What are you talking about?"

"Bridget, you've been walking around here lying to me! I keep asking you what's wrong but you won't tell me!" He put his hands on my shoulders and looked intently into my eyes like he was trying to suck the truth out of me. His voice lowered considerably. "Why won't you talk to me? Don't you know that I can sense when something's wrong with you? I know you, Bridget. I *know* you."

My breathing increased as I just stared into his eyes. Even though they were familiar to me, it was like I was looking for the first time. From the moment I met Tristan, he had a strange way of affecting me. The night at Autumn's apartment when he looked into my eyes...it was like he was *really* looking inside my soul. He made me feel like no one has ever made me feel. It was the strangest thing but back then I didn't understand it so I just dismissed it and figured that Tristan was just an intense person. But now I knew he was more than that...so much more. He had some kind of ability that I could not comprehend. The power I always said he possessed behind his baby blues was real. I was sure of it. Something inside me broke free and I couldn't contain my true beliefs and deep feelings about him any longer. I could feel my lips trembling as the words escaped my mouth. "You are *so* weird."

He obviously wasn't expecting me to say that because his eyes widened slightly and his head jerked back in shock. "What did you say?"

At this point, my voice was shaky and I was still trembling as I tried to make sense of the person standing in front of me. "I said you're weird, Tristan! You're bizarre and I don't understand you anymore!"

The intensity was back in his azure orbs and I could tell he was challenging me. "How am I bizarre?"

I quieted my voice but the fear inside me was still reflected in my voice. "You can hear me crying silently at night? How, Tristan? How can you hear me when I hardly make a sound? Why do you always wake up when I leave the bed? How can you hear what two people are whispering in a bathroom behind a closed door? Do you really sleep at night or are you just pretending to sleep?"

"I didn't say I heard *what* you were whispering, Bridget. I just said I *heard* you whispering."

"It doesn't matter! How did you hear us?!?"

"I don't know. I just did, alright?"

"No, it's not alright Tristan! What about the hand-slapping game? How did you do that? How did you keep hitting my hand without looking? How come I couldn't hit yours...not even once?" I was beginning to feel how I felt when Autumn was having strange, unexplainable dreams pertaining to me and Tristan. But his bizarre abilities pertaining to me made me feel even more uneasy. I was overwhelmed with emotions and I could feel tears on my cheeks and my vision was blurry again.

"I told you, Bridget. I could just sense when you were about to move."

"And you don't think that's weird?!? People can't just do that!" I took a breath to try and compose myself. Reliving the unexplainable moment caused me to wrap my arms around myself protectively. I looked down at the floor and murmured quietly to myself as the realization of our argument hit me. "Oh my God."

He stepped closer to me and his intoxicating yet pleasant scent engulfed me. I felt momentary comfort and I could feel myself relaxing and becoming calm. His voice was gentle when he said, "Bridget, what do you think a soul mate is?" I slowly lifted my head to look into his eyes. "That's why I'm so in-tuned with you, love. That's why I know you the way I do. I can feel what you feel and I can sense your emotions. I told you before...I'm the other half of you. We share a soul...a bond." He gestured between us. "What we have is real, darlin'. It's *real*." His voice wavered slightly when he asked, "Or don't you believe that anymore?"

I tried to keep my lips from trembling but my emotions were still overpowering me. "I *do* believe it." Tristan raised a skeptical eyebrow.

"But I still don't understand *you*. I don't understand how you can hear the way you do and how you can be as fast as you are. I don't understand the things you can do, Tristan. I still don't know how you can seduce me so easily and I can't ever resist. No one has ever been able to manipulate me the way you do. One look from you and I'm no longer in control of myself." I whispered in total trepidation and uncertainty, "It's like you bend me to your will. How do you have this power over me?" This time he didn't answer me. We stared into each other's eyes and because I was afraid something would pass between us again, I quickly looked away. Sometimes you don't ask certain questions because you know if you ask them, you'll sound utterly ridiculous. Not only that, but the question itself is completely absurd. But at this point, I was too frustrated to care and I honestly felt that anything was possible. "Are you human?"

Tristan didn't respond for a couple seconds but then he smirked and his expression seemed like he was mocking me. I was trying to be serious and I could feel myself getting angry because he wasn't taking me seriously. And the fact that he spoke in a condescending tone made the Fiery Redhead inside me want to smack the smirk right off his face. "What? You really think I'm an angel? Is that it?" This time I didn't answer because that's what I truly believed in my heart from the moment I met him. He chuckled softly but I could tell there was no real humor behind it. "You and I both know that I'm no bloody angel." All of a sudden, his voice turned hard. "Now...I want you to answer one of *my* questions. What's going on with you and Justin?"

I whipped my head up to look at him and I lied once again. "Nothing."

And once again, Tristan didn't look convinced. "I know you're attracted to him, Bridget. I mean...why else would you have asked me to shag him?"

I kept the deception alive and repeated myself in a firm tone. "Nothing is going on."

He gave me a side-long glance and narrowed his eyes slightly. "You weren't thinking about him the other night while we were making love?"

I swallowed nervously because I had a feeling he was going to reveal that he knew another one of my secrets. "Of course I was thinking about him when he spent the night." I wasn't going to put my head on the chopping block willingly so I wasn't going to tell him that I was thinking of Justin in a sexual way. But as our argument continued, my brain learned to conjure lies more quickly. This time I thought of a really good one that actually had me believing it. "I was worried, Tristan. I was worried that he was bleeding internally in the next room. And I was worried that he had a broken rib and it would pierce his lung while he slept."

Tristan crossed his arms over his chest and I noticed he didn't look like he believed my answer. When he started shaking his head and laughing, I knew he wasn't fooled. He confirmed my assumption by saying, "You can't lie for shit. Has anyone ever told you that?"

I gaped at him in pure denial. "Tristan, I'm not lying!"

And that's when he started walking circles around me again. I don't know if he was trying to intimidate me but I was getting more nervous every time he walked a full circle. He spoke to me slowly like he was interrogating me. "You want me to believe that you were so concerned for his well-being that you faked a fucking orgasm with me?"

I gasped so loudly that I almost choked. "Tristan! How..." I started shaking my head again in disbelief and I began to panic because my brain couldn't conjure a lie. When we were making love, I tried to make my fake orgasm as real as possible. How did he know it wasn't genuine? Usually men can't tell when women fake it.

He stopped right in front of me and pierced his heated blue gaze into me. I could tell he was really angry and being dead serious now. "No more lies, Bridget. I mean it. Tell me right now. What...the...fuck... is...going...on?"

I wasn't submitting to his questioning that easily. "How did you know I faked it?" I asked quietly.

He entered my personal space and spoke softly but firmly. "I told you...I *know* you. I know every part of your body, Bridget. I know how you feel when you cum. We've shagged more times than I can fucking count. Don't you think I pay attention to you? I've been paying attention to every little thing about you since I first met you. You can't fake it with me." He paused and when he whispered his next words to me, I felt an uncomfortable chill run through me. "My *soul* feels it when you cum."

At this point, I realized he wasn't going to ease up on me until I told him the truth. If he wanted my head on the block, I was ready to lay down. But not before he laid his head down too. I whispered back and I was actually surprised that I mustered the courage to challenge him. "I'll tell you my secret...if you tell me yours."

He pulled back away from me suddenly and a confused look appeared on his face. "What secret?"

"Tell me how you can do what you do."

He laughed humorlessly. "It's not a secret, Bridget. I can do it 'cause I'm connected to you. I'm sorry if you don't believe it."

"I already said I believe it."

I could tell he was getting annoyed because he turned his head away and threw his hands in the air. "See, you're lying again."

"I'm not---"

I think he finally reached his breaking point and lost his patience with me because he shouted, "If you believed it, then you wouldn't be questioning me about it!" I knew he was trying to control his anger because I watched him as he took a deep breath before he closed his eyes briefly and pinched the bridge of his nose. He spoke quietly when he said, "Look, if you're not straight with me from this point on...I'm walking out the fucking door. I mean it, Bridget 'cause I can't take your lies anymore. It's killing me 'cause I've been waiting for you to open up and talk to me but you won't. And I can sense something is wrong with you but I don't understand why you won't tell me. Why are you keeping things from me? Justin comes to our house and then you fake a fucking orgasm with me."

Tristan's face was slowly twisting in anger and he began shouting again. "For the first time since I've been with you...you faked it! I died on the inside but I didn't say anything because I was trying to convince myself that you really didn't." His voice started to crack and I could see his azure eyes becoming glassy. "Then you cry yourself to sleep and later I hear the two of you whispering in the loo. What the fuck am I supposed to think? Please tell me 'cause I'm at a loss here!" The tears that were being held behind his eyes finally began to trickle down his cheeks and I realized my deception was not only eating away at me but it was eating away at my husband too.

There was only a small space between us while we were standing in our living room. I was the one who finally closed it when I put my arms around him. I held Tristan and he continued to cry silently but he kept his intense gaze on me. I looked into his eyes and I could feel my own tears on my cheeks. It was truly amazing how we could affect each other and share our emotions. I decided I was tired of lying and it was time to put my dishonesty to rest. I prayed he would still love me and I knew I was about to lose his trust; maybe forever. Even though he was waiting for me to respond, I could see in his eyes that he was pleading with me to end the agony. I was just sorry that I was going to hurt him even more.

"Okay, baby. I'll tell you the truth. I'm not going to make any excuses for what I did. I'm just going to be honest because you deserve that. The reason I've been acting strange lately is because I've been keeping a secret that I didn't want to keep. I want you to know that I wanted to tell you my secret right after it happened but I was too afraid." I paused and took a deep breath. I tried to be brave but I failed miserably and I couldn't even look my husband in the eye when I confessed my infidelity. "That night while you were out looking for Johnny...I kissed Justin." I was scared to death to meet Tristan's eyes but I knew I had to deal with his reaction. I slowly lifted my head to look at him and I saw true emotional pain etched into his face. His face was actually red and his lips were trembling violently. His eyes were staring back at me and all I could see was disappointment and anguish. They quickly filled with tears once again and I noticed that his breathing became erratic.

He released me suddenly and staggered back a few steps as if I had pushed him away. I reached out to him. "Tristan, I'm---" But he put a hand up to silence me. He started blinking rapidly and I saw more tears begin to stream down his face. His lips parted slightly and I could hear him taking short, quick breaths like he was hyperventilating.

Then he finally spoke but it was barely above a whisper and I almost couldn't make out what he was saying. "You...you kissed him?"

I nodded and replied quietly, "I'm sorry."

He yelled again and I jumped in surprise. "Don't tell me your sorry, Bridget! Kissing is not a bloody accident! You can't accidentally kiss someone! What, did you trip and your lips landed on his?!?" I started to cry because the reality was finally setting in that Tristan now knew that I cheated on him. It seemed to hit him at the same time because he said in shaky, quiet voice, "I can't believe you would cheat on me. I would never do that to you, Bridget...*ever*." He took a couple steps closer to me and for a moment we just looked at each other and cried together. I knew the more his voice broke, the more his fragile heart was shattering. "You know how I feel about cheating. You know how it destroyed my family."

"I know, Tristan. I really *am* sorry. I wish I didn't do it. I wish I could go back in time---" He walked away and turned his back to me. Then I saw him grab his hair and I could see his shoulders shaking and I knew he was crying harder. I approached him slowly and spoke through my tears. "Please forgive me, baby. *Please*...I am *so* sorry, Tristan. Your mother forgave your father remember?"

He rounded on me and yelled, "Yeah, after twelve fucking years!"

I don't know why I started comparing our situation to his parents' but they were the only people I could draw a parallel between. I continued down that road for a moment when I went back on my word and attempted to make an excuse for my actions. "Tristan, I just kissed him. And it was a comfort kiss because I felt sorry for him. I mean, it's not like I had sex with him. Besides, you kissed him too."

My plan backfired before I could even blink. Tristan was like a loaded gun because he fired back aggressively at my lame excuse. "Only 'cause you wanted me to!" His voice ripped right through my heart when he admitted quietly, "I only kissed him 'cause you wanted me to...and I never did it behind your back."

That's when I started begging him for the first time in our relationship. "Please, Tristan. Please forgive me. I know I lost your trust---" I reached out to touch him but he moved away from me.

"First Jake...now you! I never thought it would be you, Bridget. I thought I could always trust you. You're my wife!"

"I know, I'm---"

My sentence was cut short because his next words were more of a growl as he spoke through clenched teeth. "You kissed another *fucking* bloke." His feet moved quickly and before I knew it, he was standing right in front of me again; looking down at me with an intensity that made me want to shrink back in fear. His voice turned low and deadly and it was full of contempt. I honestly felt like he hated me. "You gave my kiss to Justin while I was out defending his arse." I averted my eyes from him in total shame because I knew my infidelity was like a kick in the 'bollocks' to him. All of a sudden, he reached out and roughly wiped my mouth with his hand like he was trying to wipe Justin's kiss from my lips.

There was no way I could get a grip on my emotions because the truth of the matter was, this was the worst fight me and Tristan ever had. He moved away from me again and sat down on the sofa. Then he leaned forward with his elbows on his knees and put his head in his hands. I felt absolutely no shame when I knelt down in front of him in a desperate attempt to receive his forgiveness. For a minute, I thought I had a resolution to our problem. A ridiculous idea entered my mind and I felt that it couldn't hurt to suggest it because I was already past hurting him. "What if you go out and cheat on me? Then we'll be even."

Tristan lifted his blond head and I saw that his face was still flushed and tear-stained. His eyes were bloodshot and watery and I knew my face looked identical to his. He replied quietly, "I don't wanna cheat on you." Then his voice started to have a sharp edge to it as he continued speaking. "That's the difference between you and me. I go out and I'm not tempted by birds anymore. And believe me...they flock to me all the time when you're not around but I'm not interested in them." He whispered in a broken voice, "Because all I want is you."

Then I asked the most dreaded question: "Are you going to leave me?" Fresh tears trickled down my face and I instinctively put a hand to my belly as I remembered our unborn baby growing inside me. "I know I told you I would leave you if you ever cheated on me."

He was still whispering because he was probably emotionally drained. "I would never leave you, Bridget." I sighed softly in relief. "No matter what you do to me...I'll always stay with you." My eyes widened in shock because I wasn't expecting him to say something like that. He sniffled a couple times and tried to wipe the sadness from his eyes but it was quickly replaced with new tears. Then he set his heartbroken gaze on me again. "I love you and I can't live without you."

It was at that moment, that I knew Tristan was a better person than I was and his wonderful heart was unlike any I've ever known. I had to make this right some how. I broke his heart so it was up to me to try and mend it. I put my hands on his knees and I was honestly surprised he didn't try to kick me away from him. I knew that if I couldn't gain his trust back, I was going to try my hardest to gain his forgiveness. "Tristan...*please*...tell me what I have to do for you to forgive me. I'll do anything you want, baby. Please...I'm begging you. I know I've hurt you deeply but I had to tell you the truth. I couldn't lie to you anymore. Just like you don't like arguing with me...I don't like lying to you. I really don't and I actually wanted to cry every time I did." Tristan just looked into my eyes with the most heart wrenching expression I've ever seen. His tears still continued to flow and I felt like the worst wife in the world. He's always been so good to me and I gave into temptation with another man so easily. I was so weak and I felt so pathetic. If I was honest with myself, I wouldn't blame him if he really wanted to divorce me. I knew he took infidelity very seriously and so did I. I pleaded with him again. "Please tell me what I have to do."

He finally answered me in a broken voice that was filled with nothing but emptiness. "I'll forgive you, Bridget...but I don't want you to ever see Justin again."

I agreed immediately. "I promise I won't. I already decided earlier that I never want to see him again."

"Don't even talk to him. He's out of our lives for good. Do you understand me?"

"I understand, sweetheart. No more Justin....*ever*." I leaned in to try and kiss him but he recoiled from me again.

"No, just leave me alone," he said in weary and trembling voice. Then he leaned back against the sofa and covered his eyes with his arm. I just stared at him dejectedly and covered my mouth while I cried silently because it was the first time he rejected my affection.

I respected Tristan's wish and slowly walked upstairs to our bedroom and closed the door quietly. Then I collapsed on the bed and laid there for the rest of afternoon. I cried until my pillow was soaked with tears and my sobs exhausted my entire body. I must've cried myself to sleep and slept throughout the evening, because when I felt Tristan get in the bed with me, I opened my eyes and the bedroom was engulfed in darkness. My back was to him but I was facing the alarm clock on the nightstand and the glowing red numbers read 11:15PM.

It was quiet until I heard more soft sobbing but this time...I wasn't the one crying. I turned my body to face Tristan and when I reached out to feel his body position, he jerked away from my touch and said sharply, "Don't touch me, Bridget."

I pulled my hand back quickly but I could tell he wasn't facing me. I said his name quietly but he didn't answer me. I already knew he didn't trust me anymore but I felt like I needed a solid confirmation from him. "Baby, do you still trust me?"

It was few seconds before he answered but when he did, his voice was low and muffled. "No." I immediately turned on the waterworks and then I heard him say in a broken sad voice, "I don't have your whole heart anymore...but you still have mine."

I scooted closer to him but I still didn't touch him. "You do have my whole heart, Tristan."

"No I don't. I know that Justin has some of your heart now."

The urge to hold and console him was so strong but I didn't want to cross the invisible boundary he seemed to draw between us now. I tried to connect with him and make him believe that I was being completely truthful. "Baby, I don't love him. I swear I don't. You're the only one I love; the only one I'll *ever* love...for the rest of my life." In the back of my mind, I thought to myself: *'You lied to him before. Why should he believe you now?'* That was the consequence of breaking someone's trust.

Tristan must've felt the exact same way because he replied in his soft, boyish voice that was laced with a British accent, "I don't believe you."

I laid there next to him just looking up at the ceiling as my silent tears began to wet my pillow all over again. I listened to my brokenhearted prince cry softly into his own pillow until he cried himself to sleep the same way I did. I succumbed to the realization that I lost Tristan's trust for a man I didn't even love. If losing his trust didn't already make me feel bad, the fact that he didn't believe I didn't love Justin, made me feel worse.

Soon my mind began to wander and I started having random thoughts. A strange one in particular; how a cartoon character's conscience has two sides. One side is good and usually represented by an angelic version of the character. It always tries to persuade the character to do the right thing. The other side is bad and usually represented by a demonic version of the character. It always tries to persuade the character to do the wrong thing. But the other difference between the two sides is that the bad side works harder and tries to entice the character with the pleasures you can gain and the rewards you can reap if you do the wrong thing. For the next couple hours, the two sides of my conscience were battling to get the upper hand with me. When I finally believed that Tristan was fast asleep, I made a decision and listened to one side of my conscience.

First, I got out of bed and went downstairs to my office to write a hand-written letter to him. I pulled out some old stationary that one of my students gave me for Christmas, and I sat at my desk for a few minutes and just poured my feelings out onto the paper.

My Beloved Tristan,

I'm writing this letter to you in hopes that you will listen to what I have to say and know that I am being sincere. Words can't describe how I feel about what I've done to you; breaking your trust and breaking your heart in the process. I feel like I'm no longer worthy of your love. But since you decided to stay with me despite my infidelity, I believe we can work through this and go back to loving each other the way we were born to. I do believe you're my soul mate but I admit that what happens between us frightens me. You know me well enough to know that the unexplainable and incomprehensible always make me feel uneasy and insecure. Though I felt you mocked my belief that you are my angel, deep in my heart I believe that you are. Sometimes I wonder if you are even aware of how special you are. And sometimes I wonder if I truly deserve your love. I proved tonight that I don't. There are many things I need to consider before I can go back to being the wife I should be; the wife you need me to be. So I must leave you for awhile to reflect on my actions and ponder the ways in which I can regain your trust. I feel this is the only way to heal the ugly wound that now festers in our joined soul. All I ask is that you give me some time and I promise that I will come back to you. Please my darling...do not try to contact me.

Yours Eternally,
Bridget

Then I walked quietly back upstairs to our bedroom with my letter still in hand. I laid it gently on my tear-stained pillow and then I tip-toed out of the room without making a sound. I left the house so swiftly that even if my sounds awakened Tristan, I would already be out of Hollywood by the time he would realize I was gone. It was raining tonight and it was coming down heavily. There was a bitter chill in the air and the wind whipped and howled like an angry beast. I drove through the treacherous storm and I found it kind of ironic because the gloomy weather mirrored exactly how I felt in my heart. I made my travels north for over an hour and when I knocked on the door to my place of temporary refuge, I was greeted by a very concerned and worried face. As soon as their eyes fell upon my miserable, guilt-ridden and rain-soaked form, I humbled myself and begged them to take pity on me.

Chapter 26

My only thought after I left the house was to go to my parents' house in Sacramento. I left so quickly that I really didn't have time to pack anything. As soon as I reached the bottom of the stairwell, I grabbed my purse from the living room, my coat from the hall closet, and headed out towards my destination. My intention was absolutely clear: I wanted to get away from Tristan for awhile. I figured it would be best for the both of us if we spent some time apart. I rationalized my decision and thought of that old expression: *'Absence makes the heart grow fonder.'* I hoped that after we distanced ourselves temporarily, our souls would be in a better, more serene place. Then we could try to work through my infidelity and heal the ugly wound I caused in our marriage.

As I drove further north, the rainstorm that seemed to be chasing me finally decided to back off my heels. By the time I reached my parents' house, the pouring rain in Hollywood gave way to a clear starless night sky. Because I was in such a bad emotional state and my mind was still a little foggy, I didn't even think to use my key. I was actually glad I didn't use my key because I know it would've scared my parents to hear someone come into the house at such a late hour. I rang the doorbell and my father answered the door. He was dressed in a royal blue robe and I could see his checkered pajamas underneath. His face was filled with worry and concern as I stood there still wet and pitiful like a lost puppy. "Bridget? What are you doing here, sweetheart?"

"Hi Daddy," I said in a low, shaky voice that made me sound pathetic. I sniffled a couple times and smoothed my wet hair back; trying to make myself look presentable.

He put his arm around my shoulder to guide me inside and I found myself leaning on him for support. After he closed the door, was when I noticed my mother standing in the fully-lit foyer. She was dressed in a flowery robe but unlike my father's bare feet, she had on a pair of lavender slippers. She was fidgeting the belt on her robe and looking at me with a concerned expression. Her eyebrows knitted tightly together and she slowly walked towards me. When she finally reached me, I saw her eyes give me the once-over as she took in my ragged appearance. Then she smoothed my hair the same way I did seconds ago but in her own motherly fashion. I could hear the compassion in her voice when she spoke to me in a gentle tone. "Bridget, what's wrong darling?"

I finally lost my composure and I sobbed. As my tears began to flow, the child inside me emerged to the surface and I gave her a look that begged for the comfort only a mother can give. "Mommy." She embraced me immediately and my eyes leaked even more tears of guilt and remorse. She rubbed my back soothingly to try to calm me and I held her as if my life depended on it. The pain I felt in my heart over what I did to Tristan's heart almost caused my knees to buckle and I was thankful I had my mother as an anchor.

For a moment, I saw Tristan's face very clearly in my mind at the exact moment when I revealed my secret kiss with Justin. I've never seen him look at me with his eyes so full of anguish and heartache; not even when I tried to reason with him after his father's surprise visit to our wedding. I'll admit that after I confessed to him, part of me wanted to lie again and place the blame squarely on Justin. For a quick second, I wanted to reiterate and say: 'Actually, he kissed me. I didn't even see it coming.' I knew if I said those words, Tristan would understand because the same situation happened to him at his birthday party last year when the blonde home wrecker known as Kelly kissed him. But I couldn't say it; I couldn't lie to him anymore.

The visions of my heartbroken husband caused me to cry harder and that's when I heard my mother say, "What's wrong, honey?"

My lips were trembling as I tried to form words and provide her with an answer that she could comprehend. But all that escaped my mouth were more sobs. I took a deep breath and finally answered her in a voice that was laced with the realization of the atrocity I caused in my wonderful, loving marriage. "I hurt Tristan."

"What do you mean you hurt Tristan, sweetheart?"

Through my tears I managed to say, "I hurt him. I broke his heart."

She pulled away from me and looked into my watery eyes. Then she put her hands on my shoulders and spoke in a firm tone. "What did you do, Bridget?"

I opened my mouth to speak but my words failed me again. "I..." I couldn't tell her because I knew she'd be disappointed in me. I've always been my parents' pride and joy because I'm their only child. Receiving my mother's disapproval always made me feel insecure so I just stood there in the foyer and tried to wipe the tears from my eyes. I was grateful when she put her arm around me and we walked towards the living room.

Once we were sitting down on the sofa together, she turned to face me and took my hands in hers. Her voice was kind and reassuring as she tried to coerce the truth out of me. "Tell me what happened, sweetheart." She released one of my hands to wipe some of the tears from my cheeks. I still didn't want to tell her because confessing to Tristan took everything out of me. I didn't think I had the strength or the courage to tell another person about my betrayal. But my mother was quiet and patient and she sat there with me as I continued to sniffle and stare at my lap. I finally raised my head to meet her eyes but I was clutching my purse to my chest like it was my security.

"I cheated on Tristan."

Her eyes widened in shock and she exclaimed, "What?!? When?!? Why?!?" I thought her next question would be 'How?' but instead she just looked at me in disbelief. Then she started shaking her head and her expression changed to disappointment just as I expected. "I can't believe you would do something like that, Bridget. I'm very surprised at you." She sighed. "Why did you cheat on Tristan? What did you do? Did you sleep with another man?"

For some reason, I couldn't look her in the eye any longer. My eyes began to roam around the living room and I finally noticed my father sitting in an armchair adjacent from me. He was pretty quiet during our conversation and he was looking back at me with curiosity. I don't know why, but he was making me feel embarrassed and I didn't want him to hear the details of my marital infidelity directly from my mouth. I'd much rather him hear it from a third-party; namely my mother. Even though I sought out my parents' approval while I was growing up, I was always more afraid to disappoint my father. I guess because I've always been viewed as 'Daddy's Little Girl'. But my father knows me well and he knew his daughter only wanted to confide in her mother. He was pretty sly about it because I saw his expression change as if a thought had entered his mind which made him realize his attention was needed elsewhere; almost like he remembered he had to turn off the oven.

After he got up and left the room, I confessed to my mother quietly, "I kissed another man."

She gasped. "What?!?" She continued speaking to me firmly. "Why did you do that, Bridget? What is so bad in your marriage that you felt the need to kiss another man?"

"There's nothing wrong in our marriage, Mom. It's just...this guy... he's a friend of ours and I'm kind of attracted to him. He was hurt really badly and he came to me for help. I felt deep sympathy for him and I just..." I sighed and closed my eyes briefly. Then I gave her the same excuse I gave Tristan. "It was just a comfort kiss."

And just like Tristan, my mother was not accepting my lame excuse. "But a kiss nonetheless."

"Yeah, I know," I admitted quietly.

"Don't tell me that Tristan kicked you out of the house."

I whipped my head towards her and said loudly, "No! I left."

She turned her head slightly to give me a side-long glance. I could sense the skepticism in her voice when she asked, "Left...or ran away?"

"Ran away," I admitted again.

I had a sneaking suspicion that my mother enjoyed chastising me. "You shouldn't have done that, Bridget. You shouldn't run away from your problems. You're married now and you have to get through the bumps in your marriage by working it out with Tristan."

I should've expected this but that doesn't mean I wanted to hear it. "I know, Mom. I know."

"Do you? Then why are you here?"

"I just...I need time away for awhile. I need some time to think and I can't do it while I'm in the house with him."

All of a sudden, I felt my mother's hands on my face as she gently turned my head so that I would look at her. Her voice changed as well; it was more compassionate. "Listen to me, sweetheart. Obviously you came to us for help so I'm going to help you by giving you some sound advice. Something *is* wrong in your marriage, honey. And you and Tristan need to figure out what it is. The reason I say this is because if you really love someone, you don't give into the temptation of other men. It's alright to look; we're only human after all. But once you start acting on your attraction...there's a problem."

"But Justin...he's just so..." I sighed again as I tried to find the words to express my feelings for him. "He reminds me of Tristan so much and he's so beautiful to me." My mother's eyes widened again. "He's beautiful just like Tristan. Well, I think Tristan is the most beautiful man in the world. But Justin...he comes in at a close second. I didn't mean to kiss him." She didn't look like she believed me so I wisely retracted my statement. "Okay, maybe I *wanted* to kiss him. I just wanted to know what it felt like. I know I shouldn't have done it. Believe me, I do feel remorse and a lot of regret because I've hurt the person dearest to me. But I still wanted to kiss him so I gave into temptation and did it. That's all I can say, Mom."

"Did Tristan catch you?"

"No, I told him the truth about what happened. Not at first but he sensed something was going on and he was able to miraculously get me to confess."

"Let me ask you something, Bridget. This other man...Justin...do you have feelings for him?"

Her question caused me to swallow hard in nervousness. The truth was that I was attracted to Justin. I was attracted physically and I was very fond of him as a person. And only in my wildest fantasy could I have both him and Tristan as lovers without any jealousy between them. But I wasn't in love with Justin. He didn't have my heart because Tristan had complete and full claim over it. I just needed to convince him of that fact. "I like him as a friend but I'll admit that the idea of sleeping with him is a fantasy of mine."

"What stopped you from acting on it?" This time my eyes widened in shock. My mother gave me a look I couldn't quite place and strangely, her motherly role began to morph into that of a psychiatrist. "If you kissed him, why didn't you go all the way with your infidelity? To me, once you cross the line you can't really take it farther because you've already crossed it."

"I would never have sex with Justin without Tristan's permission." After my admission, I realized that I just opened the door and invited my mother to see a glimpse of my desire for a threesome relationship. I needed to shut the door immediately. "Look, I don't want to talk about my sexual fantasies. The point is that I wouldn't sleep with him. I love Tristan way too much to have sex with another man behind his back. The kiss didn't even last that long before I realized what I was actually doing."

All of a sudden, the phone rang. Not my cell phone which was ringing and beeping continuously as I was driving up to Sacramento. Soon after I left the house, Tristan must've awakened from his sleep and read my letter. He disobeyed my instructions and started calling and texting me nonstop. I didn't answer my phone and I ended up just turning it off. The phone in my parents' kitchen was ringing and moments later my father reappeared in the living room. "Do you want me to answer it?" He was holding the cordless phone in his hand and my mother and I were just staring at him like he was holding a loaded gun. My father quickly walked over to me as it continued to ring and he showed me the number on the Caller ID; it was Tristan's cell phone.

"It's Tristan. Don't answer it."

My mother gasped. "Bridget Raegan!"

"No, Mom! I can't talk to him right now!" Ironically, that's when the ringing stopped. My parents had voicemail as opposed to an answering machine and I was eternally grateful. I don't think I could stand hearing Tristan's voice yelling through the answering machine begging my parents to help locate me.

My father walked back out of the room and that's when my mother spoke again. But this time, her tone of voice was the same one she used when she was chastising me earlier. "You're not ready to be married." I gaped at her because I wasn't expecting that type of comment. But she wasn't fazed by my reaction and she continued to express her opinion on me and my marriage. "You're not ready to be with one man. You have a lot of thinking to do young lady; especially because you're pregnant with your husband's child. You can stay here for as long as you want but I have a feeling that Tristan will come here looking for you."

I sighed because I was already aware of that reality. "I know, Mom. This is only temporary."

Like night and day, her voice became tender once again. "You really should talk to him and tell him how you feel, honey. You should tell him why you left. He's your husband. He has a right to know."

"I told him why I left. I wrote him a letter."

She clucked her tongue and shook her head in obvious disapproval. She also resumed her reprimand. "That was cowardly, Bridget. You should've told him face-to-face."

Finally, I had enough of being the bad guy. I already knew I committed not one but *three* acts of disloyalty: kissing another man, lying about it, and then running away. But my mother continuously pointing it out to me directly was beginning to make me feel uncomfortable. "Mom, I couldn't tell him face-to-face because I knew he wouldn't let me have time away. He would've begged me to stay and work it out."

"That's exactly what you should be doing!"

Even though I hated to disappoint her, I was determined to do what I wanted to do. "I can't. I need time to think...and I need to call Autumn." I got up from the sofa. "If Tristan calls again or if anyone does and they're looking for me...just tell them you haven't seen me."

I went into my old bedroom, shut the door, and finally removed my damp jacket. I sat on the bed and retrieved my cell phone from my purse. As soon as I turned it on, it almost exploded with alerts for missed calls, voicemails, and text messages. I couldn't even access my phone book because the beeping, chiming, and notifications that were popping up on the LCD screen was continuous. When my phone finally quieted down, I was curious so I checked my missed calls and I saw that Tristan, Jake, Autumn, and Justin tried to reach me. Then I gasped in shock when I saw the phone number for Tristan's home in Brighton, England. Oh my God, he called his mother too and she was trying to reach me. I couldn't believe it. The phone rang again and the sound actually startled me. It was Jake and I already decided I wasn't going to answer it. I knew I'd have to listen to him tell me how badly his brother needs me to come back home. Jake was sent to voicemail and that's when I dialed Autumn.

When she answered the phone, she was literally hysterical. "BRIDGET! OH MY GOD! WHERE ARE YOU?!? WHAT'S GOING ON?!?"

I moved the phone a few inches from my ear. "Aut, calm down okay. And stop screaming in my ear. I called you because I need your help."

I could hear her breathing rapidly on the other end. To my relief, she lowered her voice when she spoke again. "Where are you? Tristan is at Jake's and he's a fucking mess. Oh my God. Please come back home."

I sighed because now I had to try and persuade her to choose me over her other best friend. "I'm at my parents' right now but I don't want to stay here because I know Tristan will eventually come looking for me. I need you to help me figure out where I can go so he won't find me."

Surprisingly, Autumn was completely quiet for a few seconds. Then her voice dropped considerably and she sounded even more upset. "So you're *really* trying to run away from Tristan? You don't wanna be with him anymore?"

"No, I *do* want to be with him. I just need some time away for awhile. I told him that in the letter I wrote him."

"Bridget...you can't leave. You *have* to come back." She sighed. "You don't understand what you're doing to him. He's talking some crazy ass suicidal shit, okay. He said if you don't ever come back to him...he's gonna kill himself."

I rolled my eyes because I felt Tristan was being overdramatic about this situation. "Aut, I told him I would come back. And I asked him to just give me a little time to think."

"Yeah, well he's not accepting that," she snapped.

"Obviously," I snapped back. Then I remembered that I needed her help. "Look Aut, I need you to swear that you won't tell Tristan where I am. Don't even tell him that you spoke to me."

"Bridget!"

"Please just help me hide from him for a little while. And then I'll come back to him...I promise. I would never leave him permanently. I love him too much...I really do. We had a huge fight and I need time away right now. I think I'm entitled to that. Plus, he was very angry with me and I'm surprised he doesn't feel the need to have time away from me too."

Autumn's voice was still clipped and I found myself being berated all over again. "That's the difference between you and him, Bridge. Tristan loves you so much that no matter what you do to him...he still wants to be with you. He's out of his mind if you ask me, but I guess that's just the way he feels about you. Look, I heard about what happened, okay. And you were wrong for what you did and I really shouldn't help you do anything to hurt him even more. You haven't seen him, Bridge. He's a total wreck. He came here looking for you and seeing him like that scared the shit out of me. Ryan had to calm him down 'cause he wouldn't even listen to me. He was talking about how you left him, you're not answering your phone and he has no idea where you are. He was actually shaking. He kept crying about how you guys are having a baby and how could you leave him like this."

I felt that Tristan was being a Drama King so I wasn't that concerned by her information. Since I figured Autumn wasn't going to help me with my plan, I started thinking of other friends I could call for help. She interrupted my reverie when she yelled, "How could you pick Justin over Tristan?!?"

Now I had to explain my infidelity to my best friend too. "I didn't pick him. I still want to be with Tristan. I just kissed Justin."

"Yeah, but why?!? You have Tristan! Hello! Sexy, British, I'll-protect-you-from-anyone Tristan who practically worships you and loves you more than anything in the world!"

I already had enough from my mother and I didn't feel like hearing it from Autumn too. My voice turned hard when I decided to look elsewhere for assistance. "You know what...fine, don't help me! Keep your loyalties to Tristan. I'll call Amy because I know she'll help me. I'll go and stay with her. Tristan doesn't know her phone number or where she lives. Thanks anyway." I was about to hang up when I heard her voice again.

"Okay, I'll help you!" Then I heard her sigh heavily.

"Thank you, Autumn."

"But I'm only helping you because I love you. Trust me, I don't really wanna do this but I will...for you."

"Thank you, I appreciate it."

"Ohhhh...you are *so* gonna owe me, you bitch."

I chuckled softly. "Yeah, I know."

"So I'm thinking...you can go to my parents' beach house. Do you remember where it is?"

My voice turned cheerful at the idea of a more permanent yet temporary refuge. "Yeah, I remember."

"Well, they're not staying there so it's pretty much abandoned. I mean, there's still electricity and running water, and my dad has a maid service go there a few times a month to keep it clean. But you'll need to get yourself some food 'cause the fridge is probably empty. I'll leave the key under the mat by the front door."

"Great! Thanks, Aut!"

Then she said affirmatively, "And I promise I won't tell Tristan."

"Thanks," I said quietly.

"But you know, Bridge...you really need to go back to him."

I rolled my eyes again before I sighed in exasperation. "He'll be okay, Aut."

She was quiet again and then she replied wearily, "I don't think so."

"Look, I'm turning off my phone again but I'll call you if I need you."

"Okay...bye." And then she hung up.

Something bizarre happened the moment after our conversation ended. It was almost like another call was just waiting; biding its time so it could make its way through. In my haste to turn off my phone, I accidentally pressed the flash button which clicked me over to another call. And that's when I heard Justin's boyish voice on the other end. "Bridget? Are you there?" Oh no. I was about to hang up because that would've been the wise thing to do but a part of me really wanted to talk to him. So once again, I gave into temptation.

I answered timidly, "Yes, I'm here."

"Oh...hi," he responded softly. He paused and I didn't say anything because the truth was...I didn't know what to say to him. The silence didn't last very long because then I heard him speak again. "I've been trying to reach you all night. Tristan called me earlier and he told me that you left him."

"Yeah, I did. But only temporarily...you know, to clear my head for awhile."

"You told him about what happened?"

"Yes," I said abashed. I don't know why I felt guilty about admitting that I revealed our secret.

Surprisingly, Justin didn't sound angered by my admission; he actually sounded curious. "Why did you tell him?"

I sighed tiredly. "Because it was eating away at me, Justin. It was eating away at him too. He knew something was going on between us."

Justin paused again. Then his voice was eerily quiet and his words scared me a little. "He thinks you're with me. He said he's gonna kill me if you are." Another pause. "But I'm not afraid, Bridget. You can come to me if you want."

I swallowed hard and I began to wonder about the words that were exchanged between the two of them. I was almost afraid to know but I was a curious human being by nature. "What exactly did you say to him, Justin?" I braced myself for his response when all of a sudden, he brought me back in time with him to his phone conversation with Tristan.

Justin: Hey Tristan, what's up?

[silence]

Justin: Tristan? You there?

[more silence followed by erratic breathing]

Tristan: Is Bridget with you?

Justin: [pause] Uh, no.

Tristan: You better not be lying to me. 'Cause if you are...[pause] I'm gonna fucking kill you.

Justin: [pause] Why would she be with me?

Tristan: She left me so I figured that she went to you. I know about the kiss.

Justin: Oh, so she told you?

Tristan: Yeah. How could you do that to me, Justin? After what I did for you...I defended your arse. I beat the shit out of another bloke for you. And you go behind my back and kiss my wife? I thought we were mates.

Justin: We ARE friends...well, if you still want to be.

Tristan: Are you fucking kidding me?!? I'd like to beat the shit out of YOU right about now!

Justin: I'm not gonna apologize for what I did 'cause I wanted to kiss her. I really like her.

Tristan: YOU FUCKING---

Justin: I tried to get you to see what we could have...the three of us.

Tristan: What the fuck are you on about?

Justin: I know Bridget wants it...but the problem is you.

Tristan: What?!?

Justin: Tristan...imagine it, man. You could still have Bridget anytime you want...she's your wife. But when you feel like having cock...you could have me. And in turn, you would share Bridget with me. You could have the best of both worlds. A guy and a girl at your beckoned call to fulfill all your sexual needs. And hey, who knows...maybe we could all learn to love each other.

Tristan: Wait a minute. [pause] You're trying to come between my relationship with Bridget? Is that it?

Justin: I'm not trying to come BETWEEN your relationship...I wanna be a part of it. I know Bridget is attracted to me. I mean, she chose me for you and I remember she told both of us that we were beautiful. But your jealousy and possessiveness is preventing our threesome from becoming a reality.

[silence]

Tristan: Holy shit. You're fucking mad. I'll never share Bridget with you. Not with you...not with anyone. She's mine...and only mine.

[silence]

Tristan: Why did you ring her that night? Why didn't you ring any of your other mates? Why Bridget?

Justin: I never stopped thinking about either of you. And I'm being honest when I say this...after the day I left your apartment, I never spoke to Bridget again. Even though I wanted to hear her voice again, I backed off and respected the fact that you guys were getting married. But I remembered how nice she was the night I first met her. I'll never forget her kindness. I mean, she actually persuaded me to sleep with you; a total stranger. And she was straight up with me about her reason: to help you fulfill her fantasy. I just couldn't say no to her. Look, she may be your wife but I think Bridget is a beautiful girl inside and out. I needed someone like her when I was sitting in my car bleeding all over the steering wheel. That's why I called her. I wanted her to help me and make me feel the way I felt the last time I was with her.

Tristan: Well, I told her to stay away from you. And she promised she wouldn't see or talk to you again.

Justin: If she does though, I'm not gonna turn her away.

Tristan: Stay...away...from...her. Do you fucking hear me, Justin?!?

Justin: *sigh* Yeah, loud and clear, Tristan. Look, just think about what I said, alright? Give it some real thought and try to let go of this crazy *possessiveness over Bridget. You don't own her, you know. She's not your property.*

Tristan: What part of SHE'S MINE don't you understand?

Justin: Whatever.

Tristan: *CLICK*

By the time Justin finished telling about the conversation he had with Tristan, I had already broke out in a nervous sweat. I had no idea that he was trying to persuade Tristan to have a threesome relationship. The truth of the matter was he just made my situation with Tristan even worse. Tristan was already insecure about his ability to keep me loyal to him and he didn't believe me when I told him I didn't love Justin. Now he had to worry about Justin trying to take me away from him. And I still believed that in the back of Tristan's mind, the threat of his brother Jake stepping on his toes and claiming me was still there. I knew it would eat away at him forever until he felt confident Jake had absolutely no feelings for me what-so-ever.

I had to come to Tristan's rescue and ease his worry and his sanity just a little bit. I also had to say one last goodbye to the youthful blond angel on the other end of the line. "Justin, listen to me sweetie. As long as I stay away from you...you're safe. Tristan won't come after you. But please don't tell him that you spoke to me. If he calls you again, just keep telling him that you don't know where I am and I'm not with you."

Sadness was evident in Justin's voice when he asked softly, "So...you don't wanna see me anymore? *Ever?*"

I fought back tears and spoke in a tone with unmistaken finality. "No, I don't. I'm sorry but this really is goodbye. I love Tristan and it's the only way I can keep my marriage to him. Take care of yourself, Justin. And please..." My voice cracked at the end of my farewell and I was helpless to prevent it. "Don't call me again." Before he could reply, I hung up and turned off my phone.

I had to act quickly before Tristan figured out to come looking for me here so I went into my closet and pulled out an old suitcase. I filled it with whatever clothes, hair products, dental and toiletries that I left here the last time I stayed. I said goodbye to my parents but I was careful not to tell them exactly where I was going. I figured the less people who knew of my whereabouts...the better.

I drove down to Malibu to Autumn's parents' beach house where I celebrated my 25th birthday. I pulled into the driveway and I was relieved when I found a key under the mat by the front door. When I went inside, it was pitch black and I fumbled around in the dark for a couple minutes before I found a light switch. There was a clock on the wall in the foyer and I finally realized how much time had passed since I left our house in Hollywood. My eyes widened in surprise when I saw that it would be dawn in about three hours. It was also at this moment that my body felt everything I went through that night. I was completely drained and in serious need of rest.

I carried my suitcase upstairs and approached the first bedroom I saw. After turning on the light, I saw a full-size bed in the corner by the window but there were no sheets on the bed. I was thankful there were at least two pillows. I checked the closet in the room but it was completely empty. I was about to just sleep on the bare bed but something told me to check around the house. Luckily, I found sheets and a comforter in a closet in the master bedroom. They seemed to fit the queen-size bed in the room so I guess I would be sleeping in the master bedroom of my hideaway. It wasn't long after I made the bed that I climbed into it without changing my clothes and drifted off to sleep. I couldn't recall what I dreamt about but I awakened in the early afternoon on Sunday to the sound of seagulls.

My first order of business was to go out and stock up on some food and supplies. After I showered and changed clothes, I went back downstairs and I heard the phone ringing in the kitchen. At first I was surprised the phone was still working in a house where no one stays. But if Autumn's parents kept the electricity and water on...why not the phone too? I wondered if the cable still worked because I did see a television in the living room.

When I answered the phone, I heard Autumn's frantic voice on the other end. "Bridget, Tristan is going insane now. You have to come back."

I sighed exhaustively. "Autumn---"

But I didn't get another word in. "According to Jake...Tristan is a fucking emotional mess. And Jake's been calling me and bugging me to help him find you. I'm telling you, Bridge...he's freaking out 'cause he can't console him at all. You know it's bad when Jake starts to freak out.

He's one of the most laid-back dudes I know. But don't worry, I didn't tell him anything."

"Thanks, Aut."

"You know Bridge, I really hate being in the middle of you guys like this."

I started to feel nervous because I was wondering if Autumn was going to break under the pressure and reveal my secret hideout. "I know Aut, but I need you to keep my hideout a secret. Trust me, Tristan will be alright. This is first time I've left him and he doesn't know what to do so he's panicking."

She was quiet for a moment and her next words caused a chill to run down my spine. "I don't think you're gonna stay hidden for long."

Right at that moment, my nervousness intensified threefold. I began to panic and I know it was reflected in my tone of voice. "Why?!? Are you planning to rat me out?!?"

She answered me calmly. "No, but Tristan is determined to find you." All of a sudden, she laughed. "If you really wanna leave, you should take advantage of those plane tickets that Lauren and Jake gave you."

My eyes widened as I contemplated the possibility of an overseas vacation away from my marital problems. I became excited but the feeling deflated quickly when I remembered where my ticket was. "I can't because the tickets are at home and I don't want to risk going back there."

Autumn replied sarcastically, "You didn't give this whole 'I'm-running-away-from-my-husband' plan any real thought, did you?"

I wore a thoughtful expression as I reflected on my actions the night before. "No, it was a last-minute decision really."

"I was only joking about the ticket," she said blandly. "That's crazy, Bridge! Those tickets are for you and your loving husband to take a trip *together*!"

Autumn's plan really did sound like a good idea so I had to try and persuade her to help me put it in motion. "I know Aut, but Tristan would never know I was out of the country. He probably wouldn't even notice the ticket was gone and I'd just replace it once I got back. I wouldn't be gone for long. You can come here so I can give you my house key and then you can go to our house, get my ticket and my passport, and bring it back to me."

I was actually surprised when Autumn yelled through the phone, "Are you trying to kill Tristan?!? If you go to Ireland without him, he'll go fucking psycho and me and Jake will have to deal with him!"

I humbled myself and begged her. "Pleeeeease Autumn? Pretty please? Do this for me and I'll owe you big time."

She sighed heavily and I could hear the irritation in her voice when she finally submitted to my plea. "I can't right now but I'll come by tonight, okay?"

"Thanks!"

"Bridge...are you sure you're ready to be married?" She echoed my mother's words and it caught me off-guard so I didn't respond. "Is this the life you want or do you really wanna be with Justin?"

That wasn't a difficult question so I answered immediately. "I want to be with Tristan. We're going to have a baby remember?"

She responded in a very somber tone and I finally realized that playing the role of my accomplice was affecting her emotionally. "Well, you're not acting like it. You're trying to run away from him. Don't you realize that? And in the process...you're really hurting him. Are you gonna run away every time you have a problem in your marriage?"

The fact that I had to keep repeating my reasons for leaving was becoming exhausting. But I did anyway because I really needed her help. Unfortunately, I couldn't keep the bitterness or the frustration from my voice. "I just need some time away...that's all. But Tristan can't respect that. He's bothering everyone I know to try and find out where I am. And I asked him not to. I told him I would come back to him when I was ready but like you said...he's not accepting that either. So I have to go farther away. He's not leaving me any choice, Autumn! I have to go away!"

Autumn sighed again and spoke quietly. "Fine...I'll see you tonight."

After we hung up with each other, I remembered that I had to call the principal and explain my situation to him without revealing too much information. I called him at home and told him that I needed to take a leave of absence for mental health reasons. I admitted that I didn't feel I was in any position emotionally or mentally to teach children. He was surprisingly understanding about it and he told me to take whatever time I needed.

I left the house and ventured around Malibu to find some stores where I could buy food and supplies. Once I came back to the house with my groceries, I was in the kitchen putting the food away when the house phone rang again. I didn't answer it this time because I knew it was Autumn. She probably wanted to give me the latest on my mentally unstable husband and I was in no mood to hear it.

For the rest of the afternoon, I was lounging around just contemplating where I would go once I arrived in Ireland and what I would do to help take my mind off my problems. Soon the afternoon turned into evening and I became restless with staying indoors. The air had a chilly bite to it so I grabbed my coat and walked out onto the beach.

I sat on the sand by the shore but far enough so that the cold ocean water wouldn't touch me. I wrapped my coat tighter around me and tried to sit with my knees to my chest. I noticed it was a little difficult and my body felt strange in that position. That's when I realized my slightly bulging pregnant belly was hindering me from becoming absolutely comfortable. I forgot that my stomach wasn't as flat as it used to be. I was four months pregnant and I smiled and looked down as I put a hand on the little life inside me that was still growing. I started to feel like I had some company while I was sitting alone on the beach. Someone I could talk to who would just listen and not say a word. Someone who wouldn't yell back at me, mock me, chastise me, or judge me. Just simply... listen to me.

"I don't deserve your father's love." I said in hard voice. "A person like me who could betray him so easily and disregard his love is not worthy of receiving it. I'm a weak person and I honestly don't blame him for his lack of trust in me."

My mind flashed back to the night I last stepped foot on this sand when Tristan proposed to me. I began to absentmindedly twist my wedding ring on my finger as I remembered when he first put a different ring in its place; my engagement ring that was currently nestled on my *right* ring finger. I laughed before I said, "Your father wanted to get me another wedding ring to match the engagement ring but I refused because I wanted him to keep his promise from our first Christmas in Brighton. I wanted him to turn the Claddagh from a promise ring to a wedding ring."

A weary sigh escaped my lips. "He's done so much for me and he's given me so much in my life. Your father is truly the best man I've ever known. And he's treated me better than anyone I've ever been with. His heart is so special and anyone who's lucky enough to receive it should hold it precious." Another stab of guilt pierced my heart. "Unfortunately, I failed," I said somberly.

Suddenly, the tempter known as Justin entered my thoughts. I started thinking about the question I asked him, and how he said if I wasn't with Tristan, that we would be together. "I wonder what it would be like to be with Justin," I said out loud. "He's not a bad-boy like your father and he isn't wild and untamed; at least he doesn't come across that way. Do you know what? I think your father could've been like him if he didn't live a hard life in Brighton. Not only are they similar in physical appearance, but they have similar personalities too. They're both fun, carefree, sensitive, affectionate and caring. You know, I spoke to Justin before about his life and his family, and aside from his parents divorcing when he was a kid and then his mother dying when he was a teen, he lived a life similar to mine. Actually, his life is more similar to mine than your father's."

I sighed again as I thought wistfully about the two beautiful blond angels that came into my life known as Tristan and Justin. I touched my ring again and another thought entered my mind but I expressed it to the baby. "Your father doesn't believe me, but I *do* think he's my soul mate. I know he's my other half. Even though he's not like me, I don't think he's supposed to be. Justin is more like me and most people would probably think he'd be the more sensible choice for a husband. But we're too alike, so he could never be my soul mate."

I looked up at the night sky and one lone star captured my eye. It seemed to be burning brighter than the others; almost like it wanted me to notice it. I decided to give it my attention when I continued my one-sided conversation with my unborn child. "Some people believe that a soul mate is someone you meet who is exactly like you; you act the same way, like the same things, come from similar backgrounds. But what if a true soul mate is not only the other half of your soul...but also the opposite? They are what you are *not*; the yin to your yang. And when you come together with your true soul mate; two opposites...that's what really makes you a complete person."

A cool breeze blew across the sand and I felt a few tiny grainy pebbles brush against my body. The breeze swept through my hair which partially blinded me for a moment. As I was trying to tame my long, auburn locks...I heard a voice call out to me from behind; a very familiar voice. I gasped in sheer disbelief and whipped my head around towards the voice. What I saw made me yelp in fear and my brain didn't give my body enough time to stand up so I just scooted away across the sand on my butt. I shrieked out loud into the night, "TRISTAN?!?"

He was making long strides towards me dressed in all black. It was dark on the beach except for the moon hanging above my head in the sky and the light coming from the kitchen windows in the beach house a few yards away. He reached me quickly and stood towering above me. I looked up at him with wide-eyes and I found his presence menacing but also beautiful at the same time. He looked the way he did the last time we were here together. The moonlight made his naturally golden hair look more of a silvery white-blond and his eyes remained hidden in shadow. I could still see the ivory skin on his face because the moon was casting a soft glow that seemed to surround him. At this exact moment, he looked like a wingless fallen angel.

He knelt down next to me in the sand and it was then that I could finally see his face. He had dark circles under his azure eyes and he looked tired and worn. What Autumn was telling me earlier about what he was going through because of my absence was clearly evident on his face. His lips parted and my name escaped as a whisper. I noticed him inching closer to me but I just sat there frozen in shock because I couldn't believe he found me. He reached out and I flinched unexpectedly when I felt him caress my cheek with his warm hand.

Before I knew what was happening, he moved quickly and embraced me tightly. His unique, intoxicating scent engulfed me and I was finally able to move and put my arms around him. We held each other on the beach and then he began to sob. It was heart wrenching and intense, and I could feel his entire body trembling. He shifted and began holding me by the waist so he could put his head against my belly. Then he laid his head on my lap while he cried and I instinctively began comforting him by running my fingers through his soft hair. My emotions betrayed me and I could feel tears pricking at the back of my eyes. Once again, Tristan openly exposed his raw emotions to me and I saw how truly vulnerable he was. I wouldn't let my tears fall because a feeling of utter confusion reached the surface of my consciousness and I began to wonder how he found me.

Once Tristan started to calm down and all that could be heard were the ocean waves crashing against the shore mixed with the sound of his quiet hiccups, I decided it was safe to ask. "How did you find me?" He didn't answer me and a full minute went by without a word from him. Then I thought that maybe Autumn had finally broke under the pressure of the Hathaway brothers but he didn't want to tell me. "Did Autumn tell you I was here?"

His voice was muffled because he seemed to bury himself in my lap. "No."

I gasped so loudly in shock that it actually startled Tristan because I felt him jump. He sat up slowly and just looked at me, and I looked back at him with an expression of fear and confusion. "Then who told you?"

After a beat, he replied quietly, "No one." Even though it was dark, I know he could see the look on my face. I started to shiver from head to toe and not because I was cold. He continued speaking to me in an almost detached but quiet tone. "I was lying on the floor at Jake's flat just turning my bracelet..." He pulled up one of the sleeves on his coat to reveal the ID bracelet I gave him two Christmases ago. "Thinking about you. The next thing I knew...I fell asleep. I saw a picture in my head...it was this place...and I remembered it from your birthday party last year. So I just decided to see if you were here."

I was breathing so rapidly after I listened to his bizarre explanation that I could see my breath coming out in puffs against the chilly nighttime air. Not only did I have a best friend with unexplained psychic abilities, it seemed I also had a husband that possessed something similar. I had to get some kind of confirmation from him to ease my sanity. I was still a little afraid of this new revelation so I asked meekly, "Are you psychic like Autumn?"

I saw Tristan look down and he didn't meet my eyes as he answered me. "I don't know but I've always felt different from everyone else." He finally looked up at me and I could feel the intensity of his gaze even through the dense darkness. "I've been feeling it even more since I met you and it gets stronger the longer I'm with you."

The realization of what he was actually saying finally hit me and I blurted out, "So you *have* been keeping a secret from me!"

"Yes," he murmured quietly. I sighed and before I could speak, he moved closer to me again and grabbed my upper arms. Then he started to plead with me. "Bridget, please come home with me. *Please.*"

I sighed again. "I can't, Tristan. I need time away for a little while."

"Why? Why can't we work this out together? You know how much I love you and I need to be with you."

I spoke tenderly when I replied, "Baby, I thought you wouldn't mind a little time apart from each other after I broke your heart. I thought you'd be relieved."

He started shaking his head. "No, Bridget. I don't need time apart from you. You don't understand..." He sighed heavily. "Yes, I was angry about you cheating on me but I didn't want you to go away." He leaned towards me and kissed me. His lips were so soft and I wanted him to deepen the kiss and seduce me with it. Unfortunately, he unsealed his lips from mine but he whispered against them, "I don't ever want you to go away." He pulled back and I could hear the panic in his voice as he spoke to me. "When I read your letter...I thought I was gonna fucking die. I couldn't believe you left me."

"I told you I was going to come back to you."

"Yeah, but when?!?" I put my head down in shame because Tristan had a point. I wasn't very specific on the timeframe of my sudden departure. "Then you tell me not to contact you. What the fuck?!? Don't you think I wanna know where you are...that you're safe? Darlin', you're pregnant. And have you forgotten that you're my wife?"

"No, I haven't forgotten. And I didn't tell you because I knew you'd beg me to come back."

"Yeah, you're right. 'Cause we shouldn't run away from each other." His voice turned hard when he said, "I was ringing everybody trying to find your arse." All of a sudden, I started wondering at what lengths he would've gone to find me and how long he would've searched. The next thing Tristan said was very cryptic because it was almost like he knew what I was thinking. "And I wasn't gonna stop until I found you."

I sighed in defeat. "Yeah, well you did. Are you happy now?"

He entered my personal space and his voice was dangerously low. "Happy?" Then he moved back and yelled, "Do you even know what you put me through?!? Do you even care?!? First you cheat on me and then you leave me in the middle of the fucking night! You don't say when you're coming back or where you're going! And I'm just supposed to accept that?!?" He grabbed my arms again and pierced his heated blue gaze into me. His tone of voice was firm when he said, "I'm not leaving here without you. Do you understand me, Bridget? We're leaving together and we're going home."

The Fiery Redhead emerged from inside me and I pushed his arms off. Luckily, nice Bridget decided to compromise because I really did feel guilty for putting him through so much distress. "The only way I'm coming home is if we talk about everything we're feeling and share our secrets. And we both agree not to judge each other, get angry or yell at each other."

Tristan agreed immediately. "Fine. We'll lay ourselves bare and put all our cards on the table; no matter how private or how embarrassing. All secrets between us officially end tonight. We tell each other *everything*." He took my hands in his and began rubbing them. Then he said quietly, "I just hope you're ready to hear it." I noticed that the more he rubbed my hands, the warmer I began to feel. "Love, your hands are freezing." He started to stand up but he didn't release his hold on me. "C'mon, let's go. Let's get you warmed up." I complied with my British prince and stood up, and he immediately put his arms around me as we walked back up to the beach house.

As we were leaving Malibu and heading back to our own house in Hollywood, I started to wonder about what Tristan was going to reveal to me once we 'laid ourselves bare'. I looked back in my rear-view mirror and I could see him following close behind me on his green and black motorcycle. I couldn't see his face because his head was covered by his helmet but I wondered about his facial expression and what he was thinking about. Was he wondering about what secrets I was going to reveal to him? Would it actually be new information that he didn't already know? Tristan's intuitiveness towards me was absolutely mind-boggling. I've never met anyone; my parents included, who knew me as well as he did. He could read my mind, sense my feelings and intentions, and seduce and manipulate me so easily. Now I had to add to the list of his creepy perceptive abilities: see my location in his sleep. But I was even more perplexed because I didn't feel like I knew him the same way.

Following my thoughts about Tristan and his unusual abilities, came thoughts about Autumn and her weird dreams. I wondered if she had a dream that Tristan was going to find me tonight and that's why she said I wasn't going to stay hidden for long. Because her name entered my mind, I remembered that I had to call her and tell her not drive up to Malibu since my plan to escape to Ireland was now moot. As I was fumbling in my purse for my cell phone, I glanced at the clock on the dashboard and it was already past 11PM. She told me she would come by tonight but I couldn't help but wonder if she was planning to come at all. I looked in the mirror again and Tristan was still following behind me. All of a sudden I was filled with anxiety because in less than an hour, I was finally going to know the truth behind the mystery of Tristan Caleb Hathaway.

∞

WHEN WE FINALLY ARRIVED AT our house in Hollywood, I pulled my little red Mercedes convertible into the driveway and turned off the engine. I glanced to my left and I saw that Tristan had already hopped off his motorcycle and he was removing his helmet. Our eyes met briefly before I turned my head to stare at the garage door. My mind wandered for a moment and I thought about how I ran away from him the night before; into the pouring rain and the howling wind. I remembered my conscience convinced me it would be easy to get away from him for awhile. It told me that all couples need time away from each other every now and then. It reassured me by saying I was making a wise decision and temporary separation during a stressful time is healthy for our relationship since it wasn't often that we were apart.

The other side of my conscience continued to scream at me as I peeled out of the driveway and drove off into the night. It tried desperately to convince me to turn around and get back into bed with my heartbroken husband. It pleaded with me and told me that he needed me and that he would be devastated once he learned of my disappearance. Then demonic Bridget won me over by saying my actions were totally justified because Tristan needed to get over his obsession with me. It said that if I didn't get away now, he would end up smothering me in our marriage and I'd never get to have time to myself. The bad side of my conscience told me that I should run and hide. Unfortunately, Autumn was right because

I didn't stay hidden for long before Tristan found me. But tonight...he would reveal to me how his bizarre internal navigation system worked.

A knock on the glass brought me out of my reverie and I whipped my head towards the driver's side window. Tristan was standing next to my door; tall and imposing, looking down at me and gesturing for me to get out of the car. I unlocked my door and I was surprised when he quickly grabbed the door handle and opened it. As soon as I got out of my car, he closed the door and took my hand. We walked towards the front door and once inside, he closed it behind us and immediately armed the security alarm. He turned to face me but strangely, he moved back a couple feet to lean his weight against the door. In the fully-lit foyer, his five-foot-eleven frame was dressed in all black; from his jacket to his boots but I could see remnants of sand on his jeans. His expression was intense and the look in his eyes had one clear meaning that I understood immediately: 'You're not going anywhere.'

I shifted on my feet and averted my eyes from him because he started to pierce his heated blue gaze into me. Even though I knew Tristan loved me immensely and wouldn't physically hurt me, he never hesitated to dominate me whenever the mood struck him. And I'll admit that sometimes even the Fiery Redhead inside me was afraid to take on the Blond Archangel; especially when he was really angry or being dead serious because his domination was very intimidating. The silence in the foyer was broken when I spoke quietly as to not betray the uneasiness I felt because of his burning, steady gaze. "So, where do you want to talk?" Tristan didn't respond verbally; he just walked towards me without taking his eyes off me. Then he took my hand again and I obediently followed him as he guided me upstairs to our bedroom.

We both walked towards the bed and I removed my coat. I laid it across my lap after I sat down to face him but I noticed he remained standing. He looked at me for a moment and then he began to strip off his clothing. I knitted my brows together in confusion and looked at him questioningly. "What are you doing?"

He carelessly dropped articles of clothing on the floor as he undressed and when he finally opened his mouth to speak, he responded in a soft tone. "Are you ready to talk?"

"Yes."

"Good. Then take off your clothes. I said we were gonna lay ourselves *bare*, didn't I?" I couldn't help but to smirk at him.

The bed was still unmade from the last time we were both in it so he laid on the cotton sheets with his head propped up on his elbow. He was laying on his side and he watched me silently as I removed all my clothing and joined him on the bed. I laid on my side facing him but I cradled my head on my folded arms. Something inside of me finally realized how much I missed the presence of my beautiful husband so I reached out and brushed my hand over the tattoo on his left shoulder. As soon as Tristan felt my touch, he returned the affection and glided his hand across my pregnant belly. His hand lingered there for awhile and his display of tenderness was unmistaken as he continued to gently rub our growing baby.

I put my hand on top of his and for the next couple seconds, we just gazed into each other's eyes as we connected with our unborn child. I was filled with such emotion from this simple act that I couldn't help but to smile warmly at him. Tristan smiled back at me and at that moment, I realized that I should've never left this bed the other night. His eyes shifted back to my belly but looked into my eyes when he heard me speak. "I'll go first, okay?" He nodded with a grin and I took a deep breath before I put the rest of my cards on the table. "My *other* secret is... I fantasize about having you and Justin at the same time. I wonder what it would be like to have you both as lovers. And in my fantasy, you both agree to share me equally without any jealousy. Part of the reason why I kissed him was because I wanted to know what it felt like. Another part was because I felt sympathy for him, but I'll also admit that I'm attracted to him because he reminds me so much of you."

We kept our eyes on each other as I confessed my secret. I was grateful when I didn't see a flicker of shock or surprise on his face. Then I wondered if maybe it was because he already knew this information. Before I could even ask, he read my mind again. "I had a feeling you wanted both of us. The fact that you liked to see us together sexually, really confused me at first. But then I thought maybe it was because you wanted a threesome if I agreed to it." His voice lowered when he admitted, "I know I'm the only thing preventing it from happening; me and my jealousy and possessiveness." He broke our gaze and looked down at the bed. "I just can't help feeling that way, Bridget. You know how I am and how I feel about you."

I couldn't disagree with him on that point. I already knew he didn't like to share me with anyone else. Even if he did agree to a threesome with Justin, I knew he'd only be doing it to satisfy me. Tristan has told me on numerous occasions that he'd do anything for me. He expressed that his limit was sharing me with another person sexually but I secretly knew that if I begged him enough, he would eventually give into me. But I loved him more than anyone in the world and I would never make him compromise like that. I knew if I slept with Justin...even with his permission...his heart would be suffering. I needed to reassure him that even though a threesome with him and Justin was a secret desire of mine, I would protect his heart and never ask him to make it a reality. "I know, baby. But you know, even though I desire both of you...I think I can only handle being with one man." I finished by saying with a grin, "One relationship is hard enough, don't you think?"

Tristan grinned back at me and we were both quiet for a moment. Then his expression changed to one more serious. His voice was still low when he said, "I know you chose me over him but if we weren't married and you weren't pregnant...would you have made the same choice?"

Sometimes Tristan's insecurity annoyed me, but other times...like this one...it pulled at my heart strings. My voice was tender as I continued to reassure him. "Yes, I still would've chosen you." His expression lightened right before my very eyes. He grinned widely and I saw his cute little dimple on his left cheek. He put his head down to rest on his arms so we were now eye-to-eye with each other. I reached out to caress his cheek and I could feel the slight stubble. I remembered that he's been in emotional distress the last few nights so I'm sure he wasn't thinking about shaving. My affection caused him to close his eyes in contentment. "It's because I love you, Tristan. I was telling the truth when I told you that I didn't love Justin. I'll admit that I was infatuated with him but I'm not in love with him." My caress traveled south and I brushed my fingers across his soft sensual lips. When I felt him kiss them, I smiled at his tenderness and reassured him once again. "He doesn't have my heart, baby. He has my friendship and that's it."

Tristan opened his eyes and his voice turned hard when he mumbled against my fingers, "I still don't want you to see him ever again."

I chuckled in amusement as his jealousy easily bubbled to the surface. "I know. I won't. The truth is...he's not good for our marriage."

"Yeah, it should just be me and you. Besides, you're mine and I'm not sharing you." To my surprise, Tristan reached out in a clear display of possessiveness and pulled me close to his body. He embraced me and I laughed in delight and quickly molded my body to his. I hooked one of my legs over his and as I rubbed my leg against his, the tiny blond hairs on his leg tickled my skin. I felt his naughty boy parts touch my girly ones and we both ground our hips into each other at the same time. Tristan moaned in pleasure and when his lips finally descended upon mine, I kicked myself mentally for wanting to run away from this feeling.

I felt him about to roll us over so he could lie on top of me, so I had to take control quickly. I didn't want us to get lost in each other before all our secrets were revealed. I broke the kiss and pushed lightly at his chest. He looked at me with a confused expression so I cleared my throat and gave him a friendly reminder. "Um, it's your turn now, remember? Put your cards on the table. Uhhh, I mean...the bed." I chuckled at my own wittiness.

Right at that moment, Tristan's mood changed. He released me and moved away a few inches back to his previous position. He looked a little worried and I couldn't help but wonder what he was about to tell me and why it seemed to be so difficult for him. I was filled with anxiety once again but I gave him my undivided attention. For the next minute, he didn't meet my eyes because they were fixed on my pillow and his mind seemed to be some where else. His expression changed again and he looked like he was contemplating his words. I laid there quietly and patiently, but then I decided to help him with his confession by giving him some comfort and support. I rubbed my hand in a gentle caress up and down the side of his naked body; from his shoulder down to his hip. I think my actions had the desired effect because he shivered slightly and I noticed him scoot closer to me to seek more physical attention.

When he put his arm across my waist and my eyes finally met his baby blues...I knew he was ready to talk. I was surprised when he started whispering. "Do you wanna know why I say I'm fucked in the head?" My eyes widened almost involuntarily and I nodded. "It's 'cause I am, Bridget. I'm *really* mad." I think he could tell by my confused expression that I didn't understand so he elaborated by saying, "All my life...I've felt different from everyone else. I've always felt like no one understood me. I'm not sure how to explain it to you...but I'll try." He paused again but when he said, "I don't know who I am," I swallowed hard in nervousness. I mean, how do you react to a statement like that? The best I could do was school my face into a neutral expression. "You know how people... *normal* people...have a sense of oneself? Well, I've never had that." He paused yet again and it seemed as if our eyes were locked on each other because I couldn't look away. "I think I'm someone else."

As Tristan continued to reveal his secret, I felt like I was getting to know him all over again. "Sometimes when I'm asleep, I see pictures of things and places that I know don't exist. I don't think I'm dreaming either; I think they're real. And sometimes...I hear a voice in my head."

My mouth dropped in complete shock. I didn't want to interrupt him but I couldn't help it because I was so curious. "Did you ever talk to the voice and ask it who it was?"

"I asked it a long time ago but it wouldn't tell me." He paused again and our bedroom was completely silent. He broke the silence when he finished by saying, "But I know *now*."

A chill ran down my spine and I could hear myself breathing rapidly in anticipation. I asked in an urgent tone, "Who is it?"

His voice was barely a whisper when he answered. "You."

My eyes were wide with fright and I gasped. Tristan's voice was eerily quiet and his gaze was filled with a serious intensity. It took an enormous amount of effort not to move away from him. "I hear you in my head, Bridget. The voice sounds exactly like you. I hear you when you're not even speaking to me. But it's not all the time...just once in awhile. I first realized it on the night we met. You have no idea how hard I was trying not to lose my wits. I mean, you say 'hi' to me...and your voice sounds *just* like the one I've been hearing in my head. I was scared shitless but at the same time...all I wanted was to be around you." No matter how hard I tried, I couldn't control my. I covered my mouth with my hand because I couldn't believe what he was telling me. How was this possible? Was he psychic like Autumn? Wait a minute, was she even psychic? I never really figured out her mystery either.

His hand moved from my hip and rested on my belly once again. I didn't dare interrupt him because even though I was afraid of his secret, I was highly intrigued as well. "I think that's how I know what you're thinking sometimes. I think your soul speaks to mine and I'm able to hear it. When I was a kid, your voice used to sound like a little girl." His expression lightened and he gave a short laugh. "My family thought you were my imaginary friend, but I knew you were real." Then he wore a thoughtful expression when he said, "I think your soul was the one that showed me a picture of where you were." He chuckled. "You ratted yourself out, babe."

I'll admit that it disturbed me greatly that Tristan could literally read my mind. But if that was the case, why didn't he find out about my infidelity on his own? "If you can hear my soul speak...did you hear me thinking about my kiss with Justin?"

"No. Like I said before...I only hear your voice once in awhile. And I only hear it when your soul actually speaks. Sometimes love, you're just talking to yourself. It's your own inner monologue." And just like the changing of the tides, he turned serious again. "I don't think your soul wanted me to know what you *did*, but I think it wanted me to know where you *were*. I was passed out on the floor at Jake's flat and I saw the beach house in my mind. Then I woke up, ran out of his flat, jumped on my bike, and rode to Malibu."

What Tristan was saying was so unbelievable but I knew he was telling the truth. Perplexity was filling me rapidly because I couldn't make any sense of it. And I hated when things didn't make any sense. He changed the subject all of a sudden by saying, "I don't know why I can hear so well or why I can be really fast when I wanna be. And I don't know why I heal so quickly either. When I was a kid, I would get bumps and bruises and heal completely within a couple days. Mum and Nanny were always amazed that I could heal so fast. But as I got older I thought that maybe I was just special. You know, like some people are really smart or have incredible memories."

He brought the subject back to the voice in his head when he admitted, "The only person who knows about the voice is Jake. When I was a teenager, he caught me having a conversation with you. He kept questioning me about who I was talking to, so I finally told him what was going on. But to this day, he doesn't know the voice is yours. I never told him. And I never told Mum or Nanny 'cause I didn't want them to send me to a mental institute or make me talk to a shrink. You know I hate talking to fucking strangers about what goes on in my head. Whenever

I heard your voice and my family was around, I either ignored it or whispered quietly so they couldn't hear me."

"Is that why you got so angry the day I suggested you get professional help for your obsession over me?"

"Yeah. First of all, I don't think anyone can help me. And two, I don't want anyone judging me. Sometimes you can see it, Bridget. People try to hide their judgment but their eyes always betray them."

While he was talking, I began to wonder why he never told me all of this before. My inner thoughts found their way out of my mouth when I asked, "Why didn't you ever tell me this? Why did you keep it a secret?"

Tristan sighed softly. "Bridget, where I come from...people like me are mad. They're fucked in the head. I really care about your opinion of me and I didn't want you to think I was mad. I thought if you knew, you wouldn't wanna be with me. Why would you wanna be with a man who's insane? I know how you get scared of things you don't understand. And I don't really understand it myself, so how could I explain it to you so you wouldn't be afraid?" When Tristan spoke his next words, the strength in his voice began to waver and I could tell he was getting emotional. "Bridget, I am *so* afraid to lose you. It's my biggest fear in the whole fucking world. So if keeping my insanity a secret will protect you and I'll get to keep you...then I'll do it."

I realized that the more Tristan spoke to me about his secrets and his feelings, the less fear consumed me. I wished to understand him better and I guess that's why I found myself asking him more questions. "Why do you always wake up when I leave the bed?"

"I start to feel lonely and the feeling upsets me and it wakes me out of my sleep. Before I met you, I always felt alone." I wasn't expecting him to say something like that especially knowing how popular he is. Why would he ever feel alone? He has more friends than I'll ever have in my life. Tristan exercised his recently explained mind-reading ability when he said, "Even though I have a lot of mates, I felt alone 'cause no one really understood me. I was always afraid to tell people my true feelings 'cause I didn't want them to take the piss out of me." To this day, I still can't comprehend most of the British terms that Tristan uses. He naturally sensed my confusion because he clarified by saying, "Take the piss out means 'make fun'. I hated feeling that way but since I've been with you...

I've never felt that way again. When you leave the bed, it's like my soul knows yours isn't there. I think our souls speak to each other when we sleep and mine always wants attention from yours."

I found the idea quite endearing so I smiled affectionately. My genuine smile seemed to affect Tristan's mood because he smiled back. All of a sudden, a peculiar look crossed his handsome features like he just remembered something. He lowered his voice again and whispered, "You know how sometimes I check the weather to see if it's gonna rain? I know it hardly ever does, but since I ride a bike, I wanna know ahead of time." He paused again and I saw him swallow hard like he was feeling apprehensive. His simple action caused me to start getting nervous all over again. "That storm...the night you left...I don't remember any weather forecast about that. You'd think they would warn us that was coming. I mean, how often do we get storms?" My eyes widened in shock because I remembered that I didn't hear anything about a storm coming to the Hollywood area either. Rain storms were rare so if one was coming our way, we were usually informed about it. Before I could even try to come up with an explanation, Tristan dropped another secret. "I felt like the storm was actually raging inside me. From the moment I finished reading your letter to the moment I collapsed on Jake's floor. But I really felt it when I was riding around looking for you."

Right at that moment, I felt terrible guilt for everything I put him through. Another apology was definitely in order and I tried to make him believe that I was being sincere. "I'm *so* sorry, baby. I'm sorry I put you through so much heartache and emotional distress. But I really didn't think you'd mind having some time away from me. I mean, you didn't want me to talk to you or touch you. So I thought it would best for both of us...for our souls...to just be apart for a little awhile; give us both time to think." I averted my eyes in shame as I thought back to how Autumn described Tristan's mental and emotional state after I left him. I thought about how I easily dismissed his feelings for his usual oversensitivity and overreactions. "Autumn told me how you were acting when you showed up at her apartment looking for me. She told me how bad you were crying and shaking. She said she couldn't even get through to you."

Tristan's voice was filled with emotion again and he finally expressed how badly I hurt him. "Bridget, I thought I was gonna fucking die. I kept thinking the worse; like you weren't ever gonna come back to me. I felt like I was in a nightmare. I couldn't believe you left me; especially after you admitted to cheating on me. I was thinking, 'Why would she hurt me even more?' I thought you stopped loving me." He paused and I saw tears beginning to fill his light blue eyes. He started blinking rapidly to keep them at bay and I saw him take a couple breaths to try and compose himself. His voice was still shaky when he continued speaking. "Then I started thinking that you ran off with Justin. I actually ringed him and threatened his life."

I was about to tell on myself again and reveal that I spoke to Justin but I wisely kept my trap shut. I remembered that old expression I used on Jake in the past: '*Some things are better left unsaid*' and decided to take my own advice. Instead, I brought the focus back to Autumn. "She told me you said you were going to kill yourself if I didn't come back."

Tristan gave me an intense look and it was reflected in his voice. "Yeah, I would've. I'm fucking serious. The thought of losing you and our baby drove me completely mad. I just couldn't function and I felt like I was breaking down."

My eyes began to fill with tears as I imagined the scene at Autumn's apartment. My voice trembled when I admitted, "I should've never left you, Tristan. You needed me. I should've gone home." I sobbed once and Tristan embraced me again. I sniffled and tried to compose myself but I turned into a blubbering mess. "I thought I was doing the right thing...but all I was doing was breaking your heart even more. I'm sorry, sweetheart. I'll never leave you again."

The room was quiet except for the sound of my pathetic sniffling. Tristan didn't say anything as he continued to hold me in an angel's embrace. Finally he spoke and he asked a question I wish he didn't. "How long were you planning to hide from me?"

I remembered my plan to escape to Ireland by using one of our vacation tickets that were given to both of us as a gift. I had no idea how long I would've stayed in my homeland. But I answered him truthfully when I said, "I really don't know. But not for long. I was going to keep my promise and come back to you. I would never leave you permanently."

Tristan released me and when I looked up at him again, I could see something burning in his azure eyes; it was deep and powerful and it began to enrapture me in a hypnotic spell. I don't think I blinked once as he continued speaking. The intensity had returned to Tristan's voice when he revealed yet another secret. "The longer I'm with you...the stranger I've been feeling. I feel like something wants to break out of me; it wants to be free. But I don't think I'm possessed like some *'Exorcist'* shit though. I feel like it's really a part of me; part of who I am. I mean, it's been with me all my life."

I thought back to a prediction I made about Tristan the night I confessed my infidelity and I heard myself repeating it quietly. "Maybe you're not human after all."

Tristan let out a breath through his nose as he smirked. "Trust me, I am. You know who my parents are and they're definitely human."

We were both quiet again as we gazed at each other. His masculine beauty has always been so appealing to me so I reached out and ran my fingers through his soft hair. I actually missed the feeling of his golden strands between my fingers. Tristan closed his eyes briefly as he enjoyed my loving affection. "Do you remember when you told me that some things in life just defy all logic?"

He opened his eyes and chuckled again. "Yeah, I said that 'cause my *life* defies all logic."

I smiled and spoke earnestly from my heart. "Well, I believe that too because I can't explain any of what you just told me. As much as I like things to make sense, I think I may have to just let this one go because my mind is totally baffled. Autumn has her bizarre dreams and you have an amazing gift too. You really *are* special, Tristan."

"I still believe the truth about what's going on with me is out there." He sighed heavily in frustration. "I just don't know where or how to figure it out."

My fingers were still enjoying themselves in Tristan's wheat-colored hair but soon they decided to travel south and caress his beautiful face. I moved closer to him because I wanted to feel more of my soul mate's gorgeous body against mine. I encircled my arms around him and a feeling of sheer contentment came over me as I was engulfed by his wonderful scent and his comforting warmth. I had forgotten all about my ugly betrayal which caused his broken heart. I forgot about our tears of anguish and my selfish abandonment of him. For a moment, we were lovers again. I kissed his Adam's apple tenderly and spoke softly to ease his worries. "Don't let it worry you, sweetheart. Just continue being you."

I wasn't able to ease his worry just yet because I could hear it in his voice when he replied, "But that's the thing...who am I?"

Tristan's pure vanilla skin was soft, smooth, and delicious. My lips and tongue began to ravish him with open-mouth kisses on his neck and chest. A sexual ache began to develop in the apex of my thighs so I rubbed my pussy against him in arousal. It wasn't long before he returned the gesture, and I could hear him moaning softly and feel him growing hard right between my legs. It would only be a matter of minutes before we were joined in passion. I smiled against his skin and held him as I conveyed all my love through my embrace. "You're Tristan Caleb Hathaway. My soul mate, my prince, my angel. That's who you are. And I don't ever want you to think you're fucked in the head again."

While we were holding each other I felt like Tristan had really forgiven me this time. I know he said it last night when he was crying but now I really felt like he did. He confirmed my assumption when he said, "I decided to give you another chance, darlin'. I put my full trust in you again. I realized that sometimes people deserve second chances. God knows I've been given plenty." I felt him kiss the top of my head and I began to cry silently in relief. "I don't think a comfort kiss is reason enough to destroy our marriage."

My voice was trembling because I was filled with heavy emotion. "Thank you, Tristan." I lifted my head up to look him in the eyes. Tristan smiled down at me and his long piano fingers wiped some of the tears from my cheeks. I cherished his touch and closed my eyes because I was right where I belonged. A soft sigh escaped my lips when I felt his fingers gently brush my eyelashes. "I swear I won't let you down again." I took a deep breath and swore an oath to my husband. "On my life, Tristan...I promise never to betray you again."

Tristan smoothed my hair away from my forehead and tucked a few strands behind both my ears. His smile was still as beautiful as ever. "Good, 'cause I don't think my heart will mend the next time you break it."

"It's my job to protect your heart, baby...not break it."

He searched my eyes and I held his gaze intently. How I loved getting lost in his sky blue eyes. He broke the spell when he whispered in a serious tone, "Do you really believe everything I told you?"

I responded immediately and directly from my heart. "Every word... I swear I do."

"Promise you'll keep my secret and never tell anyone."

I tilted my head up to seal my promise with a kiss. "I cross my heart."

I should've known my chaste promise kiss wouldn't satisfy his need. I guess he behaved long enough and now he was determined to have his way with me. He moved swiftly when I was least expecting it and this time he was able to roll us over so he was on top of me. My legs open instantly and his lean naked body was nestled between them in a natural position. Every part of him seemed to fit me just perfectly: his hand in mine, his manhood and my womanhood, his soul to my soul. He embraced me tightly and captured my mouth quickly. His kiss was deep and possessive; just the way I loved it. A moan escaped my throat as I felt his tongue plunder inside my mouth and reach every corner and crevice. His lips slanted over mine repeatedly and I couldn't help but to reach up and grasp the soft hair at the nape of his neck. His tongue glided across my lips and I felt him capture my bottom lip and suck it gently into his mouth.

As soon as he released it, I took his tongue prisoner and it was completely willing. I sucked on it greedily as our hips began to hump and grind against each other. Our moans of sheer pleasure became louder and louder as the passion between us began to swirl and mix with sinful lust. I could feel my pussy getting swollen the more his hardness rubbed against me. The feeling was so wonderful that I held him with equal strength and rocked my body against his. There was no space between us and I could feel every inch of him. Soon the headboard began to bang against the wall from our movements. We broke the kiss to come up for air and I could see that his lips were a little puffy from my passionate assault. I could feel myself trembling when he outlined the shape and curve of my lips with his tongue. Then he spoke softly but dominantly, "Let me do whatever I want. Submit to your prince."

I responded back in a breathless voice, "I'm your princess...my body is yours."

The next thing I knew, he took one of my hands, put it between our bodies, and made me put his erection deep inside me. He had complete control over me so I guided him in very slowly so that I could feel every inch as he entered me. I cried out in total bliss when I felt that he was all the way in; right to the base. He filled me completely and he didn't move for about five seconds. We just laid motionless and he let me relish in the feeling of our bodies being joined. It wasn't long until he started to move inside me. He started off slow and steady, but soon his thrusts became faster and more forceful. Then he put his head in the crook of my neck and just pounded straight into me without mercy. And every time he would slam into me, I would cry out in total rapture. I could feel my pussy getting wetter and he was sliding in and out of me with perfect ease.

He rose up to support himself on his arms and he moved his head to look into my eyes. We locked our gaze as we met each other stroke for stroke. Then he began talking to me in dominant tone. "You're mine, Bridget. You're fucking mine...do you hear me?"

I was breathing rapidly and trying to catch my breath at the same time. "Yes, Tristan! I'm yours!"

He cried out loudly and began panting as he thrusted inside me faster and faster. "Every fucking part of you is mine." Then all of a sudden he laid on top of me again, grabbed both my hands and held them above my head. The pleasure he was giving me was incredible and I wanted to cum so desperately. I was trying so hard to reach my peak but a part of me didn't want our love making to end just yet. I tried to relax a little so I closed my eyes and concentrated on what I was feeling in the place where we were joined. I could feel his hips rubbing against my inner thighs. As soon as I opened my legs as wide as they could go, I felt my body take him in even deeper. Tristan felt it too because he cried out again in passion and swore loudly. I could feel his raw erection driving into me harder and my sensitive pussy was tingling with pleasure all over. His lips crushed against mine again, and he held me possessively as he took my body and fucked me the way he wanted.

My eyes shot open when he rolled our joined bodies once again so that I was on top of him. I tried to sit up so I could ride my British stallion but he pulled me down against his body. "No, stay right here. I wanna hold you. Just fuck me, Bridget. Fuck me hard." He kept his legs flat on the bed which told me that he wanted me to do most of the work. I was in such an aroused state that I didn't mind in the least. Tristan lifted his hips off the bed and drove his erection up into my pussy repeatedly while he kept me in a tight embrace. I humped up and down on him in a sexual frenzy while I entangled my fingers into his hair. Our lips melted together divinely and our tongues mated fiercely. The only sound in the room was our moaning combined with the sound of the headboard hitting the wall.

Soon the pleasure became too much for me and I had to hold my gorgeous prince in my arms. A strange thing occurred because our bodies began to wrap around each other in a close and intimate lover's embrace. We held each other closely as we made love that I felt like we were becoming one. As we kissed, we began to breathe through our noses because we didn't want to detach our mouths from one another.

My sexual peak was closing in on me with great speed and I could feel myself about to jump over the edge. I had to break the kiss to tell my prince that his princess was about to cum all over his magnificent cock. But before I could speak, Tristan spoke in an urgent voice. "I want you to know...this is my favorite position. I love having you like this, Bridget." His pace was becoming erratic and I could see that he was sweating from exertion. I was sweating too and I could hear our bodies slapping against each other and the sound was turning me on even more. My womanly flower was oozing with feminine nectar and Tristan's lips met mine briefly before he said breathlessly, "Your prince is about to cum. Cum with me, princess...cum with me right now! I wanna feel your pretty twat cream all over my cock!"

In that next second, I screamed his name out loud and came in absolute ecstasy. "TRISTAN!" I granted my prince's request and gushed all over his throbbing hardness. The sensation was so intense that I yelled out again in orgasmic pleasure.

Tristan followed immediately after me and he cried out my name too. "BRIDGET!" We laid there bucking and humping against each other as the wonderful tremors of sexual pleasure rippled through our bodies at the same time. We held each other so tightly, it was a miracle that either of us could even breathe. But this was the way we usually made love. It was more than physical; it was a connection so deep and so spiritual that we felt it in our shared soul. I began to whimper and I tried to keep my body still because I wanted to feel Tristan's full release. The sensation was almost indescribable. His essence was released in powerful spurts and he filled me quickly and completely. I could feel myself leaking from the combination of my own feminine juices and Tristan's erupting manhood. I had a strong feeling that whatever I was feeling, he was feeling as well. He began to whimper from the pleasure too and he pressed his pelvis against mine and held it there by grabbing my butt. He continued his release and I didn't dare move my body a single inch until my prince's cock was completely spent. His voice was trembling with all the emotions he was feeling from his intense orgasm. "Do you love your angel? How much do you love me, darlin'?"

I mustered up as much remaining strength as I could so I could lift my head and gaze upon his beautiful face. Tristan's blue eyes were staring back at me and his near-flawless ivory skin was pleasantly flushed. A thin sheen of sweat covered his brow and I threaded my fingers through his semi-wet hair and gazed adoringly at him. He smiled and I returned the gesture and replied, "I love my angel; for all eternity, baby." I kissed his lips before I rested my head against his chest in total exhaustion.

The silence crept back into the bedroom because our breathing began to steady. I knew it wouldn't take long for us to crash land from this amazing and wild sexual high. I could already feel myself getting drowsy. I was breathing deeply because Tristan's unique masculine scent seemed intensified. I heard his voice rumble in his chest. "There's no way in hell I'd ever let Justin experience this with you. My soul will never share you, Bridget. You're my princess...forever."

I smiled at Tristan's blatant possessiveness and I responded sleepily, "I know." Even though the room was still illuminated, I closed my eyes to the sound of his heart's lullaby and I felt his embrace tighten once again. Then suddenly, a thought entered my mind: *Tristan...wrap your wings around me while I sleep.*

I felt him put his nose to my hair and I heard him inhale deeply. Then I felt him kiss the top of my head again. I was beginning to fall asleep but I heard his boyish voice that was laced with a sexy British accent whisper into my hair, "I always do, love."

Chapter 27

I CAN HONESTLY SAY THAT pregnancy is one of the most amazing feelings. It's true what they say; you really do form a special bond with your child while they're still in the womb. It's a connection unlike anything else and much different than the connection I share with Tristan. I was now at the end of my second trimester and I noticed that the more my belly grew, the more protective I was of it. I was also prone to talking to the baby a lot. Instead of my usual inner monologues, I was expressing my thoughts and opinions to the baby. I could just imagine how crazy I looked the other day when I was talking to the baby while I was grocery shopping. I was in the frozen-foods section trying to decide on an ice cream flavor and I asked out loud, "So which one do you think your father would prefer... his favorite cookies-n-cream or this new *Sundae Explosion?*" We decided to be daring and buy Tristan the *Sundae Explosion*.

But what I love the most are the times where Tristan and I bond with the baby together. Sometimes before we go to sleep, he puts headphones on my belly so the baby can listen to music for a little while. I think he's introduced our baby to every genre of music except Country & Western. Being pregnant also caused me to worry a lot more than usual and I was concerned that I wouldn't be a nurturing mother. Even though Tristan reminds me constantly that I'm already a nurturer, I was worried I wouldn't feel a bond with our baby once it was born.

I really do enjoy being pregnant, but it's not without its discomforts. Swollen ankles, heartburn, frequent bathroom visits, and backaches just to name a few. Not to mention experiencing my first case of embarrassing and painful hemorrhoids. I also gained weight, and lately I've been feeling very self-conscious about my body. Either Tristan hasn't noticed or he was avoiding the subject of my extra poundage to spare my feelings. I was just grateful that he was still interested in me sexually. I was surprised when he expressed how much he enjoyed looking at my bare swollen belly. He also admitted to me that he was very turned on by it. Well, that made *one* of us.

But I realized that the good definitely outweigh the bad. I pray every day that Tristan has given me a beautiful child and God will make them healthy. I was really looking forward to bringing our precious bundle into the world so it could finally see its mother who's been making random conversation with it, and its father who's been exposing it to British rock music.

This morning was an extremely important day because it was the day of my first ultrasound. We were also going to find out the sex of the baby. All throughout my pregnancy, Tristan insisted we were having a little girl because he had a strong belief in Autumn's dream. I'll admit that I believed her dream too but I didn't want to assume anything. That's the main reason why I haven't planned a baby shower and why the nursery is still void of any decorations or furniture. We decided not to have a unisex theme because we wanted to wait until the sex of the baby was confirmed. Today was the moment of truth and we were both anxious and excited.

I was accommodated in a very comfortable bed in one of the ultrasound rooms. Tristan was sitting next to me in an armchair and he was holding my hand for support. My belly was already exposed but it wasn't coated yet with the dreaded cold and wet goo. While we were waiting for Dr. Boykin to come in the room and perform the actual procedure, I noticed Tristan's eyes were fixed on the ultrasound monitor. I was curious as to where his mind had wandered off to, so I decided to pick his brain. "What are you thinking about?"

He finally tore his eyes away from the screen and looked at me. "I'm thinking about what I'm gonna see on that screen." A beautiful smile graced his already beautiful face. "I know it's a girl. I just know it."

His confidence in Autumn's dream was astounding. Something inside me decided to play the Devil's Advocate. "I don't know. You might see some little boy bits on the screen."

He laughed and shook his head. There was no persuading him otherwise because he was sticking to his firm belief. "Nah, Katie's inside you. I know she is." His voice lowered and the look in his eyes was one of pure affection. "I can't wait to see our baby. I can't even begin to tell you how I'm feeling right now." I felt him give my hand a tight squeeze and then rub the back of it with his thumb.

I smiled warmly at him because I was so happy we were about to share this special moment together. "I know how you feel because I feel the same way. I've been carrying the baby for over six months and I really want to see who's been moving around inside me." Tristan smiled back and then he placed his other hand on my belly. He rubbed it slowly and gently and I covered his hand with mine as we connected with our unborn child once again.

The door to our room opened and Dr. Boykin appeared. She gave us both a friendly smile and her voice was laced with enthusiasm. "So, today's the big day, huh? Are you both ready?" Tristan and I nodded and she laughed lightly before she took a seat on the other side of my bed next to the monitor. "What do you think we're going to see? You think you're having a girl?"

Tristan replied with confidence, "I know we are."

Dr. Boykin laughed again. "You sound pretty confident, Tristan."

He smiled and I saw his cute dimple on his left cheek. "Yeah, I am. I just know we're having a daughter. I can feel it, doc."

"Well, we'll see about that in a few minutes." Dr. Boykin slathered my belly with that cold wet goo without warning. I made a sound of surprise and she quickly apologized. "I'm sorry Bridget, I should've warned you first. I know it's cold." She spread the goo very generously and it peaked Tristan's curiosity because he reached out and tested some of it for himself. I watched him in amusement as he grinned and rubbed it between his fingers. I laughed out loud when he actually put it to his nose.

"It smells like medicine," he remarked. "And yeah, it is kinda cold."

Once she was done basting me like a Thanksgiving turkey, she turned on the monitor. Then she put the ultrasound wand against my belly and started moving it around. I think I was holding my breath in anticipation because the next thing she said was, "Bridget, you can breathe, you know." I let out a nervous, shaky breath and continued staring at the screen intently. I couldn't really see anything but a lot of fuzzy gray matter. Was there really a baby in all that confusion? I guess so because she exclaimed, "Oh, here's the head!" I tried squinting my eyes but I couldn't make out anything that resembled a human head.

Tristan was feeling similar because he remarked, "I don't see anything."

That's when she started drawing on the monitor. Once she did that, Tristan and I responded in unison. "Ohhhh!"

As she continued to move the wand against my belly, she showed us more of the little person who was camping out inside me. "And here's the heart. Do you see it beating?"

I responded breathlessly, "Oh my God. Yeah, I see it." I could feel myself getting emotional because I could see the beating heart and I could also see the baby moving around.

Dr. Boykin's voice was filled with joy when she exclaimed again, "Oh my, it's sucking its thumb! Can you see the little hand?" I could feel tears pricking at the back of my eyes because I saw our baby and it was really sucking its little thumb. I heard Tristan laughing beside me so I turned to look at him and I could tell he was thoroughly amused. Then her tone of voice changed. She still sounded surprised but I didn't get the same feeling as before. "Oh...oh...I see..." She paused and I held my breath again because I wasn't sure if something was wrong. Oh God, please don't let her see any deformities.

Tristan was still holding my hand and I squeezed it tightly because I could feel myself beginning to panic. She didn't finish her sentence so I asked urgently, "What is it?!?"

She stilled the wand movement and turned her head to face us. My eyes were wide as I waited for her to reveal what she saw. All of a sudden, a smile played at the corners of her mouth and her eyes focused on Tristan. "You were right." She paused again and I think she was doing it just to add to the suspense. "You're having a daughter." She smiled brightly before she turned back towards the screen again and started drawing on it. "Look, there's the vulva. I don't see any sign of a developing penis so I'm 99.9% sure you're having a girl."

After Dr. Boykin revealed the sex of our baby, I gasped in shock and turned my head swiftly to look at my husband's reaction. What I saw made my heart skip a beat. He was actually crying. Tristan's azure eyes were glassy but I could tell he was happy. When his eyes met mine, he didn't hold his tears at bay; he allowed them to fall freely. For a moment he was just looking at me with an expression of adoration and I held his gaze intently. He took my hand that he was holding, closed his eyes briefly and placed a light kiss on the inside of my wrist. While still holding my hand, he stood from his chair so he could lean over and press his lips against mine. His kiss was so tender and I couldn't help but to thread my fingers through his hair with my free hand. All I could think about was how there really was a little Katie inside me all this time… and Tristan was the one who gave her to me. And I no longer had to call our baby 'it' because her gender was finally revealed. Soon my emotions overpowered me and I could feel my own tears leaking from my eyes. When Tristan unsealed his lips from mine, he whispered affectionately, "You have no idea how much I love you."

"I love you too," I whispered back. Then I wiped the tears from his cheeks.

He sniffled once before he spoke to me again. But this time his voice was stronger and it had an undertone of smugness. "I told you Katie was inside you."

I smirked as I corrected him. "Actually…Autumn told me." We both chuckled as we thought back to her weird dream that started it all.

We were relieved when the doctor told us that Katie looked completely healthy and was growing and developing normally. She also reassured me that my weight was fine because I expressed earlier that I was concerned I may be gaining too much.

After the ultrasound, she was standing next to me while she cleaned the messy goo off my belly when Tristan asked, "We're gonna get a picture of her right?" He pointed to the monitor that was now turned off. "The ultrasound of Katie?"

She smiled fondly. "Of course. I'll make sure you get it before you leave."

Once I was clean, I sat up and pulled my shirt down to cover my belly. That's when he spoke up again. "Dr. Boykin?"

"Yes, Tristan?"

"I wanted to talk to you about something." She sat down again and Tristan moved towards the bed so he could sit next to me. We sat side-by-side facing her and she looked at him expectedly. "I was reading one of those pamphlets that you gave us a few months ago about birthing pools." I turned to look at him curiously because he never mentioned to me that he read about those. "You know...water births?"

She nodded in understanding. "Yes, yes. I know what you mean."

"Well, I was wondering...you know..." He paused and turned to look at me briefly before he turned his attention back to her. "Do you think we could have one of those? Could Bridget have Katie in one of those pools?" This request of his was much unexpected and I was completely speechless. All I could do was continue looking at him in mild shock. He must've sensed my gaze on him or maybe my inner thoughts because that's when he turned to look at me again. "Babe, I wanted to talk to you about it but first I wanted to ask Dr. Boykin if it was possible. I was thinking that we could really bond with Katie if you gave birth to her in the water."

He turned towards the doctor again. "I was online and I saw some videos on water births." He met my eyes and I saw unmistaken affection behind them. He took my hand and entwined our fingers. When he spoke again, his voice was softer. "Just imagine it darlin'...I would be right there with you...holding you in my arms while you give birth to our daughter." His smile was lovely and he tucked my hair behind my ear with tenderness. I couldn't help but smile back because I had no idea he desired such an intimate birth. "I could even help you give birth to her and I'll give you my strength if you need it. I told you that I'd be with you every step of the way...and I meant it, love. I thought you would prefer to give birth in the water rather than in a hospital bed with your legs spread wide for all to see."

I couldn't argue with Tristan on that point because I was definitely feeling uneasy about spreading my legs for the whole hospital room. Dr. Boykin filled me in on more of the details by saying, "Basically, you would be in a small pool of warm water after you go into labor. You decide what position is best for you while you deliver. From what I'm told, the water helps you to relax and it does lessen the labor pains. Plus the fact that you can get in any comfortable position you want, allows you to control the delivery. It's a very natural way to give birth. And yes...Tristan would be in the pool with you and he could support you in whichever way you see fit. The baby and the placenta are both usually delivered in the water. It doesn't hurt the baby and once Katie is born, she's quickly removed from the water and placed in your arms with the umbilical cord still attached. That's usually the moment when you and Tristan really bond with her. A midwife is usually present to assist with the delivery and administer any pain medications if you want them."

At the mention of a midwife, I had to interrupt her. I didn't want a midwife to help me bring Katie into the world; I wanted her. "Dr. Boykin, I don't want a midwife. I want *you* to be there. I want *you* to help me bring Katie into the world. You know I've always seen you as more than my doctor. I've known you for ten years." My eyes filled with unshed tears once again at the thought of her not being there. "You're like my aunt."

She smiled at me and I could see her eyes filling with tears too. Her voice wavered slightly when she replied, "Thank you, Bridget. That means a lot to me." She dabbed at her eyes and then she took a moment to compose herself. Her voice was stronger when she continued. "If that's what you want, then I'll be there for your delivery. You already have my home number." She chuckled.

I smiled appreciatively. "Thanks. So, are there birthing pools at the hospital? How does it work exactly? I mean, do I have to reserve one or something?"

Tristan seemed to have it all figured out because he jumped right in to answer my question. "There are places where you can order a pool. They're inflatable and part of a water birth kit that they deliver to your home."

I was truly amazed because he definitely did his research on the subject. Then my brows knitted in confusion when I realized what he was implying. "To our *home?*" Surely I thought he'd be rushing me to the hospital once my water broke and the contractions started.

And just when I thought he couldn't shock me any further, he replied quietly, "I want us to have Katie at home, don't you? We have plenty of space in our bedroom to set up the pool."

I should've known; Tristan was the king of shock value. I couldn't believe what I was hearing and I was utterly surprised that he wanted a home birth. But I was also touched that he wanted us to bring our first child into the world in such a meaningful way. I leaned into him and put my arm around his waist because I was filled with such love and devotion towards him. He put his arm around my shoulder and kissed the top of my head. As I inhaled deeply to take in his unique masculine scent, I took a moment to contemplate his requests. The idea of delivering Katie in the comfort of my own home, and in the arms of the person I love more than anyone in the world seemed so perfect. It didn't take me very long to come to a decision. I smiled up at him and spoke softly. "Yes, I want to have Katie at home...in the water...with you."

We were temporarily lost in each other's eyes, but Dr. Boykin's voice broke the spell. "Your due date is February 28th or March 1st, so I'll be sure to make myself available on those days."

On our way home from the ultrasound center, Tristan asked me to call Autumn and tell her that her dream has now been confirmed one-hundred percent true. I wasn't sure what kind of reaction she would have so I braced myself for it. I turned on the speakerphone and dialed her number. When I heard her pick up, I made the announcement gleefully. "Hey Aut, guess what? We just found out we're having a girl."

I guess she needed to let the news process in her head because she didn't respond for a couple seconds. But then she screamed out loud in joy and disbelief just as I expected. "OH MY GOD! ARE YOU SERIOUS?!?"

Tristan could hear her big mouth through the phone and he laughed. I laughed too and replied, "Yeah, I am. I had my first ultrasound today and we saw little Katie on the monitor. Aut, she was sucking her thumb! Can you believe it?!?"

Autumn was laughing and crying at the same time. "Oh my God, I can't believe it. I wish I could've been there. So, I'm gonna have a little niece? And you're gonna name her Katie, right?"

"Yep. Actually, we're naming her after Tristan's mom but we'll call her Katie."

"Bridge, I'm so happy for you guys." She paused and I heard her sniffling. "I am so freaking out right now...you have no idea. I can't believe my dream was right again."

"Trust me, the feeling was mutual. But it only lasted a little while... until I saw my little princess moving around."

Tristan spoke loudly so she could hear him. "I wasn't freaked! I never doubted you for a second, Aut!"

She laughed. "You have a picture of her right; from your ultrasound?"

I carefully pulled Katie's ultrasound picture out from a manila folder that was sitting on my lap. I gazed at her shadowed form adoringly as I replied, "I sure do and I can't wait to show you." Then I remembered someone else who I wanted to share the news with. "Oh! I have to tell my mom!"

"Okay, well I'll be over in a little while. Will you be home?"

"Yeah, we're on our way home now."

After we hung up with each other, I called my mom to tell her that she and Dad would have a granddaughter in a couple months. She was almost as excited as Autumn but she also said, "Honey, you should let me take you shopping for the baby now. I think I've waited long enough, don't you? Besides, it's time for you and Tristan to start working on the nursery."

That's when I remembered a little thing called a baby shower. "I'd like to have my baby shower first, Mom. You can take me shopping for whatever I don't get. And Tristan and I still have to decide on what we're going to do with Katie's nursery."

Tristan chimed in loudly, "Whatever you want, babe!"

There was silence on her end but when she finally spoke, I was surprised by what came out of her mouth and that she actually sounded worried. "You're going to invite me to your shower, aren't you?" My mother's question pulled at my heart strings. She was probably under the impression that my baby shower would just be for me and my friends. But I would never think of leaving her out. If Tristan's mom and grandmother didn't live on the other side of the Atlantic Ocean, I would invite them too. But I didn't think a baby shower for a few hours during the day was worth the trip; especially knowing how hesitant they both are about flying these days. I was confident that they wouldn't mind sending a few baby gifts through the mail. Besides, they sent gifts through the mail for our birthdays and our wedding anniversary.

I had to reassure my mother that I planned on including her. "Of course, Mom. I wouldn't leave you out. I was planning on inviting you anyway."

She seemed to sigh a breath of relief. "Oh good." Then it seemed as if she read my mind a few moments ago. "Are Tristan's mother and grandmother coming too?"

"No, they're not." I looked at Tristan when I spoke my next words. "But I'm sure they'll send us something when he tells them the news." He briefly took his eyes off the road to glance at me and nod affirmatively.

"What are you naming the baby?"

"We're naming her after Tristan's mom."

"What about her middle name? Have you decided on that yet?"

Her question caused me to knit my brow in confusion. "I don't think you understand. We're naming her after Kate so it's going to be her *full* name."

There was more silence on her end and then I heard her reply quietly, "Oh."

I couldn't help but wonder if she was disappointed or maybe even a little jealous. I felt she deserved a full explanation. "Mom, we already decided this like..." I looked over at Tristan and remembered his request to name our baby after his mother even before I knew I was pregnant. "A long time ago. Tristan wanted to name our daughter after his mom even before we found out we were pregnant. He's my husband and I love him so I want to do this for him. Plus, I love his mom too." I wanted to add that she was like my second mother but I wasn't sure if making a statement like that would upset her. Tristan glanced at me with an unreadable expression before he turned his eyes back on the road. He didn't say anything but I wondered what he was thinking. Right at that moment, I wished I possessed the same bizarre mind-reading abilities that he did.

"Okay, well...I was just wondering."

We were approaching our house when I said, "Mom, I have to go now. I'll let you know the date for the shower, okay?"

Once we got inside the house, I noticed he was heading towards the kitchen. I had a sneaking suspicion that it would be a repeat of what happened when we found out we were going to be parents. I decided to test my assumption so I asked curiously, "You're going to be on the phone for awhile, aren't you?"

He turned to look at me with a wide grin. "Hell yeah! I'm gonna tell everybody!" He walked quickly towards the kitchen and within a couple seconds, I heard him exclaiming to his mother that we were having a girl. He only spoke to her for about a minute before he met me back in the living room and handed me the cordless phone with a smile. "She wants to talk to you." And this time...I was ready to share their happiness. As expected, she and Nanny wanted to send us things for the baby. I told her that once I put a baby registry together, I would send her the link and she and Nanny could decide what they wanted to buy. I was right once again because after I gave Tristan the phone back, he was on it for at least another half-hour spreading the news of our daughter.

When Autumn arrived at our house, she greeted me with a huge congratulatory hug. She was still so excited and talking a hundred miles per minute that I could barely keep up with her. We were sitting in the living room together and I showed her the picture of Katie from the ultrasound. I watched her face intently and I could see that it was full of admiration. She remarked wistfully, "I can't wait to see what she looks like."

At that moment, I was curious about the little girl she saw in her dream and I wondered if the real Katie would turn out to look like her. Since the vision was only in Autumn's mind, I tried to get her to describe Katie in more detail. "Hey Aut, what did Katie look like in your dream? I know you said she had blonde hair and blue eyes, but what else do you remember?"

Autumn cast her hazel eyes towards the ceiling as she thought back to the dream she had many months ago. "She was about three or four years old in my dream. Her hair was long and wavy, and her eyes were the same color as Tristan's. She didn't have freckles like you but her face was a total combo of you and Tris. I remember when she smiled at me, she had a dimple on her left cheek just like him so I knew she was definitely his." Autumn's brows knitted together in confusion when she said, "I thought it was weird that she had a British accent too." She shrugged and I narrowed my eyes in suspicion because that was definitely odd. I started thinking that maybe Katie was mimicking her father's accent. Either that, or perhaps Tristan and I would move to England in the future and raise her there. "But what I remember most was how pretty she was." Her eyes finally met mine and we smiled at each other. I wished so badly that I could see the vision of Katie in her mind but I guess I would have to wait a few years. I was filled with such happiness and relief at the strong possibility that Katie would take after her beautiful father and have his attractive Nordic features.

All of a sudden, I saw the expression change on Autumn's face as quickly as you change the channels on a television. She slapped my knee and shouted excitedly, "Oooh! Your baby shower! You should let me organize it! I can start on the guest list right now!"

A look of confusion appeared on my face because I wasn't aware that baby showers were supposed to be major events. I was planning to have a small one here at the house with just a few friends and my mother. My mind flashed back to my extravagant birthday party last year when Autumn went all out on the festivities. I didn't want to make such a big deal out of my baby shower. Not to mention, I didn't want a large amount of people in my nice house; people I'd have to clean up after once the party was over. Even though I knew Autumn was an incredible party planner and hostess, I had to pass on her offer this time. I gave her knee a gentle pat before I regretfully deflated her excitement. "That's okay, Aut. I think I can handle it. Besides, I don't want a big shower and I only want to invite certain people. And I'm going to have it here at the house."

Now it was her turn to look confused. "Huh? Bridge, don't you know that the more people you invite, the more gifts you'll get? By the time it's over...you won't need to buy anything. You'll be totally covered!"

That was a nice thought and it was a very tempting idea but I still wanted to buy some of my own things for our baby. After all, I did promise my mother she could take me shopping. If everyone else bought me everything I need, what would be left for us to buy? "Yeah, I know but I still want to get some of Katie's stuff myself. Thanks, but I'll organize my own baby shower."

Her face fell and she looked dejected but it only lasted a few seconds because then she seemed to want to compromise with me. "Okay, well... will you at least let me design the invitations? You can invite whoever you want but I'll design them and send them out for you. I'll also help you set up here at the house if you want."

I was so flattered that she wanted to help that I couldn't reject her again. "Sure, you can do that! You can even help me put together my baby registry."

A bright smile instantly lit up her face and her mood shifted to exuberance once more. "Thanks! And what about the nursery? Have you and Tris decided what you're gonna do?"

Right at that moment, Tristan waltzed into the living room. He must've caught that part of our conversation because he added cryptically, "Jake said he wants to help with the nursery." He sat down next to me on the sofa. "You know he's artistic and shit so he said he wants to do something special. I told him I'd talk to you first but he said whatever you want him to do...he'll do it. I figured he'll be helping us anyway so I may as well let him put his personal touch on *something*."

Autumn was still filled with enthusiasm. "Hey, I have an idea! Let's go online and take a look at some nurseries. Maybe you'll get an idea of what you wanna do with it."

Tristan and I agreed and the two of them followed me into my personal office. We were on the computer for awhile looking at pictures of nurseries and putting together the baby registry. We decided to get the crib ourselves since it would probably be one of the more expensive items. After viewing many different ideas, we finally decided on a whimsical theme for Katie's room. Tristan pleaded with me not to go overboard with pink so I complied with his request and settled on pink, white, and green.

It wasn't long after Autumn and I started on the subject of the baby shower, that Tristan got up from his seat and made a hasty exit. I started talking about how I wanted all the decorations in the living room to be pink and girly. That's when he lost interest in the conversation and commented that he didn't feel like he was of any more use to me. Autumn and I just laughed as he closed the door behind him. I gave her full reign over the design of the invitations and I told her I wanted to invite my mom, Dr. Boykin, Becca, Lauren, Michelle, and Amy. I also told her she could help me shop for the decorations and figure out what food I would be serving.

We planned my baby shower for one month from today and when I finally informed Tristan of our plans, he surprised me by saying he would hire a caterer so I wouldn't have to cook. He remarked, "You should be doing as little work as possible, babe. Actually, you should let me and Aut set up so you can just sit back and relax. Your only job should be opening Katie's presents."

I smiled warmly at his thoughtfulness. "You know I won't sit back while you guys do all the work." He looked like he was about to object so I quickly added, "But I won't do anything too stressful." I gave him a peck on the lips to reassure him. "I promise."

Over the next few weeks, the nursery was slowly but surely coming along. Tristan and Jake did all the painting and they also put the rug down. Jake and I decided on a corner in the room where me and Katie would bond and I could breastfeed her. He told me he would do something nice for our special little mother-daughter nook. Autumn and I hung all the curtains, and we looked on in amusement while the Hathaway brothers put Katie's crib together. Between the two of them, I think they smashed their fingers with the hammer at least ten times. I've never heard more swear words come from a baby's room in all my life.

On the afternoon of my baby shower, Autumn and I had the kitchen set up with the food and drinks from the caterer. The dining room table was accented with pink and white place settings and decorations with a baby shower theme. The living room was also transformed into a very pink and girly atmosphere. We had balloons, ribbons, flower arrangements, and even a few stuffed animals. My mother showed up early to help out and her many wrapped gifts were already on the table in the living room with Autumn's. They both bought Katie a lot of things and so did Tristan's parents and his grandmother. I started to wonder if there would be anything left for me to buy after the shower was over. Tristan didn't really help because we shooed him away and he retreated to the basement to play with his toys.

When he finally came back upstairs, he entered the living room from the hallway. I was standing there making some last-minute adjustments and I glanced at him. His eyes were wide with surprise but his face wore an expression of distaste. He commented disgustedly, "Oh bloody hell. I've walked into a pink nightmare."

I turned towards him and put a hand on my hip. I lifted a haughty eyebrow in response to his rude comment about my decorations and retorted back, "Oh shut up, you. You wouldn't say that if we were having a boy and everything was blue." I watched his eyes dart around the room and he shook his head like he was trying to clear the fuzziness from his mind. I decided a little teasing was in order, so I walked over to him with a fresh-cut pink rose in hand and caressed the side of his face with the soft petals. I smiled and gave him a seductive look because I could tell he was enjoying my flirtatious gesture.

He grinned at me, and to my surprise, he took the rose from my hand. First he put it to his nose and briefly inhaled the fragrance before he placed it in my hair by tucking it above my right ear. Tristan was being so romantic, that I encircled my arms around his waist to close some of the distance between us. I thought to myself: *Where oh where did this gorgeous man truly come from?* When he leaned down to kiss me, my lips instantly melted with his and we savored each other's mouths for a short moment. Then I felt his words against my lips and his breath was a sweet whisper. "You have another guest, love."

It took a moment for me to recover because I found myself getting lost in him. He jerked his head towards the front window and I looked at him questioningly. "I don't hear anyone." That's when the doorbell rang. He looked into my eyes and at that moment, he reminded me that he possessed acute hearing. I stood there looking at him in amazement but he walked away towards the foyer to answer the door.

When he opened it, he greeted our guest by simply saying, "Just follow the pink." I heard distinct female laughter and seconds later I saw Becca come into the living room holding a few wrapped gifts in her arms.

I greeted her with a welcoming hug and then I introduced her to my mother who was waiting to take the gifts from her. Tristan came back over to me and made an unexpected announcement. "Anthony just ringed me. He got me an audition so I have to go. I'm sorry darlin', I know it's your baby shower and everything." I looked at him in confusion because didn't he know he wasn't even supposed to be here? I was about to remind him but he dropped a chaste kiss on my lips and walked away. He disappeared from my view but I heard him yell out, "Love ya babe! Have fun!"

Lauren was the next person to arrive and my mother was absolutely thrilled to meet her. Honestly, I think it was the red hair and freckles we share in common that won my mother over. I remarked that everyone says we look alike and I was pleasantly surprised when she agreed wholeheartedly. "She could've been your younger sister, Bridget." Lauren laughed joyously and it didn't take long for the two of them to warm up to each other.

The blonde beauty from The Hills known as Michelle arrived next, followed by Dr. Boykin. It was obvious that my mother and the doctor were happy to see each other. I think part of the reason was because they were the two oldest women at the baby shower. It wasn't long until they sat down together on the sofa to catch up on old times.

Amy was the last person to arrive and when I saw her, she still looked as thin and beautiful as ever. I guess it was my own self-consciousness due to my pregnancy but now I was beginning to feel like 'The Fat Friend'. Amy was ecstatic to see me and all she wanted to do was to touch my belly. She was absolutely amazed by it. When I told her it was going to get even bigger she replied excitedly, "Make sure you put up the pictures because I really want to see it! I saw the ones you have on your MySpace but I was anxious to see your belly up close."

During the party, I showed Katie's ultrasound picture to everyone. Tristan and I put the picture in its own special frame and I let all the girls pass it around. I had just started to open the gifts when Tristan came back home. He walked into the living room again and looked around in amazement when he saw that I was surrounded by gifts for our baby. All of a sudden, I heard Michelle exclaim to my left, "Hey Triscuit! You can't be here." I looked over at her and she was jerking her thumb in the direction he came in. "You have to leave."

Autumn chimed in, "Yeah, beat it you male intruder! Go on... scram!"

I started laughing but I explained to him gently, "This is my baby shower, sweetheart. You're not supposed to be here."

I could see Tristan's eyes as they settled on each of us looking back at him like he had The Plague. He wore an expression of utter confusion and it was reflected in his voice when he asked innocently, "I thought that was for bachelorette parties?"

Autumn rolled her eyes and sighed exasperatedly. "You are *so* ignorant."

Tristan scowled at her but his expression lightened as he approached us to inspect some of the already-opened gifts. He picked up the pink pacifier with the word 'Princess' that Michelle bought. He was examining it in his hands before he looked up at me with his sad puppy dog eyes. "I wanna see Katie's baby stuff too."

My mother was sitting next to me and I could feel her gaze on me. I turned to look at her but I couldn't read the message she was trying to convey through her lovely emerald eyes. Once she scooted over, I knew what she was telling me: '*Let your husband be included.*'

She patted the seat next to me which was now unoccupied. "Come here, son. Come here and sit down."

Tristan's feet moved quickly and I could tell he was excited to take his place beside me. But before he sat down, he paused his steps to give Autumn another dirty look. I swear, sometimes they really *were* like brother and sister.

Lauren handed me a gift to open and once I removed the wrapping paper, it revealed a square box which held a child-size pink and white soccer ball. All the females in the room laughed in amusement. I looked over at my fellow redhead with a smile but also with a look that was asking for an explanation. She grinned sheepishly before she explained, "It's from Jake." That explanation made perfect sense so I started laughing too. Tristan took the ball from me and the way he was admiring it with an approving expression, told me that he was absolutely elated by this particular gift.

I think Autumn could sense it too because she asked a very interesting question. "So Tris, are you gonna teach Katie how to play soccer?" Immediately after her sentence, I remembered the part of her dream where Katie was chasing after a soccer ball.

I found myself staring at Tristan intently while I waited for him to answer. He looked over at Autumn with a grin and replied cheerfully, "You know I am. My little girl is definitely gonna play footie." He turned his attention back to the ball and he wore a thoughtful expression as he continued speaking. "She's gonna be the best on her team." He laughed lightly. "Yeah...she'll be the captain of her team." He nodded to himself and I could hear the pride and wistfulness in his voice. "Katie is gonna be the next Mia Hamm."

Autumn looked over at me and we shared a knowing smile. Right at that moment, I wished even more that I could see her dream in my own mind.

After I opened all of Katie's gifts, we had dinner and dessert in the dining room. The baby shower lasted into the early evening but soon most of our guests decided to leave. Autumn was the last one to leave because she helped us bring all of Katie's gifts into her nursery. Once she finally left, Tristan and I looked around the Katie's room in astonishment because of all the stuff we had. I had my hands on my hips when I predicted, "We have our work cut out for us."

Tristan chuckled. "Yeah, I know. But we can do it. You'll see...we'll have her nursery finished in no time."

I stared at the corner that Jake and I chose and decided to see if I could get a sneak-preview from his little brother. "So, what's Jake doing to my corner? Did he tell you?"

He looked at me with a smirk. "Yeah, he told me." Then he turned away from me and moved towards the crib. I watched him as he ran his hands across the top like he was admiring it. He finally finished his sentence when he looked at me over his shoulder. "But I'm not telling *you*."

That night after we made love, Tristan was holding me in his arms. I could feel myself beginning to doze off and as always, his wonderful beating heart provided me with the perfect bedtime lullaby. The bedroom was still illuminated and I heard him speak quietly. "Bridget, don't go to sleep yet. I need to tell you something."

"What is it?" I responded sleepily.

He didn't answer me for a couple seconds. But when he did, it made me sit up in bed. "Kelly called me earlier today." I looked at him with wide-eyes and I could feel my breathing increasing. He tried to ease my worry by saying, "I didn't wanna tell you before 'cause I didn't wanna spoil your day...or your mood. But I think you should know now."

The memory of the blonde home wrecker known as Kelly made me grind my teeth in anger. I spoke through clenched teeth when I asked, "What did she want?"

"She's been calling a lot lately. She always calls from random numbers and I've been telling her to leave me the fuck alone. I thought she would've learned her lesson when Autumn beat her arse but I guess not." Suddenly, my mind was filled with worry because once again...she was threatening my relationship with Tristan. He took my hands in his in an attempt to comfort me because he could probably sense that I was getting upset. I couldn't even speak because I kept wondering why she was bothering him again. "I didn't tell you when she first started calling me 'cause I didn't want you to worry. It actually started a few months ago but now it's getting out of hand so I had to change my fucking number again."

I repeated my earlier question. "What did she want? What has she been saying?"

I could hear the annoyance in his voice when he answered me. "She wants *me*. She keeps saying that she's better for me and that I should leave you for her. She says she loves me and she hasn't stopped thinking about me. I asked her, 'What about when my mate beat the shit out of you? Were you thinking about me then?' First she tried to say that Aut didn't beat her arse which is a damn lie. I laughed out loud when she said that bollocks. But then she said she never stopped thinking about me. She keeps saying things like why can't I see that she's prettier than you. Some shit like that. She was asking me if I remember how good she was in bed. She's off her fucking rocker is what she is. I'm telling you babe... that's one mad, delusional tart."

A recent memory resurfaced and even though it gave me an uncomfortable chill, the mention of Kelly caused me to relive it. "Maybe she was the one who was driving that mysterious black car on our anniversary." Tristan's eyes widened in shock and I think I saw a flicker of something akin to fear in his face. He might've been feeling apprehensive but I was determined to catch this bitch once and for all. I vowed I would never let anyone take Tristan away from me again. "Try to call her from another phone...some random phone like maybe a pay phone. See if you can get her to mention the car. If she does, we have over ten witnesses that saw how she was terrorizing us. And you, Dane, and Ty know that she tried to knock you guys off the freeway."

My request caused Tristan to sit up in bed. It also caused the volume of his voice to rise. "Now hold on a second. There's no way in hell that stupid bint could drive like that."

I guess it was up to me to do all the detective work. "Maybe she wasn't the one driving. Maybe someone else was in the car with her. It could've been that brunette bitch. Remember her little accomplice?" Tristan started shaking his head so I finally admitted my real fear. "Tristan, she's threatening our relationship! She knows where we live and she knew your phone number. She's stalking you all over again! What if she tries to pull a *'Fatal Attraction'*?"

I was surprised when Tristan chuckled humorously because I didn't see any humor in this situation. I was about to berate him but he got his words in first. "Bridget, I'm not afraid of her. I remember when I first met her; she definitely lived up to the stereotype of a dumb blonde. It was so easy to get her into bed."

I stared intently into Tristan's eyes as I tried to make him understand the seriousness of what she was doing. Perhaps he needed a friendly reminder. "She's not that stupid if she could find out your phone number and where you live."

Unfortunately, he wasn't convinced. "Let's not get ahead of ourselves and think she had anything to do with that car, okay? I need to get proof first. And second, she could've found my address and phone number on the Web...it's not that hard." I started worrying my bottom lip between my teeth and I could feel myself beginning to tremble slightly. I've never wanted anyone to disappear off the face of the earth but I definitely wouldn't feel regret if Kelly simply vanished from existence. Tristan put his arms around me and held me close. I embraced him tightly as if I was trying to keep him safe. And in my mind, I was desperately praying for someone to watch over him. He started rubbing my back soothingly and I rested my head in the crook of his neck. His voice was soft and gentle as he tried to reassure me. "Don't worry, love. She's not a threat to us. I would never leave you for her; not in a million years. And I told you...I'll protect you from anyone. Please trust me." It wasn't *him* that I didn't trust.

Even days after Tristan's revelation, Kelly continued to haunt my thoughts. I found myself becoming paranoid and I started looking out the front window again to see if the black sports car would drive up the street. Fortunately, it never did but I couldn't stop wondering when and where she would show up in our lives again. Part of me wished Tristan had never told me she contacted him but the other part was glad he did because I didn't want to be a sitting duck. I wanted to be alert and aware in case she tried anything sneaky.

My sanity was spared and my soul was given momentary peace when we finally finished Kelly's nursery a couple weeks later. I didn't think about Kelly at all that day. Jake wanted to surprise me with my mother-daughter nook so Tristan took my hand and we went upstairs to where Jake, Lauren, and Autumn were already waiting in Katie's room. He covered my eyes with his hand once we got to the top of the stairwell and then he guided me into her room. Suddenly, he removed his hand. "Open your eyes."

I opened my eyes slowly and gasped in complete surprise. Tears of happiness filled my eyes and I covered my mouth with my hand when I saw the quaint little space my brother-in-law made for me and his unborn niece.

There was a small crystal chandelier hanging above a green lounge chair and ottoman. The chair was accented with a pink pillow and a white nursing blanket was draped along the top of the chair. There was a round end table on one side of the chair with a matching green tissue box on top and a pink basket filled with baby stuff on the other side. But what really surprised me was the tall hand-painted tree on the wall behind the chair. It stretched from the floor to the ceiling and expanded over the two adjacent walls. The bird that was perched on one of the branches looked like it was just watching over our little corner. The tree and the bird were painted in green on top of the pale pink that made up the rest of Katie's nursery. My eyes roamed around the room and I noticed that he painted more green birds in certain places on the walls. And they all looked like they were flying towards the tree.

Jake came to stand next to me and I heard him speak quietly. "So… do you like it?"

I turned towards him and my immediate reaction was to hug him tightly. In between my sniffles, I expressed my sincere gratitude at the loving and thoughtful way he added a little part of himself to Katie's nursery. "Yes, I love it. Thank you, Jake." Suddenly, I felt a tiny foot kick inside me. I gasped in surprise again and grabbed Jake's hand. I put it to my belly and I watched his expression change to match mine.

"I felt her! She kicked!"

I smiled affectionately. "Katie says thank you too." He smiled back and that's when Tristan joined us and put his hand on my belly too.

I think Katie wanted to show off and impress her father so she kicked me again. Tristan laughed in delight and exclaimed happily, "See, she's already Daddy's little footie star!"

Chapter 28

SINCE MY DUE DATE WAS late February or early March, I started my maternity leave in mid-February. During my last day of school, some of my students surprised me with some nice baby gifts for Katie. When I returned to school after having my first ultrasound, I announced the news that I was having a daughter. All of the girls in my class were pretty excited but some of the boys didn't hesitate to express that they had hoped I would help contribute to the male population. I'll admit that a part of me had wished for a little boy too. Sometimes I would imagine chasing a miniature version of Tristan around the house. But then I remembered that we're still young and we have plenty of time to try for a boy.

After classes let out, some of the faculty gave me a small baby shower in the teacher's lounge with gifts and cake. Our little celebration lasted into the early evening and it was probably around 6PM when everyone decided to go home. Between the gifts I received from my students and the gifts from my co-workers, I actually needed help carrying everything to the car. Two of my co-workers that helped me load all my baby gifts into the trunk, gave me a couple more congratulatory hugs before I got in my car and drove out of the parking lot.

It was already dark outside and I was driving down a busy main road on my way home. I let my mind wander for a moment and I began thinking about what Tristan's reaction would be after I showed him that we had even *more* presents for our little unborn princess. As I was driving, I noticed construction lights up ahead and a few cars stopped in front of me. I knew there was traffic and I didn't want to be stuck in it because I was anxious to get home after a long day. So I made a quick decision and turned a sharp right down a side-street. It was a two-lane road lined with nothing but trees on both sides and it was pretty deserted.

Suddenly, I heard a sound like an engine revving and the next thing I knew...someone came out of nowhere and hit me from behind. I really had no warning because I didn't even see any headlights and I wasn't aware that anyone was driving behind me. And I wouldn't even say that they hit me; it was more like they rammed into me. I screamed in terror and the impact was so strong that it made me lose control of the wheel and I veered off the side of the road. What was even stranger was that it was almost like the other car was pushing mine. I glanced briefly in my rear-view mirror and I could see something black connected to my rear bumper. The other car's engine was still loud and revving but I didn't focus my attention on it for too long because I tried to slam on the brakes. Unfortunately, it was already too late.

The front end of my little red convertible plowed into a tree and I immediately felt a sharp pain in my right ankle. I screamed again as the air bag deployed and my body was thrown forward with my face meeting the bag forcefully. The breath was knocked out of my lungs and when I finally pulled my face out of the airbag, I looked down to check my belly and I could see and feel the steering wheel resting on top of it.

When I looked up, I noticed my windshield was cracked severely but I was grateful that it didn't shatter completely and cover me with dangerous shards of glass. At least one of the headlights on my car was still on and I looked into the rear-view mirror again to see who hit me. I could feel my entire body trembling in fear as I watched them put their car in reverse. I could see that the car was black and it didn't have any headlights. My mind immediately flashed back to our wedding anniversary last year and I remembered the mysterious black sports car that terrorized me silently; the car with tinted windows, no license plates...and no headlights. My car shook slightly as the front end of their car detached itself from my rear bumper and the unexpected motion caused me to yelp in shock. I couldn't tear my eyes away as I watched their every move and I felt frozen because I didn't know what was going to happen next. All I could hear was shaky breaths escaping my mouth and the sound of the other person's partially mangled car as they slowly backed away from mine.

Once they were a few feet away, I stared with wide-eyes as they began to rev the engine again. Right at that moment, I had a terrible suspicion that they were going to ram into me again. Oh my God, they wanted to finish me off. I couldn't help but wonder...who was this person and why me? I turned my head to look behind me and I could see that the rear of my car was completely totaled. I even saw some of Katie's gifts exposed from the now non-existent trunk. If this mystery person rammed me again, they would probably hit my body this time. I would get pushed into my little two-seater even further or maybe even the tree itself and my pregnant belly that was protecting Katie would be smashed by the steering wheel.

Tears quickly filled my eyes and I could feel them trickling down my cheeks because I thought we were about to be killed. That's when some intense maternal instinct flowed through me and I realized that I had to try and escape. I tried to move my body but I was stuck. The steering wheel had trapped me and when I tried to move my legs, my right ankle seared with pain. I used every ounce of strength I possessed and tried to push the steering wheel off my belly but it seemed to be lodged there. Both of my legs were trapped as well and I was suddenly aware that I was a sitting duck.

I began to cry harder and I wished for the black car to spare me and my baby's life and just drive away. Then I wished for someone to come and help me. Since I thought I was about to die at any moment, I did the only thing I could think of in the few seconds I had left: I called out for Tristan. But I didn't call his name out loud. I remembered that sometimes he hears my voice in his head so I called out telepathically for my angel to save me: *'Tristan, if you can hear me...please help. I've been in an accident and I'm trapped. The person who hit me is going to ram me again and I don't know if we'll survive.'* I could hear myself sobbing as I prayed for him to hear my desperate plea in his mind. *'Please Tristan... help me and Katie.'*

I don't know if he heard me because I didn't hear him answer me in my mind. To make matters even worse, it started to rain and some of the water began seeping through the windshield. Then to my complete and utter surprise, something happened that was actually in my favor.

Instead of the black car ramming into me again, it started to drive away. Maybe the person behind the wheel took pity on me. Either that or they thought I was already dead. I knew I had to call for real help but my cell phone was in my purse. And my purse that was sitting on the passenger seat before the accident was now on the floor and I couldn't reach it.

I was trapped in my small convertible on a deserted road with no one to rescue me. I began to panic and I tried to dislodge the steering wheel again. I pushed and pushed but my actions were futile because it refused to budge. I screamed in frustration and started crying again. Then I began to yell out loud helplessly as the rain turned into a down-pour. "Help! Someone help me! I'm trapped! Help!" In a last effort to try and communicate with my soul mate, I screamed his name at the top of my lungs into the stormy night. "TRISTAN!" That's when my headlight went out and I found myself sitting in complete darkness.

A few minutes later, I saw light coming from behind me. I turned my head to see a car driving up the road. I wanted them to stop and help me so I started yelling again to get their attention. To my relief, they stopped and pulled over on the side of the road a few feet in back of me. Then seconds later, I heard rapid footsteps running through wet earth and an unfamiliar male voice asked, "Are you alright miss?"

I broke down into a sobbing mess and begged this stranger to help me. "Please help me! I'm pregnant and I'm trapped. I can't get out of the car. *Please!*" A moment later, I saw him pull out his cell phone and call 911. After he got off the phone with the emergency dispatcher, he tried to dislodge my steering wheel but he was also unsuccessful. Then he told me to try and remain calm and that help was on the way. I saw him move away from me and I thought he was leaving. I panicked at the thought of being left alone again and before I could stop myself, I reached out to grab my rescuer's arm. I pleaded with him out of total fear, "Please don't leave me!"

He gently put his hand on top of mine and his voice was kind when he replied, "Don't worry miss, I'm not leaving. Not until the ambulance and the police arrive." When I looked at his face, I noticed he was an older gentleman; probably around my father's age. He began making small-talk with me to keep me relaxed while we waited for help. It was probably about fifteen minutes into our conversation when I heard sirens in the distance. A couple minutes later, I saw many flashing lights and I actually sighed a huge breath of relief.

I wasn't freed from my vehicular prison until a fireman actually sawed the steering wheel off the dashboard. A police officer then lifted me out of my seat and when I looked back at my car; a Valentine's gift from my beloved two years ago, my heart broke when I saw that it was completely destroyed. The front and the back were smashed and the only part that was in tact was the two seats. The dashboard was bent and I could see a gaping hole where my steering wheel used to be.

Amidst all the confusion, I found myself being laid on a gurney and within a couple seconds, a stiff brace was placed around my neck. Then one Emergency Medical Technician started asking me all these health questions. I was trying to answer him the best I could but I was still trembling in fear from everything that happened to me. I told him that I was almost nine months pregnant, I had a headache and my right ankle was sore. I was also wet and shivering, but by this time, it had already stopped raining.

All of a sudden, I heard the one voice I really wanted to hear all along. I heard Tristan calling my name and I tried to turn my head towards the sound of his voice, but the neck brace was hindering me. So I called back to him and I heard his voice with his British accent arguing with someone and yelling, "That's my wife! That's my wife! Let me through!" He reached me within seconds and I saw his face looking down at me full of worry and deep concern. I watched his eyes scan my body and then I felt his warm hands caressing my face and smoothing my hair. His breathing was erratic and I knew he was in a state of panic because I could hear it in his voice even though he spoke to me quietly. "Oh Bridget. I came to you as fast as I could, love. I'm sorry I couldn't make it to you sooner." When he leaned over me to place a soft kiss on my forehead, his unique scent invaded my nostrils and I closed my eyes as it engulfed me with momentary comfort. His voice started to crack and I could see tears filling his beautiful azure eyes. "Are you alright? What happened? Talk to me, babe."

My lips were trembling as I tried to speak but I was truly relieved to be in his presence. Actually, what I really wanted was for them to take the neck brace off me and let me go home with my husband. But I knew that wasn't going to happen. I still didn't get to tell the police about the accident. I didn't even get a chance to tell Tristan because a female police officer came into my line of vision and stood next to him. She was a tall, curvy, light-skinned African-American with dark almond-shaped eyes. She wasn't wearing any makeup and the small intricate braids in her hair were pulled into a tight bun. She looked down at me and I glanced at her briefly before returning my attention back to Tristan. Judging by the look on his face, I could tell he was miffed that she interrupted us and she was standing so close to him. It was no secret that Tristan hated the police with a passion. The officer's voice was very friendly as she introduced herself. "Hello ma'am, I'm Officer Mason from the Los Angeles Police Department. What's your name?"

"Bridget Hathaway," I answered in a low, shaky voice.

"Bridget, can you tell me what happened tonight? I need to record your account of the events for my report before we take you to the hospital." Tristan remained silent as I recounted the accident to the officer but when he heard me describe the car that rammed me, I actually saw the color drain from his face. He swallowed hard and then his lips parted as he began to let out short, quick breaths. The officer must've noticed his reaction because she turned to him and asked, "Sir, are you alright?" Without looking at her, he quickly schooled his face into a neutral expression and gave her a curt nod. She turned towards me again but I saw her give Tristan a side-long glance right before she asked me, "Did you recognize the car? Have you seen it before?" I guess Tristan's attempt to mask his emotions weren't quick enough to fool perceptive Officer Mason.

"Yes. There was a black, late-model Mitsubishi Eclipse that drove by our house about six months ago. It had tinted windows, no license plates, and no headlights. It kept circling the block but every time it came around, it would stop directly in front of our house. We couldn't see who was inside and they never made themselves known. Eventually, the car went away and we haven't seen it since." Then I swallowed hard against the nervous lump in my throat. "Until tonight."

"So you're positive it was the same car?"

I've never been so sure of anything in my life. I answered her firmly and affirmatively. "Yes, I'm completely positive." Right at that moment, I remembered Tristan's experience with the black car and I tried to convey to him through my eyes that he should say something. When he averted his eyes from me, I knew he didn't want to say anything because he didn't want to talk to the police. But now was not the time to let his stubbornness and hatred get in the way. Now was our opportunity to catch Kelly once and for all. After what happened tonight, there was no doubt in my mind that she was responsible for almost taking my life and that of our unborn baby's. She knew where we lived, she knew Tristan's phone number, and now I realized that she knew where I worked because she must have been following me.

Officer Mason was writing on her clipboard before she looked up at me with a friendly smile. "Thank you for speaking with me, Bridget. I'll turn in my report to my superior and you should be hearing from our department soon to follow up." Then she gave me a gentle pat on the arm and said reassuringly, "And don't worry. You and your baby are going to be just fine."

She started to walk away and Tristan still didn't open his mouth. I could see in his face that he was contemplating something in his mind. Maybe he was debating with himself on whether he should tell the officer that the same car almost knocked him and his friends off the freeway. My accident wasn't Kelly's first attempt at trying to kill someone. I said his name quietly and his eyes met mine again. But this time I verbally pleaded with him when I whispered, *"Please* Tristan...tell her."

He gave a sigh and to my relief, he finally opened his mouth to speak. "Officer Mason."

She turned around at the sound of his voice. "Yes?"

"There's more to my wife's story." She quirked an eyebrow at his statement and quickly walked back over to us. Tristan filled her in on what happened when he and his friends followed the car. I could tell she was intrigued and when he finished speaking, she gave him a smile and her thanks. Then she said something to an EMT and that's when they started pushing my gurney towards the ambulance. I was surrounded by at least three of them and I almost lost sight of Tristan. They put me in the ambulance and I heard Tristan's stern voice when he demanded, "She's my wife and I'm riding with her." I watched him enter the back of the ambulance and his tall form was hunched over as he moved to take a seat beside me. He held my hand and leaned his head down next to mine the entire ride to the hospital.

When we arrived at the hospital, Tristan tried to follow as they rushed me into the emergency room but one of the police officers held him back and told him he couldn't go in. He immediately panicked and yelled, "Bollocks! I wanna make sure she's alright!"

The officer continued to barricade his way and told him to sit in the waiting room until the doctor came out. Tristan started arguing with him and when I saw him begin to struggle against the officer's firm grip, I became worried for his safety. I yelled out, "We'll be okay, baby! Just wait for me! Please!" I could feel my heart pounding in my chest when I heard him desperately calling my name but I lost sight of him once the emergency room doors closed.

After the doctor and nurses checked me thoroughly, they sent me for an MRI to make sure Katie was okay. Once all my tests were done, the doctor confirmed that I was fine except for a sprained ankle. He assured me that even though the airbag hit me in the face pretty hard, it actually prevented me from getting a concussion or any spinal damage. But the initial impact was the reason for my throbbing headache. I was also relieved when they finally told me that Katie was unharmed. I actually started crying in relief because she was my main concern. I wasn't sure if the steering wheel that was lodged against my belly was cutting off her circulation or pressing on any part of her tiny body. A nurse tended to my injured ankle and soon I was brought back into the emergency room.

I was still lying in a bed and they rolled me next to an elderly woman who had some tubes coming out of her nose. She looked very frail and they had her hooked up to some sort of heart monitor. The constant beeping sound confirmed that she was actually still alive. She had a head full of white hair and a deeply wrinkled face. She was asleep and for a moment I watched her thin chest slowly rise and fall with each breath she took.

Another nurse passed my bed and I asked her if I could see my husband. She laughed when I told her he would be the tall blond guy who's probably pacing impatiently in the waiting room. Within a few minutes, I saw Tristan come through the emergency room doors and head straight for me. He wore an expression of concern and when he reached my bed, he put his arms around me in a tight embrace. I held him with equal strength while he spoke in a quiet but urgent voice, "Are you okay, love?" He pulled away and before I could answer, he pressed his lips to mine. When we ended the kiss, I watched his eyes scan my face and his brows knit together in worry. He smoothed my hair away from my forehead and I saw nothing but absolute affection behind his loving gaze. "What did they say? Is Katie alright?"

I cupped his face in my hands and spoke tenderly when I reassured him. "I'm fine, baby. And Katie is fine too. I just have a sprained ankle and a killer headache. But nothing some Excedrin won't fix." I laughed lightly but I winced when a sharp pain hit me in the temple.

He smiled slightly and then he took a seat in the chair next to my bed. "I'm so glad you're both alright. I was so worried." Suddenly, his eyes became glassy with unshed tears and he quickly took my hands in his and gave them a squeeze. I knew he was really shaken up by what happened to me and I felt an intense need to comfort him.

I reached out to thread my fingers through his hair and I spoke softly. "Everything is okay, Tristan. See...I'm fine. Don't worry, sweetheart." He sniffled once and I immediately put my arms out to him. We embraced again but this time I felt his body trembling and I knew he was crying. When I heard a few more sniffles, I began to rub his back soothingly. For a moment, we just held each other and I was so eternally grateful to be in his arms.

His voice was barely above a whisper and it sounded broken when he said, "I heard you calling me, Bridget. I heard you call me for help. I was at home and I just..." He paused and took a breath. "I heard your voice in my head as clear as if you were right there talking to me." When I realized that he heard my mental plea, I closed my eyes in relief and held him closer. When he pulled away, I saw that his cheeks were wet with tears. I gently wiped them with my fingers as he continued speaking. "I didn't know where I was going. It was almost like something was guiding me. It was such a strange feeling that I can't even describe it. Then I saw the lights from the ambulance and I just knew you were there. I stopped my bike and I started praying to God that you were still alive; that I wasn't too late." He paused again and took a couple more breaths. That's when I saw the tears begin to leak from his eyes again. His voice wavered when he admitted, "I don't know what I would've done if they told me you were dead." He sobbed once and laid his head in my lap. I held him and stroked his hair while I whispered words of comfort.

The same nurse that I spoke to earlier came over to me and handed me some tissues. I continued to console Tristan and when he finally lifted his head, I wiped his tears once again with the tissue and tried to get him to calm down by changing the subject. "What about your bike? You realize that you left it at the scene, right?"

He replied nonchalantly, "They probably towed it. I don't give a shit though. I really don't. All I care about is you and Katie right now."

We were interrupted once again but this time by the sound of a choking cough coming from the woman lying in the bed next to mine. Tristan and I looked over at her and she coughed a few more times before she let out a long wheeze. I cringed involuntarily because it seemed painful. A slender, wrinkled hand reached up to wipe her dry lips and then two cataract-infested eyes looked over at us. She blinked slowly like she was trying to get her vision in focus. Tristan turned his head away back towards me and that's when I heard a quivering, raspy voice escape her throat. "*So beautiful.*" To my surprise, she smiled with a mouth absent of any teeth and I saw her eyes quickly fill with tears. But her expression didn't look sad, she actually looked...happy.

Tristan turned his attention to her again and replied kindly, "Yeah, she is." That's when I realized...she wasn't talking about me. Her eyes were fixed on him. She continued to gaze at him adoringly but I wore an expression of utter confusion.

I slowly turned my head towards Tristan and once our eyes met, I informed him quietly, "She's talking about *you*, baby." His eyes widened slightly and he whipped his head towards the old woman again. Then she finally tore her eyes away from him and looked at me. She opened her mouth and I heard her inhale like she was about to say something else. Instead, more violent coughs racked her small body and I wanted to tell her not to speak.

She wiped her lips again and they cracked when she smiled at me and finally spoke. "You're a lucky girl to have him."

I smiled back and responded fondly, "Yes, I---" But my sentence was cut short because all of a sudden, she took a quaking breath and closed her eyes. My mouth opened in shock when I heard the heart monitor flat line. Oh my God, the little old lady was dying right before my eyes! Within a matter of seconds, the doctor and some nurses rushed to her bedside and before I knew what was happening, they pulled the curtain shut and blocked her from my view. Tristan and I just stared at each other with identical expressions of disbelief. I heard random voices coming from behind the curtain as I stared into Tristan's cerulean eyes. *'We're losing her... She's failing... I'm trying doctor, I'm trying...'*

As Tristan's gaze penetrated me straight through to our shared soul, I began to wonder what the woman saw. What was *so* beautiful? Was she just commenting on his physical attractiveness...or did she see something else? Suddenly, I gaped at him in shock and at the exact same moment, I saw his expression change. He actually looked unnerved; like my stare was making him uncomfortable. He broke our gaze to look down at the bed and then he whispered quietly, "Don't look at me like that. Don't look at me like you don't know me." But I couldn't stop because I couldn't believe what just happened.

Then I heard the most dreadful words coming from the other side of the curtain. *'We lost her... She's gone... Someone call it... Time of death, 10:56PM...'* I gasped because I realized that the old woman saw something about Tristan right before she died. But what did she see? I wanted to ask him directly but no words would come forth from my lips because I was too afraid. Tristan's head was still down but I saw his blue eyes look up at me. His voice sounded detached and it actually frightened me a little because it was the same as it was that night on the soccer field. "You know me, Bridget." As soon as he said that, I thought to myself: *'Do I? This is the same man who admitted to me that he didn't even know who he was.'*

Eventually, they let me go home but Tristan had to call us a taxi because we had no mode of transportation. My car was completely obliterated and his bike was probably sitting in an impound lot somewhere. As soon as we got through the front door, the first thing out of his mouth was, "I'm ringing Jake. I'm gonna see if I can find that fucking car again."

I couldn't believe he just said that to his injured, traumatized, and pregnant wife. I was leaning on him for support on one side with a crutch on the other. I looked up at him with incredulity and exclaimed, "No Tristan! I need you here with me! Please don't leave me tonight!" I could feel myself on the verge of extreme panic at the thought of him leaving me to try and find Kelly to exact his revenge. I'll admit that I wanted revenge too but mine was along the lines of long-term imprisonment.

To my surprise, he lifted me in his arms which caused me to accidentally drop my crutch. It hit the hardwood floor with a loud bang that echoed throughout the foyer. He kissed me firmly before he said, "Okay, love. I won't leave you." He started walking and he surprised me even further when he carried my big, almost-nine-months-pregnant ass up the stairs. I tried to tell him to put me down before he hurt his back or worse...dropped me, but he completely ignored my demand. Once we got to the bedroom, he laid me down on the bed gently and I noticed he didn't look affected from carrying me; he wasn't even out of breath. Then he casually sat on the bed next to me and helped me get undressed for the night. "It's a good thing you started your maternity leave. You'll be in the house and I can keep an eye on you." I smirked because it wasn't as if he didn't do that already.

The next morning, something occurred for the first time in our relationship: Tristan had breakfast delivered. The reason for this was because he wouldn't allow me to stand and cook. After watching me hobble around the kitchen for a couple minutes just bringing the food from the refrigerator to the counter, he ordered me to sit in the living room. I tried to argue with him that we needed to eat but he insisted that he would take care of it. Tristan can't cook so I said jokingly, "Oh, so we're going to have cold cereal then?"

He laughed dryly and then he said, "No, I'll just order take-away." Thankfully, the diner a couple blocks away from us had delivery.

After breakfast, I was sitting in the living room watching television when I heard the doorbell. I tried to get up and answer the door but I saw a flash of blond pass the entryway to the living room and head straight for the front door. I heard hushed voices and then I saw Tristan and another tall, blond, but older man enter the room and approach me. He was dressed in a navy sports coat that was open and revealed a white button-down shirt with the top unbuttoned. His shirt was tucked into a pair of casual blue jeans and he was wearing dark oxford shoes. He gave me friendly smile with straight, white teeth and made a point of showing me the badge that was pinned to his belt. I also noticed he was holding a manila folder in his hand. "Hello Mrs. Hathaway, I'm Detective Grace. I'm here to speak to you about your accident yesterday." Tristan moved away from him to sit down next to me on the sofa.

I smiled back and replied politely, "Hello. Please have a seat." I gestured to the armchair that was adjacent to the sofa. I'll admit that I was a little surprised that a detective showed up at our house. I'll also admit that I was very relieved because I really hoped he would be able to catch Kelly once and for all.

He sat in the armchair and then he opened the folder and pulled out a photograph. He laid it on the coffee table in front of me and Tristan and said, "We found the car that hit you last night; a late-model, black Mitsubishi Eclipse. It was found on the side of the road about twenty-five miles from the scene of the accident. It was also on fire." I picked up the photograph and I could see the black sports car was turned into a charred metal wreck. "There were no occupants and like you said in your statement Mrs. Hathaway...no license plates. We checked the VIN and found out that the car was reported stolen from Oakland about six months ago."

Right at that moment, Tristan and I looked at each other because it was six months ago when we had our wedding anniversary. Det. Grace noticed our exchange and said, "I read the police report. You've seen the car before?" I looked over at him but he was reading something in the folder. He kept his blue eyes on whatever he was reading as he spoke again. "Ah yes, at your...wedding anniversary; six months ago. Is that correct?" He pulled out a pen from one of his inner jacket pockets and gave us an expected look.

"Yes, that's correct," I replied affirmatively.

"And you don't know who was driving the car? Did you get a look at the person who hit you last night?"

"No, I didn't see anyone but..." I finally told the detective what I've been suspecting all along. "I have an idea who it is." He immediately started scribbling something in his folder and then he looked back up at me. I looked at Tristan but I noticed he was just looking at the floor. If he wasn't going to share the truth with the detective, he wasn't going to deter me from doing it. "There's this girl...Kelly. I don't know her last name. Do you, Tristan?" He didn't respond so I nudged him with my elbow to garner his attention.

"No," he replied quietly.

"She's been stalking my husband. Actually, she's been stalking him for..." I nudged him again. "How long has it been, sweetie?"

"Almost three fucking years," he murmured. I looked over at Det. Grace and his eyebrows lifted in mild surprise.

"The first time I ever saw her was at his birthday party two years ago. She came uninvited." I told the detective my account of the events during Tristan's 24th birthday party and I described Kelly and her unnamed brunette 'accomplice' to the best of my memory. I also made Tristan tell him what he knew about her since he's had more contact with her than I have. I was really surprised when I learned how she's been constantly invading his life for the past few years. I was even more surprised by the fact that he was so hesitant to talk about it. We gave the detective all the information we had and Tristan even told him that she's still been calling him; even after he changed his phone number for the second time.

"Tristan, I'd like to run a check on your cell phone records to see if we can find the locations she's been calling him from."

Tristan didn't answer him for at least a full minute until I pleaded with him through my eyes. "Yeah, whatever," he mumbled quietly without looking at the detective.

"I'm also going to dig up the police report from your party. I want to check and see if the bar & grill had any video surveillance of Kelly and her friend." Then he turned his attention towards me and said, "I'm working on your case, Mrs. Hathaway and---"

He kept addressing me as 'Mrs. Hathaway' and for some reason I felt like Tristan's mother; it was just so formal. "Please call me 'Bridget'," I said with a warm smile.

He smiled back and that's when I noticed for the first time that he was handsome. Because of his physical attractiveness, I found myself feeling more comfortable speaking to him. "My apologies, Bridget. As I was saying...I'm working on your case and I'll try to find this Kelly person and ask her a few questions."

"Well, I can give you the names of the people who witnessed her drive by our house during our anniversary. But they didn't see any more than I did." I turned my attention towards Tristan again when I spoke my next words because I was hoping he would offer more information. "Two of the witnesses were actually with Tristan when she tried to knock them off the freeway. You see Det. Grace, my accident wasn't the first time she attempted vehicular manslaughter."

He nodded and tapped his pen against his chin. "I see." Then he cast his eyes down and scribbled something else in his folder. "Yes, that would be very helpful." His eyes settled on Tristan when he asked, "Tristan, can you tell me the names of the two witnesses who were in the car with you that night?" I turned to look at Tristan and he was fidgeting his hands apprehensively. He was also hesitating to answer again but after a few seconds, he finally told the detective what he wanted to know.

After Det. Grace left our house, Tristan walked back into the living room. He joined me on the sofa again and I couldn't contain my curiosity or my frustration any longer. "Tristan, what's wrong with you? Why wouldn't you talk to him? Don't you understand that he's trying to help us? He's trying to help us catch Kelly so we can end this once and for all. Aren't you sick of her bothering you? Don't you want her out of our lives?"

I could hear the irritation in his voice when he answered me. "I don't trust the police. You know that, Bridget. We still don't even have proof that she had anything to do with that car. I wanna be sure I find the right person responsible for almost killing you. But if she is the one responsible, then I wanna deal with her *myself*." All of a sudden, he shouted, "Fuck the pigs! I don't need their bloody help!" My eyes were wide as I sat there in shock after his unexpected outburst. I was so perplexed by his behavior that I couldn't even say anything to him.

I almost jumped out of my skin when his cell phone rang because the sound startled me. He was still pissed off about the detective dropping by so he answered his phone sharply without checking the Caller ID. "What?!?" Then something strange happened. His face turned red and his jaw dropped. In the next second, he slowly pulled the phone away from his ear and I saw him swallow hard. I was beginning to feel very uneasy because then his face twisted into anger. Right at that moment, I knew he was *royally* pissed off; even more than before. He turned his head towards me and spoke in a dangerously low voice. "That was Kelly. She asked me if you were alright." I gasped in shock and covered my mouth with my hand. My hand began to tremble when he finished with, "Then she laughed and hung up."

I hated to be the one to say 'I told you so', so instead I asked quietly, "Is that proof enough?"

Tristan stood up abruptly I could see that he had his phone in a tight grip. His voice was dripping with venom when he growled loudly, "That's it! That's *fucking* it!"

I didn't dare say one word because the Blond Archangel had emerged. I just stared up at him in fear from my frozen seated position and watched him press a few buttons on his cell phone. A second later, I heard a sweet female voice coming through the speaker on the other end.

"Yes, Tristan?"

Strangely, Tristan's tone of voice changed to match hers. He was actually very friendly and his tone was casual and conversational. "Hi Kelly, why'd you hang up like that, darlin'? I wanted to talk to you." Right at that moment, I knew he was trying to set her up.

"Oh really?"

"Yeah, I haven't seen you in a long time and I've been thinking about what you said. You know, that we should be together."

When she giggled, she definitely sounded like she was a little out of touch with reality. "You want to be with me?"

"Yeah, I do. So, I'm thinking...we should meet up somewhere. Would you meet with me?"

Kelly was quiet for a moment and then she said haughtily, "I don't think your wife would appreciate that." She paused again and then she asked curiously, "Is she there?" Her voice changed and she sounded accusing but yet the situation was humorous to her. "Am I on speaker, Tristan?"

Tristan's voice might have been friendly but his facial expression was anything but. I could tell it was taking him a tremendous amount of effort not to cuss her out in his usual British bad-boy style. He lied quite impressively. "No, she's not here. I wouldn't be ringing you if she was. Do you think I'm daft? I don't want her to find out that I'm talking to you. So what do you say...do you wanna get together? I know it's early but I really wanna see you, love." Oh, the icing on the cake was always his sentimental endearment. I had my fingers crossed that she was going to melt from his charms.

To my misfortune, she rejected him easily. "I'm sorry, honey. I can't see you right now. I'm away at the moment."

"Oh yeah? Where?"

She giggled again and she sounded even more insane. "Ohhhh...I'm somewhere relaxing with my thoughts."

Tristan was determined so he tried to persuade her again. "How about I meet you there? Are you far away?" She didn't answer him this time. She just laughed and I could tell he was getting frustrated. It was reflected in his voice when he finally decided to stop playing this little game with her. "How did you get my number again?"

Her voice was low when she purred, "I can't tell you, darling."

"Did you get it from your brunette mate? The one who was with you at my birthday party?"

She laughed again and replied lightly, "Are you trying to play detective, Tristan?" She continued to mock him through the phone. "Maybe that should be your next role." I was watching his face and the muscle in his jaw was so pronounced that I knew he was practically grinding his teeth together in anger.

"Tell me where you are," he demanded. Then I jumped in surprise because he yelled, "How did you get my number?!? Tell me you fucking cunt! Where are you?!?"

She laughed louder but it sounded more like a witch's cackle. "I have to go now, my love. I probably won't see you for awhile. But when I do..." She sighed wistfully. "I'll look my best for you. I'll make you see that I'm so much prettier than that ugly freckled-face bitch you married." Before Tristan could cuss her out again, she hung up. That's when he realized his temper got the best of him and ruined his plan to entangle Kelly in his manipulative trap. The Archangel threw his cell phone against the wall with brute force and it shattered to pieces. Then he grabbed his hair in frustration and started pacing the living room. I could see him taking deep breaths as he tried to control his anger.

I thawed myself from my seat and limped over to him. "Let's call Det. Grace and tell him what just happened."

Tristan was breathing hard and I watched his eyes dart back and forth like he was thinking about something. He answered me in a hard quiet voice. "No, he has what he needs. I'm not gonna tell him anything else."

"Tristan---"

"But what I *am* gonna do is get video surveillance for our house. She knows where we live and now she's threatening my family." He pointed towards the front window. "The street is as far as she's ever gonna get to our house. I'm through fucking around with her." Before I could even get another word in, he walked out of the living room. He didn't leave the house but I had no idea where he was going.

I hobbled back over to the sofa and sat on the reclining part so I could prop my ankle up. I started thinking about what I just heard between him and Kelly. She really *was* a crazy bitch. I started imagining what I would say to her once the police finally caught her insane ass. That is... right before I punched her fucking lights out. First she tried to get me to break up with Tristan and almost succeeded. Then she tried to kill me and almost succeeded again. I wasn't stupid and I knew exactly what she was doing. Her objective was Tristan and what does one do when there is an obstacle in the way of getting the objective? There's only one answer: get rid of the obstacle. She tried twice and I had a sneaking suspicion she wasn't going to stop until I was no longer in her way. I have to admit, persistence is one thing we had in common. But what she probably didn't realize was that I wasn't going to stop working with the authorities until they caught her.

Tristan approached me about a half-hour later and announced, "They're coming to install the video surveillance in about an hour."

I looked at him with a confused expression. "Who?'"

"The security company I just hired. I told you I was getting it, didn't I?"

I was flabbergasted that he was taking this so seriously, that I almost choked on my words. "Yeah, but I didn't know you were doing it already." My mind shifted gears suddenly and I pleaded with him when I said, "Tristan, we need to get a restraining order against Kelly."

This time he looked confused. "How are we gonna do that, babe? We don't know her last name and we don't know where she lives. Are we just gonna ask for all birds with long blonde hair and brown eyes to be prohibited from coming within fifty feet of us?" My hope deflated because Tristan was right. How would we get a restraining order when we didn't have any information on her?

Forty-five minutes later the doorbell rang again but this time it was the security installation crew. They came with monitors, cameras, and long black cables. I felt helpless as I just watched them walk back and forth past the entryway to the living room. Truth be told, being nearly nine months pregnant and moving around on a bum ankle was painful for me. They were doing something upstairs too because I heard drilling and they were continuously going up and down the stairs. I finally got up and hobbled around to see exactly where they were installing everything. I met Tristan upstairs and he seemed to be overseeing the progress.

By the time they were finished, we had security monitors set up in our bedroom behind some big wooden cabinet that looked like an entertainment center. The monitors were linked to video surveillance cameras outside the house. I was absolutely amazed at how Tristan was able to get someone to come on such short notice. I couldn't help but wonder how much he paid them. One of the security guys showed us how everything works and then Tristan signed the receipt before the guy left. Then he turned to me and said almost as an afterthought, "Oh, and from now on...if you go out...I'm going with you."

At this point, I felt he was taking our security and safety a little too far. "Tristan, I don't need a bodyguard, alright?"

I was sitting on the bed and he stood right in front of me and pierced his gaze into me. I'll admit that his intensity made me want to scoot away from him. "You want me to put my trust in the detective? Fine, I will. But until he catches that mad tart, it's *my* job to protect you. What happened last night...that ain't gonna happen again. Do you understand me? I'm not gonna let it happen. She crossed the fucking line so no more games...this is serious now."

Right at that moment, the realization of what was going on in our once-happy lives hit me full on. I could feel myself getting so upset that I feared I would go into premature labor. Before I knew it, I broke down and started crying. I just wanted Kelly to go away for good. Was that too much to ask? She didn't even have to go away for good; just get out of our lives. Why wouldn't she just find some other guy to stalk and leave my Tristan alone? She told him that she would see him again but I didn't want her to see him again. I didn't want her to come near him or even talk to him...*ever*. He was mine...my prince...my angel and I wanted him to be safe. Tristan said he wanted to protect me but I wanted to protect him.

He sat next to me and embraced me tightly while I sobbed uncontrollably into his t-shirt. He started rubbing my back and said quietly, "Bridget, please don't think I'm evil for saying this but..." He pulled away from me and when I looked up at his face, he wore a humorless expression. "I wanna kill her." I gasped in shock at his bold admission but he wasn't fazed by my reaction. "She tried to kill you and now...I wanna kill *her*."

Now, I've heard Tristan threaten to kill people before but now I knew he was being dead serious. The last thing I wanted was for my husband to become a cold-blooded murderer. I shook my head vehemently and shouted, "No, Tristan! Let the police handle it."

He heaved a heavy sigh and I could detect defeat in his voice. "Maybe we should move. Just sell the house and pack up everything."

Oh no, he was *not* letting her win. I wasn't going to let that blonde home wrecker drive us out of our new house; a house we haven't even turned into a true home yet. "No, this is our home and we're not going anywhere. She's the one that's going away. Just let Det. Grace work on our case. They'll catch her sooner or later."

"I'm worried it may be too late," he replied wearily. "You were right, Bridget. She *is* a real threat."

My voice softened as I tried to reassure him. "I trust that they'll find her and arrest her. Just give them some time. Even if they can't trace the car back to her, she's stalking you and there are laws against that."

Tristan sighed heavily again. "Okay, whatever you say, babe." All of sudden, his expression changed like he just remembered something. "We need to get another car. I don't have time to wait around for the insurance company to pay us. I ringed Mum and Dad and told them everything. They wired us some money so we can get another one. Aut's on her way over to take us to the Volvo dealer. We may as well get it now." I'll admit that my spirits were lifted momentarily at the idea of buying a new car. Although I was saddened that I no longer had the first and best Valentine's gift Tristan ever gave me, I was still a little excited to get our official Hathaway Family Mobile.

Autumn was so upset and concerned about what happened to me last night that she offered to stay with us for awhile and look after me. I agreed with her suggestion because I didn't want Tristan keeping a hawk eye on me 24/7. As we were driving home in our brand new, 2008 passion red Volvo V50, we stopped at the impound lot to pick up Tristan's bike. Then he and Autumn followed me as I drove the rest of the way home by myself. When we got inside, she set herself up in the guest room.

We didn't hear back from Det. Grace until almost three days later. This time I greeted him at the door and he followed me into our living room once again to fill us in on the latest details regarding our case. Autumn was at the store so she wasn't present but I planned to tell her everything once she returned. I was anxious to know what he found out and if he actually spoke to Kelly. Tristan was even more anxious because he asked gruffly, "So, did you catch the fucking bint?"

Det. Grace started scratching his head. When he gave a small sigh, I could tell right away that he was going to deliver bad news. He confirmed my assumption because he replied, "The name she gave to the police during the altercation at the bar & grill was false. We don't know her friend's name because she fled the scene before the police arrived." Tristan swore loudly and then he got up from his seat. He began pacing the room as the detective continued speaking. "Also, the restaurant didn't have video surveillance at the time so we have no photo of Kelly or her friend. After reviewing the records from Tristan's cell phone, most of the numbers she contacted him from are now disconnected. And the active numbers are random pay phones throughout California. But we're still working on trying to find out the last persons the disconnected numbers were registered to."

Tristan yelled out again, "It's like she's a fucking ghost! No one can catch her!" He turned to me with his light blue eyes ablaze. "What did I tell you, Bridget?!? I told you the bloody pigs wouldn't be able to help us! I'm the only one that can end this!"

Det. Grace put his hands up and spoke calmly. "Now just wait a minute, Tristan. I also came here to ask your permission to tap your phones; particularly your cell phone and your house phone."

Tristan responded sharply, "I have another phone number...*again*. She hasn't ringed me on it...*yet*."

"Well, I'm hoping she won't. But still...it would be a good idea to let us tap the phones; just for awhile so we can monitor them. If she *does* call, we'll be able to trace it easily."

I looked over at Tristan and he was trembling in anger from head to toe. I knew he hated accepting the police's help in any way, shape, or form. His dislike for them was embedded deep inside him and I knew me and Katie were the only reasons why he was agreeing to all this. He wanted to protect his family. He reluctantly gave the detective permission to tap our phones and they even tapped my cell phone in case she started harassing me too.

Two weeks went by without a word or a sign from the elusive Kelly. And for awhile...I foolishly let myself believe it was over.

Chapter 29

WHEN I WOKE UP ON the morning of Saturday, February 28th, I didn't feel any maternal sense or instinct that Katie was ready to leave the comfort of my warm, protective womb. Dr. Boykin said that today or tomorrow would be my due date but for some reason, I didn't believe today was the day. Tristan didn't share my belief and he put his faith in the doctor. He was convinced that before this day was over, it would no longer be just the two of us. Today we would become a family of three.

The previous night, I called my parents, Autumn, Jake and Lauren and told them that tomorrow could be the big day. I reminded them that it wasn't one-hundred percent guaranteed but if they wanted to, they could come over to wait and see if I went into labor. That morning while I was making breakfast, Tristan wasted no time setting up everything in our bedroom in preparation for my delivery.

After we ate, he guided me upstairs because he wanted me to inspect his hard work. I was really impressed when I saw that he already inflated our oval-shaped, blue vinyl birthing pool. It was sitting a couple feet from our bed on a large sheet of protective floor plastic. I saw the electric air pump he used neatly tucked into a corner. He even unraveled the water hose and ran it from one of the faucets in the master bathroom to the pool. All the necessary contents of the birthing kit were laid out on the bed: the underwater flashlight, debris net, floating thermometer, and the handheld water mirror. But what truly touched my heart was when I saw that he laid out some baby items for Katie; like a small diaper, and her thermal pink wrap with matching newborn gown and beanie.

I heard the doorbell in the late morning and Tristan was walking next to me as I went to answer the door. Autumn was the first to arrive and she was extremely excited and totally animated. She came inside and stood in the foyer with an expression of pure glee. "Bridge, where's your camcorder?!? I wanna catch the whole thing on video!"

Her enthusiasm rubbed off on me immediately and I smiled. "Wait, you're not going to ask me to put it on YouTube, are you?"

She laughed. "Of course! Or you could put it on your MySpace."

Her idea seemed to spark Tristan's interest because he voiced his opinion immediately. "Yeah, that's a good idea Aut!" He looked over at me and his expression matched hers. "I wanted to get it on video anyway but I forgot I'd be in the pool with you. I didn't think about who would be capturing the actual footage. You said you only wanted certain people in the room with you when you delivered, right babe?"

"Yeah, just Dr. Boykin and my mother." Right after I said that, I noticed Autumn's joyous mood disappear and her expression was crestfallen. I assumed she already knew she'd be in the room since we just established she was the video director but I guess not. I turned to her with a warm smile and put my hand on her shoulder. "Aut, I want you there too. Who else is going to hold the camcorder? My mother? She has a hard enough time just using her cell phone." I laughed lightly and when I saw her expression turn jovial once again, I knew I was able to reassure her.

Jake and Lauren arrived a couple hours after Autumn and I felt it necessary to inform them of the very small audience that was allowed to be present once I went into labor. Lauren looked a little disappointed but Jake actually looked relieved. He confirmed my assumption when he sighed a breath of relief and said, "Oh good. I really didn't wanna see it anyway. I don't think I can stomach seeing all that blood." In the corner of my eye, I saw Lauren's expression change and she seemed bothered by her boyfriend's comment. Tristan was standing right there and I was worried what Jake said may freak him out. I turned towards Tristan and I was surprised that he didn't look affected at all. But something inside me felt the need to gently remind him that it could get a little messy in the water.

"Baby, you know there will be some blood, right? I mean, I'll be giving birth and it's no picnic. You may see some things you've never seen before and they're not very pleasant."

Tristan still wasn't fazed. He put his arm around my shoulder and held me close. I nuzzled my nose into his shirt and he kissed the top of my head before he assured me that he was comfortable sharing the entire moment with me. "I know darlin', but I don't really care. I just wanna help you bring Katie into the world. You should know me by now and shit like that doesn't bother me." Just at that moment, my heart burst in devotion for him and I was glad he would be right there with me. Truthfully, I couldn't imagine any other person in the entire world that I would want to help me give birth to our daughter.

My parents arrived from Sacramento in the early afternoon and my mother made lunch for everyone. While we were eating in the dining room, I got a call from Dr. Boykin and she asked me if I went into labor yet. When I told her I didn't, she said she would still come over just in case.

After lunch, we were all sitting in the living room watching television but it seemed that I was the only person actually watching it. I felt six pairs of eyes on me and when I looked around the room, they were all watching me intently; like waiting for a timer to go off. Tristan was sitting next to me and he put his hand on my belly and began trying to coax Katie into leaving the womb. He spoke to her gently as if she was a child who was really sitting on my lap. "Do you wanna come out of there, baby girl? C'mon out and meet the fam." I heard a few chuckles and I couldn't help but to smile.

I put my hand on top of his and looked into his eyes. "You know, today might not be the day. It might be tomorrow."

He slowly rubbed my belly as he spoke to me and once again he was adamant in his belief. "No, it's gonna be today...I can feel it. She'll come out when she's ready but I know it's gonna be today." Tristan's words caused me to remember back to how certain he was that we were having a girl. I started to think of the possibility that maybe his senses were in some way in-tune to Katie. Right at that moment, I decided to put my faith in him and Dr. Boykin and I hoped that I would give birth before the day was over. I even took a page from Tristan's book and started talking to Katie too. I told her how much her family wanted to meet her and how she had a special nursery just waiting for her.

Since everyone in the room had their attention on me, their scrutiny was beginning to make me feel uncomfortable. I decided to get out of the house, so I stood up with the intention of talking a slow walk around the backyard. Naturally, my action caught Tristan's attention. "Babe, where are you going?"

"I'm just going outside to walk for a little while. I need to get out of the house." What I really wanted to say was: 'I need to get away from you all staring at me like you're waiting for me to pop.'

I don't know what made me think I could get away by myself because Tristan stood up immediately. "I'll come with you." He smiled so beautifully at me and when I saw his cute little dimple on his left cheek, I just couldn't reject him.

We left everyone in the living room and went through the kitchen and out the French doors to the back patio. We took a leisurely stroll hand-in-hand around the perimeter of the backyard and then we walked around our new in-ground pool. I laughed quietly to myself when I remembered how Tristan celebrated after the pool was ready for swimming last December. I was kneeling next to the edge; just passing my hand back-and-forth through the clear water when I noticed he was heading towards the diving board. When I saw him stand on it, I called out to him in surprise but it was already too late. He dove into the water fully-clothed. Even though the pool could be heated, it wasn't heated when he jumped in and I know the water was freezing cold. He yelled out in shock when he emerged from the surface but a smile quickly lit up his face and his boisterous laughter sounded so good to my ears.

Tristan's voice brought me back to the present and he must've heard my inner thoughts because he said quietly, "Yeah, the water was freezing. I don't know what I was thinking." I looked up at him and smiled and he gave me a knowing smile in return. Then he changed the subject. "I really wanna see Katie. I hope it happens soon. I've been waiting for this day ever since we found out you were pregnant." He gently pulled me close to him and placed a soft kiss on my forehead.

I found myself agreeing with him wholeheartedly. "Yeah, me too."

We stopped in front of the steps that lead into the water. "Sometimes I think about swimming with Katie. You know, when she's bigger. I wanna teach her how to swim." He gestured towards the pool slide. "Why do you think I got a slide and a diving board instead of that fake rock pool with the jacuzzi?" I gave him an expected look because I was curiously awaiting his answer. "'Cause I wanted our pool to be fun. I want our kids to enjoy it." One thing I really loved about Tristan... he always thought ahead. His voice sounded wistful when he said, "I wanna see Katie sliding down the slide; laughing all the way down." I was watching his face and he wore a thoughtful expression so I had a sneaking suspicion he was imagining the scene. For a moment, I wished I could see exactly what he was seeing because I wondered how he envisioned Katie when she grew up.

All of a sudden, I felt a cramp in my lower abdomen. The discomfort caused me to gasp and I put my hand there. That's when my water broke. Within seconds, it soaked through my panties and my heather-gray sweatpants. I felt the warm liquid run down my legs and even into my lounge slippers. My breathing increased when I realized my water breaking was the beginning of labor. I looked up at Tristan with wide-eyes and he was looking down at me in total shock. Once again, we were one with our emotions. He exclaimed loudly, "Oh shit! It's time, babe! It's time!"

He was absolutely right. I replied breathlessly, "Tristan, oh my God!" Before I could even blink, I found myself being picked up in his strong arms. He carried me quickly towards the back door and I was even more surprised when he opened it while still holding me. Surely I thought he'd be banging on it urgently for someone inside to let us in.

Once we were in the kitchen, he shouted, "It's time! Someone fill the pool and call the doctor!"

I saw Autumn's bleach-blonde head run into the kitchen first with Lauren and Jake in-tow. Her eyes were wide and she responded quickly. "I'm on it!" Then she dashed out of sight and I heard her run up the stairs in haste.

When I saw Dr. Boykin appear in the kitchen, I actually sighed a breath of relief. "I'm already here, Tristan."

Tristan moved swiftly and everyone followed behind us. Before he reached the stairs, he turned his head and spoke a friendly reminder over his shoulder. "Only Sharon and Dr. Boykin are allowed upstairs."

My father, Lauren, and Jake halted their steps but my mother and Dr. Boykin continued following us. When we got to the bedroom, I saw Autumn kneeling next to the pool as it was being filled with water. She was holding the thermometer in the water and she looked up and gave me a kind smile. "Don't worry, the water is the right temperature. I'll check it again once it's full."

Tristan sat me down on the bed and when his eyes met mine, he started smoothing my hair away from my forehead and speaking to me softly. "Are you ready, love? Are you ready to do this?"

I took a couple deep breaths because I could feel myself getting nervous. He kissed me and his lips stayed connected to mine for a few seconds. His unique, masculine scent engulfed my senses and I felt myself becoming calmer. When he unsealed his lips from mine, I nodded affirmatively. "Yeah, I'm ready."

"Don't be afraid, darlin'. I'll be there with you. I'll hold you in my arms through it all and I promise not to let go." The look in Tristan's eyes was one of pure affection and I smiled warmly and caressed his cheek.

Dr. Boykin interrupted our sentimental moment by saying, "You should get undressed, Bridget. The pool will be full in a matter of minutes." I turned towards her and I noticed she set up a little baby station at the foot of the bed. I saw a small weight scale and some other medical supplies laid out on a medium-sized folding table.

I was about to lift my shirt over my head when suddenly, a pain unlike anything I've ever experienced hit me in the same spot where I had the cramp. I quickly grabbed my abdomen and sucked some air between my teeth. I had to assume that was a contraction. I thought to myself: *Oh my God, this is what I'm going to have to deal with?!?* Dr. Boykin stood next to Tristan and they were both looking at me with deep concern. I guess my actions and my expression gave me away because she asked, "Are you having contractions, Bridget?"

Another one hit me and I squeezed my eyes shut and groaned in pain. I felt like lying down and curling into a ball but I knew I couldn't. I couldn't even speak because this contraction seemed to last longer than the first one. All I could do was nod. Then I heard her say, "Good, I'm going to start timing them. Tristan, I want you to help Bridget get undressed and into the pool." My eyes were still closed because I was secretly praying the pain would go away.

I felt Tristan's warm hands caressing my face and then I heard his quiet voice. "Just breathe, babe. Remember your breathing?" I opened my eyes because I felt him removing my clothes. Then I remembered the breathing I learned when he and I attended one of our Lamaze childbirth classes.

My mother sat next to me and started rubbing my back in an attempt to soothe me. "Tristan is right, honey. You need to breathe; in through your nose and out your mouth...slowly. And try to keep it steady."

The doctor asked, "When you have your next contraction, I want you to tell me."

I nodded again as I tried to control my breathing but it was impossible because the pain was so severe. I was still breathing erratically and I closed my eyes again. I just wanted to scream between feeling the contraction and Tristan struggling to remove my clothes while I remained in a seated position. To my relief, the pain began to subside and I was able to regulate my breathing more effectively. Before I knew it, I was sitting on the bed stark naked. I stood up slowly with Tristan supporting me on one side and my mother on the other. Autumn also came to stand next to me and she announced finally, "The pool is all ready for you and Tristan now."

I looked up and gave her a strangled smile. "Thanks, Aut."

She moved to the side where Tristan was supporting me and said, "Let me help her, Tris. You get in the pool." Tristan didn't need to be told twice because he had no qualms allowing her to take his position.

Then to my complete and utter surprise, he hastily stripped down to his birthday suit right in front of us. His action caught all the female attention because nobody moved a muscle but him. I wasn't concerned about Autumn seeing him naked because it was nothing new to her. I also wasn't concerned about Dr. Boykin because she's a doctor. But I gaped at him when I realized my *mother* was looking at his gorgeous nude form. "Tristan!" I shrieked.

He gave me a confused look and shrugged. "What?"

I heard my mother chuckle and when I turned to look at her, her eyes were roaming up-and-down my husband appreciatively. "*Very* nice," she said in a low, amused voice.

I was standing right next to the pool when I saw him get in first and sit with his back against the side. I informed him gently, "Tristan, I'm the one who has to be naked...not *you*."

He seemed very comfortable in the water and he looked up at me with a roguish grin. "If you're naked, then I'm gonna be naked."

I got into the pool and I was relieved that the water was so warm. I was really hoping it would help lessen the pain from the contractions because I needed all the help I could get. Tristan reached his arms out to me and I sat down between his legs with my back against his chest. Right at that moment, I felt another contraction and I moaned loud and deep like a suffering animal. Oh my God, it hurt *so* badly. Tristan immediately put his arms around me and the contractions continued. According to the doctor, they were getting closer together.

Soon, I couldn't stay in one position and I moved away from Tristan to sit in the middle of the pool. I was taught pain management in Lamaze class but all my teachings went out the window because the pain was excruciating. I was breathing hard and groaning as stab after stab of hot, searing pain tore through my lower abdomen. I tried not to yell out loud so I started biting my bottom lip. My mother noticed what I was doing and scolded me loudly, "Bridget, don't do that! You'll end up biting right through your lip!"

Okay fine, I won't bite my lip. I yelled out instead, "Oh God!" and I started rocking back and forth. Tristan moved from his previous position and was now sitting right next to me. He was rubbing my back and for a minute, I put my head on his shoulder and yelled in agony. "Oh my God! Tristan!" He encircled his arms around me in comfort and for some reason, I took a deep breath and submerged my entire head under the water. I don't know why I did it but pain of this caliber makes you do strange things.

Instead of screaming, I blew bubbles under the water and when I resurfaced, I sucked a huge amount of air into my lungs. Tristan smoothed my hair back away from my forehead and when I looked at him, he was just staring intently into my eyes. He spoke quietly again. "Breathe, darlin'. You can do it...try to breathe." Katie wasn't showing my body any mercy but I tried my hardest to regulate my breathing again.

I heard Autumn's friendly, reassuring voice. "You're doing great, Bridge. You're doing great." I looked up at her and she was sitting on the bed pointing the camcorder at me and Tristan.

Then Dr. Boykin approached the pool and leaned towards me. "Bridget, I want you to lay back and spread your legs so I can feel how dilated you are." I laid back and she put her gloved hand inside me. Suddenly her expression turned to one of surprise and her eyebrows shot upwards. "Oooohh-oh-oh-oh! You're ready, sweetie. You're ready to start pushing. Now is the time for you to deliver your baby."

Tristan moved away from me and I watched him sit back against the wall of the pool again. His expression was intense while he commanded me gently, "Come here, love. We can do it. Just let me help you."

The pain was bearing down on me now and I wanted the labor to be over. I could feel my body beginning to tremble and I was about five seconds away from asking for some pain medication. But I obediently moved into Tristan's embrace once more. Dr. Boykin spoke to me again. "When you feel a contraction, that's when you should push." She was still leaning over the pool and I saw the flashlight and the mirror in her hand.

I felt Tristan move his hands down and they were now resting between my open thighs. He whispered in my ear, "I'll catch her, darlin'. I'll be able to feel when she's coming. We can do this together. Do you trust me?"

"Yes, baby. I trust you," I responded quietly. Right at that moment, I knew he wanted the birth to be a moment shared only between me and him.

And so it began. Another mind-shattering contraction hit me and I yelled out. And just when I thought the pain couldn't get any worse... it did when I started pushing. How in the world did women go through natural child birth without any drugs? Now I wanted to beg someone to knock me out with a horse tranquilizer and just take Katie out of me while I'm unconscious. Forget holding her as soon as she's born. I'll bond with her when I wake up. I could feel her spreading my body inside and the pain was horrific. The contractions were nonstop and each time I pushed, I could feel her moving further down. That's when I started crying from the pain. Tristan was in back of me whispering words of encouragement and comfort but I really couldn't hear him because all I could focus on was the pain. That's probably why I turned into a sobbing mess and started pleading with the doctor. "I can't do it. I can't. It hurts soooo much." At this point, the lower part of my abdomen was on fire.

Dr. Boykin tried to help me by saying, "You can move around, Bridget. You can get into another position; maybe one that's more comfortable."

I was still blubbering when I responded, "No, I can't. I can't move. It hurts too much." An unfamiliar sound filled my ears and the entire bedroom. Then I realized the sound was actually me wailing out loud in agony.

Tristan decided to take control of the situation and he also gave me a pep-talk. "Bridget, you can do it. I know you, love. You're stronger than me. You can do this." His arms embraced me once again and he spoke firmly but quietly. "Try to push through the pain. Keep telling yourself... it's the only way to bring Katie into the world." His voice lowered even more when he asked, "Am I still your angel?"

"Yes," I whispered. I was desperately looking for some way that he could ease my pain and suddenly a thought entered my mind: *Wrap your wings around me. Please.*

"Close your eyes, love." I closed my eyes and I felt his embrace tighten. Then something strange happened: all I could hear was Tristan's voice. It was so weird but it was like we were all alone in a dark room and every other sight and sound was blocked out. "Forget the other people in the room. It's just me and you now. The pain will keep coming but you have to try and overcome it. Think about Katie. Now's the time, Bridget. It's time for Katie to join us." I felt his hands slip between my thighs again. "I need you to push, darlin'. Push our daughter out." I wasn't feeling any pain while he was speaking to me but then another contraction hit and a bore down on his hands and gave one, long, hard push. That's when he said, "Open your eyes."

My eyes shot open and I saw Dr. Boykin holding the flashlight and the mirror under the water. "I see the head! You're doing great, Bridget. Come on now...you can do it." My mother was kneeling next to the doctor and her hands were clasp tight as she looked on silently.

I pushed again and I actually felt part of Katie break through me. I gasped and cried out loudly in pain once again. My entire body was shaking in Tristan's arms and I felt him touch me under the water. He whispered, "I can feel her head. She's right there."

An animalistic growl escaped my throat as I pushed harder than ever. I felt like the lower half of me was being split in two. The doctor was telling me I was almost there and I was praying to God she was telling the truth. Oh, how I wanted this agonizing ordeal to be over. Tristan wanted another child in the future but I don't think I could go through this again. I took a moment to catch my breath and that's when I heard his voice again. He whispered directly in my ear, "If you give me one good push this time, I'll pull her gently. C'mon, sweets...you can do it. Let me help you bring Katie into the world now." I knew my limits and I didn't have much left in me so I told myself: *This is it. You either push her out now or suffer even longer.*

If Katie wanted to come out, I wasn't going to hinder her any further. I pushed with all my might and I felt Tristan tugging her at the same time. It was happening just the way we both wanted; we were giving birth to our daughter together. Her entire body slipped through me and the pain intensified for a few seconds. I looked down between my legs and I saw the color red tinge the cloudy water. I yelled out loud after one last push and that's when I finally felt Tristan pull our baby from my body. Right at that moment, the pain turned into a dull throb and I couldn't help but to sob in relief. I gasped again and tried to catch my breath but I couldn't because I was crying so intensely. Then I heard Tristan exclaim in sheer happiness, "I got her! She's in my hands!" I reached down and we pulled our daughter from the water.

The first thing I saw was the top of a small head covered completely with hair. We held Katie up just to make sure she was a girl and once it was confirmed, I cradled her gently in my arms. Upon closer inspection, I realized her hair wasn't red like mine; it was blonde like Tristan's. Since it was wet, it was a darker blonde but what I noticed even more was how much hair she had. My eyes were wide because I couldn't believe what I was seeing and neither could anyone else. My mother pointed it out first. "Oh my goodness! Look at all that hair! I can't believe it!"

Autumn laughed. "Wow, I've never seen a baby with a full head of hair like that. And she's blonde like Tristan!"

My eyes connected with Autumn's hazel ones and we shared yet another knowing smile. I was thinking about how every aspect of her dream was coming true so far. I still wondered about Katie's British accent and when I would find out the reason behind that.

One of Tristan's arms was under mine and the other reached up to stroke her hair. I could see the umbilical cord still attached to her and the end of it disappeared under the water. His voice was full of emotion and I could tell he was crying. "My daughter...my little princess. She's beautiful just like her mother." Then he kissed me on the cheek. "You did it, love. You did it."

I turned my head slightly and kissed him on the lips because I realized I couldn't have done it without his support. Tristan really did give me his strength because I was the one who wanted to give up. I smiled lovingly before I corrected his statement. "No my love...we did it." Then I remembered something else of great importance and I felt an urgent need to make him aware. "Baby, when Katie was still inside me and you said you felt her...your touch was the first she ever felt. She felt her father's touch."

He smiled back at me and I saw his azure eyes glisten with tears of joy. We both turned our attention to the newest member of our family and as I gazed at the little wonder in my arms, I realized he was right. She was beautiful...just like her *father*. I was trembling and crying because I couldn't believe she was finally with us.

Dr. Boykin moved right next to us on the outside of the pool so she could quickly examine Katie. Then she stuck this thing in Katie's mouth that made a soft sucking sound and that's when we heard the sound we were all waiting to here: the baby's first cry. Katie cried for at least a full minute before she settled down. I was pleasantly surprised that she only calmed down once Tristan whispered soothing words to her. I couldn't help but smile because she was already 'Daddy's Little Girl'. When she opened her eyes and looked up at us, we both gasped in surprise. Her eyes were blue but not the exact color of Tristan's. But I knew deep inside that they would eventually change to match his beautiful shade. I also noticed in addition to his hair, she had his perfect nose. I pointed this fact out to him when I said, "She has your nose."

Tristan chuckled. "No, she doesn't."

I looked up at him and smirked. "You have an elfin nose."

"I have a *what?*"

I looked back at Katie and touched the tip of her tiny nose. "Do you see that? That's a little elfin nose." I looked into my beloved's eyes again. "That's *your* nose."

Everyone laughed and that's when I heard Autumn's voice again. It was low and quiet like she didn't want to scare the baby. "Oh my God, you guys. She's so cute. I can't believe I'm an aunt. I am *so* gonna spoil her rotten." I looked up at her and she was kneeling next to the pool; still pointing the camcorder at us.

My mother chimed in, "That makes two of us."

Tristan retorted, "When my parents and Nanny see her, that'll make..." I looked up at him and he had his eyes cast towards the ceiling as he thought. "Five of you!" He picked up one of Katie's tiny hands and put his finger inside her palm. He made a sound of surprise when she grasped his finger and held on tight. "Whoa! She's strong! She has my finger, babe! Do you see this?" I laughed in delight when I saw that she was exhibiting another good sign that she was healthy. Her blue eyes looked around the room and Tristan remarked again, "Look how curious she is. She's just looking around at everything. And she won't let go of my finger." He chuckled in amusement and then he spoke to her softly. "Hey princess, can Daddy have his finger back?" She still held onto it so he shrugged. "I guess not."

While we continued to bond with Katie, something in the back of my mind remembered that the worse was over and there was still another female in the house who was prohibited from entering our bedroom during the delivery. I looked over at my mother and asked, "Mom, can you get Lauren please? I want her to come in now."

She nodded and then she disappeared from the room to invite my fellow redhead to join in the celebration. A few minutes later, she returned with my faux younger sister in-tow. Lauren's cinnamon eyes were wide with surprise as she approached the pool. She knelt down next to me and looked at Katie in amazement. "Wow, look at all that hair!" Katie's hair was beginning to dry and it resembled Tristan's golden color even more. Lauren covered her mouth with her hand to stifle her girly giggles. "Bridget, she is so adorable." She repeated Autumns' earlier remark when she said, "And she has blonde hair like Tristan." She reached out like she was going to touch Katie but then decided against it.

I gave her a reassuring smile. "You can touch her. It's okay."

She smiled back and reached out to gently stroke Katie's chubby cheeks. She was still touching her affectionately when she asked casually, "What was it like?"

"What? Giving birth?" She nodded. "Uh, let's see...painful!" We both laughed but when I looked down at my brand new daughter again, I added fondly, "But it was worth it."

Dr. Boykin asked me if I wanted the cord cut and when I gave her the green light, she instructed Tristan on how to do it. I was honestly surprised that he wasn't hesitant or squeamish in the least. Once he cut the cord, she clamped it and said, "Alright kiddo, you can deliver the placenta whenever you're ready."

Ugh, the placenta. The thought of it made me nauseous. I knew what was going to happen when I delivered it so I felt responsible to inform the other party in the pool with me. "Um...sweetheart, you may want to get out of the pool now because delivering the placenta will be kind of gross."

Tristan raised an eyebrow and gave me a look as if to say: *Do I look like I care?* Oh that's right. Duh, how stupid of me. I told the doctor I was ready because I wanted to get it over with. I handed Katie to my mother and I watched her coo and fuss over her just like a typical grandmother. The doctor was standing by with the debris net while I proceeded to make the pool water even more disgusting. I remembered I was being filmed so I looked over at Autumn. "Aut, turn off the camera. I don't want anyone to see this."

She obliged and immediately following the delivery, even I couldn't stand being in the pool any longer. Tristan was eerily calm and I wondered if that was his own defense mechanism. Maybe he was detaching himself from the reality of what was happening so he wouldn't scream and jump out of the pool. I was a second away from screaming myself so I said in an urgent voice, "I want to get out of here!"

Tristan and Lauren helped me to stand up and when I did, I felt like a tremendous weight had disappeared from me and I actually felt lighter. Well, that's because I was. My stomach was kind of flabby but it was definitely flatter than before. I took one last look at the water Tristan and I was sitting in and it looked like it was feeding time for sharks. I shuddered involuntarily and I was grateful when I finally stepped foot onto the plastic floor cover. It wasn't until I heard Lauren's cheeky remark, "You're not as hairy as your brother," that I remembered Tristan was naked in front of everyone.

Tristan stood proud and flashed a charming smile. "I know."

I saw that my mother handed Katie to the doctor and she was doing something with her over at the baby station. Autumn and Lauren cleaned me off with a sponge and then Dr. Boykin handed Katie to

Tristan. Katie was now wrapped in her pink blanket but her shock of wheat-colored hair was visible. I guess she didn't need her beanie after all. The doctor told me she wanted to examine me to assess if I needed any medical attention to my nether regions. My mother put a mattress-top on top of the comforter to protect it while the doctor examined me. The examination actually caused me more pain but I thanked my lucky stars when she informed me that I wouldn't need stitches. I was still having major cramps so she finally gave me some pain meds. Then I put on a pair of panties and a maternity nightgown before I rested comfortably in our bed.

Tristan had on a pair of black track pants and was slowly walking barefoot around the room with Katie. I was sitting up watching him and he seemed oblivious to everyone around him as he cradled her little body close to his bare chest. He spoke to her in a hushed voice and I couldn't help but wonder what he was saying to her.

Dr. Boykin sat next to me on the bed and told me that she took Katie's height and weight, and she even took her hand and footprints. She was holding a blank birth certificate in her hand when she asked me gently, "So, what name do I put on this?"

Tristan heard her question and he paused his steps to look over at us. His eyes met mine and we shared another loving smile. Then I announced proudly, "Katherine Elizabeth Hathaway."

It wasn't long until Tristan joined me in the bed and we bonded with Katie once again. Autumn and my mother pumped the water out of the birthing pool and soon it was cleaned, deflated, and packed away. Autumn was holding Katie when Jake and my father were finally allowed entrance into the bedroom. My father's eyes filled with tears of joy when they took sight of his first grandchild. He held her lovingly and the happiness was clearly evident in his face when I saw the crinkles on the corners of his eyes. He remarked to Tristan, "Watch out for this one. She's going to have the boys calling the house and knocking on your door in no time." He looked over at me with a very fatherly smile. "Trust me, I should know."

I smiled in return and that's when Tristan replied, "Believe me, I already know." He laughed. "But don't worry...I'll be prepared."

I was leaning against Tristan's chest and he had his arms around me. I looked up at him and asked, "Oh, so you're going to be one of *those* fathers? Scaring any boy half to death who tries to date your daughter."

"That's right, babe. Katie's not dating until she's eighteen." I laughed in amusement because his response was one of the typical overprotective father variety.

Jake was watching my father curiously as he held Katie in his arms. When my father noticed and tried to hand Katie to him, I was surprised when Jake rejected him quietly. "No, I can't. I don't know how to hold babies."

My mother stepped in immediately to remedy Jake's problem. She took Katie from my father and placed her gently in Jake's capable arms. He cradled her like she was precious, fragile glass and he seemed tickled to be holding his first and only niece. "She's a wee girl. Hullo love, I'm your uncle Jake." He must've done the same thing Tristan did earlier because then he exclaimed, "Oi! She's got my finger! And she's really strong!" He laughed lightly.

Tristan remarked sarcastically, "Yeah, tell me about it."

"I don't think she's gonna let go either. She's got me in a tight grip." He took a few steps and started walking with her as he spoke. "She's just looking around."

"She's really curious, bro."

"Oh, wait. I think she's bored with me. She looked at me for a quick second and then she turned her head. Yep, she's bored with me."

This time Autumn laughed. "That's weird 'cause she wasn't bored with me."

Jake looked over at her and replied dryly, "That's 'cause you're a female." He looked over at his girlfriend and asked curiously, "Lauren, how did she react when you spoke to her?"

Lauren smiled. "Actually, she looked right at me."

He pouted but I could tell he was amused by being ignored by his niece. He slowly walked over to me and Tristan and bent down slightly. "Please take her now. I'm afraid I may drop her." Lauren intervened and I guess she wanted more time with Katie so she held her for awhile. Jake stood close to her and smiled as they showered Katie with attention. I smiled thoughtfully and started wondering if they would have a baby of their own soon.

My meds were kicking in and I felt completely pain-free. I was also starving. I sat up and announced to no one in particular, "I'm so hungry right now. I'm in the mood for some McDonald's."

My mother, who was sitting on the bed at my feet, clucked her tongue and shook her head in disapproval. "Bridget, you know you shouldn't be eating that garbage."

"Mom, I've been good most of my pregnancy and now I want to eat some junk food. I have a taste for some nuggets, French fries, and a strawberry shake."

Autumn stood up from her seat on the bed and exclaimed once again, "I'm on it!" She was like my personal assistant today and I couldn't help but to laugh at her enthusiasm.

She was on her way out the door when I yelled out, "And a double cheeseburger!"

I heard Tristan speak quietly under his breath. "Damn."

I turned my head towards him and gave him a peck on the lips. "Don't worry, baby. I'll share my fries with you." He grinned at me and his cute dimple made an appearance for my pleasure.

My declaration of hunger caught Dr. Boykin's attention because she asked, "I wonder if Katie would feed from you now. Why don't you give it a try?"

Tristan's voice was breathless when he agreed with her. "Yeah, babe. Try it." Lauren gave Katie to me while Tristan took the liberty of opening one of the breast flaps on my maternity gown. Katie was wide awake looking around the room as I tried to tempt her with a nipple. At first she wasn't paying it any attention but soon she began to suckle.

I gasped in amazement and triumph when I felt her actually feeding from me. Tristan held me close and stroked Katie's hair that now matched his as she enjoyed her dinner. I saw the doctor beginning to pack up her belongings and I knew she was leaving. But I didn't want her to leave before I could express to her my most sincere gratitude for personally assisting us with our home birth. "Dr. Boykin?"

She looked up at me as she put something in one of her bags. "Yes, Bridget?"

I was powerless to stop the tears from forming in my eyes when I said, "Thank you for everything. I can't even begin to tell you what having you here has meant to me. You're so much better than any midwife I could've ever had."

She didn't say anything for a moment but I could tell she was humbled. She dabbed at her eyes before she finally spoke. "You're welcome, Bridget. And don't worry, I'll be back to check up on you and Katie. I don't normally do house calls but I'll gladly make an exception for you. Besides, you're like my niece. Call me if you have any problems or if you need me." She picked up one of her bags. "Oh, and I want to see you in my office in a few days. I'll need to give you and Tristan all the official medical documents for Katie. And we need to discuss her vaccinations." Everyone else gave her their thanks and said goodbye. Then my father helped her with her belongings and she closed the bedroom door behind her.

Jake called Will, Kate, and Nanny, and soon they were celebrating the news of their newborn granddaughter and great-granddaughter on the other side of the Atlantic Ocean. He exclaimed humorously to his father, "Dad, I'm telling you...she has more hair than you!" I spoke to them on the phone while Katie napped peacefully in her father's protective arms after she had her fill of milk. Kate didn't know we were naming the baby after her and when I revealed the surprise, it was a very emotional moment.

She paused for a moment before she started crying. "Ohhh Bridget, I can't believe you and Tristan would do that. You didn't have to name her after me."

Hearing her voice so heavy with emotion caused tears to prick at the back of my eyes. Before I knew it, my vision was blurry. "I love you Kate, and when Tristan told me he wanted to name her after you...there was no way I could say no." She was quiet again but I heard her soft sniffles.

"Thank you, Bridget. You've always been such a sweetheart. I love you too. I can't wait to see her. I bet she's beautiful."

"She really is, and she looks just like Tristan. She's got blonde hair!"

I could hear the cheerfulness in her voice when she said, "We're all going to take the first flight we can to California. Will is on the computer booking our tickets right now." I was filled with such happiness because I haven't seen my in-laws in a long time and I was anxious for them to meet the newest member of the Hathaway family.

Lauren and Jake stayed for awhile but soon they decided to leave too. But before they did, I asked them if they would be Katie's Godparents. Jake was stunned by my request and Lauren was surprised as well but they both happily agreed and said they would be honored.

Autumn came back with my McDonald's order, but she also brought food for everyone. My mother watched in distaste as I took pleasure in devouring every morsel of the fattening and greasy fast-food. I kept my promise and shared my French fries with my husband but he also ate most of my nuggets.

I fed Katie once more and I noticed her eyelids drooping again. We decided to put her in the nursery so we all followed Tristan as he carried her. I was holding my breath as he laid her gently in her crib because I was praying she wouldn't wake up and start crying. She twitched in her sleep but other than that, she didn't open her eyes.

Autumn whispered she had to leave and I noticed she was taking my camcorder with her because she had the carrying case slung over shoulder. "I'll call you when I upload the video to my computer. Then I'll send you the file and you can upload it on YouTube or MySpace after you guys watch it." She bent down into the crib and gave Katie a gentle kiss on the top of her sleeping blonde head before she left. "G'night my special niece."

My parents went home shortly after Autumn, and it wasn't much longer until Tristan and I decided to go to bed. Katie was still asleep and we both had a very tiring and emotional day. When our heads hit the pillow, we were out like a couple of lights.

Unfortunately, my peaceful slumber didn't last long because I heard Katie crying on the baby monitor. I woke up first and padded barefoot down the hall to her nursery. I turned on the light and I saw her crying and writhing in her crib. I picked her up gently and cradled her against my bosom. "It's okay, darling. Mommy's here." I checked her diaper and low and behold, I was about to experience my first diaper change. Luckily, because she was born a few hours ago, I didn't have to deal with the odor that usually accompanies them. She was still kind of fussy after I changed her so I wondered if she was hungry again. I sat in our mother-daughter nook that Uncle Jake made for us and watched her beautiful blue eyes look up at me as she suckled.

It was probably ten minutes into our bonding, when Tristan walked in the nursery. To my surprise, he turned off the ceiling light and turned on the small lamp that was sitting on her dresser. I looked up at him and he was looking back at me through slightly puffy and sleepy eyes. He was in his *au naturale* state and his blond hair was a messy bird's nest on top of his head. I spoke to him quietly. "Baby, go back to sleep. I can handle this. She's okay now. She just needed a diaper change and she was hungry again."

I don't know why I bothered to tell him to go back to sleep because I knew he wouldn't. I had my feet propped up on the ottoman but there was still enough room for him to sit on it. He was watching me breastfeed Katie and I could tell from his expression that the scene was affecting him emotionally. There was unmistaken adoration in his gaze and he reached out to stroke her soft baby hair that was so similar to his own. He spoke quietly too as to not disturb the peaceful ambiance in the nursery. "I can't go back to sleep without you. But I don't mind staying here with you and Katie." We shared another smile and the room was quiet and dim as we listened to Katie enjoying her late-night meal.

I was looking down at her and I started thinking about how today was just the beginning; the beginning of a life-long commitment to being her mother. There would be so many more late-night feedings and diaper changes. Not to mention, teaching her everything I could and guiding her in the right direction. My mind fast-forwarded to the future and I wondered what kind of person she'd become. How we raise her will have a lasting effect on her for the rest of her life and I was afraid to make any mistakes. An unexpected feeling of anxiety floated to the surface of my consciousness and I couldn't help but to express to my soul mate what I was truly feeling. I whispered in the dim nursery, "Tristan, I'm scared of being a parent."

He rubbed my leg through my nightgown in an attempt to comfort me. But I was surprised when he admitted, "I'm scared too. But we'll be okay 'cause we'll raise her together. And if we need help, we have our parents to help us." He chuckled softly. "We'll be lucky if we can get Mum and Nanny to leave once they see Katie." Tristan was probably right and I chuckled too. Then his expression changed and his voice took on a more serious tone. "Bridget?"

"Yes?"

He paused and averted his eyes for a moment. I was watching his face and he looked like he was contemplating his next words. Then his azure eyes darted towards me again. "I don't want you to go back to work after your maternity leave is over."

I wasn't expecting that type of request so I looked at him questioningly. "Why?"

He answered me simply, "I want you to take care of Katie."

I couldn't hide the surprise in my voice when I asked, "You want me to be a stay-at-home mom?"

"Yeah, I do. And when we have more kids, I want you to be able to be home with them. I mean, you can do other things when they're in school. You know, like shopping or take up any hobbies you want." He paused again and looked intently into my eyes. "I wanna take care of you, Bridget." Tristan rendered me speechless but I was filled with emotion because I had no idea he desired this. When he started speaking again it was like his mind was somewhere else. "I wanna put money away for our kids. I want them to go to the best schools and the best universities. And I wanna buy them nice cars when they get their license."

Tristan's thoughts of the future made me laugh and I couldn't help but to ask, "Oh, you want to spoil them too like my mother and Autumn?"

He laughed lightly before he said, "No kid of mine is gonna be a fucking brat...trust me. I'll put my foot in their arse the moment they start expecting shit from us. We'll teach them that they have to earn what they want but I'll give them things if I feel they've earned it or deserve it." He paused again and his tone was softer. "I don't want you to go back to work. I'm not forcing you. I'm only *asking* you."

At that moment, I thought of what my parents would think if I stopped working. Then I started thinking of all the money they spent on my education. I wondered if they would be disappointed in me. "Tristan, my parents spent a lot of money on my education and I've only been a teacher for five years. I haven't even begun to pay them back."

His expression changed to one of confusion. "Babe, I don't think they want you to pay them back. Sending kids to college is what parents do."

The idea of being able to be there full-time for my children was very tempting. I looked at the little one in my arms and I wanted to be the best mother to her. And if I had more time to devote to her growth and development, it would definitely be to her benefit. I was still unable to make a solid decision so I replied, "I don't know Tristan, but I'll definitely consider it." I gazed at Katie again and I was even more tempted to give up teaching other people's children and concentrate on my own. "Maybe you're right. I probably won't want to go back to work after being with Katie. I'll probably want to spend as much time with her as possible."

He smiled and gave my knee a gentle pat. "You have time to think about it." Then he reached over towards the CD player that was sitting on the end table next to me and turned on the music. I noticed Katie had released me and I could see her eyelids drooping heavily as the traditional Irish lullaby *'Gartan Mother's Lullaby'* quietly filled her whimsical nursery. The song was part of a Celtic baby CD that Nanny had given to us. I was rocking our newborn daughter to sleep while Tristan sat silently and watched. He stayed in the nursery with me and we finally laid Katie in her crib for the second time that night.

We both stood next to it and took a moment to look down at our daughter's tiny sleeping body. She just looked so perfect to me. I was so thankful and I felt so blessed because my very own fallen angel gave me the most beautiful child and God made her healthy. Tristan put his arm around my waist and his whisper was like a soft caress on my skin. "Bridget Raegan...I've never loved you more than I do right now." I looked up at him and I could see unshed tears being held behind his beautiful cerulean orbs. Right at that moment, I wondered if he heard my thoughts again.

My lips melted with his and when the kiss ended, I whispered back, "I love you too, Tristan Caleb." Then we put our arms around each other as we turned off the lamp, and let the music from Katie's homeland dance into her dreams.

That night as I lay in my angel's embrace, I pondered a life of freedom and just raising a family. Despite the indescribable pain I experienced during child birth, I decided that I would go through it all over again just to have another precious baby from the gorgeous Brit lying in bed with me. But the next time we joined each other in the birthing pool,

I hoped to grace our second child with the special name Tristan Caleb Hathaway, Jr. There was a smile of contentment on my face as I thought of expanding our little family in the future. Then I closed my eyes and finally succumbed to my own lullaby sung to me by Tristan's wonderful heart.

Chapter 30

'All God's angels come to us disguised.'

~ James Russell Lowell

JAKE AND LAUREN'S NEW HOME in Glendale, California was absolutely breathtaking. Their house was bigger than me and Tristan's and they lived in a private gated community. But unlike his younger brother, Jake didn't need his parents' assistance to purchase his huge, expensive residence. All the money he made working at the bank really paid off for him and he was currently enjoying a simpler less-demanding career. The newlyweds purchased their 4-bedroom, 3 1/2-bath Spanish house a couple months after their wedding in September. The day of Jake's marriage proposal was unforgettable. He and Lauren were at our house for a summer pool party, when he surprised her with the proposal. And right after she accepted his proposal and he stood up from his kneeling position, she looked into the eyes of her new fiancé and told him that she was three months pregnant. The expression on Jake's face was so priceless that I actually took a picture of it with Tristan's cell phone.

Tristan and I arrived at their house in the late afternoon for their Christmas Eve party. The decorations were definitely top-notch and I was truly impressed with how much detail they put into the festivities. I was also appreciative of the fact that the guest count for the party itself wasn't too overwhelming. We were standing by their nine-foot, fully-decorated, white Christmas tree and I was amazed there was still space above the bright star on top because of their high, magnificent ceilings.

I was holding Katie in my arms and she was dressed in her red velvet holiday dress with white stockings and black-and-white saddle shoes. I topped off her Christmas baby ensemble with a red silk hair band that was accented with fake holly and red berries, and little gold snowmen earrings. Tristan was smiling as he tempted his ten-month-old daughter with a Christmas cookie in the shape of a reindeer. She wasted no time grabbing the cookie with her chubby hands and munched on it in sheer delight. I could feel the cookie crumbs landing on my shoulder as I asked my brother-in-law about his drastic career change. "So Jake, how does it feel leaving the corporate world for the rewarding sanction of education?"

Jake had a frosty bottle of beer in his hand and he laughed lightly. "Even though I miss the salary, I'm actually having more fun." He smiled and wore a thoughtful expression. "I really like teaching kids." Jake coached soccer for a junior high in Glendale and I agreed with Tristan when he said it was the perfect job for his brother. If there was one person who loved 'footie' more than Tristan, it was Jake. And the opportunity to teach other people how to play was right up his alley. I smiled too as I thought back to when I last taught children; right before my maternity leave two weeks prior to Katie's birth. I finalized my decision not to return to school after my maternity leave was over. I was currently enjoying the freedom of just being a full-time wife and mother...and I loved every minute of it.

Thoughts of my old profession made me realize how quickly this year has gone by. In addition to Jake and Lauren's wedding, I attended two other special nuptials this year. After four years of dating each other exclusively, Autumn and Ryan finally tied the knot in the spring. Then to everyone's surprise, Kate and Will broke the news that they had fallen in love again and decided to give marriage another try. They wed in Brighton during the summer and attending their wedding brought back so many memories for me. As I watched them exchange their vows and new wedding rings, I thought of the day Tristan and I got married just two years ago in the same city during the same season. The subject of the elder Hathaways came up when Jake remarked, "Mum, Dad, and

Nanny are flying out for Christmas tomorrow. And Lauren's family is coming down too."

The idea of a packed house full of in-laws caused my eyebrows to shoot upwards in surprise. "Wow Jake! You're going to have a packed house. It's a good thing you have two extra bedrooms." I glanced at Lauren's pregnant belly and I remembered something else. "You would have *three* if the nursery wasn't already finished."

I heard Tristan's voice next to me. "Babe, Nanny is staying with us since we have an extra room." I looked over at him and he was brushing cookie residue off Katie's nose and cheeks. Sometimes I think she forgets where her mouth is. I don't know if Tristan thought I would object but his tone softened suddenly. "I told her she could stay."

I gave him a reassuring smile and I saw his expression lighten. "Oh, that'll be great!" I exclaimed happily. I immediately thought of Nanny's delicious culinary skills and added wistfully, "I really miss her cooking."

Lauren was playing with Katie and I noticed she slipped her another cookie when I wasn't looking. I had a good mind to take it away from her considering we didn't even have dinner yet but I weighed my options between a screaming baby and a content baby. Tristan didn't seem to mind and I didn't want to spoil Katie's obvious enjoyment so I opted for the latter kind of baby. But I made up my mind that was the last cookie she was going to have for the day. Katie's blue eyes, which were identical to her father's, lit up like the Christmas tree lights and she was ecstatic after she got another treat. She giggled happily and her gratitude affected Lauren because she laughed and pinched Katie's rosy cheeks. She rubbed her nine-months-pregnant belly when she said, "I'm telling you, Bridget. I'm about to pop at any moment."

I looked at her belly again and I couldn't help but to agree with her. "Yeah, you are."

Jake interjected, "Just don't pop right now. You're not due for a few days."

Tristan joined in on the baby subject when he announced proudly, "Katie took her first steps yesterday. We got it all on video and I'm gonna show the grands tomorrow."

The memory filled me and I looked at our daughter in amazement as she munched on her second cookie. "I'm really surprised because she's only ten months old."

Yesterday evening we were in the bedroom and I was standing in our closet trying to figure out what I wanted to wear to Jake and Lauren's party. Tristan was sitting on the bed talking to me while Katie was sitting on the floor playing with a toy. Then all of a sudden, she got bored with her toy and decided she liked something that was sitting on the closet floor next to my feet. She got up and took a couple wobbly baby-steps towards me and that's when Tristan stood up quickly and exclaimed in absolute joy. His excitement startled Katie and she fell flat on her little diapered 'bum'. I didn't waste any time when he told me to get the camcorder. I was filled with anticipation as I recorded the entire moment.

First, Tristan knelt a few feet away from her. Then he reached his arms out and beckoned her to walk towards him. Now, I thought she was going to crawl, but Katie is always ready to please her daddy. She got up again and wobbled into his arms without a single pause in her steps. Once she was in his arms, Tristan was thrilled and he picked her up and kissed both of her cheeks. I kept the camera rolling with a huge smile on my face as they snuggled each other and he showered his daughter with praise. They were definitely two-of-a-kind because Katie was truly amazing just like her father.

Autumn and Ryan were standing with us and she laughed. "Since Katie's walking now, I bet Tris will have her kicking a soccer ball in no time." This time everyone laughed because we all knew that was quite probable.

Because we were laughing, Katie giggled too. I reached up to smooth some of the soft, blonde curls on her head. "Do you know what her first word was?"

Jake guessed first. "Was it 'no'?" He grinned slyly.

I smiled because that was a very common first word for babies but our baby was anything but common. Tristan answered before I could and there was that underlying pride in his voice again. "It was 'da-da'." He kissed Katie on the cheek.

I couldn't help but to pout a little. "I was surprised she didn't say my name first."

Lauren tilted her head to the side and spoke condescendingly. "You know little girls love their daddies."

I couldn't argue with her on that point. Tristan stroked Katie's hair that matched his, and then he gently rubbed his perfect elfin nose against her tiny one. He started using his baby voice when he said to her, "That's right...you love your daddy, don't you?" Katie gave a loud squeal in happiness and gurgled at receiving her father's loving attention. She really was 'Daddy's Little Girl'.

Not only that, *she* was the star tonight. She garnered everyone's attention because Tristan and I were the only people at the party with a child. Lauren was watching Tristan and Katie with an amused expression. Without taking her eyes off them, she remarked casually, "We finally decided on a name for the baby. We're naming him Connor James."

Tristan nodded approvingly. "That's a good, strong Irish name."

I decided to tease Autumn and maybe jinx her a little so I remarked, "You know Aut...you're next in line to have a baby."

Her eyes widened and she shook her head vehemently. "No way!" she rejected loudly. "I'm better suited to be an aunt anyway."

Ryan put his arm around her shoulder and held her close. "Awww, c'mon babe. A baby wouldn't be that bad." He reached out to tickle Katie and she giggled again before she buried her head in the crook of my neck. Suddenly, the scent of sugar cookie and apple juice invaded my nostrils.

Autumn was still shaking her head. "No, Ryan. You're not knocking me up." Her boyfriend laughed and kissed her affectionately. Then she made a comment that I found to be quite cryptic. It also caused a chill to run down my spine. "Katie and Connor are gonna be more like brother and sister than cousins since they'll only be a few months apart."

Whenever Autumn makes 'predictions', I always wonder if it's because she had another one of her creepy dreams. "Did you have a dream about it or something?"

She looked at me with a grin and I noticed the pensive expression on her face. "No, it's just a feeling I have." All of a sudden, her expression changed like a light bulb went off in her head. She looked at me intently and then she extracted herself from Ryan and stood close to me. I noticed her eyes darting around the room and she seemed anxious about something. Tristan, Jake, and Ryan seemed to get into an animated male conversation about something, and Lauren was preoccupied with telling Katie how pretty she looked in her dress. That's when Autumn whispered to me, "I need to talk to you." I looked at her expectedly to signal that she should continue and then she said, "Hey Bridge, will you come outside with me while I have a smoke?" But she said it loudly like she wanted everyone to hear her. I looked at her curiously because she started giving me an intense look. When she jerked her head in a direction away from our small social gathering, I finally picked up on the hint and turned towards my husband.

"Tristan, can you take Katie for a minute? I'm going outside with Autumn for a little while." He obliged immediately and I noticed Katie became extra bouncy once she was in her daddy's arms. Before I could even turn back around towards Autumn, she grabbed my arm and started guiding me through the house.

We reached the back door and stepped onto the patio. Autumn didn't light up a cigarette; she just stood there biting her shiny black fingernails while she gave me a worried look. Finally, I couldn't take her bizarre behavior any longer. I yelled in frustration, "What Autumn?!? Why are you looking at me like that?!?"

She didn't answer me at first and she shifted on her feet nervously. "I think you should sit down."

I sat on a cushioned patio chair and pulled my red cardigan tightly around me. "Can you make this fast because it's kind of cold out here."

She took a few steps to stand right in front of me and I noticed she didn't look any calmer. "I had another weird dream last night." My eyes widened in shock and she quickly added, "It wasn't about Katie and Connor. I was telling the truth when I said I didn't have a dream about them. No, this one was about..." She paused and took a deep breath. "It was about Tristan...*again*." Now she had my undivided attention. Actually, I think I was frozen in my chair. "Look, I know he told me not to tell you anymore of my dreams but I also remember his jinx." I didn't remember what she was referring to and I guess my internal confusion was reflected on my face. "You know, when he said to tell you guys if I had a dream that one of you was gonna die."

Right at that moment, I started trembling and my breathing increased. Then I stood up abruptly and started shaking my head. "No Autumn! I don't want to hear it! I don't want to know!"

She put her hand on my shoulder because I was on my way to the door. "Bridge, wait! It's not..." She paused again and I turned around to face her. I know the terror was written all over my face so she tried to reassure me by saying, "I'm not sure if it meant one of you died but..." She shifted her eyes back and forth as she desperately tried to convince me to stay and listen to her dream. "It just felt that way." She stepped closer to me, put both her hands on my shoulders, and gave me a pleading look. "Please just listen. Then you can draw your own conclusion as to what it means because I really don't know. I'm just guessing."

Because of my current state of panic, my voice was a little more clipped than I intended. "Yeah...well, your *guesses* have been pretty accurate as of late, haven't they?"

She sighed heavily. "I know Bridge, but I really think you should hear this one."

I took a deep breath and tried my hardest to stomp down on my feeling of apprehension. It was Christmas Eve and I didn't want to think about death on such a joyous occasion. But because I'm a very curious person, I slowly walked back to the chair and sat down. Then I looked up at her with a serious expression. "Fine...go ahead."

"First let me say that it didn't feel like a dream. These kind usually don't and I feel like I'm really there.

In my dream, the scene when I got ready for bed last night replayed itself. But it was different the second time around. I'll try to explain. The second time, I was getting ready for bed again but when I walked from the bathroom to the bedroom, there was a man sitting on my bed and he was crying. And the man wasn't Ryan. I couldn't see his face but he was blond with some gray hair. He was an older man; like maybe around my dad's age. Anyway, he was crying really hard; more like sobbing, when all of a sudden...my bedroom changed to a different bedroom. Then this little blond boy walked into the room wearing pajamas. He stood in front of the man and asked, 'Grandpa, why are you crying?' The man looked up at him and said, 'I miss Grandma.' I noticed they both had British accents. The boy asked him, 'Is Grandma in heaven?' and the man said, 'Yes, she's waiting for me.' Then he hugged the boy and kissed him on the top of his head. He told the boy to go back to bed and the little boy smiled at him before he left the room. As soon as he left, I walked closer to the man 'cause I wanted to know if he could see me. Bridge, I swear...he looked right at me. And now that I could see his face, I realized it was Tristan; an older Tristan. He grinned at me with his sad eyes still wet with tears and his face still flushed. I could see that dimple on his left cheek. I was just looking at him in shock 'cause I couldn't believe it was him. But then he whispered, 'Goodbye Autumn.'

Then I woke up. I was gonna call you but I figured I'd tell you once I saw you at the party."

As I listened to Autumn's dream, all I could think about was the fact that I was going to die first. And if Tristan was around Autumn's father's age, then it meant that I died young. It saddened me greatly to think that Tristan and I weren't going to grow old together, and we weren't going to die in each other's arms like in *'The Notebook'*. But I was still curious to know what Autumn thought her dream meant. "What do you think it means?"

She gave me a look filled with sorrow because the realization probably hit her too that I was going to die before Tristan. I also think she was trying to avoid crushing my already broken spirits even more when she replied, "I don't know but maybe that was Tristan's future. It doesn't necessarily mean that's when *he* dies. I don't know why he said 'goodbye' to me." Even if she didn't know...I knew. I believed he did die that night because why else would he say 'goodbye' to her? Right at that moment, I regretted my decision to listen to her dream and I wished I would've gone back inside to rejoin the party. I mentally slapped myself for being so damn curious and wanting to know everything. Sometimes it's not good to know the future.

We were both quiet for awhile as I sat in the patio chair and let my mind take me to my own little world. I started thinking about our deaths and how there would come a time where we would be prematurely separated from each other forever. I didn't feel the tears trickling down my cheeks until I felt Autumn's fingers wipe them away. She was sitting in the chair next to me and her voice was soft and full of remorse. "I'm sorry, Bridge. I know that's not what you wanted to hear but I had to tell you. I thought you should know. I also realized something after I woke up from this dream." I finally turned my head to look at her and she gave me an apologetic smile. "I haven't had a dream about *you*. Come to think of it...I never did. They were all about Tristan. I think I'm connected to *him* and not you." Her admission caused me to look at her with intrigue. The more I thought about it, the more I realized she was right. I didn't make an appearance in any of her dreams. There was a contemplative tone in her voice when she admitted quietly, "I don't know why or how I'm connected to him, but I always felt there was something different about him. He's unlike anyone I've ever met and when I first met him, I could sense there was more to him than what I was seeing with my naked eye. Tristan's not just your average guy." She shook her head like she was trying to clear the perplexity from her mind. "I really can't explain it."

That made two of us because I felt the exact same way about Tristan. I don't know what was stranger: her bizarre dreams about him or my unexplainable soul connection to him. Autumn gave me a gentle pat on the knee before she got up and lit her cigarette. The backyard was silent because I started brooding again while she smoked a few feet away from me. She brought me out of my reverie when she said, "I think we should go back inside. You're starting to shiver." I was actually surprised because I didn't even notice.

Christmas Eve dinner was served shortly after we went back inside the house. I tried to mask my true feelings before I approached Tristan but I could tell by the concerned look on his face that he suspected something was wrong with me. I also tried to build a mental block in my mind in hopes that he wouldn't be able to hear my thoughts. I remember one day I got frustrated with him and his telepathic ability. I told him that I felt like he was invading my privacy and I asked him to stop reading my mind. To my surprise, he laughed and kindly reminded me that he wasn't. Some of my inner thoughts were actually my soul speaking and since his soul is connected to mine, there was no way for him *not* to hear me. He replied jokingly, "Tell your soul to stop speaking and then I won't hear you."

After dinner, Jake asked us to gather in his impressive theater room that seated twenty so he could share his special home video presentation on the big screen. Tristan and I sat next to each other with Katie on my lap as we enjoyed watching Jake act as director. The movies were actually a collection of all his family and friends that were shot throughout the years. I was especially tickled to see footage of the Hathaway brothers when they were children. As Jake allowed me a glimpse of when my husband was a child, I had forgotten all about Autumn's distressing dream. But relief was short-lived because another haunting memory was brought to the surface when video from Tristan's birthday party two years ago appeared on the screen. Everyone was laughing at Tristan wearing the Burger King crown but my eyes were fixed on Kelly's face in the background. I gasped in shock when I saw her brunette friend standing right next to her.

Kelly's been in hiding ever since the day Tristan called her and tried to trick her into meeting with him. She never called him again and we never saw another suspicious car driving up the street or following us around town. She really was elusive because Detective Grace had absolutely no leads. He couldn't trace anything back to her and he still couldn't locate her accomplice. Months went by and still no sign of Kelly. I let myself believe that she had finally given up on Tristan and decided to focus her energy on some other poor unsuspecting guy. Soon she disappeared from our thoughts completely and we continued to live our normal, happy, stalker-free lives.

Naturally, my reaction from seeing her face caught Tristan's attention because he leaned over towards me and whispered, "What's the matter?"

I swallowed thickly against the nervous thump in my throat. I couldn't believe I finally found evidence that could help the detective catch her. I tried to compose my excitement before I whispered back, "Didn't you see Kelly in the video from your birthday party?" His face scrunched together in confusion so I assumed he didn't. "I saw her face...and her brunette friend too!"

Tristan's eyes widened in shock but then he yelled in triumph, "Brilliant!" His expression turned devious and his eyes glinted with revenge when he said, "She won't be so elusive anymore."

I nodded in agreement. "I'll ask Jake to give me a copy of the video and then I'll give it to Det. Grace the day after tomorrow. I don't want to bother him on Christmas." Tristan smiled and reached over to give my hand a tight squeeze.

As the evening wore on, Katie became fussier so I knew she was getting sleepy. It was way past her bedtime so Tristan and I decided to leave the party. I was anxious to return tomorrow because I was looking forward to seeing Kate, Will, and Nanny again. I even called my parents and asked them if they could drive down to Glendale so we could all spend Christmas together. I was so elated when they agreed because it would be the first time my parents, Lauren's family, and Jake and Tristan's family would all be together. Before we left, Jake graciously copied the video from Tristan's birthday party onto a disc. After he handed it to me, his expression turned serious and he spoke in a hard voice. "I hope you catch that mad bint."

While we were driving home, Katie fell asleep in her car seat. I was enjoying an after-dinner candy cane and looking out the window when Tristan remarked casually, "You know babe, sometimes I watch Jake and Lauren. I watch them just to see if they have the kinda love we have."

I turned my head to look at him and he glanced at me briefly before turning his eyes back on the road. "You know how I pay attention to things and tonight I realized that they don't. I mean, I know they love each other but I can tell that soul connection isn't there." As Tristan was talking, I couldn't help but to smile because he obviously felt our love was a special kind and could not be duplicated. He confirmed my assumption when he said, "The love we have is so pure, darlin'. I don't think there's anything in the world that could destroy it. I think it's eternal; like even after we both die...we'll be together again." Suddenly, my mind shifted back to Autumn's dream and I wondered if Tristan's current conversation was more than just a coincidence. Did my soul blab my inner thoughts out loud again?

He didn't mention hearing my thoughts when he continued. "Do you know why I believe this? 'Cause we love with more than just our hearts. It's different than Lauren and Jake's; even my parents and your parents. We love with our souls. They actually speak to each other when we sleep, and when we wake up...they wanna be together again. Why do you think it's so intense every time we make love? 'Cause our souls feel it, babe. They wanna feel it...they *need* to feel it. I don't care what anyone says...you don't get any more real than that." We stopped at a red light and Tristan looked over at me. "Bridget, what we have is the *definition* of true love." He wasted no time showing me just how much he loved me when he leaned over the center console to kiss me. His kiss was deep and passionate, and we both moaned softly into each other's mouths. His tongue delved inside my moist cavern swiftly and greedily as he took pleasure in tasting the minty sweet flavor of my mouth. When our lips unsealed from one another he whispered, "Do you know how many people would kill to have the kinda love we have?"

I placed my hand on his cheek and caressed it gently. I looked lovingly into his baby blues when I remembered how blessed I was to have him. My fingers traveled south and I traced the curve of his sensual lips. I found myself mesmerized by him and I responded breathlessly, "It's the kind they write about in love stories." Tristan smiled beautifully and tried to pick up where we left off but the light changed.

We made it back home and pulled into the driveway. The automated gate slowly closed behind us and Tristan turned off the engine. I got out of the car and opened Katie's door to unbuckle our little sleeping beauty from her car seat. Tristan came around the car to stand next to me and he bent down to nuzzle my neck. Then he placed a heated kiss on my cheek before he whispered seductively, "After we put our little princess to bed...there's a bubble bath with our names on it." I looked up at him with a warm smile and he waggled his eyebrows. Suddenly, I heard an unfamiliar female voice approaching us in the driveway.

"Merry Christmas, Tristan."

Tristan and I turned around at the same time, and my eyes were wide as I stared in disbelief. The infamous Kelly was slowly making her way towards us. I couldn't believe after all this time, she mustered up enough audacity to actually come to our house. My first instinct should've been to charge forward and start beating the shit out of her but I was frozen in place like a deer caught in headlights. As I took in her disheveled appearance, her blonde hair was still waist-length but it looked stringy and unkempt. She was also extremely thin; almost emaciated and I could see the sunken hollows of her cheeks. She stood a few feet away from us wearing nothing but a sleeveless red dress which was supposed to hug a woman's curves but hung from her skinny frame like a clothes hanger. I found it odd that her breasts seemed to be disproportioned from the rest of her body. They were big and perky but it looked like she stuffed her bra. Either that or some plastic surgeon gave her a terrible boob job. She had on matching red heels and she was unsteady on her feet.

I could feel Tristan's body tense next to me and he instinctively put his arm out like he was shielding me. She raised a shaky hand to smooth her hair and she smiled widely. Her straight teeth looked a bit yellow. I could tell she was trying to make herself presentable but she failed miserably because she looked like a train wreck. Her dark eyes were fixed on Tristan when she asked, "Do you remember me?" She walked towards us with her back as straight as a board like she was trying to be conscious of her posture.

I looked up at Tristan's face and his expression was one of confusion and suspicion. He moved away from me and took a few steps towards her. It didn't take long for recognition to finally strike him. "Oh yeah, I remember you." His voice turned hard and he shouted, "You're the bitch who almost ruined my fucking life! How did you know where I lived?!?" I moved towards him because I could see that he was on the verge of attacking her. Everything about his body language suggested he was highly agitated and I knew his temper would turn volatile at any moment.

She boldly came closer to us until she was within a couple feet from where we were standing. She seemed fidgety and that's when I got a good look at her eyes. They were glassy and her pupils were dilated. Right then I knew...she was on drugs. To my surprise, she laughed and once again she sounded out of touch with reality. "Since I'm here, I may as well tell you darling. My friend Gina...the one who was with me at your birthday party...she's Anthony's daughter." Tristan gaped at her in shock. "You remember him, right? Your *former* manager. She snooped around Daddy's office and got me all the info on you; your cell number... where you live."

As she was revealing her secret, Tristan was inching closer to her and I wondered if he even realized his feet were moving. Kelly wasn't acknowledging my presence because she spoke her next words like I wasn't even there. "I found out where that freckled-face bitch worked from your emergency contact list." She chuckled low in her throat and I could detect the amusement in her voice. "That was convenient that you had the phone number to her school. Gina felt bad for ditching me at your party so she wanted to make it up to me." She smiled but it was more of a grimace and it made her look even more insane. "She promised to help me win you back."

After her admission about how she was able to stalk him all these years, Tristan yelled back at her and his voice was laced with incredulity. "Win me back?!? You never had me, you delusional tart!" I could feel the anger building inside me and I think Tristan was sharing my emotions because his fists were balled up at his sides. He was actually shaking slightly from his rage but I could tell he was trying to contain it.

Kelly seemed oblivious to Tristan's personal attack and her confession continued to pour from her mouth. "Her brother helped us steal a car so we could see where you lived."

She smiled again and gave him a look like she was expecting him to be happy about this new information. Tristan was within striking distance from her and his voice was dangerously low. "So you really *did* try to kill Bridget. It was *you* in that car. And you were the one who tried to knock me and my mates off the freeway." I knew from the tone of Tristan's voice that he wasn't really asking her; it was more like he was confirming a known fact.

Kelly giggled maniacally and I could tell she really thought this whole situation was funny. "No silly! That was Gina. She was driving that night. You guys really scared her and she freaked out." All of a sudden her expression changed to one of distaste. "But *Bridget...*" my name rolled off her tongue with disgust. "She's the only thing preventing us from being together. Can't you see that?" She stepped closer to him and gazed up into his eyes with a pleading look. She was definitely strung out on something because she had no idea Tristan was three seconds away from choking the life out of her. She spoke meekly like she was trying to make him see reason. "I tried to get her out of the way so we could be together. But then I saw the car driving up the road and I had to bail." She smiled evilly and her skeletal features made her resemble a female demon. "I really *am* sorry I couldn't finish her off."

I couldn't believe her blatant audacity and madness, and I covered my open mouth with my hand. Tristan reached his point of madness too because her last statement was the straw that broke the camel's back for him. He lunged at her and a look of surprise appeared on her face. She stumbled back across the concrete driveway until she fell on her bony ass. I grabbed Tristan by the waist and I could actually hear him growling in anger. Most people would ask why I chose to restrain him instead of letting him give Kelly what she had coming to her. But you must understand that I didn't want my husband to get arrested for assault or manslaughter. As I was holding Tristan back from ending her life, she quickly got back on her feet. She was breathing hard and staring at him in disbelief. Now would've been a good time for her to leave, but then again...she wasn't very bright and she was sky high on narcotics. In one brief moment, she made eye contact with me and I took the opportunity to ask her quietly, "How did you get past the gate?"

Hearing my voice seemed to set her off because her eyes were wide and they clearly reflected her insanity. She was like a ticking time bomb and I just made her explode. Her scream was more like an ear-piercing shrill. "SHUT UP! I HATE YOU!" I was taken back, but her scream woke up Katie and I could hear her beginning to cry in the car. I immediately started walking back towards the car to quiet her down but I could still hear Kelly speaking to Tristan in a soft, friendly voice. "If this is the life you wanted Tristan, I could've given it to you. What does she have that I don't have? Can't you see that I'm prettier than her?"

Katie was crying and fussing in her car seat. I quickly unbuckled her and then I smoothed her hair and face in an effort to try and soothe her. "It's okay, sweetie. Mommy's here."

I turned my head towards them and I saw Tristan point to the street and yell, "You better clear off before I fucking kill you! I mean it, Kelly!" Then I saw him press the remote for the gate at the end of the driveway and it slowly began to open.

Kelly ignored Tristan's demand and stood her ground. I knew she was highly unstable so I wasn't that surprised when she grabbed her hair at the scalp. She looked down at the ground and mumbled to herself. Then she looked up at Tristan with her crazy brown eyes and screamed again. "WHY TRISTAN?!? HOW COULD YOU HURT ME?!? I LOVED YOU!" This time Katie screamed and she started crying again. I tried to console her but I still had one eye on Tristan and Kelly. Finally, he had enough of her intrusion on our property and her psychotic behavior. He grabbed her quickly and I gasped in shock as I watched him push her towards the end of the driveway. While he had her in his grip, she was struggling with him and screaming obscenities at the top of her lungs.

I decided I had enough too so I reached in the front seat and pulled my cell phone from my purse. I immediately dialed emergency. "Hello 911? There's a crazy blonde woman at our house and she won't leave." I was giving them the address to our house but I was still watching Tristan as he tried to remove Kelly from our property.

They were almost at the end of the driveway where the gate was wide open, when all of a sudden she made a move and Tristan released her. He doubled over for a second and I saw him put a hand to the right side of his face. Then he turned around to look at me with an expression of disbelief. He started walking towards me and once he reached me, I could hear the surprise in his voice. "The bitch scratched me. Did you see that shit?" He pulled his hand away and I saw angry red lines across his right cheek. Kelly dug her claws into him pretty deep because the fresh scratches had already begun to bleed.

I was holding my cell phone in one hand and I reached up with the other to touch them gingerly. He winced and quickly sucked some air between his teeth. "Don't worry, baby. I called the police. They'll be here soon to take her crazy ass back to wherever she came from. Hopefully, they'll lock her up in a nuthouse and throw away the key."

Tristan and I were standing next to Katie's opened car door but his back was to Miss Crazy Ass. I glanced over his shoulder and I could see her making wide strides towards us and there was obvious determination in her step. Tristan stepped to the side of me and leaned into the car to try and calm his little princess who was still crying. Kelly was less than six feet away from us and that's when I saw the tears streaming down her cheeks. Her body was trembling and her voice was low and shaky but I'll never forget her words. "If I can't have you Tristan...no one can."

Tristan must've heard her too because he removed his body from the car and in that exact same second, I saw her reach into her bra. At that moment, I realized she really *did* stuff her bra with something. She pulled out a shiny gun and pointed it directly at his back. Oh my God. He was about to turn around and I knew exactly what she was going to do. The next events happened almost in slow motion even though I tried to act swiftly. I screamed his name. "TRISTAN!" Then I dropped my cell phone and put myself in front of him with the intention of moving him out of harm's way. Unfortunately, I've never possessed Tristan's quick reflexes and I wasn't fast enough to move us *both* out of the way.

I heard a loud bang and then I felt hot, searing pain hit me in the back and it immediately spread to my chest. I gasped and my lungs actually burned like they were filled with fire. That's when Tristan grabbed me. I clutched the front of his jacket at the same time because I felt my knees buckle from under me. Something strange happened because for a minute...I couldn't hear anything. I was surrounded by silence but I saw Tristan's light blue eyes looking back at me in terror. I couldn't do anything but stare at him and for the next couple seconds we just gazed into each other's eyes. It was almost like neither of us could believe what was happening. I felt warm wetness on my chest like someone threw a drink on me. Then suddenly my hearing returned because I heard Tristan cry out in horror, "BRIDGET! OH GOD NO!" I heard Katie scream again because now her father was screaming too.

I couldn't keep my balance and I felt my knees give way. Tristan was holding me but we both fell to the ground together. He cradled me in his arms and I glanced to my right and I saw Kelly standing there in her red high heels. Her dark eyes wide as saucers and her hand still holding the smoking silver gun. Her hand was shaking so violently that she couldn't hold the gun any longer and it dropped to the ground with a clanking noise. She was staring back at me in utter shock and the next thing I knew, she turned on her heel and I heard her rapid footsteps as she ran down the driveway. Within the next couple seconds, I heard a car engine revving and tires screeching. The blonde home wrecker peeled off down the street and my prince wailed loudly into the night.

I was having trouble breathing and I looked down at my chest. I gasped again but I choked when I saw the dark crimson blood staining the front of my cream cashmere sweater and red cardigan. I couldn't believe what I was seeing so I reached out to touch it to make sure it was real. Before I could, Tristan grabbed my hand and held it and that's when I looked up at his face. What I saw...I've never seen in my entire life. His face was filled with anguish and fear. His body was shaking and he was sobbing loudly as he rocked me gently in his arms. He spoke through his tears. "You'll be okay, love. Just stay with me."

I could hear Katie crying in the background but I could also hear the muffled voice of the 911 operator coming through my cell phone that was lying on the ground. Tristan heard it too because he quickly reached over and grabbed it. He yelled frantically, "My wife's been shot! My wife's been shot! Please help! Someone send an ambulance!" He dropped the phone from his trembling hand and pulled me close to him. His unique masculine scent smelled so good and I tried to inhale it deeply but my lungs burned with every breath I took. There was blood in my mouth and the copper taste made me want to gag.

A loud rumble from the heavens above us made me look up at the sky; past my grieving husband's tormented face. The thunder was threatening and it was mixed with cracks of lightening and white streaks that briefly illuminated the blanket of darkness. I felt wetness on my face and I knew it was more than just my tears combined with Tristan's. It started to rain and it quickly turned into a down-pour. It was so ironic that it began to storm around us right at this very moment. We were both soaked to the bone within a matter of seconds but Tristan seemed oblivious as he held me in his protective embrace. I looked at him again and even though the rainwater wet his face, I could see that his eyes were bloodshot and his lips were quivering so I knew he was still crying. I reached up to thread my fingers through his darkened blond locks and he whispered, "Don't leave me, Bridget. I need you and Katie needs her mum." His voice broke at the end and he started sobbing uncontrollably.

I gave him a sad smile and my voice wavered slightly as I tried to speak through the pain in my chest. "I know, I'm sorry."

"Why did you do it?"

That wasn't a difficult question to answer. I remembered the silent vow I made to myself after Kelly's first attempt to keep us apart. "I wasn't going to let her take you away from me again."

He smoothed my wet hair back from my forehead and then he leaned down to place a soft kiss on my lips. His lips lingered against mine for a few seconds before he pulled away. "Just hold on, darlin'. Help is coming." He looked into my eyes and his warms hands caressed my face. "Look at me, okay? Stay with me, love," he said quietly. He broke down again and it was a heart wrenching sight because I knew he was suffering. But there wasn't anything I could do. I couldn't console him this time. In between his hiccups, he managed to say, "You promised you would never leave me."

I caressed his cheek and he leaned into my touch. He closed his eyes briefly and I saw a fresh batch of tears escape his long lashes. They trickled down his cheeks and melted away with the rainwater. "I'm sorry, Tristan. I'm sorry I broke my promise."

Renowned strength crept back into his voice and I could detect a flicker of confidence. "You're not gonna die, Bridget. You're not. You're gonna see Katie grow up and we're gonna have more babies and grow old together. We're gonna die together...in each other's arms; like in '*The Notebook*' remember?"

I didn't want to die. I became angry because I didn't want Kelly to succeed in separating us. I was the one who was supposed to win. I was supposed to aid Det. Grace in her capture. I was supposed to be sitting in court when the judge threw the book at her and sentenced her to life in prison. I was supposed to spend the rest of my life with Tristan in peace and surrounded by our grandchildren.

In that instant, I thought back to Autumn's dream and I remembered that Tristan was alone. I began to wonder if this moment was when I was *supposed* to die. I'll admit, I thought I would die a lot older than twenty-seven. I also remembered that there was a slim possibility that her dream could be wrong and I feared that Tristan wouldn't make it to be an old man. There were so many times when he told me he would die without me; that he didn't want to go on with his life if I wasn't a part of it. I believed my death would cause his own, and I didn't want him to take his own life. I wanted him to be there for Katie. She needed him now more than ever and I was filled with deep regret that he would have to raise our daughter by himself. When I finally accepted the fact that I was going to die, I asked my husband to make me one last promise. "Promise me that you'll take care of Katie. Don't leave her, Tristan. She'll need you."

I could hear the sirens in the background and my poor little girl was still in her car seat crying her head off. I wanted desperately to go to her and ease her fear but I knew I couldn't. I knew I would never be able to go to her again. I was looking into Tristan's watery eyes and I saw a conflict building behind them. After a few seconds, he whispered his answer. "I promise." Then he sealed his promise with another tender kiss.

I smiled, and then...something magical happened. I gasped again and my eyes widened in astonishment because Tristan began to physically transform right before my very eyes. A soft white glow emanated from his entire body and that's when I saw them. I opened my mouth to speak but I couldn't form the words to express what I was truly seeing. I know I wasn't dreaming this time. So many nights I saw Tristan as a real angel in my dreams. I believed in my heart from the moment I met him that he was a fallen angel disguised in human form. But now, the truth was finally revealed and I realized that I was right all along. Two, large wings were spanned out from his back but they curled and wrapped around us protectively. Most of the feathers were white but I could see shades of gray that gave the wings a more natural appearance.

Tristan was sniffling and crying and he didn't seem to notice what was happening to him. I was amazed even further because at that moment, his body healed itself more rapidly than I've ever seen. The nasty scratches that Kelly inflicted on him moments ago, faded away instantly. I wanted him to know what I was seeing so I dug deep down inside me and finally found my voice. "Tristan, I can see your wings now. You really *are* a fallen angel. I knew they were there...I knew it." He was still oblivious and he continued to weep openly. I noticed that the more he cried, the more his feathers would molt. And as the feathers hit the ground, they would disappear. I was in awe at the heavenly sight before me. "They're so beautiful, sweetheart."

I think awareness finally came to him because he slowly lifted his head towards the sky and closed his eyes. He let the rain fall on him and he extended his wings to their full breadth. They were truly magnificent and my eyes feasted on his divine beauty. I believe it was at this moment that he learned of his true self. When his eyes opened, he looked down at me with unmistaken adoration behind his gaze. He gave me a weary smile and I saw the cute dimple on his left cheek. "*You're* beautiful Bridget. I love you so much."

He kissed me again and then I whispered back, "I love you too."

I was beginning to feel sleepy and I think I closed my eyes for a moment because then I heard him panic again. He yelled my name and my eyes shot open. Then he started crying and praying at the same time. "Please don't take her away from me. Please not now. I need her." I could hear the sirens getting closer but I was surrounded by Tristan and his angelic wings. His eyes locked on mine and I found myself getting lost in his beautiful cerulean pools. "Bridget, I need you to stay with me. Don't leave me yet. Your prince isn't ready to lose his princess." His voice was cracking and he cradled my head close to his chest. I looked up at him my heart broke because there was only agony etched into his face. I didn't want to leave him; I wanted to stay but the fatigue was really bearing down on me and I closed my eyes again. Right at that moment, he lost his composure once more. I couldn't see him but I could hear his erratic breathing and there was a painstaking desperate tone in his broken voice. "I'm so sorry, Bridget. I'm sorry I failed you." I could feel soft, warm kisses all over my face. "I'm sorry I couldn't protect you."

There was still a small amount of strength left in me and I slowly opened my eyes again. Sadness and guilt was evident on my prince's handsome face. I brushed my fingers gently across his lips to reassure him that he was already forgiven. He kissed them tenderly. "It's okay, baby. I protected *you*...I kept you safe." My eyelids were so heavy that it took a great amount of effort to keep my eyes open. "I'm just..." I felt like yawning; I was so tired. "I feel so sleepy."

"Bridget..."

Finally, I couldn't fight it anymore and I let my eyelids flutter close. "I'm just going to sleep for awhile."

I felt Tristan kiss my lips once more and I don't think I'll ever forget the way his lips feel pressed against mine. The fallen angel began to cry out loud in agony as he crushed me against his chest. I even felt his wings brush against my cheeks like a gentle caress. Then suddenly, I heard his voice in my ear but it was barely above a whisper and for a moment I thought I didn't hear him speak. "I'll be here when you wake up." My lungs were burning so badly and I wanted to extinguish the fire so I decided to stop breathing to see if it would ease my pain. To my relief, it worked and I felt serene and completely pain-free. I also realized that I didn't have the urge to take another breath. It felt so nice to be able to rest my eyes. I found myself slipping into unconsciousness but I heard my soul mate's guttural scream...and it carried my name. "BRIDGET!"

My soul wept and I wonder if he heard my last thoughts before I fell into a deep, peaceful sleep. *'Goodbye, Tristan. I will always love you.'*

Epilogue

'Love is something eternal; the aspect may change, but not the essence.'

~ Vincent van Gogh

I DON'T THINK I WAS asleep for very long before I heard a familiar voice awaken me from my slumber. The voice sounded close by and it spoke to me softly. "Bridget, it's time to wake up, love." My eyelids still felt heavy but I was able to slowly open my eyes. It took a moment for my vision to come into focus and I gasped in surprise when I took in the sight before me. The first thing I noticed was that it was bright and sunny and I was stark naked. A feeling of panic should've settled in immediately but instead I was filled with curiosity as to where I was and what happened to my clothing. I looked down at my bare breasts and I noticed the blood was gone from my chest; there's wasn't even a wound or a scar left behind. My body was clean and dry and I had that fresh 'after-bath' feeling.

The next thing I realized was that I was lying on an extremely comfortable and spacious four-poster bed. It felt like thousands of down feathers were underneath me and my pillow was one big cotton ball. I started to wonder if I was even lying on a mattress because it felt so light that it was almost like I was floating on air. My hands were folded on my stomach but I reached down to touch the bed just to confirm I was actually being supported by something. The bed sheets were cool, cream-colored and velvety soft to the touch. I cast my eyes down at my feet and it looked like someone had given me a pedicure while I slept. My eyes widened in surprise and I wiggled my toes because I've never seen them look so pretty. Past my feet, I saw a thick white comforter with gold stitching and it was rolled up at the end of the bed.

I didn't lift my head but my eyes darted around the beautiful unfamiliar room and I noticed it was open-air. I could see outside and the air surrounding me was calm like a warm summer day. I saw many tall trees that looked like a lush and dense forest. The sky was clear blue and filled with white fluffy clouds. I could even hear birds chirping and the sound of rushing water in the distance. I lifted my head slightly and expected to succumb to the disorientation that accompanies a dream-like state but I didn't feel that way at all. I was completely conscious and fully aware. But I had to be dreaming because I had no idea where I was. The last thing I remembered was Tristan holding me in the rain after Kelly shot me. Then I closed my eyes, he screamed my name, and my soul said 'goodbye' to him right before I fell asleep.

As I looked at the room itself, there were a few stone columns with strange and intricate carvings. It was furnished extravagantly yet other-worldly and the entire scene reminded me of '*Lord of the Rings - The Fellowship of the Ring*' when Frodo awakened in Rivendell. I thought to myself: *Am I dreaming? Have I fallen into Middle Earth?* Then I laughed inwardly as I thought: *Am I Frodo?*

Immediately following that thought, I heard someone in the room chuckle softly...and it wasn't me. Then I heard Tristan's boyish voice that was laced with a British accent. He remarked humorously, "You're a lot sexier than Frodo."

I gasped again and whipped my head towards the sound of his voice. I almost jumped out of my skin when I saw that he was right next to me. His beautiful, periwinkle blue eyes were peeking out from under his golden blond fringe and they were glinting with amusement. He was still youthful and he gave me a dazzling smile that caused his cute dimple to make an appearance on his left cheek. His head was resting on a pillow a few inches from mine and he was lying on his side just gazing at me. I was gaping at him in shock as my eyes traveled the full length of his gorgeous Adonis form. I was pleasantly surprised that I could still see his magnificent angelic wings even though they were folded behind him. I saw the tips of some of the feathers curling around his lean muscular legs. I also noticed there wasn't a single article of clothing on him either.

That's when the panic finally settled in. I came to the conclusion that I died and if Tristan was here with me; looking exactly the way I remember him...then he must have died too. A look of fear appeared on my face and my voice reflected the realization of his premature death. I exclaimed loudly, "Please tell me you didn't kill yourself!" Tristan's eyes widened slightly and the smile disappeared from his face. "You left Katie?!?" My voice started to crack and I could feel the tears pricking at the back of my eyes at the thought of Tristan leaving our daughter to become an orphan. Then I remembered the promise he made to me before I died. "You promised, Tristan!" I was powerless to prevent my tears from falling because I didn't want to believe that he would break his promise.

A look of confusion appeared on his face for the briefest moment before another smile graced his handsome features. He laughed lightly and scooted closer to me to peck me on the lips. Then he brushed the tears from my cheeks before he rested his arm across my waist. His familiar touch actually comforted me and I placed my arm on top of his. "No, I didn't leave her, darlin'. Katie's still alive and so are our grandkids." Our grandkids?!? Now it was my turn to look confused. He explained gently but in a more serious tone. "Bridget...it's been thirty years."

My mouth dropped in astonishment and it took a couple seconds for me to find my voice. "What?!? No way!" I started shaking my head in disbelief. Now I was convinced that I was dreaming. Thirty years?!? That couldn't be right. I was trying to make sense of this but it was so unbelievable that I started stuttering. "But...but...I...how?" I paused to take a breath and close my eyes. When I looked at him, I knew the perplexity I was feeling was clearly displayed on my face. "But I just woke up. That much time has passed since Kelly shot me?"

I saw Tristan flinch at the latter part of my question. He continued speaking to me in a gentle tone. "Your half of our soul was asleep. It was waiting for its other half and now that I'm here...you can wake up." He gave me a reassuring smile to try and ease my bewilderment.

It wasn't really working and I still didn't know what was going on. But for a minute, my mind flashed back to the one person who separated me from my husband and child. I couldn't keep the animosity from my voice when I asked, "What happened to Kelly...the Insane Stalking Murderer?"

"The bobbies went after her, but she was so strung out on drugs that she crashed her car and killed herself."

I'll admit I felt relieved after hearing of her demise and I think I smiled involuntarily. I'm glad her life was taken for taking mine and I hoped she wasn't in a nice place like I was. Where was I anyway? My mind shifted back to my apparent not-so-recent death and I started wondering about Tristan after I died. "What happened to you after I died?" Thinking about my death caused me to think of my other loved ones and what they went through. "What about my parents and Autumn? What about Jake?"

Right at that moment, Tristan's expression changed and I could see the sadness etched all over his face. His voice was barely above a whisper. "Please don't make me tell you." There was a desperate tone in his plea and he was losing the strength in his voice. "My worst fear in life happened 'cause I failed to protect you and I suffered a pain you can't even imagine. My agony ran deep; straight to the core of my soul. And I mourned you until it almost suffocated the remaining life out of me. Bridget, I don't---" Before I knew it, I saw his eyes begin to fill with unshed tears. "I don't wanna relive the memory." But I had a feeling it was already too late. He sobbed once and then he squeezed his eyes shut. His lips began to tremble and I watched the unmistaken emotions of pain and grief cross his features. That's when I saw a few tears escape his long blond lashes. My angel started to cry and I was immediately filled with the urge to comfort him.

I slipped my arms around his waist and his wings rested on top of them. I was expecting them to feel heavy but they weren't, and the feathers were so soft. I held him close and molded my body to his. When I felt him embrace me, I kissed his lips tenderly to console him. "It's okay, baby. You don't have to tell me. And it's not your fault, sweetheart so please don't blame yourself. I'm the one who jumped in front of the bullet." I reached up, and this time I wiped the tears from *his* cheeks.

When his eyes opened, they were looking back at me with a heartbroken gaze. He sniffled a couple times as he tried to compose himself. I placed light kisses all over his face and gently threaded my fingers through his wheat-colored locks. His hair was silky to the touch and my fingers combed through his blond strands like water. His unique, intoxicating scent invaded my nostrils and it didn't take me long to remember how wonderful his body felt pressed against mine. He opened his mouth to speak and his voice wavered slightly due to his current emotional state. "I'll just tell you what I can bear to tell you. I stayed and raised Katie and I watched her grow up. I ended up selling our house in Hollywood and moving back to Brighton to live with my family."

I gasped and covered my mouth with my hand. I couldn't stop my own tears as I thought back to our country-style English Tudor that we were just beginning to make into a true home. And all the dedication we put into it in hopes that it would be a home filled with love where we could raise our family. I could see the regret in Tristan's eyes as he gently caressed my face. I leaned into his touch and closed my eyes as he continued speaking. "I couldn't stand living in the house without you. And I couldn't walk past our parkway without breaking down. Ever since you died, I parked my bike on the street. And I never let anyone use the parkway. I had to leave, Bridget. I had to. But I kept my promise to you."

As I started thinking about what his life was like without me, I wondered if he ever found true love again. I opened my eyes and asked quietly, "Did you ever get married again?"

There was a real intensity that began to fill Tristan's azure orbs as he looked intently into my eyes. "No, I never married again. I could never love anyone the way I loved you. You're my soul mate, and in life...you only get *one*. All the love I had left...I gave to Katie." My heart almost burst at the seams because of his devotion to me. Suddenly he averted his eyes when he admitted, "I did end up going back to my old ways as a swinger." When his eyes met mine, he gave me a sheepish grin. "Hey, I'm still a male and I had sexual needs." I didn't hold that against him because I can't imagine how lonely he felt all those years. I was lucky enough not to experience that kind of heartache because he was here when I woke up, so I never longed for him. There was a serious tone in his voice when he continued. "But sex with those women was nothing compared to what we had. With them, it was just a shag. My body may have felt physical pleasure but I never felt it in my soul. That kinda pleasure I only shared with you."

There was a thoughtful expression on his face when he said, "Katie grew up surrounded by love in Brighton and I gave her everything I could." He laughed lightly and I could tell his spirits were lifting as he reminisced about our daughter. "I'll admit that she was a little spoiled by all of us. She went to Oxford and after she graduated, she became a professional football player. She plays for the Arsenal Ladies. She eventually got married to a good-looking Welsh bloke she was seeing from the university. He's a veterinarian and they have a son and a daughter: Kieran and Bridget. I have to say, it was really fun being a grandfather."

I smiled wistfully at the thought of Katie naming her own daughter after me. I was also smiling because the mystery behind her British accent in Autumn's dream was finally revealed. Tristan raised her in the same city where he was raised and I found myself thinking I would've actually preferred that she grew up there as opposed to Hollywood. It wasn't long until my happiness was quickly replaced with feelings of sadness and regret. "I missed out on so much of Katie's life," I said with my voice full of sorrow. I sighed wearily as I thought of all the time with her that I'll never get back. "Her first day of school, her first date...her first period."

Tristan chuckled. "I know, but I was there. And it'll please you to know that I let her date before she was eighteen." That made me feel slightly better and I cracked a smile. "Actually, she was fifteen." His hands cupped my face gently and there was a real tenderness in his voice. "I can share my memories with you. I know it's not the same as being there but it's all I can do."

I looked into his eyes and asked desperately, "Will I ever see Katie when it's her time?"

"I don't know, love. When people die, there are infinite places they can end up. It all depends on the person and what's in their heart."

My mind flashed back to when he told me it's been thirty years since I died. If that was true, then he was in his mid-fifties and that's a young age to die as well. I was curious about his last moments on Earth so I asked, "Tristan, how did you die?"

Surprisingly, he smirked and judging by the tone of his voice, my question seemed to amuse him. "Do you still wonder about Autumn's strange dreams?" His question caused my eyebrows to shoot upwards and I became anxious for him to finally reveal the secret. He didn't disappoint because he said, "She really *is* psychic and because of what I am, she could connect to me on a spiritual level. I've only made three *real* wishes in my life as a human, and my three wishes and her three dreams about me were connected. Before I met her, when I was a teen living in Brighton, I wished to be happy. So a few months later when I moved to The States, I met her and then later she met you online. She was the bridge between us. She had the dream about meeting me as a boy, and since she was connected to me, I told her what my heart needed to be happy. I needed you. That's why she set up our first meeting. My second wish...I wished for you to have a baby so she had a dream that she met Katie. The dream was actually telling her that my wish came true 'cause you were pregnant. Then years after you died, I wished to be with you again and she dreamt that she was there with me. I made my last wish that night and I said 'goodbye' to her. But she had the dream years before I died. She actually saw my future...the *second* time. The first time was when I was playing footie at the beach with Katie."

All of a sudden, Tristan's voice turned somber and his expression was one of sadness once again. "After awhile, the grief I felt by your death was too much for me. It actually haunted me for the rest of my life. Finally, I couldn't live without you any longer. I had Katie, my family, my grandkids, and my acting career but I wasn't really living anymore; not like I was when you were with me. I decided that Katie would be okay 'cause she has her own family now. One night, I made my third wish to be with you again. I went to sleep and left my body so I could be with you. If it wasn't for Katie, I would've left with you, Bridget; right there in our parkway...we both would've died. I only stayed 'cause I wanted to keep my promise to you. You see, when I learned of my true self, the memory of who I really am came back to me and I knew what I was capable of in my human body. And I remembered that my father gave me the choice to come home any time I wanted."

I swallowed hard and I was speechless when I realized that keeping his promise to me was the only reason we didn't die in each other's arms. I did feel relief to finally know the truth behind Autumn's bizarre dreams. But then I realized something else that still didn't make sense. "If you died when you were older, then why do you still look the way I remember you?"

"'Cause I thought you would prefer me this way."

He smiled adoringly and I immediately returned the gesture. One of Tristan's wings moved and it caught my attention. This time I didn't resist and I reached out to touch them. He extended them slightly and my eyes widened in amazement because they were such a new and unfamiliar part of him now. "They really do become you," I commented affectionately. He grinned in appreciation and I guess he wanted to show them off to me so he extended them even further. My fingers ruffled through some of the feathers and he closed his eyes as he enjoyed the sensation. My eyes roamed over the rest of his divine body and I took in the other parts of him that I was very familiar with. "You still have your tatts?"

He opened his eyes and gave me sly grin. "I'm quite fond of them so He let me keep them."

After my appraisement of his true angelic form, I was filled with such gratitude because he was here with me. The thought of being alone for all eternity frightened me and I was glad that he was the first person I laid eyes on when I awakened from my thirty-year sleep. I held him tightly and I honestly didn't want to let him go. "I'm so happy to see you, Tristan."

He held me with equal strength and I felt him rub my back in the most soothing way. "I'm happy to see you too, love. I can't even begin to tell you how much I've missed you."

Our reunion caused my emotions to overpower me and I started crying. "I thought I'd never see you again."

Tristan pulled away and when I looked into his eyes, there was nothing but pure adoration behind them. "I told you that you'd never be alone, didn't I?" He smiled again and gently wiped my tears away with his thumbs.

All of a sudden, something appeared at the foot of the bed; a soft white light that was actually swirling around in a large circle. It looked like a portal of some sort. I looked up at Tristan and asked innocently, "Should we go into the light now?"

"It's not that kinda light, sweets," he explained gently. "That light will bring you back to Earth to be reborn."

I was still confused so I repeated my question. "Should we go into it?"

"It was hard enough the first time trying to find you. I don't wanna go through that shit again."

In addition to his tattoos and British accent, I guess some other aspects about Tristan will never change. I exclaimed in surprise, "You still curse?!?"

He smiled and shrugged nonchalantly. "Eh, it's a habit."

I was curious as to what other habits he held onto so I asked, "Do you still drink and smoke too?"

He shook his head. "I can't. There's none of that stuff here."

I wasn't exactly sure where *here* was but Tristan seemed to know. I decided to pick his brain a little more. "How do you know all this?"

His jovial mood seemed to disappear because I could detect the seriousness in his voice now. "'Cause I've been here before. This is my home." My eyes widened and Tristan continued to shock me even further. "When I was here the last time, I was alone and miserable. It was thousands of years since God needed my services and mankind doesn't really believe in us anymore. My father took pity on me and released me from my duty. He sent my commander, The Archangel Michael, to deliver a message to me. Michael told me there was one human on Earth who was my true love. I was told I could stay here but be miserable forever, or if I wanted a chance to be happy and have love for all eternity, I could fall to Earth but I would be born with half a soul. My journey would be to find the other half...my soul mate. Michael reminded me that it may not be easy 'cause there are billions of people on Earth. I longed for love and companionship so badly that I took the chance and fell to be born. When you were dying, my true form was revealed to you. Only people who are dying can see me for what I truly am. Remember the old lady in the hospital?" I nodded. "She saw me. My grandfather also saw my true form before he died. I was only a child at the time. I tried to make my third wish for you to come back to life but it wasn't granted 'cause it goes against what I am."

I know Tristan could see the confusion on my face. That's probably why he took the liberty of explaining more about his history. "You see, before I fell...I was a warrior angel and my duty was in battle. I was created to fight and take lives...not bring them back." I could hear the resentment in his voice when he finished with, "I don't have the power to heal others."

What Tristan was telling me was unbelievable but now that I thought back on my life with him...it all made sense. "So the dog hearing, the rapid healing ability, and the really fast reflexes..." My eyes were wide with astonishment because I was finally learning the truth about what I suspected all along. "No wonder you were such a bad-boy and you were always quick to fight someone. You were a warrior so it was just coming naturally to you." I could see a smile playing on the corners of Tristan's mouth. He knew I was right. "I can't believe the only reason you fell was to find me." There was unconditional love behind Tristan's eyes when he reached out to caress my cheek. He didn't speak and I held his gaze as he ran his thumb gently across my bottom lip. I felt so honored that a real angel fell to Earth just to find me because I possessed the other half of his soul...and his heart.

I started thinking about our relationship and especially the intense passion between us. That's when I solved yet another of Tristan's mysteries. "I remember the way you could just enrapture me so easily with your seductive spell. I could never resist you. I always knew you had real power behind your baby blues." Tristan grinned wickedly. "I mean, the fact that you're absolutely gorgeous should've been a dead giveaway." I laughed and shook my head in amazement.

Tristan released me from his embrace and leaned over me with his arms resting on either side of my head. His voice lowered and he looked intently into my eyes again. "All of my kind has the power of seduction."

He gave me a roguish look, and true to his word, I found myself falling under his spell. I was getting lost in his sky blue eyes and I felt myself getting aroused. I wanted him inside me and I wanted him to take me swiftly and without mercy. My surroundings began to fade out of focus and all I could see was the sexy, blond, tattooed angel hovering above me. Tristan leaned his head down and pressed his lips to mine. A quiet moan escaped my throat and I closed my eyes in sheer contentment. I reached up to thread my fingers through the soft hair at the nape of his neck. I could feel a sexual ache developing in my pussy and I rubbed my thighs together instinctively. Then suddenly, he broke the spell. I was still in a daze and I was gazing up at him beneath lowered lids. "You really *were* my angel," I said breathlessly. I paused for a few seconds as I tried to clear the lust-filled fog from my mind. "I always felt it in my heart from the moment I met you."

"I still *am*, darlin'." Then he chuckled before he said, "I told you we have a real bond. I mean, our souls spoke to each other. Because I was a Fallen, my soul was able to hear and speak to yours. And I could do it regardless if I was asleep or awake; verbally or telepathically. But you were human, so you could only hear me while you were unconscious. When we were children, it was Michael who whispered to you in your sleep and told you not to speak your name. I guess he didn't want your identity revealed to me 'cause then it would've made my mission too easy. One day I revealed my name to you, but our conversations were on another plane of reality; so far away that when you woke up, you either didn't remember anything or you thought it was just a dream."

Suddenly, Tristan cast his eyes towards the marble ceiling that was painted to resemble a heavenly golden sky. His next words sounded like an afterthought. "I wonder if Michael knew I would meet Autumn." His eyes met mine again and he smiled. "'Cause you know, if I never met her...I wouldn't have found you. Autumn was like a short-cut on my path." He laughed lightly. "It's ironic to me that the one person who would help me on my journey was a Psychic with a spiritual connection to me."

Tristan was helping me to understand and full comprehension was finally coming to me. "It's all starting to make sense now." I yelled triumphantly in my head because I liked when things made sense. "So I'm actually the physical manifestation of my soul right now?" He nodded. "And you're an angel who fell to Earth and was born as Tristan Hathaway?" He didn't confirm my statement; he just tilted his head to the side in a gesture all too familiar and smiled brilliantly. And that was all the confirmation I needed. "So...what's your *real* name?"

His hands began to smooth my hair back and then he dropped a light kiss on my forehead. Our eyes met and he said softly, "I loved you as 'Tristan', so that's my name." We shared another smile and I brushed my fingers across his sensual lips. He kissed them tenderly and then he continued to reveal his secret to me. "Michael never told me about the other catch in God's deal. When I was born on Earth, my true self was hidden from my memory. But because I was one of the Fallen, my human form was actually *superhuman*. That's why I had extraordinary abilities and why I always felt different from everyone else. But of course...I didn't know why. And the longer I was with you…the other half of my soul…the stronger my powers were getting."

I was still looking at him in amazement when I replied, "I guess *you* were the one who was going to make me a believer because you knew I didn't believe in the supernatural."

"I guess so."

All this talk about angels brought back the memory of another person who I felt was a beautiful angel. "I know you probably don't want to hear this but…what about Justin? Was he a Fallen too? Is he still alive?"

To my surprise, Tristan didn't seem bothered by the mention of Justin's name. I guess now that we were together without anyone around to threaten our relationship, there was no reason for him to feel insecure any longer. "Yes, he's still alive and yes…he's like me." I gaped again because I couldn't believe my heart was right again. Tristan's brows knitted together in confusion when he said, "I don't know if he fell willingly or if he was cast out. He fell three years after I was born, so I don't know why he's on Earth. There are others like me and they're on Earth for their own reasons. They remain hidden to human eyes unless a person is dying and their soul is about to leave their body. I'm sure Justin's mum saw him for what he truly is right before she died."

All of a sudden, we were interrupted by hushed voices coming from the swirling portal at the foot of the bed. I looked down and it was almost like it was beckoning me. I felt hypnotized and I couldn't tear my eyes away as I watched the wispy white circle swirl around and around. Suddenly, I blinked and came out of my trance because Tristan lifted his wing and blocked the portal from my view. When my eyes snapped back to his, he spoke softly. "Pay no attention to the light, babe. It'll go away in a minute."

There was an affectionate look in his eyes and his head slowly descended towards mine again. Our lips melted together perfectly and right at that moment, I felt a cool breeze and it carried his wonderful masculine scent. When the kiss ended, I asked him out of sheer curiosity, "Did you do that?" A slow smile crept onto his face and he answered me wordlessly. Something sparked in my brain and I started thinking back to the rain storms; especially the night he said he felt it raging inside of him. I decided to test my theory. "Did you cause the rain too? Remember the storms?"

This time he answered me verbally. "The Fallen are one with the earthly elements and sometimes our emotions affect the atmosphere surrounding us. Not many humans are aware of that 'cause they're not aware of our existence among them." He grinned slyly when he confessed, "They're not the only ones who have a direct effect on the weather. Our effect is just a little more immediate."

I was looking at Tristan in absolute awe because there seemed to be no end to his ability to render me speechless. Now I was learning that the air around us was affected by his emotions because he's an angel. My inner thoughts found their way out of my mouth when I said excitedly, "Wow, I can't wait to see what else you can do!"

He extended his wings again and I could hear the pride in his voice. "Well, I don't have these wings for nothing, doll. You can fly with me, you know. You have nothing to be afraid of." He leaned down close to me and whispered, "Bridget, you never have to be afraid of anything ever again. Nothing and *no one* can hurt you now." Our lips connected like magnets and neither of us could resist the pleasure of savoring each other's mouths. When Tristan pulled away, he was breathless. "Ever since our first date...all it takes is one kiss from you. One kiss...and I instantly desire you."

I couldn't help but to blush from his intimate confession and that's when he finally moved himself to lay on top of me. My legs spread instinctively and he settled naturally between them. I felt his warm, hard erection rub against my pussy in just the right spot and I purred in delight. "I love you, Tristan."

I was being smoldered by hot azure flames and my angelic prince was slowly weaving his spell around my senses. "I love you too, Bridget."

He was leaning in for another taste of my mouth so I spoke my words quickly before he captured it. "Where exactly are we anyway?"

He smiled lovingly and ran his long, piano fingers through my auburn strands. "We're right where we ought to be, princess." This time when he swooped down on me, his kiss brought with it the promise of mind-blowing sex. He wrapped his, strong tattooed arms around me and held me possessively as he slanted his lips over mine repeatedly. His tongue plundered inside my mouth and he grasped my hair more firmly. He continued to dominate me and he tilted my head back slightly so his tongue could delve deeper and taste every corner and crevice. I felt his wings begin to enfold around me and the sensation was absolutely heavenly. Even though he said nothing could hurt me, I still felt safe in his embrace.

I was a curious human when I was on Earth and some aspects about me will never change. I reached up to feel where his wings were joined to his body and when I felt the muscles there, I knew they were one-hundred percent real. I massaged the base and move my hands up to touch as much of his beautiful wings as I could. To my surprise, they shuddered from my touch and his entire body trembled. Tristan ground his hips into me and moaned in pleasure so deeply that I felt the vibration from his soul to mine. I smiled inwardly because I just discovered a new erogenous zone of his.

We broke the kiss; not to come up for air, but because he whispered against my lips, "So let's just stay here and make love to each other..." I was becoming so aroused that I began to rub myself against him to try and ease the intense sexual ache developing between my legs. Tristan was eager to relieve it, but he surprised me when he rolled our bodies so that I was the one on top. He moved his head to rest next to mine and whispered sweetly in my ear one word that held so much meaning: "Forever." Then he spoke firmly. "Turn around Bridget." At first I thought he wanted me in the '69' position but then he grasped my shoulder gently to stop me. "No love, turn around with your back against my chest." I looked at him questioningly but I did as my prince commanded. I yelled out in surprise when I felt him enter my pussy from behind. Okay, that's not really what made me yell. What made me yell was when he hooked his ankles around mine which caused my legs to spread eagle, and *then* he entered me from behind. I have never been in such an openly exposed, sexual position but it felt so good and I relished the feeling of him being inside me again.

And when my angel began his incredible thrusting action, I cried out again because it felt even better. "Yes! Yes! Oh Tristan! Please don't stop! This feels so good baby, I don't want you to stop!" His head was right next to mine and I turned slightly so our lips could melt together. And as we kissed, he continued to thrust inside my pussy from the back so deliciously while my small, freckled breasts bounced freely. He surprised me once more when he reached around the front of my body and put his hand between my legs. I thought I would die all over again from the ultimate pleasure. This was the most intimate position we had ever been in. Laying on Tristan's body and having him inside me this way was an indescribable feeling. And the fact that his lovely fingers were rubbing every part of my pussy while my legs were spread wide caused me to whimper until I felt like crying.

My sexual peak was closing in on me and I knew I wouldn't last much longer. Tristan must have felt it too because he said breathlessly, "Cum with me, doll. I wanna feel you cream all over me." My body answered him immediately, and I moaned long and deep as the first wave crashed over me. My pussy tingled with pleasure all over and my legs began to shake when I released my feminine nectar. The feeling was unlike anything I've ever felt in my human life. Not to mention, Tristan's encouragement made it feel even more wonderful. He didn't stop driving into me when he whispered gently, "That's my girl, give it to me. Give me everything you have, you beautiful redhead."

We kept our ankles hooked to each other as the orgasmic wave hit him next. He yelled my name out loud, "Bridget!" And I felt him release in powerful spurts. His male essence filled me to the point where my womanly flower was overflowing. He wrapped his strong arms around me tightly and my arms immediately latched onto his. I felt his wings enfold me once again in a protective embrace while our bodies trembled together from the force of our extreme coupling. My angel was with his rose once again and when we reached our plateau of ecstasy, we sung our own personal love song straight into the heaven around us. But this time was even more special; it was magical and I knew it would be this way forever.

Now I couldn't be sure, but I think the portal finally disappeared because I could no longer hear the hushed voices. The only sound that filled my ears were our cries of passion as our souls joined at last.

While I was lost in a place of sheer bliss, my emotions overpowered me the same way they did on our wedding night and I couldn't keep my tears at bay. I literally cried from the intense orgasm Tristan had given me. I turned my head slightly because I needed to look into my beloved's eyes. My vision was blurry but I could still see his handsome face. It was flushed from exertion and his baby blues were gazing back at me with nothing but pure affection. When I finally caught my breath, the first and middle names that he was given on Earth escaped my quivering lips,

"Tristan Caleb," and my voice wavered as I begged my angel unabashedly to make the pleasure last forever. "Please don't let me go."

My eternal husband kept his beautiful azure eyes fixed on me when he responded softly, "Don't worry Rosie...I'll never let you go." I smiled lovingly when I realized he called me by the childhood name he graced me with. His unique, comforting scent engulfed my senses and blanketed my entire body and I closed my eyes in contentment. I felt him place a tender kiss on my temple and I silently thanked the Lord for blessing me with a soul mate. Then I remembered the words Tristan spoke to me on the night I died. What we share *is* the definition of true love. We are bound to each other for all eternity, and not even death could keep us from our happily ever after.

THE END

Breinigsville, PA USA
14 July 2010
241836BV00004B/13/P